James Patterson's previous international No.1 bestsellers include ALONG CAME A SPIDER, KISS THE GIRLS, JACK AND JILL, WHEN THE WIND BLOWS, POP GOES THE WEASEL, CRADLE AND ALL, ROSES ARE RED, SUZANNE'S DIARY FOR NICHOLAS, VIOLETS ARE BLUE, MIRACLE ON THE 17TH GREEN (with Peter de Jonge), 2ND CHANCE (with Andrew Gross), THE BEACH HOUSE (with Peter de Jonge), FOUR BLIND MICE, THE JESTER (with Andrew Gross), THE LAKE HOUSE, and most recently, THE BIG BAD WOLF. He resides in Florida.

Praise for James Patterson's bestselling novels:

'Makes Kay Scarpetta's lot look positively fairytale'
Mirror

'A master of the suspense genre' *Sunday Telegraph*

'Unputdownable' *The Times*

JAMES
PATTERSON

CAT AND MOUSE

1ST TO DIE

headline

CAT AND MOUSE
first published in Great Britain in 1997
by HEADLINE BOOK PUBLISHING

1ST TO DIE
first published in Great Britain in 2001
by HEADLINE BOOK PUBLISHING

First published in this omnibus edition in 2004
by HEADLINE BOOK PUBLISHING

A HEADLINE paperback

10 9 8 7 6 5 4 3 2

ISBN 0 7553 2262 2

Typeset in Palatino-Light by
Letterpart Limited, Reigate, Surrey

Printed and bound in Great Britain by
Clays Ltd, St Ives plc

Papers and cover board used by Headline are natural, recyclable
products made from wood grown in sustainable forests. The
manufacturing processes conform to the environmental
regulations of the country of origin.

HEADLINE BOOK PUBLISHING
A division of Hodder Headline
338 Euston Road
LONDON NW1 3BH

www.headline.co.uk
www.hodderheadline.com

CAT AND MOUSE

CATCH A SPIDER

ONE

Washington, D.C.

The Cross house was twenty paces away and the proximity and sight of it made Gary Soneji's skin prickle. It was Victorian-style, white-shingled, and extremely well kept. As Soneji stared across Fifth Street, he slowly bared his teeth in a sneer that could have passed for a smile. This was perfect. He had come here to murder Alex Cross and his family.

His eyes moved slowly from window to window, taking in everything from the crisp, white lace curtains to Cross's old piano on the sunporch to a Batman and Robin kite stuck in the rain gutter of the roof. *Damon's kite*, he thought.

On two occasions he caught sight of Cross's elderly

grandmother as she shuffled past one of the down-stairs windows. Nana Mama's long, purposeless life would soon be at an end. That made him feel so much better. *Enjoy every moment – stop and smell the roses,* Soneji reminded himself. *Taste the roses, eat Alex Cross's roses – flowers, stems, and thorns.*

He finally moved across Fifth Street, being careful to stay in the shadows. Then he disappeared into the thick yews and forsythia bushes that ran like sentries alongside the front of the house.

He carefully made his way to a whitewashed cellar door, which was to one side of the porch, just off the kitchen. It had a Master padlock, but he had the door open in seconds.

He was inside the Cross house!

He was in the cellar: The cellar was a clue for those who collected them. The cellar was worth a thousand words. A thousand forensic pictures, too.

It was important to everything that would happen in the very near future. The Cross murders!

There were no large windows, but Soneji decided not to take any chances by turning on the lights. He used a Maglite flashlight. Just to look around, to learn a few more things about Cross and his family, to fuel his hatred, if that was possible.

The cellar was cleanly swept, as he had expected it would be. Cross's tools were haphazardly arranged on a pegged Masonite board. A stained Georgetown ballcap was hung on a hook. Soneji put it on his own head. He couldn't resist.

He ran his hands over folded laundry laid out on a long wooden table. He felt close to the doomed family now. He despised them more than ever. He felt around the hammocks of the old woman's bra. He touched the boy's small Jockey underwear. He felt like a total creep, and he loved it.

Soneji picked up a small red reindeer sweater. It would fit Cross's little girl, Jannie. He held it to his face and tried to smell the girl. He anticipated Jannie's murder and only wished that Cross would get to see it, too.

He saw a pair of Everlast gloves and black Pony shoes tied around a hook next to a weathered old punching bag. They belonged to Cross's son, Damon, who must be nine years old now. Gary Soneji thought he would punch out the boy's heart.

Finally, he turned off the flashlight and sat all alone in the dark. Once upon a time, he had been a famous kidnapper and murderer. It was going to happen again. He was coming back with a vengeance that would blow everybody's mind.

He folded his hands in his lap and sighed. He had spun his web perfectly.

Alex Cross would soon be dead, and so would everyone he loved.

TWO

London, England.

The killer who was currently terrorizing Europe was named *Mr Smith*, no first name. It was given to him by the Boston press, and then the police had obligingly picked it up all over the world. He accepted the name, as children accept the name given by their parents, no matter how gross or disturbing or pedestrian the name might be.

Mr Smith – so be it.

Actually, he had a thing about names. He was obsessive about them. The names of his victims were burned into his mind and also into his heart.

First and foremost, there was Isabella Calais. Then came Stephanie Michaela Apt, Ursula Davies, Robert Michael Neel, and so many others.

He could recite the complete names backward and forward, as if they had been memorized for a history quiz or a bizarre round of Trivial Pursuit. That was the ticket – this chase was *trivial pursuit*, wasn't it?

So far, no one seemed to understand, no one got it. Not the fabled FBI. Not the storied Interpol, not Scotland Yard or any of the local police forces in the cities where he had committed murders.

No one understood the secret pattern of the victims, starting with Isabella Calais in Cambridge, Massachusetts, March 22, 1993, and continuing today in London.

The victim of the moment was Derek Cabott. He was a chief inspector – of all the hopelessly inane things to do with your life. He was 'hot' in London, having recently apprehended an IRA killer. His murder would electrify the town, drive everyone mad. Civilized and sophisticated London loved a gory murder as well as the next burg.

This afternoon Mr Smith was operating in the wealthy, fashionable Knightsbridge district. He was there *to study the human race* – at least that was the way the newspapers described it. The press in London and across Europe also called him by another name – *Alien*. The *prevailing* theory was that Smith was an extraterrestrial. *No human could do the things that he did*. Or so they said.

Mr Smith had to bend low to talk into Derek Cabott's ear, to be more intimate with his prey. He played music while he worked – all kinds of music.

Today's selection was the overture to *Don Giovanni*. Opera buffa felt right to him.

Opera felt right for this *live* autopsy.

'Ten minutes or so after your death,' Mr Smith said, 'flies will already have picked up the scent of gas accompanying the decomposition of your tissue. Green flies will lay the tiniest eggs within the orifices of your body. Ironically, the language reminds me of Dr Seuss – "green flies and ham." What could that mean? I don't know. It's a curious association, though.'

Derek Cabott had lost a lot of blood, but he wasn't giving up. He was a tall, rugged man with silver-blond hair. A never-say-never sort of chap. The inspector shook his head back and forth until Smith finally removed his gag.

'What is it, Derek?' he asked. 'Speak.'

'I have a wife and two children. Why are you doing this to me? Why me?' he whispered.

'Oh, let's say because you're Derek. Keep it simple and unsentimental. You, Derek, are a piece of the puzzle.'

He tugged the inspector's gag back into place. No more chitchat from Derek.

Mr Smith continued with his observations as he made his next surgical cuts and *Don Giovanni* played on.

'Near the time of death, breathing will become strained, intermittent. It's exactly what you're feeling now, as if each breath could be your last. Cessation will occur within two or three minutes,' whispered Mr Smith, whispered the dreaded *Alien*. 'Your life will end. May I be the first to congratulate you. I sincerely mean that, Derek. Believe it or not, *I envy you*. I wish I were Derek.'

PART ONE

TRAIN STATION MURDERS

CHAPTER 1

'I am the great Cornholio! Are you challenging me? I am Cornholio!' the kids chorused and giggled. Beavis and Butt-head strike again – in my neighborhood.

I bit my lip and decided to let it go. Why fight it? Why fan the fires of preadolescence?

Damon, Jannie, and I were crowded into the front seat of my old black Porsche. We needed to buy a new car, but none of us wanted to part with the Porsche. We were schooled in tradition, in the classics. We loved the old car, which we had named 'The Sardine Can' and 'Old Paintless.'

Actually, I was preoccupied at twenty to eight in the morning. Not a good way to start the day.

The night before, a thirteen-year-old girl from Ballou High School had been found in the Anacostia River. She had been shot, and then drowned. The gunshot had been to her mouth. What the coroners call a 'hole in one.'

A bizarre statistic was creating havoc with my stomach and central nervous system. *There were now more than a hundred unsolved murders of young, inner-city women committed in just the past three years.* No one had called for a major investigation. No one in power seemed to care about the dead black and Hispanic girls.

As we drove up in front of the Sojourner Truth School, I saw Christine Johnson welcoming kids and their parents as they arrived, reminding everyone that this was a community with good, caring people. She was certainly one of them.

I remembered the very first time we met. It was the previous fall and the circumstances couldn't have been any worse for either of us.

We had been thrown together – *smashed* together someone said to me once – at the homicide scene of a sweet baby girl named Shanelle Green. Christine was the principal of the school that Shanelle attended, and where I was now delivering my own kids. Jannie was new to the Truth School this semester. Damon was a grizzled veteran, a fourth grader.

'What are you mischief makers gawking at?' I turned to the kids, who were looking back and forth from my face to Christine's as if they were watching a championship tennis match.

'We're *gawking* at you, Daddy, and you're *gawking* at Christine!' Jannie said and laughed like the wicked child-witch of the North that she can be sometimes.

'She's Mrs Johnson to you,' I said as I gave Jannie my best squinting evil eye.

Jannie shrugged off my baleful look and frowned at me as only she can. 'I know that, Daddy. She's the *principal* of my school. I know exactly who she is.'

My daughter already understood many of life's important connections and mysteries. I was hoping that maybe someday she would explain them to me.

'Damon, do you have a point of view we should hear?' I asked. 'Anything you'd like to add? Care to share some good-fellowship and wit with us this morning?'

My son shook his head no, but he was smiling, too. He liked Christine Johnson just fine. Everybody did. Even Nana Mama approved, which is unheard of, and actually worried me some. Nana and I never seemed to agree about *anything*, and it's getting worse with age.

The kids were already climbing out of the car, and Jannie gave me a kiss goodbye. Christine waved and walked over.

'What a fine, upstanding father you are,' she said. Her brown eyes twinkled. 'You're going to make some lady in the neighborhood very happy one of these days. Very good with children, reasonably handsome, driving a classy sports car. My, my, my.'

'My, my, back at you,' I said. To top everything off, it was a beautiful morning in early June. Shimmering blue skies, temperature in the low seventies, the air crisp and relatively clean. Christine was wearing a soft beige suit with a blue shirt, and beige flat-heeled shoes. Be still my heart.

A smile slid across my face. There was no way to stop it, to hold it back, and besides I didn't want to. It fit with the fine day I was starting to have.

'I hope you're not teaching my kids that kind of cynicism and irony inside that fancy school of yours.'

'Of course I am, and so are all my teachers. We speak Educanto with the best of them. We're trained in cynicism, and we're all experts in irony. More important, we're excellent skeptics. I have to get inside now, so we don't miss a precious moment of indoctrination time.'

'It's too late for Damon and Jannie. I've already programmed them. A child is fed with milk and praise. They have the sunniest dispositions in the neighborhood, probably in all of Southeast, maybe in the entire city of Washington.'

'Oh we've noticed that, and we accept the challenge. Got to run. Young minds to shape and change.'

'I'll see you tonight?' I said as Christine was about to turn away and head toward the Sojourner Truth School.

'Handsome as sin, driving a nice Porsche, of course you'll see me tonight,' she said. Then she turned away and headed toward the school.

We were about to have our first 'official' date that night. Her husband, George, had died the previous winter, and now Christine felt she was ready to have dinner with me. I hadn't pushed her in any way, but I couldn't wait. Half-a-dozen years after the death of my wife, Maria, I felt as if I were coming out of a deep rut, maybe even a clinical depression. Life was looking as good as it had in a long, long time.

But as Nana Mama has often cautioned, 'Don't mistake the edge of a rut for the horizon.'

CHAPTER 2

A lex Cross is a dead man. Failure isn't an option.
Gary Soneji squinted through a telescopic sight he'd removed from a Browning automatic rifle. The scope was a rare beauty. He watched the oh-so-touching affair of the heart. He saw Alex Cross drop off his two brats and then chat with his pretty lady friend in front of the Sojourner Truth School.

Think the unthinkable, he prodded himself.

Soneji ground his front teeth as he scrunched low in the front seat of a black Jeep Cherokee. He watched Damon and Janelle scamper into the schoolyard, where they greeted their playmates with high and low fives. Years before he'd almost become famous for kidnapping two school brats right here in Washington. Those were the days, my friend! Those were the days.

For a while he'd been the dark star of television and

newspapers all over the country. Now it was going to happen again. He was sure that it was. After all, it was only fair that he be recognized as the best.

He let the aiming post of the rifle sight gently come to rest on Christine Johnson's forehead. *There, there, isn't that nice.*

She had very expressive brown eyes and a wide smile that seemed genuine from this distance. She was tall, attractive, and had a commanding presence. *The school principal.* A few loose hairs lay curled on her cheek. It was easy to see what Cross saw in her.

What a handsome couple they made, and what a tragedy this was going to be, what a damn shame. Even with all the wear and tear, Cross still looked good, impressive, a little like Muhammad Ali in his prime. His smile was dazzling.

As Christine Johnson walked away and headed towards the red-brick school building, Alex Cross suddenly glanced in the direction of Soneji's Jeep.

The tall detective seemed to be looking right into the driver's side of the windshield. Right into Soneji's eyes.

That was okay. Nothing to worry about, nothing to fear. He knew what he was doing. He wasn't taking any risks. Not here, not yet.

It was all set to start in a couple of minutes, but in his mind it had already happened. It had happened a hundred times. He knew every single move from this point until the end.

Gary Soneji started the Jeep and headed toward Union Station. The scene of the crime-to-be, the scene of his masterpiece theater.

'Think the unthinkable,' he muttered under his breath, 'then *do* the unthinkable.'

CHAPTER 3

After the last bell had rung and most of the kids were safe and sound in their classrooms, Christine Johnson took a slow walk down the long deserted corridors of the Sojourner Truth School. She did this almost every morning, and considered it one of her special treats to herself. You had to have treats sometimes, and this beat a trip to Starbucks for café latte.

The hallways were empty and pleasantly quiet – and always sparkling clean, as she felt a good school ought to be.

There had been a time when she and a few of her teachers had actually mopped the floors themselves, but now Mr Gomez and a porter named Lonnie Walker did it two nights a week, every week. Once you got good people thinking in the right way, it was amazing how many of them agreed a school should be clean and safe, and were willing to help. Once people believed the right thing could actually happen, it often did.

The corridor walls were covered with lively, colorful artwork by the kids, and everybody loved the hope and energy it produced. Christine glanced at the drawings and posters every morning, and it was always something different, another child's perspective, that caught her eye and delighted her inner person.

This particular morning, she paused to look at a simple yet dazzling crayon drawing of a little girl holding hands with her mommy and daddy in front of a new house. They all had round faces and happy smiles and a nice sense of purpose. She checked out a few illustrated stories: 'Our Community,' 'Nigeria,' 'Whaling.'

But she was out here walking for a different reason today. She was thinking about her husband, George, and how he died, and why. She wished she could bring him back and talk to him now. She wanted to hold George at least one more time. *Oh God, she needed to talk to him.*

She wandered to the far end of the hall to Room 111, which was light yellow and called *Buttercup*. The kids had named the rooms themselves, and the names changed every year in the fall. It was *their* school, after all.

Christine slowly and quietly opened the door a crack. She saw Bobbie Shaw, the second-grade teacher, scrubbing notes on the blackboard. Then she noticed row after row of mostly attentive faces, and among them Jannie Cross.

She found herself smiling as she watched Jannie, who happened to be talking to Ms Shaw. Jannie Cross was so animated and bright, and she had such a sweet perspective on the world. She was a lot like her father. *Smart, sensitive, handsome as sin.*

Christine eventually walked on. Preoccupied, she found herself climbing the concrete stairs to the second floor. Even the walls of the stairwells were decorated with projects and brightly colored artwork, which was part of the reason most of the kids believed that this was 'their school.' Once you understood something was 'yours,' you protected it, felt a part of it. It was a simple enough idea, but one that the government in Washington seemed not to get.

She felt a little silly, but she checked on Damon, too.

Of all the boys and girls at the Truth School, Damon was probably her favorite. He had been even before she met Alex. It wasn't just that Damon was bright, and verbal, and could be very charming – Damon was also a really good person. He showed it time and again with the other kids, with his teachers, and even when his little sister entered the school this past semester. He'd treated her like his best friend in the world – and maybe he already understood that *she was*.

Christine finally headed back to her office, where the usual ten-to-twelve-hour day awaited her. She was thinking about Alex now, and she supposed that was really why she had gone and looked in on his kids.

She was thinking that she wasn't looking forward to their dinner date tonight. She was afraid of tonight, a little panicky, and she thought she knew why.

CHAPTER 4

A t a little before eight in the morning, Gary Soneji strolled into Union Station, as if he owned the place. He felt tremendously good. His step quickened and his spirits seemed to rise to the height of the soaring train-station ceilings.

He knew everything there was to know about the famous train gateway for the capital. He had long admired the neoclassical façade that recalled the famed Baths of Caracalla in ancient Rome. He had studied the station's architecture for hours as a young boy. He had even visited the Great Train Store, which sold exquisite model trains and other railroad-themed souvenirs.

He could hear and feel the trains rattling down below. The marble floors actually shook as powerful Amtrak trains departed and arrived, mostly on schedule, too. The glass doors to the outside world *rumbled*, and he could hear the panes *clink* against their frames.

He loved this place, everything about it. It was truly magical. The key words for today were *train* and *cellar*, and only he understood why.

Information was power, and he had it all.

Gary Soneji thought that he might be dead within the next hour, but the idea, the image, didn't trouble him. Whatever happened was meant to, and besides, he definitely wanted to go out with a bang, not a cowardly whimper. Why the hell not? He had plans for a long and *exciting career after his death*.

Gary Soneji was wearing a lightweight black jumpsuit with a red Nike logo. He carried three bulky bags. He figured that he looked like just another yuppified traveler at the crowded train station. He appeared to be overweight and his hair was gray, for the time being. He was actually five foot ten, but the lifts in his shoes got him up to six-one today. He still had a trace of his former good looks. If somebody had wanted to guess his occupation, they might say *teacher*.

The cheap irony wasn't lost on him. He'd been a teacher once, one of the worst ever. He had been *Mr Soneji – the Spider Man*. He had kidnapped two of his own students.

He had already purchased his ticket for the Metroliner, but he didn't head for his train just yet.

Instead, Gary Soneji crossed the main lobby, hurrying away from the waiting room. He took a stairway next to the Center Café and climbed to the balcony on the second floor, which looked out on the lobby, about twenty feet below.

He gazed down and watched the lonely people streaming across the cavernous lobby. Most of these assholes had no idea how undeservedly lucky they were this particular morning. They would be safely on board their little commuter trains by the time the 'light and sound' show began in just a few minutes.

What a beautiful, beautiful place this is, Soneji thought. How many times he'd dreamed about this scene.

This very scene at Union Station!

Long streaks and spears of morning sunlight shafted down through delicate skylights. They reflected off the walls and the high gilded ceiling. The main hall before him held an information booth, a magnificent electronic train-arrival-and-departure board, the Center Café, Sfuzzi, and America restaurants.

The concourse led to a waiting area that had once been called 'the largest room in the world.' What a grand and historic venue he had chosen for today, his birthday.

Gary Soneji produced a small key from his pocket. He flipped it in the air and caught it. He opened a silver-gray metallic door that led into a room on the balcony.

He thought of it as *his room*. Finally, he had his own room – *upstairs* with everyone else. He closed the door behind him.

'Happy birthday, dear Gary, happy birthday to you.'

CHAPTER 5

This was going to be incredible, beyond anything he'd attempted so far. He could almost do this next part blindfolded, working from memory. He'd done the drill so many times. In his imagination, in his dreams. He had been looking forward to this day for more than twenty years.

He set up a folding aluminum tripod mount inside the small room, and positioned a Browning BAR on it. The rifle was a dandy, with a milspec scoping device and an electronic trigger he had customized himself.

The marble floors continued to shake as his beloved trains entered and departed the station, huge mythical beasts that came here to feed and rest. There was nowhere he'd rather be than here. He loved this moment so much.

Soneji knew everything about Union Station, and also about mass murders conducted in crowded public places. As a boy, he had obsessed on the so-called 'crimes of the century.' He had imagined himself committing such acts and becoming feared and famous. He planned perfect murders, random ones, and then he began to carry them out. He buried his first victim on a relative's farm when he was fifteen. The body still hadn't been found, not to this day.

He *was* Charles Starkweather; he *was* Bruno Richard Hauptmann; he *was* Charlie Whitman. Except that he was much smarter than any of them; and he wasn't crazy like them.

He had even appropriated a name for himself: Soneji, pronounced *Soh-nee-gee*. The name had seemed scary to him even at thirteen or fourteen. It still did. *Starkweather, Hauptmann, Whitman, Soneji.*

He had been shooting rifles since he was a boy in the deep, dark woods surrounding Princeton, New Jersey. During the past year, he'd done more shooting, more hunting, more practicing than ever before. He was primed and ready for this morning. Hell, he'd been ready for years.

Soneji sat on a metal folding chair and made himself as comfortable as he could. He pulled up a battleship-gray tarp that blended into the background of the train terminal's dark walls. He snuggled under the tarp. He was going to disappear, to be part of the scenery, *to be a sniper in a very public place. In Union Station!*

An old-fashioned-sounding train announcer was

singing out the track and time for the next Metroliner to Baltimore, Wilmington, Philadelphia, and New York's Penn Station.

Soneji smiled to himself – *that was his getaway train.*

He had his ticket, and he still planned to be on it. No problem, just book it. He'd be on the Metroliner, or bust. Nobody could stop him now, except maybe Alex Cross, and even that didn't matter anymore. His plan had contingencies for every possibility, even his own death.

Then Soneji was lost in his thoughts. His memories were his cocoon.

He had been nine years old when a student named Charles Whitman opened fire out of a tower at the University of Texas in Austin. Whitman was a former Marine, twenty-five years old. The outrageous, sensational event had galvanized him back then.

He'd collected every single story on the shootings, long pieces from *Time, Life, Newsweek,* the *New York Times,* the *Philadelphia Inquirer, The Times* of London, *Paris Match, Los Angeles Times, Baltimore Sun.* He still had the precious articles. They were at a friend's house, being held for posterity. They were *evidence – of past, present, and future crimes.*

Gary Soneji knew he was a good marksman. Not that he needed to be a crackerjack in this bustling crowd of targets. No shot he'd have to make in the train terminal would be over a hundred yards, and he was accurate at up to five hundred yards.

Now, I step out of my own nightmare and into the real

world, he thought as the moment crystallized. A cold, hard shiver ran through his body. It was delicious, tantalizing. He peered through the Browning's telescope at the busy, nervous, milling crowd.

He searched for the first victim. *Life was so much more beautiful and interesting through a target scope.*

CHAPTER 6

You are there.

He scanned the lobby with its thousands of hurrying commuters and summer vacation travelers. Not one of them had a clue about his or her mortal condition at that very moment. No one ever seemed to believe that something horrible could actually happen *to them*.

Soneji watched a lively brat-pack of students in bright blue blazers and starched white shirts. Preppies, goddamn preppies. They were giggling and running for their train with unnatural delight. He didn't like happy people at all, especially dumb-ass children who thought they had the world by the nuts.

He found that he could distinguish smells from up here: diesel fuel, lilacs and roses from the flower vendors, meat and garlic shrimp from the lobby's restaurants. The odors made him hungry.

The target circle in his customized scope had a

black site post rather than the more common bull's-eye. He preferred the post. He watched a montage of shapes and motion and colors swim in and out of death's way. This small circle of the Grim Reaper was his world now, self-contained and mesmerizing.

Soneji let the aiming post come to rest on the broad, wrinkled forehead of a weary-looking business-woman in her early- to mid-fifties. The woman was thin and nervous, with haggard eyes, pale lips. 'Say good-night, Gracie,' he whispered softly. 'Good-night, Irene. Good-night, Mrs Calabash.'

He almost pulled the trigger, almost started the morning's massacre, then he eased off at the last possible instant.

Not worthy of the first shot, he thought, chastising himself for impatience. *Not nearly special enough. Just a passing fancy. Just another middle-class cow.*

The aiming post settled in and held as if by a magnet on the lower spine of a porter pushing an uneven load of boxes and suitcases. The porter was a tall, good-looking black – *much like Alex Cross,* Soneji thought. His dark skin gleamed like mahogany furniture.

That was the attraction of the target. He liked the image, but who would get the subtle, special message other than himself? No, he had to think of others, too. This was a time to be selfless.

He moved the aiming post again, the circle of death. There was an amazing number of commuters in blue suits and black wing tips. Business sheep.

A father and teenage son floated into the circle, as if they had been put there by the hand of God.

Gary Soneji inhaled. Then he slowly exhaled. It was his shooting ritual, the one he'd practiced for so many years alone in the woods. *He had imagined doing this so many times. Taking out a perfect stranger, for no good reason.*

He gently, very gently, pulled the trigger toward the center of his eye.

His body was completely still, almost lifeless. He could feel the faint pulse in his arm, the pulse in his throat, the approximate speed of his heartbeat.

The shot made a loud cracking noise, and the sound seemed to follow the flight of the bullet down toward the lobby. Smoke spiraled upward, inches in front of the rifle barrel. Quite beautiful to observe.

The teenager's head exploded inside the telescopic circle. Beautiful. The head flew apart before his eyes. The Big Bang in miniature, no?

Then Gary Soneji pulled the trigger a second time. He murdered the father before he had a chance to grieve. He felt absolutely nothing for either of them. Not love, not hate, not pity. He didn't flinch, wince, or even blink.

There was no stopping Gary Soneji now, no turning back.

CHAPTER 7

Rush hour! Eight-twenty a.m. Jesus God Almighty, no! A madman was on the loose inside Union Station.

Sampson and I raced alongside the double lanes of stalled traffic that covered Massachusetts Avenue as far as the eye could see. *When in doubt, gallop*. The maxim of the old Foreign Legion.

Car and truck drivers honked their horns in frustration. Pedestrians were screaming, walking fast, or running away from the train station. Police squad cars were on the scene everywhere.

Up ahead on North Capitol I could see the massive, all-granite Union Station terminal with its many additions and renovations. Everything was somber and gray around the terminal except the grass, which seemed especially green.

Sampson and I flew past the new Thurgood Marshall Justice Building. We heard gunshots coming from the station. They sounded distant, muffled by the thick stone walls.

'It's for goddamn real,' Sampson said as he ran at my side. 'He's here. No doubt about it now.'

I knew he would be. An urgent call had come to my desk less than ten minutes earlier. I had picked up the phone, distracted by another message, a fax from Kyle Craig of the FBI. I was scanning Kyle's fax. He desperately needed help on his huge *Mr Smith* case. He wanted me to meet an agent, Thomas Pierce. I couldn't help Kyle this time. I was thinking of getting the hell out of the murder business, not taking on more cases, especially a serious bummer like *Mr Smith*.

I recognized the voice on the phone. 'It's Gary Soneji, Dr Cross. It really *is* me. I'm calling from Union Station. I'm just passing through D.C., and I hoped against hope that you'd like to see me again. Hurry, though. You'd better scoot if you don't want to miss me.'

Then the phone went dead. Soneji had hung up. He loved to be in control.

Now, Sampson and I were sprinting along Massachusetts Avenue. We were moving a whole lot faster than the traffic. I had abandoned my car at the corner of Third Street.

We both wore protective vests over our sport shirts. We were 'scooting,' as Soneji had advised me over the phone.

'What the hell is he doing in there?' Sampson said

through tightly gritted teeth. 'That son of a bitch has always been crazy.'

We were less than fifty yards from the terminal's glass and wood front doors. People continued to stream outside.

'He used to shoot guns as a boy,' I told Sampson. 'Used to kill pets in his neighborhood outside Princeton. He'd do sniper-kills from the woods. Nobody ever solved it at the time. He told me about the sniping when I interviewed him at Lorton Prison. Called himself the pet assassin.'

'Sounds like he graduated to people,' Sampson muttered.

We raced up the long driveway, heading toward the front entrance of the ninety-year-old terminal. Sampson and I were moving, burning up shoe leather, and it seemed like an eternity since Soneji's phone call.

There was a pause in the shooting – then it began again. Weird as hell. It definitely sounded like rifle reports coming from inside.

Cars and taxis in the train terminal's driveway were backing out, trying to get away from the scene of gunfire and madness. Commuters and day travelers were still pushing their way out of the building's front doors. I'd never been involved with a sniper situation before.

In the course of my life in Washington, I'd been inside Union Station several hundred times. Nothing like this, though. Nothing even close to this morning.

'He's got himself trapped in there. Purposely

trapped! Why the hell would he do that?' Sampson asked as we came up to the front doors.

'Worries me, too,' I said. Why had Gary Soneji called me? Why would he effectively trap himself in Union Station?

Sampson and I slipped into the lobby of Union Station. The shooting from the balcony – from up high somewhere – suddenly started up again. We both went down flat on the floor.

Had Soneji already seen us?

CHAPTER 8

I kept my head low as my eyes scanned the huge and portentous train-station lobby. I was desperately looking for Soneji. Could he see me? One of Nana's sayings was stuck in my head: *Death is nature's way of saying 'howdy.'*

Statues of Roman legionnaires stood guard all around the imposing main hall of Union Station. At one time, politically correct Pennsylvania Railroad execs had wanted the warriors fully clothed. The sculptor, Louis Saint-Gaudens, had managed to sneak by every third statue in its accurate historical condition.

I saw three people already down, probably dead, on the lobby floor. My stomach dropped. My heart beat even faster. One of the victims was a teenage boy in cutoff shorts and a Redskins practice jersey. A second victim appeared to be the father. Neither of them was moving.

Hundreds of travelers and terminal employees were trapped inside arcade shops and restaurants. Dozens of frightened people were squashed into a small Godiva Chocolates store and an open café called America.

The firing had stopped again. What was Soneji doing? And where was he? The temporary silence was maddening and spooky. There was supposed to be lots of noise here in the train terminal. Someone scraped a chair against the marble floor and the screeching sound echoed loudly.

I palmed my detective's badge at a uniformed patrolman who had barricaded himself behind an overturned café table. Sweat was pouring down the uniformed cop's face to the rolls of fat at his neck. He was only a few feet inside one of the doorways to the front lobby. He was breathing hard.

'You all right?' I asked as Sampson and I slid down behind the table. He nodded, grunted something, but I didn't believe him. His eyes were open wide with fear. I suspected he'd never been involved with a sniper either.

'Where's he firing from?' I asked the uniform. 'You seen him?'

'Hard to tell. But he's up in there somewhere, that general area.' He pointed to the south balcony that ran above the long line of doorways at the front of Union Station. Nobody was using the doors now. Soneji was in full control.

'Can't see him from down here,' Sampson snorted

at my side. 'He might be moving around, changing position. That's how a good sniper would work it.'

'Has he said anything? Made any announcements? Any demands?' I asked the patrolman.

'Nothing. He just started shooting people like he was having target practice. Four vics so far. Sucker can shoot.'

I couldn't see the fourth body. Maybe somebody, a father, mother, or friend, had pulled one of the victims in off the floor. I thought of my own family. Soneji had come to our house once. And he had called me here – invited me to his coming-out party at Union Station.

Suddenly, from up on the balcony above us, a rifle barked! The flat crack of the weapon echoed off the train station's thick walls. This was a shooting gallery with human targets.

A woman screamed inside the America restaurant. I saw her go down hard as if she'd slipped on ice. Then there were lots of moans from inside the café.

The firing stopped again. *What the hell was he doing up there?*

'Let's take him out before he goes off again,' I whispered to Sampson. 'Let's do it.'

CHAPTER 9

Our legs pumping in unison, our breath coming in harsh rasps, Sampson and I climbed a dark marble stairway to the overhanging balcony. Uniformed officers and a couple of detectives were crouched in shooting positions up there.

I saw a detective from the train-station detail, which is normally a small-crimes unit. Nothing like this, nothing even close to dealing with a sharp-shooting sniper.

'What do you know so far?' I asked. I thought the detective's name was Vincent Mazzeo, but I wasn't sure. He was pushing fifty and this was supposed to be a soft detail for him. I vaguely remembered that Mazzeo was supposed to be a pretty good guy.

'He's inside one of those anterooms. See that door over there? The space he secured has no roof cover. Maybe we can get at him from above. What do you think?'

I glanced up toward the high copper ceiling. I remembered that Union Station was supposed to be the largest covered colonnade in the United States. It sure looked it. Gary Soneji had always liked a big canvas. He had another one now.

The detective took something out of his shirt pocket. 'I got a master key. This gets us into some of the antechambers. Maybe the room he's in.'

I took the key. He wasn't going to use it. He wasn't going to play the hero. He didn't want to meet up with Gary Soneji and his sharpshooter's rifle this morning.

Another burst of gunfire suddenly came from in the anteroom.

I counted. There were six shots – just like the last time.

Like a lot of psychos, Soneji was into codes, magical words, numbers. I wondered about *sixes*. *Six, six, six*? The number hadn't come up in the past with him.

The shooting abruptly stopped again. Once more it was quiet in the station. My nerves were on edge, badly strained. There were too many people at risk here, too many to protect.

Sampson and I moved ahead. We were less than twenty feet from the anteroom where he was shooting. We pressed against the wall, Glocks out.

'You okay?' I whispered. We had been here before, similar bad situation, but that didn't make it any better.

'This is fun shit, huh, Alex? First thing in the morning,

too. Haven't even had my coffee and doughnut.'

'Next time he fires,' I said, 'we go get him. He's been firing six shots each time.'

'I noticed,' Sampson said without looking at me. He patted my leg. We took in big sips of air.

We didn't have to wait long. Soneji began another volley of shots. *Six shots. Why six shots each time?*

He knew we'd be coming for him. Hell, he'd invited me to his shooting spree.

'Here we go,' I said.

We ran across the marble-and-stone corridor. I took out the key to the anteroom, squeezed it between my index finger and thumb.

I turned the key.

Click!

The door wouldn't open! I jiggled the handle. Nothing.

'What the hell?' Sampson said behind me, anger in his voice. 'What's wrong with the door?'

'I just locked it,' I told him. *'Soneji left it open for us.'*

CHAPTER 10

Downstairs, a couple and two small children started to run. They rushed toward the glass doors and possible freedom. One of the kids tripped and went down hard on his knee. The mother dragged him forward. It was terrifying to watch, but they made it.

The firing started again!

Sampson and I burst into the anteroom, both of us crouched low, our guns drawn.

I caught a glimpse of a dark gray tarp straight ahead.

A sniper rifle pointed out from the cover and camouflage of the tarp. Soneji was underneath, hidden from view.

Sampson and I fired. Half-a-dozen gunshots thundered in the close quarters. Holes opened in the tarp. The rifle was silent.

I rushed across the small anteroom and ripped

away the tarp. I groaned – a deep, gut-wrenching sound.

No one was underneath the tarp. No Gary Soneji!

A Browning automatic rifle, spattered with blood, was strapped on a metal tripod. A timing device was attached to a rod and the trigger. The whole thing was customized. The rifle would fire at a programmed interval. Six shots, then a pause, then six more shots. No Gary Soneji.

I was already moving again. There were metal doors on the north and south walls of the small room. I yanked open the one closest to me. *I expected a trap.*

But the connecting space was empty. There was another gray metal door on the opposing wall. The door was shut. Gary Soneji still loved to play games. His favorite trick: He was the only one with the rules.

I rushed across the second room and opened door number two. Was that the game? A surprise? A booby-prize behind either door one, two, or three?

I found myself peering inside another small space, another empty chamber. No Soneji. Not a sign of him anywhere.

The room had a metal stairway – it looked as if it went to another floor. Or maybe a crawlspace above us.

I climbed the stairs, stopping and starting so he wouldn't get a clear shot from above. My heart was pounding, my legs trembling. I hoped that Sampson was close behind. I needed cover.

At the top of the stairway, a hatchway was open.

No Gary Soneji here either. I had been lured deeper and deeper into some kind of trap, into his web.

My stomach was rolling. I felt a sharp pain building up behind my eyes. Soneji was still somewhere in Union Station. He had to be. *He'd said he wanted to see me.*

CHAPTER 11

S oneji sat as calm as a small-town banker, pretending to read the *Washington Post* on the 8:45 a.m. Metroliner to Penn Station in New York. His heart was still palpitating, but none of the excitement showed on his face. He wore a gray suit, white shirt, striped blue tie – he looked just like all the rest of the commuter assholes.

He had just tripped the light fantastic, hadn't he? He had gone where few others ever would have dared. He had just outdone the legendary Charles Whitman, and this was only the beginning of his prime-time exposure. There was a saying he liked a lot. *Victory belongs to the player who makes the next-to-last mistake.*

Soneji drifted in and out of a reverie in which he returned to his beloved woods around Princeton, New Jersey. He could see himself as a boy again. He remembered everything about the dense, uneven, but often spectacularly beautiful terrain. When he was eleven, he had stolen a .22-caliber rifle from one of the surrounding farms. He kept it hidden in a rock quarry near his house. The gun was carefully wrapped in an oilcloth, foil, and burlap bags. The .22-caliber rifle was the only earthly possession that he cared about, the only thing that was truly his.

He remembered how he would scale down a steep, very rocky ravine to a quiet place where the forest floor leveled off, just past a thick tangle of bayberry prickers. There was a clearing in the hollow, and this was the site of his secret, forbidden target practice in those early years. One day he brought a rabbit's head and a calico cat from the nearby Ruocco farm. There wasn't much that a cat liked more than a fresh rabbit's head. Cats were such little ghouls. Cats were like him. To this day, they were magical for him. The way they stalked and hunted was the greatest. That was why he had given one to Dr Cross and his family.

Little Rosie.

After he had placed the severed bunny's head in the center of the clearing, he untied the neck of the burlap and let the kitty free. Even though he had punched a few airholes in the bag, the cat had almost suffocated. 'Sic 'em. Sic the bunny!' he commanded. The cat caught the scent of the fresh kill and took off in a pouncing run. Gary put the .22 rifle on his shoulder and watched. He sighted on the moving target. He caressed the trigger of his deuce-deuce, and then he fired. He was learning how to kill.

You're such an addict! He chastised himself now,
back in the present, on the Metroliner train. Little had
changed since he'd been the original Bad Boy in the
Princeton area. His stepmother – the gruesome and
untalented whore of Babylon – used to lock him in
the basement regularly back then. She would leave
him alone in the dark, sometimes for as long as ten to
twelve hours. He learned to love the darkness, to be
the darkness. He learned to love the cellar, to make it
his favorite place in the world.

Gary beat her at her own game.

*He lived in the underworld, his own private hell. He
truly believed he was the Prince of Darkness.*

Gary Soneji had to keep bringing himself back to
the present, back to Union Station and his beautiful
plan. The Metro police were searching the trains.

The police were outside right now! Alex Cross was
probably among them.

What a great start to things, and this was only the
beginning.

CHAPTER 12

He could see the police jackasses roaming the loading platforms at Union Station. They looked scared, lost and confused, and already half-beaten. That was good to know, valuable information. It set a tone for things to come.

He glanced toward a businesswoman sitting across the aisle. She looked frightened, too. Frozen. Stiff. White knuckles showing on her clenched hands. Shoulders thrown back like a military school cadet.

Soneji spoke to her. He was polite and gentle, the way he could be when he wanted to. 'I feel like this whole morning has to be a bad dream. When I was a boy, I used to go – *one, two, three, wake up!* I could bring myself out of a nightmare that way. It's sure not working today.'

The woman across the aisle nodded as if he'd said something profound. He'd made a connection with her. Gary had always been able to do that, reach out and touch somebody if he needed to. He figured he needed to now. It would look better if he was talking to a travel companion when the police came through the train car.

'One, two, three, wake up,' she said in a low voice across the aisle. 'God, I hope we're safe down here. I hope they've caught him by now. Whoever, *whatever* he is.'

'I'm sure they will,' Soneji said. 'Don't they always? Crazy people like that have a way of catching themselves.'

The woman nodded once, but didn't sound too convinced. 'They do, don't they. I'm sure you're right. I hope so. That's my prayer.'

Two D.C. police detectives were stepping inside the club car. Their faces were screwed tight. Now it would get interesting. He could see more cops approaching through the dining car, which was just one car ahead. There had to be hundreds of cops inside the terminal now. It was showtime. Act Two.

'I'm from Wilmington, Delaware. Wilmington's home.' Soneji kept talking to the woman. 'Otherwise I'd have left the station already. That's if they let us back upstairs.'

'They won't. I tried,' the woman told him. Her eyes were frozen, locked in an odd place. He loved that look. It was hard for Soneji to glance away, to focus on the approaching policemen and the threat they might present.

'We need to see identifications from everyone,' one

of the detectives was announcing. He had a deep, no-nonsense voice that got everybody's attention. 'Have IDs with pictures out when we come through. Thank you.'

The two detectives got to his row of seats. This was it, wasn't it? Funny, he didn't feel much of anything. He was ready to take both cops out.

Soneji controlled his breathing and also his heart-beat. *Control, that was the ticket.* He had control over the muscles in his face, and especially his eyes. He'd changed the color of his eyes for today. Changed his hair colour from blond to gray. Changed the shape of his face. He looked soft, bloated, as harmless as your average traveling salesman.

He showed a driver's license and Amex card in the name of Neil Stuart from Wilmington, Delaware. He also had a Visa card and a picture ID for the Sports Club in Wilmington. There was nothing memorable about the way he looked. Just another business sheep.

The detectives were checking his ID when Soneji spotted Alex Cross outside the train car. *Make my day.*

Cross was coming his way, and he was peering in through the windows at passengers. Cross was still looking pretty good. He was six three and well built. He carried himself like an athlete, and looked younger than forty-one.

Jesus, Jesus, Jesus, what a mindblower. Trip the god-damn light fantastic. I'm right here, Cross. You could almost touch me if you wanted to. Look in at me. Look at me, Cross. I command you to look at me now!

The tremendous anger and fury growing inside him was dangerous, Soneji knew. He could wait until Alex Cross was right on top of him, then pop up and put half-a-dozen shots into his face.

Six head shots. Each of the six would be well deserved for what Cross had done to him. Cross had ruined his life – no, Alex Cross had destroyed him. Cross was the reason all of this was happening now. Cross was to blame for the murders in the train station. It was all Alex Cross's fault.

Cross, Cross, Cross! Was this the end now? Was this the big finale? How could it be?

Cross looked so almighty as he walked, so above-the-fray. He had to give that to Cross, he was two or three inches taller than the other cops, smooth brown skin. *Sugar* – that's what his friend Sampson called him.

Well – he had a surprise for Sugar. Big unexpected surprise. Mindscrewer for the ages surprise.

If you catch me, Dr Cross – you catch yourself. Do you understand that? Don't worry – you will soon enough.

'Thank you, Mr Stuart,' said the detective as he handed Soneji back his credit card and the Delaware driver's license.

Soneji nodded and offered a thin smile to the detective, and then his eyes flicked back to the window.

Alex Cross was right there. *Don't look so humble, Cross. You're not that great.*

He wanted to start shooting now. He was in heat. He experienced something like hot flashes. He could do Alex Cross right now. There was no doubt about it. He hated that face, that walk, everything about the doctor-detective.

Alex Cross slowed his step. Then Cross looked right in at him. He was five feet away.

Gary Soneji slowly moved his eyes up to Cross, then very naturally over to the other detectives, then back to Cross.

Hello, Sugar.

Cross didn't recognize him. How could he? The detective looked right at his face – then he moved on. He kept on walking down the platform, picking up speed.

Cross had his back to him and it was an almost irresistibly inviting target. A detective up ahead was calling to him, motioning for Cross to come. He loved the idea of shooting Cross in the back. A cowardly murder, that was the best. That's what people really hated.

Then Soneji relaxed back into his train seat.

Cross didn't recognize me. I'm that good. I'm the best he's ever faced by far. I'll prove it, too.

Make no mistake about it. I will win.

I am going to murder Alex Cross and his family, and no one can stop it from happening.

CHAPTER 13

I t was past five-thirty in the evening before I even got to *think* about leaving Union Station. I'd been trapped inside all day, talking to witnesses, talking to Ballistics, the medical examiner, making rough sketches of the murder scene in my notepad. Sampson was pacing from about four o'clock on. I could see he was ready to blow out of there, but he was used to my thoroughness.

The FBI had arrived, and I'd gotten a call from Kyle Craig who had stayed down in Quantico working on Mr Smith. There was a mob of news reporters outside the terminal. How could it get any worse? I kept thinking, *the train has left the station*. It was one of those wordplays that gets in your head and won't leave.

I was bleary-eyed and bone-weary by day's end, but also as sad as I remembered being at a homicide scene. Of course this was no ordinary homicide scene.

I had put Soneji away, but somehow I felt responsible that he was out again.

Soneji was nothing if not methodical: He had wanted me at Union Station. Why, though? The answer to that question still wasn't apparent to me.

I finally snuck out of the station through the tunnels, to avoid the press and whatnot. I went home and showered and changed into fresh clothes.

That helped me a little. I lay on my bed and shut my eyes for ten minutes. I needed to clear my head of everything that had happened today.

It wasn't working worth a damn. I thought of calling off the night with Christine Johnson. A voice of warning was in my head. *Don't blow it. Don't scare her about The Job. She's the one*. I already sensed that Christine had problems with my work as a homicide detective. I couldn't blame her, especially not today.

Rosie the cat came in to visit. She cuddled against my chest. 'Cats are like Baptists,' I whispered to her. 'You know they raise hell, but you can't ever catch them at it.' Rosie purred agreement and chuckled to herself. We're friends like that.

When I finally came downstairs, I got 'the business' from my kids. Even Rosie joined in the fun, racing around the living room like the family's designated cheerleader.

'You look so nice, Daddy. You look *beautiful*.' Jannie winked and gave me the A-OK sign.

She was being sincere, but she was also getting a

large charge out of my 'date' for the night. She obviously delighted in the idea of my getting all dolled up just to see the principal from her school.

Damon was even worse. He saw me coming down the stairs and started giggling. Once he started, he couldn't stop. He mumbled, 'Beautiful.'

'I'll get you for this,' I told him. 'Ten times over, maybe a hundred times. Wait until you bring somebody home to meet your pops. Your day will come.'

'It's worth it,' Damon said, and continued to laugh like the little madman that he can be. His antics got Jannie going so bad that she was finally rolling around on the carpet. Rosie hopped back and forth over the two of them.

I got down on the floor, growled like Jabba the Hut, and started wrestling with the kids. As usual, they were healing me. I looked over at Nana Mama, who was standing in the doorway between the kitchen and dining room. She was strangely quiet, not joining in as she usually does.

'You want some of this, old woman?' I said as I held Damon and lightly rubbed my chin against his head.

'No, no. But you're sure nervous as Rosie tonight,' Nana said and finally started to laugh herself. 'Why, I haven't seen you like this since you were around fourteen and off to see Jeanne Allen, if I remember the name correctly. Jannie's right, though, you do look, let's say, rather dashing.'

I finally let Damon up off the floor. I stood and brushed off my snazzy dinner clothes. 'Well, I just want to thank all of you for being so supportive in my time of need.' I said it with false solemnity and a hurt look on my face.

'You're welcome!' they all chorused. 'Have a good time on your date! You look *beautiful!*'

I headed out to the car, refusing to look back and give them the satisfaction of one final taunting grin or another rousing huzzah. I did feel better, though, strangely revived.

I had promised my family, but also myself, that I was going to have some kind of normal life now. Not just a career, not a series of murder investigations. And yet as I drove away from the house, my last thought was, *Gary Soneji is out there again. What are you going to do about it?*

For starters, I was going to have a terrific, peaceful, exciting dinner with Christine Johnson.

I wasn't going to give Gary Soneji another thought for the rest of the night.

I was going to be *dashing,* if not downright *beautiful.*

CHAPTER 14

Kinkead's in Foggy Bottom is one of the best restaurants in Washington or anywhere else I've ever eaten. The food there might even be better than home, though I'd never tell Nana that. I was pulling out the stops tonight, trying to anyway, doing the best I could.

Christine and I had agreed to meet at the bar around seven. I arrived a couple of minutes before seven, and she walked in right behind me. Soul mates. So began the first date.

Hilton Felton was playing his usual seductive-as-hell jazz piano downstairs, as he did six nights a week. On the weekends, he was joined by Ephrain Woolfolk on bass. Bob Kinkead was in and out of the kitchen, garnishing and inspecting every dish. Everything seemed just right. Couldn't be better.

'This is a really terrific place. I've been wanting to come here for years,' Christine said as she looked around approvingly at the cherrywood bar, the sweeping staircase up to the main restaurant.

I had never seen her like this, all dressed up, and she was even more beautiful than I had thought. She had on a long black slip dress that showed off nicely toned shoulders. A cream-colored shawl fringed in black lace was draped over one arm. She wore a necklace made from an old-fashioned brooch that I liked a lot. She had on black flat-heeled pumps, but she was still nearly six feet tall. She smelled of flowers.

Her velvet-brown eyes were wide and sparkling with the kind of delight I suspected she saw in her children at school, but which was absent on the faces of most adults. Her smile was effortless. She seemed happy to be here.

I wanted to look like anything but a homicide detective, so I had picked out a black shirt given to me by Jannie for my birthday. She called it my 'cool guy shirt.' I also wore black slacks, a snazzy black leather belt, black loafers. I already knew that I looked 'beautiful.'

We were escorted to a cozy little booth in the mezzanine section. I usually try to keep 'physical allure' in its place, but heads turned as Christine and I walked across the dining room.

I'd completely forgotten what it was like to be out with someone and have that happen. I must admit that I sort of liked the feeling. I was remembering what it was like to be with someone you want to be with. I was also remembering what it was like to feel whole, or almost whole, or at least on the way to being whole again.

Our cozy booth overlooked Pennsylvania Avenue and also had a view of Hilton tinkering away at his piano. Kind of perfect.

'So how was your day?' Christine asked after we settled into the booth.

'Uneventful,' I said and shrugged. 'Just another day in the life of the D.C.P.D.'

Christine shrugged right back at me. 'I heard something on the radio about a shooting at Union Station. Weren't you involved just a little bit with Gary Soneji at one point in your illustrious career?'

'Sorry, I'm off-duty now,' I said to her. 'I love your dress, by the way.' *I also love that old brooch that you turned into a necklace. I like that you wore flats just in case I needed to be taller tonight, which I don't.*

'Thirty-one dollars,' she said and smiled shyly, wonderfully. The dress looked like a million on her. I thought so anyway.

I checked her eyes to see if she was all right. It had been more than six months since her husband's death, but that isn't really a lot of time. She seemed fine to me. I suspected she'd tell me if that changed.

We picked out a nice bottle of merlot. Then we shared Ipswich clams, which were full belly and a little messy, but a good start to dinner at Kinkead's. For a main dish, I had a velvety salmon stew.

Christine made an even better choice. Lobster with

buttery cabbage, bean purée and truffle oil.

All the while we ate, the two of us never shut up. Not for a minute. I hadn't felt so free and easy around someone in a long, long time.

'Damon and Jannie say you're the best principal ever. They paid me a dollar each to say that. What's your secret?' I asked Christine at one point. I found that I was fighting off an urge simply to babble when I was around her.

Christine was thoughtful for a moment before she answered. 'Well, I guess the easiest and maybe the truest answer is that it just makes me feel good to teach. The other answer I like goes something like this. If you're right-handed, it's really hard to write with your left hand. Well, most kids are *all left hand* at first. I try to always remember that. That's my secret.'

'Tell me about today at school,' I said, staring into her brown eyes, unable not to.

She was surprised by my question. 'You really want to hear about my day at school? Why?'

'I absolutely do. I don't even know why.' *Except that I love the sound of your voice. Love the way your mind works.*

'Actually, today was a great day,' she said, and her eyes lit up again. 'You sure you want to hear this, Alex? I don't want to bore you with work stuff.'

I nodded. 'I'm sure. I don't ask a whole lot of questions I don't want to hear the answers to.'

'Well then, I'll tell you about my day. Today, all the kids had to pretend they were in their seventies and eighties. The kids had to move a little more slowly than they're used to. They had to deal with infirmities, and being alone, and usually not being the center of attention. We call it *"getting under other people's skin,"* and we do it a lot at the Truth School. It's a great program and I had a great day, Alex. Thanks for asking. That's nice.'

Christine asked me about my day again, and I told her as little as possible. I didn't want to disturb her, and I didn't need to relive the day myself. We talked about jazz, and classical music, and Amy Tan's latest novel. She seemed to know about everything, and was surprised I had read *The Hundred Secret Senses*, and even more surprised that I liked it.

She talked about what it was like for her growing up in Southeast, and she told me a big secret of hers: She told me about 'Dumbo-Gumbo.'

'All through grade-school days,' Christine said, 'I was Dumbo-Gumbo. That's what some of the other kids called me. I have big ears, you see. Like Dumbo the flying elephant.'

She pulled back her hair. 'Look.'

'Very pretty,' I said to her.

She laughed. 'Don't blow your credibility. I *do* have big ears. And I do have this *big* smile, lots of teeth and *gums*.'

'So some smart-ass kid came up with Dumbo-Gumbo?'

'My brother, Dwight, did it to me. He also came up with "Gumbo Din." He still hasn't said he's sorry.'

'Well, I'm sorry for him. Your smile is dazzling, and your ears are just right.'

She laughed again. I loved to hear her laugh. I loved everything about her actually. I couldn't have been happier with our first night out.

CHAPTER 15

The time flew by like nothing at all. We talked about charter schools, a national curriculum, a Gordon Parks exhibit at the Corcoran Gallery of Art, lots of silly stuff, too. I would have guessed it was maybe nine-thirty when I happened to glance at my watch. It was actually ten to twelve.

'It's a school night,' Christine said. 'I have to go, Alex. I really do. My coach will turn into a pumpkin and all that.'

Her car was parked on Nineteenth Street and we walked there together. The streets were silent, empty, glittering under overhead lamps.

I felt as if I'd had a little too much to drink, but I knew I hadn't. I was feeling carefree, remembering what it was like to be that way.

'I'd like to do this again sometime. How about tomorrow night?' I said and started to smile. God, I liked the way this was going.

Suddenly, something was wrong. I saw a look I didn't like – sadness and concern. Christine peered into my eyes.

'I don't think so, Alex. I'm sorry,' she said. 'I'm really sorry. I thought I was ready, but I guess maybe I'm not. There's a saying – scars grow with us.'

I sucked in a breath. I wasn't expecting that. In fact, I don't remember ever having been so wrong about how I was getting along with someone. It was like a sudden punch to the chest.

'Thanks for taking me to just about the nicest restaurant I've ever been to. I'm really, really sorry. It's nothing that you did, Alex.'

Christine continued to look into my eyes. She seemed to be searching for something, and I guess not finding it.

She got into her car without saying another word. She seemed so efficient suddenly, so in control. She started it up and drove away. I stood in the empty street and watched until her car's blazing brake lights disappeared.

It's nothing that you did, Alex. I could hear her words repeating in my head.

CHAPTER 16

Bad Boy was back in Wilmington, Delaware. He had work to do here. In some ways, this might even be the best part.

Gary Soneji strolled the well-lit streets of Wilmington, seemingly without a care in the world. Why should he worry? He was skillful enough at makeup and disguises to fool the stiffs living here in Wilmington. He'd fooled them in Washington, hadn't he?

He stopped and stared at a huge, red-type-on-white poster near the train station. 'Wilmington – A Place To Be Somebody,' it read. What a terrific, unintentional joke, he thought.

So was a three-story mural of bloated whales and dolphins that looked as if it had been stolen from some beach town in Southern California. Somebody ought to hire the Wilmington town council to work on *Saturday Night Live*. They were good, real good.

He carried a duffel bag, but didn't draw any attention to himself. The people he saw on his little walk looked as if they had outfitted themselves from the pages of the Sears catalogue, circa 1961. Lots of twill that didn't exactly flatter girth; putrid-colored plaid; comfortable brown shoes on everybody.

He heard the grating mid-Atlantic accent a few times, too. 'I've got to phewn heum' ('I've got to phone home'). A plain and ugly dialect for plain and ugly thoughts.

Jesus, what a place to have lived. How the hell had he survived during those sterile years? Why had he bothered to come back now? Well, he knew the answer to that question. Soneji knew why he'd come back.

Revenge.

Payback time.

He turned off North Street and onto his old street, Central Avenue. He stopped across from a white-painted brick house. He stared at the house for a long time. It was a modest Colonial, two stories. It had belonged to Missy's grandparents originally, which was why she hadn't moved.

Click your heels together, Gary. Jesus, there's no place like home.

He opened his duffel bag and took out his weapon of choice. He was especially proud of this one. He'd been waiting for a long time to use it.

Gary Soneji finally crossed the street. He marched up to the front door as if he owned the place, just as

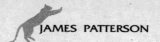

he had four years ago, the last time he'd been here, the day Alex Cross had barged into his life along with his partner, John Sampson.

The door was open – how sweet – his wife and daughter were waiting up for him, eating Poppycock and watching *Friends* on television.

'Hi. Remember me?' Soneji said in a soft voice.

They both started to scream.

His own sweet wife, Missy.

His darling little girl, Roni.

Screaming like strangers, because they knew him so well, and because they had seen his weapon.

CHAPTER 17

I f you ever began to face all the facts, you probably
wouldn't get up in the morning. The war room
inside police headquarters was filled beyond
capacity with ringing telephones, percolating computers, state-of-the-art surveillance equipment. I
wasn't fooled by all the activity or the noise. We were
still nowhere on the shootings.

First thing, I was asked to give a briefing on Soneji.
I was supposed to know him better than anyone else,
yet somehow I felt that I didn't know enough, especially now. We had what's called a roundtable. Over
the course of an hour, I shorthanded the details of his
kidnapping of two children a few years earlier in
Georgetown, his eventual capture, the dozens of
interviews we'd had at Lorton Prison prior to his
escape.

Once everybody on the task force was up to speed,
I got back to work myself. I needed to find out who

Soneji was, who he really was; and why he had decided to come back now; why he had returned to Washington.

I worked through lunch and never noticed the time. It took that long just to retrieve the mountain of data we had collected on Soneji. Around two in the afternoon, I found myself painfully aware of *pushpins* on the Big Board, where we were collecting 'important' information.

A war room just isn't a war room without pushpin maps and a large bulletin board. At the very top of our board was the name that had been given to the case by the chief of detectives. He had chosen 'Web,' since Soneji had already picked up the nickname 'Spider' in police circles. Actually, I'd coined the nickname. It came out of the complex webs he was always able to spin.

One section of the Big Board was devoted to 'civilian leads.' These were mostly reliable eyewitness accounts from the previous morning at Union Station. Another section was 'police leads,' most of which were the detectives' reports from the train terminal.

Civilian leads are 'untrained eye' reports; police leads are 'trained eye.' The thread in all of the reports so far was that no one had a good description of what Gary Soneji looked like now. Since Soneji had demonstrated unusual skill with disguises in the past, the news wasn't surprising, but it was disturbing to all of us.

Soneji's personal history was displayed on another

part of the board. A long, curling computer printout listed every jurisdiction where he had ever been charged with a crime, including several unsolved homicides from his early years in Princeton, New Jersey.

Polaroid pictures depicting the evidence we had so far were also pinned up. Captions had been written in marker on the photos. The captions read: 'known skills, Gary Soneji'; 'hiding locations, Gary Soneji'; 'physical characteristics, Gary Soneji'; 'preferred weapons, Gary Soneji.'

There was a category for 'known associates' on the board, but this was still bare. It was likely to remain that way. To my knowledge, Soneji had always worked alone. *Was that assumption still accurate?* I wondered. Had he changed since our last run-in?

Around six-thirty that night, I got a call from the FBI evidence labs in Quantico, Virginia. Curtis Waddle was a friend of mine, and knew how I felt about Soneji. He had promised he'd pass on information as fast as he got it himself.

'You sitting down, Alex? Or you pacing around with one of those insipid, state-of-the-artless cordless phones in your hand?' he asked.

'I'm pacing, Curtis. But I'm carrying around an old-fashioned phone. It's even black. Alexander Graham Bell himself would approve.'

The lab head laughed and I could picture his broad, freckled face, his frizzy red hair tied with a rubber-band in a ponytail. Curtis loves to talk, and I've found

you have to let him go on or he gets hurt and can even get a little spiteful.

'Good man, good man. Listen, Alex, I've got something here, but I don't think you're going to like it. I don't like it. I'm not even sure if we trust what we have.'

I edged in a few words. 'Uh, what do you have, Curtis?'

'The blood on the stock and barrel of the rifle at Union Station? We've got a definite match on it. Though, as I said, I don't know if I trust what we have. Kyle agrees. Guess what? It's not Soneji's blood.'

Curtis was right. I didn't like hearing that at all. I hate surprises in any murder investigation. 'What the hell does that mean? Whose blood is it then, Curtis? You know yet?'

I could hear him sigh, then blow out air in a *whoosh*. 'Alex, it's *yours*. Your blood was on the sniper rifle.'

PART TWO

MONSTER HUNT

CHAPTER 18

I t was rush hour in Penn Station in New York City when Soneji arrived. He was on time, right on schedule, for the next act. *Man, he had lived this exact moment a thousand times over before today.*

Legions of pathetic burnouts were on the way home, where they would drop onto their pillows (no goose down for these hard cases), sleep for what would seem like an instant, and then get back up the following morning and head for the trains again. Jesus – and they said *he* was crazy!

This was absolutely, positively, the best – he'd been dreaming of this moment for more than twenty years. *This very moment!*

He had planned to get to New York between five and five-thirty – and here he was. Heeere's Gary! He'd imagined himself, *saw* himself, coming up out of the deep dark tunnels at Penn Station. He knew he was going to be out-of-his-head furious when he got upstairs, too. Knew it before he began to hear the piped-in circus music, some totally insane John Philip Sousa marching band ditty, with an overlay of tinny-sounding train announcements.

'You may now board through Gate A to Track 8, Bay Head Junction,' a fatherly voice proclaimed to the clueless.

All aboard to Bay Head Junction. All aboard, you pathetic morons, you freaking robots!

He checked out a poor moke porter who wore a dazed, flat look, as if life had left him behind about thirty years ago.

'You just can't keep a bad man down,' Soneji said to the passing redcap. 'You dig? You hear what I'm saying?'

'Fuck off,' the redcap said. Gary Soneji snorted out a laugh. Man, he got such a kick out of the surly downtrodden. They were everywhere, like a league these days.

He stared at the surly redcap. He decided to punish him – to let him live.

Today's not your day to die. Your name stays in the Book of Life. Keep on walking.

He was furious – just as he knew he would be. He was seeing red. The blood rushing through his brain made a deafening, pounding sound. Not nice. Not conducive to sane, rational thought. *The blood? Had the bloodhounds figured it out yet?*

The train station was filled to the gills with shoving, pushing, and grumbling New Yorkers at their worst.

These goddamn commuters were unbelievably aggressive and irritating.

Couldn't any of them see that? Well hell, sure they could. And what did they do about it? They got even more aggressive and obnoxious.

None of them came close to approaching his own seething anger, though. Not even close. His hatred was pure. Distilled. He *was* anger. He did the things most of them only fantasized about. Their anger was fuzzy and unfocused, bursting in their bubbleheads. He saw anger clearly, and he acted upon it swiftly.

This was so fine, being inside Penn Station, creating another scene. He was really getting into the spirit now. He was noticing everything in full-blast, touchy-feely 3-D. Dunkin' Donuts, Knot Just Pretzels, Shoetrician Shoe Shine. The omnipresent rumble of the trains down below – it was just as he'd always imagined it.

He knew what would come next – and how it would all end.

Gary Soneji had a six-inch knife pressed against his leg. It was a real collector's item. Had a mother-of-pearl handle and a tight serpentine blade on both sides. 'An ornate knife for an ornate individual,' a greasy salesman had told him once upon a long time ago. 'Wrap it up!' he'd said. Had it ever since. For special occasions like today. Or once to kill an FBI agent named Roger Graham.

He passed Hudson News, with all of its glossy magazine faces staring out at the world, staring at

him, trying to work their propaganda. He was still being shoved and elbowed by his fellow commuters. Man, didn't they ever stop?

Wow! He saw a character from his dreams, from way back when he was a kid. There was *the guy*. No doubt about it. He recognized the face, the way the guy held his body, everything about him. *It was the guy in the gray-striped business getup, the one who reminded him of his father*.

'You've been asking for this for a long time!' Soneji growled at Mr Gray Stripes. 'You asked for this.'

He drove the knife blade forward, felt it sink into flesh. It was just as he had imagined it.

The businessman saw the knife plunge near his heart. A frightened, bewildered look crossed his face. Then he fell to the station floor, stone cold dead, his eyes rolled back and his mouth frozen in a silent scream.

Soneji knew what he had to do next. He pivoted, danced to his left, and cut a second victim who looked like a slacker type. The guy wore a 'Naked Lacrosse' T-shirt. The details didn't matter, but some of them stuck in his mind. He cut a black man selling *Street News*. Three for three.

The thing that really mattered was *the blood*. Soneji watched as the precious blood spilled onto the dirty, stained, and mottled concrete floor. It spattered the clothes of commuters, pooled under the bodies. The blood was a clue, a Rorschach test for the police and FBI hunters to analyze. The blood was there for Alex

Cross to try and figure out.

Gary Soneji dropped his knife. There was incredible confusion, shrieking everywhere, panic in Penn Station that finally woke the walking dead.

He looked up at the maze of maroon signs, each with neat Helvetic lettering: *Exit 31st St., Parcel Checking, Visitor Information, Eighth Avenue Subway*.

He knew the way out of Penn Station. It was all preordained. He had made this decision a thousand times before.

He scurried back down into the tunnels again. No one tried to stop him. He was the Bad Boy again. Maybe his stepmother had been right about that. His *punishment* would be to ride the New York subways.

Brrrr. Scar-ry!

CHAPTER 19

Seven that evening. I was caught in the strangest, most powerful epiphany. I felt that I was outside myself, *watching myself*. I was driving by the Sojourner Truth School, on my way home. I saw Christine Johnson's car and stopped.

I got out of my car and waited for her. I felt incredibly vulnerable. A little foolish. I hadn't expected Christine to be at the school this late.

At quarter past seven, she finally wandered out of the school. I couldn't catch my breath from the instant I spotted her. I felt like a schoolboy. Maybe that was all right, maybe it was good. At least I was feeling again.

She looked as fresh and attractive as if she'd just arrived at the school. She had on a yellow-and-blue-flowered dress cinched around her narrow waist. She wore blue sling-back heels and carried a blue bag over one shoulder. The theme song from *Waiting to*

Exhale floated into my head. I was waiting, all right.

Christine saw me, and she immediately looked troubled. She kept on walking, as if she were in a hurry to be somewhere else, anywhere else but here.

Her arms were crossed across her chest. *A bad sign,* I thought. The worst possible body language. Protective and fearful. One thing was clear already: Christine Johnson didn't want to see me.

I knew I shouldn't have come, shouldn't have stopped, but I couldn't help myself. I needed to understand what had happened when we left Kinkead's. Just that, nothing more. A simple, honest explanation, even if it hurt.

I sucked in a deep breath and walked up to her. 'Hi,' I said, 'you want to take a walk? It's a nice night.' I almost couldn't speak, and I am never at a loss for words.

'Taking a break in one of your usual twenty-hour workdays?' Christine half-smiled, tried to anyway.

I returned the smile, felt queasy all over. I shook my head. 'I'm off work.'

'I see. Sure, we can walk a little bit, a few minutes. It is a nice night, you're right.'

We turned down F Street and entered Garfield Park, which was especially pretty in the early summer. We walked in silence. Finally, we stopped near a ballfield swarming with little kids. A frenzied baseball game was in progress.

We weren't far from the Eisenhower Freeway and the *whoosh* of rush-hour traffic was steady, almost soothing. Tulip poplars were in bloom, and there was coral honeysuckle. Mothers and fathers were playing with their kids; everybody in a nice mood tonight.

This had been my neighborhood park for almost thirty years, and during the daylight hours it can almost be idyllic. Maria and I used to come here all the time when Damon was a toddler and she was pregnant with Jannie. Much of that is starting to fade away now, which is probably a good thing, but it's also sad.

Christine finally spoke. 'I'm sorry, Alex.' She had been staring at the ground, but now she raised her lovely eyes to mine. 'About the other night. The bad scene at my car. I guess I panicked. To be honest, I'm not even sure what happened.'

'Let's be honest,' I said. 'Why not?'

I could tell this was hard for her, but I needed to know how she felt. I needed more than she'd told me outside the restaurant.

'I want to try and explain,' she said. Her hands were clenched. One of her feet was tapping rapidly. Lots of bad signs.

'Maybe it's all my fault,' I said. 'I'm the one who kept asking you to dinner until—'

Christine reached out and covered my hand with hers. 'Please let me finish,' she said. The half-smile came again. 'Let me try to get this out once and for all. I was going to call you anyway. I was planning to call you tonight. I would have.

'You're nervous now, and so am I. God, am I nervous,' she said quietly. 'I know I've hurt your feelings, and I don't like that. It's the last thing I meant to do. You don't deserve to be hurt.'

Christine was shivering a little. Her voice was shaking, too, as she spoke. 'Alex, my husband died because of the kind of violence you have to live with every day. You accept that world, but I don't think I can. I'm just not that kind of person. I couldn't bear to lose someone else I was close to. Am I making sense to you? I'm feeling a little confused.'

Everything was becoming clearer to me now. Christine's husband had been killed in December. She said that there had been serious problems in the marriage, but she loved him. She had seen him shot to death in their home, seen him die. I had held her then. I was part of the murder case.

I wanted to hold her again, but I knew it was the wrong thing to do. She was still hugging herself tightly. I understood her feelings.

'Please listen to me, Christine. I'm not going to die until probably in my late eighties. I'm too stubborn and ornery to die. That would give us longer together than either of us has been alive so far. Forty-plus years. It's also a long time to avoid each other.'

Christine shook her head a little. She continued to look into my eyes. Finally, a smile peeked through.

'I *do* like the way your crazy mind works. One minute, you're Detective Cross – the next minute you're this very open, very sweet child.' She put her hands up to her face. 'Oh, God, I don't even know what I'm *saying*.'

Everything inside me said to do it, every instinct, every feeling. I slowly, carefully, reached out and took Christine into my arms. She fit so right. I could feel myself melting and I liked it. I even liked that my legs felt shaky and weak.

We kissed for the first time and Christine's mouth was soft and very sweet. Her lips pushed against mine. She didn't pull away, as I'd expected she might. I ran the tips of my fingers along one cheek, then the other.

Her skin was smooth and my fingers tingled at the tips. It was as if I had been without air for a long, long time and suddenly could breathe again. I could breathe. I felt alive.

Christine had shut her eyes, but now she opened them. Our eyes met, and held. 'Just like I imagined it,' she whispered, 'times about four hundred and fifty.'

Then the worst thing imaginable happened – my pager *beeped*.

CHAPTER 20

At six o'clock in New York City, police cruisers and EMS van sirens were wailing everywhere in the always highly congested five-block radius around Penn Station. Detective Manning Goldman parked his dark-blue Ford Taurus in front of the post office building on Eighth Avenue and ran toward the multiple-murder scene.

People stopped walking on the busy avenue to watch Goldman. Heads turned everywhere, trying to find out what was going on, and how this running man might fit in.

Goldman had long, wavy caramel-and-gray hair and a gray goatee. A gold stud glinted from one earlobe. Goldman looked more like an aging rock or jazz musician than a homicide detective.

Goldman's partner was a first-year detective named Carmine Groza. Groza had a strong build and wavy black hair, and reminded people of a young

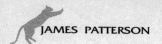

Sylvester Stallone, a comparison he hated. Goldman rarely talked to him. In his opinion, Groza had never uttered a single word worth listening to.

Groza nonetheless followed close behind his fifty-eight-year-old partner, who was currently the oldest Manhattan homicide detective working the streets, possibly the smartest, and definitely the meanest, grumpiest bastard Groza had ever met.

Goldman was known to be somewhere to the right of Pat Buchanan and Rush Limbaugh when it came to politics but, like most rumors, or what he called 'caricature assassinations,' this one was off the mark. On certain issues – the apprehension of criminals, the rights of criminals versus the rights of other citizens, and the death penalty – Goldman was definitely a radical conservative. He knew that anyone with half a brain who worked homicide for a couple of hours would come to exactly the same conclusions that he had. On the other hand, when it came to a woman's right to choose, same-sex marriages, or even Howard Stern, Goldman was as liberal as his thirty-year-old son, who just happened to be a lawyer with the ACLU. Of course, Goldman kept that to himself. The last thing he wanted was to ruin his reputation as an insufferable bastard. If he did that, he might have to talk to up-and-coming young assholes like 'Sly' Groza.

Goldman was still in good shape – better than Groza, with his steady diet of fast foods and high-octane colas and sugary teas. He ran against the tide of people streaming out of Penn Station. The murders, at least the ones he knew about so far, had taken place in and around the main waiting area of the train station.

The killer had chosen the rush hour for a reason, Goldman was thinking as the train-station waiting area came into view. Either that, or the killer just happened to go wacko at a time when the station was jam-packed with victims-to-be.

So what brought the wacko to Penn Station at rush hour? Manning Goldman wondered. He already had one scary theory that he was keeping to himself so far.

'Manning, you think he's still in here someplace?' Groza asked from behind.

Groza's habit of calling everybody by their first names, as if they were camp counselors together, really got under his skin.

Goldman ignored his partner. No, he didn't believe the killer was still in Penn Station. The killer was on the loose in New York. That bothered the hell out of him. It made him sick to his stomach, which wasn't all that hard these days, the past couple of years, actually.

Two pushcart vendors were artfully blocking the way to the crime scene. One cart was called Montego City Slickers Leather, the other From Russia With Love. He wished they would go back to Jamaica and Russia, respectively.

'NYPD. Make way. Move these ashcarts!' Goldman yelled at the vendors.

He pushed his way through the crowd of onlookers, other cops, and train-station personnel who were gathered near the body of a black man with braided hair and tattered clothing. Bloodstained copies of *Street News* were scattered around the body, so Goldman knew the dead man's occupation and his reason for being at the train station.

As he got up close, he saw that the victim was probably in his late twenties. There was an unusual amount of blood. Too much. The body was surrounded by a bright-red pool.

Goldman walked up to a man in a dark-blue suit with a blue-and-red Amtrak pin prominent on his lapel.

'Homicide Detective Goldman,' he said, flashing his shield. 'Tracks ten and eleven.' Goldman pointed at one of the overhead signs. 'What train would have come in on those tracks – just before the killings?'

The Amtrak manager consulted a thick booklet he kept in his breast pocket.

'The last train on ten . . . that would have been the Metroliner from Philly, Wilmington, Baltimore, originating in Washington.'

Goldman nodded. It was exactly what he'd been afraid of when he'd heard that a spree killer had struck at the train station, and that he was able to get away. That fact meant he was clearheaded. The killer had a plan in mind.

Goldman suspected that the Union Station and Penn Station killers might be one and the same – and that now the maniac was here in New York.

'You got any idea yet, Manning?' Groza was yapping again.

Goldman finally spoke to his partner without looking at him. 'Yeah, I was just thinking that they've got earplugs, bunghole plugs, so why not *mouth* plugs.'

Then Manning Goldman went to scare up a public phone. He had to make a call to Washington, D.C. He believed that Gary Soneji had come to New York. Maybe he was on some kind of twenty- or thirty-city spree killer tour.

Anything was a possibility these days.

CHAPTER 21

I answered my pager and it was disturbing news from the NYPD. There had been another attack at a crowded train station. It kept me at work until well past midnight.

Gary Soneji was probably in New York City. Unless he had already moved on to another city he'd targeted for murder. Boston? Chicago? Philadelphia?

When I got home, the lights were off. I found lemon meringue pie in the refrigerator and finished it off. Nana had a story about Oseola McCarty attached to the fridge door. Oseola had washed clothes for more than fifty years in Hattiesburg, Mississippi. She had saved one hundred and fifty thousand dollars and donated it to the University of Southern Mississippi. President Clinton had invited her to Washington and given her the Presidential Citizen's Medal.

The pie was excellent, but I needed something

else, another kind of nourishment. I went to see my shaman.

'You awake, old woman?' I whispered at Nana's bedroom door. She always keeps it ajar in case the kids need to talk or cuddle with her during the night. *Open twenty-four hours, just like 7-Eleven*, she always says. It was like that when I was growing up, too.

'That depends on your intentions,' I heard her voice in the dark. 'Oh, *is that you, Alex?*' she cackled and had a little coughing spell.

'Who else would it be? You tell me that? In the middle of the night at your bedroom door?'

'It could be anyone. Hugger-mugger. Housebreaker in this dangerous neighborhood of ours. Or one of my gentlemen admirers.'

It goes like that between us. Always has, always will.

'You have any particular boyfriends you want to tell me about?'

Nana cackled again. 'No, but I suspect you have a girlfriend you want to talk to me about. Let me get decent. Put on some water for my tea. There's lemon meringue pie in the fridge, at least there *was* pie. You *do* know that I have gentlemen admirers, Alex?'

'I'll put on the tea,' I said. 'The lemon meringue has already gone to pie heaven.'

A few minutes passed before Nana appeared in the kitchen. She was wearing the cutest housedress, blue stripes with big white buttons down the front. She looked as if she were ready to begin her day at half past twelve in the morning.

'I have two words for you, Alex. Marry her.'

I rolled my eyes. 'It's not what you think, old woman. It's not that simple.'

She poured some steaming tea for herself. 'Oh, it is absolutely that simple, granny son. You've got that spring in your step lately, a nice gleam in your eyes. You're *long gone*, mister. You're just the last one to hear about it. Tell me something. This is a serious question.'

I sighed. 'You're still a little high from your sweet dreams. What? Ask your silly question.'

'Well, it's this. If I was to charge you, say, ninety dollars for our sessions, *then* would you be more likely to take my fantastic advice?'

We both laughed at her sly joke, her unique brand of humor.

'Christine doesn't want to see me.'

'Oh, dear,' Nana said.

'Yeah, oh, dear. She can't see herself involved with a homicide detective.'

Nana smiled. 'The more I hear about Christine Johnson, the more I like her. Smart lady. Good head on those pretty shoulders.'

'Are you going to let me talk?' I asked.

Nana frowned and gave me her serious look. 'You always get to say what you want, just not at the exact moment you want to say it. Do you love this woman?'

'From the first time I saw her, I felt something extraordinary. Heart leads head. I know that sounds crazy.'

She shook her head and still managed to sip steaming hot tea. 'Alex, as smart as you are, you sometimes seem to get everything backwards. You don't sound crazy at all. You sound like you're better for the first time since Maria died. Will you look at the evidence that we have here? You have a spring back in your step again. Your eyes are bright and smiling. You're even being nice to me lately. Put it all together – your heart is working again.'

'She's afraid that I could die on the job. Her husband was murdered, remember?'

Nana rose from her chair at the kitchen table. She shuffled around to my side, and she stood very close to me. She was so much smaller than she used to be, and that worried me. I couldn't imagine my life without her in it.

'I love you, Alex,' she said. 'Whatever you do, I'll still love you. *Marry her*. At least live with Christine.' She laughed to herself. 'I can't believe I said that.'

Nana gave me a kiss, and then headed back to bed.

'I *do too* have suitors,' she called from the hall.

'Marry one,' I called back at her.

'I'm not in love, lemon meringue man. You are.'

CHAPTER 22

First thing in the morning, six-thirty-five to be exact, Sampson and I took the Metroliner to New York's Penn Station. It was almost as fast as driving to the airport, parking, finagling with the airlines – and besides, I wanted to do some thinking about *trains*.

A theory that Soneji was the Penn Station slasher had been advanced by the NYPD. I'd have to know more about the killings in New York, but it was the kind of high-profile situation that Soneji had been drawn to in the past.

The train ride was quiet and comfortable, and I had the opportunity to think about Soneji for much of the trip. What I couldn't reconcile was why Soneji was committing crimes that appeared to be acts of desperation. They seemed suicidal to me.

I had interviewed Soneji dozens of times after I had apprehended him a few years ago. That was the

Dunne-Goldberg case. I certainly didn't believe he was suicidal then. He was too much of an egomaniac, even a megalomaniac.

Maybe these were copycat crimes. *Whatever* he was doing now didn't track. *What had changed? Was it Soneji who was doing the killings? Was he pulling some kind of trick or stunt? Could this be a clever trap? How in hell had he gotten my blood on the sniper's rifle in Union Station?*

What kind of trap? For what reason? Soneji obsessed on his crimes. Everything had a purpose with him.

So why kill strangers in Union and Penn Stations? Why choose railroad stations?

'Oh ho, smoke's curling out of your forehead, Sugar. You aware of that?' Sampson looked over at me and made an announcement to the nice folks seated around us in the train car.

'Little wisps of white smoke! See? Right *here*. And *here*.'

He leaned in close and started hitting me with his newspaper as if he were trying to put out a small fire.

Sampson usually favors a cool deadpan delivery to slapstick. The change of pace was effective. We both started to laugh. Even the people sitting around us smiled, looking up from their newspapers, coffees, laptop computers.

'Phew. Fire seems to be out,' Sampson said and chuckled deeply. 'Man, your head is *hot* as Hades to the touch. You must have been brainstorming some powerful ideas. Am I right about that?'

'No, I was thinking about Christine,' I told Sampson.

'You lying sack. You *should* have been thinking about Christine Johnson. Then I would have had to beat the fire out someplace else. How you two doing? If I might be so bold as to ask?'

'She's great, she's the best, John. Really something else. She's smart and she's funny. Ho ho, ha ha.'

'And she's almost as good-looking as Whitney Houston, and she's sexy as hell. But none of that answers my question. What's happening with you two? You trying to hide your love on me? My spy, Ms Jannie, told me you had a date the other night. Did you have a big date and not tell me about it?'

'We went to Kinkead's for dinner. Had a good time. Good food, great company. One little minor problem, though: She's afraid I'm going to get myself killed, so she doesn't want to see me anymore. Christine's still mourning her husband.'

Sampson nodded, slid down his shades to check me out sans light filtration. 'That's interesting. Still mourning, huh? Proves she's a good lady. By the by, since you brought up the forbidden topic, something I should tell you, all-star. You ever get capped in action, your family will mourn you for an indecent length of time. Myself, I would carry the torch of grief up to and through the funeral service. That's it, though. Thought you should know. So, are you two star-crossed lovers going to have another date?'

Sampson liked to talk as if we were girlfriends in a Terry McMillan novel. We could be like that sometimes, which is unusual for men, especially two tough guys like us. He was on a roll now. 'I think you two are so cute together. Everybody does. Whole town is talking. The kids, Nana, your aunties.'

'They are, are they?'

I got up and sat down across the aisle from him. Both seats were empty. I spread out my notes on Gary Soneji and started to read them again.

'Thought you would never get the hint,' Sampson said as he stretched his wide body across both seats.

As always, there was nothing like working a job with him. Christine was wrong about my ever getting hurt. Sampson and I were going to live forever. We wouldn't even need DHEA or melatonin to help.

'We're going to get Gary Soneji's ass in a sling. Christine's going to fall hard for you, like you obviously already fell for her. Everything will be beautiful, Sugar. Way it has to be.'

I don't know why, but I couldn't quite make myself believe that.

'I know you're thinking negative shit already,' Sampson said without even looking over at me, 'but just watch. Nothing but happy endings this time.'

CHAPTER 23

Sampson and I arrived in New York City around nine o'clock in the morning. I vividly remembered an old Stevie Wonder tune about getting off the bus in New York for the first time. The mixture of hopes and fears and expectations most people associate with the city seems a universal reaction.

As we climbed the steep stone steps from the underground tracks in Penn Station, I had an insight about the case. If it was right, it would definitely tie Soneji to both train-station massacres.

'I might have something on Soneji,' I told Sampson as we approached the bright lights gleaming at the top of the stairs. He turned his head toward me but kept on climbing.

'I'm not going to guess, Alex, because my mind doesn't ever go where yours does.' Then he mumbled, 'Thank the Lord and Saviour Jesus for that. Addlehead brother.'

'You trying to keep me amused?' I asked him. I could hear music coming from the main terminal now – it sounded like Vivaldi's *The Four Seasons*.

'Actually, I'm trying not to let the fact that Gary Soneji is on this current mad-ass rampage upset my equilibrium or otherwise depress the hell out of me. Tell me what you're thinking.'

'When Soneji was at Lorton Prison, and I interviewed him, he always talked about how his stepmother kept him in the cellar of their house. He was obsessed about it.'

Sampson's head bobbed. 'Knowing Gary as we do, I can't completely blame the poor woman.'

'She would keep him down there for hours at a time, sometimes a whole day, if his father happened to be away from home. She kept the lights off, but he learned to hide candles. He would read by candlelight about kidnappers, rapists, mass murderers, all the other bad boys.'

'And so, Dr Freud? These mass killers were his boyhood role models?'

'Something like that. Gary told me that when he was in the cellar, he would fantasize about committing murders and other atrocities – *as soon as he was let out.* His idée fixe was that release from the cellar would give him back his freedom and power. He'd sit in the cellar obsessing on what he was going to do as soon as he got out. You happen to notice any cellarlike locations around here? Or maybe at Union Station?'

Sampson showed his teeth, which are large and

very white, and can give you the impression that he likes you maybe more than he does. 'The train tunnels represent the cellar of Gary's childhood house, right? When he gets out of the tunnels, all hell breaks loose. He finally takes his revenge on the world.'

'I think that's part of what's going on,' I said. 'But it's never that simple with Gary. It's a start anyway.'

We had reached the main level of Penn Station. This was probably how it had been when Soneji arrived here the night before. More and more I was thinking that the NYPD had it right. Soneji could definitely be the Penn Station killer, too.

I saw a mob of travelers lingering beneath the slipping numbers of the Train Departures board. I could almost see Gary Soneji standing where I was now, taking it all in – *released from the cellar to be Bad Boy again! Still wanting to do famous crimes and succeeding beyond his craziest dreams.*

'Dr Cross, I presume.'

I heard my name as Sampson and I wandered into the brightly lit waiting area of the station. A bearded man with a gold ear stud was smiling at his small joke. He extended his hand.

'I'm Detective Manning Goldman. Good of you to come. Gary Soneji was here yesterday.' He said it with absolute certainty.

CHAPTER 24

Sampson and I shook hands with Goldman and also his partner, a younger detective who appeared to defer to Goldman. Manning Goldman wore a bright-blue sports shirt with three of the buttons undone. He had on a ribbed undershirt that exposed silver and reddish-gold chest hairs sprouting toward his chin. His partner was dressed from head to toe in black. Talk about your odd couples, but I still preferred Oscar and Felix.

Goldman started in on what he knew about the Penn Station stabbings. The New York detective was high-energy, a rapid-fire talker. He used his hands constantly, and appeared confident about his abilities and opinions. The fact that he'd called us in on his case was proof of that. He wasn't threatened by us.

'We know that the killer came up the stairs at track

ten here, just like the two of you just did. We've talked to three witnesses who may have seen him on the Metroliner from Washington,' Goldman explained. His swarthy, dark-haired partner never said a word. 'And yet, we don't have a good ID of him – each witness gave a different description – which doesn't make any sense to me. You have any ideas on that one?'

'If it's Soneji, he's good with makeup and disguises. He's devious and clever. He enjoys fooling people, especially the police. Do you know where he got on the train?' I asked.

Goldman consulted a black leather notebook. 'The stops for that particular train were D.C., Baltimore, Philadelphia, Wilmington, Princeton Junction, and New York. We assumed he got on in D.C.'

I glanced at Sampson, then back at the NYPD detectives. 'Soneji used to live in Wilmington with his wife and little girl. He was originally from the Princeton area.'

'That's information we didn't have,' Goldman said. I couldn't help noticing that he was talking only to me, as if Sampson and Groza weren't even there. It was peculiar, and made it uncomfortable for the rest of us.

'Get me a schedule for yesterday's Metroliner, the one that arrived at five-ten. I want to double-check the stops,' he barked at Groza. The younger detective skulked off to do Goldman's bidding.

'We heard there were three stabbings, three

deaths?' Sampson finally spoke. I knew that he'd been sizing up Goldman. He'd probably come to the conclusion that the detective was a New York asshole of the first order.

'That's what it says on the front pages of all the daily newspapers,' Goldman cracked out of the side of his mouth. It was a nasty remark, delivered curtly.

'The reason I was asking—' Sampson started to say, still keeping his cool.

Goldman cut him off with a rude swipe of the hand. 'Let me show you the sites of the stabbings,' he said as he turned his attention back to me. 'Maybe it will jog something else you know about Soneji.'

'Detective Sampson asked you a question,' I said.

'Yeah, but it was a pointless question. I don't have time for p.c. crap or pointless questions. Like I said, let's move on. Soneji is on the loose in my town.'

'You know much about knives? You cover a lot of stabbings?' Sampson asked. I could tell that he was starting to lose it. He towered over Manning Goldman. Actually, both of us did.

'Yeah, I've covered quite a few stabbings,' Goldman said. 'I also know where you're going. It's extremely unlikely for Soneji to be able to kill three out of three with a knife. Well, the knife he used had a double serpentine blade, extremely sharp. He cut each victim like some surgeon from NYU Medical Center. Oh, yeah, he tipped the knife with potassium cyanide. Kill you in under a minute. I was getting to that.'

Sampson backed off. The mention of poison on the knife was news to us. John knew we needed to hear what Goldman had to say. We couldn't let this get personal here in New York. Not yet anyway.

'Soneji have any history with knives?' Goldman asked. He was talking to me again. 'Poisons?'

I understood that he wanted to pump me, to use me. I didn't have a problem with it. Give and take is as good as it gets on most multijurisdictional cases.

'Knives? He once killed an FBI agent with a knife. Poisons? I don't know. I wouldn't be surprised. He also shot an assortment of handguns and rifles while he was growing up. Soneji likes to kill, Detective Goldman. He's a quick study, so he could have picked it up. Guns and knives, and poisons, too.'

'Believe me, he did pick it up. He was in and out of here in a couple of minutes. Left three dead bodies just like *that*.' Goldman snapped his fingers.

'Was there much blood at the scene?' I asked Goldman. It was the question I'd had on my mind all the way from Washington.

'There was a *helluva* lot of blood. He cut each victim deep. Slashed two of their throats. Why?'

'There could be an angle connected with all the blood.' I told Goldman one of my findings at Union Station. 'The sniper in D.C. made a mess. I'm pretty sure Soneji did it on purpose. He used hollow-points. He also left traces of my blood on his weapon,' I revealed to Goldman.

He probably even knows I'm here in New York, I thought. *And I'm not completely sure who is tracking whom.*

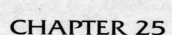

CHAPTER 25

For the next hour, Goldman, with his partner practically walking up his heels, showed us around Penn Station, particularly the three stabbing sites. The body markings were still on the floor, and the cordoned-off areas were causing more than the usual congestion in the terminal.

After we finished with a survey of the station, the NYPD detectives took us up to the street level, where it was believed Soneji had caught a cab headed uptown.

I studied Goldman, watched him work. He was actually pretty good. The way he walked around was interesting. His nose was poised just a little higher than those of the rest of the general population. His posture made him look haughty, in spite of the odd way he was dressed.

'I would have guessed he'd use the subway to escape,' I offered as we stood out on noisy Eighth

Avenue. Above our heads, a sign announced that Kiss was appearing at Madison Square Garden. Shame I'd have to miss it.

Goldman smiled broadly. 'I had the same thought. Witnesses are split on which way he went. I was curious whether you'd have an option. I think Soneji used the subway, too.'

'Trains have a special significance for him. I think trains are part of his ritual. He wanted a set of trains as a kid, but never got it.'

'Ah, *quod erat demonstrandum,*' Goldman said and smirked. 'So now he kills people in train stations. Makes perfect sense to me. Wonder he didn't blow up the whole fucking train.'

Even Sampson laughed at Goldman's delivery on that one.

After we had finished the tour of Penn Station and the surrounding streets, we made a trip down-town to One Police Plaza. By four o'clock I knew what the NYPD had going – at least everything that Manning Goldman was prepared to tell me at this time.

I was almost sure that Gary Soneji was the Penn Station killer. I personally contacted Boston, Philly, and Baltimore and suggested tactfully that they pay attention to the train terminals. I passed on the same advice to Kyle Craig and the FBI.

'We're going to head back to Washington,' I finally told Goldman and Groza. 'Thanks for calling us in on this. This helps a lot.'

'I'll call if there's anything. You do the same, hey?' Manning Goldman put out his hand, and we shook. 'I'm pretty sure we haven't heard the last of Gary Soneji.'

I nodded. I was sure of it, too.

CHAPTER 26

In his mind, Gary Soneji lay down beside Charles Joseph Whitman on the roof of the University of Texas tower, circa 1966.

All in his goddamn incredible mind!

He had been up there with Charlie Whitman *many, many times before* – ever since 1966, when the spree killer had become one of his boyhood idols. Over the years, other killers had captured his imagination, but none were like Charlie Whitman. Whitman was an American original, and there weren't many of those left.

Let's see now, Soneji ran down the names of his favorites: James Herberty, who had opened fire without warning inside the McDonald's in San Ysidio, California. He had killed twenty-one, killed them at an even faster clip than they could dish out greasy hamburgers. Soneji had actually copycatted the McDonald's shootings a few years earlier. That was when he'd first met Cross face to face.

Another of his personal favorites was postman Patrick Sherill, who'd blown away fourteen co-workers in Edmond, Oklahoma, and also probably started the postman-as-madman paranoia. More recently, he had admired the handiwork of Martin Bryant at the Port Arthur penal colony in Tasmania. Then there was Thomas Watt Hamilton, who invaded the mind space of virtually everyone on the planet after his shooting spree at a primary school in Dunblane, Scotland.

Gary Soneji desperately wanted to invade everybody's mind space, to become a large, disturbing icon on the world's Internet. He was going to do it, too. He had everything figured out.

Charlie Whitman was still his sentimental favorite, though. Whitman was the original, the 'madman in the tower.' A Bad Boy down there in Texas.

God, how many times had he lain on that same tower, in the blazing August sun, along with Bad Boy Charlie?

All in his incredible mind!

Whitman had been a twenty-five-year-old student of architectural engineering at the University of Texas when he'd gone tapioca pudding. He'd brought an arsenal up onto the observation deck of the limestone tower that soared three hundred feet above the campus, and where he must have felt like God.

Just before he'd gone up in the clock tower, he had murdered his wife and mother. Whitman had made

Charlie Starkweather look like a piker and a real chump that afternoon in Texas. The same could be said for Dickie Hickock and Perry Smith, the white-trash punks Truman Capote immortalized in his book *In Cold Blood*. Charles Whitman made those two look like crap, too.

Soneji never forgot the actual passage from the *Time* magazine story on the Texas tower shootings. He knew it word for word: *'Like many mass murderers, Charles Whitman had been an exemplary boy, the kind that neighborhood mothers hold up as a model to their own recalcitrant youngsters. He was a Roman Catholic altar boy, and a newspaper delivery boy.'*

Cool goddamn beans.

Another master of disguise, right. Nobody had known what Charlie was thinking, or what he was ultimately going to pull off.

He had carefully positioned himself under the VI numeral of the tower's clock. Then Charles Whitman opened fire at 11:48 in the morning. Beside him on the six-foot runway that went around the tower were a machete, a Bowie knife, a 6mm Remington bolt-action rifle, a 35mm Remington, a Luger pistol, and a .357 Smith & Wesson revolver.

The local and state police fired thousands of rounds up onto the tower, almost shooting out the entire face of the clock – but it took over an hour and a half to bring an end to Charlie Whitman. The whole world marveled at his audacity, his unique outlook and perspective. The whole goddamn world took notice.

Someone was pounding on the door of Soneji's hotel room! The sound brought him back to the here and now. He suddenly remembered where he was.

He was in New York City, in Room 419 of the Plaza, which he always used to read about as a kid. He had always fantasized about coming by train to New York and staying at the Plaza. *Well, here he was.*

'Who's there?' he called from the bed. He pulled a semiautomatic from under the covers. Aimed it at the peephole in the door.

'Maid service,' an accented Spanish female voice said. 'Would you like your bed turned down?'

'No, I'm comfortable as is,' Soneji said and smiled to himself. *Well actually, señorita, I'm preparing to make the NYPD look like the amateurs that cops usually are. You can forget the bed turndown and keep your chocolate mints, too. It's too late to try and make up to me now.*

On second thoughts – 'Hey! You can bring me some of those chocolate mints. I like those little mints. I need a little sweet treat.'

Gary Soneji sat back against the headboard and continued to smile as the maid unlocked the door and entered. He thought about doing her, boffing the scaggy hotel maid, but he figured that wasn't such a good idea. He wanted to spend one night at the Plaza. He'd been looking forward to it for years. It wasn't worth the risk.

The thing that he loved the most, what made it so

perfect, was that nobody had any idea where this was going.

Nobody would guess the end to this one.

Not Alex Cross, not anybody.

CHAPTER 27

I vowed I would not let Soneji wear me down this time. I wouldn't let Soneji take possession of my soul again.

I managed to get home from New York in time for a late dinner with Nana and the kids. Damon, Jannie, and I cleaned up downstairs and then we set the table in the dining room. Keith Jarrett was playing ever so sweetly in the background. This was nice. This was the way it was supposed to be and there was a message in that for me.

'I'm so impressed, Daddy,' Jannie commented as we circled the table, putting out the 'good' silverware, and also glasses and dinner plates I'd picked out years ago with my wife, Maria. 'You went all the way to New York. You came all the way back again. You're here for dinner. Very good, Daddy.'

She beamed and giggled and patted me on my arm as we worked. I was a good father tonight. Jannie approved. She bought my act completely.

I took a small formal bow. 'Thank you, my darling daughter. Now this trip to New York I was on, about how far would you say that might be?'

'Kilometers or miles?' Damon broke in from the other side of the table, where he was folding napkins like fans, the way they do in fancy restaurants. Damon can be quite the little scene stealer.

'Either measurement would be fine,' I told him.

'Approximately two hundred forty-eight miles, one way,' Jannie answered. 'Howzat?'

I opened my eyes as wide as I could, made a funny face, and let my eyes roll up into my forehead. I can still steal a scene or two myself. 'Now, *I'm* impressed. Very good, Jannie.'

She took a little bow and then did a mock curtsy. 'I asked Nana how far it was this morning,' she confessed. 'Is that okay?'

'That's cool,' Damon offered his thought on his sister's moral code. 'It's called research, Velcro.'

'Yeah, that's cool, Baby,' I said, and we all laughed at her cleverness and sense of fun.

'Round-trip, it's four hundred ninety-six miles,' Damon said.

'You two are . . . smart!' I exclaimed in a loud, playful voice. 'You're both smarty pants, smart alecks, smarties of the highest order!'

'What's going on in there? What am I missing out on?' Nana finally called from the kitchen, which was overflowing with good smells from her cooking. She doesn't like to miss anything. Ever. To my knowledge, she just about never has.

'G. E. College Bowl,' I called out to her.

'You will lose your shirt, Alex, if you play against those two young scholars,' she warned. 'Their hunger for knowledge knows no bounds. Their knowledge is fast becoming encyclopedic.'

'En-cy-clo-pedic!' Jannie grinned.

'Cakewalk!' she said then, and did the lively old dance that had originated back in plantation times. I'd taught it to her one day at the piano. The cakewalk music form was actually a forerunner of modern jazz. It had fused polyrhythms from West Africa with classical melodies and also marches from Europe.

Back in plantation days, whoever did the dance best on a given night won a cake. Thus the phrase 'that takes the cake.'

All of this Jannie knew, and also how to actually do the damn dance in high style, and with a contemporary twist or two. She can also do James Brown's famous Elephant Walk and Michael Jackson's Moonwalk.

After dinner, we did the dishes and then we had our biweekly boxing lesson in the basement. Damon and Jannie are not only smart, they're tough little weasels. Nobody in school picks on those two. 'Brains and a wicked left hook!' Jannie brags to me sometimes. 'Hard combination to beat.'

We finally retired to the living room after the Wednesday-night fights. Rosie the cat was curled up on Jannie's lap. We were watching a little of the Orioles baseball game on television when Soneji slid into my head again.

Of all the killers I had ever gone up against, he was the scariest. Soneji was single-minded, obsessive, but he was also completely whacked-out, and that's the proper medical term I learned years ago at Johns Hopkins. He had a powerful imagination fueled by anger, and he acted on his fantasies.

Months back, Soneji had called to tell me that he'd left a cat at our house, a little present. He knew that we had adopted her, and loved little Rosie very much. He said that every time I saw Rosie the cat, I should think: *Gary's in the house, Gary is right there.*

I had figured that Gary had seen the stray cat at our house, and just made up a nasty story. Gary loved to lie, especially when his lies hurt people. That night, though, with Soneji running out of control again, I had a bad thought about Rosie. It frightened the hell out of me.

Gary is in the house. Gary is right here.

I nearly threw the cat out of the house, but that wasn't an option, so I waited until morning to do what had to be done with Rosie. *Goddamn Soneji. What in hell did he want from me? What did he want from my family?*

What could he have done to Rosie before he left her at our house?

CHAPTER 28

I felt like a traitor to my kids and also to poor little Rosie. I was feeling subhuman as I drove thirty-six miles to Quantico the next morning. I was betraying the kids' trust and possibly doing a terrible thing, but I didn't see that I had any other choice.

At the start of our trip, I had Rosie trapped in one of those despicable, metal-wire pet carriers. The poor thing cried and meowed and scratched so hard at the cage and at me that I finally had to let her out.

'You be good now,' I gave her a mild warning. Then I said, 'Oh, go ahead and raise hell if you want to.'

Rosie proceeded to lay a huge guilt trip on me, to make me feel miserable. Obviously, she'd learned this lesson well from Damon and Jannie. Of course, she had no idea how angry she ought to be at me. But maybe she did. Cats are intuitive.

I was fearful that the beautiful red-and-brown Abyssinian would have to be destroyed, possibly this morning. I didn't know how I could ever explain it to the kids.

'Don't scratch up the car seats. And don't you dare jump on top of my head!' I warned Rosie, but in a pleasant, conciliatory voice.

She meowed a few times, and then we had a more or less peaceful and pleasant ride to the FBI quarters in Quantico. I had already spoken to Chet Elliott in the Bureau's SAS or Scientific Analysis Section. He was waiting for Rosie and me. I was carrying the cat in one arm, with her cage dangling from the other.

Now things were going to get very hard. To make things worse, Rosie got up on her hind legs and nuzzled my face. I looked into her beautiful green eyes and I could hardly stand it.

Chet was outfitted in protective gear: a white lab coat, white plastic gloves, even gold-tinted goggles. He looked like the king of the geeks. He peered at Rosie, then at me and said, 'Weird science.'

'Now what happens?' I asked Chet. My heart had sunk to the floorboards when I'd spotted him in his protective gear. He was taking this seriously.

'You go over to Admin,' he said. 'Kyle Craig wants to see you. Says it's important. Of course, everything with Kyle is important as hell and can't wait another second. I know he's crazed about Mr Smith. We all are. Smith is the craziest fucker yet, Alex.'

'What happens to Rosie?' I asked.

'First step, some X-rays. Hopefully, little Red here isn't a walking bomb, compliments of our friend

Soneji. If she isn't, we'll pursue toxicology. Examine her for the presence of drugs or poison in the tissues and fluids. You run along. Go see Uncle Kyle. Red and I will be just fine. I'll try to do right by her, Alex. We're all cat-people in my family. I'm a cat-person, can't you tell? I understand about these things.'

He nodded his head and then flipped down his swimmer-style goggles. Rosie rubbed up against him, so I figured she knew he was okay. So far, anyway.

It was later that worried me, and almost brought tears to my eyes.

CHAPTER 29

I went to see what Kyle had on his mind, though I thought I knew what it was. I dreaded the confrontation, the war of the wills that the two of us sometimes get into. Kyle wanted to talk about his Mr Smith case. Smith was a violent killer who had murdered more than a dozen people in America and Europe. Kyle said it was the ugliest, most chilling spree he had ever seen, and Kyle isn't known for hyperbole.

His office was on the top floor of the Academy Building, but he was working out of a crisis room in the basement of Admin. From what he'd told me, Kyle was practically camping out inside the war room, with its huge Big Board, state-of-the-art computers, phones, and a whole lot of FBI personnel, none of whom looked too happy on the morning of my visit.

The Big Board read: MR SMITH 17 – GOOD GUYS 0, in bright-red letters.

'Looks like you're in your glory again. Nowhere to go but up,' I said. Kyle was sitting at a big walnut desk, lost in study of the evidence board, at least he seemed to be.

I already knew about the case – more than I wanted to. 'Smith' had started his string of gory murders in Cambridge, Massachusetts. He had then moved on to Europe, where he was currently blazing a bewildering trail.

Smith's work was so strange and kinky and *unhinged* that it was seriously discussed in the media that he might be an alien, as in a visitor from outer space. At any rate, 'Smith' definitely seemed inhuman. No human could have committed the monstrosities that he had. That was the working theory.

'I thought you'd never get here,' Kyle said when he saw me.

I raised my hands defensively. 'Can't help. Won't do it, Kyle. First, because I'm already overloaded with Soneji. Second, because I'm losing my family on account of my work habits.'

Kyle nodded. 'All right, all right. I hear you. I see the larger picture. I even understand and sympathize, to a degree. But since you're here, with a little time on your hands, I do need to talk to you about Mr Smith. Believe me, Alex, you've never seen anything like this. You've got to be a little curious.'

'I'm not. In fact, I'm going to leave now. Walk right out that door I came in.'

'We've got an unbelievably ugly problem on our

hands, Alex. Just let me talk, and you listen. Just *listen*,' Kyle pleaded.

I relented, but just a little. 'I'll listen. That's all. I'm not getting involved with this.'

Kyle made a small, ceremonial bow in my direction. 'Just listen,' Kyle said. 'Listen and keep an open mind, Alex. This is going to blow your mind, I guarantee it. It's blown mine.'

Then Kyle proceeded to tell me about an agent named Thomas Pierce. Pierce was in charge of the Mr Smith case. What *was* intriguing was that Smith had brutally murdered Pierce's fiancée some years back.

'Thomas Pierce is the most thorough investigator and the most brilliant person I've ever met,' Kyle told me. 'At first, we wouldn't let him anywhere near the Smith case, for obvious reasons. He worked it on his own. He made progress where we hadn't. Finally, he made it clear that if he couldn't work on Smith, he'd leave the Bureau. He even threatened to try and solve the case on his own.'

'You put him on the case?' I asked Kyle.

'He's very persuasive. In the end, he made his case to the director. He sold Burns. Pierce is logical, and he's creative. He can analyze a problem like nobody I've ever seen. He's been fanatical on Mr Smith. Works eighteen- and twenty-hour days.'

'But even Pierce can't crack this case,' I said and pointed at the Big Board.

Kyle nodded. 'We're finally getting close, Alex. I desperately need your input. And I want you to meet

Thomas Pierce. You have to meet Pierce.'

'I said I'd listen,' I told Kyle. 'But I don't have to meet anyone.'

Nearly four hours later, Kyle finally let me out of his clutches. He *had* blown my mind, all right – about Mr Smith *and* about Thomas Pierce – but I wasn't getting involved. I couldn't.

I finally made my way back to SAS to check on Rosie. Chet Elliott was able to see me right away. He was still wearing his lab coat, gloves, and the gold-tinted goggles. His slow-gaited walk toward me said *bad news*. I didn't want to hear it.

Then he surprised me and grinned. 'We don't see anything wrong with her, Alex. I don't think Soneji did anything to her. He was just mind-humping you. We checked her for volatile compounds – nada. Then for nonvolatile organic compounds that would be unusual in her system – also negative. Forensic serology took some blood. You ought to leave Red with us for a couple of days, but I doubt we'll find anything. You can leave her here, period, if you like. She's a really cool cat.'

'I know.' I nodded and breathed a sigh of relief. 'Can I see her?' I asked Chet.

'Sure can. She's been asking for you all morning. I don't know why, but she seems to like you.'

'She knows I'm a cool cat, too.' I smiled.

He took me back to see Rosie. She was being kept in a small cage, and she looked pissed as hell. I'd brought her here, hadn't I? I might as well have administered the lab tests myself.

'Not my fault,' I explained as best I could. 'Blame that nutcase Gary Soneji, not me. Don't look at me like that.'

She finally let me pick her up and she even nuzzled my cheek. 'You're being a very brave good girl,' I whispered. 'I owe you one, and I always pay my debts.'

She purred and finally licked my cheek with her sandpaper tongue. *Sweet lady, Rosie O'Grady.*

CHAPTER 30

London, England.

Mr Smith was dressed like an anonymous street person in a ripped and soiled black anorak. The killer was walking quickly along Lower Regent Street in the direction of Piccadilly Circus.

Going to the Circus, oh boy, oh boy! He was thinking. His cynicism was as thick and heavy as the air in London.

No one seemed to notice him in the late-afternoon crowds. No one paid much attention to the poor in any of the large, 'civilized' capitals. Mr Smith had noticed that, and used it to his advantage.

He hurried along with his duffel bag until he finally reached Piccadilly, where the crowds were even denser.

His attentive eyes took in the usual traffic snarl, which could be expected at the hub of five major streets. He also saw Tower Records, McDonald's, the Trocadero, far too many neon ads. Backpackers and camera-hounds were everywhere on the street and sidewalks.

And a single alien creature – himself.

One being who didn't fit in any way with the others.

Mr Smith suddenly felt so alone, incredibly lonely in the middle of all these people in London town.

He set down the long, heavy duffel bag directly under the famous statue in the Circus – *Eros*. Still, no one was paying attention to him.

He left the bag sitting there, and he walked toward Haymarket.

When he was a few blocks away, he called the police, as he always did. The message was simple, clear, to the point. *Their time was up.*

'Inspector Derek Cabott is in Piccadilly Circus. He's in a gray duffel bag. What's left of him. You blew it. Cheers.'

CHAPTER 31

Sondra Greenberg of Interpol spotted Thomas Pierce as he walked toward the crime scene at the center of Piccadilly Circus. Pierce stood out in a crowd, even one like this.

Thomas Pierce was tall; his long blond hair was pulled back in a ponytail; and he usually wore dark glasses. He did not look like your typical FBI agent, and, in fact, Pierce was nothing like any agent Greenberg had ever met or worked with.

'What's all the excitement about?' he asked as he got up close. 'Mr Smith out for his weekly kill. Nothing so unusual.' His habitual sarcasm was at work.

Sondra looked around at the packed crowd at the homicide scene and shook her head. There were press reporters and television news trucks everywhere.

'What's being done by the local geniuses? The police?' said Pierce.

'They're canvassing. *Obviously*, Smith has been here.'

'The bobbies want to know if anyone saw a little green man? Blood dripping from his little green teeth?'

'Exactly, Thomas. Have a look?'

Pierce smiled and it was entirely captivating. Definitely not the American FBI's usual style. 'You said that like, *spot of tea? . . . Have a look?*'

Greenberg shook her head of dark curls. She was nearly as tall as Pierce, and pretty in a tough sort of way. She always tried to be nice to Pierce. Actually, it wasn't hard.

'I guess I'm finally becoming jaded,' she said. 'I wonder why.'

They walked toward the crime scene, which was almost directly under the towering, waxed aluminum figure of Eros. One of London's favorite landmarks, Eros was also the symbol for the *Evening Standard*. Although people believed the statue was a representation of erotic love, it had actually been commissioned as a symbol for Christian charity.

Thomas Pierce flashed his ID and walked up to the 'body bag' that Mr Smith had used to transport the remains of Chief Inspector Cabott.

'It's as if he's *living* a Gothic novel,' Sondra Greenberg said. She was kneeling beside Pierce. Actually, they looked like a team, even like a couple.

'Smith called you here, too – to London? Left voice-mail?' Pierce asked her.

Greenberg nodded. 'What do you think of the body? The latest kill? Smith packed the bag with body parts in the most careful and concise way. Like you would if you had to get everything into a suitcase.'

Thomas Pierce frowned. 'Freak, goddamn butcher.'

'Why Piccadilly? A hub of London. Why under Eros?'

'He's leaving clues for us, obvious clues. We just don't understand,' Thomas Pierce said as he continued to shake his head.

'Right you are, Thomas. Because we don't speak Martian.'

CHAPTER 32

*C*rime marches on and on.

Sampson and I drove to Wilmington, Delaware, the following morning. We had visited the city made famous by the Duponts during the original manhunt for Gary Soneji a few years before. I had the Porsche floored the entire ride, which took a couple of hours.

I had already received some very good news that morning. We'd solved one of the case's nagging mysteries. I had checked with the blood bank at St Anthony's. A pint of my blood was missing from our family's supply. Someone had taken the trouble to break in and take my blood. *Gary Soneji? Who else? He continued to show me that nothing was safe in my life.*

'Soneji' was actually a pseudonym Gary had used as part of a plan to kidnap two children in Washington. The strange name had stuck in news stories, and that was the name the FBI and media used now. His real name was Gary Murphy. He had lived in Wilmington with his wife, Meredith, who was called Missy. They had one daughter, Roni.

Actually, Soneji was the name Gary had appropriated when he fantasized about his crimes as a young boy locked in the cellar of his house. He claimed to have been sexually abused by a neighbor in Princeton, a grade-school teacher named Martin Soneji. I suspected serious problems with a relative, possibly his paternal grandfather.

We arrived at the house on Central Avenue at a little past ten in the morning. The pretty street was deserted, except for a small boy with Rollerblades. He was trying them out on his front lawn. There should have been local police surveillance here, but, for some reason, there wasn't. At least I didn't see any sign of it yet.

'Man, this perfect little street kills me,' Sampson said. 'I still keep looking for Jimmy Stewart to pop out of one of these houses.'

'Just as long as Soneji doesn't,' I muttered.

The cars parked up and down Central Avenue were almost all American makes, which seemed quaint nowadays: Chevys, Olds, Fords, some Dodge Ram pickup trucks.

Meredith Murphy wasn't answering her phone that morning, which didn't surprise me.

'I feel sorry for Mrs Murphy and especially the little girl,' I told Sampson as we pulled up in front of the house. 'Missy Murphy had no idea who Gary really was.'

Sampson nodded. 'I remember they seemed nice enough. Maybe too nice. Gary fooled them. Ole Gary the Fooler.'

There were lights burning in the house. A white Chevy Lumina was parked in the driveway. The street was as quiet and peaceful as I remembered it from our last visit, when the peacefulness had been short-lived.

We got out of the Porsche and headed toward the front door of the house. I touched the butt of my Glock as we walked. I couldn't help thinking that Soneji could be waiting, setting some kind of trap for Sampson and me.

The neighborhood, the entire town, still reminded me of the 1950s. The house was well kept and looked as if it had recently been painted. That had been part of Gary's careful façade. It was the perfect hiding place: a sweet little house on Central Avenue, with a white picket fence and a stone walkway bisecting the front lawn.

'So what do you figure is going on with Soneji?' Sampson asked as we came up to the front door. 'He's changed some, don't you think? He's not the careful planner I remember. More impulsive.'

It seemed that way. 'Not everything's changed. He's still playing parts, acting. But he's on a rampage like nothing I've seen before. He doesn't seem to care if he's caught. Yet everything he does is planned. He *escapes.*'

'And why is that, Dr Freud?'

'That's what we're here to find out. And that's why we're going to Lorton Prison tomorrow. Something weird is going on, even for Gary Soneji.'

I rang the front doorbell. Sampson and I waited for Missy Murphy on the porch. We didn't fit into the small-town-America neighborhood, but that wasn't so unusual. We didn't exactly fit into our own neighborhood back in D.C. either. That morning we were both wearing dark clothes and dark glasses, looking like musicians in somebody's blues band.

'Hmm, no answer,' I muttered.

'Lights blazing inside,' Sampson said. 'Somebody must be here. Maybe they just don't want to talk to Men in Black.'

'Ms Murphy,' I called out in a loud voice, in case someone was inside, but not answering the door. 'Ms Murphy, open the door. It's Alex Cross from Washington. We're not leaving without talking to you.'

'Nobody home at the Bates Motel,' Sampson grunted.

He wandered around the side of the house, and I followed close behind. The lawn had been cut recently and the hedges trimmed. Everything looked so neat and clean and so harmless.

I went to the back door, the kitchen, if I remembered. I wondered if he could be hiding inside. Anything was possible with Soneji – the more twisted and unlikely, the better for his ego.

Things about my last visit were flashing back. Nasty

memories. It was Roni's birthday party. She was seven. Gary Soneji had been inside the house that time, but he had managed to escape. A regular Houdini. A very smart, very creepy creep.

Soneji could be inside now. Why did I have the unsettling feeling that I was walking into a trap?

I waited on the back porch, not sure what to do next. I rang the bell. Something was definitely wrong about the case, everything about it was wrong. Soneji here in Wilmington? Why here? Why kill people in Union and Penn Stations?

'Alex!' Sampson shouted. 'Alex! Over here! Come quick. Alex, *now*!'

I hurried across the yard with my heart in my throat. Sampson was down on all fours. He was crouched in front of a doghouse that was painted white, and shingled to look like the main residence. What in hell was inside the doghouse?

As I got closer, I could see a thick black cloud of flies.

Then I heard the buzzing.

CHAPTER 33

'Oh, goddamn it, Alex, look at what that madman did. Look at what he did to her!'

I wanted to avert my eyes, but I had to look. I crouched down low beside Sampson. Both of us were batting away horse flies and other unpleasant, crawling insects. White larvae were all over everything – the doghouse, the lawn. I held a handkerchief bunched over my nose and mouth, but it wasn't enough to stifle the putrid smell. My eyes began to water.

'What the hell is wrong with him?' Sampson said. 'Where does he get his insane ideas?'

Propped up inside the doghouse was the body of a golden retriever, or what remained of it. Blood was spattered everywhere on the wooden walls. The dog had been decapitated.

Firmly attached to the dog's neck was the head of

Meredith Murphy. Her head was propped perfectly, even though it was too large proportionately for the retriever's body. The effect was beyond grotesque. It reminded me of the old Mr Potato Head toys. Meredith Murphy's open eyes stared out at me.

I had met Meredith Murphy only once, and that had been almost four years before. I wondered what she could have done to enrage Soneji like this. He had never talked much about his wife during our sessions. He had despised her, though. I remembered his nicknames for her: 'Simple Cipher,' 'The Headless Hausfrau,' 'Blonde Cow.'

'What the hell is going on inside that sick, sorry son of a bitch's head? You understand this?' Sampson muttered through his handkerchief-covered mouth.

I thought that I understood psychotic rage states, and I had seen a few of Soneji's, but nothing prepared me for the past few days. The current murders were extreme, and bloody. They were also clustered, happening much too frequently.

I had the grim feeling Soneji couldn't turn off his rage, not even after a new kill. None of the murders satisfied his need anymore.

'Oh, God.' I rose to my feet. 'John, his little girl,' I said. 'His daughter, Roni. What has he done with her?'

The two of us searched the wooded half-lot, including a copse of bent, wind-battered evergreens on the northeast side of the house. No Roni. No other bodies, or grossly severed parts, or other grisly surprises.

We looked for the girl in the two-car garage. Then in the tight, musty crawlspace under the back porch. We checked the trio of metal garbage cans neatly lined alongside the garage. Nothing anywhere. Where was Roni Murphy? Had he taken her with him? Had Soneji kidnapped his daughter?

I headed back toward the house, with Sampson a step or two behind me. I broke the window in the kitchen door, unlocked it, and rushed inside. I feared the worst. Another murdered child?

'Go easy, man. Take it slow in here,' Sampson whispered from behind. He knew how I got when children were involved. He also sensed this could be a trap Soneji had set. It was a perfect place for one.

'Roni!' I called out. 'Roni, are you in here? Roni, can you hear me?'

I remembered her face from the last time I'd been in this house. I could have drawn her picture if I had to.

Gary had told me once that Roni was the only thing that mattered in his life, the only good thing he'd ever done. At the time, I believed him. I was probably projecting my feelings for my own kids. Maybe I was fooled into thinking that Soneji had some kind of conscience and feelings because that was what I wanted to believe.

'Roni! It's the police. You can come out now, honey. Roni Murphy, are you in here? Roni?'

'Roni!' Sampson joined in, his deep voice just as loud as mine, maybe louder.

Sampson and I covered the downstairs, throwing open every door and closet as we went. Calling out her name. Dear God, I was praying now. It was sort of a prayer anyway. *Gary – not your own little girl. You don't have to kill her to show us how bad you are, how angry. We get the message. We understand.*

I ran upstairs, taking the creaking wooden steps two at a time. Sampson was close behind me, a shadow. It usually doesn't show on his face, but he gets as upset as I do. Neither of us is jaded yet.

I could hear it in his voice, in the shallow way he was breathing. 'Roni! Are you up here? Are you hiding somewhere?' he called out.

'Roni! It's the police. You're safe now, Roni! You can come out.'

Someone had ransacked the master bedroom. Someone had invaded this space, desecrated it, broken every piece of furniture, overturned beds and bureaus.

'You remember her, John?' I asked as we checked the rest of the bedrooms.

'I remember her pretty good,' Sampson said in a soft voice. 'Cute little girl.'

'Oh, no – *nooo* . . .'

Suddenly I was running down the hallway, back down the stairs. I raced through the kitchen and pulled open a hollow-core door between the refrigerator and a four-burner stove.

We both hurried down into the basement, into the *cellar* of the house.

My heart was out of control, *beating, banging, thudding* loudly inside my chest. I didn't want to be here, to see any more of Soneji's handiwork, his nasty surprises.

The cellar of his house.

The symbolic place of all Gary's childhood nightmares.

The cellar.

Blood.

Trains.

The cellar in the Murphy house was small and neat. I looked around. *The trains were gone!* There had been a train set down here the first time we came to the house.

I didn't see any signs of the girl, though. Nothing looked out of place. We threw open work cabinets. Sampson yanked open the washer, then the clothes dryer.

There was an unpainted wooden door to one side of the water heater and a fiberglass laundry sink. There was no sign of blood in the sink, no blood-stained clothes. Was there a way outside? Had the little girl run away when her father came to the house?

The closet! I yanked open the door.

Roni Murphy was bound with rope and gagged with old rags. Her blue eyes were large with fear. She was alive!

She was shaking badly. He didn't kill her, but he had killed her childhood, just as his had been killed. A few years before, he had done the same thing with a girl called Maggie Rose.

'Oh, sweet girl,' I whispered as I untied her and took out the cloth gag her father had stuffed into her mouth. 'Everything is all right now. Everything is okay, Roni. You're okay now.'

What I didn't say was, *Your father loved you enough not to kill you – but he wants to kill everything and everyone else.*

'You're okay, you're okay, baby. Everything is okay,' I lied to the poor little girl. 'Everything is okay now.'

Sure it is.

CHAPTER 34

O nce upon a long time ago, Nana Mama had been the one who had taught me to play the piano.

In those days, the old upright sat like a constant invitation to make music in our family room. One afternoon after school, she heard me trying to play a little boogie-woogie. I was eleven years old at the time. I remember it well, as if it were yesterday.

Nana swept in like a soft breeze and sat next to me on the piano bench, just the way I do now with Jannie and Damon.

'I think you're a little ahead of yourself with that cool jazz stuff, Alex. Let me show you something beautiful. Let me show you where you might start your music career.'

She made me practice my Czerny finger exercises every day until I was ready to play and appreciate Mozart, Beethoven, Handel, Haydn – all from Nana

Mama. She taught me to play from age eleven until I was eighteen, when I left for school at Georgetown and then Johns Hopkins. By that time, I was ready to play that cool jazz stuff, and to know what I was playing, and even know why I liked what I liked.

When I came home from Delaware, very late, I found Nana on the porch and she was playing the piano. I hadn't heard her play like that in many years.

She didn't hear me come in, so I stood in the doorway and watched her for several minutes. She was playing Mozart and she still had a feeling for the music that she loved. She'd once told me how sad it was that no one knew where Mozart was buried.

When she finished, I whispered, 'Bravo. Bravo. That's just beautiful.'

Nana turned to me. 'Silly old woman,' she said and wiped away a tear I hadn't been able to see from where I was standing.

'Not silly at all,' I said. I sat down and held her in my arms on the piano bench. 'Old yes, really old and cranky, but never silly.'

'I was just thinking,' she said, 'about that third movement in Mozart's Piano Concerto No. 21, and then I had a memory of how I used to be able to play it, a long, long time ago.' She sighed. 'So I had myself a nice cry. Felt real good, too.'

'Sorry to intrude,' I said as I continued to hold her close.

JAMES PATTERSON

'I love you, Alex,' my grandmother whispered. 'Can you still play "Clair de Lune"? Play Debussy for me.'

And so with Nana Mama close beside me, I played.

CHAPTER 35

The groan-and-grunt work continued the following morning.

First thing, Kyle faxed me several stories about his agent, Thomas Pierce. The stories came from cities where Mr Smith had committed murders: Atlanta, St Louis, Seattle, San Francisco, London, Hamburg, Frankfurt, Rome. Pierce had helped to capture a murderer in Fort Lauderdale in the spring, unrelated to Smith.

Other headlines: *For Thomas Pierce, The Crime Scene Is in the Mind; Murder Expert Here in St Louis; Thomas Pierce – Getting into Killers' Heads; Not All Pattern Killers Are Brilliant – But Agent Thomas Pierce Is; Murders of the Mind, the Most Chilling Murders of All.*

If I didn't know better, I'd have thought Kyle was trying to make me jealous of Pierce. I wasn't jealous. I didn't have the time for it right now.

A little before noon, I drove out to Lorton Prison, one of my least favorite places in the charted universe.

Everything moves slowly inside a high-security federal prison. It is like being held underwater, like being drowned by unseen human hands. It happens over days, over years, sometimes over decades.

At an administrative max facility, prisoners are kept in their cells twenty-two to twenty-three hours a day. The boredom is incomprehensible to anyone who hasn't served time. *It is not imaginable.* Gary Soneji told me that, created the drowning metaphor when I interviewed him years back at Lorton.

He also thanked me for giving him the experience of being in prison, and he said that one day he would reciprocate if he possibly could. More and more, I had the sense that my time had come, and I had to guess what the excruciating payback might be.

It was not imaginable.

I could almost feel myself drowning as I paced inside a small administrative room near the warden's office on the fifth floor at Lorton.

I was waiting for a double-murderer named Jamal Autry. Autry claimed to have important information about Soneji. He was known inside Lorton as the Real Deal. He was a predator, a three-hundred-pound pimp who had murdered two teenage prostitutes in Baltimore.

The Real Deal was brought to me in restraints. He was escorted into the small, tidy office by two armed guards with billy clubs.

'You Alex Cross? Gah-damn. Now ain't that some-thin',' Jamal Autry said with a middle-South twang.

He smiled crookedly when he spoke. The lower half of his face sagged like the mouth and jaw of a bottom feeder. He had strange, uneven piggy eyes that were hard to look at. He continued to smile as if he were about to be paroled today, or had just won the inmates' lottery.

I told the two guards that I wanted to talk to Autry alone. Even though he was in restraints, they departed reluctantly. I wasn't afraid of this big load, though. I wasn't a helpless teenage girl he could beat up on.

'Sorry, I missed the joke,' I finally said to Autry. 'Don't quite know why it is that you're smiling.'

'Awhh, don't worry 'bout it, man. You get the joke okay. Eventually,' he said with his slow drawl. 'You'll get the joke, Dr Cross. See, *it's on you.*'

I shrugged. 'You asked to see me, Autry. You want something out of this and so do I. I'm not here for your jokes or your private amusement. You want to go back to your cell, just turn the hell around.'

Jamal Autry continued to smile, but he sat down on one of two chairs left for us. 'We boff want something,' he said. He began to make serious eye contact with me. He had the don't-mess-with-me look now. His smile evaporated.

'Tell me what you've got to trade. We'll see where it goes,' I said. 'Best I can do for you.'

'Soneji said you a hard-ass. Smart for a cop. We'll

see what we see,' he drawled.

I ignored the bullshit that flowed so easily from his over-large mouth. I couldn't help thinking about the two sixteen-year-old girls he'd murdered. I imagined him smiling at them, too. Giving them the look. 'The two of you talked sometimes? Soneji was a friend of yours?' I asked him.

Autry shook his head. The look stayed fixed. His piggy eyes never left mine. 'Naw, man. Only talked when he needed somethin'. Soneji rather sit in his cell, stare out into far space, like Mars or someplace. Soneji got no friends in here. Not me, not anybody else.'

Autry leaned forward in his chair. He had something to tell me. Obviously, he thought it was worth a lot. He lowered his voice as if there were someone in the room besides the two of us.

Someone like Gary Soneji, I couldn't help thinking.

CHAPTER 36

'Lookit, Soneji didn't have no friends in here. He didn't need nobody. Man had a guest in his attic. Know what I mean? Only talked to me when he wanted something.'

'What kind of things did you do for Soneji?' I asked.

'Soneji had simple needs. Cigars, fuck-books, mustard for his Froot-Loops. He paid to keep certain individuals away. Soneji always had money.'

I thought about that. Who gave Gary Soneji money while he was in Lorton? It wouldn't have come from his wife – at least I didn't think so. His grandfather was still alive in New Jersey. Maybe the money had come from his grandfather. He had only one friend that I knew of, but that had been way back when he was a teenager.

Jamal Autry continued his bigmouthed spiel. 'Check it out, man. Protection Gary bought from me was good – the best. Best anybody could do in here.'

'I'm not sure I follow you,' I said. 'Spell it out for me, Jamal. I want all the details.'

'You can protect *some* of the people *some* of the time. That's all it is. There was another prisoner here, name of Shareef Thomas. Real crazy nigger, originally from New York City. Ran with two other crazy niggers – Goofy and Coco Loco. Shareef's out now, but when he inside, Shareef did whatever the hell he wanted. Only way you control Shareef, you cap him. *Twice*, just to make sure.'

Autry was getting interesting. He definitely had something to trade. 'What was Gary Soneji's connection with Shareef?' I asked.

'Soneji tried to cap Shareef. Paid the money. But Shareef was smart. Shareef was lucky, too.'

'Why did Soneji want to kill Shareef Thomas?'

Autry stared at me with his cold eyes. 'We have a deal, right? I get privileges for this?'

'You have my full attention, Jamal. I'm here, I'm listening to you. Tell me what happened between Shareef Thomas and Soneji.'

'Soneji wanted to kill Shareef 'cause Shareef was fuckin' him. Not just one time either. He wanted Gary to know he was *the man*. He was the one man even crazier than Soneji in here.'

I shook my head and leaned forward to listen. He had my attention, but something wasn't tracking for me. 'Gary was separated from the prison population. Maximum security. How the hell did Thomas get to him?'

'Gah-damn, I told you, things get done in here. Things always get done. Don't be fooled what you hear on the outside, man. That's the way it is, way it's always been.'

I stared into Autry's eyes. 'So you took Soneji's money for protection, and Shareef Thomas got to him anyway? There's more, isn't there?'

I sensed that Autry was relishing his own punch line, or maybe he just liked having the power over me.

'There's more, yeah. Shareef gave Gary Soneji the Fever. Soneji has the bug, man. He's dying. Your old friend Gary Soneji is dying. He got *the message* from God.'

The news hit me like a sucker punch. I didn't let it show, didn't give away any advantage, but Jamal Autry had just made some sense of everything Soneji had done so far. He had also shaken me to the quick. *Soneji has the Fever. He has AIDS. Gary Soneji is dying. He has nothing to lose anymore.*

Was Autry telling the truth or not? Big question, important question.

I shook my head. 'I don't believe you, Autry. Why the hell should I?' I said.

He looked offended, which was part of his act. 'Believe what you want. But you *ought* to believe. Gary got the message to me in here. Gary *contacted* me this week, two days ago. Gary let me know he has the Fever.'

We had come full circle. Autry knew that he had me

from the minute he walked into the room. Now I got to hear the punch line of his joke – the one he'd promised at the start. First, though, I had to be his straight man for a little while longer.

'Why? Why would he tell you he's dying?' I played my part.

'Soneji said you'd come here asking questions. He knew you were coming. He knows you, man – better than you know him. Soneji wanted me to give you the message personally. He gave me the message, just for you. *He said to tell you that.*'

Jamal Autry smiled his crooked smile again. 'What do you say now, Dr Cross? You get what you come here for?'

I had what I needed all right. Gary Soneji was dying. He wanted me to follow him into hell. He was on a rampage with nothing to lose, nothing to fear from anyone.

CHAPTER 37

When I got home from Lorton Prison I called Christine Johnson. I needed to see her. I needed to get away from the case. I held my breath as I asked her to dinner at Georgia Brown's on McPherson Square. She surprised me – she said yes.

Still on pins and needles, but kind of liking the feeling, I showed up at her place with a single red rose. Christine smiled beautifully, took the rose and put it in water as if it were an expensive arrangement.

She was wearing a gray calf-length skirt and a matching soft gray V-necked blouse. She looked stunning again. We talked about our respective days on the drive to the restaurant. I liked her day a lot better than mine.

We were hungry, and started with hot buttermilk biscuits slathered with peach butter. The day was definitely improving. Christine ordered Carolina shrimp and grits. I got the Carolina Perlau – red rice, thick chunks of duck, shrimp, and sausage.

'No one has given me a rose in a long time,' she told me. 'I love that you thought to do that.'

'You're being too nice to me tonight,' I said as we started to eat.

She tilted her head to one side and looked at me from an odd angle. She did that now and again. 'Why do you say that I'm being too nice?'

'Well, you can tell I'm not exactly the best company tonight. It's what you're afraid of, isn't it? That I can't turn off my job.'

She took a sip of wine. Shook her head. Finally she smiled, and the smile was so down-to-earth. 'You're *so* honest. But you have a good sense of humor about it. Actually, I hadn't noticed that you weren't operating at one hundred and ten percent.'

'I've been distant and into myself all night,' I said. 'The kids say I get twilight zoned.'

She laughed and rolled her eyes. 'Stop it, stop it. You are the least into-yourself man I think I've ever met. I'm having a very nice time here. I was planning on a bowl of Corn Pops for my dinner at home.'

'Corn Pops and milk are good. Curl up in bed with a movie or book. Nothing wrong with that.'

'That was my plan. I finally gave in and started *The Horse Whisperer*. I'm glad you called and spoiled it for me, took me out of my own twilight zone.'

'You must really think I'm crazy,' Christine said and smiled a little later during dinner. 'Lawdy, Miss

Clawdy, I believe I *am* crazy.'

I laughed. 'For going out with me? Absolutely crazy.'

'No, for telling you I didn't think we should see each other, and now late dinner at Georgia Brown's. Forsaking my Corn Pops and *Horse Whisperer*.'

I looked into her eyes, and I wanted to stay right there for a very long time, at least until Georgia Brown's asked us to leave. 'What happened? What changed?' I asked.

'I stopped being afraid,' she said. 'Well, almost stopped. But I'm getting there.'

'Yeah, maybe we both are. I was afraid, too.'

'That's nice to hear. I'm glad you told me. I couldn't imagine that you get afraid.'

I drove Christine home from Georgia Brown's around midnight. As we rode on the John Hansen Highway, all I could think about was touching her hair, stroking the side of her cheek, maybe a few other things. Yes, definitely a few other things.

I walked Christine to her front door and I could hardly breathe. Again. My hand was lightly on her elbow. She had her house key clasped in her hand.

I could smell her perfume. She told me it was called Gardenia Passion, and I liked it a lot. Our shoes softly scraped the cement.

Suddenly, Christine turned and put her arms around me. The movement was graceful, but she took me by surprise.

'I have to find something out,' she said.

Christine kissed me, just as we had a few days before. We kissed sweetly at first, then harder. Her lips were soft and moist against mine, then firmer, more urgent. I could feel her breasts press against me; then her stomach, her strong legs.

She opened her eyes, looked at me, and she smiled. I loved that natural smile – loved it. *That smile – no other one*.

She gently pulled herself away from me. I felt the separation and I didn't want her to go. I sensed, I knew, I should leave it at that.

Christine opened her front door and slowly backed inside. I didn't want her to go in just yet. I wanted to know what she was thinking, all her thoughts.

'The first kiss wasn't an accident,' she whispered.

'No, it wasn't an accident,' I said.

CHAPTER 38

Gary Soneji was in the cellar again.
Whose dank, dark cellar was it, though?
That was the $64,000 question.

He didn't know what time it was, but it had to be very early in the morning. The house upstairs was as quiet as death. He liked that image, the rub of it inside his mind.

He loved it in the dark. He went back to being a small boy. He could still feel it, as if it had happened only yesterday. His stepmother's name was Fiona Morrison, and she was pretty, and everybody believed she was a good person, a good friend and neighbor, a good mother. It was all a lie! She had locked him away like a hateful animal – *no*, worse than an animal! He remembered shivering in the cellar, and peeing in his pants in the beginning, and sitting in his own urine as it turned from warm to icy cold. He remembered the feeling that he wasn't like the rest of his family. He wasn't like anybody else. There was nothing about him that anybody could love. There was nothing good about him. He had no inner core.

He sat in the dark cellar now and wondered if he was where he thought he was.

Which reality was he living in?

Which fantasy?

Which horror story?

He reached around on the floor in the dark. *Hmmm*. He wasn't in the cellar in the old Princeton house. He could tell he wasn't. Here the cold cement floor was smooth. And the smell was different. Dusty and musty. Where was he?

He turned on his flashlight. Ahhh!

No one was going to believe this one! No one would guess whose house this was, whose cellar he was hiding in now.

Soneji pushed himself up off the floor. He felt slightly nauseated and achy, but he ignored the feeling. The pain was incidental. He was ready to go upstairs now.

No one would believe what he was going to do next. How outrageous.

He was several steps ahead of everybody else.

He was way ahead.

As always.

CHAPTER 39

Soneji entered the living room and saw the correct time on the Sony television's digital clock. It showed 3:24 in the morning. Another witching hour.

Once he reached the upstairs part of the house, he decided to crawl on his hands and knees.

The plan was good. Damn it, he *wasn't* worthless and useless. He hadn't deserved to be locked in the cellar. Tears welled in his eyes and they felt hot and all too familiar. His stepmother always called him a crybaby, a little pansy, a fairy. She never stopped calling him names, until he fried her mouth open in a scream.

The tears burned his cheeks as they ran down under his shirt collar. He was dying, and he didn't deserve to die. He didn't deserve any of this. So now someone had to pay.

He was silent and careful as he threaded his way

through the house, slithering on his belly like a snake. The floorboards underneath him didn't even creak as he moved forward. The darkness felt charged with electricity and infinite possibilities.

He thought about how frightened people were of intruders inside their houses and apartments. They ought to be afraid, too. There were monsters preying just outside their locked doors, often watching their windows at night. There were Peeping Garys in every town, small and large. And there were thousands more, twisted perverts, just waiting to come inside and feast. The people in their so-called safe houses were monster-fodder.

He noticed that the upstairs part of the house had green walls. *Green walls. What luck!* Soneji had read somewhere that hospital operating walls were often painted green. If the walls were white, doctors and nurses sometimes saw ghost images of the ongoing operation, the blood and gore. It was called the 'ghosting effect,' and green walls masked the blood.

No more intruding thoughts, no matter how relevant, Soneji told himself. No more interruptions. Be perfectly calm, be careful. The next few minutes were the dangerous ones.

This particular house was dangerous – which was why the game was so much fun, such a mind trip.

The bedroom door was slightly ajar. Soneji slowly, patiently, inched it open.

He heard a man softly snoring. He saw another

digital clock on a bedside table. *Three-twenty-three*. He had *lost* time.

He rose to his full height. He was finally out of the cellar, and he felt an incredible surge of anger now. He felt rage, and it was justified.

Gary Soneji angrily sprang forward at the figure in bed. He clasped a metal pipe tightly in both his hands. He raised it like an ax. He swung the pipe down as hard as he could.

'Detective Goldman, so nice to meet you,' he whispered.

CHAPTER 40

The Job was always there, waiting for me to catch up, demanding everything I could give it, and then demanding some more.

The next morning I found myself hurrying back to New York. The FBI had provided me with a helicopter. Kyle Craig was a good friend, but he was also working his tricks on me. I knew it, and he knew I did. Kyle was hoping that I would eventually get involved in the Mr Smith case, that I would meet agent Thomas Pierce. I knew that I wouldn't. Not for now anyway, maybe not ever. I had to meet Gary Soneji again first.

I arrived before 8:30 a.m. at the busy New York City heliport in the East Twenties. Some people call it 'the New York Hellport.' The Bureau's black Belljet floated in low over the congested FDR Drive and the East River. The plane dropped down as if it owned the city, but that was just FBI arrogance. No one could own New York – except maybe Gary Soneji.

Detective Carmine Groza was there to meet me and we got into his unmarked Mercury Marquis. We sped up the FDR Drive to the exit for the Major Deegan. As we crossed over into the Bronx, I remembered a funny line from the poet Ogden Nash: 'The Bronx, no thonx.' I needed some more funny lines in my life.

I still had the irritating noise of the helicopter's rotor blades roaring inside my head. It made me think of the nasty *buzzing* in the doghouse in Wilmington. Everything was happening too fast again. Gary Soneji had us off balance, the way he liked it, the way he always worked his nastiness.

Soneji got in your face, applied intense pressure, and then waited for you to make a crucial mistake. I was trying not to make one right now, not to end up like Manning Goldman.

The latest homicide scene was up in Riverdale. Detective Groza talked nervously as he drove the Deegan. His chattering reminded me of an old line I try to live by – *never miss a good chance to shut up*.

Logically, the Riverdale area should be part of Manhattan, he said, but it was actually part of the Bronx. To confuse matters further, Riverdale was the site of Manhattan College, a small private school having no affiliation with either Manhattan or the Bronx. New York's mayor, Rudy Giuliani, had attended Manhattan, Groza said.

I listened to the detective's idle chitchat until I felt he had talked himself out. He seemed a different man from the one I'd met earlier in the week at Penn Station when he was partnered with Manning Goldman.

'Are you okay?' I finally asked him. I had never lost a partner, but I had come close with Sampson. He had been stabbed in the back. That happened in North Carolina, of all places. My niece, Naomi, had been kidnapped. I have counseled detectives who have lost partners, and it's never an easy thing.

'I didn't really like Manning Goldman,' Groza admitted, 'but I respected things he did as a detective. No one should die the way he did.'

'No, no one should die like that,' I agreed. *No one was safe*. Not the wealthy, certainly not the poor, and not even the police. It was a continuing refrain in my life, the scariest truth of our age.

We finally turned off the crowded Deegan Expressway and got onto an even busier, much noisier Broadway. Detective Groza was clearly shook up that morning. I didn't show it, but so was I.

Gary Soneji was showing us how easy it was for him to get into a cop's home.

CHAPTER 41

Manning Goldman's house was located in an upscale part of Riverdale known as Fieldstone. The area was surprisingly attractive – for the Bronx. Police cruisers and a flock of television vans and trucks were parked on the narrow and pretty residential streets. A FOX-TV helicopter hovered over the trees, peeking through the branches and leaves.

The Goldman house was more modest than the Tudors around it. Still, it seemed a nice place to live. Not a typical cop's neighborhood, but Manning Goldman hadn't been a typical cop.

'Goldman's father was a big doctor in Mamaroneck,' Groza continued to chatter. 'When he passed away, Manning came into some money. He was the black sheep in his family, the rebel – a cop. Both of his brothers are dentists in Florida.'

I didn't like the look and feel of the crime scene,

and I was still two blocks away. There were too many blue-and-whites and official-looking city cars. Too much help, too much interference.

'The mayor was up here early. He's a pisser. He's all right, though,' Groza said. 'A cop gets killed in New York, it's a huge thing. Big news, lots of media.'

'Especially when a detective gets killed right in his own home,' I said.

Groza finally parked on the tree-lined street, about a block from the Goldman house. Birds chattered away, oblivious to death.

As I walked toward the crime scene, I enjoyed one aspect of the day, at least, the anonymity I felt in New York. In Washington, many reporters know who I am. If I'm at a homicide scene, it's usually a particularly nasty one, a big case, a violent crime.

Detective Carmine Groza and I were ignored as we walked through the crowd of looky-loos up to the Goldman house. Groza introduced me around inside and I was allowed to see the bedroom where Manning Goldman had been brutally murdered. The NYPD cops all seemed to know who I was and why I was there. I heard Soneji's name muttered a couple of times. Bad news travels fast.

The detective's body had already been removed from the house, and I didn't like arriving at the murder scene so late. Several NYPD techies were working the room. *Goldman's blood was everywhere*. It was splattered on the bed, the walls, the beige-carpeted floor, the desk and bookcases, and even on a gold menorah. I already knew why Soneji was so interested in spilling blood now – his blood was deadly.

I could feel Gary Soneji here in Goldman's room, *I could see him,* and it stunned me that I could imagine his presence so strongly, physically and emotionally. I remembered a time when Soneji had entered my home in the night with a knife. *Why would he come here?* I wondered. *Was he warning me, playing with my head?*

'He definitely wanted to make a high-profile statement,' I muttered, more to myself than to Carmine Groza. 'He knew that Goldman was running the case in New York. He's showing us that he's in complete control.'

There was something else, though. There had to be more to this than I was seeing so far. I paced around the bedroom. I noticed that the computer on the desk was turned on.

I spoke to one of the techies, a thin man with a small, grim mouth. Perfect for homicide scenes. 'The computer was on when they found Detective Goldman?' I asked.

'Yeah. The Mac was on. It's been dusted.'

I glanced at Groza. 'We know he's looking for Shareef Thomas, and that Thomas was originally from New York. He's supposed to be back here now. Maybe he made Goldman pull up Thomas's file before he killed him.'

For once Detective Groza didn't answer. He was

quiet and unresponsive. I wasn't completely certain myself. Still, I trusted my instincts, especially when it came to Soneji. I was following in his bloody footsteps and I didn't think I was too far behind.

CHAPTER 42

The surprisingly hospitable New York police had gotten me a room for the night at the Marriott Hotel on Forty-second Street. They were already checking on Shareef Thomas for me. What could be done was being taken care of, but Soneji was on the loose for another night on the town.

Shareef Thomas had lived in D.C., but he was originally from Brooklyn. I was fairly certain Soneji had followed him here. Hadn't he told me as much through Jamal Autry at Lorton Prison? He had a score to settle with Thomas, and Soneji settled his old scores. I ought to know.

At eight-thirty I finally left Police Plaza, and I was physically whipped. I was driven uptown in a squad car. I'd packed a duffel bag, so I was set for a couple of days, if it came to that. I hoped that it wouldn't. I like New York City under the right circumstances, but this was hardly Fifth Avenue Christmas shopping in

December, or a Yankee World Series game in the fall.

Around nine, I called home and got our automatic answering machine – Jannie. She said, 'Is this E.T.? You calling *home*?' She's cute like that. She must have known the phone call would be from me. I always call, no matter what.

'How are you, my sweet one? Light of my life?' Just the sound of her voice made me miss her, miss being home with my family.

'Sampson came by. He was checking on us. We were supposed to do boxing tonight. Remember, Daddy?' Jannie played her part with a heavy hand, but it worked. 'Bip, bip, bam. Bam, bam, bip,' she said, creating a vivid picture out of sound.

'Did you and Damon practice anyway?' I asked. I was imagining her face as we talked. Damon's face. Nana's too. The kitchen where Jannie was talking. I missed having supper with my family.

'We sure did. I knocked his block right off. I put out his lights for the night. But it's not the same without you. Nobody to show off for.'

'You just have to show off for yourself,' I told her.

'I know, Daddy. That's what I did. I showed off for myself, and myself said good show.'

I laughed out loud into the phone receiver. 'I'm sorry about missing the boxing lesson with you two pit bulls. Sorry, sorry, sorry,' I said in a bluesy, sing-song voice. 'Sorry, sorry, sorry, sorry.'

'That's what you *always* say,' Jannie whispered, and I could hear the crackle of hurt in her voice. 'Someday, it's not going to work anymore. Mark my words. Remember where you heard it first. Remember, remember, remember.'

I took her counsel to heart in the lonely New York City hotel room as I ate a room-service burger and looked out over Times Square. I remembered an old joke among shrinks: '*Schizophrenia beats eating alone.*' I thought about my kids, and about Christine Johnson, and then about Soneji and Manning Goldman, murdered in his own house. I tried to read a few pages of *Angela's Ashes*, which I'd packed in my bag. I couldn't handle the beautifully described Limerick ghetto that night.

I called Christine when I thought I had my head screwed on straight. We talked for almost an hour. Easy, effortless talk. Something was changing between us. I asked her if she wanted to spend some time together that weekend, maybe in New York if I still had to be here. It took some nerve for me to ask. I wondered if she could hear it in my voice.

Christine surprised me again. She wanted to come to New York. She laughed and said she could do some early Christmas shopping in July, but I had to *promise* to make time for her.

I promised.

I must have slept some finally, because I woke in a strange bed, in a stranger town, wrapped in my bedsheets as if I were trapped in a straitjacket.

I had a strange, discomforting thought. Gary Soneji is tracking *me*. It's not the other way round.

CHAPTER 43

*H*e was the Angel of Death. He had known that since he was eleven or twelve years old. He had killed someone back then, just to see if he could do it. The police had never found the body. Not to this day. Only he knew where all the bodies were buried, and he wasn't telling.

Suddenly, Gary Soneji drifted back to reality, to the present moment in New York City.

Christ, I'm snickering and laughing to myself inside this bar on the East Side. I might have even been talking to myself.

The bartender at Dowd & McGoey's had already spotted him, talking to himself, nearly in a trance. The sneaky, red-haired Irish prick was pretending to polish beer glasses, but all the time he was watching out of the corner of his eye. *When Irish eyes are spying.*

Soneji immediately beckoned the barman over with a wave and a shy smile. 'Don't worry, I'm cutting myself off. Starting to get a little out of control here. What do I owe you, Michael?' The name was emblazoned on the barman's shirt tag.

The phoney, apologetic act seemed to work okay, so he settled his bill and left. He walked south for several blocks on First Avenue, then west on East Fiftieth Street.

He saw a crowded spot called Tatou. It looked promising. He remembered his mission: He needed a place to stay the night in New York, someplace safe. The Plaza hadn't really been such a good idea.

Tatou was filled to the rafters with a lively crowd come to talk, rubberneck, eat and drink. The first floor was a supper club; the second floor was set up for dancing. *What was the scene here about?* he wondered. He needed to understand. Attitude was the answer he came up with. Stylish businessmen and professional women in their thirties and forties came to Tatou, probably straight from work in midtown. It was a Thursday night. Most of them were trying to set up something interesting for the weekend.

Soneji ordered a white wine and he began to eye the men and women lined up along the bar. They looked so perfectly in tune with the times, so desperately cool. *Pick me, choose me, somebody please notice me*, they seemed to plead.

He chatted up a pair of lady lawyers who, unfortunately, were joined at the hip. They reminded him of the strange girls in the French movie *La Cérémonie*. He learned that Theresa and Jessie had been roommates for the past eleven years. Jesus! They were both thirty-six. Their clocks were ticking very loudly. They worked out religiously at the Vertical Club on Sixty-first Street. Summered in Bridge-hampton, a mile from the water. They were all wrong for him and, apparently, for everyone else at the bar.

Soneji moved on. He was starting to feel a little pressure. The police knew he was using disguises. Only not what he might look like on a given day. Yesterday, he was a dark-haired Spanish-looking man in his mid-forties. Today, he was blond, bearded, and fit right in at Tatou. Tomorrow, who knew? He could make a dumb mistake, though. He could be picked up and everything would end.

He met an advertising art director, a creative direc-tor in a large ad factory on Lexington Avenue. Jean Summerhill was originally from Atlanta, she told him. She was small and very slim, with blonde hair, lots of it. She wore a single trendy braid down one side, and he could tell she was full of herself. In an odd way, she reminded him of his Meredith, his Missy. Jean Summerhill had her own place, a condo. She lived alone, in the seventies.

She was too pretty to be in here alone, looking for company in all the wrong places, but Soneji under-stood why once they'd talked: Jean Summerhill was too smart, too strong and individualistic for most men. She scared men off without meaning to, or even knowing that she had.

She didn't scare him, though. They talked easily, the way strangers sometimes do at a bar. Nothing to lose, nothing to risk. She was very down-to-earth. A woman with a need to be seen as 'nice'; unlucky in love, though. He told her that and, since it was what she wanted to hear, Jean Summerhill seemed to believe him.

'You're easy to talk to,' she said over their third or fourth drink. 'You're very calm. Centered, right?'

'Yeah, I am a little boring,' Soneji said. He knew he was anything but that. 'Maybe that's why my wife left me. Missy fell for a rich man, her boss on Wall Street. We both cried the night that she told me. Now she lives in a big apartment over on Beekman Place. Real fancy digs.' He smiled. 'We're still friends. I just saw Missy recently.'

Jean looked into his eyes. There was something sad about the look. 'You know what I like about you,' she said, 'it's that you're not afraid of me.'

Gary Soneji smiled. 'No, I guess I'm not.'

'And I'm not afraid of you either,' Jean Summerhill whispered.

'That's the way it should be,' Soneji said. 'Just don't lose your head over me. Promise?'

'I'll do my best.'

The two of them left Tatou and went to her condo together.

CHAPTER 44

I stood all alone on Forty-second Street in Manhattan, anxiously waiting for Carmine Groza to show. The homicide detective finally picked me up at the front entrance of the Marriott. I jumped into his car and we headed to Brooklyn. Something good had finally happened on the case, something promising.

Shareef Thomas had been spotted at a crackhouse in the Bedford-Stuyvesant section of Brooklyn. Did Gary Soneji know where Thomas was, too? How much, if anything, had he learned from Manning Goldman's computer files?

At seven on Saturday morning, traffic in the city was a joy to behold. We raced west to east across Manhattan in less than ten minutes. We crossed the East River on the Brooklyn Bridge. The sun was just coming up over a group of tall apartment buildings. It was a blinding yellow fireball that gave me an instant headache.

We arrived in Bed-Stuy a little before seven-thirty. I'd heard of the Brooklyn neighborhood, and its tough reputation. It was mostly deserted at that time of the morning. Racist cops in D.C. have a nasty way of describing this kind of inner-city area. They call them 'self-cleaning ovens.' You just close the door and let it clean itself. Let it burn. Nana Mama has another word for America's mostly neglectful social programs for the inner cities: genocide.

The local bodega had a handpainted sign scrawled in red letters on yellow: FIRST STREET DELI AND TOBACCO, OPEN 24 HOURS. The store was closed. So much for the sign.

Parked in front of the deserted deli was a maroon-and-tan van. The vehicle had silver-tinted windows and a 'moonlight over Miami' scene painted on the side panels. A lone female addict slogged along in a knock-kneed swaying walk. She was the only person on the street when we arrived.

The building that Shareef Thomas was in turned out to be two-storied, with faded gray shingles and some broken windows. It looked as if it had been condemned a long time ago. Thomas was still inside the crackhouse. Groza and I settled in to wait. We were hoping Gary Soneji might show up.

I slid down into a corner of the front seat. In the distance, I could see a peeling billboard high above a red-brick building: COP SHOT $10,000 REWARD. Not a good omen, but a fair warning.

The neighborhood began to wake up and show its

character around nine or so. A couple of elderly women in blousy white dresses walked hand in hand toward the Pentecostal church up the street. They made me think of Nana and her buddies back in D.C. Made me miss being home for the weekend, too.

A girl of six or seven was playing jump rope down the street. I noticed she was using salvaged electrical wire. She moved in a kind of listless trance.

It made me sad to watch the little sweetheart play. I wondered what would become of her? What chance did she have to make it out of here? I thought of Jannie and Damon and how they were probably 'disappointed' in me for being away on Saturday morning. *Saturday is our day off, Daddy. We only have Saturdays and Sundays to be together.*

Time passed slowly. It almost always does on surveillance. I had a thought about the neighborhood – *tragedy can be addictive, too.* A couple of suspicious-looking guys in sleeveless T-shirts and cutoff shorts pulled up in an unmarked black truck around ten-thirty. They set up shop, selling watermelons, corn on the cob, tomatoes, and collard greens on the street. The melons were piled high in the scummy gutter.

It was almost eleven o'clock now and I was worried. Our information might be wrong. Paranoia was starting to run a little wild in my head. Maybe Gary Soneji had already visited the crackhouse. He was good at disguises. He might even be in there now.

I opened the car door and got out. The heat rushed at me and I felt as if I were stepping into a blast oven.

Still, it was good to be out of the car, the cramped quarters.

'What are you doing?' Groza asked. He seemed prepared to sit in the car all day, playing everything by the book, waiting for Soneji to show.

'Trust me,' I said.

CHAPTER 45

I took off my white shirt and tied it loosely around my waist. I narrowed my eyes, let them go in and out of focus.

Groza called out: 'Alex.' I ignored him and I began to shuffle toward the dilapidated crackhouse. I figured I looked the street-junkie part okay. It wasn't too hard. God knows I'd seen it played enough times in my own neighborhood. My older brother was a junkie before he died.

The crackhouse was being operated out of an abandoned building on a dead-end corner. It was pretty much standard operating procedure in all big cities I have visited: D.C., Baltimore, Philly, Miami, New York. Makes you wonder.

As I opened the graffiti-painted front door, I saw that the place was definitely bottom of the barrel, even for crackhouses. This was end-of-the-line time. Shareef Thomas had the Virus, too.

Debris was scattered everywhere across the grimy, stained floor. Empty soda cans and beer bottles. Fast-food wrappers from Wendy's and Roy's and Kentucky Fried. Crack vials. Hanger wires used to clean out crack pipes. Hot time, summer in the city.

I figured that a down-and-out dump like this would be run by a single 'clerk.' You pay the guy two or three dollars for a space on the floor. You can also buy syringes, pipes, papers, butane lighters, and maybe even a soda pop or cerveza.

'Fuck-it' and 'AIDS' and 'Junkies of the World' were scrawled across the walls. There was also a thick, smoky fog that seemed allergic to the sunlight. The stink was fetid, worse than walking around in a city dump.

It was incredibly quiet, strangely serene, though. I noticed everything at a glance, but no Shareef Thomas. No Gary Soneji either. At least I didn't see him yet.

A Latino-looking man with a shoulder holster over a soiled 'Bacardi' T-shirt was in charge of the early-morning shift. He was barely awake, but still managed to look in control of the place. He had an ageless face and a thick mustache.

It looked as if Shareef Thomas had definitely fallen down a few notches. If he was here, he was hanging with the low end of the low. Was Shareef dying? Or just hiding? Did he know Soneji might be looking for him?

'What do you want, chief?' the Latino man asked in

a low grumble. His eyes were thin slits.

'Little peace and quiet,' I said. I kept it respectful. As if this were church, which it was for some people.

I handed him two crumpled bills and he turned away with the money. 'In there,' he said.

I looked past him into the main room, and I felt as if a hand were clutching my heart and squeezing it tight.

About ten or twelve men and a couple of women were sitting or sprawled on the floor and on a few soiled, incredibly thin mattresses. The pipeheads were mostly staring into space, doing nothing, and doing it well. It was as if they were slowly fading or evaporating into the smoke and dust.

No one noticed me, which was okay, which was good. Nobody much cared who came or left this hellhole. I still hadn't spotted Shareef. Or Soneji.

It was as dark as a moonless night in the main room of the crackhouse. No lights except for an occasional match being struck. The sound of the match-head strike, then a long, extended hiss.

I was looking for Thomas, but I was also carefully playing my part. Just another strung-out junkie pipehead. Looking for a spot to smoke, to nod out in peace, not here to bother anyone.

I spotted Shareef Thomas on one of the mattresses, near the rear of the dark, dingy room. I recognized him from pictures I'd studied at Lorton. *I forced my eyes away from him.*

My heart started to pump like crazy. Could Soneji

be here, too? Sometimes he seemed like a phantom or ghost to me. I wondered if there was a door back out. I had to find a place to sit down before Thomas became suspicious of me.

I made it to a wall and started to slide down to the floor. I watched Shareef Thomas out of the corner of my eye. Then all kinds of unexpected madness and chaos broke out inside the crackhouse.

The front door was thrown open and Groza and two uniforms burst in. So much for trust. 'Muhfucker,' a man near me woke up and moaned in the smoky shadows.

'Police! Don't move!' Carmine Groza yelled. 'Nobody move. Everybody stay cool!' He sounded like a street cop anyway.

My eyes stayed glued to Shareef Thomas. He was already getting up off the mattress, where he'd been content as a cat just a few seconds ago. Maybe he wasn't stoned at all. Maybe he *was* hiding.

I grabbed for the Glock under my rolled-up shirt, tucked at the small of my back. I brought it around in front of me. I hoped against hope I wouldn't have to use it in these close quarters.

Thomas raised a shotgun that must have been hidden alongside his mattress. The other pipeheads seemed unable to move and get out of the way. Every red-rimmed eye in the room was opened wide with fear.

Thomas's Street Sweeper exploded! Groza and the uniformed cops hit the floor, all three of them. I couldn't tell if anyone had been hit up front.

The Latino at the door yelled, 'Cut this shit out! Cut the shit!' He was down low on the floor himself, screaming without raising his head into the line of fire.

'Thomas!' I yelled at the top of my voice.

Shareef Thomas was moving with surprising speed and alertness. Quick, sure reflexes, even under the influence. He turned the shotgun on me. His dark eyes glared.

There is nothing to compare with the sight of a shotgun pointed right at you. I had no choice now. I squeezed the trigger of the Glock.

Shareef Thomas took a thunderbolt in his right shoulder. He spun hard left, but he didn't go down. He pivoted smoothly. He'd been here before. So had I.

I fired a second time, hit him in the throat or lower jaw. Thomas flew back and crashed into the paper-thin walls. The whole building shook. His eyeballs flipped back and his mouth sagged open wide. He was gone before he hit the crackhouse floor.

I had killed our only connection to Gary Soneji.

CHAPTER 46

I heard Carmine Groza shouting into his radio. The words chilled me. 'Officer down at 412 Macon. *Officer down!'*

I had never been on the scene when another officer was killed. As I got to the front of the crackhouse, though, I was certain one of the uniforms was going to die. Why had Groza come in here like that? Why had he brought in patrolmen with him? Well, it didn't matter much now.

The uniformed man lay on his back on the littered floor near the front door. His eyes were already glazed and I thought he was in shock. Blood was trickling from the corner of his mouth.

The shotgun had done its horrifying work, just as it would have done me. Blood was splashed on the walls and across the scarred wooden floor. A scorched pattern of bullet holes was tattooed in the wall above the patrolman's body. There was nothing any of us could do for him.

I stood near Groza, still holding my Glock. I was clenching and unclenching my teeth. I was trying not to be angry with Groza for overreacting and causing this to happen. I had to get myself under control before I spoke.

The uniformed cop to my left was muttering 'Christ, Christ,' over and over again. I could see how traumatized he was. The uniformed man kept wiping his hand across his forehead and over his eyes, as if to wipe out the bloody scene.

EMS arrived in a matter of minutes. We watched while two medics tried desperately to save the patrolman's life. He was young and looked to be only in his mid-twenties. His reddish hair was in a short brush-cut. The front of his dark-blue shirt was soaked with blood.

In the rear of the crackhouse another medic was trying to save Shareef Thomas, but I already knew that Thomas was gone.

I finally spoke to Groza, low and serious. 'We know that Thomas is dead, but there's no reason Soneji has to know. This could be how we get to him. If Soneji *thought* Thomas was alive at a New York hospital.'

Groza nodded. 'Let me talk to somebody downtown. Maybe we could take Thomas to a hospital. Maybe we could get the word to the press. It's worth a shot.'

Detective Groza didn't sound very good and he

didn't look too good. I was sure I didn't either. I could still see the ominous billboard in the distance: COP SHOT $10,000 REWARD.

CHAPTER 47

No one in the police manhunt would ever guess the beginning, the middle, but especially the end. None of them could imagine where this was heading, where it had been going from the first moment inside Union Station.

Gary Soneji had all the information, all the power. He was getting famous again. He was somebody. He was on the news at ten-minute intervals.

It didn't much matter that they were showing pictures of him. Nobody knew what he looked like today, or yesterday, or tomorrow. They couldn't go around and arrest everyone in New York, could they?

He left the late Jean Summerhill's apartment around noon. The pretty lady had definitely lost her head over him. Just like Missy in Wilmington. He used her key and locked up tight. He walked west on Seventy-third Street until he got to Fifth, then he turned south. The train was back on the track again.

He bought a cup of black coffee in a cardboard container with Greek gods all over the sides. The coffee was absolute New York City swill, but he slowly sipped it anyway. He wanted to go on another rampage right here on Fifth Avenue. He really wanted to go for it. He imagined a massacre, and he could already see the *live* news stories on CBS, ABC, CNN, FOX.

Speaking of news stories, Alex Cross had been on TV that morning. Cross and the NYPD had nabbed Shareef Thomas. Well hooray for them. It proved they could follow instructions at least.

As he passed chic, well-dressed New Yorkers, Soneji couldn't help thinking how smart he was, how much brighter than any of these uptight assholes. If any of these snooty bastards could get inside his head, just for a minute, then they'd know.

No one could, though, no one had ever been able to. No one could guess.

Not the beginning, the middle, or the end.

He was getting very angry now, almost uncontrollably so. He could feel the rage surging as he walked the overcrowded streets. He almost couldn't see straight. Bile rose in his throat.

He flung his coffee, almost a full cup of the steamy liquid, at a passing businessman. He laughed right in the shocked, outraged face. He howled at the sight of coffee dripping from the New Yorker's aquiline nose, his squarish chin. Dark coffee stained the expensive shirt and tie.

Gary Soneji could do anything he wanted to, and most often, he did.

Just you watch.

CHAPTER 48

A t seven that night, I was back in Penn Station. It wasn't the usual commuter crowd, so it wasn't too bad on Saturdays. The murders that had taken place at Union Station in Washington, and here, were spinning around in my mind. The dark train tunnels were the 'cellar' to Soneji, symbols of his tortured boyhood. I had figured out that much of the delusionary puzzle. When Soneji came up and out of the cellar, he exploded at the world in a murderous rage . . .

I saw Christine coming up the stairs from the train tunnels.

I began to smile in spite of the locale. I smiled, and shifted my weight from foot to foot, almost dancing. I felt light-headed and excited, filled with hope and desire that I hadn't felt in a long time. She had really come.

Christine was carrying a small black bag with

'Sojourner Truth School' printed on it. She was traveling light. She looked beautiful, proud, more desirable than ever, if that was possible. She was wearing a white short-sleeved dress with a jewel neckline and her usual flats in black patent leather. I noticed people looking at her. They always did.

We kissed in a corner of the train station, keeping our privacy as best we could. Our bodies pressed together and I could feel her warmth, her bones, her flesh. I heard the bag she was carrying drop at her feet.

Her brown eyes looked into mine and they were wide and questioning at first, but then became very soft and light. 'I was a little afraid you wouldn't be here,' she said. 'I had visions of you off on some police emergency, and me standing here alone in the middle of Penn Station.'

'There's no way I would let that happen,' I said to her. 'I'm so glad you're here.'

We kissed again, pressing even harder together. I didn't want to stop kissing Christine, holding her tightly. I wanted to take her where we could be alone. My body nearly convulsed. It was that bad, that good.

'I tried,' she said and grinned, 'but I couldn't stay away from you. New York scares me a little, but here I am.'

'We're going to have a great time. You'll see.'

'You promise? Will it be unforgettable?' she teased me.

'Unforgettable. I promise,' I said.

I held her tightly in my arms. I couldn't let her go.

CHAPTER 49

The beginning of 'unforgettable' felt like this, looked like this, sounded like this.

The Rainbow Room at eight-thirty on a Saturday night. Christine and I waltzed off the glitzy elevator, arm in arm. We were immediately swept into another era, another lifestyle, maybe another life. A fancy silver-on-black placard near the elevator door read: 'The Rainbow Room, Step into an MGM Musical.' Hundreds of minispotlights kicked off from the dazzling chrome and crystal. It was over the top, and just about perfect.

'I'm not sure if I'm dressed right for an MGM musical, but I don't particularly care. What a wonderful idea,' Christine said as we made our way past overdone, outrageous-looking ushers and usherettes. We were directed to a desk that looked down onto the deco ballroom but also had panoramic views of New York. The room was jam-packed on a Saturday night; every table and the dance floor was filled.

Christine was dressed in a simple black sheath. She wore the same necklace, made from an old-fashioned brooch, that she wore at Kinkead's. It had belonged to her grandmother. Because I'm six-three, she wasn't afraid to wear dressier shoes with high heels, rather than her comfortable flats. I had never realized it before, but I liked being with a woman who was nearly as tall as I am.

I had dressed up, too. I'd chosen a charcoal-gray, summer-weight suit, crisp white shirt, blue silk tie. For tonight anyway, I was definitely not a police detective from D.C. I didn't look like Dr Alex Cross from Southeast. Maybe more like Denzel Washington playing the part of Jay Gatsby. I liked the feeling, for a night on the town anyway. Maybe even for a whole weekend.

We were escorted to a table in front of a large window that overlooked the glittering East Side of Manhattan. A five-piece Latin band was onstage, and they were cooking pretty good. The slowly revolving dance floor was still full. People were having a fine time, lots of people dancing the night away.

'It's funny, beautiful, and ridiculous, and I think it's as special as anywhere I've been,' Christine said once we were seated. 'That's about all the superlatives you're going to hear from me tonight.'

'You haven't even seen me dance,' I said.

'I already know that you can dance.' Christine laughed and told me, 'Women always know which men can dance, and which men can't.'

We ordered drinks, straight Scotch for me, Harvey's Bristol Cream for Christine. We picked out a bottle of sauvignon blanc, and then spent a few delicious minutes just taking in the spectacle of the Rainbow Room.

The Latin combo was replaced by a 'big band combo,' which played swing and even took a swipe at the blues. A whole lot of people still knew how to jitterbug and waltz and even tango, and some of them were pretty good.

'You ever been here before?' I asked Christine as the waiter came with our drinks.

'Only while I was watching *The Prince of Tides* alone in my bedroom at home,' she said and smiled again. 'How about you? Come here often, sailor?'

'Just the one time I was chasing down this split-personality ax-murderer in New York. He went right out that picture window over there. Third from the left.'

Christine laughed. 'I wouldn't be surprised if it was true, Alex. I wouldn't be a bit surprised.'

The band started to play 'Moonglow,' which is a pretty song, and we had to get up and dance. Gravity just pulled us. At that moment, I couldn't think of too many things in the world I wanted to do more than hold Christine in my arms. Actually, I couldn't think of anything at all.

At some point in time, Christine and I had agreed to take a risk and see what would happen. We'd both lost people we loved. We knew what it meant to be hurt, and yet here we were, ready to go out on the dance floor of life again. I think I'd wanted to slow-dance with Christine from the very first time I saw her at the Sojourner Truth School.

Now, I tucked her in close and my left arm encircled her waist. My right hand clasped hers. I felt her soft intake of breath. I could tell she was a little nervous, too.

I started to hum softly. I might have been floating a little, too. My lips touched hers and my eyes closed. I could feel the silk of her dress under my fingers. And yes, I could dance pretty well, but so could she.

'Look at me,' she whispered, and I opened my eyes. She was right. It was much better that way.

'What's going on here? What *is* this? I don't think I've ever felt like this, Alex.'

'Neither have I. But I could get used to it. I know that I like it.'

I lightly brushed her cheek with my fingers. The music was working and Christine seemed to flow with me. Graceful, moonlit choreography. All my body parts were moving. I was finding it hard to breathe.

Christine and I were in harmony together. We both could dance well enough, but together it was something special. I moved slowly and smoothly with her. The palm of her hand felt magnetized to mine. I spun her slowly, a playful half-turn underneath my arm.

We came back together and our lips were inches

apart. I could feel the warmth of her body right through my clothes. Our lips met again, for just an instant, and the music stopped. Another song began.

'Now *that* is a hard act to follow,' she said as we sashayed back to our table after the slow-dance. 'I knew you could dance. Never a doubt in my mind. But I didn't know you could *dance*.'

'You haven't seen anything. Wait until they play a samba,' I told her. I was still holding her hand, couldn't let go. Didn't want to.

'I *think* I can samba,' she said.

We danced a lot, we held hands constantly, and I think we even ate dinner. We definitely danced some more, and I could not let go of Christine's hand. She couldn't let go of mine. We talked nonstop, and later, I couldn't remember most of what had been said. I think that happens high above New York City in the Rainbow Room.

The first time I looked at my watch all night it was nearly one o'clock and I couldn't believe it. That same mysterious time-loss thing had happened a couple of times when I'd been with Christine. I paid our bill, our *big* bill, and I noticed that the Rainbow Room was nearly empty. Where had everybody gone?

'Can you keep a secret?' Christine whispered as we were going down to the lobby in the walnut-paneled elevator. We were alone in the car with its soft yellow light. I was holding her in my arms.

'I keep lots of secrets,' I said.

'Well, here it is,' Christine said as we reached the

bottom floor with just the lightest *bump*. She held me inside after the door had opened. She wasn't going to let me out of the softly lit elevator until she finished saying what she had to say.

'I really like that you got me my own room at the Astor,' she said. 'But Alex, I don't think I'll be needing it. Is that okay?'

We stood very still in the elevator and began to kiss again. The doors shut, and the elevator slowly climbed back up to the roof. So we kissed going up, and we kissed on the way back down to the lobby, and it wasn't nearly a long-enough round-trip.

'You know what, though?' she finally said as we reached the ground floor of Rockefeller Center a second time.

'What, though?' I asked her.

'That's what's *supposed* to happen when you go to the Rainbow Room.'

CHAPTER 50

I t *was* unforgettable. Just like the magical Nat King
Cole song, and the more recent version with
Natalie Cole.

We were standing at the door to my hotel room,
and I was completely lost in the moment. I had let go
of Christine's hand to open the door – and I was *lost*.
I fumbled the key slightly and missed the lock. She
gently placed her hand on mine and we glided the
key into the lock, turned the tumblers together.

An eternity of seconds passed, at least it seemed
that way. I knew that I would never forget any of this.
I wouldn't let skepticism or cynicism diminish it
either.

I knew what was happening to me. I was feeling
the dizzying effect of a return to intimacy. I hadn't
realized how much I'd missed it. I had let myself be
numb, let myself live numb for the past few years. It's
easy enough to do, so easy that you don't even realize

your life has become a deep rut.

The hotel door slowly opened, and I had the thought that the two of us were giving up something of our past now. Christine turned to me at the threshold. I heard the faint swish of her silk dress.

Her beautiful face tilted toward mine. I reached for her and balanced her chin with my fingertips. I felt as if I hadn't been able to breathe properly all night, not from the moment she'd arrived at Penn Station.

'Musician's hands. Piano player fingers,' she said. 'I love the way you touch me. I always knew I would. I'm not afraid anymore, Alex.'

'I'm glad. Neither am I.'

The heavy wooden door of the hotel room seemed to close all by itself.

It didn't really matter where we were right now, I was thinking. The twinkling lights outside, or maybe a boat gliding by on the river, gave the impression that the floor was gently moving, much as the dance floor at the Rainbow Room had moved under our feet.

I had switched hotels for the weekend, moving to the Astor on Manhattan's East Side. I'd wanted someplace special. The room was on the twelfth floor, facing out on the river.

We were drawn to the picture window, attracted by the strobing lights of the New York skyline to the southeast. We watched the silent, strangely beautiful movement of traffic passing the United Nations, moving toward the Brooklyn Bridge.

I remembered taking the bridge earlier today on

our way to a crackhouse in Brooklyn. It seemed so long ago. I saw the face of Shareef Thomas, then the dead policeman's, then Soneji's, but I shut down those images immediately. I wasn't a police detective here. Christine's lips were on my skin, lightly bussing my throat.

'Where did you go just now? You went away, didn't you?' she whispered. 'You were in a dark place.'

'Just for a few seconds.' I confessed the truth, my flaw. 'A flashback from work. It's gone.' I was holding her hand again.

She kissed me lightly on the cheek, a paper-thin kiss, then very lightly on the lips. 'You can't lie, can you, Alex? Not even tiny white lies.'

'I try not to. I don't like lies. If I lie to you, then who am I?' I said and smiled. 'What's the point?'

'I love that about you,' she whispered. 'Lots of other things, too. I find something else every time I'm with you.'

I nuzzled the top of her head, then I kissed Christine's forehead, her cheek, her lips, and finally the sweet hollow of her throat. She was trembling a little. So was I. Thank God that neither of us was afraid, right. I could feel the pulse tripping under her skin.

'You're so beautiful,' I whispered. 'Do you know that?'

'I'm way too tall, too thin. *You're* the beautiful one. You are, you know. Everybody says so.'

Everything felt electric and so right. It seemed a miracle that we had found each other, and now we were here together. I was so glad, felt so lucky, that she had decided to take a chance with me, that I had taken a chance, too.

'Look in the mirror there. See how beautiful you are,' she said. 'You have the sweetest face. You *are* trouble though, aren't you, Alex?'

'I won't give you too much trouble tonight,' I said.

I wanted to undress her, to do everything for and to Christine. A funny word, strange word was in my head, *rapture*. She slid her hand over the front of my pants and felt how hard I was.

'Hmmm,' she whispered and smiled.

I began to unzip her dress. I couldn't remember wanting to be with someone like this, not for a long time anyway. I ran my hand over her face, memorizing every part, every feature. Christine's skin was so soft and silky underneath my fingers.

We started to dance again, right there in the hotel room. There wasn't any music, but we had our own. My hand pressed just below her waist, folding her in close to me.

Moonlit choreography again. We slowly rocked back and forth, back and forth, a sensuous cha-cha-cha next to the broad picture window. I held her buttocks in the palms of my hands. She wiggled into a position she liked. I liked it, too. A whole lot.

'You dance real good, Alex. I just knew you would.'

Christine reached down and tugged at my belt until the prong came free. She unzipped me, lightly fondled me. I loved her touch, anywhere, everywhere.

Her lips were on my skin again. Everything about her was erotic, irresistible, unforgettable.

We both knew to do this slowly, no need to hurry anything tonight. Rushing would spoil this, and it mustn't be spoiled in any way.

I held the thought that we'd both been here before, but never like this. We were in this very special place for the first time. This would only happen one time.

My kisses slowly swept over her shoulders and I could feel her breasts rising and falling against me. I felt the flatness of her stomach, and her legs pressing. I cupped Christine's breasts in my hands. Suddenly I wanted everything, all of her at once.

I sank to my knees. I ran my hands up and down her soft legs, along her waist.

I rose to my feet. I unzipped her black sheath the rest of the way and it trailed down her long arms to the floor. It made a shimmering black puddle surrounding her ankles, her slender feet.

Finally, when there were no more clothes and we looked at each other, Christine watched my eyes and I watched hers. Her eyes shamelessly traveled down my chest, past my waist. I was still highly aroused. I wanted to be inside her so much.

She took a half-step back. I couldn't breathe. I could hardly bear this. But I didn't want it to stop. I was feeling again, remembering how to feel, remembering how good it could be.

She pulled her hair to one side, behind one ear. Such a simple, graceful movement.

'Do that again,' I smiled.

She laughed and repeated the movement with her hair. 'Anything that you want.

'Stay there,' she whispered. 'Don't move, Alex. Don't come closer – we might both catch fire. I mean it.'

'This could take the rest of the weekend,' I said and started to laugh.

'I hope it does.'

I heard the tiniest *click*.

Was that the door to our room?

Had I closed it?

Was someone out there?

Jesus, no.

CHAPTER 51

Suddenly nervous and paranoid, I peered back at the door to the hotel room. It was closed and locked tight. Nobody there, nothing to worry about. Christine and I were safe here. Nothing bad was going to happen to either of us tonight.

Still, the moment of fear and doubt had raised the hairs on my neck. Soneji has a habit of doing that to me. *Damn it, what did he want from me?*

'What's wrong, Alex? You just left me again.' Christine touched me, brought me back. Her fingers were like feathers on the side of my cheek. 'Just be here with me, Alex.'

'I'm here. I just thought I heard something.'

'I know you did. No one is there. You locked the door behind us. We're fine. It's okay, it's okay.'

I pulled Christine close against my body again and she felt electric and incredibly warm. I drew her down onto the bed and rolled over her, holding my weight on the palms of my hands. I dipped and kissed her sweet face again, then each of her breasts; I pulled at the nipples with my lips, licked them with my tongue. I kissed between her legs, down her long legs, her slender ankles, her toes. *Just be here with me, Alex.*

She arched herself toward me and she gasped, but she was smiling radiantly. She was moving her body against me and we had already found a nice rhythm. We were both breathing faster and faster.

'Please, do it now,' she whispered, her teeth biting into my shoulder near the clavicle. 'Please now, *right now*. I want you inside.' She rubbed my sides with the palms of her hands. She rubbed me like kindling sticks.

A fire ignited. I could feel it spreading through my body. I entered her for the first time. I slid inside slowly, but I went as deep as I could go. My heart was pounding, my legs felt weak. My stomach was taut and I was so hard it hurt.

I was all the way inside Christine. I knew I'd wanted to be here for a long time. I had the thought that I was made for this, for being in this bed with this woman.

Gracefully and athletically, she rolled on top of me and sat up proud and tall. We began to rock slowly like that. I felt our bodies surge and peak, surge and peak, surge.

I heard my own voice crying yes, yes, yes. Then I realized it was both our voices.

Then Christine said something so magical. She whispered, *'You're the one.'*

PART THREE

THE CELLAR OF CELLARS

CHAPTER 52

Paris, France.

Dr Abel Sante was thirty-five years old, with longish black hair, boyish good looks, and a beautiful girlfriend named Regina Becker, who was a painter, and a very good one, he thought. He had just left Regina's apartment, and was winding his way home on the back streets of the sixth arrondissement at around midnight.

The narrow streets were quiet and empty and he loved this time of day for collecting his thoughts, or sometimes for not thinking at all. Abel Sante was musing on the death of a young woman earlier today, a patient of his, twenty-six years old. She had a loving husband and two beautiful daughters. He had a perspective about death that he thought was a good one: Why should leaving the world, and rejoining the cosmos, be any scarier than entering the world, which wasn't very scary at all?

Dr Sante didn't know where the man, a street person in a soiled gray jacket and torn, baggy jeans, had come from. Suddenly the man was at his side, nearly attached to his elbow.

'Beautiful,' the man said.

'I'm sorry, excuse me?' Abel Sante said, startled, coming out of his inner thoughts in a hurry.

'It's a beautiful night and our city is so perfect for a late walk.'

'Yes, well it's been nice meeting you,' Sante said to the street person. He'd noticed that the man's French was slightly accented. Perhaps he was English, or even American.

'You shouldn't have left her apartment. Should have stayed the night. A gentleman always stays the night – unless of course he's asked to leave.'

Dr Abel Sante's back and neck stiffened. He took his hands from his trouser pockets. Suddenly he was afraid, very much so.

He shoved the street person away with his left elbow.

'What are you talking about? Why don't you just get out of here?'

'I'm talking about you and Regina. Regina Becker, the painter. Her work's not bad, but not good enough, I'm afraid.'

'Get the hell away from me.'

Abel Sante quickened his pace. He was only a block from his home. The other man, the street person, kept up with him easily. He was larger, more athletic than Sante had noticed at first.

'You should have given her babies. That's my opinion.'

'Get away. Go!'

Suddenly, Sante had both fists raised and clasped tightly. This was insane! He was ready to fight, if he had to. He hadn't fought in twenty years, but he was strong and in good shape.

The street person swung out and knocked him down. He did it easily, as if it were nothing at all.

Dr Sante's pulse was racing rapidly. He couldn't see very well out of his left eye, where he'd been struck.

'Are you a complete maniac? Are you out of your mind?' he screamed at the man, who suddenly looked powerful and impressive, even in the soiled clothes.

'Yes, of course,' the man answered. 'Of course I'm out of my mind. *I'm Mr Smith* – and you're next.'

CHAPTER 53

Gary Soneji hurried like a truly horrifying city rat through the low dark tunnels that wind like intestines beneath New York's Bellevue Hospital. The fetid odor of dried blood and disinfectants made him feel sick. He didn't like the reminders of sickness and death surrounding him.

No matter, though, he was properly revved for today. He was wired, flying high. *He was Death. And Death was not taking a holiday in New York.*

He had outfitted himself for his big morning: crisply pressed white pants, white lab coat, white sneakers; a laminated hospital photo ID around his neck on a beaded silver chain.

He was here on morning rounds. Bellevue. *This was his idea of rounds anyway!*

There was no way to stop any of this: his train from hell, his destiny, his last hurrah. No one could stop it because no one would ever figure out where the last train was headed. Only he knew that, only Soneji himself could call it off.

He wondered how much of the puzzle Cross had already pieced together. Cross wasn't in his class as a thinker, but the psychologist and detective wasn't without crude instincts in certain specialized areas. Maybe he was underestimating Dr Cross, as he had once before. Could he be caught now? Perhaps, but it really didn't matter. The game would continue to its end without him. That was the beauty of it, the evil of what he had done.

Gary Soneji stepped into a stainless-steel elevator in the basement of the well-known Manhattan hospital. A pair of porters shared the narrow car with him, and Soneji had a moment of paranoia. They might be New York cops working undercover.

The NYPD actually had an office on the main floor of the hospital. It was there under 'normal' circumstances. *Bellevue. Jesus, what a sensational madhouse this was. A hospital with a police station inside.*

He eyed the porters with a casual and disinterested city-cool look. *They can't be policemen,* he thought. *Nobody could look that dumb.* They were what they looked like – slow-moving, slow-thinking hospital morons.

One of them was pushing around a stainless-steel cart with *two* bum wheels. It was a wonder that any patient ever made it out of a New York City hospital alive. Hospitals here were run with about the same personnel standards as a McDonald's restaurant, probably less.

He knew one patient who wasn't going to leave Bellevue alive. The news reports said that Shareef Thomas was being kept here by the police. Well, Thomas was going to suffer before he left this so-called 'vale of tears.' Shareef was about to undergo a world of suffering.

Gary Soneji stepped out of the elevator onto the first floor. He sighed with relief. The two porters went about their business. They weren't cops. No, they were dumber and dumbest.

Canes, wheelchairs, and metal walkers were everywhere. The hospital artifacts reminded him of his own mortality. The halls on the first floor were painted off-white, the doors and radiators were a shade of pink like old gum. Up ahead was a strange coffee shop, dimly lit like a subway passageway. *If you ate in that place*, he thought to himself, *they ought to lock you up in Bellevue!*

As he walked from the elevator, Soneji caught his own reflection in a stainless-steel pillar. *The master of a thousand faces*, he couldn't help thinking. It was true. His own stepmother wouldn't recognize him now, and if she did, she would scream her bloody lungs out. She'd know he'd come all the way to hell to get her.

He walked down the corridor, singing very softly in a reggae lilt, 'I shot the Shareef, but I did not shoot the dep-u-tee.'

No one paid him any mind. Gary Soneji fit right in at Bellevue.

CHAPTER 54

Soneji had a perfect memory, so he would recall everything about this morning. He would be able to play it back for himself with incredible detail. This was true for all of his murders. He scanned the narrow, high-ceilinged hallways as if he had a surveillance camera mounted where his head was. His powers of concentration gave him a huge advantage. He was almost supernaturally aware of everything going on around him.

A security guard was riffing with young black males outside the coffee shop. They were all mental defectives for sure, the toy cops especially.

No threat there.

Silly baseball caps were bobbing everywhere. New Jork Janquis. San Francisco Jints. San Jose Sharks. None of the ball-cap wearers looked as if they could play ball worth spit. Or harm, or stop him.

The Hospital Police Office was up ahead. The lights

were out, though. Nobody home right now. So where were the hospital patrol cops? Were they waiting for him someplace? Why didn't he see any of them? Was that the first sign of trouble?

At the inpatient elevator, a sign read: ID REQUIRED. Soneji had his ready. For today's masquerade, he was Francis Michael Nicolo, R.N.

A framed poster was on the wall: Patients' Rights and Responsibilities. Signs stared out from behind fuzzy Plexiglas everywhere he looked. It was worse than a New York highway: Radiology, Urology, Hematology. *I'm sick, too,* Soneji wanted to yell out to the powers that be. *I'm as sick as anybody in here. I'm dying. Nobody cares. Nobody has ever cared.*

He took the central elevator to four. No problems so far, no hassles. No police. He got off at his stop, pumped to see Shareef Thomas again, to see the look of shock and fear on his face.

The hallway on four had a hollowed-out basement feel to it. Nothing seemed to absorb sound. The whole building felt as if it were made entirely of concrete.

Soneji peered down the corridor to where he knew Shareef was being kept. His room was at the far end of the building. Isolated for safety, right? So this was the high-and-mighty NYPD in action. What a joke. Everything was a joke, if you thought about it long and hard enough.

Soneji lowered his head and started to walk toward Shareef Thomas's hospital room.

He had bribed a hospital security guard who brought the meals up to four and was aware of the tight security. He was as dead now as Robert Fishenauer, the supervisor who had helped Soneji escape from prison.

CHAPTER 55

Carmine Groza and I were inside the private hospital room waiting for Soneji, hoping that he would show. We had been here for hours. How would I know what Soneji looked like now? That was a problem, but we would take them one at a time.

We never heard a noise at the door. Suddenly it was swinging open. Soneji exploded into the room, expecting to find Shareef Thomas. He stared at Groza and me.

His hair was dyed silver-gray and combed straight back. He looked like a man in his fifties or early sixties – but the height was about right. His light-blue eyes widened as he looked at me. It was the eyes that I recognized first.

He smiled the same disdainful and dismissive smirk I'd seen so many times, sometimes in my nightmares. He thought he was so damn superior to the rest of us. He *knew* it.

Soneji said only two words: 'Even better.'

'New York police! Freeze,' Groza barked a warning in an authoritative tone.

Soneji continued to smirk as if this surprise reception pleased him no end, as if he'd planned it himself. His confidence, his arrogance, were incredible to behold.

He's wearing a bulletproof vest – my mind registered a bulge around his upper body. *He's protected. He's ready for whatever we do.*

There was something clasped tightly in his left hand. I couldn't tell what. He'd entered the room with the arm half-raised.

He flipped a small green bottle in his hand toward Groza and me. Just the *flip* of his hand. The bottle clinked as it hit the wooden floor. It bounced a second time. Suddenly I understood . . . but too late, seconds too late.

'Bomb!' I yelled at Groza. 'Hit the floor! Get down!'

Groza and I dove away from the bed and the caroming green bottle. We managed to put up sitting chairs as shields. The flash inside the room was incredibly bright, a splintered shock of white light with an afterglow of the brightest yellow. Then everything around us seemed to catch fire.

For a second or two, I was blinded. Then I felt as if I were burning up. My trousers and shoes were engulfed in flames. I covered my face, mouth, and eyes with my hands. 'Jesus, God,' Groza screamed.

I could hear a sizzle, like bacon on a grill. I prayed it

wasn't me that was cooking. Then I was choking and gurgling and so was Groza. Flames burst and danced across my shirt, and through it all I could hear Soneji. He was laughing at us.

'Welcome to hell, Cross,' he said. 'Burn, baby, burn.'

CHAPTER 56

Groza and I stripped the bed of blankets and sheets and beat out our burning trousers. We were lucky, at least I hoped we were. We smothered the flames. The ones on our legs and shoes.

'He wanted to burn Thomas alive,' I told Groza. 'He's got *another* firebomb. I saw another green bottle, at least one.'

We hobbled as best we could down the hospital corridor, chasing after Soneji. Two other detectives were already down outside, wounded. Soneji *was* a phantom.

We followed him down several twisting flights of back stairs. The sound of the footrace echoed loudly on the stairway. My eyes were watering, but I could see okay.

Groza alerted and clued in other detectives on his two-way. 'Suspect has a firebomb! Soneji has a bomb.

Probably a knife also. Use extreme care.'

'What the hell does he want?' the detective yelled at me as we kept moving. 'What the hell's he going to do now?'

'I think he wants to die,' I gasped. 'And he wants to be even more famous. Go out with a bang. That's his way. Maybe right here at Bellevue.'

Attention was what Gary Soneji had always craved. From his boyhood years, he'd been obsessed with stories of 'crimes of the century.' I was sure that Soneji wanted to die now, but he had to do it with a huge noise. He wanted to control his own death.

I was wheezing and out of breath when we finally got to the lobby floor. Smoke had seared my throat, but otherwise I was doing okay. My brain was fuzzy and unclear about what to do next.

I saw a blur of hectic movement ahead, maybe thirty yards across the front lobby.

I pushed through the nervous crowd trying to exit the building. Word had spread about the fire upstairs. The flow of people in and out of Bellevue was always as steady as at a subway turnstile, and that was *before* a bomb went off inside.

I made it onto the stoop in front of the hospital. It was raining hard, gray and awful outside. I looked everywhere for Soneji.

A cluster of hospital staff and visitors were under the front awning, smoking cigarettes. They seemed unaware of the emergency situation, or maybe these workers were just used to them. The brick path leading away from the building was crowded with more pedestrians coming and going in the downpour. The umbrellas were blocking my vision.

Where the hell had Gary Soneji gone? Where could he have disappeared to? I had the sinking feeling that I'd lost him again. I couldn't stand any more of this.

Out on First Avenue, food vendors under colorful umbrellas stained with dirt were peddling gyros, hot dogs, and New York-style pretzels.

No Soneji anywhere.

I kept searching, frantically looking up and down the busy, noisy street. I couldn't let him get away. I would never get another chance as good as this. There was an opening in the crowd. I could see for maybe half a block.

There he was!

Soneji was moving with a small clique of pedestrians headed north on the sidewalk. I started to go after him. Groza was still with me. We both had our guns out. We couldn't risk a shot in the crowds, though. Lots of mothers and children and elderly people, patients coming and going from the hospital.

Soneji peered to the left, the right, and then behind. He saw us coming. I was sure he'd seen me.

He was improvising his escape, a way out of the extreme and dangerous mess. The sequence of recent events showed deterioration in his thinking. He was losing his sharpness and clarity. *That's why he's ready to die now. He's tired of dying slowly. He's losing his mind. He can't bear it.*

A Con Ed crew had blocked off half the intersection. Hard hats bobbed in the rain. Traffic was trying to maneuver around the roadwork, nonstop honkers everywhere.

I saw Soneji make a sudden break from the crowd. What the hell? He was running toward First Avenue, racing down the slippery street. He was weaving, running in a full sprint.

I watched as Gary Soneji spun quickly to his right. *Do us all a favor. Go down!* He ran along the side of a white and blue city bus that had stopped for passengers.

He was still slipping, sliding. He almost fell. Then he was inside the goddamn bus.

The bus was standing-room only. I could see Soneji frantically waving his arms, screaming orders at the other passengers. *Jesus, God, he's got a bomb on that city bus.*

CHAPTER 57

Detective Groza staggered up beside me. His face was smudged with soot and his flowing black hair was singed. He signaled wildly for a car, waving both arms. A police sedan pulled up beside us and we jumped inside.

'You all right?' I asked him.

'I guess so. I'm here. Let's go get him.'

We followed the bus up First Avenue, weaving in and out of traffic, siren full blast. We almost hit a cab, missed by inches, if that.

'You sure he's got another bomb?'

I nodded. 'At least one. Remember the Mad Bomber in New York? Soneji probably does. The Mad Bomber was famous.'

Everything was crazy and surreal. The rain was coming down harder, making loud bangs on the sedan's roof.

'He has hostages.' Groza spoke into the two-way

on the dash. 'He's on a city bus heading up First Avenue. He appears to have a bomb. The bus is an M-15. All cars stay on the bus. Do not intercept at this point. He has a goddamn bomb on the M-15 bus.'

I counted half-a-dozen blue-and-whites already in pursuit. The city bus was stopping for red lights, but it was no longer picking up passengers. People standing in the rain, bypassed at stops, waved their arms angrily at the M-15. None of them understood how lucky they were that the bus doors didn't open for them.

'Try to get close,' I told the driver. 'I want to talk to him. Want to see if he'll talk anyway. It's worth a try.'

The police sedan accelerated, then weaved on the wet streets. We were getting closer, inching alongside the white and blue bus. A poster advertised the musical *The Phantom of the Opera* in bold type. *A real live phantom was on board the bus.* Gary Soneji was back in the spotlight that he loved. He was playing New York now.

I had the side window of the car rolled down. Rain and wind attacked my face, but I could see Soneji inside the bus. *Jesus, he was still improvising* – he had somebody's child, a bundle of pink-and-blue cradled in his arm. He was screaming orders, his free arm swinging in angry circles.

I leaned as far as I could outside the car. 'Gary!' I yelled. 'What do you want?' I called out again, fighting the traffic noise, the loud roar of the bus. '*Gary! It's Alex Cross!*'

Passengers inside the bus were looking out at me. They were terrified, beyond terror, actually.

At Forty-second Street and First, the bus made a sudden, sweeping left turn!

I looked at Groza. 'This the regular route?'

'No way,' he said. 'He's making his own route up as he goes.'

'What's on Forty-second Street? What's up ahead? Where the hell could he be going?'

Groza threw up his hands in desperation. 'Times Square is across town, home of the skells, the city's worst derelicts and losers. Theater district's there, too. Port Authority Bus Terminal. We're coming up on Grand Central Station.'

'Then he's going to Grand Central,' I told Groza. 'I'm sure of it. This is the way he wants it. In a train station!' Another cellar, a glorious one that went on for city blocks. *The cellar of cellars.*

Gary Soneji was already out of the bus and running on Forty-second Street. He was headed toward Grand Central Station, headed toward home. He was still carrying the baby in one arm, swinging it loosely, showing us how little he cared about the child's life.

Goddamn him to hell. He was on the homestretch, and only he knew what that meant.

CHAPTER 58

I made my way down the crowded stone-and-mortar passageway from Forty-second Street. It emptied into an even busier Grand Central Station. Thousands of already harried commuters were arriving for work in the midtown area. They had no idea how truly bad their day was about to become.

Grand Central is the New York end for the New York Central, the New York, New Haven, and Hartford trains and a few others. And for three IRT subway lines. Lexington Avenue, Times Square–Grand Central Shuttle, and Queens. The terminal covers three blocks between Forty-second and Forty-fifth Streets. Forty-one tracks are on the upper level and twenty-six on the lower, which narrows to a single four-track line to Ninety-sixth Street.

The lower level is a huge labyrinth, one of the largest anywhere in the world.

Gary's cellar.

I continued to push against the densely packed rush-hour crowd. I made it through a waiting room, then emerged into the cavernous and spectacular main concourse. Construction work was in progress everywhere. Giant cloth posters for Pan Am Airlines and American Express and Nike sneakers hung down over the walls. The gates to dozens of tracks were visible from where I stood.

Detective Groza caught up with me in the concourse. We were both running on adrenaline. 'He's still got the baby,' he huffed. 'Somebody spotted him running down to the next level.'

Leading a merry chase, right? Gary Soneji was heading to the cellar. That wouldn't be good for the thousands of people crowding inside the building. He had a bomb, and maybe more than one.

I led Groza down more steep stairs, under a lit sign that said OYSTER BAR ON THIS LEVEL. The entire station was still under massive construction and renovation, which only added to the confusion. We pushed past crowded bakeries and delis. Plenty to eat here while you waited for your train, or possibly to be blown up.

Detective Groza and I reached the next level. We entered a spacious arcade, surrounded by more railway-track doorways. Signs pointed the way to the subways, to the Times Square Shuttle.

Groza had a two-way cupped near his ear. He was getting up-to-the-second reports from around the station. 'He's down in the tunnels. We're close,' he told me.

Groza and I raced down another steep deck of stone steps. We ran side by side. It was unbearably hot down below and we were sweating. The building was vibrating. The gray stone walls and the floor shook beneath our feet. We were in hell now, the only question was, which circle?

I finally saw Gary Soneji up ahead. Then he disappeared again. He still had the baby, or maybe it was just the pink-and-blue blanket puffed in his arms.

He was back in sight. Then he *stopped* suddenly. Soneji turned and stared down the tunnel. He wasn't afraid of anything anymore. I could see it in his eyes.

'Dr Cross,' he yelled. 'You follow directions beautifully.'

CHAPTER 59

Soneji's dark secret still worked, still held true for him: Whatever would make people intensely angry, whatever would make them inconsolably sad, whatever would hurt them – *that's what he did.*

Soneji watched Alex Cross approaching. *Tall and arrogant black bastard. Are you ready to die, too, Cross?*

Right when your life seems so promising. Your young children growing up. And your beautiful new lover.

Because that's what's going to happen. You're going to die for what you did to me. You can't stop it from happening.

Alex Cross kept walking toward him, parading across the concrete train platform. He didn't look afraid. Cross definitely walked the talk. That was his strength, but it was also his folly.

Soneji felt as if he were floating in space right now. He felt so free, as if nothing could hurt him anywhere. He could be exactly who he wanted to be, act as he wished. He'd spent his life trying to get here.

Alex Cross was getting closer and closer. He called out a question across the train platform. It was always a question with Cross.

'What do you want, Gary? What the hell do you want from us?'

'Shut your hole! What do you think I want?' Soneji shouted back. 'You! I finally caught *you*.'

CHAPTER 60

I heard what Soneji said, but it didn't matter anymore. The thing between us was going down now. I kept coming toward him. One way or the other, this was the end.

I walked down a flight of three or four stone steps. I couldn't take my eyes off Soneji. I couldn't. I refused to give up now.

Smoke from the hospital fire was in my lungs. The air in the train tunnel didn't help. I began to cough.

Could this be the end of Soneji? I almost couldn't believe it. What the hell did he mean *he finally caught me*?

'Don't anybody move. Stop! Not another step!' Soneji yelled. He had a gun. The baby. 'I'll tell you who moves, and who doesn't. That includes you, Cross. So *just stop walking*.'

I stopped. No one else moved. It was incredibly quiet on the train platform, deep in the bowels of

Grand Central. There were probably twenty people close enough to Soneji to be injured by a bomb.

He held the baby from the bus up high, and that had everybody's attention. Detectives and uniformed police stood paralyzed in the wide doorways around the train tunnel. We were all helpless, powerless to do anything to stop Soneji. We had to listen to him.

He began to turn in a small, tight, frenzied circle. His body twirled around and around. A strange whirling dervish. He was clutching the infant in one arm, holding the tiny baby like a doll. I had no idea what had become of the child's mother.

Soneji almost seemed in a trance. He looked crazy now – maybe he was. 'The good Dr Cross is here,' he yelled down the platform. 'How much do you know? How much do you *think* you know? Let *me* ask the questions for a change.'

'I don't know enough, Gary,' I said, keeping my answer as low-key as possible. Not playing to the crowd, *his* crowd. 'I guess you still like an audience.'

'Why yes, I do, Dr Cross. I love an appreciative crowd. What's the point of a great performance with no one to see it? I crave the look in all of your eyes, your fear, your hatred.' He continued to turn, to spin as if he were playing a theater-in-the-round. 'You'd all like to kill me. You're all killers, too!' he screeched.

Soneji did another slow spin around, his gun pointed out, the baby cradled in his left arm. The infant wasn't crying, and that worried me sick. The bomb could be in a pocket of his trousers. It was somewhere. I hoped it wasn't in the baby's blanket.

'You're back there in the cellar? Aren't you?' I said. At one time I had believed Gary Soneji was schizophrenic. Then I was certain he wasn't. Right now, I wasn't sure of anything.

He gestured with his free arm at the underground caverns. He continued to walk slowly toward the rear of the platform. We couldn't stop him. 'As a kid, this is where I always dreamed I would escape to. Take a big, fast train to Grand Central Station in New York City. Get away clean and free. *Escape* from everything.'

'You've done it. You finally won. Isn't that why you led us here? To catch you?' I said.

'I'm *not* done. Not even close. I'm not finished with you yet, Cross,' he sneered.

There was his threat again. It made my stomach drop to hear him talk like that. 'What about me?' I called. 'You keep making threats. I don't see any action.'

Soneji stopped moving. He stopped backing toward the rear of the platform. Everyone was watching him now, probably thinking none of this was real. I wasn't even sure if I did.

'This doesn't end here, Cross. *I'm coming for you*, even from the grave if I have to. There's no way you can stop this. You remember that! Don't you forget now! I'm sure you won't.'

Then Soneji did something I would never understand. His left arm shot up. He threw the baby high in the air. The people watching gasped as the child tumbled forward.

They sighed audibly as a man fifteen feet down the platform caught the baby perfectly.

Then, the infant started to cry.

'Gary, no!' I shouted at Soneji. He was running again.

'Are you ready to die, Dr Cross?' he screamed back at me. *'Are you ready?'*

CHAPTER 61

Soneji disappeared through a silver, metallic door at the rear of the platform. He was quick, and he had surprise on his side. Gunshots rang out – Groza fired – but I didn't think Soneji had been hit.

'There's more tunnels back there, lots of train tracks down here,' Groza told me. 'We're walking into a dark, dirty maze.'

'Yeah, well let's go anyway,' I said. 'Gary loves it down here. We'll make the best of it.'

I noticed a maintenance worker and grabbed his flashlight. I pulled out my Glock. Seventeen shots. Groza had a .357 Magnum. Six more rounds. How many shots would it take to kill Soneji? Would he ever die?

'He's wearing a goddamn vest,' Groza said.

'Yeah, I saw that.' I clicked the safety off the Glock. 'He's a Boy Scout – *always prepared*.'

I opened the door through which Soneji had

disappeared, and it was suddenly as dark as a tomb. I leveled the barrel of the Glock in front of me and continued forward. This was the cellar, all right, his private hell on a very large scale.

Are you ready to die, Dr Cross?

There's no way you can stop it from happening.

I bobbed and weaved as best I could and the light from the flashlight shook all over the walls. I could see dim light, dusty lamps up ahead, so I turned off the flash. My lungs hurt. I couldn't breathe very well, but maybe some of the physical distress was claustrophobia and terror.

I didn't like it in his cellar. This is how Gary must have felt when he was just a boy. Was he telling us that? Letting us experience it?

'Jesus,' Groza muttered at my back. I figured that he felt what I felt, disoriented and afraid. The wind howled from somewhere inside the tunnel. We couldn't see much of anything up ahead.

You had to use your imagination in the dark, I was thinking as I proceeded forward. Soneji had learned how to do that as a boy. There were voices behind us now, but they were distant. The ghostly voices echoed off the walls. Nobody was hurrying to catch up with Soneji in the dark, dingy tunnel.

The brakes of a train screeched on the other side of the blackened stone walls. The subway was down here, just parallel to us. There was a stench of garbage and waste that kept getting worse the farther we walked.

I knew that street people lived in some of these

tunnels. The NYPD had a Homeless Unit to deal with them.

'Anything there?' Groza muttered, fear and uncertainty in his voice. 'You see anything?'

'Nothing,' I whispered. I didn't want to make any more noise than we had to. I sucked in another harsh breath. I heard a train whistle on the other side of the stone walls.

There was dim light in parts of the tunnel. A scrim of garbage lay underfoot, discarded fast-food wrappers, torn and grossly soiled clothing. I had already seen a couple of oversized rats scurrying alongside my feet, out food shopping in the Big Apple.

Then I heard a scream right on top of me. My neck and back stiffened. It was Groza! He went down. I had no idea what had hit him. He didn't make another sound, didn't move on the tunnel floor.

I whirled around. Couldn't see anyone at first. The darkness seemed to swirl.

I caught a flash of Soneji's face. One eye and half his mouth in dark profile. He hit me before I could get the Glock up. Soneji screamed – a brutal, primal yell. No recognizable words.

He hit me with tremendous power. A punch to the left temple. I remembered how incredibly strong he was, and how crazy he had become. My ears rang, and my head was spinning. My legs were wobbly. He'd almost taken me out with the first punch. Maybe he could have. But he wanted to punish me, wanted his revenge, his payback.

He screamed again – this time inches from my face.

Hurt him back, I told myself. *Hurt him now, or you won't get another chance.*

Soneji's strength was as brutal as it had been the last time we met, especially fighting in close like this. He had me wrapped in his arms and I could smell his breath. He tried to crush me with his arms. White lights flickered and danced before my eyes. I was nearly out on my feet.

He screamed again. I butted with my head. It took him by surprise. His grip loosened, and I broke away for a second.

I threw the hardest punch of my life and heard the crunch of his jaw. Soneji didn't go down! What did it take to hurt him?

He came at me again, and I struck his left cheek. I felt bone crush under my fist. He screamed, then moaned, but he didn't fall, didn't stop coming after me.

'You can't hurt me,' he gasped, growled. 'You're going to die. You can't stop it from happening. You can't stop this now.'

Gary Soneji came at me again. I finally got the Glock out and raised it. *Hurt him, hurt him, kill him right now.*

I fired! And although it happened fast, it seemed like slow-motion to me. I thought I could *feel* the gunshot travel through Soneji's body. The shot bulldozed through his lower jaw. It must have blown his tongue away, his teeth.

What remained of Soneji reached out to me, tried to hold on, to claw at my face and throat. I pushed him away. *Hurt him, hurt him, kill him.*

He staggered several steps down the darkened tunnel. I don't know where he got the strength. I was too tired to chase him, but I knew I didn't have to.

He fell toward the stone floor. He dropped like a deadweight. As he hit the ground, the bomb in his pocket ignited. Gary Soneji exploded in flames. The tunnel behind him was illuminated for at least a hundred feet.

Soneji screamed for a few seconds, then he burned in silence – a human torch in his cellar. He had gone straight to hell.

It was finally over.

CHAPTER 62

The Japanese have a saying – after victory, tighten your helmet cord. I tried to keep that in mind.

I was back in Washington early on Tuesday, and I spent the whole day at home with Nana and the kids and with Rosie the cat. The morning started when the kids prepared what they called a 'bubba-bath' for me. It got better from there. Not only didn't I tighten my helmet cord, I took the damn thing off.

I tried not to be upset by Soneji's horrible death, or his threat against me. I'd lived with worse from him in the past. Much worse. Soneji was dead and gone from all of our lives. I had seen him blown to hell with my own eyes. I'd helped blow him there.

Still, I could hear his voice, his warning, his threat at different times during my day at home.

You're going to die. You can't stop it from happening.

I'm coming for you, from the grave if I have to.

Kyle Craig called from Quantico to congratulate me

and ask how I was doing. Kyle still had an ulterior motive. He tried to suck me into his Mr Smith case, but I told him no. Definitely no way. I didn't have the heart for Mr Smith right now. He wanted me to meet his superagent Thomas Pierce. He asked if I'd read his faxes on Pierce. *No*.

That night I went to Christine's house, and I knew I had made the right decision about Mr Smith and the FBI's continuing problems with the case. I didn't spend the night because of the kids, but I could have. I wanted to. 'You promised you'd be around until we were both at least in our eighties. This is a pretty good start,' she said when I was leaving for the night.

On Wednesday, I had to go to the office to start closing down the Soneji case. I wasn't thrilled that I had killed him, but I was glad it was over. Everything but the blasted paperwork.

I got home from work around six. I was in the mood for another 'bubba-bath,' maybe some boxing lessons, a night with Christine.

I walked in the front door of my house – and all hell broke loose.

CHAPTER 63

Nana and the kids were standing before me in the living room. Sampson, several detective friends, neighbors, my aunties, a few uncles, and all of their kids were with them. Jannie and Damon started the group yell on cue, 'Surprise, Daddy! Surprise party!' Then everybody else in kingdom come joined in. 'Surprise, Alex, surprise!'

'Who's Alex? Who's Daddy?' I played dumb at the door. 'What the hell is going on here?'

Toward the back of the room I could see Christine, at least her smiling face. I waved at her, even as I was being hugged and pounded on the back and shoulders by all my best friends in the world.

I thought Damon was acting a little too respectful, so I swooped him up in my arms (this was probably the last year I would be able to do it) and we hollered assorted sports and war cries, which seemed to fit the party scene.

It's not usually a very charitable idea to celebrate the death of another human being but, in this case, I thought a party was a terrific idea. It was an appropriate and fitting way to end what had been a sad and scary time for all of us. Somebody had hung a droopy, badly hand-painted banner over the doorway between the living room and dining area. The banner read: *Congratulations, Alex! Better luck next lifetime, Gary S!*

Sampson led me into the backyard, where even more friends were waiting in ambush. Sampson had on baggy black shorts, a pair of combat boots, and his shades. He wore a beat-up Homicide cap and had a silver loop in one ear. He was definitely ready to party, and so was I.

Detectives from all around D.C. had come to offer their hearty congratulations, but also to eat my food and drink my liquor.

Succulent kabobs and racks of baby-back ribs were arranged beside homemade breads, rolls, and an impressive array of hot-sauce bottles. It made my eyes water just to look at the feast. Aluminum tubs overflowed with beer and ale and soda pop on ice. There was fresh corn on the cob, colorful fruit salads, and summer pastas by the bowlful.

Sampson grabbed my arm tight, and hollered so I could hear him over the noise of joyful voices and also Toni Braxton wailing her heart out on the CD player. 'You party on, Sugar. Say hello to all your other guests, all your peeps. I plan to be here until closing time.'

'I'll catch you later,' I told him. 'Nice boots, nice shorts, nice legs.'

'Thank you, thank you, thank you. You got that son of a bitch, Alex! You did the right thing. May his evil, hair-bag ass burn and rot in hell. I'm just sorry I wasn't there with you.'

Christine had taken a quiet spot in the corner of the yard under our shade tree. She was talking with my favorite aunt, Tia, and my sister-in-law, Cilla. It was like her to put herself last on the greeting line.

I kissed Tia and Cilla, and then reached out and gave Christine a hug. I held her and didn't want to let go. 'Thank you for coming here for all this madness,' I said. 'You're the best surprise of all.'

She kissed me, and then we pulled apart. I think we were overly conscious that Damon and Jannie had never seen us together. Not like this anyway.

'Oh shit,' I muttered. 'Look there.'

The two little devil-demons *were* watching us. Damon winked outrageously, and Jannie made an okay sign with her busy and quick little fingers.

'They're way, way ahead of us,' Christine said and laughed. 'Figures, Alex. We should have known.'

'Why don't you two head on up to bed?' I kidded the kids.

'It's only six o'clock, Daddy!' Jannie yelped, but she was grinning and laughing and so was everybody else.

It was a wild, let-loose party and everybody quickly got into the spirit. The monkey of Gary Soneji was finally off my back. I spotted Nana talking to some of my police friends.

I heard what she was saying as I passed. It was pure Nana Mama. 'There is *no* history that I know of that has led from slavery to freedom, but there is sure a history from the slingshot to the Uzi,' she said to her audience of homicide detectives. My friends were grinning and nodding their heads as if they understood what she was saying, where she was coming from. I did. For better or for worse, Nana Mama had taught me how to think.

On the lighter side there was dancing to everything, from Marsalis to hip-hop. Nana even danced some. Sampson ran the barbecue in the backyard, featuring hot-and-spicy sausages, barbecued chicken, and more ribs than you would need for a Redskins tailgate party.

I was called upon to play a few tunes, so I banged out ''S Wonderful,' and then a jazzy version of 'Ja – da, ja – da, ja – da, jing, jing, jing.'

'Here's a stupid little melody,' Jannie hammed it up at my side, 'but it's so *soothing* and *appealing* to me.'

I grabbed some slow-dances with Christine as the sun set and the night progressed. The fit of our bodies was still magical and right. Just as I remembered it from the Rainbow Room. She seemed amazingly comfortable with my family and friends. I could tell that they *approved* of her big time.

I sang along with a Seal tune as we danced in the

moonlight. 'No, we're never going to survive – Unless – We get a little cra-azy.'

'Seal would be sooo proud,' she whispered in my ear.

'Mmm. Sure he would.'

'You are such a good, smooth dancer,' she said against my cheek.

'For a gumshoe and a flatfoot,' I said. 'I only dance with you, though.'

She laughed, and then punched my side. 'Don't you lie! I *saw* you dancing with John Sampson.'

'Yes, but it didn't mean anything. It was only for the cheap sex.'

Christine laughed and I could feel a small quiver in her stomach. It reminded me of how much life she had in her. It reminded me that she wanted kids, and that she ought to have them. I remembered every-thing about our night at the Rainbow Room, and afterward at the Astor. I felt as if I had known her forever. *She's the one, Alex.*

'I have summer school in the morning,' Christine finally told me. It was already past midnight. 'I brought my car. I'm okay. I've been drinking kiddie cocktails mostly. You enjoy your party, Alex.'

'You sure?'

Her voice was firm. 'Absolutely. I'm fine. I'm cool. And I'm outta here.'

We kissed for a long time, and when we had to come up for air, we both laughed. I walked her out to her car. 'Let me drive you home at least,' I protested as

I stood with my arms around her. 'I want to. I insist.'

'No, then my car would still be here. *Please* enjoy your party. Be with your friends. You can see me tomorrow, if you like. I'd like that. I won't take no for an answer.'

We kissed again, and then Christine got in her car and drove away to Mitchellville.

I missed her already.

CHAPTER 64

I could still feel Christine's body against me, smell her new Donna Karan perfume, hear the special music of her voice. Sometimes you just get lucky in life. Sometimes the universe takes care of you pretty good. I wandered back to the party taking place in my house.

Several of my detective friends were still hanging out, including Sampson. There was a joke going around about Soneji having 'angel lust.' 'Angel lust' was what they called cadavers at the morgue with an erection. The party was going *there*.

Sampson and I drank way too much beer, and then some B&B on the back-porch steps – after everyone else was long gone.

'Now *that* was a hell of a party,' Two-John said. 'The all-singing, all-dancing model.'

'It was pretty damn good. Of course, we are still *standing*. Sitting up anyway. I feel real good, but I'm going to feel pretty bad.'

Sampson was grinning and his shades were placed slightly crooked on his face. His huge elbows rested on his knees. You could strike a match on his arms or legs, probably even on his head.

'I'm proud of you, man. We all are. You definitely got the twenty-thousand-pound gorilla off your back. I haven't seen you smiling so much in a long, long while. More I see of Ms Christine Johnson, the more I like her, and I liked her to begin with.'

We were on the porch steps, looking over Nana's garden of wildflowers, her roses that bloomed so abundantly, and garden-lilies, looking over the remains of the party, all that food and booze.

It was late. It was already tomorrow. The wildflower garden had been there since we were little kids. The smell of bone meal and fresh dirt seemed particularly ageless and reassuring that night.

'You remember the first summer we met?' I asked John. 'You called me watermelon-ass, which burned me, because it was complete bullshit. I had a tight butt, even then.'

'We tangled good in Nana's garden, right in the brierpatch over yonder. I couldn't believe you would tangle with me. Nobody else would do that, still don't. Even back then you didn't know your limitations.'

I smiled at Sampson. He finally had taken off his shades. It always surprises me how sensitive and warm his eyes are. 'You call me watermelon-ass, we'll tangle again.'

Sampson continued to nod and grin. Come to think of it, I hadn't seen him smiling so much in a long while. Life was good tonight. The best it had been in a while.

'You really like Ms Christine. I think you've found yourself another special person. I'm sure of it. You're down for the count, champ.'

'You jealous?' I asked him.

'Yeah, of course I am. Damn straight. Christine is all that and a bag of chips. But I would just fuck it up if I ever found somebody sweet and nice like that. You're easy to be with, Sugar. Always have been, even when you had your little watermelon-ass. Tough when you have to be, but you can show your feelings, too. Whatever it is, Christine likes you a lot. Almost as much as you like her.'

Sampson pushed himself up off the sagging back-porch step, which I needed to replace soon.

'God willing, I'm going to walk on home. Actually, I'm going to Cee Walker's house. The beautiful diva left the party a little early, but she was kind enough to give me a key. I'll be back, pick up my car in the morning. Best not to drive when you can hardly walk.'

'Best not to,' I agreed. 'Thanks for the party.'

Sampson waved good-bye, saluted, and then he went round the corner of the house, which he bumped on the way out.

I was alone on the back-porch steps, staring out over Nana's moonlit garden, smiling like the fool I can be sometimes, but maybe not often enough.

I heard Sampson call out. Then his deep laugh came from the front of the house.

'Good night, watermelon-ass.'

CHAPTER 65

I came fully awake, and I wondered what I was
afraid of, what the hell was happening here. My
first conscious fear was that *I was having a heart
attack in my own bed*.

I was spacey and woozy, still flying high from the
party. My heart was beating loudly, thundering in my
chest.

I thought that I had heard a deep, low, pounding
noise from somewhere inside the house. The noise
was *close*. It sounded as if a heavy weight, maybe a
club, had been striking something down the hallway.

My eyes weren't adjusted to the darkness yet. I
listened for another noise.

I was frightened. I couldn't remember where I left
my Glock last night. What could possibly make that
heavy *pounding* sound inside the house?

I listened with all the concentration I could
command.

The refrigerator purred down in the kitchen.

A distant truck changed gears on the mean streets.

Still, something about that sound, the pounding noise, bothered me a lot. *Had there even been a sound? I wondered. Was it just the first warnings of a powerful headache coming on?*

Before I realized what was happening, a shadowy figure rose from the other side of the bed.

Soneji! He's kept his promise. He's here in the house!

'Aaagghhgghh!' the attacker screamed and swung at me with a large club of some sort.

I tried to roll, but my body and mind weren't cooperating. I'd had too much to drink, too much party, too much fun.

I felt a powerful blow to my shoulder. My whole body went numb. I tried to scream, but suddenly I had no voice. I couldn't scream. I could barely move.

The club descended swiftly again – this time it struck my lower back.

Someone was trying to beat me to death. Jesus, God. I thought of the loud pounding sounds. *Had he gone to Nana's room first? Damon and Jannie's? What was happening in our house?*

I reached for him and managed to grab his arm. I yanked hard and he shrieked again, a high-pitched sound, but definitely a man's voice.

Soneji? How could it be? I'd seen him die in the tunnels of Grand Central Station.

What was happening to me? Who was in my bedroom?

Who was upstairs in our house?

'Jannie? Damon? . . .' I finally mumbled, tried to call to them. *'Nana? Nana?'*

I began scratching at his chest, his arms, felt something sticky, probably drawing blood. Then my left wrist went numb. I was fighting with only one arm now, and barely able to do that.

'Who are you? What are you doing? *Damon! Damon!'* I called out again. Much louder this time.

He broke loose and I fell out of the bed, face first. The floor came at me hard, *struck*, and my face went numb.

My whole body was on fire. I began to throw up on the carpet.

The bat, the sledgehammer, the crowbar – whatever in hell it was – came down again and seemed to split me in two. I was burning up with pain.

I could feel and smell blood everywhere around me on the floor. My blood?

'I told you there was no way to stop me!' he screamed. 'I told you.'

I looked up and saw his gun, thought I recognized the face looming above me. *Gary Soneji? Could it possibly be Soneji? How could that possibly be? It couldn't!*

He began shooting. I understood that I was dying, and I didn't want to die. I wanted to run, to see my kids one more time. Just one more look at them.

I knew I couldn't stop the attack. Knew there

was nothing I could do to stop this horror from happening.

I thought of Nana and Jannie, Damon, Christine. My heart ached for them.

Then I let God do His will.

PART FOUR

THOMAS PIERCE

CHAPTER 66

Matthew Lewis happily drove the graveyard shift on the city bus line that traveled along East Capitol Street in D.C. He was absently whistling a Marvin Gaye song, 'What's Goin' On,' as he piloted his bus through the night.

He had driven the same route for nineteen years and was mostly glad to have the work. He also enjoyed the solitude. Lewis had always been a fairly deep thinker, according to his friends and Alva, his wife of twenty years. He was a history buff, and interested in government, sometimes a little sociology, too. He had developed the interests in his native Jamaica and had kept up with them.

For the past few months, he had been listening to self-improvement tapes from an outfit called the Teaching Company, in Virginia. As he rode along East Capitol at five in the morning, he was really getting into an excellent lecture called 'The Good King – the

American Presidency Since the Depression.' Sometimes he'd knock off two or three lectures in a single night, or maybe he'd listen to a particularly good tape a couple of times in a night.

He saw the sudden movement out of the corner of his eye. He swerved the steering wheel. The brakes screeched. His bus skidded hard right and wound up diagonally across East Capitol.

The bus emitted a loud hiss. There wasn't any traffic coming, thank goodness, just a string of green lights as far as he could see.

Matthew Lewis threw open the bus doors and climbed out. He hoped he'd missed whoever, or whatever, had run into the street.

He wasn't sure, though, and he was afraid of what he might find. Except for the drone of his tape inside the bus, it was quiet. This was so weird and as bad as can be, he thought to himself.

Then he saw an elderly black woman lying in the street. She was wearing a long blue-striped bathrobe. Her robe was open and he could see her red nightgown. Her feet were bare. His heart bucked dangerously.

He ran across the street to help her, and thought he was going to be sick. In his headlights he saw that her nightgown wasn't red. It was bright-red blood, all over her. The sight was gruesome and awful. It wasn't the worst thing he'd encountered in his years on the night route, but it was right up there.

The woman's eyes were open and she was still

conscious. She reached out a frail, thin arm toward him. *Must be domestic violence,* he thought. *Or maybe a robbery at her home.*

'Please help us,' Nana Mama whispered. 'Please help us.'

CHAPTER 67

Fifth Street was blocked off and completely barricaded to traffic. John Sampson abandoned his black Nissan and ran the rest of the way to Alex's house. Police cruiser and ambulance sirens were wailing everywhere on the familiar street that he almost thought of as his own.

Sampson ran as he never had before, in the grip of the coldest fear of his life. His feet pounded heavily on the sidewalk stones. His heart felt heavy, ready to break. He couldn't catch a breath, and he was certain he would throw up if he didn't stop running this second. The hangover from the night before had dulled his senses, but not nearly enough.

Metro police personnel were still arriving at the confused, noisy, throbbing scene. Sampson pushed his way past the neighborhood looky-loos. His contempt for them had never been more obvious or more intense. People were crying everywhere Sampson looked – people he knew, neighbors and friends of Alex. He heard Alex's name being spoken in whispers.

As he reached the familiar wooden picket fence that surrounded the Cross property, he heard something that turned his stomach inside out. He had to steady himself against the whitewashed fence.

'They're all dead inside. The whole Cross family gone,' a pock-faced woman in the crowd was shooting off her mouth. She looked like a character from the TV show *Cops*, had the same crude lack of sensitivity.

He spun round toward the source of the words, toward the hurt. Sampson gave the woman a glazed look and pushed forward into the yard, past collapsible sawhorses and yellow crime-scene tape.

He took the front porch steps in two long, athletic strides, and nearly collided with EMS medics hurrying a litter out of the living room.

Sampson stopped cold on the Crosses' front porch. He couldn't believe any of this. Little Jannie was on the litter and she looked so small. He bent over, and then collapsed hard on his knees. The porch shook beneath his weight.

A low moan escaped his mouth. He was no longer strong, no longer brave. His heart was breaking and he choked back a sob.

When she saw him, Jannie started to cry. 'Uncle John, Uncle John.' She said his name in the tiniest, saddest, hurt voice.

Jannie isn't dead, Jannie is alive, Sampson thought,

and the words almost tumbled out of his mouth. He wanted to shout the truth to the looky-loos. *Stop your damn rumors and lies!* He wanted to know everything, all at once, but that just wasn't possible.

Sampson leaned in close to Jannie, his goddaughter, whom he loved as if she were his own child. Her nightgown was smeared with blood. The coppery smell of blood was strong and he was almost sick again.

More blood ribboned through Jannie's tight, carefully braided hair. She was so proud of her braids, her beautiful hair. *Oh, dear God. How could this happen? How could it be? He remembered her singing 'Ja – da, ja – da,' just the night before.*

'You're okay, baby,' Sampson whispered, the words catching like barbed wire in his throat. 'I'm going to be back here with you in a minute. You're okay, Jannie. I need to run upstairs. I'll be right back, baby. Be right back. Promise you.'

'What about Damon? What about my daddy?' Jannie whimpered as she softly cried.

Her eyes were wide with fear, with a terror that made Sampson's heart break all over again. She was just a little girl. How could anyone do this?

'Everybody's okay, baby. They're okay,' Sampson whispered again. His tongue was thick, his mouth as dry as sandpaper. He could barely get out the words. *Everybody's okay, baby.* He prayed that was true.

The EMS medics did their best to wave Sampson away, and they carried Jannie down to a waiting ambulance. More ambulances were still arriving in front, and more police cruisers as well.

He pushed his way into the house, which was crowded with police – both street officers and detectives. When the first alarm came, half of the precinct must have rushed over to the Cross house. He had never seen so many cops in one place.

He was late as usual – the *late* John Sampson, Alex liked to call him. He'd slept at a woman's house, Cee Walker's, and couldn't be reached right away. His beeper was off, taking a night off after Alex's party – after the big celebration.

Someone knew Alex would have his guard down, Sampson thought, being a homicide detective already. *Who knew? Who did this terrible thing?*

What in the name of God happened here?

CHAPTER 68

Sampson bolted up the narrow, twisting stairs to the second floor of the house. He wanted to shout above the blaring noise, the buzz of the incipient police investigation, to yell Alex's name, to see him appear out of one of the bed-rooms.

He had way too much to drink the night before and he was reeling, feeling shaky, rubbery all over. He rushed into Damon's room and let out a deep moan. The boy was being transferred from his bed to a litter. Damon looked so much like his father, so much like Alex when he was Damon's age.

He looked worse than Jannie. The side of his face was beaten raw. One of Damon's eyes was closed, swollen to twice its size. Deep purple and scarlet bruises were around the eye. There were contusions and lacerations.

Gary Soneji was dead – he'd gone down in Grand

Central Station. He couldn't have done this horrible thing at Alex's house.

And yet, he had promised that he would!

Nothing made sense to Sampson yet. He wished he were dreaming this nightmare, but knew he wasn't.

A detective named Rakeem Powell grabbed him by the shoulder, grabbed him hard and shook him. 'Damon's all right, John. Somebody came in here, beat the living hell out of the kids. Looks like he just used fists. Hard punches. Didn't mean to kill them, though, or maybe the cowardly fuck couldn't finish the job. Who the hell knows at this point. Damon's all right. *John?* Are you all right?'

Sampson pushed Rakeem away, threw him off impatiently. 'What about Alex? Nana?'

'Nana was beaten bad. Bus driver found her on the street, took her to St Tony's. She's conscious, but she's an old woman. Skin rips when they're old. Alex got shot in his bedroom, John. They're up there with him.'

'Who's in there?' Sampson groaned. He was close to tears, and he never cried. He couldn't help himself now, couldn't hide his feelings.

'Christ, who isn't?' Rakeem said and shook his head. 'EMS, us, FBI. Kyle Craig is here.'

Sampson broke away from Rakeem Powell and lunged toward the bedroom. *Everybody wasn't dead inside the house – but Alex had been shot. Somebody came here to get him! Who could it have been?*

Sampson tried to go into Alex's bedroom, but he

was held back by men he didn't know – probably FBI from the look of them.

Kyle Craig was in the room. He knew that much. The FBI was here already. 'Tell Kyle I'm here,' he told the men at the door. 'Tell Kyle Craig it's Sampson.'

One of the FBI agents ducked inside. Kyle came out immediately, pushed his way into the hall to Sampson.

'Kyle, what the hell?' Sampson tried to talk. '*Kyle*, what happened?'

'He's been shot twice. Shot and beaten,' Kyle said. 'I need to talk to you, John. Listen to me, just *listen* to me, will you?'

CHAPTER 69

Sampson tried to hold back his fears, his true feelings, tried to control the chaos in his mind. Detectives and police personnel were clustered at the bedroom door in the narrow hallway. A couple of them were crying. Others were trying not to.

None of this could be happening!

Sampson turned away from the bedroom. He was afraid he was going to lose it, something he never did. Kyle hadn't stopped talking, but he couldn't really follow what Kyle was saying. He couldn't concentrate on the FBI man's words.

He inhaled deeply, trying to fight off the reverberations of shock. It *was* shock, wasn't it? Then hot tears started to stream down his cheeks. He didn't care if Kyle saw. The pain in his heart cut so deep, cut right to the bone. His nerve endings were already rubbed raw. Never anything like this before.

'Listen to me, John,' Kyle said, but Sampson wasn't listening.

Sampson's body slumped heavily against the wall. He asked Kyle how he'd gotten here so fast. Kyle had an answer, always an answer for everything. Still – nothing was really making sense to Sampson, not a word of it.

He was looking at something over the FBI man's shoulder. Sampson couldn't believe it. Through the window, he could see an FBI helicopter. It was landing in the vacant lot just across Fifth Street. Things were getting stranger and stranger.

A figure lurched out of the helicopter, crouched under the rotor blades, then started toward the Cross house. It almost seemed as if he were levitating above the blowing grass in the yard.

The man was tall and slender, with dark sunglasses, the kind with small round lenses. His long blond hair was bound in a ponytail. He didn't look like FBI.

There was definitely something different about him, something radical for the Bureau. He almost looked angry as he pushed the looky-loos away. He also looked as if he were in charge, at least in charge of himself.

Now . . . what was this? Sampson thought. *What's going on here?*

'Who the hell is that?' he asked Kyle Craig. 'Who is that, Kyle? Who is that goddamn ponytailed asshole?'

CHAPTER 70

My name is Thomas Pierce, but the press usually call me 'Doc.' I was once a medical student at Harvard. I graduated, but never worked a day in a hospital, never practiced medicine. Now I'm part of the Behavioral Science Unit of the FBI. I'm thirty-three years old. Truthfully, the only place I might look like a 'Doc' is in an episode of the TV show *E.R.*

I was rushed from the training compound at Quantico to Washington early that morning. I had been ordered to investigate the attack on Dr Alex Cross and members of his immediate family. To be candid, I didn't want to be involved in the case for a number of reasons. Most important, I was already part of a difficult investigation, one that had drained nearly all of my energy – the Mr Smith case.

Instinctively, I knew that some people would be angry with me because of the shooting of Alex Cross and my being at the crime scene so quickly. I knew with absolute certainty I would be seen as opportunistic, when that couldn't be farther from the truth.

There was nothing I could do about it now. The Bureau wanted me there. So I put it out of my mind. I tried to anyway. I was performing my job, the same as Dr Cross would have done for me under comparably unfortunate circumstances.

I was certain of one thing, though, from the moment I arrived. I knew I looked as shocked and outraged as anyone else standing sentinel in the crowd gathered at the house on Fifth Street. I probably looked angry to some of them. I *was* angry. My mind was full of chaos, fear of the unknown, fear of failure, too. I was close to the state of mind described as 'toast.' Too many days, weeks, months in a row with Mr Smith. Now this new bit of blasphemy.

I had listened to Alex Cross speak once at a profiler seminar at the University of Chicago. He had made an impression. I hoped that he would live, but the reports were all bad. Nothing I'd heard so far left room for hope.

I figured that was why they'd brought me in on the case right away. The vicious attack on Cross would mean major headlines, and put intense pressure on both the Washington police and the Bureau. I was there on Fifth Street for the simplest of reasons – to relieve the pressure.

I felt an unpleasant aura, residue from the recent violence, as I approached the tidy, white-shingled

Cross house. Some policemen I passed were red-eyed and a few seemed almost to be in shock. It was all very strange and disquieting.

I wondered if Alex Cross had died since I had left Quantico. I already had a sixth sense for the terrible and unexpected violence that had taken place inside the modest, peaceful-looking house. I wished that none of the others were at the crime scene, so I could absorb everything without all these distractions.

That was what I had been brought here to do. Observe the scene of unbelievable mayhem. Get a gut feeling for what might have happened in the early hours of the morning. Figure everything out quickly and efficiently.

Out of the corner of my eye, I saw Kyle Craig coming out of the house. He was in a hurry, as he always is. I sighed. *Now it begins, now it begins.*

Kyle crossed Fifth Street in a quick jog. He came up to me and we shook hands. I was glad to see him. Kyle is smart and very organized, and also supportive of those he works with. He's famous for getting things done.

'They just moved Alex,' he said. 'He's hanging on.'

'What's the prognosis? Tell me, Kyle.' I needed to know everything. I was there to collect facts. This was the start of it.

Kyle averted his eyes. 'Not good. They say he won't live. They're sure he won't live.'

CHAPTER 71

The press corps intercepted Kyle and me as we headed toward the Cross house. There were already a couple dozen reporters and cameramen at the scene. The vultures effectively blocked our way, wouldn't let us pass. They knew who Kyle was and possibly they knew about me, too.

'Why is the FBI already involved?' one of them shouted above the street noise and general commotion. Two news helicopters fluttered overhead. They loved this sort of disaster. 'We hear this is connected to the Soneji case. Is that true?'

'Let me talk to them,' Kyle whispered close to my ear.

I shook my head. 'They'll want to talk to me about it anyway. They'll find out who I am. Let's get the silly shit over with.'

Kyle frowned, but then he nodded slowly. I tried to control my impatience as I walked toward the horde of reporters.

I waved my hands over my head and that quieted some of them. The media are extremely visual, I've learned the hard way, even the print journalists, the so-called wordsmiths. They all watch far too many movies. Visual signals work best with them.

'I'll answer your questions,' I volunteered and served up a thin smile, 'as best I can anyway.'

'First question, who are you?' a man with a scraggly red beard and Salvation Army store taste in clothes hollered from the front of the pack. He looked like the reclusive novelist Thomas Harris, and maybe he was.

'That's an easy one,' I answered, 'I'm Thomas Pierce. I'm with BSU.'

That quieted the reporters for a moment. Those who didn't recognize my face knew the name. The fact that I'd been brought in on the Cross case was news in itself. Camera flashes exploded in front of me, but I was used to them by now.

'Is Alex Cross still alive?' someone called out. I had expected that to be the *first* question, but there's no way to predict with the press corps.

'Dr Cross is alive. As you can see, I just got here, so I don't know much. So far, we have no suspects, no theories, no leads, nothing particularly interesting to talk about,' I said.

'What about the Mr Smith case,' a woman reporter shouted at me. She was a dark-haired anchor-person type, perky as a chipmunk. 'Are you putting Mr Smith on hold now? How can you work two big cases? What's up, Doc?' the reporter said and smiled. She was obviously smarter and wittier than she looked.

I winced, rolled my eyes, and smiled back at her. 'No suspects, no theories, no leads, nothing interesting to talk about,' I repeated. 'I have to go inside. The interview's over. Thanks for your concern. I know it's genuine in this god-awful case. I admire Alex Cross, too.'

'Did you say admire or admired?' another reporter shouted at me from the back.

'Why did they bring you in on this, Mr Pierce? Is Mr Smith involved?'

I couldn't help arching my eyebrows at the question. I felt an unpleasant itch in my brain. 'I'm here because I get lucky sometimes, all right? Maybe I'll get lucky again. I have to go into the trenches now. I promise that I'll tell you if and when we have anything. I sincerely doubt that Mr Smith attacked Alex Cross last night. And I said *admire*, present tense.'

I pulled Kyle Craig out of there with me, holding on to his arm for support as much as anything. He grinned as soon as we had our backs to the horde.

'That was pretty goddamn good,' he said. 'I think you managed to confuse the hell out of them, even beyond the usual blank stares.'

'Mad dogs of the fourth estate,' I shrugged. 'Smears of blood on their lips and cheeks. They couldn't care less about Cross or his family. Not one question about the kids. Edison said, "We don't know a millionth of one percent about *anything*!" The press doesn't get that. They want everything in black-and-white. They mistake simplicity and simplemindedness for the truth.'

'Make nice with the D.C. police,' Kyle cajoled, or maybe he was giving me a friendly warning. 'This is an emotional time for them. That's Detective John Sampson on the porch. He's a friend of Alex. Alex's closest friend in fact.'

'Great,' I muttered. 'Just who I don't want to see right now.'

I glanced at Detective Sampson. He looked like a bad storm about to happen. *I didn't want to be here. Didn't want or need any of this.*

Kyle patted my shoulder. 'We need you on this one. Soneji promised this would happen,' he suddenly told me. 'He *predicted* it.'

I stared at Kyle Craig. He'd delivered his stunning thunderbolt of news in his usual deadpan, under-stated way, sort of like Sam Shepard on Quaalude.

'Say again? What was that last bit?'

'Gary Soneji warned Alex that he'd get him, even if he died. Soneji said he couldn't be stopped. It looks like he made good on his promise. I want you to tell me how. Tell me how Soneji did it. *That's* why you're here, Thomas.'

CHAPTER 72

M y nerves were already on edge. My awareness was heightened to a level I found
almost painful. I couldn't believe I was here
in Washington, involved in this case. *Tell me how Gary
Soneji did this?* Tell me how it could have happened.
That's all I had to do.

The press had one thing right. It's fair to say that I
am the FBI's current hotshot profiler. I should be used
to graphic, violent crime scenes, but I'm not. It stirs
up too much white noise, too many memories of
Isabella. *Of Isabella and myself. Of another time and
place, another life.*

I have a sixth sense, which is nothing paranormal,
nothing like that at all. It's just that I can process
raw information and data better than most people,
better than most policemen anyway. I feel things
very powerfully, and sometimes my 'felt' hunches
have been useful not only to the FBI but also to

Interpol and Scotland Yard.

My methods differ radically from the Federal Bureau's famed investigative process, however. In spite of what they say, the Bureau's Behavioral Science Unit believes in formalistic investigation with much less room for surprising hunches. I subscribe to a belief in the widest possible array of hunches and instincts, followed by the most exacting science.

The FBI and I are polar opposites, yet to their credit they continue to use me. Until I screw up badly, which I could do at any moment. Like right now.

I had been working hard at Quantico, reporting in on the gruesome and complex 'Mr Smith' investigation, when the news arrived about the attack on Cross. Actually, I had been in Quantico for less than a day, having just returned from England where 'Smith' was blazing his killer trail and I was in lukewarm pursuit.

Now I was in Washington, at the center of a raging storm over the Cross family attack. I looked at my watch, a TAG Heuer 6000 given to me by Isabella, the only material possession I really care about. It was a few minutes past eight when I entered the Cross frontyard. I noted the time. Something about it bothered me, but I wasn't sure what it was yet.

I stopped beside a battered and rusting EMS truck. The roof lights were flashing, the rear doors thrown open. I looked inside and saw a boy – it had to be Damon Cross.

The boy had been badly beaten. His face and arms

were bloody, but he was alert and talking in a soft voice to the medics, who tried to be gentle and comforting.

'Why wouldn't he have killed the children? Why just thrash out at them?' Kyle said. We had the same mind-set on that question.

'His heart wasn't in it.' I said the first thing that came into my head, the first *feeling* I had. 'He was compelled to make a symbolic gesture toward the Cross children, but no more than that.'

I turned to look at Kyle. 'I don't know, Kyle. Maybe he was frightened. Or in a hurry. Maybe he was afraid of waking Cross.' All of those thoughts invaded my mind, almost in an instant. *I felt as if I had briefly met the attacker.*

I looked up at the old house, the Cross house. 'Okay, let's go to the bedroom, if you don't mind. I want to see it before the techies do their number in there. I need to see Alex Cross's room. I don't know, but I think something is seriously fucked-up here. This certainly wasn't done by Gary Soneji *or* his ghost.'

'How do you know that?' Kyle grabbed my arm and made eye contact. 'How can you know for sure?'

'Soneji would have killed the two kids and the grandmother.'

CHAPTER 73

Alex Cross's blood was spattered everywhere in the corner bedroom. I could see where a bullet had exited through the window directly behind Cross's bed. The glass fracture was clean and the radial lines even: The shooter had fired from a standing position, directly across the bed. I made my first notes, and also a quick sketch of the small, unadorned bedroom.

There was other 'evidence.' A shoe print had been discovered near the cellar. The Metro police were working on a 'walking picture' of the assailant. A white male had been spotted around midnight in the mostly black neighborhood. For a moment, I was almost glad I'd been rushed up here from Virginia. There was so much raw data to take in and process, almost too much. The mussed bed, where Cross had apparently slept on top of a hand-sewn quilt. Photos of his children on the walls.

Alex Cross had been moved to St Anthony's Hospital, but his bedroom was intact, just the way the mysterious assailant had left it.

Had he left the room like this on purpose? Was this his first message to us?

Of course it was.

I looked at the papers still out on Cross's small work desk. They were notes on Gary Soneji. They had been left undisturbed by the assailant. Was that important?

Someone had taped a short poem to the wall over the desk. *Wealth covers sins – the poor/Are naked as a pin.*

Cross had been reading a book called *Push*, a novel. A piece of lined yellow paper was stuck inside, so I read it: *Write the talented author about her wonderful book!*

The time I spent in the room passed like a snap of the fingers, almost a mind fugue. I drank several cups of coffee. I remembered a line from the offbeat TV show *Twin Peaks*, 'Damn fine cup of coffee, and hot!'

I had been inside Cross's bedroom for almost an hour and a half, lost in forensic detail, hooked on the case in spite of myself. It was a nasty and disturbing puzzle, but a very intriguing one. Everything about the case was intense, and highly unusual.

I heard footsteps thumping outside in the hallway and looked up, my concentration interrupted. The bedroom door suddenly swung open and thudded against the wall.

Kyle Craig popped his head inside. He looked concerned. His face was white as chalk. Something had happened. 'I have to go right now. Alex has gone into cardiac arrest!'

CHAPTER 74

'I'll go with you,' I said to Kyle. I could tell that Kyle badly needed company. I wanted to see Alex Cross before he died, if that was what it had come to, and it sounded like it, felt like it to me.

On the ride over to St Anthony's I gently questioned Kyle about the extent of Dr Cross's injuries and the tenor of concern at the hospital. I also made a guess about the cause of the cardiac arrest.

'It sounds like it's due to blood loss. There's a lot of blood in the bedroom. It's all over the sheets, the floor, the walls. Soneji was obsessed with blood, right? I heard that at Quantico before I left this morning.'

Kyle was quiet for a moment in the car, and then he asked the question I expected. I'm sometimes a step or two ahead in conversations.

'Do you ever miss it, not being a doctor anymore?'
I shook my head, frowned a little. 'I really don't.

Something delicate and essential broke inside me when Isabella died. It will never be repaired, Kyle, at least I don't think so. I couldn't be a doctor now. I find it hard to believe in healing anymore.'

'I'm sorry,' he whispered solemnly.

'And I'm sorry about your friend. I'm sorry about Alex Cross,' I said to him.

In the spring of 1993, I had just graduated from Harvard Medical School. My life seemed to be spiraling upward at dizzying speed, when the woman I loved more than life itself was murdered in our apartment in Cambridge. Isabella Calais was my lover, and she was my best friend. She was one of the first victims of 'Mr Smith.'

After the murder, I never showed up at Massachusetts General, where I'd been accepted as an intern. I didn't even contact them. I knew I would never practice medicine. In an odd way, my life had ended with Isabella's, at least that was how I saw it.

Eighteen months after the murder, I was accepted into the FBI's Behavioral Science Unit, what some wags call the 'b.s. group.' It was what I wanted to do, what I needed to do. Once I had proved myself in the BSU, I asked to be put on the Mr Smith case. My superiors fought the move at first, but finally they gave in.

'Maybe you'll change your mind one day,' Kyle said. I had a feeling that he personally believed I would. Kyle likes to believe that everyone thinks as he does: With perfectly clear logic and a minimum of emotional baggage.

'I don't think so,' I told him, without sounding argumentative, or even too firm on the point. 'Who knows, though?'

'Maybe after you finally catch Smith.' He persisted with his point.

'Yes, maybe then,' I said.

'You don't think Smith—' he started to say, but then backed off from the absurd notion that Mr Smith could be involved with the attack here in Washington.

'No,' I said, 'I do not. Smith couldn't have made this attack. They would all be dead and mutilated if he had.'

CHAPTER 75

A t St Anthony's Hospital, I left Kyle and roamed about playing 'Doc.' It didn't feel too bad to be working in a hospital, contemplating what it might have been like. I tried to find out as much as I could about Alex Cross's condition, and his chances of surviving his wounds.

The staff nurses and doctors were surprised that I understood so much about trauma and gunshot wounds, but no one pressed me as to how or why. They were too busy trying to save Alex Cross's life. He had done pro bono work at the hospital for years and no one there could bear to let him die. Even the porters liked and respected Cross, calling him a 'regular brother.'

I learned that the cardiac arrest had been caused by the loss of blood, as I had guessed. According to the doctor in charge, Alex Cross had gone into massive arrest minutes after he arrived at the E.R. His blood pressure had dipped dangerously low: 60 over 0.

The staff's prognosis was that he could probably die during the surgery necessary to repair his massive internal injuries, but that he would definitely die without the surgery. The more I heard, the more I was certain they were right. An old saying of my mother's ran through my head, 'May his body rise to heaven, before the devil finds out he's dead.'

Kyle caught up with me in the busy and chaotic hallway on the fourth floor at St Anthony's. A lot of people working there knew Cross personally. They were all visibly upset and helpless to do anything about it. The hospital scene was raw and emotional, and I couldn't help being swept up in the tragedy, even more so than I had been at the Cross house.

Kyle was still pale, his brow furrowed and punctu-ated by blisters of sweat. His eyes had a distant look as he gazed down the hospital corridor. 'What did you find out? I know you've been poking around,' he said. He rightly suspected that I would have already con-ducted my own mini-investigation. He knew my style, even my motto: Assume nothing, question everything.

'He's in surgery now. He's not expected to make it.' I gave him the bad news. Unsentimental, the way I knew he wanted it. 'That's what the doctors believe. But what the hell do doctors know?' I added.

'Is that what you think?' Kyle asked.

The pupils of his eyes were the tiniest, darkest points. He was taking this as badly as I'd seen him react to anything since I'd known him. He was being very emotional for Kyle. I understood how close he and Cross had been.

I sighed and shut my eyes. I wondered if I should tell him what I really thought. Finally, I opened them. I said, 'It might be better if he doesn't make it, Kyle.'

CHAPTER 76

'C'mon with me,' he said, pulling me along. 'I want you to meet someone. C'mon.'

I followed Kyle down one floor to a room on three. The patient in the room was an elderly black woman.

Her head was swathed in Webril, a stretchy woven bandage. The head bandage resembled a turban. A few wisps of gray hair hung loose from the dressing. Telfa bandages covered the abrasions on her face.

There were two IV lines, 'cut downs,' one for blood and one for fluids and antibiotics. She was hooked to a cardiac monitor.

She looked up at us as if we were intruders, but then she recognized Kyle.

'How is Alex? Tell me the truth,' she said in a hoarse, nearly whispering voice that still managed to be firm. 'No one here will tell me the truth. Will you, Kyle?'

'He's in surgery now, Nana. We won't know anything until he comes out,' Kyle said, 'and maybe not
even then.'

The elderly woman's eyes narrowed. She shook her
head sadly.

'I asked you for the truth. I deserve at least that
much. *Now, how is Alex?* Kyle, is Alex still alive?'

Kyle sighed loudly. It was a weary sound, and a sad
one. He and Alex Cross had been working together
for years.

'Alex's condition is extremely grave,' I said, as gently
as I could. 'That means—'

'I know what grave means,' she said. 'I taught
school for forty-seven years. English, history, Boolean
algebra.'

'I'm sorry,' I said, 'I didn't mean to sound condescending.' I paused for a second or two, then continued to answer her question.

'The internal injuries involve a kind of "ripping,"
probably with a high degree of contamination to the
wounds. The most serious wound is to his abdomen.
The shot passed through the liver and apparently
nicked the common hepatic artery. That's what I was
told. The bullet lodged in the rear of the stomach,
where it's now pressing onto the spinal column.'

She winced, but she was listening intently, waiting
for me to finish. I was thinking that if Alex Cross was
anything near as strong as this woman, as willful,
then he must be something special as a detective.

I went on.

'Because of the nick to the artery there was considerable blood loss. The contents of the stomach itself and the small bowel can be sources of E. coli infection. There's a danger of inflammation of the abdominal cavity – peritonitis, and possibly pancreatitis, all of which can be fatal. The gunshot wound is the *injury*, the infection is the *complication*. The second shot went through his left wrist, but missed the radial artery and exited, without shattering bone. That's what we know so far. That's the truth.'

I stopped at that point. My eyes never left those of the elderly woman, and hers never left mine.

'Thank you,' she said in a resigned whisper. 'I appreciate that you didn't condescend to me. Are you a doctor here at the hospital? You speak as if you were.'

I shook my head. 'No, I'm not. I'm with the FBI. I studied to be a doctor.'

Her eyes widened and seemed even more alert than when we had come in. I sensed that she had tremendous reserves of strength. 'Alex is a doctor *and* a detective.'

'I'm a detective, too,' I said.

'I'm Nana Mama. I'm Alex's grandmother. What's your name?'

'Thomas,' I told her. 'My name is Thomas Pierce.'

'Well, thank you for speaking the truth.'

CHAPTER 77

Paris, France.

The police would never admit it, but *Mr Smith had control of Paris now. He had taken the city by storm and only he knew why.* The news of his fearsome presence spread along boulevard Saint-Michel, and then rue de Vaugirard. This sort of thing wasn't supposed to happen in the '*très luxe*' sixth arrondissement.

The seductively chic shops along boulevard Saint-Michel lured tourists and Parisians alike. The Panthéon and beautiful Jardin du Luxembourg were nearby. Lurid murders weren't supposed to happen here.

Clerks from the expensive shops were the first to leave their posts and hurriedly walk or run toward No. 11 rue de Vaugirard. They wanted to *see* Smith, or at least his handiwork. They wanted to see the so-called alien with their own eyes.

Shoppers and even owners left the fashionable clothing shops and cafés. If they didn't walk up rue de Vaugirard, they at least looked down to where several police black-and-whites and also an army bus were parked. High above the eerie scene, pigeons fluttered and squawked. They seemed to want to see the famous criminal as well.

Across Saint-Michel stood the Sorbonne, with its foreboding chapel, its huge clock, its open cobble-stone terrace. A second bus filled with soldiers was parked in the plaza. Students tentatively wandered up rue Champollion to have a look-see. The tiny street had been named after Jean-François Champollion, the French Egyptologist who had discovered the key to Egyptian hieroglyphics while deciphering the Rosetta stone.

A police inspector named René Girard shook his head as he pulled onto rue Champollion and saw the crowd. Girard understood the common man's sick fascination with 'Mr Smith.' It was the fear of the unknown, especially fear of sudden, horrible death, that drew people's interest to these bizarre murders. Mr Smith had gained a reputation because his actions were so completely incomprehensible. He actually did seem to be an 'alien.' Few people could conceive of another human acting as Smith routinely did.

The inspector let his eyes wander. He took in the electronic sign hanging at the Lycée St Louis corner.

Today it advertised 'Tour de France Femina' and also something called 'Formation d'artistes.' More madness, he thought, He coughed out a cynical laugh.

He noticed a sidewalk artist contemplating his sidewalk chalk masterpiece. The man was oblivious to the police emergency. The same could be said of a homeless woman blithely washing her breakfast dishes in the public fountain.

Good for both of them. They passed Girard's test for sanity in the modern age.

As he climbed the gray-stone stairway leading to a blue-painted door, he was tempted to turn toward the crowd of onlookers massed on rue de Vaugirard, and to scream, 'Go back to your little chores and your even smaller lives. Go see an art movie at Cinéma Champollion. This has nothing whatsoever to do with you. Smith takes only interesting and deserving specimens – so you people have absolutely nothing to worry about.'

That morning, one of the finest young surgeons at L'École Pratique de Médecine had been reported missing. If Mr Smith's pattern held, within a couple of days the surgeon would be found dead and mutilated. That was the way it had been with all the other victims. It was the only strand that represented anything like a repeating pattern. *Death by mutilation.*

Girard nodded and said hello to two flics and another low-ranking inspector inside the surgeon's expensively furnished apartment. The place was magnificent, filled with antique furniture, expensive art, with a view of the Sorbonne.

Well, the golden boy of L'École Pratique de Méde-cine had finally gotten a bad break. Yes, things had suddenly gotten very bleak for Dr Abel Sante.

'Nothing, no sign of a struggle?' Girard asked the closest flic as he entered the apartment.

'Not a trace, just like the others. The poor rich bastard is gone, though. He's disappeared, and Mr Smith has him.'

'He's probably in Smith's space capsule,' the other flic said, a youngish man with longish red hair and trendy sunglasses.

Girard turned brusquely. '*You!* Get the hell out of here! Go out on the street with the rest of the madmen and the goddamned pigeons! I would hope Mr Smith might take *you* for his *space capsule* but, unfortunately, I suspect his standards are too high.'

Having said his piece and banished the offending police officer, the inspector went to examine the handiwork of Mr Smith. He had a *procès-verbal* to write up. He had to make some sense out of the madness somehow. All of France, all of Europe, waited to hear the latest news.

CHAPTER 78

FBI headquarters in Washington is located on Pennsylvania Avenue between Ninth and Tenth Streets. I spent from four until almost seven in a BOGSAAT with a half-dozen special agents, including Kyle Craig. BOGSAAT is a *bunch of guys sitting around a table*. We vigorously discussed the Cross attack inside a Strategic Ops Center conference room.

At seven that night, we learned that Alex Cross had made it through the first round of surgery. A cheer went up around the table. I told Kyle that I wanted to go back to St Anthony's Hospital.

'I need to see Alex Cross,' I told him. 'I really do need to see him, even if he can't talk. No matter what condition he's in.'

Twenty minutes later, I was in an elevator headed to the sixth floor of St Anthony's. It was quieter there than the rest of the building. The high floor was a little spooky, especially under the circumstances.

I entered a private recovery room near the center of the semidarkened floor. I was too late. Someone was already in there with Cross.

Detective John Sampson was standing vigil by the bed of his friend. Sampson was tall and powerful, at least six foot six, but he looked incredibly weary, as if he were ready to fall over from exhaustion and the long day's stress.

Sampson finally looked at me, nodded slightly, then turned his attention back to Dr Cross. His eyes were a strange mixture of anger and sadness. I sensed that he knew what was going to happen here.

Alex Cross was hooked up to so many machines it was a visceral shock to see him. I knew that he was in his early forties. He looked younger than his age. That was the only good news.

I studied the charts at the base of the bed. He had suffered severe-moderate blood loss secondary to the tearing of the radial artery. He had a collapsed lung, numerous contusions, hematomas, and lacerations. The left wrist had been injured. There was blood poisoning, and the morbidity of the injuries put him on the 'could be about to check out' list.

Alex Cross was conscious, and I stared into his brown eyes for a long time. What secrets were hidden there? What did he know? Had he actually seen the face of his assailant? *Who did this to you? Not Soneji. Who dared to go into your bedroom?*

He couldn't talk and I could see nothing in his eyes. No awareness that I was there with Detective

Sampson. He didn't seem to recognize Sampson either. Sad.

Dr Cross was getting excellent care at St Anthony's. The hospital bed had a Stryker frame attached to it. The injured wrist was encased in an Elastoplast cast and the arm was anchored to a trapeze bar. He was receiving oxygen through a clear tube that ran into an outlet in the wall. A fancy monitor called a Slave scope was providing pulse, temp, blood pressure, and EKG readings.

'Why don't you leave him alone?' Sampson finally spoke after a few minutes. 'Why don't you leave both of us? You can't help here. Please, go.'

I nodded, but continued to look into the eyes of Alex Cross for a few more seconds. Unfortunately, he had nothing to tell me.

I finally left Cross and Sampson alone. I wondered if I would ever see Alex Cross again. I doubted that I would. I didn't believe in miracles anymore.

CHAPTER 79

That night, I couldn't get Mr Smith out of my head, as usual, and now Alex Cross and his family were residing there as well. I kept revisiting different scenes from the hospital, and from the Cross house. Who had entered the house? Who had Gary Soneji gotten to? That had to be it.

The crisscrossing flashbacks were maddening and running out of control. I didn't like the feeling, and I didn't know if I could conduct an investigation, still less two, under these stressful, almost claustrophobic, conditions.

It had been twenty-four hours from hell. I had flown to the United States from London. I'd landed at National Airport, in D.C., and gone to Quantico, Virginia. Then I had been rushed back to Washington where I worked until ten in the evening on the Cross puzzle.

To make things worse, if they could get any worse, I

found I couldn't sleep when I finally got to my room at the Washington Hilton & Towers. My mind was in a chaotic state that steadfastly refused sleep.

I didn't like the working hypothesis on Cross that I had heard from the FBI investigators at headquarters that night. They were stuck in their usual rut: They were like slow students who scan classroom ceilings for answers. Actually, most police investigators reminded me of Einstein's incisive definition of insanity. I had first heard it at Harvard: *'Endlessly repeating the same process, hoping for a different result.'*

I kept flashing back to the upstairs bedroom where Alex Cross had been brutally attacked. I was looking for something – but what was it? I could see his blood spattered on the walls, on the curtains, the sheets, the throw rug. *What was I missing? Something?*

I couldn't sleep, goddamnit.

I tried work as a sedative. It was my usual antidote. I had already begun extensive notes and sketches on the scene of the attack. I got up and wrote some more. My PowerBook was beside me, always at the ready. My stomach wouldn't stop rolling and my head throbbed in a maddening way.

I typed: *Could Gary Soneji possibly still be alive? Don't rule anything out yet, not even the most absurd possibility.*

Exhume Soneji's body if necessary.

Read Cross's book – Along Came a Spider.

Visit Lorton Prison, where Soneji was held.

I pushed aside my computer after an hour's work. It was nearly two in the morning. My head felt stuffed, as if I had a terrible, nagging cold. I still couldn't sleep. I was thirty-three years old; I was already beginning to feel like an old man.

I kept seeing the bloody bedroom at the Cross house. No one can imagine what it's like to live with such imagery day and night. I saw Alex Cross – the way he looked at St Anthony's Hospital. Then I was remembering victims of Mr Smith, his 'studies,' as he called them.

The terrifying scenes play on and on and on in my head. Always leading to the same place, the same conclusion.

I can see another bedroom. It is the apartment Isabella and I shared in Cambridge, Massachusetts.

With total clarity, I remembered running down the narrow hallway that terrible night. I remember my heart pushing into my throat, feeling larger than a clenched fist. I remember every pounding step that I took, everything I saw along the way.

I finally saw Isabella, and I thought it must be a dream, a terrible nightmare.

Isabella was in our bed, and I knew that she was dead. No one could have survived the butchery I witnessed there. No one did survive – neither of us.

Isabella had been savagely murdered at twenty-three, in the prime of her life, before she could be a mother, a wife, the anthropologist she'd dreamed of becoming. I couldn't help myself, couldn't stop. I bent

and held what was left of Isabella, *what was left*.

How can I ever forget any of it? How can I turn that sight off in my mind?

The simple answer is, I cannot.

CHAPTER 80

I was on the hunt again, the loneliest road on this earth. Truthfully, there wasn't much else that had sustained me during the past four years, not since Isabella's death.

The moment I awoke in the morning, I called St Anthony's Hospital. Alex Cross was alive, but in a coma. His condition was listed as extremely critical. I wondered if John Sampson had remained at his bedside. I suspected he had.

By nine in the morning, I was back at the Cross house. I needed to study the scene in much greater depth, to gather every fact, every splinter and fragment. I tried to organize everything I knew, or thought I knew at this early stage of the investigation. I was reminded of a maxim that was frequently used at Quantico: All truths are half-truths and possibly not even that.

A fiendish 'ghoul' had supposedly struck back from the

grave and attacked a well-known policeman and his family in their home. The ghoul had warned Dr Cross that he would come. There was no way to stop it from happening. It was the ultimate in cruel and effective revenge.

For some reason, though, the assailant had failed to execute. None of the family members, or even Alex Cross, had been killed. That was the perplexing and most baffling part of the puzzle for me. That was the key!

I arrived at the cellar in the Cross house just before eleven in the morning. I had asked the Metro police and FBI technicians not to mess around down there until I was finished with my survey of the other floors. My data gathering, my science, was a methodical step-by-step process.

The attacker had hidden himself (herself?) in the basement while a party had been in progress upstairs and in the backyard. There was a partial footprint near the entryway to the cellar. It was a size nine. It wasn't much to go on, not unless the perpetrator had wanted us to find the print.

One thing struck me right away. *Gary Soneji had been locked in a cellar as a child. He'd been excluded from family activities in the rest of the house. He'd been physically abused in the cellar. Just like the one in the Cross house.*

The attacker had definitely hidden in the cellar. That couldn't be a coincidence.

Had he known about Gary Soneji's explicit warning to Cross? That possibility was disturbing as hell. I didn't want to settle on any theories or premature conclusions yet. I just needed to collect as much raw data and information as I could. Possibly because I'd been to medical school, I approached cases as a clinical scientist would.

Collect all the data first. Always the data.

It was quiet in the cellar, and I could focus and concentrate all of my attention on my surroundings. I tried to imagine the attacker lurking here during the party, and then afterward, as the house grew quiet, until Alex Cross finally went to bed.

The attacker was a coward.

He wasn't in a rage state. He was methodical.

It was not a crime of passion.

The intruder had struck out at each of the children first, but not fatally. He had beaten Alex Cross's grandmother, but had spared her. *Why?* Only Alex Cross was meant to die and so far even that hadn't happened.

Had the attacker failed? Where was the intruder now?

Was he still in Washington? Checking out the Cross house right now? Or at St Anthony's Hospital, where the Metro police were guarding Alex Cross.

As I passed an ancient coal stove, I noticed the metal door was slightly ajar. I poked it open with my handkerchief and peered inside. I couldn't see very well and took out a penlight. There were inches of ash that were light gray in color. Someone had burned a flammable substance recently, possibly newspapers or magazines.

Why start a fire in the middle of summer? I wondered.

A small hand shovel was on a worktable near the stove. I used the shovel to sift through the ashes.

I carefully scraped along the stove's bottom.

I heard a *clink*. A metal-against-metal noise.

I scooped out a shovelful of ash. Something came with the ash. It was hard, heavier. My expectations weren't high. I was still just collecting data, anything and everything, even the contents of an old stove. I emptied the ashes onto the worktable in a pile, then smoothed it out.

I saw what the small shovel had struck. I flipped over the new evidence with the tip of the shovel. *Yes*, I said to myself. I finally had something, the first bit of evidence.

It was Alex Cross's detective shield, and it was burned and charred.

Someone wanted us to find the shield.

The intruder wants to play! I thought. *This is cat and mouse.*

CHAPTER 81

Ile-de-France.

Dr Abel Sante was normally a calm and collected man. He was widely known in the medical community to be erudite, but surprisingly down-to-earth. He was a nice man, too, a gentle physician.

Now he desperately tried to put his mind somewhere other than where his body was. Just about anywhere else in the universe would do just fine.

He had already spent several hours remembering minute details from his pleasant, almost idyllic, boyhood in Rennes; then his university years at the Sorbonne and L'École Pratique de Médecine; he had replayed tennis and golf sporting events; he had relived his seven-year love affair with Regina Becker – dear, sweet Regina.

He needed to be somewhere else, to exist anywhere else but where he actually was. He needed to exist in the past, or even the future, but not in the present. He was reminded of *The English Patient* – both the book and the movie. He was Count Almasy now, wasn't he? Only his torture was even worse than Almasy's horribly burned flesh. He was in the grasp of Mr Smith.

He thought about Regina constantly now, and he realized that he loved her fiercely, and what a fool he'd been not to marry her years ago. What an arrogant bastard, and what a huge fool!

How dearly he wanted to live now, and to see Regina again. Life seemed so damned precious to him at this moment, in this terrible place, under these monstrous conditions.

No, this wasn't a good way to be thinking. It brought him down – it brought him back to reality, to the present. *No, no no! Go somewhere else in your mind. Anywhere but here.*

The present line of thought brought him to this tiny compartment, this infinitesimal **x** on the globe where he was now a prisoner, and where no one could possibly find him. Not the flics, not Interpol, not the entire French Army, or the English, or the Americans, or the Israelis!

Dr Sante could easily imagine the furor and outrage, the panic continuing in Paris and throughout

France. NOTED PHYSICIAN AND TEACHER ABDUCTED! The headline in *Le Monde* would read something like that. Or, NEW MR SMITH HORROR IN PARIS.

He was the horror! He was certain that tens of thousands of police, as well as the army, were searching for him now. Of course, every hour he was missing, his chances for survival grew dimmer. He knew that from reading past articles about Mr Smith's unearthly abductions, and what had happened to the victims.

Why me? God Almighty, he couldn't stand this infernal monologue anymore.

He couldn't stand this nearly-upside-down position, this terribly cramped space, for one more second.

He just couldn't bear it. Not one more second!

Not one more second!

Not one more second!

He couldn't breathe!

He was going to die in here.

Right here, in a goddamn dumbwaiter. Stuck between floors, in a godforsaken house in Ile-de-France somewhere on the outskirts of Paris.

Mr Smith had put him in the dumbwaiter, stuffed him inside like a bundle of dirty laundry, and then left him there – for God only knew how long. It seemed like hours, at least several hours, but Abel Sante really wasn't sure anymore.

The excruciating pain came and went, but mostly it rushed through his body in powerful waves. His neck, his shoulders, and his chest ached so badly, beyond belief, beyond his tolerance for pain. The feeling was as if he'd been slowly crushed into a squarish heap. If he hadn't been claustrophobic before, he was now.

But that wasn't the worst part of this. No, it wasn't the worst. The most terrifying thing was that he knew what all of France wanted to know, what the whole world wanted to know.

He knew certain things about Mr Smith's identity. He knew precisely how he talked. He believed that Mr Smith might be a philosopher, perhaps a university professor or student.

He had even *seen* Mr Smith.

He had looked out from the dumbwaiter – upside down, no less – and stared into Smith's hard, cold eyes, seen his nose, his lips.

Mr Smith saw that.

Now there was no hope for him.

'Damn you, Smith. Damn you to hell. I know your shitty secret. I know everything now. You *are* a fucking alien! *You aren't human.*'

CHAPTER 82

'You really think we're going to track down this son of a bitch? You think this guy is dumb?'

John Sampson asked me point-blank, challenging me. He was dressed all in black, and he wore Ray-Ban sunglasses. He looked as if he were already in mourning. The two of us were flying an FBI Belljet helicopter from Washington to Princeton, New Jersey. We were supposed to work together for a while.

'You think Gary Soneji did this somehow? Think he's Houdini? You think maybe he's still alive?' Sampson went on. 'What the hell do you think?'

'I don't know yet,' I sighed. 'I'm still collecting data. It's the only way I know how to work. No, I don't *think* Soneji did it. He's always worked alone before this. Always.'

I knew that Gary Soneji had grown up in New Jersey, then gone on to become one of the most savage murderers of the times. It didn't seem as if his run were over yet. Soneji was part of the ongoing mystery.

Alex Cross's notes on Soneji were extensive. I was finding useful and interesting insights all through the notes, and I was less than a third of the way through. I had already decided that Cross was a sharp police detective but an even better psychologist. His hypotheses and hunches weren't merely clever and imaginative; they were often right. There's an important difference in that, which many people fail to see, especially people in medium-high places.

I looked up from my reading.

'I've had some luck with difficult killers before. All except the one I really want to catch,' I told Sampson.

He nodded, but his eyes stayed locked onto mine. 'This Mr Smith something of a cult hero now? Over in Europe, especially, the Continent, London, Paris, Frankfurt.'

I wasn't surprised that Sampson was aware of the ongoing case. The tabloids had made Mr Smith their latest icon. The stories were certainly compelling reading. They played up the angle that Smith might be an alien. Even newspapers like the *New York Times* and *The Times* of London had run stories stating that police authorities believed Smith might be an extra-terrestrial being who had come here to study humans. To *grok*, as it were.

'Smith has become the evil E.T. Something for *X-Files* fans to contemplate between TV episodes.

Who knows, perhaps Mr Smith *is* a visitor from outer space, at least from some other parallel world. He doesn't have anything in common with human beings, I can vouch for that. I've visited the murder scenes.'

Sampson nodded. 'Gary Soneji didn't have much in common with the human race,' he said in his deep, strangely quiet voice. 'Soneji was from another planet, too. He's an ALF, alien life-form.'

'I'm not sure he fits the same psychological profile as Smith.'

'Why is that?' he asked. His eyes narrowed. 'You think your mass killer is smarter than our mass killer?'

'I'm not saying that. Gary Soneji was very bright, but he made mistakes. So far, Mr Smith hasn't made any.'

'And that's why you're going to solve this hinky mystery? Because Gary Soneji makes mistakes?'

'I'm not making predictions,' I told Sampson. 'I know better than that. So do you.'

'Did Gary Soneji make a mistake at Alex's house?' he suddenly asked, his dark eyes penetrating.

I sighed out loud. 'I think someone did.'

The helicopter was settling down to land outside Princeton. A thin line of cars silently streamed past the airfield on a state highway. People watched us from the cars. It could safely be assumed that everything had started here. The house where Gary Soneji had been raised was less than six miles away.

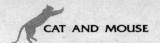

This was the monster's original lair.

'You're sure Soneji's not still alive?' John Sampson asked one more time. 'Are you absolutely sure about that?'

'No,' I finally said. 'I'm not sure of anything yet.'

CHAPTER 83

*A*ssume nothing, question everything.

As we set down in the small private airfield, I could feel the hair on the back of my neck standing on end. *What was wrong here? What was I feeling about the Cross case?*

Beyond the thin ribbons of landing strip were acre upon acre of pine forests and hills. The beauty of the countryside, the incredible shades of green, reminded me of something Cézanne had once said: 'When color is at its richest, form is at its fullest.' I never looked at the world in quite the same way after hearing that.

Gary Soneji was brought up near here, I thought to myself. *Was it possible that he could still be alive? No, I didn't believe that. But could there be connections?*

We were met in New Jersey by two field agents who brought a blue Lincoln sedan for our use. Sampson and I proceeded first to Rocky Hill where

Soneji grew up, and then over to Lambertville to see his grandfather. I knew that Sampson and Alex Cross had been to Princeton less than a week ago. Still, I had questions of my own, theories that needed field-testing.

I also wanted to see the entire area where Gary Soneji had grown up, where his madness had been inflicted and nurtured. Mostly I wanted to talk with someone neither Cross nor Sampson had spent much time investigating, a brand-new suspect.

Assume nothing, question everything . . . and everyone.

Seventy-five-year-old Walter Murphy, Gary's grandfather, was waiting for us on a long, white-washed porch. He didn't ask us inside his house.

The porch had a nice view out from the farmhouse. I saw multiflora rose everywhere, an impenetrable bramble. The nearby barn was also over-run by sumac and poison ivy. I guessed that the grandfather was letting this happen.

I could feel Gary Soneji at his grandfather's farm, I felt him everywhere.

According to Walter Murphy, he'd had no inkling that Gary was capable of murder. Not at any time. Not a clue.

'Some days I think I've gotten used to what's happened, but then suddenly it's fresh and incomprehensible to me all over again,' he told us as the mid-day breeze ruffled his longish white hair.

'Did you stay close to Gary as he got older?' I asked cautiously. I was studying his build, which was large.

His arms were thick and looked as if they could still do physical damage.

'I remember long talks with Gary from the time he was a boy right up until it was alleged he'd kidnapped those two children in Washington.' *Alleged.*

'And you were taken by surprise?' I said. 'You had no idea?'

Walter Murphy looked directly at me – for the first time. I knew that he resented my tone, the irony in it. How angry could I make him? How much of a temper did the old man have?

I leaned in and listened more closely. I watched every gesture, every tic. *Collected the data.*

'Gary always wanted to fit in, just like everybody else does,' he said abruptly. 'He trusted me because he knew I accepted him for what he was.'

'What was it about Gary that needed to be accepted?'

The old man shifted his eyes to the peaceful-looking pine woods surrounding the farm. *I could feel Soneji in those woods. It was as if he were watching us.*

'He could be hostile at times, I'll admit. His tongue was sharp, double-barbed. Gary had an air of superiority that ruffled some tail feathers.'

I kept at Walter Murphy, didn't give him space to breathe. 'But not when he was around you?' I asked. 'He didn't ruffle your feathers?'

The old man's clear blue eyes returned from their trip into the woods. 'No, we were always close. I know we were, even if the expensive shrinks say it wasn't possible for Gary to feel love, to feel anything for anybody. I was never the target for any of his temper explosions.'

That was a fascinating revelation, but I sensed it was a lie. I glanced at Sampson. He was looking at me in a new way.

'These explosions at other people, were they ever premeditated?' I asked.

'Well, you know damn well he burned down his father and stepmother's house. They were in it. So were his stepbrother and stepsister. He was supposed to be away at school. He was an honor student at the Peddie School in Highstown. He was making friends there.'

'Did you ever meet any of the friends from Peddie?' The quickening tempo of my questions made Walter Murphy uneasy. Did he have his grandson's temper?

A spark flared in the old man's eyes. Unmistakable anger was there now. Maybe the real Walter Murphy was appearing.

'No, he never brought his friends from school around here. I suppose you're suggesting that he didn't have friends, that he just wanted to seem more normal than he was. Is that your two-bit analysis? Are you a forensic psychologist, by the way? Is that your game?'

'Trains?' I said.

I wanted to see where Walter Murphy would go with it. This was important, a test, a moment of truth and reckoning.

C'mon, old man. Trains?

He looked off into the woods again, still serene and beautiful. 'Mmm. I'd forgotten, hadn't thought of the trains in a while. Fiona's son, her real son, had an expensive set of Lionel trains. Gary wasn't allowed to even be in the same room with them. When he was ten or eleven, the train set disappeared. The whole damn set, gone.'

'What happened to the train set?'

Walter Murphy almost smiled. 'They all knew Gary had taken it. Destroyed it, or maybe buried it somewhere. They spent an entire summer questioning him as to the train set's whereabouts, but he never told them squat. They grounded him for the summer and he still never told.'

'It was his secret, his power over them.' I offered a little more 'two-bit analysis.'

I was beginning to feel certain disturbing things about Gary and his grandfather. I was starting to know Soneji and maybe, in the process, getting closer to whoever had attacked the Cross house in Washington. Quantico was researching possible copycat theories. I liked the partner angle – except for the fact that Soneji had never had one before.

Who had crept into Cross's house? And how?

'I was reading some of Dr Cross's detective logs on the way here,' I told the grandfather. 'Gary had a recurring nightmare. It took place here on your farm. Are you aware of it? Gary's nightmare at your farm?'

Walter Murphy shook his head. He was blinking

his eyes, twitching. He knew something.

'I'd like your permission to do something here,' I finally said. 'I'll need two shovels. Picks, if you have them.'

'And if I say no?' He raised his voice suddenly. It was the first time he'd been openly uncooperative.

And then it struck me. The old man is acting, too. That's why he understood so much about Gary. He looks off into the trees to set his mind and gain control for the next few lines he has to deliver. *The grandfather is an actor! Just not as good as Gary.*

'Then we'll get a search warrant,' I told him. 'Make no mistake. We will do the search anyway.'

CHAPTER 84

'What the hell is this all about?' Sampson asked as we trudged from the ramshackle barn to a gray fieldstone fireplace that stood in an open clearing. 'You think this is how we catch the Bug-Eyed Monster? Beating up on this old man?'

Both of us carried old metal shovels, and I had a rusted pickax also.

'I told you – *data*. I'm a scientist by training. Trust me for about half an hour. The old man is tougher than he looks.'

The stone fireplace had been built for family cookouts a long time ago, but apparently had not been used in recent years. Sumac and other vines were creeping over the fireplace, as if to make it disappear.

Just beyond the fireplace was a rotting, wooden-plank picnic table with splintered benches on either side. Pines, oaks, and sugar maples were everywhere.

'Gary had a recurring dream. That's what brought me here. This is where the dream takes place. Near the fireplace and the picnic table at Grandpa Walter's farm. It's quite horrible. The dream comes up several times in the notes Alex made on Soneji when he was inside Lorton Prison.'

'Where Gary should have been *cooked*, until he was crispy on the outside, slightly pink toward the center,' Sampson said.

I laughed at his dark humor. It was the first light moment I'd had in a long time and it felt good to share it with someone.

I picked out a spot midway between the old fireplace and a towering oak tree that canted toward the farmhouse. I drove the pickax into the ground, drove it hard and deep. *Gary Soneji. His aura, his profound evil. His paternal granddaddy. More data.*

'In his bizarre dreams,' I told Sampson, 'Gary committed a gruesome murder when he was a young boy. He *may* have buried the victim out here. He wasn't sure himself. He felt he couldn't separate dreams from reality sometimes. Let's spend a little time searching for Soneji's ancient burial ground. Maybe we're about to enter Gary's earliest nightmare.'

'Maybe I don't want to enter Gary Soneji's earliest nightmare,' Sampson said, laughing again. The tension between us was definitely breaking some. This was better.

I lifted the pickax high and swung down with great force. I repeated the action again and again, until I found a smooth, comfortable, working rhythm.

Sampson looked surprised as he watched me handle the pick. 'You've done this kind of fieldwork before, boy,' he said, and began to dig at my side.

'Yes, I lived on a farm in El Toro, California. My father, his father, and my grandfather's father were all small-town doctors. But they continued to live on our family horse farm. I was supposed to go back there to set up practice, but then I never finished my medical training.'

The two of us were hard at work now. Good, honest work: looking for old bodies, searching for ghosts from Gary Soneji's past. Trying to goad Grandfather Murphy.

We took off our shirts, and soon both of us were covered with sweat and dust.

'This was like a *gentleman's* farm? Back in California? The one you lived on as a boy?'

I snorted out a laugh as I pictured the *gentleman's* farm. 'It was a very small farm. We had to struggle to keep it going. My family didn't believe a doctor should get rich taking care of other people. "You shouldn't take a profit from other people's misery," my father said. He still believes that.'

'Huh. So your whole family's weird?'

'That's a reasonably accurate portrait.'

CHAPTER 85

As I continued to dig in Walter Murphy's yard, I thought back to our farm in Southern California. I could still vividly see the large red barn and two small corrals.

When I lived there we owned six horses. Two were breeding stallions, Fadl and Rithsar. Every morning I took rake, pitchfork, and wheelbarrow, and I cleared the stalls; and then made my trip to the manure pile. I put down lime and straw, washed out and refilled the water buckets, made minor repairs. Every single morning of my youth. So yes, I knew how to handle a shovel and pickax.

It took Sampson and me half an hour before we had a shallow ditch stretching toward the ancient oak tree in the Murphy yard. The sprawling tree had been mentioned several times in Gary's recounting of his dreams.

I had almost expected Walter Murphy to call the

police on us, but it didn't happen. I half-expected Soneji to suddenly appear. That didn't happen either.

'Too bad old Gary didn't just leave us a map.' Sampson grunted and groaned under the hot, beating sun.

'He was very specific about his dream. I think he wanted Alex to come out here. Alex, or somebody else.'

'Somebody else did. The two of us. Ho shit, there's something down here. Something under my feet,' Sampson said.

I moved around toward his spot in the trench. The two of us continued to dig, picking up the pace. We worked side by side, sweating profusely. *Data*, I reminded myself. *It's all just data on the way to an answer. The beginning of a solution.*

And then I recognized the fragments we had uncovered in the shallow grave, in Gary's hiding place near the fireplace.

'Jesus Christ, I don't believe it. Oh God, Jesus!' Sampson said.

'Animal bones. Looks like the skull and upper thigh bone of a medium-sized dog,' I said to Sampson.

'Lots of bones!' he added.

We continued to dig even faster. Our breathing was harsh and labored. We had been digging in the summer heat for nearly an hour. It was in the nineties, sticky-hot, and claustrophobic. We were in a hole up to our waists.

'Shit! Here we go again. You recognize this from

any of your med-school anatomy classes?' Sampson asked.

We were looking down at fragments from a human skeleton. 'It's the scapula and mandible. It could be a young boy or girl,' I told him.

'So this is the handiwork of young Gary? This Gary's first kill? Another kid?'

'I don't know for sure. Let's not forget about Grandpa Walter. Let's keep looking. If it is Gary, maybe he left a sign. These would be his earliest souvenirs. They would have been precious to him.'

We kept on digging and, minutes later, we found another cache. Only the sound of our labored breathing broke the silence.

There were more bones, possibly from a large animal, possibly a deer, but probably human.

And there was something else, a definite sign from young Gary. It had been wrapped in tinfoil, which I now carefully removed.

It was a Lionel locomotive, undoubtedly one he had stolen from his stepbrother.

The toy train that launched a hundred deaths.

CHAPTER 86

Christine Johnson knew she had to go to the Sojourner Truth School, but once she got there, she wasn't sure she was ready for work yet. She was nervous, distracted, and not herself. Maybe school would help to get her mind off Alex, though.

She stopped at Laura Dixon's first-grade class on her morning walk. Laura was one of her best friends in the world, and her classes were stimulating and fun. Besides, first graders were so damn cute to be around. 'Laura's babies,' she called them. Or, 'Laura's cuddly kittens and perky puppies.'

'Oh, *look* who it is, look who's come to visit. Aren't we the luckiest first-grade class in the whole world!' the teacher cried when she spotted Christine at the door.

Laura was just a smidgen over five foot tall, but she was still a very *big* girl, large at the hips and breasts.

Christine couldn't keep from smiling at her friend's greeting. Trouble was, she was also incredibly close to tears. She realized she *wasn't* ready for school.

'Good morning, Ms Johnson!' the first graders chorused like a practiced glee club. God, they were wonderful! So bright and enthusiastic, sweet and good.

'Good morning back at you,' Christine beamed. There, she felt a little better. A big letter *B* was scrawled on the blackboard, as well as Laura's sketches of a *B*umblebee *B*uzzing around *B*atman and a *B*ig *B*lue *B*oat.

'Don't let me interrupt progress,' she said. 'I'm just here for a little refresher course. *B* is for *B*eautiful *B*eginnings, *B*abies.'

The class laughed, and she felt *connected* with them, thank God. It was at times like this when she dearly wished she had kids of her own. She loved the first graders, loved kids, and, at thirty-two, it was definitely time.

Then, out of nowhere, an image flashed from the terrible scene a few days earlier. Alex being moved from his house on Fifth Street to one of the ambulances! She had been called to the scene by neighbors, friends of hers. Alex was conscious. He said, 'Christine, you look so beautiful. Always.' And then they took him away from her.

The image from that morning and his final words made her shiver to remember. The Chinese had a saying that had been in her mind for a while, troubling her: *Society prepares the crime; the criminal only commits it.*

'Are you all right?' Laura Dixon was at her side, had seen Christine falter at the door.

'Excuse us, ladies and gentlemen,' she said to her class. 'Ms Johnson and I have to chat for a minute right outside the door. You may chat as well. Quietly. Like the ladies and gentlemen that you are, I trust.'

Then Laura took Christine's arm and walked her out into the deserted hallway.

'Do I look *that* bad?' Christine asked. 'Does it show all over my face, Laura?'

Laura hugged her tightly and the heat from her friend's ample body felt good. Laura *was* good.

'Don't you try to be so *goddamn* strong, don't try to be so brave,' Laura said. 'Have you heard anything more, sweetheart? Tell Laura. Talk to me.'

Christine mumbled into Laura's hair. It felt so good to hold her, to hold on to someone. 'Still listed as critical. Still no visitors. Unless you happen to be high up in the Metro police or the FBI.'

'Christine, Christine,' Laura whispered softly. 'What am I going to do with you?'

'What, Laura? I'm okay now. I really am.'

'You are so strong, girl. You are about the best person I have ever met. I love you dearly. That's all I'll say for right now.'

'That's enough. Thank you,' Christine said. She felt a little better, not quite so hollowed-out and empty, but the feeling didn't last very long.

She started to walk back to her office.

As she turned down the east corridor, she spotted the FBI's Kyle Craig waiting for her near her office. She hurried down the hallway toward him. *This is not good*, she told herself. *Oh dear God, no. Why is Kyle here? What does he have to tell me?*

'Kyle, what is it?' Her voice trembled and nearly went out of control.

'I have to talk to you,' he said, taking her hand. 'Please, just listen. Come inside your office, Christine.'

CHAPTER 87

That night, back in my room at the Marriott in Princeton, I couldn't sleep again. It was two cases running concurrently in my mind. I skimmed several chapters from a rather pedestrian book about trains, just to gather *data*.

I was starting to familiarize myself with the vocabulary of trains: vestibules, step boxes, roomettes, annunciators, the deadman control. I knew that trains were a key part to the mystery I had been asked to solve.

What part had Gary Soneji played in the attack at Alex Cross's house?

Who was his partner?

I went to work at my PowerBook, which I'd set up on the hotel-room desk. As I would later relate to Kyle Craig, I no sooner sat down than the specially designed alarm in the computer started to *beep*. A fax was waiting for me.

I knew instantly what it was – Smith was calling. He had been contacting me for over a year, on a regular basis. Who was tracking whom? I sometimes asked myself.

The message was classic Smith. I read it, line by line.

Paris – Wednesday.

In Foucault's Discipline and Punish, *the philosopher suggests that in the modern age we are moving from individual punishment to a paradigm of generalized punishment. I, for one, believe that this is an unfortunate happenstance. Do you see where I might be going with this line of thinking, and what my ultimate mission might be?*

I'm missing you over here on the Continent, missing you terribly. Alex Cross isn't worth your valuable time and energy.

I've taken one here in Paris in your honor – a doctor! A doctor, a surgeon, just like you wanted to be once upon a time.

Always,

Mr Smith.

CHAPTER 88

This was the way the killer communicated with me for more than a year. Fax or e-mail messages arrived on the PowerBook at any time of day or night. I would then transmit them to the FBI. Mr Smith was so contemporary, a creature of the nineties.

I relayed the fax to the Behavioral Science Unit at Quantico. Several of the profilers were still working. I could visualize the scene of consternation and frustration. My trip to France was approved.

Kyle Craig telephoned my room at the Marriott a few minutes after the fax had been relayed to Quantico. Mr Smith was giving me another window of opportunity to catch him, usually only a day or so, but sometimes only hours. Smith was challenging me to save the kidnapped doctor in Paris.

And yes, I did believe Mr Smith was far superior to Gary Soneji. Both his mind and his methodology outstripped Soneji's more primitive approach.

I was carrying my travel bag and computer when I saw John Sampson. He was outside in the parking lot of the hotel. It was a little past midnight. I wondered what he'd been up to in Princeton that night.

'What the hell is this, Pierce? Where do you think you're going?' he said in a loud, angry voice. He towered over me in the parking lot. His shadow stretched out thirty or forty feet from the lights of the building.

'Smith contacted me about thirty minutes ago. He does this just before he makes a kill. He gives me a location and challenges me to stop the murder.'

Sampson's nostrils flared. He was shaking his head from side to side. There was only one case in his mind.

'So you're just dropping what we're working on here? You weren't even going to tell me, were you? Just leave Princeton in the dead of night.' His eyes were cold and unfriendly. I had lost his trust.

'John, I left a message explaining everything to you. It's at the front desk. I already spoke to Kyle. I'll surely be back in a few days. Smith never takes long. He knows it's too dangerous. I need time to think about this case anyway.'

Sampson frowned and he continued to shake his head. 'You said it was important to visit Lorton Prison. You said Lorton is the one place where Soneji could have gotten somebody to do his dirty work. His partner probably came from Lorton.'

'I still plan to visit Lorton Prison. Right now, I have

to try and prevent a murder. Smith abducted a doctor in Paris. He's dedicating the kill to me.'

John Sampson wasn't impressed with anything I'd said.

'Trust me a little,' I said, but he turned and walked away.

I didn't get a chance to tell him the other thing, the part that bothered me the most. I hadn't told Kyle Craig either.

Isabella had come from Paris. Paris was her home. I hadn't been there since her murder.

Mr Smith knew that.

CHAPTER 89

It was a beautiful spot, and Mr Smith wanted to spoil it, to ruin it forever inside his mind. The small stone house with its earth-grouted walls and white-shuttered windows and country-lace curtains was peaceful and idyllic. The garden was surrounded by twig fencing. Under a lone apple tree sat a long wooden table, where friends, family, and neighbors might gather to eat and talk.

Smith carefully spread out pages from *Paris Monde* across the linoleum floor of the spacious farmhouse kitchen. Patti Smith – not a relation – was screeching from his CD player. She sang 'Summer Cannibals,' and the blatant irony wasn't lost on him.

The newspaper front page screamed as well – *Mr Smith Takes Surgeon Captive in Paris!*

And so he had, so he had.

The *idée fixe* that had captured the public's fancy and fear was that Mr Smith might be an alien visitor roaming and ravaging the earth for dark, unknown, perhaps *unknowable* reasons. He didn't share any traits with humans, the lurid news stories reasoned. He was described as 'not of the earth,' 'incapable of any human emotion.'

His name – Mr Smith – came from 'Valentine Michael Smith,' a visitor from Mars in Robert Heinlein's science-fiction novel, *Stranger in a Strange Land*. The book had always been a cult favorite. *Stranger* was the single book in Charles Manson's backpack when he was captured in California.

He studied the French surgeon lying nearly unconscious on the kitchen floor. One FBI report stated that 'Mr Smith seems to appreciate beauty. He has a human artist's eye for composition. Observe the studied way in which he arranges the corpses.'

A human artist's eye for beauty and composition. Yes, that was true enough. He had loved beauty once, lived for it, actually. The artful arrangements were one of the clues he left for his . . . *his followers*.

Patti Smith finished her song, and the Doors immediately came on. 'People Are Strange.' The moldy oldie was wonderful mood music as well.

Smith let his gaze wander around the country kitchen. One entire wall was a stone fireplace. Another wall was white tile, with antique shelves that held copper pots, white café au lait bowls, antique jam jars, or *confitures fines*, as they were called here. He knew that, knew just about everything about everything. There was an antique black cast-iron stove with brass knobs. And a large white porcelain sink. Adjacent to the sink, just above a butcher-block worktable, hung an impressive array of kitchen knives. The knives were beautiful, absolutely perfect in every way.

He was avoiding looking at the victim, wasn't he?

He knew that he was. He always did.

Finally, he lowered his eyes and looked into the victim's.

So this was Abel Sante.

This was lucky number nineteen.

CHAPTER 90

The victim was a very successful thirty-five-year-old surgeon. He was good-looking in a Gallic sort of way, in excellent shape even without very much meat left on his bones. He seemed a nice person, an 'honorable' man, a 'good' doctor.

What was human? What exactly was human-ness? Mr Smith wondered. That was the fundamental question he still had, after physical exams like this, in nearly a dozen countries around the world.

What was human? What, exactly, did the word mean?

Could he finally find an answer here in this French country kitchen? The philosopher Heidegger believed the *self is revealed* by what we truly care about. Was Heidegger onto something? What was it that Mr Smith truly cared about? That was a fair question to ask.

The French surgeon's hands were tightly tied behind his back. The ankles were bound to the hands;

the knees were bent back toward the head. The remaining length of rope was attached to the neck in a noose.

Abel Sante had already realized that any struggling, any thrashing about, created intense strangulation pressure. As the legs eventually tired, they would become numb and painful. The urge to straighten them would be overpowering. If he did this, it would induce self-strangulation.

Mr Smith was ready. He was on a schedule. The autopsy would start at the top of the body, then work its way down. The correct order: neck, spine, chest. Then abdomen, pelvic organs, genitalia. The head and brain would be examined last, in order to allow the blood to drain as much as possible – *for maximum viewing.*

Dr Sante screamed, but no one could hear him out here. It was an ungodly sound and almost made Smith scream, too.

He entered the chest via a classic 'Y' incision. The first cut went across the chest from shoulder to shoulder, continued over the breasts, then traveled from the tip of the sternum. He cut down the entire length of the abdomen to the pubic area.

The brutal murder of an innocent surgeon named Abel Sante.

Absolutely inhuman, he thought to himself.

Abel Sante – he was the key to everything, and none of the police masterminds could figure it out. None of them were worth shit as detectives, as investigators, as anything. It was so simple, if only they would use their minds.

Abel Sante.

Abel Sante.

Abel Sante.

The autopsy finished, Mr Smith lay down on the kitchen floor with what was left of poor Dr Sante. He did this with every victim. Mr Smith hugged the bleeding corpse against his own body. He whispered and sighed, whispered and sighed. It was always like this.

And then, Smith sobbed loudly. 'I'm so sorry. I'm so sorry. Please forgive me. Somebody forgive me,' he moaned in the deserted farmhouse.

Abel Sante.

Abel Sante.

Abel Sante.

Didn't anyone get it?

CHAPTER 91

On the American Airlines flight to Europe, I noticed that mine was the only overhead lamp glaring as the flight droned over the Atlantic.

Occasionally, one of the stewardesses stopped to offer coffee or liquor. But for the most part, I just stared into the blackness of the night.

There had never been a mass killer to match Mr Smith's unique approach to violence, not from a scientific vantage point anyway. That was one thing the Behavioral Science Unit at Quantico and I agreed on. Even the contrarians at Interpol, the international clearinghouse for police information, agreed with us.

In point of fact, the community of forensic psychologists is, or at least had been, in relative agreement about the different repeat- or pattern-murderer types; and also the chief characteristics of their disorders. I found myself reviewing the data as I flew.

Schizoid personality disorder types, as they are currently called, tend to be introverted and indifferent to social relationships. This freak is a classic loner. He tends to have no close friends or close relationships, except possibly family. He exhibits an inability to show affection in acceptable ways. He usually chooses solitary activities for his free time. He has little or no interest in sex.

Narcissists are different. They exhibit little or no concern for anyone but themselves, though they sometimes pretend to care about others. True narcissists can't empathize. They have an inflated sense of self, can become highly unstable if criticized, and feel they are entitled to special treatment. They are preoccupied with grandiose feelings of success, power, beauty, and love.

Avoidant personality disorder types usually won't get involved with other people unless they're completely sure of acceptance. These types avoid jobs and situations involving social contact. They are usually quiet and embarrass easily. They're considered 'sneaky dangerous.'

Sadistic personality disorder types are the ultimate in badness, as destructive individuals go. They habitually use violence and cruelty to establish control. They enjoy inflicting physical and psychological pain. They like to tell lies, simply for the purpose of inflicting pain. They are obsessed with involving violence, torture, and especially the death of others.

As I said, all of this ran through my mind as I sat in

my airplane seat high over the Atlantic. What interested me mostly, though, was the conclusion I'd reached about Mr Smith, and which I had recently shared with Kyle Craig at Quantico.

At different times during the long and complex investigation, Mr Smith *had fit all four of these classic murderer types*. He would seem to fit one personality disorder type almost perfectly – then change into another – back and forth at whim. He might even be a fifth type of psychopathic killer, a whole new breed of disorder type.

Perhaps the tabloids were right about Mr Smith, and he *was* an alien. He wasn't like any other human. I knew that. *He had murdered Isabella*.

This was really why I couldn't sleep on the flight to Paris. It was why I could never sleep anymore.

CHAPTER 92

W ho could ever begin to forget the cold-
blooded murder of a loved one? I couldn't.
Nothing has diminished its vividness or
unreality in four years. It goes like this, exactly the
way I told it to the Cambridge police.

It is around two in the morning, and I use my key to
open the front door of our two-bedroom apartment on
Inman Street in Cambridge. Suddenly, I stop. I have the
sense that something is wrong in the apartment.

Details inside are particularly memorable. I will
never forget any of it. A poster in our foyer: *Language
is more than speech*. Isabella is a closet linguist, a lover
of words and word games. So am I. It's an important
connection between us.

A favorite Noguchi rice-paper lamp of Isabella's.

Her treasured paperbacks from home, most of
them Folio. White uniform spines with black lettering,
so perfect and neat.

I'd had a few glasses of wine at Jillian's with some other medical students, recent graduates like myself. We were letting off steam after too many days and nights and weeks and years in the Harvard pressure cooker. We were comparing notes about the hospitals each of us would be working at in the fall. We were promising to stay in touch, knowing that we probably wouldn't.

The group included three of my best friends through medical school. Maria Jane Ruocco, who would be working at Children's Hospital in Boston; Chris Sharp, who was soon off to Beth Israel; Michael Fescoe, who had landed a prize internship at N.Y.U. I had been fortunate, too. I was headed to Massachusetts General, one of the best teaching hospitals in the world. My future was assured.

I was high from the wine, but not close to being drunk, when I got home. I was in a good mood, unusually carefree. Odd, guilty detail – I was horny for Isabella. *Free.* I remember singing 'With or Without You' on the way back in my car, a ten-year-old Volvo befitting my economic status as a med student.

I vividly remember standing in the foyer, seconds after I flicked on the hall lights. Isabella's Coach purse is on the floor. The contents are scattered about in a three- or four-foot radius. Very, very strange.

Loose change, her favorite Georg Jensen earrings, lipstick, assorted makeup containers, compact, cinnamon gum – all there on the floor.

Why didn't Isabella pick up her purse? Is she pissed at me for going out with my med-school chums?

That wouldn't be like Isabella. She is an open woman, liberal-minded to a fault.

I start back through the narrow, winding apartment, looking for her everywhere. The apartment is laid out railroad-style, small rooms on a tight track leading to a single window that looks onto Inman Street.

Some of our secondhand scuba equipment is sitting in the hall. We had been planning a trip to California. Two air tanks, weight belts, wet suits, two sets of rubber fins clutter the hallway.

I grab a speargun – just in case. *In case of what?* I have no idea. How could I?

I become more and more frantic, and then afraid. 'Isabella!' I call at the top of my voice. *'Isabella?* Where are you?'

Then I stop, everything in the world seems to stop. I let go of the speargun, let it fall, crash and clatter against the bare hardwood floor.

What I see in our bedroom will never leave me. I can still *see, smell,* even *taste,* every obscene detail. Maybe this is when my sixth sense is born, the strange feeling that is so much a part of my life now.

'Oh God! Oh Jesus, no!' I scream loud enough for the couple who live above us to hear. *This isn't Isabella,* I remember thinking. Those words of total disbelief. I may have actually spoken them aloud. *Not Isabella. It couldn't be Isabella. Not like this.*

And yet – I recognize the flowing auburn hair that I so love to stroke, to brush; the pouting lips that can make me smile, make me laugh out loud, or sometimes duck for cover; a fan-shaped, mother-of-pearl barrette Isabella wears when she wants to look particularly coquettish.

Everything in my life has changed in a heartbeat, or lack of one. I check for signs of breathing, a sign of life. I can feel no pulse in the femoral or carotid arteries. Not a beat. Nothing at all. *Not Isabella. This can't be happening.*

Cyanosis, a bluish coloration of the lips, nail beds, and skin is already taking place. Blood is pooled on the underside of her body. The bowels and bladder have relaxed, but these bodily secretions are nothing to me. They are nothing under the circumstances.

Isabella's beautiful skin looks waxy, almost translucent, as if it isn't her after all. Her pale-green eyes have already lost their liquid and are flattening out. They can no longer see me, can they? I realize they will never look at me again.

The Cambridge police arrive at the apartment somehow. They are everywhere all at once, looking as shocked as I know I look. My neighbors from the building are there, trying to comfort me, trying to calm me, trying not to be sick themselves.

Isabella is gone. We never even got to say good-bye. Isabella is dead, and I can't bring myself to believe it. An old James Taylor lyric, one of our favorites, weaved through my head: *'But I always thought that I'd see you, one more time again.'* The song was 'Fire and Rain.' It was our song. It still is.

A terrible fiend was loose in Cambridge. He had struck less than a dozen blocks from Harvard University. He would soon receive a name: *Mr Smith*, a literary allusion that could have happened only in a university town like Cambridge.

The worst thing, what I would never forget or forgive – the final thing – *Mr Smith had cut out Isabella's heart.*

My reverie ended. My plane was landing at Charles de Gaulle Airport. I was in Paris.

So was Smith.

CHAPTER 93

I checked into the Hôtel de la Seine. Up in my room, I called St Anthony's Hospital in Washington. Alex Cross was still in a grave condition. I purposely avoided meeting with the French police or the crisis team. The local police are never any help anyway. I preferred to work alone, and did so for half a day.

Meanwhile, Mr Smith contacted the Sûreté. He always did it this way; a call to the local police, a personal affront to everyone involved in chasing him. Bad news, always terrible news. *All of you have failed to catch me. You've failed, Pierce.*

He had revealed where the body of Dr Abel Sante could be found. He taunted us, called us pathetic losers and incompetents. He always mocked us after a kill.

The French police, as well as members of Interpol, were gathered in large numbers at the entrance to the

Parc de Montsouris. It was ten after one in the morning when I arrived there.

Because of the possibility of crowds of onlookers and the press, the CRS, a special force of the Paris police, had been called in to secure the scene.

I spotted an inspector from Interpol whom I knew and waved in her direction. Sondra Greenberg was nearly as obsessed about catching Mr Smith as I was. She was stubborn, excellent at her job. She had as good a chance as anyone of catching Mr Smith.

Sondra looked particularly tense and uneasy as she walked toward me. 'I don't think we need all these people, all this *help*,' I said smiling thinly. 'It shouldn't be too damn hard to find the body, Sandy. He told us where to look.'

'I agree with you,' she said, 'but you know the French. This was the way they decided it should be done. *Le grand* search party for *le grand* alien space criminal.' A cynical smile twisted along the side of her mouth. 'Good to see you, Thomas. Shall we begin our little hunt? How is your French, by the way?'

'*Il n'y a rien à voir, Madame, rentrez chez vous!*'

Sandy laughed out of the side of her mouth. Some of the French policemen were looking at us as if we were both crazy. 'I will *like hell* go home. Fine, though. *You* can tell the flics what we'd like them to do. And then they'll do the exact opposite, I'm quite sure.'

'Of course they will. They're French.'

Sondra was a tall brunette, willowy on top but with heavy legs, almost as if two body types had been fused. She was British, witty and bright, yet tolerant, even of Americans. She was devoutly Jewish and militantly gay. I enjoyed working with her, even at times like this.

I walked into the Parc de Montsouris with Sandy Greenberg, arm in arm. Once more into the fray.

'Why do you think he sends us *both* messages? Why does he want us both here?' she mused as we tramped across damp lawns that glistened under streetlamps.

'We're the stars in his weird galaxy. That's my theory anyway. We're also authority figures. Perhaps he likes to taunt authority. He might even have a modicum of respect for us.'

'I sincerely doubt that,' Sandy said.

'Then perhaps he likes showing us up, making himself feel superior. How about that theory?'

'I rather like it, actually. He could be watching us right now. I know he's an egomaniac of the highest order. *Hello there, Mr Smith from planet Mars. Are you watching? Enjoying the hell out of this?* God, I hate that creepy bastard!'

I peered around at the dark elm trees. There was plenty of cover here if someone wanted to observe us.

'Perhaps he's here. He might be able to change shapes, you know. He could be that *balayeur des rues*, or that gendarme, or even that *fille de trottoir* in disguise,' I said.

We began to search at quarter past one. At two in the morning, we still hadn't located the body of Dr

Abel Sante. It was strange and worrisome to everyone in the search party. It was obvious to me that Smith wanted to make it hard for us to locate the body. He had never done that before. He usually discarded bodies the way people throw away gum wrappers. *What was Smith up to?*

The Paris newspapers had evidently gotten a tip that we were searching the small park. They wanted a hearty serving of blood and guts for their breakfast editions. TV helicopters hovered like vultures overhead. Police barricades had been set up out on the street. We had everything except a victim.

The crowd of onlookers already numbered in the hundreds – and it was two o'clock in the morning. Sandy peered out at them. 'Mr Smith's sodding fan club,' she sneered. 'What a time! What a civilization! Cicero said that, you know.'

My beeper went off at half-past two. The noise startled Sandy and me. Then hers went off. *Dueling beepers. What a world, indeed.*

I had received a fax or a voice-mail or an e-mail. I was certain it was Smith. I looked at Sandy.

'What the hell is he pulling this time?' she said. She looked frightened. 'Or maybe it's a *she* – what is *she* pulling?'

We removed our laptops from our shoulder bags.

Sandy was already checking her machine for messages. I got to mine first.

Pierce, the fax read, *welcome back to the real work, to the real chase. I lied to you. That was your punishment for unfaithfulness. I wanted to embarrass you, whatever that means. I wanted to remind you that you can't trust me, or anyone else – not even your friend, Ms Greenberg. Besides, I really don't like the French. I've thoroughly enjoyed torturing them here tonight.*

Poor Dr Abel Sante is at the Buttes-Chaumont Park. He's up near the temple. I swear it. I promise you.

Trust me. Ha, ha! Isn't that the quaint sound you humans make when you laugh? I can't quite make the sound myself. You see, I've never actually laughed.

Always,

Mr Smith.

Sandy Greenberg was shaking her head, muttering curses in the night air. She had gotten the message, too.

'Buttes-Chaumont Park,' she repeated the location. Then she added, 'He says that I shouldn't trust you. *Ha, ha!* Isn't that the quaint sound we humans make when we laugh?'

CHAPTER 94

The huge, unwieldy search team swept across Paris to the northeast, heading toward the Buttes-Chaumont Park. The syncopated wail of police sirens was a disturbing, fearsome noise. Mr Smith still had Paris in an uproar in the early-morning hours.

'He's in control now,' I said to Sandy Greenberg as we sped along dark Parisian streets in a blue Citroën I had rented. The car tires made a ripping sound on the smooth road surface. The noise fit with everything else that was happening. 'Smith is in his glory, however ephemeral it may turn out to be. This is his time, his moment,' I rattled on.

The English investigator frowned. 'Thomas, you continue to ascribe human emotions to Smith. When are you going to get it through your skull that we're looking for a *little green man*.'

'I'm an empirical investigator. I'll believe it only

when I *see* a little green man with blood dripping from his little green mouth.'

Neither of us had ever given a millisecond's credence to the 'alien' theories, but space-visitor jokes were definitely a part of the dark humor of this manhunt. It helped to keep us going, knowing that we would soon be at a particularly monstrous and disturbing murder scene.

It was nearly three in the morning when we arrived at the Buttes-Chaumont. What difference did the late hour make to me? I never slept anymore.

The park was deserted, but brightly lit with streetlamps and police and army searchlights. A low, bluish-gray fog had settled in, but there was still enough visibility for our search. The Buttes-Chaumont is an enormous area, not unlike Central Park in New York. Back in the mid-1800s, a man-made lake was dug there and fed by the St Martin's Canal. A mountain of rocks was then constructed, and it is full of caves and waterfalls now. The foliage is dense almost anywhere you choose to roam, or perhaps to hide a body.

It took only a few minutes before a police radio message came for us. Dr Sante had been located not far from where we had entered the park. Mr Smith was finished playing with us. For now.

Sandy and I got out of the patrol car at the gardener's house near the temple and we began to climb the steep stone steps. The flics and French soldiers around us weren't just tired and shell-shocked, they looked afraid. The body-recovery scene would stay with all of them for the rest of their lives. I had read John Webster's *The White Devil* while I was an undergrad at Harvard. Webster's weird seventeenth-century creation was filled with devils, demons, and werewolves – *all of them human*. I believed Mr Smith was a human demon. The worst kind.

We pushed our way forward through thick bushes and brush. I could hear the low, pitiful whine of search dogs nearby. Then I saw four high-strung, shivering animals leading the way.

Predictably, the new crime scene was a unique one. It was quite beautiful, with an expansive view of Montmartre and Saint-Denis. During the day, people came here to stroll, climb, walk pets, live life as it should be lived. The park closed at 11:00 p.m. for safety reasons.

'Up ahead,' Sandy whispered. 'There's something.'

I could see soldiers and police loitering in small groups. Mr Smith had definitely been here. A dozen or more 'packets,' each wrapped in newspaper, were carefully laid out on a sloping patch of grass.

'Are we sure this is it?' one of the inspectors asked me in French. His name was Girard. 'What the hell is this? Is he making a joke?'

'It is not a joke, I can promise you that. Unwrap one of the bundles. Any one will do,' I instructed the French policeman. He just looked at me as if I were mad.

'As they say in America,' Girard said in French, 'this is your show.'

'Do you speak English?' I spit out the words.

'Yes, I do,' he answered brusquely.

'Good. Go fuck yourself,' I said.

I walked over to the eerie pile of 'packages,' or perhaps 'gifts' was the better word. There were a variety of shapes, each packet meticulously wrapped in newspaper. Mr Smith the artiste. A large round packet looked as if it might be a head.

'French butcher shop. That's his motif for tonight. It's all just meat to him,' I muttered to Sandy Greenberg. 'He's mocking the French police.'

I carefully unwrapped the newspaper with plastic gloves. 'Christ Jesus, Sandy.'

It wasn't quite a head – *only half a head.*

Dr Abel Sante's head had been cleanly separated from the rest of the body, like an expensive cut of meat. It was sliced in half. The face was washed, the skin carefully pulled away. Only half of Sante's mouth screamed at us – a single eye reflected a moment of ultimate terror.

'You're right. It *is* just meat to him,' Sandy said. 'How can you stand being right about him all the time?'

'I can't,' I whispered. 'I can't stand it at all.'

CHAPTER 95

Outside Washington, an FBI sedan stopped to pick up Christine Johnson at her apartment. She was ready and waiting, standing vigil just inside the front door. She was hugging herself, always hugging herself lately, always on the edge of fear. She'd had two glasses of red wine and had to force herself to stop at two.

As she hurried to the car she kept glancing around to see if a reporter was staking out her apartment. They were like hounds on a fresh trail. Persistent, sometimes unbelievably insensitive and rude.

A black agent whom she knew, a smart, nice man named Charles Dampier, hopped out and held the car's back door open for her. 'Good evening, Ms Johnson,' he said as politely as one of her students at school. She thought that he had a little crush on her. She was used to men acting like that, but tried to be kind.

'Thank you,' she said as she got into the gray-leather backseat. 'Good evening, guys,' she said to Charles and the driver, a man named Joseph Denjeau.

During the ride, no one spoke. The agents had obviously been instructed not to make small talk unless she initiated it. *Strange, cold world they live in,* Christine thought to herself. *And now I guess I live there, too. I don't think I like it at all.*

She had taken a bath before the agents arrived. She sat in the tub with her red wine and reviewed her life. She understood the good, bad, and ugly about herself pretty well. She knew she had always been a little afraid to jump off the deep end in the past, but she'd wanted to, and she'd gotten oh-so-close. There was definitely a streak of wildness inside her, *good* wildness, too. She had actually left George for six months during the early years of their marriage. She'd flown to San Francisco and studied photography at Berkeley, lived in a tiny apartment in the hills. She had loved the solitude for a while, the time for thinking, the simple act of recording the beauty of life with her camera every day.

She had come back to George, taught, and eventually got the job at the Sojourner Truth School. Maybe it was being around the children, but she absolutely loved it at the school. God, she loved kids, and she was good with them, too. She wanted children of her own so badly.

Her mind was all over the place tonight. Probably the late hour, and the second glass of merlot. The dark

Ford sedan cruised along deserted streets at midnight. It was the usual route, almost always the same trail from Mitchellville to D.C. She wondered if that was wise, but figured they knew how to do their jobs.

Occasionally Christine glanced around, to see if they were being followed. She felt a little silly doing it. Couldn't help it, though.

She was part of a case that was important to the press now. And dangerous, too. They had absolutely no respect for her privacy or feelings. Reporters would show up at the school and try to question other teachers. They called her at home so frequently that she finally changed her number to an unlisted one.

She heard the *whoop* of nearby police or ambulance sirens and the unpleasant sound brought her out of her reverie. She sighed. She was almost there now.

She shut her eyes and took deep, slow breaths. She dropped her head down near her chest. She was tired and thought she needed a good cry.

'Are you all right, Ms Johnson?' agent Dampier inquired. *He's got eyes in the back of his head. He's been watching me*, Christine thought. *He's watching everything that happens, but I guess that's good.*

'I'm fine.' She opened her eyes and offered a smile. 'Just a little tired is all. Too many early mornings and late nights.'

Agent Dampier hesitated, then he said, 'I'm sorry it has to be this way.'

'Thank you,' she whispered. 'You make it a lot easier for me with your kindness. And *you're* a real good driver,' she kidded agent Denjeau, who mostly kept quiet, but laughed now.

The FBI sedan hurtled down a steep concrete ramp and entered the building from the rear. This was a delivery entrance, she knew by now. She noticed that she was hugging herself again. Everything about the nightly trip seemed so unreal to her.

Both agents escorted her upstairs, right to the door, at which point they stepped back and she entered alone.

She gently closed the door and leaned against it. Her heart was pounding – it was always this way.

'Hello, Christine,' Alex said, and she went and held him so tight, *so tight,* and everything was suddenly so much better. Everything made sense again.

CHAPTER 96

My first morning back in Washington, I decided to visit the Cross house on Fifth Street again. I needed to look over Cross's notes on Gary Soneji one more time. I had a deepening sense that Alex Cross knew his assailant, had met the person at some time before the vicious attack.

As I drove to the house through the crowded D.C. streets I went over the physical evidence again. The first really significant clue was that the bedroom where Cross was attacked had been tightly controlled. There was little or no evidence of chaos, of someone being out of his mind. There was ample evidence that the assailant was in what is called a cold rage.

The other significant factor was the evidence of 'overkill' in the bedroom. Cross had been struck half-a-dozen times before he was shot. That would seem to conflict with the tight control at the crime scene, but I didn't think so: Whoever came to the house had a deep hatred for Cross.

Once inside the house, the attacker operated as Soneji would have. The assailant had hidden in the cellar. Then he copycatted an earlier attack Soneji had made at the house. No weapons had been found, so the attacker was definitely clearheaded. No souvenirs had been taken from Cross's room.

Alex Cross's detective shield had been left behind. The attacker wanted it found. What did that tell me – that the killer was proud of what he had accomplished?

Finally, I kept returning to the single most striking and meaningful clue so far. It had jumped at me from the first moment I arrived on Fifth Street and began to collect data.

The attacker had left Alex Cross and his family alive. Even if Cross died, the assailant had departed from the house with the knowledge that Cross was still breathing.

Why would the intruder do that? He could have killed Cross. Or was it always part of a plan to leave Cross alive? If so, why?

Solve that mystery, answer that question – case solved.

CHAPTER 97

The house was quiet, and it had a sad and empty feeling, as houses do when a big, important piece of the family is missing.

I could see Nana Mama working feverishly in her kitchen. The smell of baking bread, roast chicken, and baked sweet potatoes flowed through the house, and it was soothing and reassuring. She was lost in her cooking, and I didn't want to disturb her.

'Is she okay?' I asked Sampson. He had agreed to meet me at the house, though I could tell he was still angry about my leaving the case for a few days.

He shrugged his shoulders. 'She won't accept that Alex isn't coming back, if that's what you mean,' he said. 'If he dies, I don't know what will happen to her.'

Sampson and I climbed the stairs in silence. We were in the hallway when the Cross children appeared out of a side bedroom.

I hadn't formally met Damon and Jannie, but I had

heard about them. Both children were beautiful, though still showing bruises from the attack. They had inherited Alex's good looks. They had bright eyes and their intelligence showed.

'This is Mr Pierce,' Sampson said, 'he's a friend of ours. He's one of the good guys.'

'I'm working with Sampson,' I told them. 'Trying to help him.'

'Is he, Uncle John?' the little girl asked. The boy just stared at me – not angry, but wary of strangers. I could see his father in Damon's wide brown eyes.

'Yes, he is working with me, and he's very good at it,' Sampson said. He surprised me with the compliment.

Jannie stepped up close to me. She was the most beautiful little girl, even with the lacerations and a bruise the size of a baseball on her cheek and neck. Her mother must have been a beautiful woman.

She reached out and shook my hand. 'Well, you can't be as good as my daddy, but you can use my daddy's bedroom,' she said, 'but only until he comes back home.'

I thanked Jannie, and nodded respectfully at Damon. Then I spent the next hour and a half going over Cross's extensive notes and files on Gary Soneji. *I was looking for Soneji's partner.* The files dated back over four years. I was convinced that whoever attacked Alex Cross didn't do it randomly. There had to be a powerful connection with Soneji, *who claimed to always work alone.* It was a knotty problem and the profilers at Quantico weren't making headway with it either.

When I finally trudged back downstairs, Sampson and Nana were both in the kitchen. The uncluttered and practical-looking room was cozy and warm. It brought back memories of Isabella, who had loved to cook and was good at it, too, memories of our home and life together.

Nana looked up at me, her eyes as incisive as I remembered. 'I remember you,' she said. 'You were the one who told me the truth. Are you close to anything yet? Will you solve this terrible thing?' she asked.

'No, I haven't solved it, Nana.' I told her the truth again. 'But I think Alex might have. Gary Soneji might have had a partner all along.'

CHAPTER 98

A recurring thought was playing constantly inside my head: *Who can you trust? Who can you really believe? I used to have somebody –* Isabella.

John Sampson and I boarded an FBI Belljet Ranger around eleven the following morning. We had packed for a couple of days' stay.

'So who is this partner of Soneji's? When do I get to meet him?' Sampson asked during the flight.

'You already have,' I told him.

We arrived in Princeton before noon and went to see a man named Simon Conklin. Sampson and Cross had questioned him before. Alex Cross had written several pages of notes on Conklin during the investigation of the sensational kidnapping of two young children a few years back: Maggie Rose Dunne and Michael 'Shrimpie' Goldberg. The FBI had never really followed up on the extensive reports at the time. They wanted the high-profile kidnapping case closed.

I'd read the notes through a couple of times now. Simon Conklin and Gary had grown up on the same country road, a few miles outside the town of Princeton. The two friends thought of themselves as 'superior' to other kids, and even to most adults. Gary had called himself and Conklin the 'great ones.' They were reminiscent of Leopold and Loeb, two highly intelligent teens who had committed a famous thrill killing in Chicago one year.

As boys, Simon Conklin and Gary had decided that life was nothing more than a cock-and-bull 'story' conveniently cooked up by the people in charge. Either you followed the 'story' written by the society you lived in, or you set out to write your own.

Cross double-underscored in the notes that *Gary had been in the bottom fifth of his class at Princeton High School, before he transferred to the Peddie School. Simon Conklin had been number one, and gone on to Princeton University.*

A few minutes past noon, Sampson and I stepped out into the dirt-and-gravel parking lot of a dreary little strip mall between Princeton and Trenton, New Jersey. It was hot and humid and everything looked bleached out by the sun.

'Princeton education sure worked out well for Conklin,' Sampson said with sarcasm in his voice. 'I'm really impressed.'

For the past two years, Simon Conklin had managed an adult bookstore in the dilapidated strip mall. The store was located in a single-story, red-brick building. The front door was painted black and so were the padlocks. The sign read ADULT.

'What's your feeling about Simon Conklin? Do you remember much about him?' I asked as we walked toward the front door. I suspected there was a back way out, but I didn't think he would run on us.

'Oh, Simon Says is definitely a world-class freaka-zoid. He was high on my Unabomber list at one time. Has an alibi for the night Alex was attacked.'

'He would,' I muttered. 'Of course he would. He's a clever boy. Don't ever forget that.'

We walked inside the seedy, grungy store and flashed our badges. Conklin stepped out from behind a raised counter. He was tall and gangly and painfully thin. His milky-brown eyes were distant, as if he were someplace else. He was instantly unlikable.

He had on faded black jeans and a studded black leather vest, no shirt under the vest. If I hadn't known a few Harvard flameouts myself, I wouldn't have imagined he had graduated from Princeton and ended up like this. All around him were pleasure kits, masturbators, dildos, pumps, restraints. Simon Conklin seemed right in his element.

'I'm starting to enjoy these unexpected visits from you assholes. I didn't at first, but now I'm getting into them,' he said. 'I remember you, Detective Sampson. But *you're* new to the traveling team. You must be Alex

Cross's unworthy replacement.'

'Not really,' I said. 'Just haven't felt like coming around to this shithole until now.'

Conklin snorted, a phlegmy sound that wasn't quite a laugh. 'You haven't felt like it. That means you have feelings that you occasionally act on. How quaint. Then you *must* be with the FBI's Criminal Investigative Analysis Program. Am I right?'

I looked away from him and checked out the rest of the store.

'Hi,' I said to a man perusing a rack with Spanish Fly Powder, Sta-Hard, and the like. 'Find anything you like today? Are you from the Princeton area? I'm Thomas Pierce with the FBI.'

The man mumbled something unintelligible into his chin and then he scurried out, letting a blast of sunlight inside.

'Ouch. That's not nice,' Conklin said. He snorted again, not quite a laugh.

'I'm not very nice sometimes,' I said to him.

Conklin responded with a jaw-cracking yawn. 'When Alex Cross got shot, I was with a friend all night. Your very thorough cohorts already spoke to my squeeze, Dana. We were at a party in Hopewell till around midnight. Lots and lots of witnesses.'

I nodded, looked as bored as he did. 'On another, more promising subject, tell me what happened to Gary's trains? The ones he stole from his stepbrother?'

Conklin wasn't smiling anymore. 'Look, actually I'm getting a little tired of the bullshit. The repetition bores me and I'm not into ancient history. Gary and I were friends until we were around twelve years old. After that, we never spent time together. He had his friends, and so did I. *The end*. Now get the hell out of here.'

I shook my head. 'No, no, Gary never had any other friends. He only had time for the "great ones." He believed you were one of them. He told that to Alex Cross. I think you were Gary's friend until he died. That's why you hated Dr Cross. You had a reason to attack his house. You had a motive, Conklin, and you're the *only* one who did.'

Conklin snorted out of his nose and the side of his mouth again. 'And if you can prove that, then I go directly to jail. I do not pass Go. But you can't prove it. *Dana. Hopewell. Several witnesses*. Bye-bye, assholes.'

I walked out the front door of the adult bookstore. I stood in the blazing heat of the parking lot and waited for Sampson to catch up with me.

'What the hell is going on? Why did you just walk out like that?' he asked.

'Maybe Conklin is the leader,' I said. 'Maybe Soneji was *the follower*.'

CHAPTER 99

Sooner or later almost every police investigation becomes a game of cat and mouse. The difficult, long-running ones always do. First you have to decide, though: *Who is the cat? Who is the mouse?*

For the next few days, Sampson and I kept Simon Conklin under surveillance. We let him know we were there, waiting and watching, always just around the next corner, and the corner after that. I wanted to see if we could pressure Conklin into a telling action, or even a mistake.

Conklin's reply was an occasional jaunty salute with his middle finger. That was fine. We were registering on his radar. He knew we were there, always there, watching. I could tell we were unnerving him, and I was just beginning to play the game.

John Sampson had to return to Washington after a few days. I had expected that. The D.C. police department couldn't let him work the case indefinitely.

Besides, Alex Cross and his family needed Sampson in Washington.

I was alone in Princeton, the way I liked it, actually.

Simon Conklin left his house on Tuesday night. After some maneuvering of my own, I followed in my Ford Escort. I let him see me early on. Then I dropped back in the heavy traffic out near the malls, and I let him go free.

I drove straight back to his house and parked off the main road, which is hidden from sight by thick scrub pines and brambles. I walked through the dense woods as quickly as I could. I knew I might not have a lot of time.

No flashlight, no lights of any kind. I knew where I was going now. I was pumped up and ready. I had figured it all out. I understood the game now, and my part in it. My sixth sense was active.

The house was brick and wood and it had a quirky hexagonal window in the front. Loose, chipped, aqua-colored shutters occasionally banged against the house. It was more than a mile from the closest neighbor. No one would see me break in through the kitchen door.

I was aware that Simon Conklin might circle back behind me – if he was as bright as he thought he was. I wasn't worried about that. I had a working theory about Conklin and his visit to Cross's house. I needed to test it out.

I suddenly thought about Mr Smith as I was picking the lock. *Smith was obsessed with studying people, with breaking and entering into their lives.*

The inside of the house was absolutely unbearable: Simon Conklin's place smelled like Salvation Army furniture laced with BO and immersed in a McDonald's deep fryer. No, it was actually worse than that. I held a handkerchief over my nose and mouth as I began to search the filthy lair. I was afraid that I might find a body in here. Anything was possible.

Every room and every object was coated with dust and grime. The best that could be said of Simon Conklin was that he was an avid reader. Volumes were spread open in every room, half-a-dozen on his bed alone.

He seemed to favor sociology, philosophy, and psychology: Marx, Jung, Bruno Bettelheim, Malraux, Jean Baudrillard. Three unpainted floor-to-ceiling bookcases were crammed with books piled horizontally. My initial impression of the place was that it had already been ransacked by someone.

All of this fit with what had really happened at Alex Cross's house.

Over Conklin's rumpled, unmade bed was a framed Vargas girl, signed by the model, with a lipstick kiss next to the butt.

A rifle was stashed under the bed. It was a Browning BAR – the same model Gary Soneji had used in Washington. A smile slowly broke across my face.

Simon Conklin knew the rifle was circumstantial evidence, that it proved nothing about his guilt or innocence. *He wanted it found. He wanted Cross's badge found. He liked to play games. Of course he did.*

I climbed down creaking wooden stairs to the basement. I kept the house lights off and used only my penlight.

There were no windows in the cellar. There was dust and cobwebs, and a loudly dripping sink. Curled photographic prints were clipped to strings dangling from the ceiling.

My heart was beating in double time. I examined the dangling pictures. They were photos of Simon Conklin himself, different pics of the auteur cavorting in the buff. They appeared to have been taken inside the house.

I shined the light haphazardly around the basement, glancing everywhere. The floor was dirt and there were large rocks on which the old house was built. Ancient medical equipment was stored: a walker, an aluminum-framed potty, an oxygen tank with hoses and gauges still attached, a glucose monitor.

My eyes trailed over to the far side, the southern wall of the house. *Gary Soneji's train set!*

I was in the house of Gary's best friend, his only friend in the world, the man who had attacked Alex Cross and his family in Washington. I was certain of it. I was certain I had solved the case.

I was better than Alex Cross.

There, I've said it.

The truth begins.

Who is the cat? Who is the mouse?

PART FIVE

CAT AND MOUSE

CHAPTER 100

A dozen of the best FBI agents available stood in an informal grouping on the airfield in Quantico, Virginia. Directly behind them, two jet-black helicopters were waiting for takeoff. The agents couldn't have looked more solemn or attentive, but also puzzled.

As I stood before them, my legs were shaking and my knees were hitting together. I had never been more nervous, more unsure of myself. I had also never been more focused on a murder case.

'For those of you who don't know me,' I said, pausing not for effect, but because of nerves, 'I'm Alex Cross.'

I tried to let them see that physically I was fine. I wore loose-fitting khaki trousers and a long-sleeved navy-blue cotton knit shirt open at the collar. I was doing my best to disguise a mess of bruises and lacerations.

A lot of troubling mysteries had to unfold now. Mysteries about the savage, cowardly attack at my house in Washington – and who had done it; dizzying mysteries about the mass-murderer Mr Smith; and about Thomas Pierce of the FBI.

I could see by their faces that some of the agents remained confused. They clearly looked as if they'd been blind-sided by my appearance.

I couldn't blame them, but I also knew that what had happened was necessary. It seemed like the only way to catch a terrifying and diabolical killer. That was the plan, and the plan was all-consuming.

'As you can all see, rumors of my imminent demise have been greatly exaggerated. I'm just fine, actually,' I said and cracked a smile. That seemed to break the ice a little with the agents.

'The official statements out of St Anthony's Hospital – "not expected to live," "very grave condition," "highly unusual for someone in Dr Cross's condition to pull through" – were overstatements, and sometimes outright lies. The releases were manufactured for Thomas Pierce's benefit. The releases were a hoax. If you want to blame someone, blame Kyle Craig,' I said.

'Yes, definitely blame me,' Kyle said. He was standing at my side, along with John Sampson and Sondra Greenberg from Interpol. 'Alex didn't want to go this way. Actually, he didn't want any involvement at all, if my memory serves me.'

'That's right, but now I am involved. I'm in this up

to my eyebrows. Soon you will be, too. Kyle and I are going to tell you everything.'

I took a breath, then I continued. My nervousness was mostly gone.

'Four years ago, a recent Harvard Medical School grad named Thomas Pierce discovered his girlfriend murdered in their apartment in Cambridge. That was the police finding at the time. It was later corroborated by the Bureau. Let me tell you about the actual murder. Now let me tell you what Kyle and I believe really happened. This is how it went down that night in Cambridge.'

CHAPTER 101

Thomas Pierce had spent the early part of the night out drinking with friends at a bar called Jillian's in Cambridge. The friends were recent med-school graduates and they'd been drinking hard since about two in the afternoon.

Pierce had invited Isabella to the bar, but she'd turned him down and told him to have fun, let off some steam. He deserved it. That night, as he had been doing for the past six months, a doctor named Martin Straw came over to the apartment Isabella and Pierce shared. Straw and Isabella were having an affair. He had promised he would leave his wife and children for her.

Isabella was asleep when Pierce got to the apartment on Inman Street. He knew that Dr Martin Straw had been there earlier. He had seen Straw and Isabella together at other times. He'd followed them on several occasions around Cambridge and also on day trips out into the countryside.

As he opened the front door of his apartment, he could feel, in every inch of his body, that Martin Straw had been there. Straw's scent was unmistakable, and Thomas Pierce wanted to scream. He had never cheated on Isabella, never even come close.

She was fast asleep in their bed. He stood over her for several moments and she never stirred. He had always loved the way she slept, loved watching her like this. He had always mistaken her sleeping pose for innocence.

He could tell that Isabella had been drinking wine. He smelled the sweet odor from where he stood.

She had on perfume that night. For Martin Straw.

It was Jean Patou's Joy – very expensive. He had bought it for her the previous Christmas.

Thomas Pierce began to cry, to sob into his hands.

Isabella's long auburn hair was loose and strands and bunches flowed free on the pillows. For Martin Straw.

Martin Straw always lay on the left side of the bed. He had a deviated septum that he should have tended to, but doctors put off operations, too. He couldn't breathe very well out of the right nostril.

Thomas Pierce knew this. He had *studied* Straw, tried to understand him, his so-called humanity.

Pierce knew he had to act now, knew that he couldn't take too much time.

He fell on Isabella with all his weight, his force, his power. His tools were ready. She struggled, but he held her down. He clutched her long, swanlike throat with his strong hands. He wedged his feet under the mattress for leverage.

The struggle exposed her bare breasts and he was reminded of how 'sexy' and 'absolutely beautiful' Isabella was; how they were 'perfect together'; 'Cambridge's very own Romeo and Juliet.' What bullshit it was. A sorry myth. The perception of people who couldn't see straight. She didn't really love him, but how he had loved her. Isabella made him *feel* for the one and only time in his life.

Thomas Pierce looked down at her. Isabella's eyes were like sandblasted mirrors. Her small, beautiful mouth fell open to one side. Her skin still felt satin-soft to his touch.

She was helpless now, but she could see what was happening. Isabella was aware of her crimes and the punishment to come.

'I don't know what I'm doing,' he finally said. 'It's as if I'm outside myself, watching. And yet . . . I can't tell you how alive I feel right now.'

Every newspaper, the news magazines, TV, and radio reported what happened in gruesome detail, but nothing like what really happened, what it was like in the bedroom, staring into Isabella's eyes as he murdered her.

He cut out Isabella's heart.

He held her heart in his hands, still pumping, still alive, and watched it die.

Then he impaled her heart on a spear from the scuba equipment.

He *'pierced'* her heart. That was the clue he left. The very first clue.

He had the feeling, the sixth sense, that he actually watched Isabella's spirit leave her body. Then he thought he felt his own soul depart. He believed that he died that night, too.

Smith was born from death that night in Cambridge. *Thomas Pierce was Mr Smith.*

CHAPTER 102

'Thomas Pierce *is* Mr Smith,' I said to the agents gathered at Quantico. 'If any of you still doubt that, even a little bit, please don't. It could be dangerous to you and everyone else on this team. Pierce is Smith, and he's murdered nineteen people so far. He will murder again.'

I had been speaking for several moments, but now I stopped. There was a question from the group. Actually, there were several questions. I couldn't blame them – I was full of questions myself.

'Can I backtrack for just a second here? Your family *was* attacked?' a young crew-cut agent asked. 'You *did* sustain injuries?'

'There *was* an attack at my house. For reasons that we don't understand yet, the intruder stopped short of murder. My family is all right. Believe me, I want to understand about the attack, and the intruder, more than anyone does. I want that bastard, whoever he is.'

I held up my cast for all of them to see. 'I took a bullet in my wrist. A second entered my abdomen, but passed through. The hepatic artery was not nicked, as was reported. I was definitely banged-up, but my EKG never showed "a pattern of decreased activity." That was for Pierce's benefit. Kyle? You want to fill in some more of the holes you helped create?'

This was Kyle Craig's master plan, and he spoke to the agents.

'Alex is right about Pierce. He is a cold-blooded killer and what we hope to do tonight is dangerous. It's unusual, but this situation warrants it. For the past several weeks, Interpol and the Bureau have been trying to set a foolproof trap for the elusive Mr Smith, who we believe to be Thomas Pierce,' Kyle repeated. 'We haven't been able to catch him at anything conclusive, and we don't want to do something that might spook him, make him run.'

'He's one scary, spooky son of a bitch, I'll tell you that much,' John Sampson said from his place along-side me. I could tell he was holding back, keeping his anger inside. 'And the bastard is *very careful*. I never caught him in anything close to a slipup while I was working with him. Pierce played his part perfectly.'

'So did you, John.' Kyle offered a compliment. 'Detective Sampson has been in on the ruse, too,' he explained.

A few hours earlier, Sampson had been with Pierce in New Jersey. He knew him better than I did, though not as well as Kyle or Sondra Greenberg of Interpol, who had originally profiled Pierce, and was with us now at Quantico.

'How is he acting, Sondra?' Kyle asked Greenberg. 'What have you noticed?'

The Interpol inspector was a tall, impressive-looking woman. She'd been working the case for nearly two years in Europe. 'Thomas Pierce is an arrogant bastard. Believe me, he's laughing at all of us. He's one hundred percent sure of himself. He's also high-strung. He never stops looking over his shoulder. Sometimes, I don't think he's human either. I do believe he's going to blow soon. The pressure we've applied is working.'

'That's becoming more evident.' Kyle picked up the thread. 'Pierce was very cool in the beginning. He had everyone fooled. He was as professional as any agent we've ever had. Early on, no one in the Cambridge police believed he had murdered Isabella Calais. He never made a mistake. His grief over her death was astonishing.'

'He's for real, ladies and gents.' Sampson spoke up again. 'He's smart as hell. Pretty good investigator, too. His instincts are sharp and he's disciplined. He did his homework, and he went right to Simon Conklin. I think he's competing with Alex.'

'So do I.' Kyle nodded at Sampson. 'He's very complex. We probably don't know the half of it yet. That's what scares me.'

Kyle had come to me about Mr Smith before the Soneji shooting spree had started. We had talked again when I'd taken Rosie to Quantico for tests. I worked with him on an unofficial basis. I helped with the profile on Thomas Pierce, along with Sondra Greenberg. When I was shot at my house, Kyle rushed to Washington out of concern. But the attack was nowhere near as bad as everyone thought, or as we led them to believe.

It was Kyle who decided to take a big chance. So far, Pierce was running free. Maybe if he brought him in on the case, on *my* case? It would be a way to watch him, to put pressure on Pierce. Kyle believed that Pierce wouldn't be able to resist. Big ego, tremendous confidence. Kyle was right.

'Pierce is going to blow,' Sondra Greenberg said again. 'I'm telling you. I don't know everything that's going on in his head, but he's close to the limit.'

I agreed with Greenberg. 'I'll tell you what could happen next. The two personas are starting to fuse. Mr Smith and Thomas Pierce could merge soon. Actually, it's the Thomas Pierce part of his personality that seems to be diminishing. I think he just might have *Mr Smith take out Simon Conklin*.'

Sampson leaned into me and whispered, 'I think it's time that you met Mr Pierce *and* Mr Smith.'

CHAPTER 103

This was it. The end. It had to be.

Everything we could think of was tightly in place by seven o'clock that night in Princeton. Thomas Pierce had proved to be elusive in the past, almost illusory. He kept mysteriously slipping in and out of his role as 'Mr Smith.' But he was clearly about to blow.

How he accomplished his black magic, no one knew. There were never any witnesses. No one was left alive.

Kyle Craig's fear was that we would never catch Pierce in the act, never be able to hold him for more than forty-eight hours. Kyle was convinced that Pierce was smarter than Gary Soneji, cleverer than any of us.

Kyle had objected to Thomas Pierce's assignment to the Mr Smith case, but he'd been over-ruled. He had watched Pierce, listened to him, and became more and more convinced that Pierce was involved – at least with the death of Isabella Calais.

Pierce never seemed to make a mistake, though. He covered all of his tracks. Then a break came. Pierce was seen in Frankfurt, Germany, on the same day a victim disappeared there. Pierce was supposed to be in Rome.

It was enough for Kyle to approve a search of Pierce's apartment in Cambridge. Nothing was found. Kyle brought in computer experts. They *suspected* that Pierce might be sending himself messages, supposedly from Smith, but there was no proof. Then Pierce was seen in Paris on the day Dr Abel Sante disappeared. His logs stated that he was in London all day. It was circumstantial, but Kyle knew he had his killer.

So did I.

Now we needed concrete proof.

Nearly fifty FBI agents were in the Princeton area, which seemed like the last place in the world where a shocking crime ought to occur, or a notorious murder spree end.

Sampson and I waited in the front seat of a dark sedan parked on an anonymous-looking street. We weren't part of the main surveillance team, but we stayed close. We were never more than a mile, or at most two, from Pierce. Sampson was restless and irritable through the early night. It had gotten excruciatingly personal between him and Pierce.

I had a very personal reason to be in Princeton myself. I wanted a crack at Simon Conklin. Unfortunately, Pierce was between me and Conklin for now.

We were a few blocks from the Marriott in town where Pierce was staying.

'Quite a plan,' Sampson mumbled as we sat and waited.

'The FBI tried just about everything else. Kyle thinks this will work. He feels Pierce couldn't resist solving the attack at my house. It's the ultimate competition for him. Who knows?'

Sampson's eyes narrowed. I knew the look – sharp, comprehending. 'Yeah, and you had no part in any of the hinky shit, right?'

'Maybe I did offer a suggestion about why the setup might be attractive to Thomas Pierce, to his huge ego. Or why he might be cocky enough to get caught.'

Sampson rolled his eyes back into his forehead, the way he'd been doing since we were about ten years old. 'Yeah, maybe you did. By the way, he's an even bigger pain in the ass than you are to work with. Anal as shit, to coin a phrase.'

We waited on the side street in Princeton as night blanketed the university town. It was déjà vu all over again. John Sampson and Alex Cross on a stakeout duty.

'You still love me,' Sampson said and grinned. He doesn't get giddy too often, but when he does – watch out. 'You do love me, Sugar?'

I put my hand high on his thigh. 'Sure do, big fellow.'

He punched me in the shoulder – *hard*. My arm

went numb. My fingers tingled. The man can *hit*.

'I want to put the hurt on Thomas Pierce! I'm going to put the hurt on Pierce!' Sampson yelled out in the car.

'Put the hurt on Thomas Pierce,' I yelled with him. 'And Mr Smith, too!'

'Put the hurt on Mr Smith and Mr Pierce,' we sang in unison, doing our imitation of the *Bad Boy* movie.

Yeah!

We were back. Same as it ever was.

CHAPTER 104

Thomas Pierce felt that he was invincible, that he couldn't be stopped.

He waited in the dark, trancelike, without moving. He was thinking about Isabella, seeing her beautiful face, seeing her smile, hearing her voice. He stayed like that until the living-room light was switched on and he saw Simon Conklin.

'Intruder in the house,' Pierce whispered. 'Sound familiar? Ring any bells for you, Conklin?'

He held a .357 Magnum pointed directly at Conklin's forehead. He could blow him right out the front door and down the porch stairs.

'What the—?' Conklin was blinky-eyed in the bright light. Then his dark eyes grew beady and hard. 'This is unlawful entry!' Conklin screamed. 'You have no right to be here in my house. Get the hell out!'

Pierce couldn't hold back a smile. He definitely *got* the humor in life, but sometimes he didn't take enough pleasure in it. He got up out of the chair, holding the gun perfectly still in front of him.

There wasn't much space to move in the living room, which was filled with tall stacks of newspapers, books, clippings, and magazines. Everything was categorized by date and subject. He was pretty sure that not-so-Simple Simon had an obsessive-compulsive disorder.

'Downstairs. We're going to your basement,' he said. 'Down to *the cellar.*'

The light was already on downstairs. Thomas Pierce had gotten everything ready. An old cot was set up in the center of the crowded basement room. He had cleared away stacks of survivalist and sci-fi books to make room for the cot.

He wasn't sure, but he thought Conklin's obsession had to do with the end of the human race. He hoarded books, journals, and newspaper stories that supported his pathological idea. The cover of a science journal was taped to the cellar wall. It read: 'Sex Changes in Fish – A Look at Simultaneous and Sequential Hermaphrodites.'

'What the hell?' Simon Conklin yelled when he saw what Pierce had done.

'That's what they all say,' Thomas Pierce said and shoved him. Conklin stumbled down a couple of stairs.

'You think I'm afraid of you?' Conklin whirled and snarled. 'I'm not afraid of you.'

Pierce nodded his head once and cocked an eyebrow. 'I hear you, and I'm going to straighten that out right now.'

He shoved Conklin hard again and watched him tumble down the rest of the stairs. Pierce walked slowly down toward the heap. 'You *starting* to get afraid of me now?' he asked.

He whacked Conklin with the side of the Magnum and watched as blood spit from Simon Conklin's head. 'You starting to get afraid now?'

He bent down and put his mouth close to Conklin's hairy ear.

'You don't understand very much about pain. I know that about you,' he whispered. 'You don't have much in the way of guts either. You were the one in the Cross house, but you *couldn't* kill Alex Cross, could you? You *couldn't* kill his family. You punked out at his house. You blew it. That's what I *already know*.'

Thomas Pierce was enjoying the confrontation, the satisfaction of it. He was curious about what made Simon Conklin tick. He wanted to 'study' Conklin, to understand his humanity. To know Simon Conklin was to know something about himself.

He stayed in Conklin's face. 'First, I want you to *tell* me that you're the one who snuck into Alex Cross's house. *You did it!* Now just tell me you did it. What you say here will *not* be held against you, and will *not* be used in a court of law. It's just between us.'

Simon Conklin looked at him as if he were a complete madman. *How perceptive.*

'You're crazy. You can't do this. This won't matter in court,' Conklin squealed.

Pierce's eyes widened in disbelief. He looked at

Conklin as if *he* were the madman. 'Didn't I just say precisely that? Weren't you listening? Am I talking to myself here? No, it won't matter in *their* court. This is *my* court. So far, you're losing your case, Simple Simon. You're smart, though. I'm confident you can do a much better job over the next few hours.'

Simon Conklin gasped. A shiny, stainless-steel scalpel was pointed at his chest.

CHAPTER 105

'**L**ook at me! Would you focus on what I'm saying, Simon. I'm not another gray suit from the FBI . . . I have important questions to ask. I want you to answer them truthfully. You *were* the one at Cross's house! You attacked Cross. Let's proceed from there.'

With a swift move of his left arm, Pierce pulled Conklin roughly up off the cellar floor. His physical strength was a shock to Conklin.

Pierce put his scalpel down and hog-tied Conklin to the cot with rope.

Pierce leaned in close to Simon Conklin once he was tied down and helpless. 'Here's a news flash – I don't like your superior attitude. Believe me, *you aren't superior*. Somehow, and this amazes me, I don't think I've made myself clear yet. You're a *specimen*, Simon. Let me show you something creepy.'

'Don't!' Conklin screeched. He was helpless as

Pierce made a sudden incision in the upper chest. He couldn't believe what was happening. Simon Conklin screamed.

'Can you concentrate better now, Simon? See what's on the table here? It's your tape recorder. I just want you to confess. Tell me what happened inside Dr Cross's house. I want to hear everything.'

'Leave me alone,' Conklin whispered weakly.

'No! That's not going to happen. You will never be alone again. All right, forget the scalpel and the tape recorder. I want you to focus on *this*. Ordinary can of Coca-Cola. *Your Coke*, Simon.'

He shook the bright-red can, shook it up good, and popped it open. Then he pulled Conklin's head back. Grabbed a handful of long, greasy hair. Pierce pushed the harmless-looking can under Conklin's nostrils.

The soda exploded upward, fizz, bubbles, sugary-brown water. It shot up Conklin's nose and toward the brain. It was an army interrogator's trick. Excruciatingly painful, and it always worked.

Simon Conklin choked horribly. He couldn't stop coughing, gagging.

'I hope you appreciate the kind of resourcefulness I'm showing. I can work with any household object. Are you ready to confess? Or would you like some more Coke?'

Simon Conklin's eyes were wider than they had ever been before. 'I'll *say* whatever you want! Just please stop.'

Thomas Pierce shook his head back and forth. 'I

just want the truth. I want the facts. I want to know I solved the case that Alex Cross couldn't.'

He turned on the tape recorder and held it under Conklin's bearded chin. 'Tell me what happened.'

'I was the one who attacked Cross and his family. Yes, yes, it was me,' Simon Conklin said in a choked voice that made each word sound even more emotional. 'Gary made me. He said if I didn't, somebody would come for me. They'd torture and kill me. Somebody he knew from Lorton Prison. That's the truth, I swear it is. Gary was the leader, not me!'

Thomas Pierce was suddenly almost tender, his voice soft and soothing. 'I figured that, Simon. I'm not stupid. So Gary made you do it. Now, when you got to the Cross house, you couldn't kill him, could you? You'd fantasized about it, but then you couldn't do it.'

Simon Conklin nodded. He was exhausted and frightened. He wondered if Gary had sent this madman and thought that maybe he had.

Pierce motioned with the Coke can for him to keep going. He took a hit of the Coke as he listened. 'Go on, Simon. Tell me all about you and Gary.'

Conklin was crying, bawling like a child, but he was talking. 'We got beat up a lot when we were kids. We were inseparable. I was there when Gary burned down his own house. His stepmother was inside with her two kids. So was his father. I watched over the two kids he kidnapped in D.C. I was the one at Cross's house. You were right! It might as well have been Gary. He planned everything.'

Pierce finally took away the tape recorder and shut it off. 'That's much better, Simon. I do believe you.'

What Simon Conklin had just said seemed like a good break point – somewhere to end. The investigation was over. He'd proved he was better than Alex Cross.

'I'm going to tell you something. Something amazing, Simon. You'll appreciate this, I think.'

He raised the scalpel and Simon Conklin tried to squirm away. He knew what was coming.

'Gary Soneji was a pussycat compared to me,' Thomas Pierce said. '*I'm Mr Smith.*'

CHAPTER 106

Sampson and I rushed through Princeton, breaking just about every speed limit. The agents trailing Thomas Pierce had temporarily lost him. The elusive Pierce, or was it Mr Smith – was on the loose. They thought they had him again, at Simon Conklin's. Everything was chaos.

Moments after we arrived, Kyle gave the signal to move in on the house. Sampson and I were supposed to be *Jafos* at the scene – *just a fucking observer*. Sondra Greenberg was there. She was a *Jafo*, too.

A half-dozen FBI agents, Sampson, myself, and Sondra hurried through the yard. We split up. Some went in the front and others through the back of the ramshackle house. We were moving quickly and efficiently, handguns and rifles out. Everybody wore windbreakers with 'FBI' printed large on the back.

'I think he's here,' I told Sampson. 'I think we're about to meet Mr Smith!'

The living room was darker and gloomier than I remembered from an earlier visit. We didn't see anyone yet, neither Pierce nor Simon Conklin nor Mr Smith. The house looked as if it had been ransacked and it smelled terrible.

Kyle gave a hand signal and we fanned out, hurrying through the house. Everything was tense and unsettling.

'See no evil, hear no evil,' Sampson muttered at my side, 'but it's here all the same.'

I wanted Pierce to go down, but I wanted to get Simon Conklin even more. I figured it was Conklin who had come into my house and attacked my family. I needed five minutes alone with Conklin. Therapy time – for me. Maybe we could talk about Gary Soneji, about the 'great ones,' as they called themselves.

An agent called out – '*The basement! Down here! Hurry!*'

I was out of breath and hurting already. My right side burned like hell. I followed the others down the narrow, twisting stairs. 'Awhh Jesus,' I heard Kyle say from his position up ahead.

I saw Simon Conklin lying spread-eagled across an old striped-blue mattress on the floor. The man who had attacked me and my family had been mutilated. Thanks to countless anatomy classes at Johns Hopkins, I was better prepared than the others for the gruesome murder scene. Simon Conklin's chest, stomach, and pelvic area had been cut open, as if a crackerjack medical examiner had just performed an on-the-scene autopsy.

'He's been gutted,' an FBI agent muttered, and turned away from the body. 'Why in the name of God?'

Simon Conklin had no face. A bold incision had been made at the top of his skull. The cut went through the scalp and clear down to the bone. Then the scalp had been pulled down over the front of the face.

Conklin's long black hair hung from his scalp to where the chin should have been. It looked like a beard. I suspected that this meant something to Pierce. *What did obliterating a face mean to him, if anything?*

There was an unpainted wooden door in the cellar, another way out, but none of the agents stationed outside had seen him leave. Several agents were trying to chase down Pierce. I stayed inside with the mutilated corpse. I couldn't have run down Nana Mama right then. For the first time in my life, I understood what it would be like to be physically old.

'He did this in just a couple of minutes?' Kyle Craig asked. 'Alex, could he work this fast?'

'If he's as crazy as I think he is, yeah, he could have. Don't forget he did this in med school, not to mention his other victims. He has to be incredibly strong, Kyle. He didn't have morgue tools, no electric saws. He used a knife, and his hands.'

I was standing close to the mattress, staring down

at what remained of Simon Conklin. I thought of the cowardly attack on me, on my family. I'd wanted him caught, but not like this. Nobody deserved this. Only in Dante were such fierce punishments imposed on the damned.

I leaned in closer and peered at the remains of Simon Conklin. *Why was Thomas Pierce so angry at Conklin? Why had he punished Conklin like this?*

The basement of the house was eerily quiet. Sondra Greenberg looked pale, and was leaning against a cellar wall. I would have thought she'd be used to the murder scenes, but maybe that wasn't possible for anybody.

I had to clear my throat before I could speak again. 'He cut away the front quadrant of the skull,' I said. 'He performed a frontal craniotomy. It looks like Thomas Pierce is practicing medicine again.'

CHAPTER 107

I had known Kyle Craig for ten years, and been his friend for nearly that long. I had never seen him so troubled and disconsolate about a case before, no matter how difficult or gruesome. The Thomas Pierce investigation had ruined his career, or at least he thought so, and maybe he was right.

'How the hell does he keep slipping away?' I said. We were still in Princeton the next morning, having breakfast at PJ's Pancake House. The food was excellent, but I just wasn't hungry.

'That's the worst part of it – he knows everything we would do. He anticipates our actions and procedures. He was one of us.'

'Maybe he *is* an alien,' I said to Kyle, who nodded wearily.

Kyle ate the remainder of his soft, runny eggs in silence. His face was bent low over his plate. He wasn't aware how comically depressed he looked.

'Those eggs must be real good.' I finally broke the silence with something other than the scraping sound of Kyle's fork on the plate.

He looked up at me with his usual deadpan look. 'I really messed this up, Alex. I should have taken Pierce in when I had the chance. We talked about it down in Quantico.'

'You would have had to let him go, release him in a few hours. Then what would you do? You couldn't keep Pierce under surveillance forever.'

'Director Burns wanted to sanction Pierce, take him out, but I strongly disagreed. I thought I could get him. I told Burns I would.'

I shook my head. I couldn't believe what I'd just heard. 'The Director of the FBI approved a sanction on Pierce? Jesus.'

Kyle ran his tongue back and forth over his teeth. 'Yes, and not just Burns. This went all the way to the attorney general's office. God knows where else. I had them convinced Pierce was Mr Smith. Somehow the idea of an FBI field agent who's also a multiple killer didn't sit very well with them. We'll never catch him now. There's no real pattern, Alex, at least nothing to follow. No way to trace him. He's laughing at us.'

'Yeah, he probably is,' I agreed. 'He's definitely competitive on some level. He likes to feel superior. There's a whole lot more to this, though.'

I had been thinking about the possibility of some kind of abstract or artistic pattern since I'd first heard about the complicated case. I was well aware of the theory that each of the murders was different, and worse, seemed arbitrary. That would make Pierce almost impossible to catch. The more I thought about the series of murders, though, and especially about Thomas Pierce's history, the more I suspected that there had to be a pattern, a mission behind all of this. The FBI had simply missed it. Now I was missing it, too.

'What do you want to do, Alex?' Kyle finally asked. 'I understand if you're not going to work this one, if you're not up to it.'

I thought about my family back home, about Christine Johnson and the things we'd talked over, but I didn't see how I could step away from this awful case right now. I was also somewhat afraid of retribution from Pierce. There was no way to predict how he might react now.

'I'll stay with you for a few days. I'll be around, Kyle. No promises beyond that. Shit, I *hate* that I said that. Damn it!' I pounded the table and the plates and flatware jumped.

For the first time that morning, Kyle offered up half a smile. 'So, what's your plan? Tell me what you're going to do.'

I shook my head back and forth. I still couldn't believe I was doing this. 'My plan is as follows. I'm going home to Washington, and that's non-negotiable. Tomorrow or the next day, I'll fly up to Boston. I want to see Pierce's apartment. He wanted to see my house, didn't he? Then, we'll see, Kyle.

Please keep your evidence-gatherers on a leash before I get to his apartment. *Look, photograph*, but don't move anything around: Mr Smith is a very orderly man. I want to see how Pierce's place looks, how he arranged it for us.'

Kyle was back to the deadpan look, superserious, which I actually prefer. 'We're not going to get him, Alex. He's been given a warning. He'll be more careful from now on. Maybe he'll disappear like some killers do, just vanish off the face of the earth.'

'That would be nice,' I said, 'but I don't think it's going to happen. There *is* a pattern, Kyle. We just haven't found it.'

CHAPTER 108

As they say in the wild, Wild West, you have to get right back on the horse that threw you. I spent two days back in Washington, but it seemed more like a couple of hours. Everybody was mad at me for getting into the hunt. Nana, the kids, Christine. So be it.

I took the first flight into Boston and was at Thomas Pierce's apartment in Cambridge by nine in the morning. Reluctantly, the dragonslayer was back in play.

Kyle Craig's original plan to catch Pierce was one of the most audacious ever to come out of the usually conservative Federal Bureau, but it probably had to be. The question now – had Thomas Pierce been able to get out of the Princeton area somehow? Or was he still down there?

Had he circled back to Boston? Fled to Europe? Nobody knew for sure. It was also possible that we might not hear from Pierce, or from Mr Smith, for a long time.

There was a pattern. We just had to find it.

Pierce and Isabella Calais had lived together for three years in the second-floor apartment of a town house in Cambridge. The front door of the place opened onto the kitchen. Then came a long railroad-style hallway. The apartment was a revelation. *There were memories and reminders of Isabella Calais everywhere.*

It was strange and overwhelming, as if she still lived here and might suddenly appear from one of the rooms.

There were photographs of her in every single room. I counted more than twenty pictures of Isabella on my first pass, a quick sight-seeing tour of the apartment.

How could Pierce bear to have this woman's face everywhere, looking at him, staring silently, accusing him of the most unspeakable murder?

In the pictures, Isabella Calais has the most beautiful auburn hair, worn long and perfectly shaped. She has a lovely face and the sweetest, natural smile. It was easy to see how he could have loved her. But her brown eyes had a far-off look in some of the pictures, as if she weren't quite there.

Everything about their apartment made my head spin, my insides, too. Was Pierce trying to tell us, or maybe tell himself, that he felt absolutely nothing – no guilt, no sadness, no love in his heart?

As I thought about it, I was overwhelmed with sadness myself. I could imagine the torture that must be his life every day – never to experience real love or deep feelings. In his crazed mind did Pierce think that by dissecting each of his victims he would find the answer to himself?

Maybe the opposite was true.

Was it possible that Pierce needed to feel her presence, to *feel* everything with the greatest intensity imaginable? Had Thomas Pierce loved Isabella Calais more than he'd thought he was capable of loving anyone? Had Pierce felt redeemed by their love? When he'd learned of her affair with a doctor named Martin Straw, had it driven him to madness and the most unspeakable of acts: The murder of the only person he had ever loved?

Why were her pictures still looming everywhere in the apartment? Why had Thomas Pierce been torturing himself with this constant reminder?

Isabella Calais was watching me as I moved through every room in the apartment. What was she trying to say?

'Who is he, Isabella?' I whispered. 'What is he up to?'

CHAPTER 109

I began a more detailed search of the apartment. I paid careful attention not just to Isabella's things, but to Pierce's, too. Since both had been students, I wasn't surprised by the academic texts and papers lying about.

I found a curious test-tube rack of corked vials of sand. Each vial was labeled with the name of a different beach: Laguna, Montauk, Normandy, Parma, Virgin Gorda, Oahu. I thought about the curious notion that Pierce had bottled something so vast, infinite, and random to give it order and substance.

So what was his organizing principle for Mr Smith's murders? What would explain them?

There were GT Zaskar mountain bikes stored inside the apartment and two GT Machete helmets. Isabella and Thomas biked together through New Hampshire and across into Vermont. More and more, I was sure that he had loved her deeply. Then his love had turned to a hatred so intense few of us could imagine it.

I recalled that the first Cambridge police reports had convincingly described Pierce's grief at the murder scene as 'impossible to fake.' One of the detectives had written, 'He is shocked, surprised, utterly heartbroken. Thomas Pierce not considered a suspect at this time.'

What else, what else? There had to be a clue here. There had to be a pattern.

A framed quote was hung in the hallway. *Without God, We Are Condemned To Be Free*. Was it Sartre? I thought so. I wondered whose thinking it really represented. Did Pierce take it seriously himself or was he making a joke? *Condemned* was a word that interested me. Was Thomas Pierce a condemned man?

In the master bedroom there was a bookcase with a well-preserved, three-volume set of H. L. Mencken's *The American Language*. It rested on the top shelf. Obviously, this was a prized possession. Maybe it had been a gift? I remembered that Pierce had been a dual major as an undergraduate: biology and philosophy. Philosophy texts were everywhere in the apartment. I read the spines: Jacques Derrida, Foucault, Jean Baudrillard, Heidegger, Habermas, Sartre.

There were several dictionaries as well: French, German, English, Italian, and Spanish. A compact, two-volume set of the *Oxford English Dictionary* had type so small it came with a magnifying glass.

There was a framed diagram of the human voice

mechanism directly over Pierce's work desk. And a quote: *'Language is more than speech.'* Several books by the linguist and activist Noam Chomsky were on his desk. What I remembered about Chomsky was that he had suggested a complex biological component of language acquisition. He had a view of the mind as a set of mental organs. I *think* that was Chomsky.

I wondered what, if anything, Noam Chomsky or the diagram of the human voice mechanism had to do with Smith, or the death of Isabella Calais.

I was lost in my thoughts, when I was startled by a loud *buzzing* noise. It came from the kitchen at the other end of the hall.

I thought I was alone in the apartment, and the buzzing spooked me. I took my Glock from its shoulder holster and started down the long, narrow hallway. Then I began to run.

I entered the kitchen with my gun in position and then understood what the buzzing was. I had brought along a PowerBook that Pierce had left in his hotel room in Princeton. *Left on purpose? Left as another clue?* A special alarm on the laptop personal computer was the source of the noise.

Had he sent a message to us? A fax or voice-mail? Or perhaps someone was sending a message to Pierce? Who would be sending him messages?

I checked voice-mail first.

It was Pierce.

His voice was strong and steady and almost soothing. It was the voice of someone in control of himself and the situation. It was eerie under the circumstances, to be hearing it alone in his apartment.

Dr Cross – at least I suspect it's you I've reached. This is the kind of message I used to receive when I was tracking Smith.

Of course, I was using the messages for misdirection, sending them myself. I wanted to mislead the police, the FBI. Who knows, maybe I still do.

At any rate, here's your very first message – Anthony Bruno, Brielle, New Jersey.

Why don't you come to the seashore and join me for a swim? Have you arrived at any conclusions about Isabella yet? She is important to all of this. You're right to be in Cambridge.

Smith/Pierce

CHAPTER 110

The FBI provided me with a helicopter out of Logan International Airport to fly me to Brielle, New Jersey. I was on board the Disorient Express and there was no getting off.

I spent the flight obsessing about Pierce, his apartment, Isabella Calais, *their* apartment, his studies in biology and modern philosophy, Noam Chomsky. I wouldn't have thought it possible, wouldn't have dreamed it possible, but Pierce was already eclipsing Gary Soneji and Simon Conklin. I despised everything about Pierce. Seeing the pictures of Isabella Calais had done it for me.

Alien? I wrote on the foolscap pad lying across my lap. *He identifies with descriptor.*

Alienated? Alienated from what? Idyllic upbringing in California. Doesn't fit any of the psychopathic profiles we used before. He's an original. He secretly enjoys that, doesn't he?

No discernible pattern to murders that links with a psychological motive.

Murders seem haphazard and arbitrary! He revels in his own originality.

Dr Sante, Simon Conklin, now Anthony Bruno. Why them? Does Conklin count?

Seems impossible to predict Thomas Pierce's next move. His next kill.

Why go south toward the New Jersey Shore?

It had occurred to me that he was originally from a shore town. Pierce had grown up near Laguna Beach in Southern California. Was he going home, in a manner of speaking? Was the New Jersey Shore as close to home as he could get – as close as he dared go?

I now had a reasonable amount of information about his background in California before he came east. He had lived on a working farm not far from the famous Irvine Ranch properties. Three generations of doctors in the family. Good, hard-working people. His siblings were all doing well, and not one of them would ever dream that Thomas was capable of any of this mayhem and murder.

FBI says Mr Smith is disorganized, chaotic, unpredict-able, I scribbled in my pad.

What if they're wrong? Pierce is responsible for much of their data about Smith. Pierce created Mr Smith, then did the profile on him.

I kept revisiting his and Isabella's apartment in my

mind. The place was so very neat and organized. The home had a definite *organizing principle*. It revolved around Isabella – her pictures, clothes, even her perfume bottles had been left in place. The smell of L'Air du Temps and Je Reviens permeated their bedroom to this day.

Thomas Pierce had loved her. *Pierce had loved*. Pierce had felt passion and emotion. That was another thing the FBI was wrong about. He'd killed because he thought he was losing her, and he couldn't bear it. Was Isabella the only person who had ever loved Pierce?

Another small piece of the puzzle suddenly fell into place. I was so struck by it that I said it aloud in the helicopter. *'Her heart on a spear!'*

He had 'pierced' her heart! Jesus Christ! He had confessed to the very first murder! He had confessed!

He'd left a clue, but the police missed it. What else were we missing? What was he up to now? What did 'Mr Smith' represent inside his mind? Was everything representational for him? Symbolic? Artistic? Was he creating a kind of language for us to follow? Or was it even simpler? He had 'pierced' her heart. Pierce wanted to be caught. Caught and punished.

Crime and punishment.

Why couldn't we catch him?

I landed in New Jersey around five at night. Kyle Craig was waiting for me. Kyle was sitting on the hood of a dark-blue town car. He was drinking

Samuel Adams beer out of a bottle.

'You find Anthony Bruno yet?' I called out as I walked toward him. 'You find the body?'

CHAPTER 111

Mr Smith goes to the seashore. Sounded like an unimaginative children's story.

There was enough moonlight for Thomas Pierce to make his way along the long stretch of glowing white sand at Point Pleasant Beach. He was carrying a corpse, what was left of it. He had Anthony Bruno loaded on his back and shoulders.

He walked just south of popular Jenkinson's Pier and the much newer Seaquarium. The boarded-up arcades of the amusement park were tightly packed along the beach shoulder. The small, grayish buildings looked forlorn and mute in their shuttered state.

As usual, music ran through his head – first Elvis Costello's 'Clubland,' then Beethoven's Piano Sonata No. 21, then 'Mother Mother' by Tracy Bonham. The savage beast inside him wasn't calmed, not even close, but at least he could feel a beat.

It was quarter to four in the morning and even the

surf-casting fishermen weren't out yet. He'd seen only one police patrol car so far. The police in the tiny beach town were a joke anyway.

Mr Smith against the Keystone Cops.

This whole funky seashore area reminded him of Laguna Beach, at least the *tourista* parts of Laguna. He could still picture the surf shops that dotted the Pacific Coast Highway back home – the Southern California artifacts: Flogo sandals, Stussy T's, neoprene gloves and wet suits, beach boots, the unmistakable smell of board wax.

He was physically strong – had a workingman's build. He carried Anthony Bruno over one shoulder without much effort. He had cut out all the vital parts, so there wasn't much of Anthony anymore. Anthony was a shell. No heart, liver, intestines, lungs, or brain.

Thomas Pierce thought about the FBI's continuing search. The Bureau's fabled 'manhunts' were overrated – a holdover from the glory days of John Dillinger and Bonnie and Clyde. He knew this to be so after years of observing the Bureau chase Mr Smith. They would never have caught Smith, not in a hundred years.

The FBI was looking for him in all the wrong places. They would surely have 'numbers,' meaning excessive force, their trademark maneuver. They would be all over the airports, probably expecting him to head back to Europe. And what about the wild cards in the search, people like Alex Cross? Cross had made his bones, no doubt about that. Maybe Cross was more than he seemed to be. Pierce had never believed Kyle when Kyle told him that Cross might not survive the attack on his house. He knew it was a ploy. At any rate, he relished the thought of Dr Cross being in on this, too. He liked the competition.

The dead weight on his back and shoulder was starting to get heavy. It was almost morning, close to daybreak. It wouldn't do to be found lugging a disemboweled corpse across Point Pleasant Beach.

He carried Anthony Bruno another fifty yards to a glistening white lifeguard's chair. He climbed the creaking rungs of the chair, and propped the body in the seat.

The remains of the corpse were naked and exposed for the world to see. Quite a sight. *Anthony was a clue.* If anybody on the search team had half a brain and was using it properly.

'I'm not an alien. Do any of you follow that?' Pierce shouted above the ocean's steady roar.

'I'm human. I'm perfectly normal. I'm just like you.'

CHAPTER 112

I t was all a mind game, wasn't it – Pierce against the rest of us.

While I had been at his apartment in Boston, a team of FBI agents went out to Southern California to meet with Thomas Pierce's family. The mother and father still lived on the same farm, between Laguna and El Toro, where Thomas Pierce had grown up.

Henry Pierce practiced medicine, mostly among the indigent farmworkers in the area. His lifestyle was modest and the reputation of the family impeccable. Pierce had an older brother and sister, doctors in Northern California, who were also well regarded and worked with the poor.

Not a person the profilers spoke to could imagine Thomas a murderer. He'd always been a good son and brother, a gifted student who seemed to have close friends and no enemies.

Thomas Pierce fit no brief for a pattern killer that I was familiar with. He was an original.

'Impeccable' was a word that jumped out of the FBI profiler reports. Maybe Pierce didn't want to be impeccable.

I re-reviewed the news articles and clippings about Pierce from the time of Isabella Calais's gruesome murder. I was keeping track of the more perplexing notions on three-by-five index cards. The packet was growing rapidly.

Laguna Beach – commercial shore town. Parts similar to Point Pleasant and Bay Head. Had Pierce killed in Laguna in the past? Had the disease now spread to the Northeast?

Pierce's father was a doctor. Pierce didn't 'make it' to Dr Pierce, but as a med student he had performed autopsies.

Looking for his humanity when he kills? Studying humans because he fears he has no human qualities himself?

He had a dual major as an undergrad: biology and philosophy. Fan of the linguist Noam Chomsky. Or is it Chomsky's political writings that turn Pierce on? Plays word and math games on his PowerBook.

What were we all missing so far?

What was I missing?

Why was Thomas Pierce killing all of these people?

He was 'impeccable,' wasn't he?

CHAPTER 113

Pierce stole a forest-green BMW convertible in the expensive, quaint, quite lovely shore town of Bay Head, New Jersey. On the corner of East Avenue and Harris Street, a prime location, he hot-wired and grabbed the vehicle as slickly as a pickpocket working the boardwalks down at Point Pleasant Beach. He was so good at this, overqualified for the scut work.

He drove west through Brick Town at moderate speeds, to the Garden State Parkway. He played music all the way – Talking Heads, Alanis Morissette, Melissa Etheridge, Blind Faith. Music helped him to *feel something*. It always had, from the time he'd been a boy. An hour and a quarter later he entered Atlantic City.

He sighed with pleasure. He loved it instantly – the shameless tawdriness, the grubbiness, the tattered sinfulness, the soullessness of the place. He felt as if he were 'home,' and he wondered if the FBI geniuses had linked the Jersey Shore to Laguna Beach yet?

Entering Atlantic City, he had half-expected to see a beautifully maintained expanse of lawn sloping down to the ocean. Surfers with peroxided, gnarly hair; volleyball played around the clock.

But no, no, this was New Jersey. Southern California, his real home, was thousands of miles away. He mustn't get confused now.

He checked into Bally's Park Place. Up in his room, he started to make phone calls. He wanted to 'order in.' He stood at a picture window and watched the ghostly waves of the Atlantic punish the beach again and again. Far down the beach he could see Trump Plaza. The audacious and ridiculous penthouse apartments were perched on the main building, like a space shuttle ready to take off.

Yes, ladies and gentlemen, of course there was a pattern. Why couldn't anyone figure it out? Why did he always have to be misunderstood?

At two in the morning, Thomas Pierce sent the trackers another voice-mail message: *Inez in Atlantic City.*

CHAPTER 114

*G**oddamn him!* Half a day after we recovered the body of Anthony Bruno, we got the next message from Pierce. He had taken another one already.

We were on the move immediately. Two dozen of us rushed to Atlantic City and prayed he was still there, that someone named Inez hadn't already been butchered and 'studied' by Mr Smith and discarded like the evening trash.

Giant billboards screamed all along the Atlantic City Expressway. Caesars Atlantic City, Harrah's, Merv Griffin's Resorts Casino Hotel, Trump's Castle, Trump Taj Mahal. Call 1-800-GAMBLER. Now *that* was funny.

Inez, Atlantic City, I kept hearing inside my head. *Sounds like Isabella*.

We set up shop in the FBI field office, which was only a few blocks from the old Steel Pier and the so-called 'Great Wooden Way.' There were usually only four agents in the small office. Their expertise was organized crime and gambling, and they weren't considered movers and shakers inside the Bureau. They weren't prepared for a savage, unpredictable killer who had once been a very good agent.

Someone had bought a stack of newspapers and they were piled high on the conference table. The New York, Philly, and Jersey headline writers were having a field day with this one.

ALIEN KILLER VISITS JERSEY SHORE . . . FBI KILLER-DILLER IN ATLANTIC CITY . . . MR SMITH MANHUNT: Hundreds of Federal agents flock to New Jersey Shore . . . MONSTER ON THE LOOSE IN NEW JERSEY!

Sampson came up to the beach from Washington. He wanted Pierce as badly as any of us. He, Kyle, and I worked together, brainstorming over what Pierce-Mr Smith might do next. Sondra Greenberg from Interpol worked with us, too. She was seriously jet-lagged, and had deep circles under her eyes, but she knew Pierce and had been at most of the European murder sites.

'He's not a goddamn split personality?' Sampson asked. 'Smith and Pierce?'

I shook my head. 'He seems to be in control of his faculties at all times. He created "Smith" to serve some other purpose.'

'I agree with Alex,' Sondra Greenberg said from across the table, 'but *what* is the sodding purpose?'

'Whatever it was, it worked,' Kyle joined in. 'He had

us chasing Mr Smith halfway around the world. We're still chasing. No one has ever jerked around the Bureau like this.'

'Not even the great Herbert Hoover?' Sondra said and winked.

'Well,' Kyle softened, 'as a pure psychopath, Hoover was in a class by himself.'

I was up and pacing again. My side was hurting, but I didn't want anyone to know about it. They would try to send me home, make me miss the fun. I let myself ramble – sometimes it works.

'He's trying to tell us something. He's communicating in some strange way. *Inez*? The name reminds us of Isabella. He's obsessed with Isabella. You should see the apartment in Cambridge. Is Inez a substitute for Isabella? Is Atlantic City a substitute for Laguna Beach? Has he brought Isabella home? Why bring Isabella home?'

It went on and on like that: wild hunches, free association, insecurity, fear, unbearable frustration. As far as I could tell nothing worthwhile was said all day and late into the night, but who could really tell.

Pierce didn't try to make further contact. There were no more voice messages. That surprised us a little. Kyle was afraid he'd moved on, and that he would keep moving until he drove us completely insane. Six of us stayed in the field office throughout the night and into the early morning. We slept in our clothes, on chairs, tables, and the floor.

I paced inside the office, and occasionally outside

on the glittery, fog-laden boardwalk. As a last desperate resort, I bought a bag of Fralinger's salt water taffy and tried to get sick to my stomach.

What kind of logic system is he using? Mr Smith is his creation, his Mr Hyde. What is Smith's mission? Why is he here? I wondered, occasionally talking to myself as I strolled the mostly deserted boardwalk.

Inez is Isabella?

It couldn't be that simple. Pierce wouldn't make it simple for us.

Inez is not Isabella. There was only one Isabella. So why does Pierce keep killing again and again?

I found myself at the corner of Park Place and Boardwalk, and that finally brought a smile. *Monopoly. Another kind of game? Is that it?*

I wandered back to the FBI field office and got some sleep. But not nearly enough. A few hours at most.

Pierce was here.

So was Mr Smith.

CHAPTER 115

A flat, still sandy, still meadowy region ... a superb range of ocean beach – miles and miles of it. The bright sun, the sparkling waves, the foam, the view – a sail here and there in the distance. Walt Whitman had written that about Atlantic City a hundred years before. His words were inscribed on the wall of a pizza-and-hotdog stand now. Whitman would have been stricken to see his words on such a backdrop.

I went by myself for another stroll on the Atlantic City boardwalk around ten o'clock. It was Saturday, and so hot and sunny that the eroding beach was already dotted with swimmers and sunbathers.

We still hadn't found Inez. We didn't have a single clue. We didn't even know who she was.

I had the uncomfortable feeling that Thomas Pierce was watching us, or that I might suddenly come upon him in the dense, sweltering crowds. I had my pager just in case he tried to contact us at the field office.

There was nothing else to be done right now. Pierce-Mr Smith was in control of the situation and our lives. A madman was in control of the planet. It seemed like it anyway.

I stopped near Steeplechase Pier and the Resorts Casino Hotel. People were playing under a hot sun in the high, rolling surf. They seemed to be enjoying themselves and didn't appear to have a care in the world. How nice for them.

This was the way it should be, and it reminded me of Jannie and Damon, my own family, and of Christine. She desperately wanted me to leave this job and I couldn't blame her. I didn't know if I could walk away from police work, though. I wondered why that was so. *Physician, heal thyself.* Maybe I would someday soon.

As I continued my walk along the boardwalk, I tried to convince myself that everything that could be done to catch Pierce was being done. I passed a Fralinger's, and a James Candy store. And the old Peanut Shoppe, where a costumed Mr Peanut was stumbling about in the mid-ninety-degree heat.

I had to smile as I saw the Ripley's Believe It Or Not Museum up ahead, where you could see a lock of George Washington's hair, and a roulette table made of jelly beans. No, *I could not believe it.* I didn't think anyone on the crisis team could, but here we were.

I was jolted out of my thoughts by the beeper

vibrating against my leg. I ran to a nearby phone and called in.

Pierce had left another message. Kyle and Sampson were already out on the boardwalk. Pierce was near the Steel Pier. He claimed that Inez was with him! *He said we could still save them!*

Pierce specifically said *them*.

I shouldn't have been running around like this. My side began to throb and hurt like hell. I'd never been out of shape like this, not in my life, and I didn't like the feeling. I hadn't felt so vulnerable and relatively helpless before.

Finally, I realized: *I'm actually afraid of Pierce, and of Mr Smith.*

By the time I got near the Steel Pier, my clothes were dripping wet and I was breathing hard. I pulled off my sport shirt and waded out into the crowd bare-chested. I pushed my way past old-style jitneys and newer step vans, past tandem bikes and joggers.

I was taped and bandaged and I must have looked like an escapee from a local E.R. Even so, it was hard to stand out on a beach like the one at Atlantic City. An ice-cream man hauling a box on his shoulder cried out, 'Hitch your tongue to a sleigh ride! Get your Fudgie Wudgies here!'

Was Thomas Pierce watching us and laughing? He could be the ice-cream man, or anyone else in this frenetic mob scene.

I cupped my hands over my eyes and looked up and down the beach. I spotted policemen and FBI agents wading into the crowd. There must have been at least fifty thousand sunbathers on the beach. I could faintly hear electronic bells from the slot machines in one of the nearby hotels.

Inez. Atlantic City. Jesus!

A madman on the loose near the famous Steel Pier.

I looked for Sampson or Kyle, but I didn't see either of them. I searched for Pierce, and for Inez, and for Mr Smith.

I heard a loud voice, and it stopped me in my tracks. *'This is the FBI.'*

CHAPTER 116

he voice boomed over a loudspeaker. Probably
from one of the hotels, or maybe a police
hookup. 'This is the FBI,' Kyle Craig announced.
'Some of our agents are on the beach now. Cooperate with them and also with the Atlantic City
police. Do whatever they ask. There's no reason for
undue concern. Please cooperate with police officers.'

The huge crowd became strangely quiet. Everyone
was staring around, looking for the FBI. No, there was
no reason for *undue concern* – not unless we actually
found Pierce. Not unless we discovered Mr Smith
operating on somebody in the middle of this beach
crowd.

I made my way toward the famous amusement
pier, where as a young boy I had actually seen the
famous diving horse. People were standing out in the
low surf, just looking in toward shore. It reminded me
of the movie *Jaws*.

Thomas Pierce was in control here.

A black Belljet helicopter hovered less than seventy yards from shore. A second helicopter came into view from the northeast. It swept in close to the first, then fluttered away in the direction of the Taj Mahal Hotel complex. I could make out sharpshooters positioned in the helicopters.

So could Pierce, and so could the people on the beach. I knew there were FBI marksmen in the nearby hotels. Pierce would know that. Pierce was FBI. He knew everything we did. That was his edge and he was using it against us. He was winning.

There was a disturbance up closer to the pier. People were pushing forward to see, while others were moving away as fast as they could. I moved forward.

The beach crowd's noise level was building again. En Vogue played from somebody's blaster. The smell of cotton candy and beer and hotdogs was thick in the air. I began to run toward the Steel Pier, remembering the diving horse and Lucy the Elephant from Margate, better times a long time ago.

I saw Sampson and Kyle up ahead.

They were bending over something. *Oh God. Oh God, no. Inez, Atlantic City!* My pulse raced out of control.

This was not good.

A dark-haired teenage girl was sobbing against an older man's chest. Others gawked at the dead body, which had been clumsily wrapped in beach blankets.

I couldn't imagine how it had gotten here – but there it was.

Inez, Atlantic City. It had to be her.

The murdered woman had long bleach-blonde hair and looked to be in her early twenties. It was hard to tell now. Her skin was purplish and waxy. The eyes had flattened because of a loss of fluid. Her lips and nail beds were pale. He had operated on Inez: The ribs and cartilage had been cut away, exposing her lungs, esophagus, trachea, and heart.

Inez sounds like Isabella.

Pierce knew that.

He hadn't taken out Inez's heart.

The ovaries and fallopian tubes were neatly laid out beside the body. The tubes looked like a set of ear-rings and a necklace.

Suddenly, sunbathers were pointing to something out over the ocean.

I turned and I looked up, shading my eyes with one hand.

A prop plane was lazily making its way down the shoreline from the north. It was the kind of plane you rented for commercial messages. Most of the messages on forty-foot banners hyped the hotels, local bars, area restaurants and casinos.

A banner waved behind a sputtering plane that was getting closer and closer. I couldn't believe what I was reading. It was another message.

Mr Smith is gone for now! Wave good-bye.

CHAPTER 117

Early the next morning, I headed home to Washington. I needed to see the kids, needed to sleep in my own bed, to be far, far away from Thomas Pierce and his monstrous creation – *Mr Smith*.

Inez had turned out to be an escort from a local service. Pierce had called her to his room at Bally's Park Place. I was starting to believe that Pierce could *find intimacy only with his victims now*, but what else was driving him to commit these horrifying murders? Why Inez? Why the Jersey Shore?

I had to escape for a couple of days, or even a few hours, if that was all I could get. At least we hadn't already gotten another name, another location to rush off to.

I called Christine from Atlantic City and asked her if she wanted to have dinner with my family that night. She said yes, she'd like that a lot. She said she'd 'be there with bells on.' That sounded unbelievably good to me. The best medicine I could imagine for what ailed me.

I kept the sound of her voice in my head all the way home to Washington. She would be there with bells on.

Damon, Jannie, and I spent a hectic morning getting ready for the party. We shopped for groceries at Citronella, and then at the Giant. *Veni, vidi, Visa.*

I had *almost* put Pierce-Smith out of my mind, but I still had my Glock in an ankle holster to go grocery shopping.

At the Giant, Damon scouted on ahead to find some R.C. Cola and tortilla chips. Jannie and I had a chance to talk the talk. I knew she was dying to *bzzz-bzzz-bzzz*. I can always tell. She has a fine, over-active imagination, and I couldn't wait to hear what was on her little mind.

Jannie was in charge of pushing the shopping cart, and the metal handle of the cart was just above her eye level. She stared at the immense array of cereals in our aisle, looking for the best deals. Nana Mama had taught her the fine art of grocery shopping, and she can do most of the math in her head.

'Talk to me,' I said. 'My time is your time. Daddy's home.'

'For today.' She sent a hummer right past my ear, brushed me right back from home plate with a high, hard one.

'It's not easy being green,' I said. It was an old favorite line between us, compliments of Kermit the Frog. She shrugged it off today. No sale. No easy deals.

'You and Damon mad at me?' I asked in my most soothing tones. 'Tell me the truth, girlfriend.'

She softened a little. 'Oh, it's not so much that, Daddy. You're doing the best you can,' she said, and finally looked my way. 'You're trying, right? It's just hard when you go away from home. I get lonely for you. It's not the same when you're away.'

I shook my head, smiled, and wondered where she got much of her thinking from. Nana Mama swore that Jannie has a mind of her own.

'You okay with our dinner plans?' I asked, treading carefully.

'Oh *ab*-solutely.' She suddenly beamed. 'That's not a problem at all. I *love* dinner parties.'

'Damon? Is he okay with Christine coming over tonight?' I asked my confidante.

'He's a little scared 'cause she's the principal of our school. But he's cool, too. You know Damon. He's the man.'

I nodded. 'He *is* cool. So dinner's not a problem? You're not even a little scared?'

Jannie shook her head. 'Nope. Not because of that. Dinners can't scare me. Dinner is dinner.'

Man, she was smart, and so subtle for her age. It was like talking to a very wise adult. She was already a poet, and a philosopher, too. She was going to be competition for Maya Angelou and Toni Morrison one day. I loved that about her.

'Do you have to keep going after him? After this bum Mr Smith?' Jannie finally asked me. 'I guess you do.' She answered her own question.

I echoed her earlier line. 'I'm doing the best I can.'

Jannie stood up on her tippy-toes. I bent low to her, but not as far as I used to. She kissed me on the cheek, a nice *smacker*, as she calls the kisses.

'You're the bee's knees,' she said. It was one of Nana's favorite things to say and she'd adopted it.

'Boo!' Damon peeked around the soda-pop aisle at the two of us. His head was framed against a red, white, and blue sea of Pepsi bottles and cans. I pulled Damon close, and I kissed him on the cheek, too. I kissed the top of his head, held him in a way I would have liked my father to have held me a long time ago. We made a little spectacle of ourselves in the grocery-store aisle. Nice spectacle.

God, I loved the two of them, and what a continued dilemma it presented. The Glock on my ankle weighed a ton and felt as hot as a poker from a fire. I wanted to take it off and never put the weapon on again.

I knew I wouldn't, though. Thomas Pierce was still out there somewhere, and Mr Smith, and all the rest of them. For some reason I felt it was my responsibility to make them all go away, to make things a little safer for everyone.

'Earth to Daddy,' Jannie said. She had a small frown on her face. 'See? You went away again. You were with Mr Smith, weren't you?'

CHAPTER 118

*C*hristine can save you. If anyone can, if it's possible
for you to be salvaged at this point in your life.

I got to her place around six-thirty that
night. I'd told her I would pick her up out in Mitchellville. My side was hurting again, and I definitely felt
like damaged goods, but I wouldn't have missed this
for anything.

She came to the front door in a bright-tangerine
sundress and heeled espadrilles. She looked slightly
beyond great. She wore a bar pin with tiny silver bells.
She *did* have bells on.

'Bells.' I smiled.

'You bet. You thought I was kidding.'

I took her in my arms right there on the red-brick
front stoop, with blooming red and white impatiens
and climbing roses all around us. I hugged Christine
tightly against my chest and we started to kiss.

I was lost in her sweet, soft mouth, in her arms. My

hands flew up to her face, lightly tracing her cheek-bones, her nose, her eyelids.

The shock of intimacy was rare and overwhelming. So good, so fine, and missing for such a long time.

I opened my eyes and saw that she was looking at me. She had the most expressive eyes I'd ever seen. 'I love the way you hold me, Alex,' she whispered, but her eyes said much more. 'I love your touch.'

We backed into the house, kissing again.

'Do we have time?' She laughed.

'Shhh. Only a crazy person wouldn't. We're not crazy.'

'Of course we are.'

The bright-tangerine sundress fell away to the floor. I liked the feel of shantung, but Christine's bare skin felt even better. She was wearing Shalimar and I liked that, too. I had the feeling that I had been here before with her, maybe in a dream. It was as if I had been imagining this moment for a long time and now it was here.

She helped me with her white-lace demibra. We slid down the matching panties, two pairs of hands working together. Then we were naked, except for the fine rope necklace with a fire opal around her neck. I remembered a poem, something magical about the nakedness of lovers, but with just a touch of jewelry to set it off. Baudelaire? I bit gently into her shoulder. She bit back.

I was so hard it hurt, but the pain was exquisite, the pain had its own raw power. I loved this woman completely, and I was also turned on by her, every inch of her being.

'You know,' I whispered, 'you're driving me a little crazy.'

'Oh. Just a little?'

I let my lips trail down along her breasts, her stomach. She was lightly scented with perfume. I kissed between her legs and she began to gently call my name, then not so gently. I entered Christine as we stood against the cream living-room wall, as we seemed to push our bodies *into* the wall.

'I love you,' I whispered.

'I love you, Alex.'

She was strong and gentle and graceful, all at the same time. We danced, but not in the metaphorical sense. We really *danced*.

I loved the sound of her voice, the softest cry, the song she sang when she was with me like this.

Then I was singing, too. I had found my voice again, for the first time in many years. I don't know how long we were like that. Time wasn't part of this. Something in it was eternal, and something was so very real and right now in the present.

Christine and I were soaking wet. Even the wall behind me was slippery and wet. The wild ride at the beginning, the rocking and rolling, had transformed itself into a slower rhythm that was even stronger. I knew that no life was right without this kind of passion.

I was barely moving inside her. She tightened

around me and I thought I could feel the edges of her. I surged deeper and Christine seemed to swell around me. We began to move into each other, trying to get closer. We shuddered, and got closer still.

Christine climaxed, and then the two of us came together. We danced and we sang. I felt myself melting into Christine and we were both whispering *yes, yes, yes, yes, yes, yes*. No one could touch us here, not Thomas Pierce, no one.

'Hey, did I tell you I loved you?'

'Yes, but tell me again.'

CHAPTER 119

Kids are so damn much smarter than we usually give them credit for. Kids know just about everything, and they often know it before we do.

'You two are *late*! You have a flat tire – or were you just smooching?' Jannie wanted to know as we came in the front door. She can say some outrageous things and get away with them. She knows it, and pushes the envelope every chance she gets.

'We were smooching,' I said. 'Satisfied?'

'Yes I am.' Jannie smiled. 'Actually, you're not even late. You're right on time. Perfect timing.'

Dinner with Nana and the children wasn't an anti-climax. It was such a sweet, funny time. It was what being home is all about. We all pitched in and set the table, served the food, then ate with reckless abandon. The meal was swordfish steaks, scalloped potatoes, summer peas, buttermilk biscuits. Everything was served piping hot, expertly prepared by Nana, Jannie, and Damon. Dessert was Nana's world-famous lemon meringue pie. She made it specially for Christine.

I believe the simple yet complex word that I'm searching for is *joy*.

It was so obvious around the dinner table. I could see it in the bright and lively eyes of Nana and Damon and Jannie. I had already seen it in Christine's eyes. I watched her at dinner and I had the thought that she could have been somebody famous in Washington, anything she wanted to be. She chose to be a teacher, and I loved that about her.

We repeated stories that had been in the family for years, and are always repeated at such occasions. Nana was lively and funny all through the night. She gave us her best advice on aging: 'If you can't recall it, forget it.'

Later on, I played the piano and sang rhythm-and-blues songs. My wrist gave me trouble but I was doing OK. Jannie showed off and did the cakewalk to a jazzy version of 'Blueberry Hill.' Even Nana did a minute of jitterbugging, protesting, 'I really can't dance, I never could dance,' as she did just beautifully.

One moment, one picture, sticks out in my mind, and I'm sure it will be there until the day I die. It was just after we'd finished dinner and were cleaning up the kitchen.

I was washing dishes in the sink, and as I reached to get another platter I stopped in midturn, frozen in the moment.

Jannie was in Christine's arms, and the two of them looked just beautiful together. I had no idea how she had gotten there, but they were both laughing and it was so natural and real. As I never had before, I knew and understood that Jannie and Damon were missing so much without a mother.

Joy – that's the word. So easy to say, so hard to find in life sometimes.

In the morning, I had to go back to work.

I was still the dragonslayer.

CHAPTER 120

I shut myself away to think, to quietly obsess about Thomas Pierce and Mr Smith.

I made suggestions to Kyle Craig about moves that Pierce might make, and precautions he should think about taking. Agents were dispatched to watch Pierce's apartment in Cambridge. Agents camped out at his parents' house outside Laguna Beach, and even at the gravesite of Isabella Calais.

Pierce had been passionately in love with Isabella Calais! She had been the only one for him! Isabella and Thomas Pierce! That was the key – Pierce's obsessive love for her.

He's suffering from unbearable guilt, I wrote in my notepad.

If my hypothesis is right, then what clues are missing?

Back at Quantico, a team of FBI profilers was trying to solve the problem on paper. They had all worked closely with Pierce in the BSU. Absolutely nothing in

Pierce's background was consistent with the psycho-pathic killers they had dealt with before. Pierce had never been abused, either physically or sexually. There was no violence of any kind in his background. At least not as far as anyone knew. There was no warn-ing, no hint of madness, no sign until he blew sky-high. *He was an original. There had never been a monster anything like him. There were no precedents.*

I wrote: *Thomas Pierce was deeply in love. You are in love, too.*

What would it mean to murder the only person in the world who you loved?

CHAPTER 121

I couldn't manage any sympathy, or even a modicum of clinical empathy, for Pierce. I despised him, and his cruel, cold-blooded murders, more than I had any of the other killers I had taken down – even Soneji. Kyle Craig and Sampson felt the same, and so did most of the Federal Bureau, especially the good folks in Behavioral Science. We were the ones in a rage state now. We were obsessed with stopping Pierce. Was he using that to beat our brains in?

The following day, I worked at home again. I locked myself away with my computer, several books, and my crime-scene notepads. The only time I took off was to walk Damon and Jannie to school, and then have a quick breakfast with Nana.

My mouth was full of poached egg and toast when she leaned across the kitchen table and launched one of her famous sneak attacks on me.

'Am I correct in saying that you don't want to

discuss your murder case with me?' she asked.

'I'd rather talk about the weather or just about anything else. Your garden looks beautiful. Your hair looks nice.'

'We all like Christine very much, Alex. She's knocked our socks off. In case you wanted to know but forgot to ask. She's the best thing that's happened to you since Maria. So, what are you going to do about it? What are your plans?'

I rolled my eyes back, but I had to smile at Nana's dawn offensive. 'First, I'm going to finish this delicious breakfast you fixed. Then I have some dicey work to do upstairs. How's that?'

'You mustn't lose her, Alex. Don't do that,' Nana advised and warned at the same time. 'You won't listen to a decrepit old woman, though. What do I know about anything? I just cook and clean around here.'

'And talk,' I said with my mouth full. 'Don't forget talk, old woman.'

'Not just talk, sonny boy. Pretty sound psychological analysis, necessary cheerleading at times, and expert guidance counseling.'

'I have a game plan,' I said, and left it at that.

'You better have a winning game plan.' Nana got the last word in. 'Alex, if you lose her, you will never get over it.'

The walk with the kids and even talking with Nana revitalized me. I felt clear and alert as I worked at my old rolltop for the rest of the morning.

I had started to cover the bedroom walls with notes and theories, and the beginnings of *even more theories* about Thomas Pierce. The pushpin parade had taken control. From the looks of the room, it seemed as if I knew what I was doing, but contrary to popular opinion, looks are almost always deceiving. I had hundreds of clues, and yet I didn't have a clue.

I remembered something Mr Smith had written in one of his messages to Pierce, which Pierce had then passed on to the FBI. *The god within us is the one that gives the laws and can change the laws. And God is within us.*

The words had seemed familiar to me, and I finally tracked down the source. The quote was from Joseph Campbell, the American mythologist and folklorist who had taught at Harvard when Pierce was a student there.

I was trying different perspectives to the puzzle. Two entry points in particular interested me.

First, Pierce was curious about language. He had studied linguistics at Harvard. He admired Noam Chomsky. What about language and words, then?

Second, Pierce was extremely organized. He had created the false impression that Mr Smith was disorganized. He had purposely misled the FBI and Interpol.

Pierce was leaving clues from the start. Some of them were obvious.

He wants to be caught. So why doesn't he stop himself?

Murder. Punishment. Was Thomas Pierce punishing

himself, or was he punishing everybody else? Right now, he was certainly punishing the hell out of me. Maybe I deserved it.

Around three o'clock, I took a stroll and picked up Damon and Jannie at the Sojourner Truth School. Not that they needed someone to walk them home. I just missed the hell out of them. I needed to see them, couldn't keep myself away.

Besides, my head ached and I wanted to get out of the house, away from all of my thoughts.

I saw Christine in the schoolyard. She was surrounded by little children. I remembered that she wanted to have kids herself. She looked so happy, and I could see that the kids loved to be around her. Who in their right mind wouldn't? She made it look so natural to be turning jump rope in a navy business suit.

She smiled when she saw me approaching across the schoolyard full of kids. The smile warmed the cockles of my heart, and all my other cockles as well.

'Look who's taking a break for air,' she said, 'three potato, four.'

'When I was in high school,' I told her as she continued to turn her end of a Day-Glo pink jump rope, 'I had a girlfriend over at John Carroll. This was in my sophomore and junior years.'

'Mmm, hmmm. Nice Catholic girl? White blouse, plaid skirt, saddle shoes?'

'She was very nice. Actually, she's a botanist now. See, nice? I used to walk all the way over to South

Carolina Avenue just on the off chance I might see
Jeanne for a couple of minutes after she finished
school. I was seriously smitten.'

'Must have been the saddle shoes. Are you trying to
tell me that you're smitten again?' Christine laughed.
The kids couldn't quite hear us, but they were laughing anyway.

'I am way beyond smitten. I am smote.'

'Well that's good,' she said and continued to turn
the pink rope and smile at her kids, 'because so am I.
And when this case is over, Alex—'

'Anything you want, just say the word.'

Her eyes brightened even more than was usual. 'A
weekend away from everything. Maybe at a country
inn, but anywhere remote will do just fine.'

I wanted to hold Christine so much. I wanted to
kiss her right there, but that wasn't going to happen
in the crowded schoolyard.

'It's a date,' I said. 'It's a promise.'

'I'll hold you to it. *Smote*, that's good. We can try
that on our weekend away.'

CHAPTER 122

Back home, I worked on the Pierce case until supper time. I ate a quick meal of hamburgers and summer squash with Nana and the kids. I took some more heavy heat for being an incurable and unrepentant workaholic. Nana cut me a slice of pie, and I retreated to my room again. Well fed, but deeply unsatisfied.

I couldn't help it – I was worried. Thomas Pierce might already have grabbed another victim. He could be performing an 'autopsy' tonight. He could send us a message at any time.

I reread the notes I had plastered on the bedroom wall. I felt as if the answer were on the tip of my tongue and it was driving me crazy. People's lives hung in the balance.

He had 'pierced' the heart of Isabella Calais.

His apartment in Cambridge was an obsessive shrine to her memory.

He had returned 'home' when he went to Point Pleasant Beach. The opportunity to catch him was there – if we were smart enough, if we were as good as he was.

What were we missing, the FBI and me?

I played more word games with the assortment of clues.

He always 'pierces' his victims. I wondered if he was impotent or had become impotent, unable to have a sexual relationship with Isabella.

Mr Smith operates like a doctor – which Pierce nearly was – which his father and his siblings are. He had failed as a doctor.

I went to bed early, around eleven, but I couldn't sleep. I guess I'd just wanted to try and turn the case off. I finally called Christine and we talked for about an hour. As we talked and I listened to the music of her voice, I couldn't help thinking about Pierce and Isabella Calais.

Pierce had loved her. Obsessive love. What would happen if I lost Christine now? What happened to Pierce after the murder? Had he gone mad?

After I got off the phone, I went back at the case again. For a while, I thought his pattern might have something to do with Homer's *Odyssey*. He was heading home after a series of tragedies and misfortunes? *No, that wasn't it.*

What the hell was the key to his code? If he wanted to drive all of us mad, it was working.

I began to play with the names of the victims, starting with Isabella and ending with Inez. *I goes full* circle to *I*? Full circle? Circles? I looked at the clock on the desk – it was almost one-thirty in the morning, but I kept at it.

I wrote – *I*.

I. Was that something? It could be a start. The personal pronoun *I*? I tried a few combinations with the letters of the names.

I – S – U ... R

C – A – D ...

I – A – D ...

I stopped after the next three letters: IMU. I stared at the page. I remembered 'pierced,' the obviousness of it. The simplest wordplay.

Isabella, Michaela, Ursula. Those were the names of the first three victims – in order. *Jesus Christ!*

I looked at the names of all the victims – in order of the murders. I looked at the first, last, and middle names. I began mixing and matching the names. My heart was pounding. There was something here. Pierce had left us another clue, a series of clues, actually.

It was right there in front of us all the time. No one got it, because Smith's crimes appeared to be without any pattern. But Pierce had started that theory himself.

I continued to write, using either the first or last or middle names of the victims. It started IMU. Then *R*, for Robert. *D* for Dwyer. Was there a subpattern for selecting the name? It could be an arithmetic sequence.

There was a pattern to Pierce-Smith, after all. His mission began that very first night in Cambridge, Massachusetts. He *was* insane, but I had caught on to his pattern. It started with his love of wordplay.

Thomas Pierce wanted to be caught! But then something changed. He had become ambivalent about his capture. Why?

I looked at what I had assembled. 'Son of a bitch,' I muttered. 'Isn't this something. He has a ritual.'

I – Isabella Calais.

M – Stephanie Michaela Apt.

U – Ursula Davies.

R – Robert Michael Neel.

D – Brigid Dwyer.

E – Mary Ellen Klauk.

R – Robin Anne Schwartz.

E – Clark Daniel Ebel.

D – David Hale.

I – Isadore Morris.

S – Theresa Anne Secrest.

A – Elizabeth Allison Gragnano.

B – Barbara Maddalena.

E – Edwin Mueller.

L – Laurie Garnier.

L – Lewis Lavine.

A – Andrew Klauk.

C – Inspector Derek Cabott.

A – Dr Abel Sante.

L – Simon Lewis Conklin.

A – Anthony Bruno.

I – Inez Marquez.

S – ?

It read: I MURDERED ISABELLA CALAIS.

He had made it so easy for us. He was taunting us from the very beginning. Pierce wanted to be stopped, wanted to be caught. So why the hell hadn't he stopped himself? Why had the string of brutal murders gone on and on?

I MURDERED ISABELLA CALAIS.

The murders were a confession, and maybe Pierce was almost finished. Then what would happen? And who was *S*?

Was it Smith himself? Did S stand for Smith?

Would he symbolically murder Smith? Then Mr Smith would disappear forever?

I called Kyle Craig and then Sampson, and I told them what I had found. It was past two in the morning, and neither of them was overjoyed to hear my voice or the news. They didn't know what to do with the word jumble and neither did I.

'I'm not sure what it gives us,' Kyle said, 'what it proves, Alex.'

'I'm not either. Not yet. It does tell us he's going to kill someone with an *S* in his name.'

'George Steinbrenner,' Kyle mumbled. 'Strom Thurmond. Sting.'

'Go back to sleep,' I said.

My head was doing loops. Sleep wasn't an option for me. I half-expected to get another message from Pierce, maybe even that night. He was mocking us.

He had been from the beginning.

I wanted to get a message to him. Maybe I ought to communicate with Pierce through the newspapers or TV? We needed to get off the defensive and attack instead.

I lay in the darkness of my bedroom. *Could S be Mr Smith?* I wondered. My head was throbbing. I was past being exhausted. I finally drifted off toward sleep. I was falling off the edge – when I grabbed hold.

I bolted up in bed. I was wide-awake now.

'*S* isn't Smith.'

I knew who *S* was.

CHAPTER 123

Thomas Pierce was in Concord, Massachusetts.
Mr Smith was here, too.
I was finally inside his head.

Sampson and I were ready on a cozy, picturesque side street near the house of Dr Martin Straw, the man who had been Isabella's lover. Martin Straw was *S* in the puzzle.

The FBI had a trap set for Pierce at the house. They didn't bring huge numbers of agents this time. They were afraid of tipping off Pierce. Kyle Craig was gun-shy and he had every reason to be. Or maybe there was something else going on?

We waited for the better part of the morning and early afternoon. Concord was a self-contained, somewhat constrained town that seemed to be aging gracefully. The Thoreau and Alcott homes were here somewhere nearby. Every other house seemed to have a historical-looking plaque with a date on it.

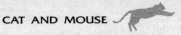

We waited for Pierce. And then waited some more. The dreaded *stakeout in Podunk* dragged on and on. Maybe I was wrong about *S*.

A voice finally came over the radio in our car. It was Kyle. 'We've spotted Pierce. He's here. But something's wrong, Alex. He's headed back toward Route Two,' Kyle said. 'He's not going to Dr Straw's. He saw something he didn't like.'

Sampson looked over at me. 'I told you he was careful. Good instincts. He *is* a goddamn Martian, Alex.'

'He spotted something,' I said. 'He's as good as Kyle always said. He knows how the Bureau works, and he saw something.'

Kyle and his team had wanted to let Pierce enter the Straw house before they took him down. Dr Straw, his wife, and children had been moved from the place. We needed solid evidence against Pierce, as much as we could get. We could lose the case if we got Thomas Pierce to court without it. We definitely could lose.

A message crackled over the shortwave. 'He's headed toward Route Two. Something spooked him. He's on the run!'

'He has a shortwave! He's intercepting us!' I grabbed the mike and warned Kyle. 'No more talk on the radio. Pierce is listening. That's how he spotted us.'

I started the engine and gunned the sedan away from the curb. I pushed the speed up to sixty on heavily populated Lowell Road. We were actually closer to Route 2 than the others. We still might be able to cut Pierce off.

A shiny, silver BMW passed us, coming from the opposite direction on the road. The driver sat on her horn as we sped by. I couldn't blame her. Sixty was a dangerous speed on the narrow village street. Everything was going crazy again, caroming out of control at the whim of a madman.

'There he is!' Sampson yelled.

Pierce's car was heading into Concord Center, the most congested area of town. He was moving way too fast.

We sped past Colonial-style houses, then upscale shops, and finally approached Monument Square. I caught glimpses of the Town House, Concord Inn, the Masons' Hall – then a sign for Route 62 – another for Route 2.

Our sedan whisked by car after car on the village streets. Brakes screeched around us. Other cars honked, justifiably angry and afraid of the car chase in progress.

Sampson was holding his breath and so was I. There's a joke about black men being pulled over illegally in suburban areas. The *DWB* violation. Driving while black. We were up to seventy inside the city limits.

We made it in one piece out of the town center – Walden Street – Main – then back onto Lowell Road approaching the highway.

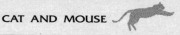

I whipped around onto Route 2 and nearly spun out of control. My wrist was still weak. The pedal was down to the floor. This was our best chance to get Thomas Pierce, maybe our last chance. Up ahead, Pierce knew this was it, too.

I was doing close to ninety now on Route 2, passing cars as if they were standing still. Pierce's Thunderbird must have been pushing eighty-five. He'd spotted us early in the chase.

'We're catching this squirrely bastard now!' Sampson hollered at me. 'Pierce goes down!'

We hit a deep pothole and the car momentarily left the road. We landed with a jarring *thud*. The wound in my side screamed. My head hurt. Sampson kept hollering in my ear about Pierce going down.

I could see his dark Thunderbird bobbing and weaving up ahead. Just a couple of car lengths separated us.

He's a planner, I warned myself. *He knew this might happen.*

I finally caught up to Pierce and pulled alongside him. Both cars were doing close to ninety. Pierce took a quick glance over at us.

I felt strangely exhilarated. Adrenaline powered through my body. *Maybe we had him*. For a second or two, I was as totally insane as Pierce.

Pierce saluted with his right hand. 'Dr Cross,' he called through the open window, 'we finally meet!'

CHAPTER 124

'I know about the FBI sanction!' Pierce yelled over the whistle and roar of the wind. He looked cool and collected, oblivious to reality. 'Go ahead, Cross. I want you to do it. Take me out, Cross!'

'There's no sanction order!' I yelled back. 'Pull your car over! No one's going to shoot you.'

Pierce grinned – his best killer smile. His blond hair was tied in a tight ponytail. He had on a black turtleneck. He looked successful – a local lawyer, shop owner, doctor. 'Doc.'

'Why do you think the FBI brought such a small unit,' he yelled. 'Terminate with prejudice. Ask your friend Kyle Craig. That's why they wanted me *inside* Straw's house!'

Was I talking to Thomas Pierce?

Or was this Mr Smith?

Was there a difference anymore?

He threw his head back and roared with laughter. It

was one of the oddest, craziest things I've ever seen. The look on his face, the body language, his calmness. He was daring us to shoot him at ninety miles an hour on Route 2 outside Concord, Massachusetts. He wanted to crash and burn.

We hit a stretch of highway with thick fir woods on either side. Two of the FBI cars caught up. They were pinned on Pierce's tail, pushing, taunting him. Had the Bureau come here planning to kill Pierce?

If they were going to take him, this was a good place – a secluded pocket away from most commuter traffic and houses.

This was the place to terminate Thomas Pierce.

Now was the time.

'You know what we have to do,' Sampson said to me.

He's killed more than twenty people that we know of, I was thinking, trying to rationalize. *He'll never give up.*

'Pull over,' I yelled at Pierce again.

'I murdered Isabella Calais,' he screamed at me. His face was crimson. 'I can't stop myself. I don't want to stop. I like it! I found out I like it, Cross!'

'Pull the hell over,' Sampson's voice boomed. He had his Glock up and aimed at Pierce. 'You butcher! You piece of shit!'

'I murdered Isabella Calais and I can't stop the killing. You hear what I'm saying, Cross? I murdered Isabella Calais, and I can't stop the killing.'

I understood the chilling message. I'd gotten it the first time.

He was adding more letters to his list of victims. Pierce was creating a new, longer code: I murdered Isabella Calais, and I can't stop the killing. If he got away, he'd kill again and again. Maybe Thomas Pierce *wasn't* human, after all. He'd already intimated that he was his own god.

Pierce had an automatic out. He fired at us.

I yanked the steering wheel hard to the left with my right arm, trying desperately to get us out of the line of fire. Our car leaned hard on its left front and rear wheels. Everything was blurred and out of focus. I gripped the wheel. I thought we were going over.

Pierce's Thunderbird shot off Route 2, rocketing down a side road. I don't know how he made the turnoff at the speed he was traveling. Maybe he didn't care whether he made it or not.

I managed to set our sedan back down on all four wheels. The FBI cars following Pierce shot past the turn. None of us could stop. Next came a ragged ballet of skidding stops and U-turns, the screech and whine of tires and brakes. We'd lost sight of Pierce. He was behind us.

We raced back to the turnoff, then down a twisting, chevroned country road. We found the Thunderbird abandoned about two miles from Route 2.

My heart was thudding hard inside my chest. *Pierce wasn't in the car. Pierce wasn't here.*

The woods on both sides of the road were thick and offered lots of cover. Sampson and I climbed out of our car.

We hurried back into the dense thicket of fir trees, Glocks out. It was almost impossible to get through the underbrush. There was no sign of Thomas Pierce anywhere.

Pierce was gone.

CHAPTER 125

*T*homas Pierce *had vanished into thin air again. I was almost convinced he might actually live in a parallel world. Maybe he* was *an alien.*

Sampson and I were headed to Logan International Airport. We were going home to Washington. Rush-hour traffic in Boston wasn't cooperating with the plan.

We were still half a mile from the Callahan Tunnel, gridlocked in a line that was barely moving. Grunting and groaning cars and trucks surrounded us. Boston was rubbing our faces in our failure.

'Metaphor for our cause. The whole goddamn manhunt for Pierce,' Sampson said about the traffic jumble, the mess. A good thing about Sampson – he gets either stoic or funny when things go really badly. He refuses to wallow in shit. He swims right out of it.

'I'm getting an idea,' I told him, giving him some warning.

'I knew you were flying around somewhere in your private universe. Knew you weren't really here, sitting in this car with me, listening to what I'm saying.'

'We'd just be stuck here in the tunnel traffic if we stayed put.'

Sampson nodded. 'Uh-huh. We're in Boston. Don't want to have to come back tomorrow, follow up on one of your hunches then. Best to do it now. Chase those wild geese while the chasing is good. I don't like you driving.'

I pulled out of the tight lane of stalled traffic. 'There's just one wild goose that I can think to chase.'

'You going to tell me where we're headed? I need to put my vest back on?'

'Depends on what you think of my hunches.'

I followed forest-green signs toward Storrow Drive, heading out of Boston the way we came. Traffic was heavy in that direction, too. There were too many people everywhere you went these days, too much crowding, and too much chaos, too much stress on everybody.

'Better put your vest back on,' I told Sampson.

He didn't argue with me. Sampson reached into the backseat and fished around for our vests.

I wiggled into my own vest as I drove. 'I think Thomas Pierce wants this to end. I think he's ready now. I saw it in his eyes.'

'So, he had his chance back there in Concord. "*Pull off the road. Pull over, Pierce!*" You remember any of that? Sound familiar, Alex?'

I glanced at Sampson. 'He needs to be in control. *S* was for Straw, but *S* is also for *Smith*. It's important to him that he finish this.'

Out of the corner of my eye I could see Sampson staring. 'And? So? What the hell is that supposed to mean?'

'He wants to end on *S*. It's magical for him. It's the way he has it figured, the way it has to be. It's his mind game, and he plays it obsessively. He can't stop playing. He told us that. He's still playing.'

Sampson was clearly having trouble with this. We had just missed capturing Pierce an hour ago. Would he put himself at risk again? 'You think he's that crazy?'

'I think he's that crazy, John. I'm sure of it.'

CHAPTER 126

Half-a-dozen police squad cars were gathered on Inman Street in Cambridge. The blue-and-white cruisers were outside the apartment where Thomas Pierce and Isabella Calais had once lived, where Isabella had been murdered four years before.

EMS ambulances were parked near the graystone front stoop. Sirens bleated and wailed. If we hadn't turned around at the Callahan Tunnel we would have missed it.

Sampson and I showed our detective shields and kept on moving forward in a hurry. Nobody stopped us. Nobody could have.

Pierce was upstairs.

So was Mr Smith.

The game had come full circle.

'Somebody called in a homicide in progress,' one of the Cambridge uniforms told us on the way up the stone front stairs. 'I hear they got the guy cornered upstairs. Wackadoo of the first order.'

'We know all about him,' Sampson said.

The elevator was stuck so Sampson and I took the stairs to the second floor.

'You think Pierce called all this heat on himself?' Sampson asked as we hurried up the stairs. I was beyond being out of breath, beyond pain, beyond shock or surprise.

This is how he wants it to end.

I didn't know what to make of Thomas Pierce. He had numbed me, and all the rest of us. I was drifting beyond thought, at least logical ideas. There had never been a killer like Pierce. Not even close. He was the most *alienated* human being I'd ever met. Not alien, *alienated*.

'You still with me, Alex?' I felt Sampson's hand gripping my shoulder.

'Sorry,' I said. 'At first, I thought Pierce couldn't feel anything, that he was just another psychopath. Cold rage, arbitrary murders.'

'And now?'

I was inside Pierce's head.

'Now I'm wondering whether Pierce maybe feels *everything*. I think that's what drove him mad. This one can *feel*.'

The Cambridge police were gathered everywhere in the small, twisty hallway. The local cops looked shell-shocked and wild-eyed. A photograph of Isabella stared out from the foyer. She looked beautiful, almost regal, and so very sad.

'Welcome to the wild, wacky world of Thomas Pierce,' Sampson said.

A Cambridge detective explained the situation to us. He had silver-blond hair, an ageless hatchet face. He spoke in a low, confidential tone, almost a whisper. 'Pierce is in the bedroom at the far end of the hall. Barricaded himself in there.'

'The master bedroom, his and Isabella's room,' I said.

The detective nodded. 'Right, the master bedroom. I worked the original murder. I hate the prick. I saw what he did to her.'

'What's he doing in the bedroom?' I asked.

The detective shook his head. 'We think he's going to kill himself. He doesn't care to explain himself to us peons. He's got a gun. The powers-that-be are trying to decide whether to go in.'

'He hurt anybody?' Sampson spoke up.

The Cambridge detective shook his head. 'No, not that we know of. Not yet.'

Sampson's eyes narrowed. 'Then maybe we shouldn't interfere.'

We walked down the narrow hallway to where several more detectives were talking among themselves. A couple of them were arguing and pointing toward the bedroom.

This is how he wants it. He's still in control.

'I'm Alex Cross,' I told the detective-lieutenant on the scene. He knew who I was. 'What has he said so far?'

The lieutenant was sweating. He was a bruiser, and a good thirty pounds over his fighting weight. 'Told us that he killed Isabella Calais, confessed. I think we knew that already. Said he was going to kill himself.' He rubbed his chin with his left hand. 'We're trying to decide if we care. The FBI is on the way.'

I pulled away from the lieutenant.

'Pierce,' I called down the hallway. The talking going on outside the bedroom suddenly stopped. 'Pierce! It's Alex Cross,' I called again. 'I want to come in, Pierce!'

I felt a chill. It was too quiet. Not a sound. Then I heard Pierce from the bedroom. He sounded tired and weak. Maybe it was an act. Who knew what he would pull next?

'Come in if you want. Just you, Cross.'

'Let him go,' Sampson whispered from behind. 'Alex, let it go for once.'

I turned to him. 'I wish I could.'

I pushed through the group of policemen at the end of the hallway. I remembered the poster that hung there: *Without God, We Are Condemned To Be Free*. Was that what this was about?

I took out my gun and slowly inched open the bedroom door. I wasn't prepared for what I saw.

Thomas Pierce was sprawled on the bed he had once shared with Isabella Calais.

He held a gleaming, razor-sharp scalpel in his hand.

CHAPTER 127

*T*homas Pierce's chest was cut wide open. He had ripped himself apart as he would a corpse at an autopsy. He was still alive, but barely. It was incredible that he was conscious and alert.

Pierce spoke to me. I don't know how, but he did. 'You've never seen Mr Smith's handiwork before?'

I shook my head in disbelief. I had never seen anything like this, not in all my years in Violent Crimes or Homicide. Flaps of skin hung over Pierce's rib cage, exposing translucent muscle and tendons. I was afraid, repulsed, shocked – all at the same time.

Thomas Pierce was Mr Smith's victim. His last?

'Don't come any closer. Just stay there,' he said. It was a command.

'Who am I talking to? Thomas Pierce, or Mr Smith?'

Pierce shrugged. 'Don't play shrink games with me. I'm smarter than you are.'

I nodded. Why argue with him – with Pierce, or was it Mr Smith?

'I murdered Isabella Calais,' he said slowly. His eyes became hooded. He almost looked in a trance. 'I murdered Isabella Calais.'

He pressed the scalpel to his chest, ready to stab himself again, to *pierce*. I wanted to turn away, but I couldn't.

This man wants to cut into his own heart, I thought to myself. *Everything has come full circle to this. Is Mr Smith S? Of course he is.*

'You never got rid of any of Isabella's things,' I said. 'You kept her pictures up.'

Pierce nodded. 'Yes, Dr Cross. I was mourning her, wasn't I?'

'That's what I thought at first. It's what the people at the Behavioral Science Unit at Quantico believed. But then I finally got it.'

'What did you get? Tell me all about myself,' Pierce mocked. He was lucid. His mind still worked quickly.

'The other murders – you didn't want to kill any of them, did you?'

Thomas Pierce glared. He focused on me with a sheer act of will. His arrogance reminded me of Soneji. 'So why did I?'

'You were punishing yourself. Each murder was a re-enactment of Isabella's death. You repeated the ritual over and over. You suffered her death each time you killed.'

Thomas Pierce moaned. 'Ohhh, ohhh, I murdered her here. In this bed! . . . Can you imagine? Of course you can't. No one can.'

He raised the scalpel above his body.

'Pierce, don't!'

I had to do something. I rushed him. I threw myself at him, and the scalpel jammed into my right palm. I screamed in pain as Pierce pulled it out.

I grabbed at the folded yellow-and-white-flowered comforter and pressed it against Pierce's chest. He was fighting me, flopping around like a man having a seizure.

'Alex, no. Alex, look out!' I heard Sampson call out from behind me. I could see him out of the corner of my eye. He was moving fast toward the bed. 'Alex, the scalpel!' he yelled.

Pierce was still struggling beneath me. He screamed obscenities. His strength was amazing. I didn't know where the scalpel was, or if he still had it.

'Let Smith kill Pierce!' he screeched.

'No,' I yelled back. 'I want you alive.'

Then the unthinkable – again.

Sampson fired from point-blank range. The explosion was deafening in the small bedroom. Thomas Pierce's body convulsed on the bed. Both his legs kicked high in the air. He screeched like a badly wounded animal. He sounded inhuman – like an *alien*.

Sampson fired a second time. A strange guttural sound came from Pierce's throat. His eyes rolled way back in his head. The whites showed. The scalpel dropped from his hand.

I shook my head. 'No, John. No more. Pierce is dead. Mr Smith is dead, too. May he rest in hell.'

CHAPTER 128

I was drained of all feeling, slightly wounded and bandaged, but at least I got home safe and sound and in time to say good night to the kids. Damon and Jannie now had their own rooms. They both wanted it that way. Nana had given Jannie her room on the second floor. Nana had moved down to the smaller bedroom near the kitchen, which suited her fine.

I was so glad to be there, to be home again.

'Somebody's been decorating in here,' I said as I peeked into Jannie's new digs. It surprised her that I was home from the wars. Her face lit up like a jack-o'-lantern on Halloween.

'I did it myself.' Jannie pumped up her arms and 'made muscles' for me. 'Nana helped me hang the new curtains, though. We made them on the sewing machine. You like?'

'You're the hostess with the mostest. I guess I

missed all the fun,' I told her.

'You sure did,' Jannie said and laughed. 'C'mere you,' she teased.

I went over to my little girl, and she gave me one of the sweetest hugs in the long and sometimes illustrious history of fathers and daughters.

Then I went to Damon's room, and because it had been both Damon and Jannie's room for so long, I was taken aback, shook up with the change.

Damon had chosen a sporting decor with monster and comedy movie accents. Manly, yet sensitive. I liked what he'd done to his room. It was pure Damon.

'You've got to help me with *my* room,' I told him.

'We missed our boxing lesson tonight,' he said, not in the tone of a major complaint, just setting the record straight.

'You want to go downstairs now?' I raised my fists. 'I'll go a round or two with you, Buster Douglas.'

Damon laughed out loud. 'You think you can take me? I don't *think so*.'

We settled for wrestling on his bed, but I had to agree to a double boxing lesson in the basement the following night. Actually, I couldn't wait. Damon was growing up too fast. So was Jannie. I couldn't have been happier with either of them.

And Christine. I could call her now, see her tomorrow. There was a saying I liked: *Heart leads head*. With Christine, I felt whole again. I felt connected to the eternal river and all that good stuff. I had missed that feeling for too many years.

I was a lucky man.

I had made it home again.

EPILOGUE

BY THE SEA, BY THE SEA

CHAPTER 129

D amon, Jannie, Nana, Christine, and I arrived at Bermuda International Airport on Sunday, the twenty-fifth of August.

I remember a scene from the airport perfectly – Christine and Jannie were standing on the passport line, holding hands and singing 'Ja – da, ja – da.' It was a mind-photo to have and to hold.

We were blessed with good weather, the very best imaginable. It was sunny and blue-skied every day. The days belonged to the kids. We went swimming and snorkeling at Elbow and Horseshoe Bay, and raced mopeds along the Middle Road.

The nights belonged to Christine and me, and we hit the good spots, and hit them hard – the Terrace Bar at the Palm Reef, the Gazebo Lounge at the Princess, the Clay House Inn. I loved being with her more than ever. I felt whole again. I kept remembering the first time I had seen her in the schoolyard at

Sojourner Truth. *She's the one, Alex. She's the one.*

One morning, I found her walking in the garden with flowers strewn in her hair. 'There's an old saying,' she told me. 'If you have only two pennies, buy a loaf of bread with one, and a lily with the other.'

The kids and I went back to Horseshoe Bay that afternoon. They couldn't get enough of the deep blue sea. Christine took a moped trip into Hamilton to pick up mementos for a few of the teachers at Sojourner Truth. Around five, Damon, Jannie, and I finally returned to the Belmont Hotel, which sat like a sentinel on lush green hills framed by china-blue skies. All around were pastel-colored cottages with white roofs. Nana was sitting out on the porch talking to her new best friends. Paradise regained, I thought.

As I stared out at the perfect blue sky, I regretted that Christine wasn't there to share it. I missed her in that short a time. I hugged the kids and we were all smiling at the obvious.

'You miss her,' Jannie whispered. 'That's good, Daddy. That's very nice.'

When Christine still hadn't returned by six, I struggled between waiting for her at the hotel or driving into Hamilton myself. Maybe she'd had an accident. *Those damn mopeds*, I thought, having found them fun and safe just the day before.

I spotted a tall, slender woman entering through the front gates of the Belmont. I sighed in relief, but as I hurried down the front stairs, I saw that it wasn't Christine.

Christine still hadn't returned, or called the hotel, by six-thirty. Or by seven.

I called the police.

CHAPTER 130

Inspector Patrick Busby arrived at seven-thirty. He told me that visitors often lost track of the time and themselves in Bermuda. There were also occasional moped accidents. He promised me that Christine would show up with a mild 'road rash,' or a slightly turned ankle.

I wouldn't have any of it. The inspector and I rode together between the hotel and Hamilton, and then we toured the streets of the capital city. I was silent as I stared out of the car, hoping to get a glimpse of Christine shopping on some side street.

When she still hadn't turned up by nine, Inspector Busby reluctantly agreed that Christine might be missing. He wanted to know if we'd had any kind of argument or disagreement.

'I'm a homicide detective in Washington, D.C.,' I finally told him. I'd been holding it back because I didn't want this to get territorial. 'I've been involved with high-profile cases involving mass murderers.'

'I see,' Busby said. He was a small, neat black man with a pencil mustache. He looked more like a fussy schoolteacher than a cop. 'Are there any other surprises I should know about, detective?'

'No, that's it. But you see why I'm worried.'

'Yes, I see the reason for your concern. I will put out a missing-persons report.'

I sighed heavily, then went up and talked to the kids and Nana. I tried my best not to alarm them, but Damon and Jannie started to cry. And then Nana Mama did, too.

We had learned nothing more about Christine's whereabouts by midnight. Inspector Busby finally left the hotel at quarter past twelve. He was kind enough to give me his home number and asked me to call right away if I heard from Christine.

At three, I was still up and pacing my hotel room. I had just gotten off the phone with Quantico. The FBI was cross-checking my homicide cases to see if anyone had connections with Bermuda, or anywhere in the Caribbean. They probably wouldn't get back to me until later in the morning.

I stood before tall dormer windows and stared out at black shapes against the moonlit sky and remembered how Christine felt in my arms. I felt incredibly helpless and alone.

I hugged myself tightly. The pain was like a solid column that went from my chest all the way up into my head. I could see her face, her beautiful smile. I remembered dancing with her at the Rainbow Room.

Was Christine out there somewhere on the island? She had to be. I prayed that she was safe. I refused to have any other thought.

The telephone in the room rang, a short burst, at a little past four in the morning. My heart was in my throat.

I rushed across the room and grabbed the phone before the second ring. My hand was trembling.

The strange, muffled voice scared me: 'You have an e-mail.' I couldn't think straight. I couldn't think at all. Then I recognized what it was.

I had brought my laptop personal computer, but left it in the closet.

Who knew that I had my computer here? Who knew a small detail like that about me? Who had been watching me? Watching us?

I couldn't breathe. I couldn't stand it. Finally, I yanked open the closet door. I grabbed the computer, hooked it up, and logged on. I scrolled down the e-mail to the last message.

It was short and very concise.

'*She's safe for now. We have her.*'

It was worse than anything I could imagine. Each word was branded into my brain, repeating over and over.

She's safe for now.

We have her.

1ST
TO DIE

My thanks to the following people, whose hard work and expertise helped in the writing of this book:

Dr Greg Zorman, Chief of Neurosurgery, Lakeland Hospital, Fort Lauderdale, Florida, who I'd like on my side in a crisis.

The lovely and talented Fern Galperin, Mary Jordan, Barbara Groszewski and Irene Markocki.

Prologue

Inspector
Lindsay Boxer

Chapter I

It is an unusually warm night in August, but I'm shivering badly as I stand on the substantial gray stone terrace outside my apartment. I'm looking out over glorious San Francisco and I have my service revolver pressed against the side of my temple.

'Goddamn You, God!' I whisper. Quite a sentiment, but appropriate and just, I think to myself.

I hear Sweet Martha whimpering. I turn and see she is watching me through the glass doors that lead to the terrace. She knows something is wrong. 'It's okay,' I call to her through the door. 'Everything's fine. Go lie down, girl.'

Martha won't leave, though, won't look away. She's a kind, loyal friend who's been nuzzling me good night every single night for the past six years. As I stare into the Border Collie's eyes, I think that maybe I should go inside and call the girls. Claire, Cindy, and Jill would be here almost before I hung up the phone. They would hold me, hug me, say all the right things. *You're special,*

Lindsay. Everybody loves you, Lindsay.

Only I'm pretty sure that I'd be back out here tomorrow night, or the night after. I just don't see a way out of this mess. I have thought it all through a hundred times. I can be as logical as hell but I am also highly emotional, obviously. That was my strength as an Inspector with the San Francisco Police Department. It is a rare combination, and I think it is why I was more successful than any of the males in Homicide. Of course, none of them are up here getting ready to blow their brains out with their own guns.

I lightly brush the barrel of the revolver down my cheek and then up to my temple again. Oh God, oh God, oh God. I am reminded of *soft hands*, of Chris, and that starts me crying.

Lots of images are coming way too fast for me to handle.

The terrible, indelible honeymoon murders that have terrified our city, mixed with close-ups of my mom and even a few flashes of my father. My best girls – Claire, Cindy, and Jill – our crazy club. I can even see myself – the way I used to be, anyway. Nobody ever, *ever* thought that I looked like an Inspector, the only woman Homicide Inspector in the entire SFPD. My friends always said I was more like Helen Hunt married to Paul Reiser in *Mad About You*. I was married once. I was no Helen Hunt; he sure was no Paul Reiser.

This is so hard, so bad, so wrong. It's so unlike me. I keep seeing David and Melanie Brandt, the first couple who were killed in the Mandarin Suite of the Grand Hyatt. I see that horrifying hotel room where they died senselessly and needlessly.

That was the beginning.

Book One

David and Melanie

Chapter One

Beautiful long-stemmed red roses filled the hotel suite – the perfect gifts, really. *Everything* was perfect.

There might be a luckier man somewhere on the planet, David Brandt thought, as he wrapped his arms around Melanie, his new bride. Somewhere in Yemen, maybe – some Allah-praising farmer with a second goat. But certainly not in all of San Francisco.

The couple looked out from the living room of the Grand Hyatt's Mandarin Suite. They could see the lights of Berkeley off in the distance, Alcatraz, the graceful outline of the lit-up Golden Gate Bridge.

'It's incredible,' Melanie beamed. 'I wouldn't change a single thing about today.'

'Me neither,' he whispered. 'Well, maybe I wouldn't have invited my parents.' They both laughed.

Only moments before, they had bid farewell to the last of the 300 guests in the hotel's ballroom. The wedding was finally over – the toasts, the dancing, the schmoozing, the photographed kisses over the cake. Now it was just the two of them. Both were twenty-nine years old and had the rest of their lives ahead of them.

David reached for a pair of filled champagne glasses he had set on a lacquered table. 'A toast,' he declared, 'to the second-luckiest man alive.'

'The second?' she said, and smiled in pretended shock. 'Who's the first?'

They looped arms and took a long, luxurious sip from the refreshing crystal. 'This farmer with two goats. I'll tell you later,' he said.

'I have something for you,' David suddenly remembered. He had already given her the perfect five-carat diamond on her finger, which he knew she wore only to please his folks. He went to his tuxedo jacket, which was draped over a high-backed chair in the living room, and returned with a jewelry box from Bulgari.

'No, David,' Melanie protested. '*You're* my gift.'

'Open it, anyway,' he said to her. 'This, you'll like.'

She lifted the lid. Inside a suede pouch was a pair of earrings; large silver rings around a pair of whimsical moons made from diamonds.

'They're how I think of you,' he said.

Melanie held the moons against the lobes of her ears. They were perfect, and so was she.

'It's you who pulls my tides,' David whispered.

They kissed, and he unfastened the zipper of her dress, letting the neckline fall just below her shoulders. He kissed her neck. Then the top of her breasts.

There was a knock on the door of the suite.

'Champagne,' called a voice from outside.

For a moment, David thought of just yelling, 'Leave it there!' All evening, he had longed to peel away the dress from his wife's soft white shoulders.

'Oh, go get it,' Melanie said, dangling the earrings in front of his eyes. 'I'll put these on.'

She wiggled out of his grasp, backing toward the Mandarin's master bathroom, a smile in her liquid brown eyes. *God, he loved those eyes.*

As he went to the door, David was thinking he wouldn't trade places with anybody in the world.

Not even for a second goat.

Chapter Two

Phillip Campbell had imagined this moment, this exquisite scene, so many times. He knew it would be the groom who opened the door. He stepped into the room.

'Congratulations,' Campbell muttered, handing over the champagne. He stared at the man in the open tuxedo shirt and black tie dangling around his neck.

David Brandt barely looked at him as he inspected the brightly ribboned box. Krug. Clos du Mesnil, 1989.

'What is the worst thing anyone has ever done?' Campbell murmured to himself. 'Am I capable of doing it? Do I have what it takes?'

'Any card?' the groom said, fumbling in his pants pocket for a tip.

'Only this, sir.'

Campbell stepped forward and plunged a knife deeply into the groom's chest, between the third and fourth rib, the closest route to the heart.

'For the man who has everything,' Campbell said. He

pushed his way into the room and slammed the door shut with a swift kick. He spun David Brandt around and shoved his back against the door and powered the blade in deeper.

The groom stiffened in a spasm of shock and pain. Guttural sounds escaped from his chest – tiny, gurgling, choking breaths. His eyes bulged in disbelief.

This is amazing, Campbell thought. He could actually feel the groom's strength leaking away. The man had just experienced one of the great moments of his life and now, minutes later, he was dying.

Why?

Campbell stepped back and the groom's body crumpled to the floor. The room tilted like a listing boat. Then everything began to speed up and run together. He felt as if he were watching a flickering newsreel. Awesome. Nothing like he had expected.

Campbell heard the wife's voice and had the presence of mind to pull the blade out of David Brandt's chest.

He rushed to intercept her as she came from the bedroom, still in her long, lacy gown.

'David?' she said, with an expectant smile that turned to shock at the sight of Campbell. 'Where's David? Who are you?'

Her eyes traveled over him, terror-ridden, fixing on his face, the knife blade, then moving to her husband's body on the floor.

'*Oh, my God! David!*' she screamed. '*Oh David, David!*'

Campbell wanted to remember her like this. The frozen,

wide-eyed look. The promise and hope that just moments ago had shined so brightly were now shattered.

The words poured from his mouth. 'You want to know why? Well, *so do I.*'

'What have you done?' Melanie said hoarsely. She struggled to understand. Her terrified eyes darted back and forth, sweeping the room for a way out.

She made a sudden dash for the living-room door. Campbell grabbed her wrist and brought the bloody knife up to her throat.

'Please,' she whimpered, her eyes frozen. 'Please don't kill me.'

'The truth is, Melanie, I'm here to save you.' He smiled into her quivering face as he stepped close.

Campbell lowered the blade and sliced into her. The slender body jolted up with a sudden cry. Her eyes flickered like a weak electric bulb. A deathly rattle shot through her. 'Why?' her begging eyes pleaded. 'Why?'

It took a full minute for him to regain his breath. The smell of Melanie Brandt's blood was deep in his nostrils. He almost couldn't believe what he had done.

Why?

He carried the bride's body back into the bedroom and placed her on the bed. She was beautiful, with delicate features. And so young. He remembered when he had first seen her and how he had been taken with her then. She had thought the whole world was in front of her.

He rubbed his hand against the smooth surface of her cheek and cupped one of her earrings – a smiling moon.

'What is the worst thing anyone has ever done?' Phillip Campbell asked himself again, heart pounding in his chest.

Was this it? Had he just done it?

'Not yet,' a voice inside answered. 'Not quite yet.'

Slowly, he lifted the bride's beautiful white wedding dress.

Chapter Three

It was a little before eight-thirty on a Monday morning in June, one of those chilly, gray summer mornings for which San Francisco is famous. I was starting the week off badly, flipping through old copies of the *New Yorker* while waiting for my GP, Dr Roy Orenthaler, to free up.

I'd been seeing Dr Roy, as I still sometimes called him, ever since I was a sociology major at San Francisco State University, and I obligingly came in once a year for my check-up. That was last Tuesday. To my surprise, he called at the end of the week and asked me to stop in today before work.

I had a busy day ahead of me: two open cases and a deposition to deliver at district court. I was hoping I could be at my desk by nine.

'Ms Boxer,' the receptionist finally called to me, 'the doctor will see you now.'

I followed her into his office.

Generally, Orenthaler greeted me with some

well-intended stab at police humor, such as, 'So if you're here, who's out on the street after *them*?' I was now thirty-four, and for the past two years, lead Inspector on the Homicide detail out of the Hall of Justice.

But today, he rose stiffly and uttered a solemn, '*Good morning.*' He motioned me to the chair across from his desk. Uh-oh.

Up until then, my philosophy on doctors was simple. When one of them gave you that deep, concerned look and told you to take a seat, three things could happen. Only one of them was bad. They were either asking you out, getting ready to lay on some bad news, or they'd just spent a fortune re-upholstering the furniture.

'I want to show you something,' Orenthaler began. He held an X-ray up against a light, pointed to splotches of tiny ghostlike spheres in a current of smaller pellets. 'This is a blow-up of the blood smear we took from you. The larger globules are erythrocytes. Red blood cells.'

'They seem happy,' I joked, nervously.

'Those are, Lindsay,' the doctor said, without a trace of a smile. 'Problem is, you don't have many.'

I fixed on his eyes, hoping they would relax, and that we'd move on to something trivial like, 'You better start cutting down those long hours.'

'There's a condition,' Orenthaler went on, 'called Negli's aplastic anemia. It's rare. Basically, the body no longer manufactures red blood cells.' He held up an X-ray photo. 'This is what a normal blood work-up looks like.'

On this one, the dark background looked like the intersection of Market and Powell at 5:00 p.m. – a virtual traffic jam of compressed, energetic spheres. Speedy messengers all carrying oxygen to parts of someone else's body. In contrast, mine looked about as densely packed as a political headquarters two hours after the candidate had conceded.

'This is treatable, right?' I asked him. More like, I was telling him.

'It's treatable,' Orenthaler said, after a pause. 'But it's serious.'

A week ago, I had come in simply because my eyes were runny and blotchy and I'd discovered some blood in my panties; and every day, by three, I was suddenly feeling like some iron-deficient gnome was inside me siphoning off my energy. Me, of the regular double shifts and fourteen-hour days. Six weeks accrued vacation.

'How serious are we talking about?' I asked, my voice catching.

'Red blood cells are vital to the body's process of oxygenation,' Orenthaler began to explain. 'Hemopoiesis, the formation of blood cells in the bone marrow.'

'Dr Roy, this isn't a medical conference. Please tell me how serious it is.'

'What is it you want to hear? Diagnosis or possibility?'

'I want to hear the truth.'

Orenthaler nodded. He got up and came around the desk and took my hand. 'Then here's the truth, my dear. What you have is life-threatening.'

'Life-threatening?' My heart stopped. My throat was as dry as parchment.

'Fatal, Lindsay.'

Chapter Four

The cold, blunt sound of the word hit me like a hollow-point shell between the eyes.

Fatal.

I waited for Dr Roy to tell me this was all some kind of sick joke. That he had my X-ray mixed up with someone else's.

'But, I want to send you to a hematologist,' he went on. 'Like a lot of diseases, there are stages. Stage One is when there's a mild depletion of cells. It can be treated with monthly transfusions. Stage Two is when there's a systematic shortage of red cells. Stage Three would require hospitalization – a bone-marrow transplant. Potentially, the removal of your spleen.'

'So where am *I*?' I asked, sucking in a cramped lungful of air.

'Your erythrocytic count is barely two hundred per cc of raw blood. That puts you on the cusp.'

'The cusp?'

'The cusp,' the doctor said, 'between Stages Two and Three.'

There comes a point in everybody's life when you realize the stakes have suddenly changed. The carefree ride of your life slams into a stone wall; all those years of merely bouncing along, life taking you where you want to go, abruptly ends. In my job, I see this moment forced on people all the time.

Welcome to mine.

'So what does this mean?' I asked weakly. The room was spinning a little now.

'What it means, my dear, is that you're going to have to undergo a prolonged regimen of intensive treatment.'

I shook my head. 'What does it mean for my job?'

I'd been in Homicide for six years now, the past two as lead Homicide Inspector. With any luck, when my Lieutenant was up for promotion, I'd be in line for his job. The Department needed strong women. They could go far. Until that moment, I had thought that I would go far.

'Right now,' the doctor said, 'I don't think it means anything. As long as you feel strong while you're undergoing treatment, you can continue work. In fact, it might even be good therapy.'

Suddenly, I was suffocating.

'I want to give you the name of a hematologist, Dr Victor Medved,' Orenthaler said.

He went on about the doctor's credentials, but I was no longer hearing him. I was thinking, Who am I going to tell? Mom had died ten years before, from breast cancer. Dad had been out of the picture since I was thirteen. I had a sister, Cat, but she was living a nice, neat life down in

Newport Beach; and for her, just making a right turn on red brought on a moment of crisis.

The doctor pushed the referral toward me. 'I know you, Lindsay. You'll pretend this is something you can fix by working harder – but you can't. This is deadly serious. I want you to call him *today*.'

Suddenly my beeper sounded. I fumbled for it in my bag and looked at the number. It was the office – Jacobi.

'I need a phone,' I said.

Orenthaler shot me a reproving look.

'Like you said . . .' I forced a nervous smile. 'Therapy.'

He nodded to the phone on his desk and left the room. I went through the motions of dialing my partner.

'Fun's over, Boxer,' Jacobi's gruff voice came on the line. 'We got a double one-eight-oh. The Grand Hyatt.'

My head was spinning with what the doctor had told me. In a fog, I must not have responded.

'You hear me, Boxer?' Jacobi asked. 'Worktime. You on the way?'

'Yeah,' I finally said.

'And wear something nice,' my partner grunted. 'Like you would to a wedding.'

Chapter Five

How I got from Dr Orenthaler's office, out in Noe Valley, all the way to the Hyatt in Union Square, I don't remember. I kept hearing the doctor's words sounding over and over in my head. *'In severe cases, Negli's can be fatal.'*

All I know is that barely twelve minutes after Jacobi's call, my ten-year-old Bronco screeched to a halt in front of the hotel's atrium entrance.

The street was ablaze with police activity. Jesus, what the hell had happened? The entire block between Sutter and Union Square had been cordoned off by a barricade of black-and-whites. In the entrance, a cluster of uniforms checked people going in and out, waving the crowd of onlookers away.

I badged my way into the lobby. Two uniformed cops whom I recognized were standing in front: Murray, a potbellied cop in the last year of his hitch, and his younger partner, Vasquez. I asked Murray to bring me up to speed.

'What I been told is that there's two VIPs murdered on the thirtieth floor. All the brainpower's up there now.'

'Who's presiding?' I asked, feeling my energies returning.

'Right now, I guess you are, Inspector.'

'In that case, I want all exits to the hotel immediately shut down. And get a list from the manager of all guests and staff. No one goes in or out unless they're on that list.'

Seconds later, I was riding up to the thirtieth floor.

The trail of cops and official personnel led me down the hall to a set of open double doors marked *Mandarin Suite*. There I ran into Charlie Clapper, the Crime Scene Unit crew chief, lugging in his heavy cases with two techs. Clapper being here himself meant this *was* big.

Through the open double doors, I saw roses first – they were everywhere. Then I spotted Jacobi.

'Watch your heels, Inspector,' he called loudly across the room.

My partner was forty-seven, but looked ten years older. His hair was white and he was beginning to go bald. His face always seemed on the verge of a smirk over some tasteless wisecrack. He and I had worked together for two and a half years. I was senior, Inspector/Sergeant, though he had seven years on me in the Department. He reported to me.

Stepping inside, I almost tripped across the legs of Body Number One, the groom. He was lying just inside the door, crumpled up in a heap, wearing an open tuxedo shirt. Blood matted the hair on his chest. I took a deep breath.

'May I present Mr David Brandt,' Jacobi intoned, with a crooked smile. 'Mrs David Brandt's in there.' He gestured toward the bedroom. 'Guess things went downhill for them quicker than most.'

I knelt down and took a long, hard look at the dead groom. He was handsome, with short, dark, tousled hair and a soft jaw, but the wide, apoplectic eyes locked open and the rivulet of dried blood on his chin marred the features. Behind him, his tuxedo jacket lay on the floor.

'Who found them?' I asked, checking his pocket for a wallet.

'Assistant manager. They were supposed to fly to Bali this morning. The island, not the casino, Boxer. For these two, assistant managers do wake-up calls.'

I opened the wallet: a New York driver's license with the groom's smiling face. Platinum cards, several hundred-dollar bills.

I got up and looked around the suite. It opened up into a stylishly decorated museum of Oriental art: celadon dragons, chairs and couches pictured with Imperial court scenes. The roses, of course. I was more the cozy bed-and-breakfast type, but if you were into making a statement, this was about as substantial a statement as you could make.

'Let's meet the bride,' Jacobi said.

I followed through a set of open double doors into the master bedroom and stopped. The bride lay on her back on a large canopy bed.

I'd been to a hundred homicides and could radar in on

the body as quick as anyone, but this I wasn't prepared for. It sent a wave of compassion racing down my spine.

The bride was still in her wedding dress.

Chapter Six

You never see so many murder victims that it stops making you hurt, but this one was especially hard to look at.

She was so young and beautiful: calm, tranquil, and undisturbed, except for the three crimson flowers of blood spread on her white chest. She looked as if she was a sleeping princess awaiting her prince, but her prince was in the other room, his guts spilled over the floor.

'Whad'ya want for thirty-five hundred bucks a night?' Jacobi shrugged. 'The whole fairy tale?'

It was taking everything I had just to keep my grip on what I had to do. I glared, as if a single, venomous look could shut Jacobi down.

'Jeez, Boxer, what's goin' on?' His face sagged. 'It was just a joke.'

Whatever it was, his childlike, remorseful expression brought me back. The bride was wearing a large diamond on her right hand and fancy earrings on her ears. Whatever the killer's motive, it wasn't robbery.

A tech from the ME's office was about to begin his initial examination. 'Looks like three stab wounds,' he said. 'She must've showed a lot of heart. He got the groom with one.'

What flashed through my mind was that fully 90 per cent of all homicides were about money or sex. This one didn't seem to be about money.

'When's the last time anyone saw them?' I asked.

'A little after ten last night. That's when the humongous reception ended downstairs.'

'And not after that?'

'I know this isn't exactly your terrain, Boxer,' Jacobi said. He broke into a grin. 'But generally people don't see the bride and groom for a while after the party.'

I smiled thinly, stood up, looked back across the large, lavish suite. 'So surprise me, Jacobi. Who springs for a room like this?'

'The groom's father is some Wall Street big shot from back East. He and his wife are down in a room on the twelfth floor. I was told it was quite a shindig downstairs. Up here, too. Look at all these goddamn roses.'

I went back over to the groom, and spotted what looked like a gift box of champagne on a marble console near the door. There was a spray of blood all over it.

'Assistant manager noticed it,' Jacobi said. 'My guess is, whoever did this brought it in with him.'

'They see anyone around?'

'Yeah, a lot of people in tuxes. It was a wedding, right?'

I read the champagne bottle label. 'Krug. Clos du Mesnil, 1989.'

'That tell you something?' Jacobi asked.

'Only that the killer has good taste.'

I looked at the blood-smeared tuxedo jacket. There was a single slash mark on the side where the fatal knife wound had gone through.

'I figure the killer must've stripped it off after he stabbed him,' Jacobi shrugged.

'Why the hell would he do that?' I muttered out loud.

'Dunno. We'll have to ask him.'

Charlie Clapper was eyeing me to see if it was okay to get started. I nodded him in. Then I went back over to the bride. I had a bad, bad feeling about this one. If it's not about money, then it must be to do with sex.

I lifted the fancy tulle lining of her skirt. The coldest, bitterest confirmation sliced through me.

The bride's panties had been pulled down and were dangling off one foot.

A fierce anger rose in my chest. I looked into the young woman's eyes. Everything had been ahead of her, every hope and dream. Now she was a slaughtered corpse, defiled, possibly raped on her wedding night.

As I stood there, blinking, I suddenly realized that I was crying.

'Warren, I want you to speak with the groom's parents,' I said. 'I want everyone who was on this floor last night interviewed. If they've checked out, I want them traced. And a list of all hotel staff on duty last night.'

I knew if I didn't get out now, I couldn't hold back the tide any longer. 'Now, Warren. Please . . . now.'

I avoided his eyes as I skirted past him out of the suite.

'What the hell's wrong with Boxer?' Charlie Clapper asked.

'You know women,' I heard Jacobi reply. 'They always cry at weddings.'

Chapter Seven

Phillip Campbell was walking along Powell Street toward Union Square and the Hyatt. The police had actually blockaded the street and the crowd outside the hotel was growing quickly. The howling screams of police and emergency vehicles filled the air. This was so unlike civilized and respectable San Francisco. He loved it!

Campbell almost couldn't believe he was headed back to the crime scene. He just couldn't help himself. Being here again helped him to relive the night before. As he walked closer and closer on Powell, his adrenaline surged, his heart pounded, almost out of control.

He edged through the mob that populated the final block outside the Hyatt. He heard the rumors swirling through the crowd, mostly well-dressed business people, their faces creased with anguish and pain. There were rumors of a fire at the hotel, a jumper, a homicide, a suicide, but nothing came close to the horror of the actual event.

Finally, he got close enough so that he could watch the San Francisco police at work. A couple of them were surveying the crowd, *looking for him*. He wasn't worried about being discovered, not at all. It just wasn't going to happen. He was too unlikely, probably in the bottom 5 per cent of the people the police might suspect. That comforted him, thrilled him actually.

God, he had done it – caused all of this to happen, and he was only just beginning. He had never experienced anything like this feeling, and neither had the city of San Francisco.

A businessman was coming out of the Hyatt and reporters and other people were asking him questions as if he were a major celebrity. The man was in his early thirties and he smirked knowingly. He had what they all wanted, and he knew it. He was lording it over everyone, enjoying his pitiful moment of fame.

'It was a couple – murdered in the penthouse,' he could overhear the man saying. 'They were on their honeymoon. Sad, huh?'

The crowd around Phillip Campbell gasped, and his heart soared.

Chapter Eight

What a scene! Cindy Thomas pushed her way through the murmuring crowd, the looky-loos surrounding the Grand Hyatt. Then she groaned at the sight of the line of cops blocking the way.

There must've been a hundred onlookers tightly pressed around the entrance: tourists carrying cameras, businesspeople on their way to work; others were flashing press credentials and shouting, trying to talk their way in. Across the street, a television news van was already setting up with the backdrop of the hotel's façade.

After two years spent covering local interest on the Metro desk of the *Chronicle*, Cindy could feel a story that might jump-start her career. This one made the hairs on her neck stand up.

'Homicide down at the Grand Hyatt,' her city editor, Sid Glass, informed her, after a staffer picked up the police transmission. Suzie Fitzpatrick and Tom Stone, the *Chronicle*'s usual crime reporters, were both on assignment. 'Get right down there,' her boss barked, to her amazement. He didn't have to say it twice.

But now, outside the Hyatt, Cindy felt her brief run of luck had come to an end.

The street was barricaded. More news crews were pulling up by the second. If she didn't come up with something now, Fitzpatrick or Stone would soon be handed the story. What she needed was inside. And here she was, out on the curb.

She spotted a line of limos and went up to the first one – a big beige stretch. She rapped on the window. The driver looked up over his paper, the *Chronicle* of course, and lowered the window as she caught his eye.

'You waiting for Steadman?' Cindy asked.

'Uh-uh,' the driver replied. 'Eddleson.'

'Sorry, sorry,' she waved. But inside she was beaming. *This was her way in.*

She lingered in the crowd a few seconds longer, then elbowed her way to the front. A young patrolman blocked her path. 'Excuse me,' said Cindy, looking harried. 'I've got a meeting in the hotel.'

'Name?'

'Eddleson. He's expecting me.'

The entrance cop paged through a computer printout fastened to a clipboard. 'You have a room number?'

Cindy shook her head. 'He said to meet him in the Grill Room at eleven.' The Grill Room at the Hyatt was the scene of some of San Francisco's best power breakfasts.

The entrance cop gave her a careful once-over. In her black leather jacket, jeans, sandals from Earthsake, Cindy figured she didn't look the part of someone arriving for a power brunch.

'My meeting,' said Cindy, tapping her watch. 'Eddleson.'

Distractedly, the cop waved her through.

She was inside. The high glass atrium rose around her, gold columns reaching to the third floor. It gave her a giggle, all that high-priced talent and recognizable faces still outside on the street.

And Cindy Thomas was first in. Now she only had to figure out what to do.

The place was definitely buzzing: cops, businessmen checking out, tour groups, crimson-suited hotel staff. The chief said it was a homicide. A daring one, given the hotel's prominent reputation. But she didn't know which floor, or when it took place. She didn't even know if it involved a guest.

She may be inside, but she didn't know shit.

Cindy spotted a cluster of suitcases unattended on the far side of the lobby. They looked like they were part of some large tour. A bellhop was dragging them outside. She wandered over and knelt by one of the bags, as if she were taking something out.

A second bellhop passed by. 'Need a taxi?'

Cindy shook her head no. 'Someone's picking me up.' Then, sweeping a view of the chaos, she rolled her eyes. 'I just woke up. What did I miss?'

'You haven't heard? You must be the only one. We had some fireworks in the hotel last night.'

Cindy widened her eyes.

'Two murders. On thirty.' He lowered his voice as if he were letting her in on the secret of her life. 'You happen to run into that big wedding last night? It was the bride and groom. Someone broke in on them in the Mandarin Suite.'

'Jesus!' Cindy pulled back.

'Sure you don't need these brought out to the front?' the bellhop checked.

Cindy forced a smile. 'Thanks. I'll wait in here.'

On the far side of the lobby, she noticed another elevator opening. A bellhop came out, wheeling a cart of luggage. It must be a service elevator. From what she could see, the cops hadn't blocked it off.

She wound through the lobby traffic toward the elevator, punched the button and the shiny gold doors opened. Thank God, it was empty. Just as quickly, Cindy jumped in and the door closed. She couldn't believe it. She couldn't believe what she was doing. She pressed 30.

The Mandarin Suite.

A double homicide.

Her story.

Chapter Nine

As the elevator came to a stop, Cindy held her breath. Her heart was pumping like a turbine. She was on 30. She was in. She was really doing this.

The doors had opened to a remote corner of the floor. She thanked God there wasn't a cop waiting in front of them. A buzz of activity was coming from the other side of the hall. All she had to do was follow the noise.

As she hurried down the hallway, the voices grew louder. Two men in yellow jackets bearing CSU in large black letters walked past her. At the end of a corridor, a group of cops and investigators stood in front of an open double doorway marked *Mandarin Suite*.

She wasn't only inside; she was right in the fucking middle of it.

Squaring her shoulders resolutely, Cindy made her way toward the double doors. The cops weren't even looking in her direction; they were letting in police staff who had come from the main elevators.

She had made it all the way. The Mandarin Suite. She

could see inside. It was huge, opulent. Roses were every-where. Then her heart stopped. She thought she might be sick.

The groom, in a bloodstained tuxedo shirt, lay unmoving on the floor.

Cindy's legs buckled. She had never seen a murder victim before. She wanted to lean forward, to let her eyes memorize every detail, but her body wouldn't move.

'Who the hell are you?' a brusque voice suddenly demanded. A large, angry cop was staring directly at her face.

All of a sudden, she was grabbed and pushed hard against the wall. It hurt. In a panic, Cindy nervously pointed to her bag and her wallet, where a pictured Press credential was displayed.

The angry cop began leafing through her IDs and credit cards as if they were junk mail.

'Jesus,' the thick-necked patrolman scowled with a face like a slobbering Doberman. 'She's a reporter.'

'How in hell did you get up here?' his partner came over and demanded.

'Get her the hell out,' Doberman barked to him. 'And keep the ID. She won't get within a mile of a police briefing for the next twelve months.'

As his partner dragged her by the arm to the main elevator bank, over her shoulder Cindy got a final glimpse of the dead man's legs splayed near the door. It was awful – terrifying, and sad. She was shaking.

'Show this *reporter* the front door,' the officer instructed a third cop manning the elevator. He flicked her Press ID as if it were a playing card. 'Hope losing this was worth the ride up.'

As the doors closed, a voice yelled, '*Hold it!*'

A tall woman in a powder-blue T-shirt and brocade vest with a badge fastened to her waist stepped in. She was nice-looking, with sandy-blonde hair, but she was clearly upset. She let out a deep sigh as the doors closed.

'Rough in there, Inspector?' the cop accompanying Cindy inquired.

'Yeah,' the woman said simply, not even turning her head.

The word 'Inspector' went off like a flash in Cindy's mind. She couldn't believe it. The scene must be beyond awful for an Inspector to be that upset. As the elevator descended, she rode the entire thirty floors just blinking her eyes and looking straight ahead.

When the doors opened to the lobby, the woman in the blue T-shirt rushed off.

'You see the front door?' the cop said to Cindy. 'Go through it. Don't come back.'

As soon as the elevator doors had closed, she spun around and scanned the vast lobby for sight of the Inspector. She caught a flash of her going into the ladies' room.

Cindy hurriedly followed her in. The place was empty – there were just the two of them in there.

The detective stood in front of a mirror. She looked close to six foot tall, slender, and impressive. To Cindy's amazement, it was clear she had been crying. Jesus, Jesus. She was back on the inside again. What had the Inspector seen to get her so upset?

'You okay?' Cindy finally inquired, in a soft voice.

The woman tensed up when she realized she wasn't alone. But she had this look on her face, as if she were on the verge of letting it all out. 'You're that reporter, aren't you? You're the one who got upstairs.'

Cindy let out a breath and nodded.

'So how did you make it all the way up there?'

'I don't know. Luck, maybe.'

The detective pulled out a tissue and dabbed at her eyes. 'Well, I'm afraid your luck's over, if you're looking for something from me.'

'I didn't mean that,' Cindy said. 'You sure you're all right?'

The cop turned around. Her eyes shouted, *'I've got nothing to say to you!'* but they lied. It was as if she needed to do exactly that, talk to someone, more than anything in the world.

It was one of those strange moments when Cindy knew there was something under the surface. If the roles just shifted, and she had the chance, the two of them might even become friends.

Cindy reached into her pocket, pulled out a card, and placed it on the sink counter in front of the detective. 'If ever you want to talk . . .'

The color came back into the Inspector's pretty face. She hesitated, then gave Cindy the faintest glimmer of a smile.

Cindy smiled in return. 'As long as I'm here . . .' She went up to the sink and took out her makeup kit, catching the policewoman's eye in the mirror.

'Nice vest,' she said.

Chapter Ten

I work out of the Hall of Justice. The Hall, as we referred to the gray, ten-story granite slab that housed the city's Department of Justice, was located just west of the freeway on Sixth and Bryant. If the building itself, and its faded antiseptic halls, didn't communicate that law enforcement lacked a total sense of style, the surrounding neighborhood surely did. It consisted of handpainted bailbondsman shacks, autoparts stores, parking lots, and dingy cafés.

Whatever ailed you, you could find at the Hall: Auto Theft, Sex Crimes, Robbery. The District Attorney was on eight, with cubicles filled with bright young prosecutors. A floor of holding cells on ten. One-stop shopping, arrest to arraignment. Next door, we even had the morgue.

After a hasty, bare-bones news conference, Jacobi and I agreed to meet upstairs and go over what we had so far.

The twelve of us who covered Homicide for the entire city shared a twenty-by-thirty squad room lit by the glare of harsh fluorescent lights. My desk was choice – by the window, overlooking the entrance ramp to the freeway. It was always crammed with folders, stacks of photos, Department releases. The one really personal item on it was a Plexiglas cube my first partner had given me. It was inscribed with the words *You can't tell which way the train went by looking at the tracks.*

I made myself a cup of tea and met Jacobi in Interrogation Room One. I drew two columns on a freestanding chalkboard: one for what we knew, one for what we had to check out.

Jacobi's initial talk with the groom's parents had produced nothing. The father was a big-time Wall Street guy who ran a firm that handled international buyouts. He said that he and his wife had stayed until the last guest had left, and 'walked the kids upstairs'. They didn't have an enemy in the world. No debts, addictions, threats. Nothing to provoke such a horrible, unthinkable act.

A canvass of guests on the thirtieth floor was slightly more successful. A couple from Chicago noticed a man lingering in the hallway near the Mandarin Suite last night around ten-thirty. They described him as medium build, with short dark hair and said he wore a dark suit or maybe a tuxedo. He was carrying what may have been a box of liquor in his hands.

Later, two used tea bags and two empty push-through Pepcids on the table were the clearest signs that we'd been bouncing these questions back and forth for several hours. It was quarter past seven. Our shift had ended at five.

'No date tonight, Lindsay?' Jacobi finally asked.

'I get all the dates I want, Warren.'

'Right, like I said – no date tonight.'

Without knocking, our Lieutenant, Sam Roth, whom we called 'Cheery', stuck his head into the room. He tossed a copy of the afternoon *Chronicle* across the table. 'You see this?'

The boldface headline announced: WEDDING NIGHT MASSACRE AT HYATT. I read aloud from the front page: ' "Under a stunning view of the Bay, in a world only the rich would know, the body of the twenty-nine-year-old groom lay curled up near the door." '

He knotted his brow. 'What did we invite this reporter in for – a house tour of the crime scene? She knows the names, maps out the scene.'

The byline read *Cindy Thomas*. I thought of the card in my purse. *Cindy Goddamn Thomas*. 'Maybe I should call her up and ask *her* if we got any leads,' Roth went on sarcastically.

'You want to come on in?' I asked. 'Look at the board. We could use the help.'

Roth just stood there, chewing on his puffy lower lip. He was about to close the door behind him, but he turned back. 'Lindsay, be in my office at a quarter of nine tomorrow. We need to lay this thing out carefully. For now, it's yours.' Then he shut the door.

I sat back on the table. A heavy weight seemed to be pressing me into the floor. The whole day had passed. I hadn't found a single moment to deal with my own news.

'You okay?' Jacobi asked.

I looked at him, on the verge of letting it all out, or maybe crying again.

'That was a tough crime scene,' he said, at the door. 'You should go home, take a bath or something.'

I smiled at him, grateful for a sudden, out-of-character sensitivity.

After he left, I faced the blank columns of the board. I felt so weak and empty I could barely push myself up. Slowly, the events of the day, my visit to Orenthaler, wove their way back into my mind. My head spun with his warning: 'Fatal, Lindsay.'

Then I was hit with the crushing realization. It was going on eight o'clock, and I had never called Orenthaler's specialist.

Chapter Eleven

That night when I got home, I did sort of take Jacobi's advice.

First, I walked my dog, Sweet Martha. Two of my neighbors take care of Martha during the day, but she's always ready for our nightly romp. After the walk, I kicked off my Aerosole pumps, tossed my gun and clothes on the bed, and took a long, hot shower, bringing in a Killian's with me.

The image of David and Melanie Brandt washed away for the night; they could sleep. But there was still Orenthaler, and Negli's. And the call to the specialist I had dreaded the whole day, and never made.

No matter how many times I lifted my face into the hot spray, I could not rinse the long day away. My life had changed. I was no longer just fighting murderers on the street. I was fighting for my life.

When I got out, I ran a brush through my hair and looked at myself for a long time in the mirror. A thought came into my mind that rarely occurred to me: I was pretty. Not a beauty, but cute. Tall, almost five-ten; decent shape for somebody who occasionally binges on beer and butterscotch praline ice cream. I had these animated, bright brown eyes. I didn't back down.

How could it be that I was going to die?

Tonight, my eyes were different, though. Scared. Everything seemed different. 'Surf the waves,' I heard a voice inside me. 'Stand tall. You always stand tall.'

As much as I tried to press it back, the question formed. *Why me?*

I threw on a pair of sweats, tied up my hair in a short ponytail and went into the kitchen to boil water for pasta and heat up a sauce I had placed in the fridge a couple of nights before. While it simmered I put on a CD, Sarah McLachlan, and sat at the kitchen counter with a glass of day-old Bianco red. I petted Sweet Martha as the music played.

Ever since my divorce became final two years ago, I've lived alone. *I hate living alone.* I love people, friends. I used to love my husband Tom more than life itself – until he left me, saying, 'Lindsay, I can't explain it. I love you, but I have to leave. I need to find somebody else. There's nothing else to say.'

I guess he was being truthful, but it was the dumbest, saddest thing I've ever heard. Broke my heart into a million pieces. It's still broken. So even though I hate living alone – except for Sweet Martha, of course – I'm afraid to be with somebody again. What if they suddenly stop loving me? I couldn't take it. So I turn down, or shoot down, just about every man who comes anywhere near me.

But God, I hate being alone.

Especially this night.

My mother had died from breast cancer when I was just out of college. I had transferred back to the city school from Berkeley to assist her, and help take care of my younger sister, Cat. Like most things in her life, even Dad walking out, Mom dealt with her illness only when it was too late to do anything about it.

I had seen my father only twice since I was thirteen. He wore a uniform for twenty years in Central. Was known as a pretty good cop. He used to go down to this bar, the Alibi, and stay for the Giants game after his shift. Sometimes he took me, 'his little mascot', for the boys to admire.

When the sauce was ready I poured it over fusilli and dragged the plate and a salad out to my terrace. Martha tagged along. She's been my shadow since I adopted her from the Border Collie Rescue Society. I live on Potrero Hill, in a renovated blue Michaelian townhouse with a view of the Bay. Not the fancy view like the one from the Mandarin Suite.

I propped my feet up on a neighboring chair and balanced the plate on my lap. Across the Bay, the lights of Oakland glimmered like a thousand unsympathetic eyes.

I looked out at the galaxy of flashing lights, felt my

eyes well up, and for the second time today, realized that I was crying. Martha nuzzled me gently, then she finished the fusilli for me.

Chapter Twelve

Quarter to nine the next morning, I was rapping at the fogged window of Lieutenant Roth's office at the Hall. Roth is fond of me – I'm like another daughter, he says. He has no idea how condescending he can be. I'm tempted to tell Roth that I'm fond of him, too – *like a grandfather*.

I was expecting a crowd – at least a couple of suits from Internal Affairs, or maybe Captain Welting, who oversaw the Bureau of Inspectors – but, as he motioned me in, there was only one other person in the room.

The stranger was a nice-looking type dressed in a chambray shirt and striped tie, with short, dark hair and strong shoulders. He had a handsome, intelligent face that seemed to come to life as I walked in, but it only meant one thing to me:

Polished brass. Someone from the Department's press corps, or City Hall.

I had the uneasy feeling they'd been talking about me.

On the way over, I had rehearsed a convincing rebuttal

about the breach in press security – how I'd arrived late on the scene myself, and the real issue was the crime. But Roth surprised me. ' "Wedding Bell Blues", they're calling it,' he said, tossing the morning's *Chronicle* in my face.

'I saw it,' I replied, relieved to focus back on the case.

He looked at Mr City Hall. 'We'll be reading about this one every step of the way. Both kids were rich, Ivy League, popular. Sort of like young Kennedy and that blonde wife of his – their tragedy.'

'Who they were doesn't matter to me,' I answered back. 'Listen, Sam, about yesterday . . .'

He stopped me with his hand. 'Forget about yesterday. Chief Mercer's already been on the line with me. This case has his full attention.' He glanced at the smartly dressed political type in the corner. 'Anyway, he wants there to be close reins on this case. What happened on other high-profile investigations can't happen here.' Then he said to me, 'We're changing the rules on this one.'

Suddenly, the air in the room got thick with the uneasy feel of a set-up.

Then Mr City Hall stepped forward. I noticed his eyes bore the experienced lines of someone who had put in his time. 'The Mayor and Chief Mercer thought we might handle this investigation as an interdepartmental alliance. That is, if you were up to working with someone new,' he said.

'New?' My eyes bounced back and forth between the two, ultimately settling on Roth.

'Meet your new partner,' Roth announced.

'I'm getting royally screwed,' the voice inside me declared. 'They wouldn't do this to a man.'

'Chris Raleigh,' Mr City Hall Hotshot said, extending his hand.

I didn't reach out to take it.

'For the past few years,' Roth went on, 'Inspector Raleigh has worked as a Community Action liaison with the Mayor's office. He specializes in managing potentially sensitive cases.'

'Managing?'

Raleigh rolled his eyes at me. He was trying to be self-effacing. 'Containing . . . controlling the damage . . . healing any wounds in the community afterwards.'

'Oh,' I shot back, 'I see. You're a marketing man.'

He smiled. Every part of him oozed a practiced, confident air I associated with the types who sat around large tables at City Hall.

'Before that,' Roth went on, 'Chris was a District Captain over in Northern.'

'That's Embassy Row,' I sniffed. Everybody joked about the blue-blooded Northern district that ranged from Nob Hill to Pacific Heights. Hot crimes there were society women who heard noises outside their townhouses and late-arriving tourists locked out of their bed and breakfasts.

'We also handled traffic around the Presidio,' Raleigh countered with another smile.

I ignored him. I turned to Roth. 'What about Warren?' He and I had shared every case for the past two years.

'Jacobi'll be reassigned. I've got a plum job for him, and his big mouth.'

I didn't like leaving my partner behind, dumb-ass wise-cracks and all. But Jacobi was his own worst enemy.

To my surprise, Raleigh asked, 'You okay with this, Inspector?'

I didn't really have a choice. I nodded yes. 'If you don't get in the way. Besides, you wear nicer ties than Jacobi.'

'Father's Day present,' he beamed. I couldn't believe I felt a tremor of disappointment shooting through me. Jesus, Lindsay. I didn't see a ring. *Lindsay!*

'I'm taking you off all other assignments,' Roth announced. 'No conflicting obligations. Jacobi can handle the back-end, if he wants to stay on the case.'

'So who's in charge?' I asked Cheery. I was senior partner to Jacobi; I was used to running my own cases.

Cheery chortled, 'He works with the Mayor. He's an ex-District Captain. Who do you think's in charge?'

'How about – in the field, you lead?' Raleigh suggested. 'What we do with what we find is mine.'

I hesitated, giving him an evaluating stare. God, he was so smooth.

Roth looked at me. 'You want me to ask Jacobi if he's got similar reservations?'

Raleigh met my eyes. 'Look, I'll let you know when we can't work it out.'

It was as good a negotiation as I was going to get. The deal had changed. But at least I kept my case. 'So what do I call you? Captain?'

With a casual ease, Raleigh wrapped a light brown sports coat over his shoulder and reached for the door. 'Try my name. I've been a civilian now for five years.'

'Okay, Raleigh,' I said, with a faint smile. 'You ever get to see a dead body while you were in Northern?'

Chapter Thirteen

The joke in Homicide about the morgue was that in spite of the lousy climate, the place was good for business. There's nothing like the sharp smell of formaldehyde or the depressing sheen of hospital-tiled halls to make the drudgery of chasing down dead leads seem like inspired work.

But as they say, that's where the bodies are.

That, and I got to see my buddy, Claire.

There wasn't much to say about Claire Washburn, except that she was brilliant, totally accomplished, and absolutely my best friend in the world. For six years, she had been the city's Chief Medical Examiner, which everyone in Homicide knew was as under-deserving a title as there was, since she virtually ran the office for Anthony Righetti. Righetti is her overbearing, power-thumping, credit-stealing boss, but Claire rarely complains.

In our book, Claire is the Office of the Coroner. Maybe the idea of a female ME still didn't cut it, even in San Francisco.

Female, and black.

When Raleigh and I arrived, we were ushered into Claire's office. She was wearing her white doctor's coat with the nickname *Butterfly* embroidered on the upper-left pocket.

The first thing you noticed about Claire was that she was carrying fifty pounds she didn't need, and had, since the day I met her. 'I'm in shape,' she always laughed. 'Round's a shape.'

The second was her bright, confident demeanor. You knew she couldn't give a damn. She had the body of a Brahman, the mind of a hawk, *and* the gentle soul of a butterfly.

As we walked in, she gave me a weary but satisfied smile, as if she'd been up working most of the night. I introduced Raleigh, and Claire flashed me an impressed wag of the eyes.

Whatever I had accumulated over the years in street smarts, she threw off in natural wisdom. How she balanced the demands of her job, and placating her credit-seeking boss, with raising two teenage kids was a marvel. And her marriage to Edmund, who played bass drum for the San Francisco Symphony Orchestra, gave me faith that the institution still had some hope.

'I've been expecting you,' she said as we hugged. 'I called you last night from here. Didn't you get the message?'

With her comforting arms around me, a flood of emotion welled up. I wanted to tell her everything. If it weren't for Raleigh, I think I would've spilled it all out –

Orenthaler, Negli's – right there.

'I was beat,' I answered back. 'And beat up. Long, tough day.'

'Don't tell me,' Raleigh chuckled, 'you guys have met.'

'Standard autopsy preparation,' grinned Claire, as we pulled apart. 'Don't they teach you that stuff down at City Hall?'

He playfully spread his arms.

'Uh-uh,' said Claire, squeezing my shoulder, 'this you gotta earn. Anyway,' she regained a tone of seriousness, 'I finished the preliminaries just this morning. You want to see the bodies?'

I nodded yes.

'Just be prepared, these two don't make much of an advertisement for *Modern Bride*.'

She led us through a series of closed compression doors towards the Vault, the large refrigerated room where the bodies were stored.

I walked ahead with Claire, who pulled me close and whispered, 'Let me guess. You gave Jacobi a kiss on the nose, and all of a sudden this charming prince appeared.'

'He works for the Mayor, Claire,' I smiled back. 'They sent him here to make sure I don't faint at the first sign of blood.'

'In that case,' she replied, pushing the heavy door to the Vault open, 'you better hold on tight to that man.'

Chapter Fourteen

I had been having very close encounters with dead bodies for six years now. But what I saw sent a shiver of revulsion racing through me.

The mutilated bodies of the bride and groom were lying side by side. They were on retractable gurneys, their faces frozen in the horrifying moment of their deaths.

David and Melanie Brandt.

In their stark, ghostly expressions was the strongest statement I have ever seen that life may not be governed by anything fair or clement. I locked on the face of Melanie. Yesterday, in her wedding dress, she had seemed somehow tragic and tranquil. Today, in her slashed, naked starkness, her body was snarled in a freeze-frame of grotesque horror. Everything I had buried deep yesterday rushed to the surface.

Six years in Homicide, and I had never turned away. But I turned away now.

I felt Claire bolstering my arm, and leaned into it. To my surprise, it turned out to be Raleigh. I righted myself with a mixture of anger and embarrassment. 'Thanks,' I exhaled. 'I'm okay.'

'I've been doing this job eight years,' Claire said quietly, 'and this one, I wanted to turn away myself.'

She picked up a folder on an examining table across from David Brandt, then pointed to the raw, gaping knife wound on the left side of his chest. 'He was stabbed once in the right ventricle. You can see here how the blade pierced the juncture between the fourth rib and the sternum on the way in. Ruptured the A-V node, which provides the heart's electrical powering. Technically, he arrested.'

'He died of a heart attack?' Raleigh asked.

She pulled a pair of tight surgical gloves over her hands and red-lacquered nails. 'Electro-mechanical dissociation. Just a fancy way of describing what happens when you get stabbed in the heart.'

'What about the weapon?' I spoke up.

'At this point, all I know is that it was a standard, straight-edged blade. No distinguishing marks or entry pattern. One thing I can tell you is that the killer was of medium height – anywhere from five-seven to five-ten – and right-handed, based on the angle of impact. You can see here the path of the incision is angled slightly upwards. Here,' she said, poking around the wound. 'The groom was six feet. On his wife, who was five-five, the angle of the first incision was slanted in a downward path.'

I checked the groom's hands and arms for abrasions. 'Any signs of a struggle?'

'Couldn't. The poor man was scared right out of his mind.'

I nodded, as my eyes fell on the groom's face.

Claire shook her head. 'That's not exactly what I meant. Charlie Clapper's boys scraped up samples of a fluid from the groom's shoes and the hardwood floor in the foyer where he was found.' She held up a small vial containing droplets of a cloudy liquid.

Raleigh and I stared at it, uncomprehending.

'Urine,' explained Claire. 'The poor man apparently went in his pants. Must have been a gusher.' She pulled the white sheet back over David Brandt's face and shook her head. 'I figure that's one secret we can keep to ourselves.

'Unfortunately,' she sighed, 'things didn't happen nearly as swiftly for the bride.' She led us over to the bride's gurney. 'Maybe she surprised him. There are marks on her hands and wrists that indicate a struggle. Here,' she pointed to a reddened abrasion on her neck. 'I tried to lift some tissue from under her nails, but we'll see what comes back. Anyway, the first wound was in the upper abdomen and tore through the lungs. With time, given the loss of blood, she might have died from that.'

She pointed to a second and third ugly incision under the left breast in a similar location as the groom's. 'Her pericardium was filled with so much blood you could've wrung it out like a wet dishrag.'

'You're getting technical again,' I said.

'The tissue-like membrane around the heart. Blood collects in this space and compresses the muscle so that the heart can no longer fill with blood from the main return. Ultimately, it ends up strangling itself.'

The image of the bride's heart choking on her own blood chilled me. 'It's almost as if he wanted to duplicate the wounds,' I said, studying the knife-entry points.

'I thought of that,' said Claire. 'Straight line to the heart.'

Raleigh furrowed his brow. 'So the killer could be professional?'

Claire shrugged. 'By the technical pattern of the wounds, perhaps. But I don't think so.'

There was a hesitancy in her voice. I looked up and fixed on her grim eyes. 'So what I need to know is, was she sexually molested?'

She swallowed. 'There are clear signs of some sort of post-mortem penetration. The vaginal mucosa was severely extended, and I found small lacerations around the introitus.'

My body stiffened in rage. 'So she was raped.'

'*If* she was raped,' Claire replied, 'it was a very bad deal. The vaginal cavity was as wide as I've ever seen it. Honestly, I don't think we're talking penile entry at all.'

'Blunt instrument?' Raleigh asked.

'Possibly . . . but there are abrasions along the vaginal walls consistent with some kind of ring.' Claire took in a breath. 'Personally, I'd go with a fist.'

The angry, shocking nature of Melanie Brandt's death made me shiver again. A fist. It had a savage finality to it. Her assailant wasn't just trying to act out his nightmare, he wanted to shame her as well. Why?

'If you can handle one more, follow me,' Claire said.

She led us out through a swinging door into an adjoining lab. On an apron of white sterile paper lay the blood-smeared tuxedo jacket we had found next to the groom.

Claire picked it up by the collar. 'Clapper loaned it to me. Of course, the obvious thing was to confirm whose blood was actually on it.'

The left front panel was slashed through with the fatal incision and sprayed with dark blotches of blood. 'This is where it starts to get really interesting,' Claire informed us. 'You see, it wasn't just David Brandt's blood that I found on the front of the jacket.'

Raleigh and I gaped in surprise.

'The killer's?' he said, wide-eyed.

She shook her head. 'No – the bride's.'

I made a fast mental recollection of the crime scene. The groom had been killed at the door; his wife, thirty feet away in the master bedroom.

'How could the bride's blood get on his jacket?' I said, confused.

'I struggled with the same thing. So I went back and lined up the jacket against the groom's torso. The slash mark didn't quite match up with his wound. Look, the groom's wound was here. Fourth rib. The slash marks on the jacket are three inches higher. Checking further, the damned jacket isn't even the same brand as the pants. This is Joseph Abboud.'

Claire winked, seeing the gears of my brain shift into place.

The jacket wasn't the groom's. It belonged to the man who killed him.

Claire rounded her eyes. 'Ain't no professional I know would leave that behind.'

'He could've been just trying to utilize the wedding as a cover,' Raleigh replied.

An even more chilling possibility had already struck me. 'He could have been a guest.'

Chapter Fifteen

A t the offices of the *San Francisco Chronicle*, Cindy Thomas's frantic brain was just barely staying ahead of her fingers.

The afternoon deadline was only an hour away.

From the bellhop at the Hyatt, she had been able to obtain the names of two guests who had attended the Brandt wedding and who were still at the hotel. After running down there again last night, she was able to put together a heart-wrenching, tragic account – complete with vows, toasts, and a romantic last dance – of the bride and groom's final agonizing moments.

All the other reporters were still piecing together the sparse details released by the police. But she was ahead so far. She was winning, and it felt great. She was also certain this was the best writing she'd done since arriving at the *Chronicle*, and maybe since she'd been an undergraduate at Michigan.

At the paper, Cindy's coup at the Hyatt had turned her into an instant celebrity. People she scarcely knew were suddenly stopping and congratulating her. Even the publisher, whom she rarely saw on the Metro floor, came down to find out who she was.

Metro was covering some demonstration in Mill Valley about a construction rerouting that had built up traffic near a school zone.

She was writing the front page.

As she typed, she noticed Sidney Glass, her city editor, coming up to her desk. Glass was known at the newspaper as El Sid. He parked himself across from her with a stiff sigh. 'We need to talk.'

Her fingers slowly settled to a halt as she looked up.

'I've got two very pissed-off senior crime reporters itching to get into this. Suzie's at City Hall awaiting a statement by the Police Chief and the Mayor. Stone's put together profiles on both families. They have twenty years and two Pulitzers between them. And it is their beat.'

Cindy felt her heart nearly come to a stop. 'What did you tell them?' she asked.

In El Sid's hardened eyes, she could see the greedy jaws of the first-team crime staff, senior reporters with their own researchers trying to elbow their way in and carve this story up. *Her* story.

'Show me what you've got,' the city editor finally said. He got up, peered over her shoulder, read a few lines off the computer screen. 'A lot of it's okay. You probably know that. "Anguished" belongs over here,' he pointed out. 'It modifies "bride's father". Nothing pisses Ida Morris off like misplaced modifiers and inversions.'

Cindy could feel herself blushing. 'I know, I know. I'm trying to get this in. Deadline's at—'

'I know when deadline is,' the editor glowered. 'But down here, if you can get it in, you can get it in right.'

He studied Cindy for what seemed an interminable duration, a deep, assessing stare that kept her on edge.

'Especially if you intend to stay on this thing.' Glass's generally implacable face twitched, and he *almost* smiled at her. 'I told them it was yours, Thomas.'

Cindy repressed an urge to hug the cranky, domineering editor right on the bullpen floor. 'You want me at City Hall?' she asked.

'The real story's in that hotel suite. Go back to the Hyatt.'

El Sid, his hands, as always, thrust into his trouser pockets, began to walk away.

But a moment later, he turned back. ''Course, if you intend to stay on this story, you'd better find a police source on the inside – and quick.'

Chapter Sixteen

After leaving the morgue, Raleigh and I walked back to the office, mostly in silence. Lots of details about the murders were bothering me. Why would the killer take away the victim's jacket? Why leave the champagne bottle? It made no sense.

'We've got a sex crime now. Bad one.' I finally turned to him on the asphalt walkway leading to the Hall. 'I want to run the autopsy results through Milt Fanning and the FBI computers. We also need to meet with the bride's parents. We'll need a history on anyone she may have been involved with before David. And a list of everyone at that wedding.'

'Why don't we wait for some confirmation on that one,' my new partner said, 'before we go all out on that angle.'

I stopped walking and stared at him. 'You want to see if anybody checked in for a bloody jacket with Lost and Found? I don't understand. What's your concern?'

'My concern,' Raleigh said, 'is that I don't want the Department intruding on the grief of the families with a lot of hypotheticals until we have more to go on. We may or may not have the killer's jacket. He may or may not have been a guest.'

'Who do you think it belonged to – the rabbi?'

He flashed me a quick smile. 'It could've been left there to set us off.'

His tone seemed suddenly different. 'You're backing off?'

'I'm not backing off,' he said. 'But until we have a lead of some sort, every old boyfriend of the bride or casualty of some corporate downsizing Gerald Brandt had a hand in could be rolled out as a possible suspect. I'd rather the spotlight wasn't aimed back at them unless we have something firm to go on.'

Here it was. The spiel. Packaging, containment. Brandt and Chancellor Weil were VIPs. Find us the bad guys, Lindsay. Just don't put the Department at any risk along the way.

I chuffed back, 'I thought the possibility that the killer could've been at that wedding *was* what we had to go on.'

'All I'm suggesting, Lindsay, is let's get some confirmation before we begin ripping into the sexlife of the best man.'

I nodded, all the while fixing in on his eyes. 'In the meantime, *Chris*, we'll just follow up on our *other* really strong leads.'

We stood there in edgy silence.

'All right, why do you think the killer changed jackets with the groom?' I asked him.

He leaned back against the edge of a stone retaining

wall. 'My guess is that he was wearing it when he killed them. It was covered with blood. He had to get out undetected. The groom's jacket was lying around. So he just switched.'

'So you figure he went to all that trouble making the slash marks and all, thinking no one would notice. Different size, different maker. That it would just slip by. Raleigh, *why did he leave it behind*? Why wouldn't he stuff the bloody jacket into a bag? Or roll it under his new jacket?'

'Okay,' Raleigh sighed. 'I don't know. Your guess is?'

I didn't know why he had left it behind, but a chilling idea was beginning to form in the back of my mind. 'Possibility one,' I answered, 'he panicked. Maybe the phone rang or someone knocked at the door.'

'On their wedding night?'

'You're starting to sound like my *ex*-partner.'

I started toward the Hall, and he caught up. He held the glass doors open for me. As I walked through, he took my arm. 'And number two?'

I stood there, staring squarely into his eyes, trying to assess just how far I could go with him. 'What's your real expertise here, anyway?' I asked.

He smiled, his look confident and secure. 'I used to be married.'

I didn't reply. Possibility two: the killer was signing his murders. He was toying with us – purposely leaving clues. One-off crime-of-passion killers didn't leave clues like the jacket. Professionals didn't, either.

Serial killers left clues.

Chapter Seventeen

The window that Phillip Campbell was staring out of had a startling view of the Bay, but he didn't really notice the sights. He was lost in his thoughts.

It's finally started. Everything is in play, he was thinking. The city on the Bay will never be the same, will it? I will never be the same. This was complicated – not what it seemed to be but beautiful in its own way.

He had closed his office door, as he always did when he was absorbed in research. Lately, he had stopped catching lunch with his co-workers. They bored him. Their lives were filled with petty concerns. The stock market. The Giants and 49ers. Where they were headed on vacation. They had such shallow, simple, middle-class dreams. His were soaring. He was like the moguls thinking up their new, new things over in Silicon Valley.

Anyway, that was all in the past. Now, he had a secret. The biggest secret in the world.

He pushed his business papers to the corner of his desk.

This is the old world, he thought. The old me. The bore. The worker bee.

He unlocked the top left drawer of his desk. Behind the usual personal clutter was a small, gray lockbox. It was barely large enough to hold a packet of three- by five-inch cards.

This is my world now.

He thought back to the Hyatt. The bride's beautiful porcelain face, the blossoms of blood on her chest. He still couldn't believe what had taken place. The sharp *crack* of the knife ripping through cartilage. The gasp of her last breath. And his, of course.

What were their names? Oh Jesus Christ, he'd forgotten. No, he hadn't! The Brandts. They were all over the newspapers and the TV news.

With a key off his chain, he opened the small box. What spilled out into the room was the intoxicating spell of his dreams.

A stack of index cards. Neat and orderly. Alphabetically arranged. One by one, he skimmed through them. New names . . . *DeGeorge* . . . *King* . . . *Merced* . . . *Passeneau* . . . *Peterson*.

All the brides and grooms.

Chapter Eighteen

Several urgent messages were on my desk when I got back from the morgue. Good – urgent was appropriate.

Charlie Clapper from CSU. Preliminary report in. Some reporters – from the AP, local television stations. Even the woman from the *Chronicle* who had left me her card.

I picked at a grilled chicken and pear salad I had brought up as I dialed Clapper back. 'Only good news, please,' I joked, as his voice came on the phone.

'In that case, I can give you a nine hundred number. For two bucks a minute they'll tell you anything you want to hear.'

I could hear it in the tone of his voice. 'You got nothing?'

'Tons of partials, Lindsay,' the CSU chief sighed, meaning inconclusive prints his team had lifted from the room. 'The bride's, the groom's, the assistant manager's, housekeeping's.'

'You dusted the bodies?' I pressed. The killer had pulled

Melanie Brandt up off the floor. 'And the box of champagne?'

'Of course. Nothing. Somebody was careful.'

'What about off the floor? Fibers, shoeprints?'

'Besides the pee.' Clapper laughed. 'You think I'm holding out on you? You're cute, Lindsay, but I get off on bagging killers more. Meanwhile, I've got someone running that tux under the microscope. I'll let you know. Roger Wilco.'

'Thanks, Charlie,' I muttered disappointedly.

Flipping further through my stack of messages, Cindy Thomas's name came to the top. I wasn't normally in the habit of phoning back reporters in the middle of an ongoing investigation, but this one had been smart and cool making her way up to the crime scene, yet kind in backing off when she had me cornered in the bathroom.

I found her at her desk. 'Thanks for calling me back, Inspector,' she said, in an appreciative tone.

'I owe you, I guess. Thanks for cutting me some slack at the hotel.'

'Happens to us all. But I have to ask, do you always react so personally at a crime scene? You're a homicide detective, right?'

I didn't have the time or heart to get into a battle of wits, so I used Jacobi's line. 'It was a wedding – I always cry at them. What can I do for you, Ms Thomas?'

'Please, call me Cindy. Actually, I'm about to do you another favor. When I reach five, maybe you'll do one for me.'

'This is a homicide we have here, a very bad one. We're not going to play Let's Make a Deal. And if we meet again, you'll find I'm not at my cheeriest when I feel indebted.'

'I guess that's what I was hoping for,' she admitted. 'I wanted to hear your spin on the bride and groom.'

'Doesn't Tom Stone cover homicide for the *Chronicle*?' I asked.

I heard her take in a breath. 'I won't lie to you. I normally handle Local Interest out of Metro.'

'Well, you got yourself a real story now. MARRIAGE MADE IN HEAVEN ENDS UP IN HELL. You're quick out of the gate.'

'Truth is, Inspector,' her voice grew softer, 'I'd never seen anything like that before. Seeing David Brandt lying there, on his wedding night . . . I know what you must think, but it's not just about the story. I'd like to help any way I can.'

'I appreciate that, but since we've got all these eager people with badges walking around here, we ought to give them a shot, don't you think? Anyway, you should know that you sneaking your way up to the thirtieth floor didn't exactly get me invited to the Commissioner's for brunch. I had tactical responsibility at the crime scene.'

'I never thought I'd actually make it through.'

'So we've established we don't know who owes whom here. But since it's my dime . . .'

The reporter's voice took on a businesslike tone. 'I called to get your reaction to a story we're going to break later today. You know the groom's father runs a buyout firm. Our business editor pulled off Bloomberg that they backed out of a proposed agreement at the last minute with the third largest Russian automaker, Kolya-Novgorod. Brandt was providing up to two hundred million dollars for a significant stake. Kolya's one of those Russian conglomerates taken over by a new branch of black-market capitalists. Without the cash, I'm told it's virtually bankrupt. My source tells me the mood got very fractious.'

I laughed. 'Fractious, Ms Thomas? I might be getting a little fractious myself.'

'Apparently, some of the Russians were left hanging with their Uncle Vanyas out.'

I smiled again. 'Conspiracy to commit murder is a federal crime,' I told her. 'If there's something to it, you should make the call to Justice.'

'I just thought I'd let you know. In the meantime, you want to throw me a comment on any other possibilities you're looking into?'

'Sure. I'd feel safe in saying that they're "ongoing".'

'Thanks,' she sighed. 'Have you narrowed into any other suspects yet?'

'This is what they tell you to ask at the *Chronicle*? You know I can't divulge that.'

'Off the record. No attribution. As a friend.'

As I listened, I remembered when I was a recruit trying to elbow my way in. How the police world was barred, closed off, until someone opened up the tiniest crack to let me crawl through. 'Like I said, Ms Thomas,' my tone was less severe now, 'no promises.'

'Cindy,' the reporter said. 'At least call me Cindy. For the next time you get cornered in the bathroom with your guard down.'

'Okay, *Cindy*. I'll be sure to keep you in mind.'

Chapter Nineteen

I didn't want to go home. And I knew I couldn't stay at the Hall any longer. I grabbed my bag, rushed down to the underground garage, started up my trusty-dusty Bronco without a clear sense of where I was headed, then I just drove – Fourth, Third, on Mission, past the Moscone Center – cafés, closed-up shops. All the way down toward the Embarcadero.

I wrapped around Battery, heading away from the Bay. I had nowhere to go, but my hands seemed to act on their own, leading me somewhere. Flashes of the murdered bride and groom flickered in my head. Echoes of Orenthaler. I had finally called Dr Medved for an appointment.

I was approaching Sutter, and I turned. Suddenly, I knew where I was heading. I pulled onto Powell, close to Union Square, and within minutes I found myself in front of the brightly lit entrance of the Hyatt.

I badged the manager, and took the elevator up to the thirtieth floor.

A single uniformed guard sat in front of the Mandarin

Suite. I recognized him – it was David Hale out of Central. He stood up as he saw me approach. 'Nowhere to go, Inspector?'

A crisscrossing barrier of yellow tape blocked the entrance to the Mandarin Suite. Hale gave me the key. I peeled off a band or two and slipped under the rest. I turned the lock and I was inside.

If you've never wandered alone at the site of a freshly committed murder, you don't really know the feeling of restless unease. The room seemed to whisper with the dark ghosts of David and Melanie Brandt.

I was sure I had missed something. I was also sure it was here. *What could it be?*

The suite was pretty much as I left it two days before. The Oriental carpet in the living room was gone to Clapper's lab, but body positions and blood sites were clearly marked out with blue chalk.

I looked at the spot where David Brandt had died. In my mind, I retraced what had likely taken place.

They are toasting each other. I knew that from the half-filled champagne glasses on a table near the terrace. Maybe he just gave her the earrings. The open box was on the master bathroom counter.

There's a knock. David Brandt goes to answer. I could feel secrets buzzing in the thick air, alive with horror.

The killer comes in, carrying the wine. Maybe David knows him – maybe he just left him an hour before at the reception. The knife comes out. Only one thrust. The groom is pinned against the door, apoplectic. It happens so fast that he cannot scream. 'Poor man pees right in his pants,' Claire had said.

Where is the bride? Maybe she's in the bathroom. (The jewelry box.) Maybe she went to put on the earrings.

The killer hunts through the suite. He intercepts the bride, coming out unsuspectingly.

I envision Melanie Brandt – radiant, full of joy. He sees it, too. Was it someone she knew? Had she just left him? Did Melanie know her killer?

There's a Navajo saying, Even the still wind has a voice. In the quiet, confessing hotel room, I listen.

Tell me, Melanie. *I am here for you*. I'm listening.

My skin tingles with the chill of resurrecting each detail of the murder. She fights, tries to run away. (The bruises and small abrasions on her arms and neck.) The killer stabs her at the foot of the bed. He is horrified, yet wildly excited about what he has done. She doesn't die immediately. He has no choice. He has to stab her again. And once more.

When he is finished, he carries her to the bed. Carries, not drags. There is no sign of blood trailing behind. This is important. He is gentle with her. It makes me think he knows her.

Maybe he once loved Melanie? He folds her arms on her waist in a restful pose. A princess sleeping. Maybe he pretends what has taken place is only a bad dream.

Nowhere in the room do I feel the clinical pattern of professionals or hired killers. Or even someone who has killed before.

I'm listening.

A ferocious anger rises up in his blood. He realizes he will never see her again. His princess . . .

He's so angry. He wants to lie down with her this one time. Feel her. But he cannot – that would defile her. Yet he must have her! So he lifts her dress. Uses his fist.

It is all screaming at me, but I'm sure there is one last thing I am not seeing. What am I missing? What has everyone missed so far?

I step over to the bed. I picture Melanie, her horrifying stab wounds, but her face is calm, unaccusing. He leaves her like that. He doesn't take the earrings. He doesn't take the huge diamond ring.

Then it hit me with the power of a train exploding from a dark tunnel!

Rings.

I ran my mind over the mental image of her lying there. Her delicate, blood-smeared hands. *The diamond was still there, but . . . Jesus! Was it possible?*

I ran back to the door and brought to mind the crumpled body of the groom.

They were married just a few hours before. They had just completed their vows. But they weren't wearing gold bands.

Wedding rings.

The killer doesn't take the earrings, I realized.

He takes the rings.

Chapter Twenty

Nine the next morning, I was in the office of Dr Victor Medved, a pleasant, smallish man with a narrow, chiseled face who, with a trace of an Eastern European accent, scared the hell out of me.

'Negli's is a killer,' he stated evenly. 'It robs the body of its ability to transport oxygen. In the beginning, the symptoms are listlessness, a weakening of the immune system, and some light-headedness. Ultimately, you may experience similar brain dysfunction to a stroke and begin to lose mental capacity as well.'

He got up, walked over to me, cradled my face in his gentle hands. He stared at me through thick glasses. 'You're already looking peaked,' he said, pressing my cheeks with his thumbs.

'Always takes me a while for the blood to get hopping in the mornings,' I said with a smile, trying to mask the fear in my heart.

'Well, in three months,' Dr Medved said, 'unless we reverse it, you will look like a ghost. A pretty ghost, but a ghost all the same.' He went back to his desk and picked up my chart. 'I see you are a police detective.'

'Homicide,' I told him.

'Then there should be no reason to go forward under any delusions. I don't mean to upset you – aplastic anemia *can* be reversed. Up to thirty per cent of patients respond to a regimen of bi-weekly transfusions of packed red blood cells. Of those who do not respond, a similar percentage can be ultimately treated through a bone-marrow transfer. But this involves a painful process of chemotherapy first in order to boost up the white cells.'

I stiffened. Orenthaler's nightmarish predictions were coming true. 'Is there any way to know who responds to the treatment?'

Medved clasped his palms together and shook his head. 'The only way is to begin. Then we see.'

'I'm on an important case. Dr Orenthaler said I could continue to work.'

Medved pursed his lips skeptically. 'You may continue as long as you feel the strength.'

I had a moment of despair. How long could I hide this? Who could I tell? 'If it works, will there be a rapid improvement?' I asked with some hope.

He frowned. 'This is not like popping aspirin for a headache. I'm afraid we're in this for the long haul.'

The long haul. I thought of Roth's likely response. My chances at Lieutenant.

This is it, Lindsay. This is the greatest challenge of your life.

'And if it doesn't work, how long before things start to . . .'

'Start to get worse? Let us attack this with optimism and hope. We'll discuss that as we go along.'

Everything was thrown open now. The case, my career, all the goals of my life. The stakes had changed. I was walking around with a time bomb ticking in my chest, tightly wound, incendiary. And the fuse was disappearing slowly.

I closed my eyes briefly, then asked, 'When do we start?'

He scribbled down the details of an office in the same building. Third floor. Moffet Outpatient Services. There was no date.

'If it's all the same to you,' he said, 'I'd like to start right now.'

Chapter Twenty-One

The story about Gerald Brandt's aborted business deal with the Russian car manufacturers had broken. It was on every newsstand – bold headline reading GROOM'S FATHER MAY HAVE TRIGGERED RUSSIAN WRATH.

The *Chronicle* reported that the FBI was seriously looking into the matter. *Great.*

Two half-liter bags of hemoglobin-enriched blood were pumping through me as I finally reached my desk about ten-thirty. It took everything I had to push the image of the thick, crimson blood slowly dripping into my veins from my mind.

When Roth called my name, the usual disgruntled glower was all over his face. '*Chronicle* says it's the Russians. The FBI seems to agree.' He leaned over my desk and thrust a copy of the morning's paper at me.

'I saw it. Don't let the FBI in on this,' I said. 'This is our case.'

I told him about last night, my going back to the crime scene. How I was pretty sure the sexual assault on the corpse, the bloody jacket, the missing rings, added up to a single, obsessed killer.

'It's not some Russian professional. He put his fist inside her,' I reminded him. 'He did this on her wedding night.'

'You want me to tell the Feds to back off,' Roth said, 'because you have strong feelings about the case?'

'This is a *murder* case. A kinky, very nasty sex crime, not some international conspiracy.'

'Maybe the Russian killer needed proof. Or maybe he *was* a sex maniac.'

'Proof of what? Every paper and TV station in the country carried the story. Anyway, don't the Russki hitters usually cut off the finger, too?'

Roth rattled a frustrated sigh. His face showed more than its usual tic of agitation.

'I've got to run,' I said. I shot my fist in the air and hoped that Roth got the joke.

Gerald Brandt was still at the Hyatt, waiting for his son's body to be released. I went to his suite and found him there alone.

'You see the papers?' I asked him as we sat at the umbrellaed table on the terrace.

'The papers, Bloomberg, some woman reporter from the *Chronicle* calling in all night. What they're suggesting is total madness,' he said.

'Your son's death was an act of madness, Mr Brandt. You want me to be straight with you when it comes to the investigation?'

'What do you mean, Inspector Boxer?'

'You were asked the other day if you knew anyone who might want to cause you harm—'

'And I told your detective, *not in this way*,' he said quietly.

'You don't think certain factions in Russia might be a little angry at you for pulling out of their deal?'

'We don't deal with factions, Ms Boxer.' His voice was stronger now. 'Kolya's shareholders include some of the most powerful men in this country. Anyway, you make me feel like I'm a suspect. It was business. Negotiations. In what we do, we deal with this sort of thing every week. David's death has nothing to do with Kolya.'

'Mr Brandt, how can you be so sure? Your son and his wife are dead.'

'Because negotiations *never broke off*, Detective. That was a ruse we used for the media. We closed on the deal last night.'

He stood up and I knew my interview was over.

My next call was to Claire. I ached to talk to her, anyway. I craved my daily Claire fix. I also needed help on the case.

When I phoned, her secretary said she was in the middle of a conference call and could I please hold.

'Forensic specialists,' Claire grumbled as she came on the line. 'Listen to this ... some guy's driving sixty in a thirty-five zone, rams into an elderly man in a Lexus, double-parked, waiting for his wife. DOA. Now the driver's tying up the guy's estate with a suit that the victim was illegally parked. All each side wants is to grab a piece of the estate, experts included. Righetti's pushing me in 'cause the case is being written up in an AAFS journal.

Some of these bastards, you give them a penny for their thoughts, you know what you get?'

'Change,' I answered with a smile. Claire *was* funny.

'You got it. I've got about thirty-one seconds. How you doing?' she inquired. 'I love you, sweetheart. I miss you. What do you *want*, Lindsay?'

I hesitated, part of me wishing I could let the whole thing burst out, but all I asked was if the Brandts were wearing any wedding bands when they were brought in.

'To my knowledge, no,' she replied. 'We inventoried earrings and a diamond as large as an eyeball. But no wedding bands. I noticed that myself. In fact, that's why I was calling you last night.'

'Great minds think alike,' I said.

'Busy minds, at least,' she countered. 'How's your grisly, godawful case coming on?'

I sighed. 'I don't know. Next thing we have to do is go through three hundred guests to see if any might've been carrying any special grudges. You saw how this is being played up in the press. Russian revenge. The FBI's creeping around and Chief Mercer's barking in Roth's ear to put a *real* detective on it. Speaking of which, I have Jacobi out trying to trace down the jacket. Other than that, the case is moving along smoothly.'

Claire laughed. 'Stick with it, sweetie. If anyone can solve these murders, it's you.'

'I wish it were only that . . .' I let my voice drop.

'Is everything all right?' Claire came back. 'You don't sound your usual chatty, irreverent self.'

'Actually, I need to talk with you. Maybe we can get together later?'

'Sure,' Claire said. 'Oh damn . . . I teach at four today. And we've got Reggie's graduation tonight. Can it keep a day? I could drive in for brunch on Sunday.'

'Of course it can,' I said, swallowing my disappointment. 'Sunday would be great. I'd like that.'

I hung up with a smile. For a moment, I actually felt better about things. Just making the date with Claire made it seem as if a weight had been lifted off my shoulders. Sunday would give me some time to prepare, about how I was going to deal with the treatment, and my job.

Raleigh wandered up. 'You want to grab a coffee?'

I thought he was needling me about what time I'd come in. He must have sensed my resentment.

He wagged a legal-sized manila envelope in my face and shrugged. 'It's the Brandts' wedding list. I thought you'd want to see who made the cut.'

Chapter Twenty-Two

We went down to Roma's, one of those stucco-on-stucco, high-ceilinged, Euro-style coffee joints across the street from the Hall. I prefer Peet's, but Roma's is closer.

I ordered a tea, while Raleigh came back with some fancy mocha latte and a slice of homemade pumpkin bread that he pushed in front of me.

'You ever wonder how these places make any money?' he asked.

'What?' I looked at him.

'There's one on every corner. They all serve the same thing and their average sale's gotta be, what . . . two dollars and thirty-five cents?'

'This isn't a *date*, Raleigh,' I snapped. 'Let's go through the list.'

'Maybe closer to three or three-fifty. Lucky if the places *gross* four hundred thousand.'

'Raleigh, please,' I said, losing patience.

He pushed the envelope toward me.

I opened it and fanned out eight or nine pages of names and addresses bearing Chancellor Weil's office crest. I recognized some of the guests on the groom's side immediately. Bert Rosen, former Secretary of the Treasury of the United States. Sumner Smith, some billionaire who had made his money in the eighties through big-time LBOs. Chip Stein, of E-flix, Spielberg's buddy. Maggie Sontero, the hot SoHo designer from New York. Lots of big names and big trouble.

From the bride's side, there were several prominent names from the San Francisco area. Mayor Fernandez for one. Arthur Abrams, the prominent local attorney. I had gone up against his firm once or twice in the witness box, testifying in homicide cases. Willie Upton, Superintendent of Public Schools.

Raleigh pulled his seat over to me. Side by side we scanned the rest of the list, which contained columns of impressive-sounding couples with the titles of 'Dr' or 'Honorable' in front of their names.

It was a long, unrevealing, seemingly impenetrable list.

I don't know what I expected – just *something* to jump out at me. Some name resonating with a culpability even the families didn't recognize.

Raleigh let out a worrisome breath. 'This list is *scary*. You take the first fifty, I'll take the second, we'll give the balance to Jacobi. We'll all meet back here in two weeks and see what we've got.'

The prospect of hammering away at these people – each one horrified and indignant at our inquiries – didn't fill me with joy or high hopes.

'You think Mayor Fernandez might be a sex killer?' I muttered.

'I do.'

What came out of me next was a complete surprise. 'So you said you were married?'

If we were going to be thrown together we might as well get it out. And the truth was, I was curious.

Raleigh nodded after a short pause. I thought I saw pain in his eyes. 'Actually, I still am. Our divorce is coming up next month. Seventeen years.'

I flashed him a sympathetic wag of my eyes. 'I'm sorry. Let's stop the Q and A.'

'It's okay. Things happen. Suddenly, it seemed we were just traveling in different circles. To be more precise, Marion fell in love with the guy who owned the real-estate office where she worked. It's an old story. I guess I never quite learned which fork to use.'

'I could've saved you some pain,' I said. 'It goes left to right. Are there kids?'

'Two great boys. Fourteen and twelve. Jason is the jock. Teddy's the brain. Set up a home page for his sixth-grade class. I get them every other weekend. Lights of my life, Lindsay.'

I could actually see Raleigh as Superdad. Kicking the ball around on Saturdays, installing the computer in the den. On top of it, the guy did have affectionate eyes. It was gradually dawning on me that he wasn't the enemy.

'I guess,' he grinned back at me, 'getting the order of forks right didn't exactly help you, either. You're divorced, right?'

'Oohh. Somebody's been checking around,' I said. 'I was just out of the Police Academy. Tom was in his second year of law school at Berkeley. At first, he was going to go criminal. We had sort of a Carville and Matalin thing going. I imagined me testifying, Tom Terrific socking it to me on the cross. Ultimately, he opted for corporate.'

'And?'

'It was his picture, not mine. I wasn't ready for the country club. It's an old story, right?' I smiled. 'The truth is, he walked out on me. Kind of broke my heart into tiny pieces.'

'Sounds like we've got some things in common,' Raleigh said gently. He did have nice eyes. *Stop it, Lindsay.*

'If you must know,' I replied, deadpan, 'for the past six months I've been having this torrid affair with Warren Jacobi.'

Raleigh laughed and pretended to look surprised. 'Jeez, Jacobi doesn't seem like your type. What's the fatal attraction?'

I thought of my ex-husband Tom, then one other man I had been sort of serious about. What always attracted me when I let someone get close. 'Soft hands. And, I guess, a soft heart.'

'So whad'ya think?' Raleigh said. 'You put a few home-made jams on the shelves, give the coffees some sexier names – Arabian Breeze, Sirocco. You think we can hike up the average sale?'

'Why are you going through this, Raleigh?'

He gave me a look that was sort of between an embarrassed grin and a sparkle in his clear, blue eyes. 'I've been doing police work for sixteen years. So you get to think-ing . . . I have this favorite place. Up in Tahoe. Maybe one of these franchises . . .'

'Sorry, I don't see you behind the counter picking out the muffins.'

'Nicest thing you've said to me so far.'

I got up, tucked the envelope under my arm and headed toward the door. 'On second thought, you might make a better baker than a cop.'

'That's my girl,' he smiled. 'Wiseguy answer for every-thing. Keep those defenses up.'

As we left the shop, I softened and said to him, 'I have this favorite place, too.'

'Maybe you'll show me one day.'

'Maybe I will.'

I was surprised by Raleigh – live and learn – he was actually a nice guy. I wondered if he had soft hands.

Chapter Twenty-Three

When Rebecca Passeneau looked at herself in the full splendor of her wedding dress, she knew that she was no longer her mother's little girl. *You're my baby.* She had heard those words from her very first days on the planet.

With three older brothers it wasn't so hard to imagine why. Her mother had always wanted a girl – Daddy, too – but as the years went on they assumed their time had passed. The oldest – Ben, the daredevil – had been killed before she was born. Her parents were crushed. They couldn't even think of more children. Then, miraculously, Becky came.

'*My baby!*' she heard her mother exclaim from where she stood behind Becky.

'Oh, Mom,' her daughter sighed, but she also smiled.

She continued to look at herself. She was beautiful. In her long white strapless dress, an avalanche of tulle, she shone like the most lovely and beautiful thing in the world. Michael would be so happy. With all the arrangements – the hotel in Napa, the flowers, the last-minute alterations to the dress – she had never thought this day would actually come. But now it was almost here. *Saturday.*

Ms Perkins, the department manager at Saks, could only stand and admire. 'You're gonna knock 'em dead, sweetheart.'

Becky spun around, catching herself in every view of the three-paneled mirror. She grinned. 'I will, won't I?'

'Your father and I want you to have something,' her mother said.

She reached into her purse and pulled out a small suede jewelry pouch. In it was her diamond brooch, a four-carat oval on a string of pearls, passed on from her own mother. She stepped closer to Becky, clasped the strand around her neck.

'It's gorgeous,' the girl gasped. 'Oh, *Mom.*'

'It was given to me on my wedding day,' her mother said. 'It has brought me a beautiful life. Now it's for you.'

Becky Passeneau stood there in the spell of the mirror. The glorious dress, the diamond in the hollow of her throat.

She finally stepped off the alteration platform and hugged her mother. 'I love you, Mom. You're the best.'

'Now it's complete,' her mother said, with a tear in her eye.

'No, not quite,' said Ms Perkins. She ran into the back and hurriedly returned with a bouquet of flowers. Imitations, sales accessories, but at the moment they looked like the most resplendent blossoms in the world.

She gave them to Becky, who hopped back up on the platform, hugging them to her. She saw her beaming smile reflected three times. They all stood there and admired.

'Now you are complete,' Ms Perkins approved.

Standing nearby in Saks, watching Becky model her stunning dress, Phillip Campbell couldn't have agreed more.

'Your big day is almost here,' he whispered softly. 'You look beautiful.'

Chapter Twenty-Four

The following morning, Milt Fanning from the FBI Sex Crime Unit reported in. His computer had popped up a handful of related crimes, but he was letting me know that none of them was a strong lead.

They had started by plugging in fists used in the act of sexual assault and that produced several cases, mostly gay crimes. One was in connection with a couple of murdered prostitutes in Compton that dated back to 1992, but Nicholas Chito was serving twenty-five years to life in San Quentin.

There had been several hotel murders, even one involving newlyweds in Ohio, in which the groom opened up the womb of his beloved with a 30-30 when he discovered he wasn't the first. But there was nothing local or still outstanding, nothing tangible to give us a direction.

I was disappointed, but not surprised. Everything we had uncovered so far convinced me that when David and Melanie Brandt ran into their killer at the Hyatt, it wasn't the first time they had met.

I saw Jacobi wandering in from outside. For two days, he had been avoiding me – running down his assignments – specifically the searches for the champagne and the jacket. After two years, I knew that when Jacobi wasn't needling me, it meant he wasn't happy.

'How's the search going?' I asked.

He flashed me a tight-lipped smirk. 'Chin and Murphy are out calling every fricking wine store in a forty-mile radius. You think any of these guys keep track of this sort of thing? They all tell me that bottle could've been ordered from anywhere in the country. Then there's mail order to consider. The Internet. Cripes!'

I knew it was a long shot. How many people pay two hundred bucks for a bottle of champagne?

'Still,' he finally faced me, 'we came up with some names.'

As if to torture me, Jacobi leafed through his notepad to what must've been page thirty. Then he squinted, cleared his throat, saying, 'Yeah, here we go . . . Golden State Wine Shop, on Crescent. *Krug. Clos du Mesnil*,' he pronounced, bludgeoning the French. 'Nineteen eighty-nine. Someone ordered a case of the stuff last March. Name of Roy C. Shoen.'

'You check him out?'

He nodded. 'Never heard of any Brandt. He's a dentist. I guess rich dentists like fancy wine, too.' He flipped over the page. 'Then there's Vineyard Wines in Mill Valley. Murphy handled it.' For the first time in a couple of days he really smiled at me. 'The guy who bought the wine was named Murphy, too. Regular customer there. Threw a dinner party for his wife's birthday. You want to give me a morning off I'll check him out, but I thought I'd send Murphy himself. Just for the laugh.'

'Any luck with the tuxedo jacket?'

'We called the manufacturer. Fifteen stores in the area sell this brand – if it even came from around here. We're bringing in their local rep. Tracking down the owner of this thing . . . it ain't gonna be easy.'

'While you're out there,' I teased him, 'see if you can pick yourself up a decent tie.'

'Ho, ho. So how you getting along without me?' Jacobi inquired, but I could see the disappointment all over his face. Made me feel bad.

'I'm coping.' Then, seriously, 'I'm sorry, Warren. You know that I didn't ask for this guy.'

He nodded self-consciously. 'You want me to check out everyone we dig up who's into fancy champagne?'

I shook my head. I got up, dropped a copy of the Brandt wedding list on his desk. 'What I want you to do is check and see if they match against this list.'

He leafed through the pages, whistling at a few of the more prominent names. 'Too bad, Boxer. No Shoen or Murphy. Maybe we'll just have to wait and take a shot at Couple Number Two.'

A chill ran through me. 'What makes you say that?' I asked. Jacobi was a pain in the ass, but he was a good cop with a good nose for sniffing out a pattern.

'We're looking for a spiffy dresser who likes to get dirty with dead brides, right?'

I nodded. I remembered something my first partner had told me. *'Never wrestle with a pig, Lindsay. You both get dirty. And the pig likes it.'*

'I figure it's gotta be hard for a guy like that to find a date,' said Jacobi.

Chapter Twenty-Five

T he first week of the Bride and Groom investigation was gone. Unbelievable.

Jacobi's team pounded the jacket-and-champagne search, but so far they had come up empty. Raleigh and I had spoken to twenty guests, from the Mayor to the groom's best friend. All of them were numb and sickened, but unable to put their finger on any one thing that might move us along.

All I could focus on was that we needed something firm – fast – before this guy who took the rings would kill again.

I underwent my second transfusion. As I watched the thick red blood drip into my veins, I prayed it was making me stronger, but was it? It had the slow, steady beat of a ticking clock.

And the clock *was* ticking. Mine, Chief Mercer's.

Saturday at six, Jacobi folded his pad, put on his sports jacket, and tucked his gun into his belt. 'See ya, Boxer,' he said.

Raleigh stopped by before heading out. 'I owe you a beer. You want to collect?'

A beer would be nice, I thought. I was even growing used to Raleigh's company. But something told me if I went with him now, I'd let everything out: Negli's, my treatments, the fear in my heart.

I shook my head. 'Think I'll stick around,' I said politely.

'You got plans tomorrow?'

'Yeah. I'm meeting Claire, then I'll come in here. What about you?'

'Jason's in a soccer tournament in Palo Alto. I'm taking both boys down.'

'Sounds nice.' It did sound nice. It had the truth of something I might miss out on in life.

'I'll be back tomorrow evening.' He had given me his beeper the first day we hooked up. 'I'm an hour away. Call if anything comes up.'

With Raleigh gone, my corner of the squad room became shrouded in silence. The investigation was shut down for the night. One or two of the night staff were chatting in the outside hall.

I had never felt so lonely. Yet somehow I knew that if I went home now, I'd be leaving behind some vital nexus to the case, to Melanie. Failing some unsaid promise I had made. One more look, I told myself. One more pass.

Why would the killer take the rings?

A wave of exhaustion washed its way through my veins. My new fighting cells were stealing my strength even as they defended me, and multiplied. The cavalry, charging into the rescue. Hope attacking doubt. It seemed crazy.

I had to let David and Melanie sleep for the night. I

bound the thick crime file up in its elastic cord and placed it in the gray bin marked *Open Cases*. Next to similar files, with similar names.

Then I sat at my desk in the dark squad room for a couple of minutes more. I started to cry.

Book Two

The Women's Murder Club

Chapter Twenty-Six

Becky DeGeorge, in the bloom of her first full day as Michael's wife, walked out of the hotel lobby, holding her husband's hand. She breathed in the cool night air, the first fresh air she had inhaled all day.

In the brief span of their marriage, she and Michael had made love several times and taken two steamy showers together. They poked their heads out for an obligatory, but at last, final brunch with the families. They begged off the trip to Opus One, scurried back upstairs, and popped a last bottle of champagne. Michael put on a sex video and they both played out some unusual and exciting roles as they watched the film. He seemed to have several fantasies about wearing women's clothes.

Tomorrow, they'd be off to Mazatlan, for another heavenly week exploring all those sexy spots on his body she had yet to find. Who knows, maybe they'd even come out once or twice to see the dolphins.

So far, she decided, things were going very well.

They were headed to the French Laundry, the finest

restaurant in Napa. Everyone said it was *the* place to eat, and they had booked the reservation almost six months in advance. Becky's mouth watered as she dreamed of some fabulous sequence of tastes: foie gras, wild berry duck, all washed down with an expensive champagne.

On the short walk to the car, a black limo pulled up alongside them. The passenger window opened and a uniformed driver stuck his head out. 'Mr and Mrs DeGeorge?'

They looked at each other, puzzled, then smiled. 'That's us.'

'I'm at your service,' the driver announced. 'Compliments of the hotel.'

Becky was ecstatic. 'You mean for us?' Once, in her job as a legal secretary, at a big closing, she had ridden in a fabulous stretch; but she was jammed in the back seat with four preoccupied lawyers.

'Booked and paid for the night,' the driver said, and winked.

The newlyweds exchanged a bright, exclamatory look.

'No one mentioned anything about this,' said Michael, who seemed pleased with the notion that he was thought of as a VIP.

Becky peeked inside. 'Oh, Michael!' There were lush leather back seats and a polished mahogany bar with crystal glasses, and the lights were dimmed to a romantic glow. There was even a bottle of Chardonnay on ice. She thought of pulling up to the most fashionable restaurant in Napa in this wonderful car.

'C'mon, honey,' she laughed, almost pulling him in. 'It'll be a trip.'

'I can be waiting at the restaurant when you come out,' the driver said, 'and as it happens, you're talking to someone who knows the most scenic routes through Napa.'

She saw Michael's mild hesitation begin to crack. 'Don't you want to take your princess in style?'

Just as it was when she had first smiled his way in the office, just as it was in bed last night, she saw him slowly come around. He was a little cautious sometimes. Accountants often were. But she'd always found ways of loosening him up.

'Whatever Mrs DeGeorge wants,' Michael finally said.

Chapter Twenty-Seven

'Just married?' Phillip Campbell asked, his heart jumping. The bright lights of oncoming cars shot through him like X-rays, exposing his innermost desires.

'Twenty-six hours, eleven minutes and . . . forty-five seconds,' Becky chirped.

Campbell's heart pounded loudly. She was perfect. They were perfect together. *Even better than he had hoped.*

The road was blank and seemed directionless, but he knew where he was going. 'Help yourself to a drink,' he invited them. 'That's a Palmeyer in the bucket. Some people think it's the best in the valley.'

As he drove, the killer's nerves were taut and excited. *What is the worst thing anyone has ever done? Can I do it again? More to the point, can I ever* stop *doing it?*

He glanced back and saw Becky and Michael pouring the Palmeyer wine. He heard the clink of raised glasses, then something about years of good luck. With a chill in his heart, he watched them kiss. He hated every smug, deluded pore in their bodies. 'Don't you want to take your princess in style?' Huh! He fingered the gun resting in his lap. He was changing murder weapons.

After a while, Campbell turned the limo up a steep hill off the main road.

'Where're we heading, driver?' The husband's voice came from the back.

He glanced in the mirror and smiled confidently at the DeGeorges. 'I thought I'd take you the scenic way. Best views in the valley. And I'll still have you to the restaurant by eight.'

'We don't want to be late,' the groom warned sheepishly. 'These reservations were harder to get than the damn hotel.'

'Oh, c'mon, honey,' Becky chimed in with perfect timing.

'Things start to open up just ahead,' he told them. 'It's real pretty. In the meantime, relax. Put on some music. I'll show you the best views . . . very romantic.'

He pushed a button, and a thin band of pulsing lights began to shoot around the roof of the back compartment, a soft, seductive light show.

'Oooh,' Becky said, as the lights came on. 'This is *so* great.'

'I'll put up the privacy screen for the rest of the trip. You're only newlyweds once. Feel free to do whatever. Just look at it as your night.'

He left the screen slightly open, so he could still see and hear them as he drove deeper into the hills. They were nuzzling now, sharing kisses. The groom's hand was moving up Becky's thigh. She pushed her pelvis into him.

The road became bumpy and, at intermittent points, the rough split concrete gave way to gravelly dirt. They were climbing. On both sides, the slopes were patterned with grids of darkened vines.

Becky's teasing laughter gave way to a steady rhythm of deep-throated sighs. Phillip Campbell's breath began to race. Only inches away, he could hear her panting. A warm, velvety sensation began to burn in his thighs, as it had a week ago at the Grand Hyatt. Michael was entering Becky and she moaned.

What is the worst thing?

At a clearing, he pulled the car to a stop, turned the headlights off. He took the gun and pulled back the double-clicking action.

Then he lowered the privacy screen.

In the ambient light, there was Becky, her black cocktail dress pulled up around her waist.

'Bravo!' he exclaimed.

They looked up, startled.

He saw a flicker of fear in the bride's eyes. She tried to cover herself.

Only then did the killer recognize that the warm flood burning his thighs and his knees was his own urine.

He emptied the gun into Becky and Michael DeGeorge.

Chapter Twenty-Eight

That Sunday morning, I woke for the first time all week with a sense of hopefulness. It's the way I am . . . or *was*.

It was clear and beautiful outside; the Bay was shimmering as if it were thrilled, too. And it was the day of my brunch with Claire. My confession to her.

Sunday mornings I had this place I always went to. My favorite place, I had told Raleigh.

First I drove downtown, to the Marina Green, in my tights, and jogged in the shadow of the bridge. Mornings like this, I felt infused with everything that was beautiful about living in San Francisco. The brown coast of Marin, the noises of the Bay, even Alcatraz, standing guard.

I ran my usual three-plus miles south of the harbor, then up the 212 stone stairs, into Fort Mason Park. Even with Negli's I could still do it. This morning it seemed to be letting me free.

I jogged past yelping dogs running loose, lovers on a morning walk, gray-clad, bald-headed Chinese men bickering over mah-jongg. I always went to the same spot, high on the cliff, looking east over the Bay. It was 7:45.

No one knew I came here. Or why. Like every Sunday, I came upon a small group practicing their t'ai chi. They were mostly Chinese, led, as every week, by the same old man in a gray knit cap and sweater vest. I huffed to a stop and joined in as I had every Sunday for the past ten years, since my mother died.

They didn't know me. What I did. Who I was. I didn't know them. The old man gave me the same quick, welcoming nod he always did.

There's a passage in Thoreau: 'Time is but the stream I go a-fishing in. I drink at it, but while I drink, I see the sandy bottom and detect how shallow it is. Its current slides away, but eternity remains. I would drink deeper, fish in the sky, whose bottom is pebbly with stars.'

I guess I've read that a hundred times. It's the way I feel up here. Part of the stream.

No Negli's.

No crimes, no faces twisted in death.

No Bride and Groom murders.

I did my Morning Swan, my Dragon, and I felt as light and free as I did before Orenthaler first dropped the news on me.

The leader nodded. No one asked me if I was well. Or how the week was. I just welcomed the day, and knew that I was lucky to have it.

My favorite place.

I got home just before eleven, a half-finished coffee and the Sunday *Chronicle* in my arms. I figured I'd poke through the Metro section, see if there was anything on the case from my new best friend Cindy Thomas. Then I'd take a shower, and be ready by noon to go meet Claire.

It was 11:25 when the phone rang. To my surprise, the voice on the line was Raleigh's.

'You dressed?' he asked.

'Sort of. Why? I have plans.'

'Cancel them. I'm picking you up. We're going to Napa.'

'Napa?' There was no trace of anything light or playful in his voice. 'What's up?'

'I went in this morning just to check. While I was there, someone named Hartwig got transferred from Central Dispatch. He's a Lieutenant in Napa. He's got some couple out there who are missing. They're newlyweds on their honeymoon.'

Chapter Twenty-Nine

By the time I called Claire to cancel, showered, put my wet hair under a turned-back Giants cap, and threw on some clothes, Raleigh's white Explorer was beeping me from below.

When I got downstairs, I couldn't help but notice him looking me over – wet hair, jeans, black leather jacket. 'You look nice, Boxer.' He smiled as he put the car in gear.

He was casually dressed in crumpled khakis and a faded blue polo shirt. He looked nice, too, but I wasn't going to say it.

'This isn't a date, Raleigh,' I told him.

'You keep saying that,' he shrugged, then stepped down on the gas.

An hour and fifteen minutes later, we pulled up to the Napa Highlands Inn, the exact time, I noted, I was supposed to be pouring my heart out to Claire.

The inn turned out to be one of those fancy, high-end spas I always dreamed about going to. It was tucked into the mountains on Stag's Leap Road. With its main lodge built of stacked giant redwoods and arcing windows of tempered glass, the guests here were not exactly into self-denial.

Two green-and-white police units were parked in the rotary outside the hotel's entrance. In the lobby, we were directed to the manager's office where a nervous, red-haired management type, who seemed just a few days out of the training program, was standing with a couple of local cops.

'I'm Hartwig,' said a tall, lanky man in street clothes. He was holding a paper cup from Starbucks. 'Sorry to bust up your weekend,' he apologized in a friendly drawl.

He passed us a wedding photo of the missing couple. It was enclosed in one of those Plexiglas 'shaky toys' with the Golden Gate Bridge in the foreground. 'Party favor,' he sighed. 'Mr and Mrs Michael DeGeorge. From down your way. They both worked in the city at a large accounting firm. Married on Friday night.'

Actually, it was a sweet photo. She, bright-eyed, with thick brown hair; he, ruddy and serious-looking, wire-rimmed glasses.

'So when were they last seen?' I asked.

'Seven-forty-five last night. Hotel staff saw them come down on their way to dinner at the French Laundry,' Hartwig said. 'The concierge wrote them out directions, but they never showed.'

'They drove off to go to dinner and were never heard from again?'

Hartwig kept rubbing the side of his face. 'The manager

said they checked in the day before in a gold Lexus. Door staff confirm they drove it briefly that afternoon.'

'Yeah?' I nodded, fast-forwarding him.

'Car's still in the lot.'

I asked, 'Any messages from the outside we should know about?'

Hartwig went back to a desk and handed me a small stack of slips. I skipped through them. *Mom. Dad. Julie and Sam. Vicki and Don. Bon voyage.*

'We thoroughly searched the grounds around the property. Then we widened the search. It's sort of like your murder down there. Big wedding, celebration. Then *poof*, they're gone.'

'Sort of like our thing,' I agreed, 'except we had *bodies*.'

The Napa cop's face tightened. 'Believe me, I didn't call you guys all the way out here just to help us with the missing-persons forms.'

'What makes you so sure?' Raleigh asked.

' 'Cause the concierge did receive one call last night. It was from the restaurant, confirming their reservations.'

'So?'

Hartwig took a sip of his coffee before he met our eyes. 'No one at the French Laundry made that call.'

Chapter Thirty

The honeymoon couple had received no unusual visitors, scheduled no other conflicting side trips. The reservation at the French Laundry had been just for two.

What made this all the more grave was that they had missed their scheduled flight to Mexico.

While Raleigh poked around outside, I made a quick check of their room. There was this enormous redwood bed neatly turned down, a suitcase laid out, clothes stacked, toiletries. Lots of flowers – mostly roses. Maybe Becky DeGeorge had brought them from the reception.

There was nothing to indicate that the DeGeorges weren't set to board their plane the next morning.

I caught up with Raleigh outside. He was talking with a bellhop who was apparently the last person who saw the DeGeorges leave.

When it was just the two of us, Raleigh said, 'A couple of the local guys and I swept a hundred yards into the woods.' He shook his head in exasperation. 'Not even a footprint. I looked around the car, too. It's locked. No blood, no sign of a struggle. But *something* happens to them out here. Someone accosts them. Twenty, thirty yards from the hotel.'

I took a frustrated 360-degree scan of the driveway and the nearby parking lot. A local police cruiser was set up outside the property gate. 'Not accosts them. Too risky – it's in plain view. Maybe someone picked them up.'

'The reservations are only for two,' he countered. 'And the guy at the front door insists they were headed to their car.'

'Then they *vanish*?'

Our attention was diverted by the swoosh of a long black limousine turning into the resort's pebbly driveway. It pulled up under the redwood overhang in front of the entrance.

Raleigh and I watched the hotel door open and the doorman emerge rolling a trolley of bags. The driver of the limo hopped out to open the trunk.

It hit us both at the same time.

'It's a long shot,' said Raleigh, meeting my eyes.

'Maybe,' I agreed, 'but it would explain how someone gained access without diverting anyone's attention. I think we should check if any limos have been reported stolen lately in the Bay area.'

Another car turned into the driveway, a silver Mazda, and parked near the far end of the circle. To my dismay, a woman in cargo pants and a University of Michigan sweatshirt jumped out.

'Raleigh, you said one of your particular skills was containment, didn't you?'

He looked at me as if I had asked Dr Kevorkian, 'You're sort of good at mixing chemicals, aren't you?'

'Okay,' I said, eyeing the approaching figure, 'contain this.'

Walking up to us was Cindy Thomas.

Chapter Thirty-One

'**E**ither you've got the sharpest nose for a story I've ever seen,' I said to her angrily, 'or I may start to think of you as a murder suspect.'

This was the second time Cindy Thomas had intruded into the middle of a possible crime scene.

'Don't tell me I'm stepping on some inter-office romance?' she quipped.

That made me steaming mad. We had a developing situation here. If it got out prematurely, it would hurt any chance the Department had to control this case. I could just imagine the nightmare headlines I'd be seeing: BRIDE AND GROOM KILLER STRIKES AGAIN. And Roth would be livid. This would be the second time I had failed to control the crime scene with the same reporter.

'Who's your friend?' Raleigh asked.

'Cindy Thomas,' she announced, extending her hand. 'And you?'

'Cindy's with the *Chronicle*,' I alerted him.

Raleigh did a startled double-take, left in midshake like

a fired worker holding the hand of his replacement.

'Listen very clearly, Ms Thomas,' I said firmly. 'I don't know if you've been around long enough to develop a sense for how this is supposed to work, but if you're planning on doing anything except telling me why you're here, then pack up your little reporter's kit and drive away. You're definitely gonna make the Department's shit list in a hurry.'

'*Cindy*,' she reminded me, 'but first, the much more interesting question is, why am I out here bumping into you?'

Raleigh and I both glared at her with deepening impatience. 'Why are you here?' I pressed.

'All right.' She took a breath and pursed her lips. 'You two shooting down here on a Sunday; Captain Raleigh kicking around the woods and the parking lot; your grilling the hotel staff; both of you looking stumped. I have to figure it all starts to add up. Like the fact that the place hasn't been cordoned off, so no crime's been committed yet. That someone could be missing. Since we all know what you two are working on, it's not a far reach to assume it might be a couple who just got married. Possibly, that our Bride and Groom killer found himself Number Two.'

My eyes were wide, worried.

'Either that,' she smiled, 'or I've grossly misjudged things and you guys are just here zin-tasting for the Department's wine club.'

'You picked up all that from watching us?' I asked her.

'Honestly? No.' She nodded toward the hotel gate. 'Most

of it was from the big-mouth local cop I was yapping with out there.'

Without meaning to, I started to smile.

'Seriously, you realize you can't run with anything here,' Raleigh said.

'Another dead bride and groom? Same MO,' she snorted with resolve. 'Damn right I'm going to run with it.'

I was starting to see the situation going straight down-hill. 'One thing I'd *strongly* consider would be to get in your car and just drive back into town.'

'Would you say that to Fitzpatrick or Stone?'

'If you went back to town, then I really *would* owe you one.'

She smiled thinly. 'You're kidding, aren't you? You want me to just walk away?'

'Yeah, just walk away.'

Cindy shook her head. 'Sorry. One, I'd probably get fired and two, there's just no way I could let this pass.'

'What if I drove back with you?' I said, spur of the moment. 'What if you can have pretty much what you're looking for, be on the inside, and give me some considera-tion at the same time.'

Raleigh's eyes almost bulged out of his head, but I gave him my best let-me-handle-this expression.

'When this story does break,' Cindy insisted, 'it's gonna be larger than any of us can control.'

'And when it does, it'll be *yours*.'

Her eyes narrowed. She was rolling around in her head whether she could trust me. 'You mean from you, exclusive?'

I waited for Raleigh to object. To my amazement, he went along.

'You said Chief Mercer was handling all the releases,' Cindy pressed.

'He is. All the *public* ones.'

I looked at Raleigh with my nerves leaping around like a Mexican jumping bean. If I couldn't trust him, then when we got back to town, I could be facing maximum rebuke. I would have Roth at my desk, or worse, Mercer. But I already felt I could trust him.

'So *I'm* gonna catch a ride back to town with Ms Thomas,' I said, waiting for his response.

'*Cindy*,' the reporter repeated, with renewed determination.

Raleigh began to nod in a gradual, acquiescent way. 'I'll finish up with Hartwig. I'll talk to you soon, Lindsay. Ms Thomas, an unexpected pleasure.'

I shot him a grateful smile. Then I took the reporter by the arm and said, 'C'mon, *Cindy*, I'm gonna explain the rules along the way.'

Chapter Thirty-Two

I don't know why I did it.

It was risky and rash, precisely the opposite of whatever had gotten me as far as I was. Maybe I just wanted to say *Screw it*, in the face of authority. To Roth, Mercer. To play things my own way. Maybe the case was widening, and I just wanted to keep the illusion that it was in my control.

Or maybe all I wanted to do was let someone else in.

'Before we go anywhere,' I said, grasping Cindy's wrist as she started up the car, 'I need to know something. How did you find out about what was going on down here?'

She took a deep breath. 'So far, all that's happened is you've pushed me away from the story of my career. Now I have to give up my sources, too?'

'Anything we do from here on is dependent on it.'

'I'd kind of prefer it if I can keep you guessing,' Cindy said.

'If this is gonna work, it's gotta be based on trust.'

'Then trust goes two ways, doesn't it, Detective?'

We sat there, baking in the hot Mazda littered with empty fast-food drink cups, sort of squaring off.

'Okay,' I finally relented. I gave her what little we knew about why we were in Napa that afternoon. The DeGeorges missing in action. That they had been married Friday night. The possibility that they were Couple Number Two. 'None of this goes to print,' I insisted, 'until we have confirmation. Then I'll give you the okay.'

Her eyes beamed with her suppositions suddenly confirmed.

'Now it's your turn. There was no press down here, even local. How did you get onto this?'

Cindy put the Mazda in gear. 'I told you I was from Metro,' she said, as the car putted out onto the main road, 'and that I've been fighting to stay on this story. My boss gave me the weekend to come up with something solid on this biggie. You had already brushed me off, so I parked myself down your street since yesterday and waited for something to turn up.'

'You followed me?'

'Pretty desperate, huh? But effective.'

I scrolled back over the past two days. 'To the movies. To the marina this morning?'

She blushed slightly. 'I was about to call it quits when your partner came by. I just tagged along for the ride.'

I pressed myself back in my seat and started to laugh. 'Not so desperate,' I muttered. 'Bad guys've been falling for it for years.' I was both embarrassed and relieved.

On the drive back to town, I explained the rules of our

agreement. I had done this before, when a reporter got too close on a story and threatened an investigation. Cindy couldn't go out with this story until we had confirmation. When we did, I'd make sure she had it first. I'd keep her ahead of the story, but just slightly ahead.

'There's a catch,' I said firmly. 'What we have now is what you would call a prioritized relationship. It goes past anything you already have – with your boyfriend or someone at work. Even your boss. Anything I give you is totally between us, and it stays with us, until I give you the okay to run with it.'

Cindy nodded, but I wanted to make sure she understood.

'Your boss asks you where any of this comes from, you just shrug. Some big shot in the Department . . . I don't care if it's Chief Mercer himself . . . parks his limo outside your door and calls you in about some leak, you say, "Thanks for the ride." The District Attorney's office calls you down to a grand jury, asks you to give up your sources, and a judge slaps you into a cell. You just make sure you bring enough reading material to fill the time.'

'I understand,' Cindy said. I could see in her eyes that she did.

The rest of the trip we talked about ourselves, our jobs, hobbies, and an unexpected development began to take shape. I started to like Cindy.

She asked me how long I'd been a cop, and I took her through more of the story than I had planned to. How my father was a police officer, and how he'd left when I was thirteen. How I was sociology at SF State. How I wanted to prove I could make a difference in a man's world. How a lot of who I was and what I did was simply trying to prove I belonged.

She came back that she was sociology, too, at Michigan. And before we even hit Marin, we had discovered a few other startling things we had in common.

Her younger brother was born on my birthday, 5 October. She was also into yoga, and the woman who had first taught me, years before in South San Francisco, was now instructing her in Corte Madera. We both liked to read travel books, and mysteries – Sue Grafton, Patricia Cornwell, Elizabeth George. We *loved* Gordon's *House of Fine Eats*.

Cindy's father had died early – some seventeen years ago – eerily, when she was only thirteen, too.

But the most chilling coincidence, the one that went right through me, was that he died of leukemia, cousin of the same degenerating disease that was coursing through me.

I thought of telling her my secret, but I stopped short. That was Claire's to hear. But as we drew close to the Golden Gate, I had a premonition I was riding with someone I was meant to be with, and definitely someone I liked to be with.

Approaching the city, I called Claire. It was hours after we were supposed to meet, but she still seemed eager to get together – and I had a lot to share. We agreed to keep our date at Susie's, this time for an early dinner instead of a brunch. When she pressed me for what I had found during the day, I told her, 'I'll fill you in when I get there.'

Then I did the second thing that surprised me that day. I asked, 'Do you mind if I bring a friend?'

Chapter Thirty-Three

Cindy and I were already into our second margarita by the time Claire walked in. From ten feet away, her smile seemed to brighten the entire room. I stood up and gave her a big hug.

'Couldn't wait for the old mom?' she said, eyeing the array of empty glasses.

'It's been a long day,' I sighed. 'Say hey to Cindy.'

'Pleasure,' said Claire brightly, grasping Cindy's hand. Though the date was planned for just her and me, Claire was one of those people who rolled easily with whatever came up.

'Lindsay's been telling me all about you,' Cindy said, over the din.

'Most of it's true, unless she's been saying I'm some kind of crackerjack forensic pathologist,' Claire said, grinning.

'Actually, all she's been saying is that you're a real good friend.'

Susie's was a bright, festive café with faux-painted walls and pretty good Caribbean food. They played a little reggae, a little jazz. It was a place where you could kick back, talk, shout, even shoot a rack of pool.

Our regular waitress, Loretta, came up, and we swayed Claire into a margarita for herself and another round of spicy, jerked wings for us.

'Tell me about Reggie's graduation,' I said.

Claire stole a wing from our bowl and wistfully shook her head. 'It's nice to know after all those years of school, they can actually say a few words that aren't "phat" or "it's the bomb". They looked like a bunch of street-struttin' kids auditioning for the Grammys, but the Principal swears they'll come out of it in time for their college interviews.'

'If they don't, there's always the Academy,' I grinned, feeling light-headed.

Claire smiled. 'I'm glad to see *you* looking up. When we spoke the other day, it sounded like Cheery was treading those big, ugly shoes of his all over your toes.'

'Cheery?' asked Cindy.

'My boss. We call him Cheery 'cause he inspires us with his humanistic concern for those entrusted to his command.'

'Oh, I thought you were talking about my city editor,' snickered Cindy. 'The guy's only truly happy when he can threaten someone with their benefits. He has *no clue* how demeaning and condescending he is.'

'Cindy's with the *Chronicle*,' I said to Claire, seeing her react with surprise. There was an undeclared no-fly zone between the force and the press. To cross it, as a reporter, you had to earn your place.

'Writing your memoirs, child?' Claire asked me, with a guarded smile.

'Maybe.' The short version. But with lots to tell.

Claire's margarita arrived, and we raised our glasses.

'To the powers that be,' I toasted.

Cindy laughed. 'Powers that be full of shit, powers that be pompous jerks, powers that be trying to keep you down.'

Claire yelped in approval, and we clinked glasses as if we were old friends.

'Y'know, when I first came to the paper,' Cindy said, nibbling a wing, 'one of the senior guys told me it was this particular editor's birthday. So I e-mail him this Happy Birthday message. I figure, him being my boss and all, it's a way to break the ice, maybe get a smile out of him. Later that day, the jerk calls me in. He's all polite and smiley. He's got bushy eyebrows as big as squirrels' tails. He nods me into the seat across from him. I'm thinking, Hey . . . the guy's human like everybody else.'

Claire smiled. Enthusiastically, I drained the last of my second drink.

'So, then the bastard narrows his eyes and says, "Thomas, in the next hour and a half, I have sixty reporters trying to take everything that doesn't make sense in this fucking world and somehow cram it into forty pages. But it's reassuring to know that while everyone else is madly rushing against the clock, you've got the time to paste a happy little smiley face on my day." He ended up assigning me a week of picking a winner from a fifth grade *Why I Want to Be an Editor for a Day* contest.'

I laughed, and coughed up a little of my drink. 'Goes under the heading of, No Good Deed Goes Unpunished. What did you do?'

Cindy had a great smile. 'E-mail it was the boss's birthday to every guy in the Department. Jerks were slumping out of his office with their faces white all day.'

Loretta came around again, and we ordered meals: chicken in a fiery sauce, fajitas, and a large salad to share. Three Dos Equis to go with them. We poured this lethal Jamaican hot sauce, Toasty Lady, on our wings and watched Cindy's eyes glaze over from the first fiery blast.

'Rite of initiation,' I grinned. 'Now you're one of the girls.'

'It's either the hot sauce, or a tattoo,' Claire announced, straight-faced.

Cindy scrunched up her eyes, in an evaluating sort of way, then turned around and rolled up the sleeve of her T-shirt. She exposed two small G clefs etched on the back of her shoulder. 'The downside of a classical education,' she said, with a crooked smile.

My eyes met Claire's – and both of us hooted with approval.

Then Claire yanked up her own shirt with a blush. Just below her ample brown waist, she revealed the outline of a tiny butterfly.

'Lindsay dared me one day,' she told Cindy. 'After you broke up with that prosecutor from San Jose, remember, honey? We went down to Big Sur overnight, just the girls, to let off some steam. Ended up coming back with these.'

'So where's yours?' Cindy turned to me.

'Can't show you.' I shook my head.

'C'mon,' she protested. 'Let's see it.'

With a sigh, I rolled onto my left buttock and patted my right. 'It's a one-inch gecko, with this really cute little tail. When I push some suspect up against a wall, if he's giving me a hard time, I tell him I'll stick it in his face so tight it's gonna seem as large as Godzilla.'

A warm silence fell over us. For a moment, the faces of David and Melanie Brandt, even Negli's, seemed a million miles away. We were just having fun.

I felt something happening, something that hadn't happened in a long time, that I desperately needed.

I felt connected.

Chapter Thirty-Four

'So now that we're all friends,' said Claire, after we had gone through another plateful of ribs, 'how'd the two of you meet up, anyway? Last I heard, you were going out to Napa to check on some missing newlyweds.'

Michael and Becky DeGeorge, who a moment ago had seemed so far away, came hurtling back with a crash.

I had so much to tell her, but the day had changed so subtly from what I had planned. I almost felt deceitful, withholding, filling her in on what had taken place in Napa, yet leaving out the important development that was going on inside of me.

Claire took it in, digesting it all with that sharp mind of hers. She had consulted on several serial-homicide cases, both as a lead examiner and an expert witness.

An idea was rolling through my head. In my weakened condition, I didn't relish the responsibility of running a media-intensive investigation into multiple homicides. What I came back with surprised even me.

'How'd you like to lend me some help?'

'Help?' Claire blinked with surprise. 'How?'

'This thing is about to explode, Claire,' I said. 'If there's a Bride and Groom killer out there, the attention will be national. We all have an interest in this case. Maybe we could meet like this. The three of us . . . off the record.'

Claire looked at me warily. 'You're suggesting we do this on our own?'

'We've got the top guns of the ME's office, Homicide, even the press, eye-deep in margaritas at this table.' The more I thought it out, the more I knew it could work.

We could reassemble whatever clues came out of the official investigation, share what we had, cut through the political cover-your-ass and the bureaucracy. Three women, who would get a kick from showing up the male orthodoxy. More important, we shared a heartfelt empathy for the victims.

Suddenly, the idea seemed lit with brilliance.

Claire shook her head in an incredulous way.

'C'mon,' I encouraged her, 'you don't think it would work? You don't think we'd be good at this?'

'That's not it at all,' she replied. 'It's just that I've known you for ten years, and never once, on anything, have I heard you ask for help.'

'Then feel very surprised,' I said, looking her straight in the eye, ' 'cause I'm asking for it now.'

I tried to let her see that something was troubling me, something maybe larger than the case. That I wasn't sure I could handle it. That I could use the help. That there was more to it.

Claire gradually broke into the slimmest, acquiescent grin. 'In margaritas veritas. I'm in.'

I beamed back, grateful, then turned to Cindy. 'How about you? You in?'

She stammered, 'I have no idea what Sid Glass would say – but fuck him. I'm in.'

We clinked glasses.

The Women's Murder Club was born.

Chapter Thirty-Five

The next morning, I arrived at the office straight from an eight o'clock transfusion, feeling light-headed, slightly woozy. First thing I did was scan the morning *Chronicle*. To my relief, there was nothing on the front page about anything relating to the disappearance in Napa. Cindy had kept her word.

I noticed Raleigh coming out of Roth's office. His sleeves were rolled up, exposing his thick forearms. He gave me a guarded smile – one that told me that behind it was his discomfort at my cutting a deal yesterday with Cindy. With a flick of his brown eyes, he motioned me outside to the corridor.

'We have to talk,' he said, as we huddled near the staircase.

'Listen, Raleigh,' I exhaled, 'I'm really sorry about yesterday. I thought it would buy us some time.'

His dark eyes smoldered. 'Maybe you should tell me why she was worth compromising control of this case.'

I shrugged. 'You see anything about Napa in the papers this morning?'

'You contramanded a direct order from the Chief of Police. If that doesn't leave you in a hole, it sure digs one for me.'

'So you'd rather be digging out of a story in the *Chronicle* about a serial killer?'

He backed against the wall. 'That's Mercer's call.'

A policeman I knew skipped up the stairs past us, grunting hello. I barely nodded back.

'Okay,' I said, 'so how do you want to play it? You want me to go in and spill my guts to Sam Roth? If so, I will.'

He hesitated. I could see he was torn, clicking through the consequences. After what seemed like a minute, he shook his head. 'What's the point now?'

I felt a wave of relief. I touched his arm and smiled at him for a couple of long beats. 'Thanks.'

'Lindsay,' he added, 'I checked with the State Highway Patrol. There's no record of any limos reported stolen in the past week.'

That news, the dead end that it represented, discouraged me.

A voice shouted out from the squad room. 'Boxer out there?'

'I'm here,' I hollered back.

It was Paul Chin, one of the bright efficient junior grades assigned to our team. 'There's a Lieutenant Frank Hartwig on the line. Says you know him.'

I ran back in, grabbed the phone on our civilian clerk's desk. 'This is Lindsay Boxer.'

'We found them, Inspector,' Hartwig said.

Chapter Thirty-Six

'Caretaker discovered them,' Hartwig muttered, with a grim shake of his head. He was guiding us up a dirt path leading to a small Napa winery. 'I hope you're ready for this. It's the worst thing I've ever seen. They were killed making love.'

Raleigh and I had rushed up to St Helena, turning east off 29, 'the wine road', onto Hawk Crest Road until it wound high into the mountains, no longer paved. We finally came upon an obscure wooden sign: *Sparrow Ridge*.

'Caretaker comes up here twice a week. Found them at seven this morning. The place is no longer in regular use,' Hartwig continued. I could tell he was nervous, shook up.

The winery was barely more than a large corrugated shed filled with shiny, state-of-the-art equipment: crushers, fermenting tanks, staggered rows of stacked, aging barrels.

'You're probably used to this sort of homicide,' Hartwig said, as we walked in. The sharp, rancid smell hit our nostrils. My stomach rolled. No, I felt like telling him, you never get used to homicide scenes.

They were killed making love.

Several members of the local SCU team were huddled over the open bay of a large, stainless steel grape presser. They were inspecting two splattered mounds. The mounds were the bodies of Michael and Becky DeGeorge.

'Awhh, shit, Lindsay,' Raleigh muttered.

The husband, in a blazer and khakis, stared up at us. A dime-sized penetration cut the center of his forehead. His wife, whose black dress was pushed up to her neck, was thrown on top of him. White-eyed fear was frozen on her face. Her bra was pulled down to her waist, and I could see blood-spattered breasts. Her panties were down to her knees.

It was an ugly, nauseating sight. 'You have an approximate time?' I asked Hartwig. He looked close to being sick.

'From the degeneration of the wounds, the ME thinks they've been dead twenty-four to thirty-six hours. They were killed the same night they disappeared. Jesus, they were just kids.'

I stared at the sad, bloodied body of the wife, and my eyes fell to her hands.

Nothing there. No wedding band.

'You said they were killed in the act?' I muttered. 'You're sure about that?'

Hartwig nodded to the assistant medical examiner. He gently rolled Becky DeGeorge's body off her husband.

Sticking out of Michael DeGeorge's unfastened khakis was a perfectly preserved remainder of his final erection.

A smoldering rage ripped through me. The DeGeorges were just kids. Both were in their twenties, like the Brandts. Who would do such a terrible thing?

'You can see over here how they were dragged,' Hartwig said, pointing to smears of dried blood visible on the pitched, concrete floor. The smears led to car tracks that were clearly delineated in the sparsely traveled soil. A couple of sheriff's men were marking off the tracks in yellow tape.

Raleigh bent down and studied them. 'Wide wheel base, but fourteen-inch tires. The tread is good, kept up. An SUV would have sixteen-inch wheels. I would guess it was some kind of large, luxury sedan.'

'I thought you were just a desk cop?' I said to him.

He grinned. 'I spent a summer in college working in the pit crew on the NASCAR circuit. I can change a tire faster than a beer man at 3Com can change a twenty. My guess would be, a Caddy. Or a Lincoln.' Limo, his eyes were saying.

My own mind was racing through what Claire had said last night. *Link the crimes.*

It was uncommon for a pattern killer to switch methods. Sexual killers liked closeness to their victims: strangulation, bludgeoning, knives. They wanted to feel their victims struggle, expire. They liked to invade a victim's home. Shooting was detached, clinical. It provided no thrill.

For a moment, I wondered if there were two crimes going on. Copycat killers. It couldn't be.

No one else knew about the rings.

I went over to Becky DeGeorge as the doctor was zipping her up in the body bag. I gazed down into her eyes. They were making love. Did he force them? Did he surprise them?

A sexual psycho who changes his methods. A killer who leaves clues.

What did he leave here?

What were we missing?

Chapter Thirty-Seven

Fresh air filled my lungs as soon as we stepped outside. Chris Raleigh, Hartwig, and I walked down the barren dirt road. The grid of the valley floor stretched out below us. Rows of fallow grapes hugged each side. We were silent. Shell-shocked.

A scary idea shot through me. We were a thousand feet up, totally isolated. Something didn't sit right. 'Why here, Hartwig?'

'How about it's remote and no one ever comes up here?'

'What I meant,' I said, 'is why *here* – this particular spot. Who knows about this place?'

'There's isolated property all up and down these slopes. The consortiums have eaten up the valley floor. These properties take more work than capital. They represent labors of love. Check the listings. Dozens of them dry up every season. Anyone around here knows places like this.'

'The first killings were in the city. Yet he knew exactly where to come. Who owns this plot?'

Hartwig shook his head. 'Dunno.'

'I'd find out. And I would also make another pass through their room. Someone had them targeted, knew all their plans. We'll take a look at their travel brochures, business cards – see if there's anything from any limousine services.'

From below I heard the sound of a large vehicle climbing up the gravel road and caught sight of a white San Francisco Medical Examiner's Bronco pulling to a stop.

Claire Washburn was behind the wheel. I had asked her down – in the hope of matching evidence to both crime scenes.

I opened her door and said gratefully, 'Thanks for coming, sweetie.'

Claire solemnly shook her head. 'I only wish they had turned up differently. It's a call I never like to receive.' She pulled her heavy frame out of the car with surprising ease. 'I have a meeting later back in town, but I thought I'd look over the crime scene, introduce myself to the presiding on-site.'

I introduced Claire to Frank Hartwig. 'Your ME is Bill Toll, isn't he?' she asked with authority.

He blinked warily, clearly nervous. First, he had Raleigh and me down here as consults. But he had asked us in. Now, the San Francisco ME pulls up.

'Relax, I already patched through to his cell phone,' Claire said. 'He's expecting me.' She spotted the medical team standing over the yellow bags. 'Why don't I go take a look.'

Trying to hold on to some sense of order, Hartwig followed closely behind.

Raleigh came and stood next to me. He looked pale and stressed.

'You okay?' I asked.

He shook his head. He kept his eyes fixed on the shed where the bodies had been dumped.

I remembered how he had steadied me at the morgue. 'Been a while since you took in a really bad one?'

'That's not it,' he said, with the same unsettled look. 'I just want you to know that wherever this leads, it's not about interfacing with City Hall. Or containment. Lindsay, I want this guy.'

I was already there in my head. This wasn't about the big collar. Or my shot at Lieutenant. Or even fighting Negli's.

We stood there side by side for a while.

'Not that either of us,' he finally said, breaking the silence, 'is in much of a position to be the last line of defense for the institution of marriage.'

Chapter Thirty-Eight

Phillip Campbell had driven since the first light of dawn, setting out in the bulky, rented stretch limo. He was nervous, wired – and he absolutely loved it.

Chewing up the miles in a steady, purposeful daze, crossing the Bay Bridge and continuing east on 80, he finally broke free of the morning traffic near Vallejo, and maintained a vigilant sixty on the speedometer as he headed east.

He didn't want to be stopped.

The papers called him a monster. Psychotic, sociopathic. Expert witnesses on TV analyzed his motives, his past, his future possible murders.

They knew nothing. They were all wrong. They'll only find what I want them to find, he thought. They'll only see what I want them to see.

From the Nevada border, it was a short drive down into Reno, which he considered a vulgar, aging cowboy town. He stayed on the highway, avoiding the Strip with its wide, stucco-lined boulevards of gas stations, gun dealerships, pawnshops. You could get anything here without a lot of questions. It was the place to come to buy a gun, or unload a car, or both.

Out by the Convention Center, he turned into Lumpy's. He pulled the car up to an open area in the lot, recovered the folded paperwork from the glove compartment and breathed a sigh of relief.

The limo was spotless. All day yesterday, he had cleaned and polished it, scrubbing out the bloodstains until the last trace of evidence was gone. It was as if Michael and Becky DeGeorge had never existed.

In minutes he had paid for the car and called a cab to take him to the airport.

At the airport, he checked in, looked through a San Francisco paper at a newsstand. There was nothing about Becky and Michael. He made his way to the gate, buying on the way a bottle of Fruitopia apricot drink and a vegetarian wrap at a fast-food counter.

He checked in at Gate 31, Reno Air to San Francisco, took a seat, and started eating his lunch.

An attractive young woman sat next to him. Blonde hair, tight ass, just tawdry-looking enough to attract his eye. She wore a gold chain around her neck with her name on it in script – *Brandee* – and a tiny diamond ring.

He smiled a quick, inadvertent greeting.

She pulled out a Kipling knapsack, took a swig from a plastic water bottle, and produced a paperback, *Memoirs of a Geisha*. It interested him that, of all things, she was reading about a woman in bondage. These were promising signs.

'Good book?' He smiled her way.

'That's what everyone says,' she replied. 'I'm just starting.'

He leaned over and breathed in the cheap, citrusy scent of her perfume.

'Hard to believe,' he went on, 'it was written by a man.'

'I'll let you know.' She flipped a few pages, then added, 'My fiancé gave it to me.'

Phillip Campbell felt the short thin hairs on his arms stand up on edge.

His heart began to throb. He ran a tremulous finger along the edge of his goatee.

'Oh – when's the big day?'

Chapter Thirty-Nine

Raleigh drove back to town in our car. I hung around and caught a ride with Claire. I needed to tell her what was going on with me. Claire and I have been best friends for years. We talk at least once every day. I *knew* why I was having trouble telling her about my illness – I didn't want to hurt her. Or to burden Claire with my problems. I loved her so much.

As the ME's van bumped down the mountain road, I asked if she had been able to pick anything up at the murder scene.

'There was definitely sexual activity going on before they were killed,' she replied confidently. 'I could see labial distending around the vagina. Secretions on her thighs. This is guesswork – I only had a few minutes – but I think the husband was shot first, Lindsay. The one clean wound to the head suggests he was dispatched without resistance, head on. The wounds on Rebecca indicate something else. She was shot from the rear – through the shoulder-blades, the neck. From a distance, I would estimate, of no more than three-to-five feet. If the semen matches up, and they were in the act when it took place, it suggests that she was on top. That would mean someone had to get in fairly close, unobserved, while they were at it. Come up at them from behind. Since you said they didn't use their own car that night, they were obviously on their way somewhere. I think it's consistent with your theory that they were in some kind of vehicle when this took place, the killer in the front seat. So why not a limousine?'

'That's all?' I shook my head and smiled at Claire.

'Like I said, I only had a few minutes. Anyway, it was your theory. If it ends up proving out, all I did was connect the dots.'

We drove on a bit. I was still fumbling for the right words. Claire asked, 'So how's the new partner?'

I flashed her an affirming nod. 'Turns out he's okay. He's backed me up with Roth and Mercer.'

'And you were so sure he was only a watchdog from the Mayor's office.'

'So I was wrong.'

'Wouldn't be the first time you ended up wrong about a guy,' Claire said.

I wrinkled my face in pretended offense and ignored her grin.

'Anyway, watchdog or not,' Claire continued, 'he's a damn sight better to look at than Jacobi.'

'Smarter, too. When we drove up to Napa yesterday, I flipped on the stereo in his Explorer. A tape of *The Shipping News* came on.'

'So,' Claire went on, with a look of inquisitiveness, 'anything going down?'

'You mean other than four innocent people being killed?'

'I mean with Chris Raleigh, Lindsay! He's working out of the Mayor's office, he's a hunk, and your social calendar isn't exactly Gwyneth Paltrow's. You can't tell me he's not your type.'

'We've been wrapped up in the case, Claire.'

'Yeah,' she chortled. 'He's not married, right?'

'C'mon,' I pleaded. 'I'm just not ready.'

As she winked at me, I found myself imagining something going on with Raleigh. If I had driven back with *him* the other day from Napa, instead of Cindy. If I had asked him up, it being nothing but a lonely Sunday, thrown together something out of the fridge. Shared a beer on the terrace as the sun melted into the Bay. In my mind, I caught him checking me over again. *You look good, Boxer.* He had noticed. Truth was, I had noticed things about him, too. Like his patient, sensitive eyes.

Even as I sat there pretending I could fall in love with someone, the daydream crashed. Life was slowly leaking out of me.

Something with Raleigh, or anyone, just wasn't a possibility now.

I flashed a glance at Claire, who was pulling the car onto 101, and I took a deep breath.

'You ever hear of something called Negli's aplastic anemia?' I asked.

Chapter Forty

It came out of the blue, so unexpectedly that it didn't even dawn on Claire what I had just said.

She answered as if she were fielding a medical question in her lab. 'Blood disorder. Pretty rare, serious. The body stops producing erythrocytes.'

'Red blood cells,' I said.

Claire glanced at me. 'Why? It's not Cat?' referring to my sister.

I shook my head. I sat rigid and stared straight ahead. My eyes were glassy. It was probably the long pause that caused it to slowly sink in.

Claire whispered, 'Not you?'

An awful stillness took hold in the car.

'Oh, Lindsay.' Claire's jaw dropped. She pulled the Bronco onto the shoulder of road and immediately reached out and hugged me. 'What has your doctor told you?'

'That it's serious. That it can be fatal.'

I saw the gravity of that wash over her face. The hurt, the

pain. Claire was a doctor, a pathologist. She had taken in what was at stake before I even met her eyes.

I told her that I was already undergoing packed red cell transfusions twice a week.

'That's why you wanted to get together the other day?' she declared. 'Oh, Lindsay. Why couldn't you just tell me?'

None of my past reasoning seemed clear now. 'I wanted to so much, but I was afraid. Maybe even more to admit it to myself. Then I allowed myself to get wrapped up in the case.'

'Does anyone know? Jacobi? Roth?'

I shook my head.

'Raleigh?'

I took a breath. 'Still think I'm ready for Mr Right?'

'You poor baby,' Claire said softly. 'Oh Lindsay, Lindsay, Lindsay.'

Her body was shaking. I could feel it. I *had* hurt her.

Suddenly, I let it all go – fear and shame and uncertainty rushing through me. I held onto Claire, and I realized she was all that kept me from hurtling out of control. I started to cry, and then we both did. It felt good, though. I wasn't alone anymore.

'I'm here for you, sweetheart,' Claire whispered. 'I love you, girl.'

Chapter Forty-One

The murder in Napa changed everything.

There were blistering attacks on the way the SFPD was trying to solve the case. We took heat from everywhere.

Sensational headlines announced the handiwork of a sadistic, deranged, completely new kind of killer. Out-of-town news crews buzzed around the Hall. Tragic wedding pictures and wrenching family scenes were the lead on every TV newscast.

The task force that I was heading was meeting twice a day. Two other Inspectors from SCU and a forensic psychologist were added on. We had to provide our files for the FBI. The investigation was no longer confined to some embittered figure lurking in David or Melanie Brandt's past. It had grown larger, deeper, more tragic and foreboding.

Canvassing area wine shops, Jacobi's team had unearthed a few names, nothing more.

The bloody jacket was coming up empty, too. The problem was, the tux style was from four to five years ago. Of the fifteen Bay Area stores, not one maintained records of manufacturers' styles, so it was virtually impossible to trace. We had to go over their records invoice by invoice.

Mercer tripled our investigators.

The killer was choosing his victims with careful precision. Both murders took place within a day of their marriage; both reflected specific knowledge of the victims, their lodgings, their itineraries. Both couples still had all of their valuables: watches, wallets, jewelry. The only things missing were the wedding rings.

He had dumped the DeGeorges in a seemingly isolated place, but one where they were sure to be found. He had left other blockbuster clues for us to follow up. It didn't make sense.

The killer knows exactly what he's doing, I thought. He knows what you're doing, too. *Link the crimes.*

I had to find the common denominator. How he knew his victims. How he knew so much about them.

Raleigh and I divided up the possibilities. He took whoever booked the Brandts' and the DeGeorges' itineraries: travel agencies, limo services, hotels. I took guests at both weddings. Ultimately, we would find some link between the crimes.

'If we don't make progress soon,' Raleigh grumbled, 'there'll be a lot of priests and rabbis in this town with a shitload of dead time. What's this maniac after?'

I didn't say, but I thought I knew. He was after happiness, dreams, expectations. He was trying to destroy the one thing that kept all of us going – hope.

Chapter Forty-Two

That night, Claire Washburn took a cup of tea into her bedroom, quietly closed the door, and started to cry again. 'Goddamn it, Lindsay,' she muttered. 'You could have trusted me.'

She needed to be alone. All that evening, she had been moody and distracted. And it wasn't like her. On Mondays, an off-night for the symphony, Edmund always cooked. It was one of their rituals, a family night – Dad in the kitchen, the boys clean up afterwards. Tonight he cooked their favorite meal, chicken in capers and vinegar. But nothing went right, and it was her fault.

One thought was pounding in her. She was a doctor, a doctor who dealt only in death. Never once had she saved a life. She was a doctor who did not heal.

Claire opened her closet, put on flannel pajamas, went into the bathroom and carefully cleansed her smooth brown face. She looked at herself.

She was not beautiful, at least not in the shape society taught us to admire. She was large and soft and round, her shapeless waist merging with her hips. Even her hands – her well-trained, efficient hands that controlled delicate instruments all day – were pudgy and full.

The only thing light about her, her husband always said, was when she was on the dance floor.

Yet, in her own eyes, she had always felt blessed and radiant. Because she had made it up from a tough, mostly black neighborhood in San Francisco to become a doctor. Because she was loved. Because she was taught to give love. Because she had everything in her life that she ever wanted.

It didn't seem fair. Lindsay was the one who attacked life, and now it was seeping out of her. She couldn't even think of it in a professional way, as a doctor, where she viewed the inevitability of disease with a clinical detachment. It pained her as a friend.

The doctor who could not heal.

After he finished helping the boys with the dishes, Edmund came in. He sat on the bed beside her.

'You're sick, kitty kat,' he said, with a hand that kneaded her shoulder. 'Whenever you curl up before nine o'clock, I know you're getting sick.'

She shook her head. 'I'm not sick, Edmund.'

'Then what is it? This grotesque case?'

Claire raised a hand. 'It's Lindsay. I rode back from Napa with her yesterday. She told me the most awful news. She's got a rare blood disorder, a form of anemia. It's called Negli's aplastic.'

'It's severe, this Negli's anemia?'

Claire nodded, her eyes dim. 'Damned severe.'

'Oh, God,' Edmund muttered. 'Poor Lindsay.' He took her hand and they sat there for a moment in stunned silence.

Claire finally spoke. 'I'm a doctor. I see death every day. I know the causes and symptoms, the science inside out. But *I can't heal.*'

'You heal us all the time,' Edmund said quietly. 'You heal me every day of my life. But there are times when even all your love and even your amazing intelligence can't change things.'

She nestled her body in his strong arms and smiled. 'You're pretty smart for a guy who plays the drums. So then what the hell *can* we do?'

'Just this,' he said, wrapping his arms around her.

He held Claire tightly for a long time, and she knew he thought she was the most beautiful woman in the whole world. That helped.

Chapter Forty-Three

The following afternoon, I got my first glimpse of the killer's face.

Chris Raleigh was talking to the people who had handled the travel arrangements of both sets of victims while I was checking into who had planned their weddings.

There were two different companies. For the DeGeorges, White Lace. For the Brandts, a fancy consultant, Miriam Campbell. That wasn't the link.

I was at my desk when the duty clerk patched through a call. It was Claire, phoning from her lab. She had just returned from examining the bodies of the victims with the County Coroner in Napa. She sounded excited.

'Get down here,' she said. 'And hurry.'

'You found a link,' I said immediately. 'Rebecca DeGeorge was sexually disturbed?'

'Lindsay, we're dealing with one sick dude.'

Minutes later, when I met her in the lab, Claire told me, 'They were *definitely* in the act when they were killed. Semen traces found in Rebecca DeGeorge matched those I scraped off her husband. And the angle of the wounds confirmed what I suspected. She was shot from behind. Rebecca's blood was all over her husband's clothes. She was straddling him . . . but that's not why I asked you down.'

She fixed her large wide eyes on me, and I could tell it was something more important.

'I thought it best to keep this quiet,' she said. 'Only the local ME and I know.'

'Know what? Tell me, for God's sake!' In the lab, I spotted a microscope on a counter and one of those airtight Petri dishes I remembered from high-school chemistry.

'As with the first victims,' she said excitedly, 'there was additional sexual disturbance of the corpse. Only this time, it wasn't so obvious. The labia was normal, what you would expect, post-intercourse, and there were no internal abrasions like with the first bride. Bill Toll missed it . . . but I was *looking* for signs of additional abuse. And there it was, and inside the vagina, sort of shouting, "Come and get me, Claire!" '

She picked up the Petri dish and a tweezer, and gently removed the top. From out of the clear dish she lifted a single, half-inch reddish-gray hair.

'It's not the husband's?'

Claire shook her head. 'Look for yourself.'

She flicked on the microscope. I leaned in, and against the brilliant white background of the lens, I saw two hairs: one thin, shiny, black-brown; the other, short, curly, sickle-shaped.

'You're looking at two sections from Michael DeGeorge,' she explained. 'The long one's from his head. The other is genital.'

Then she placed the hair from the Petri dish on another slide and inserted it in the microscope lens bay, side by side with the others. My pulse was starting to race. I thought I knew where she was going with this.

The new hair was reddish-gray in hue and twice the size in thickness. It had tiny filaments twisted around the cortex. It clearly belonged to someone else.

'It's neither cranial nor pubic. *It's from a beard.*' Claire announced, leaning over me.

I pulled back from the scope and looked at her, shocked.

The killer's facial hair had turned up in Becky DeGeorge's vagina.

'Post-mortem,' she said, to drive it home.

Chapter Forty-Four

As Claire said, we were piecing our killer together, step by step. His height, his face, his fetishes. The way he murdered.

Now I had to figure out how he was tracking his victims.

Raleigh and I were going full force on the travel and wedding-planner thing. We had fifteen detectives out there following up leads. Now that we had a facial characteristic, we went back to the guests, combing them for a guy with a beard who might have been seen strolling around.

I felt confident some aspect of this widening search would yield results. One of the guests would have noticed someone. Or there'd be a travel agent in common, a link somewhere. Or one of Jacobi's searches would come up with a match.

The following morning, Hartwig called in. 'Sparrow Ridge Vineyards . . . it's owned by a group here known as Black Hawk Partners. A local guy, Ed Lester, an attorney, puts together real-estate partnerships.'

'You know where he was over the weekend?'

'Yeah, I checked. Portland. He ran in a marathon there. I caught him when he got back to the office. He was definitely in Portland.'

I still felt certain whoever had dumped the bodies there hadn't stumbled on the remote vineyard by accident. It meant something to the killer. 'He owns this place outright?'

'Nope. Black Hawk put together deals. They bring in outside money from well-heeled guys down your way – people who want to break into the wine game. Lester acts as the managing partner.'

'So who's he partnered with on this one?'

'I don't know. Investors.'

I sucked in my breath, trying to remain patient. '*Which* investors?'

'Generally, investors who want to remain private. Listen, Inspector, I know where you're heading, but this guy only deals with pretty established people. Believe me, anyone could've found that dump site. Real-estate agents, someone who'd checked it out, anyone local. I have to deal with these people long after you're gone.'

I cradled the phone in my neck and spun around in my seat toward the window. 'This is a multiple-murder investigation, Lieutenant, the worst I've ever seen. The dump site is three miles up a deserted dirt road. Anyone riding around in the dark with two bodies could've safely dumped them anytime before. Whoever did this had to know the vineyard was there. And I don't think it's a local. I don't think he would draw attention so close to where he lives.'

I paused to let my words sink in. 'Come back to me when you know who Lester's partners were.' I hung up on Hartwig.

Some of my optimism began to unravel.

Raleigh turned up nothing on the travel agents. The Brandts had booked through Travel Ventures, a society agent that catered to a high-end crowd. The DeGeorges used Journeytime, out of Los Altos, where Michael DeGeorge worked.

We had people scour through the personnel records. There was no connection between the two firms: no cooperative arrangements, not a single travel agent who had worked for both of them. It was possible someone had tapped into their systems, said the manager of Journeytime. But finding that was next to impossible.

My end was equally disappointing. I had the files from both wedding planners. Engravers, bands, photographers, caterers, florists. Nothing matched up. The Brandts and the DeGeorges lived in two separate worlds. How the killer was identifying the victims remained a mystery. I hadn't found a single clue.

Chapter Forty-Five

I called Claire and Cindy together for a second meeting of the girls. This time, the mood was decidedly different. There was no laughter or high fives. No festive margaritas. Two more people were dead. We had no suspects, only a widening case. Clues that were rapidly leading nowhere. Intense pressure coming down on all of us.

Claire was first to arrive. She hugged me and asked how I was feeling.

'I don't know,' I admitted. I had gone through three treatments. Sometimes I felt strong. At other times, especially in the afternoon, I felt like a ghost of myself. 'Medved said he'd review my red cell count next week.'

Cindy arrived next. She was wearing a halter under a man's plaid shirt, a pair of embroidered jeans. She was very pretty, and city-cool. I hadn't spoken to her since Monday, when I let her run with the story of the second killings. Even holding her story back that one day, she still scooped the city.

'I guess I'm buying,' she announced. She tossed us a new business card with the bright red logo of the *Chronicle* on it. I read the card: *Cindy Thomas, Reporter, Metro Crime Desk.*

We toasted her with warm congratulations, then we roasted her a little, just to keep her ego in balance. What else are friends for?

I told them that the travel agents and wedding planners had led nowhere. 'A couple of things really bother me,' I said. 'The gun, for instance. Sexual killers don't usually change their methods. The methods are part of the sexual thrill.'

'It's a strange combination,' agreed Claire. 'He's so in control when he plans his strikes. He seems to know everything. Where they're married, their hotel room numbers, what their honeymoon itinerary is. How to get away. Yet, when he kills, he's close to rage. It's not enough to merely kill them. He has to *defile*.'

I nodded. 'That's the key. He's striking at weddings; something about them is intolerable to him. But I think his obsession's with the brides. Both of the grooms were dispatched quickly. It's as if they didn't even matter to him. But the brides . . . that's his real fascination.'

I pondered on this for a moment. 'So where would this guy go,' I asked aloud, 'to scout potential victims? If you wanted to kill brides, where would you check them out?'

'They had to choose a ring,' suggested Claire. 'A jeweler.'

'Or City Hall,' volunteered Cindy. 'They'd need a license.'

I looked at her and chuckled. 'It sure would fit if a government employee was the one behind this.'

'Postal employee.' Claire and Cindy spoke simultaneously.

'Photographers,' said Claire.

I could see a twisted bastard hiding behind the lens. They were all good possibilities. It only required legs and manpower to check them before the killer struck again.

'This bride business isn't exactly my expertise,' I said to Claire. 'That's why you're here.'

'What happened to all that three sharp cookies crap?' she laughed. 'And the part about my being a top-notch ME?'

There was a ripple of frustrated laughter around the table. We took another sip of beer. The Women's Murder Club. This was good. No men allowed.

'Where's the goddamn link?' I fretted. 'He *wants* us to find it. That's why he's leaving clues. He wants us to uncover the link.'

Everyone was silent, lost in thought.

'I can feel it,' I went on. 'In the ceremony, the celebration, he finds something that drives him into psychopathic rage. Something he needs to stamp out. Is it hope, innocence? The husbands he kills right away, as I've said. But the brides? How does he find the brides?'

'If he's living in this twisted dreamworld,' said Cindy, thinking aloud, 'he would go to where the fantasy was the strongest, the most vivid. He might want to build up his anger by observing them in an unsuspecting state.'

Then Claire looked at us with a spark in her eye. 'I was thinking, I'd go where they bought their wedding dresses. That's where I would pick the victims out.'

Chapter Forty-Six

When I got to work the following morning, there was a fax from Hartwig listing the partners at Sparrow Ridge. I gave them to Jacobi to check. Then I called my contacts at both wedding planners, White Lace and Miriam Campbell.

I wasn't expecting much. So far, everything had come back empty. Then, to my shock, both planners confirmed it.

Melanie Brandt and Becky DeGeorge *had* bought their dresses at the same place.

The Bridal Boutique at Saks.

It was the first tangible link between the two cases. It could lead to nothing, but I felt in my bones it had the real, promising sensation of something good.

I was at Saks by the time the store opened at ten. The Bridal Boutique was on the third floor, tucked away in a corner next to Gifts and Fine China.

I caught Maryanne Perkins as she was arriving for the day, a cup of steaming coffee in her hand. The Department

Manager was a stylish, affable woman of about fifty, just the type who would work with brides for twenty years. She had someone cover for her and sat down with me in a cluttered back room filled with magazine photos of brides.

'I was devastated when I heard about it.' She shook her head, ashen-faced. 'Melanie was just here, two weeks ago.' She stared at me, glassily. 'She was so beautiful . . . my brides are like my children, Inspector. I feel as if I've lost one of my own.'

'One?' I fixed on her eyes. 'You haven't heard?'

'Heard what?'

I told Maryanne Perkins about Rebecca Passeneau, the late Mrs DeGeorge.

Shock and horror swept over her face. Her green eyes bulged, welled with a rush of tears. She stared through me as if she were looking into the wall. 'Oh, my God . . .' She took in a heart-jolting breath. 'My husband and I were at our cabin in Modesto for a few days. Young Becky was just in here with her Mom. Oh, my God. What's going on here, Inspector?'

An immediate flood of questions tumbled out. Who would know about their customers? Other salespersons? Managers? The killer had been sighted as a male. Did any men work in the department?

Each of them elicited a disbelieving, negative response from Maryanne Perkins. The staff had all been together for a minimum of eight years. No males. *Just like our murder club.*

She leaned back in her chair, scrolling her memory for

any details that she could recall. 'We were admiring her. Becky . . . she was stunning. It was as if she had never thought of herself in quite that way, but seeing herself in her dress, it suddenly became clear. Her mother had given her this brooch – pearls, diamonds – and I ran back to the office for flowers. That's when I noticed someone. Standing over there,' she pointed. 'He was staring in Becky's direction. I remember thinking, See, even he thinks you're beautiful. I remember now.'

Frantically, I took down a description: late forties, maybe younger. 'I didn't get a really good look,' the bridal manager said. 'He had a beard.'

I was sure it was him! It confirmed that Claire was right. Saks had to be where he found his victims, where he tracked them.

I pressed her hard. 'How would anyone find out details about someone's wedding? Dates, locations – where they would honeymoon?'

'We collect that information,' Maryanne Perkins said, 'when the girls choose a gown. Some of it we need to know to help us, like dates, deadlines. And, it just helps us get a feel for the bride. Most of them register with us as well.'

A feel for the bride.

'Who has access to this information?'

She shook her head. 'Just us . . . me and my assistants. It's a small department. Sometimes we share it with Fine China and Gifts.'

I felt I was finally close. My heart was slamming inside

my chest. 'I need to see a copy of anything you have on Melanie Brandt and Becky DeGeorge, and every customer you're currently working with.' *He was spotting his potential victims here, wasn't he?* There was a good chance he would come back. Someone on the store's list could be next in line.

I saw Ms Perkins's jaw drop again. She appeared to be focusing on a horrible sight. 'There's something else you'll want to know.'

'What?'

'About a month ago, after inventory, we noticed that our folder on the brides was missing.'

Chapter Forty-Seven

A s soon as I got back to the Hall, I did two things: I
called Claire and Cindy and told them what I'd found
out at Saks, then I went to find Raleigh.

I shared everything with Chris, and we decided to put
a woman detective from the Sex Crime Unit inside the
department store. I sent a sketch artist over to see
Maryanne Perkins at Saks.

Then Chris shared something important with me. Roth
and Mercer had handed over our case files to the FBI.

I felt a knifing pain deep in my chest. I rushed into the
bathroom, closed the door behind me, pressed my back
against the cold, chipped tile. *Goddamn, son-of-a-bitch*,
controlling men. *Goddamn Roth and Mercer!*

I stared at my face in the mirror. My cheeks were
flushed. My skin was burning.

The FBI! This was my case – and Claire's, Cindy's, and
Raleigh's. It meant more to me than any other I'd ever
worked on.

Suddenly, my legs felt wobbly. Negli's? The doctor said

I'd be feeling fits of nausea or light-headedness. I had my fourth transfusion scheduled at the hematology clinic at five-thirty.

An overwhelming emptiness tugged at me, alternating between anger and fear. I was just starting to crack this thing. I didn't need outsiders in dark suits and tie pins buzzing around with a clumsy, alternative investigation.

I blinked into the mirror. My skin, apart from the burning cheeks, looked pallid and lifeless. My eyes were watery and gray. My whole body seemed drained of color.

I stared at myself until a familiar voice came alive inside me. *'Come on. Get yourself together, Lindsay. You win – you always win.'*

I splashed cold water on my face. The flashing sweat on my neck began to subside.

You're allowed *one* of these, I told myself with a thin smile. *Just don't do that again.*

I looked at my watch. It was four-twenty. I had to be at the clinic soon. I'd start on the names tomorrow. After applying a few dabs of makeup, I made my way back to my desk. To my chagrin, Raleigh wandered up.

'Now you can manage *their* fall-out,' I snapped unnecessarily, referring to the FBI.

'I didn't know,' he said mildly. 'As soon as I did, I told you.'

'Yeah,' I nodded. 'Right.'

Raleigh got up, came around and sat on the edge of my desk, facing me. 'Something's wrong, isn't it? Tell me. Please.' How did he know? Maybe he was a lot better detective than I gave him credit for.

For a moment, I really wanted to tell him. God, I wanted it to come out. Then Raleigh did something totally unexpected. He flashed one of those trusting smiles that I couldn't help but give myself over to. Then he pulled me out of my chair and gave me a hug.

I was so surprised I didn't even resist. I was quivering jelly in his arms. It wasn't quite sexual, but no burst of passion had ever rippled through me more powerfully.

Raleigh held me until the anxiety had slowly melted away. Right there, in the fucking squad room. I didn't know what to do, but I didn't want to pull back. Or have him let me go.

'I could write you up for this,' I finally mumbled into his shoulder.

He didn't move. 'You want a pen?'

Slowly, I pulled myself away. Every nerve in my body felt as if it had retreated from a tense state of alert. 'Thanks,' I muttered, with appreciation.

'You didn't seem yourself,' he said gently. 'Shift's almost done. Want to talk about it over coffee? Just coffee, Lindsay, *not a date.*'

I looked at my watch again and suddenly saw that it was almost five o'clock. I was late for my appointment.

I gave him a look that I hoped reflected, *Ask me again*, but said, 'I can't. Gotta go.'

Chapter Forty-Eight

The pretty smiling reservation clerk politely nodded for the next person in line. 'Welcome to the Lakefront Hilton, sir.'

Phillip Campbell stepped up to the counter. He noticed her name, Kaylin. Bright-eyed, bushy-bushed Kaylin. He smiled back, flirted subtly. He handed her a confirmation slip.

'First time with us, Mr Campbell?' the desk clerk asked in a high-pitched chirp.

He beamed, let her know that it was.

As she punched in his reservation, he followed her movements, thoughtfully stroking the rough hairs of his beard. He wanted her to notice. To remember his face – maybe something he had said. One day, when some diligent FBI agent came by with a drawing or photograph, he wanted this chirpy little squirrel to think back and recall this moment in a close and chilling way. He wanted her to remember everything.

As had the saleswoman in the Bridal Boutique at Saks.

'Here for a visit to the museum, Mr Campbell?' Kaylin asked, as she typed.

'For the Voskuhl wedding,' he volunteered.

'Everyone's saying that,' she smiled.

He followed the click of her peach-colored nails against the keys as she typed in his reservation. 'I've got you a deluxe room with a beautiful view,' she said, handing him a key, then added: 'Enjoy the wedding. And have a nice stay.'

'I will,' Campbell said pleasantly. Before he turned away, he caught her eye and said, 'Speaking of weddings – I like your ring.'

Upstairs, he pulled the curtains aside and, as promised, before him was a sweeping view.

Of Cleveland, Ohio.

Chapter Forty-Nine

I *saw him, that bastard. What was he doing here?*

In a large, fast-moving crowd, on Lower Market. Just a quick movement in the throng fighting its way toward the Ferry.

My blood froze with the sight of him.

He was wearing an open blue shirt, a brown corduroy jacket. He looked like some college professor. On any other day, I could have passed him by, never noticed. He was thin, gaunt, totally unremarkable in every way but one.

It was the reddish-brown beard.

His head bobbed in and out of the rushing crowd. I followed, unable to narrow the distance.

'Police!' I shouted, over the din. My cry dissolved into the hurrying, unheeding crowd. At any moment I might lose him.

I didn't know his name – I only knew his victims. *Melanie Brandt. Rebecca DeGeorge.*

Suddenly, he stopped. He bucked against the flow,

turned right toward me. His face seemed illuminated, shining against a dark background like one of those medieval Russian icons. Amid the commotion, our eyes met.

There was a moment of captured, enlightened recognition, frozen apart from the chaos of the crowd. He knew that it was me. That I was the one after him.

Then, to my horror, he fled; the crowd engulfed him, swept him away.

'*Stop!*' I shouted. 'I'll shoot!' A cold sweat broke out on my neck. I drew my gun. '*Get down!*' I cried, but the rush-hour crowd pushed on, shielding him. I was going to lose him. The killer was getting away.

I raised the gun, focused on the image of his red beard. He turned – with the sneer of someone who had totally outwitted me. I drew a breath, steadied my aim. As if in slow motion, every face in the crowd turned toward me, too.

I stepped back. In horror, I lowered the gun.

Every face in the crowd had the same red beard.

I must have been dreaming. I found myself at my kitchen counter, blinking into swirling circles in my Chardonnay. There was a familiar calm in my apartment. No rushing crowds, no fleeing faces. Only Sweet Martha lounging on her futon.

A pot of boiling water was steaming on the stove. I had my favorite sauce ready to go – ricotta, zucchini, basil. A CD was on, Tori Amos.

Only an hour ago, I had tubes and IV lines sticking out of me. My heart kept pace to the metronome-like rhythm of a monitor's steady beep.

Damn it, I wanted my old life back. My old, favorite dreams. I wanted Jacobi's sarcasm, Sam Roth's scorn, jogging on the Marina Green. I wanted kids, too – even if it meant I had to get married again.

Suddenly, the downstairs buzzer rang. Who would be here now? I shuffled over and said, 'Who is it?'

'I thought you had somewhere to go?' a static voice replied.

It was Raleigh.

Chapter Fifty

'**W**hat're you doing here?' I called back in surprise. I was pleased, but suddenly tingling with nerves. My hair was pulled up, I was in an old Berkeley T-shirt that I sometimes slept in, and I felt drained and anxious from my transfusion. My little place was a mess.

'Can I come up?' Raleigh said.

'This business or personal?' I asked. 'We don't have to go back to Napa, do we?'

'Not tonight.' I heard him laugh. 'This time I brought my own.'

I didn't quite understand that, but I buzzed him up. Then I ran back to the kitchen, turned the heat down on the pasta and, in the same breath, threw a couple of pillows from the floor onto the couch and transferred a pile of magazines to a chair in the kitchen.

I put some lip gloss on and shook out my hair as the doorbell rang.

Raleigh was in an open shirt and baggy khakis. He was carrying a bottle of wine – Kunde. Very nice. He tossed me an apologetic smile. 'I hope you don't mind me barging in.'

'Nobody barges in here. I let you in,' I said. 'What're you doing here anyway?'

He laughed. 'I was in the neighborhood.'

'The neighborhood, huh? You live across the Bay.'

He nodded, abandoning his alibi without much resistance. 'I just wanted to make sure you were okay. You didn't seem yourself back at the station.'

'That's nice, Raleigh,' I said, looking into his eyes.

'So? Are you?'

'So. I was just feeling a little overwhelmed. Roth. This FBI thing. I'm fine now. Really.'

'Glad to hear it,' he said. 'Hey – something smells good.'

'I was just throwing some pasta together.' I paused, thinking about what I wanted to say next. 'You had dinner?'

He shook his head. 'No, no. I don't want to intrude.'

'That why you came with the wine?'

He gave me one of those irresistible smiles. 'If you weren't home, I have a corner of Second and Brannan I always head to.'

I smiled back and finally held open the door.

When Raleigh came into my apartment, he looked around with sort of an impressed nod, gazing at some of the pottery, a black-and-gold satin baseball jacket from Willie Mays, my terrace with its view of the Bay. He held out the bottle.

'There's one already open on the counter,' I said. 'Pour yourself a glass. I'll check on the food.'

I went into the kitchen, reminding myself that I had just

come from the outpatient clinic for a serious disease, and we were partners, anyway. With an irrepressible flicker of excitement, I took out an extra setting.

'Number twenty-four, Giants?' he called to me. 'This warm-up jacket is the real thing?'

'Willie Mays. My father gave it to me for my tenth birthday. He wanted a boy. I kept it all these years.'

He came into the kitchen, spun a stool around at the counter. While I stirred the penne he poured himself a glass of wine. 'You always cook for yourself like this?'

'Old habit,' I said. 'Growing up, my mother worked late. I had a sister six years younger. Sometimes my mother didn't get home till eight. From the time I can remember, I had to make dinner.'

'Where was your dad?'

'Left us,' I said, whipping together some mustard, grape-seed oil, balsamic, and lemon into a vinaigrette for the salad. 'When I was thirteen.'

'So your mother brought you up?'

'You could say. Sometimes I feel like I brought myself up.'

'Until you got married.'

'Yeah, then I sort of brought him up, too.' I smiled. 'You're pretty nosy, Raleigh.'

'Cops generally are. Didn't you know that?'

'Yeah. Real cops.'

Raleigh feigned being hurt. 'What can I help you with?' he offered.

'You can grate,' I said and grinned. I pushed a block of

Parmesan and a metal grater his way.

We sat there, he grating, me waiting for the pasta to cook. Sweet Martha padded into the kitchen and let Raleigh pet her.

'You didn't seem yourself this afternoon,' he said, as he stroked Martha's head. 'Usually, you handle Roth's bullshit without even blinking. Seemed like there was something wrong.'

'Nothing's wrong,' I lied. 'At least not now. If you were asking.'

I leaned against the counter and looked at him. He was my partner, but even more than that, he was a person I thought I could trust. It had been a long, hard time since I had put my trust in anybody whose gender started with an *m*. Maybe, in a different time . . . I was thinking.

Tori Amos's haunting voice hung in the air.

'You like to dance?' Raleigh suddenly asked.

I looked at him, really surprised. 'I don't dance, I cook.' I stammered a little.

'You don't dance . . . you cook?' Raleigh repeated, scrunching up his brow.

'Yeah. You know what they say about cooking.'

He looked around. 'What *I'd* say is that it doesn't seem to be working. Maybe you should try dancing.'

The music was soft and languorous, and as much as I tried to deny it, part of me just yearned to be held.

Without my even saying yes, my goddamn partner took my hand and pulled me from around the counter. I wanted to hold back, but a soft, surrendering voice inside me said,

'Just go with it, Lindsay. He's okay. You know you trust him.'

So I gave in, and let Chris Raleigh hold me. I liked being in his arms.

At first we sort of stood there, swaying stiffly. Then I found myself letting my head fall on his shoulder, and feeling like nothing could ail me there, at least not for a while.

'This isn't a date,' I muttered, and let myself drift to a real nice place where I felt love and hope and dreams were still there to reach for.

'To tell the truth,' I told Raleigh. 'I'm glad you stopped by.'

'Me too.'

Then I felt him put his arms around me, hold me close. A tingle raced down my spine, one that I almost didn't recognize anymore.

'You've got it, don't you, Raleigh?' I said dreamily.

'What's that, Lindsay?'

Soft hands.

Chapter Fifty-One

K athy and James Voskuhl were having their first dance – and to break with tradition it was a rocker.

The loud, driving beat of 'La Bamba' jolted through the brightly lit atrium of the Rock and Roll Hall of Fame in Cleveland.

'Everybody!' the groom shouted. 'Rock and roll! Join us!'

Hip young girls in dyed hair and wearing shiny green and red prom dresses – sixties style – swung around on the dance floor, their partners in retro silk shirts, Travolta-like. The bride and groom, having changed into party garb, joined in, butting thighs, whooping, arms in the air.

It almost ruined everything, Phillip Campbell thought. He had wanted her in white. And here she was, sweaty red-streaked hair, cat's-eye-shaped glasses, a tight green dress.

This time, Kathy, you've gone too far.

Forty tables, each with the likeness of some rock-and-roll icon as a centerpiece, filled out the Great Hall of the museum. A glittery banner that hung from the glass roof proclaimed: *James and Kathy.*

After a loud crescendo the music stopped. A throng of sweaty wedding guests milled back toward their tables, fanning themselves. Waiters in black waistcoats scurried about the room, filling wine glasses.

The bride went over and embraced a happy tuxedoed couple. Mom and Dad. Phillip Campbell couldn't take his eyes off her. He saw her father give her a loving look, as if to say: 'We've come through a lot, honey, but now everything will be all right. Now you're part of the club, trust funds, and Country Day, little peach-haired grandkids.'

The groom wandered over and whispered something in Kathy's ear. She squeezed his arm, flashing him a smile that was both affectionate and coy. As he walked away, the tips of her fingers lingered, as if she were saying, 'I'll be right along.'

With a hitch of his belt, the groom drifted out of the main hall. He glanced back once or twice, and Kathy waved.

Campbell decided to follow, hanging back at a safe distance. He went down a wide, well-lit corridor off the atrium. Halfway down, James Voskuhl opened a door and went in. The men's room.

The killer moved forward. No one else was in the hall. He felt an irrepressible urge building with force. His fingers made their way into his jacket pocket, touched the cold heel of the gun. He flicked the safety off. He could no longer control what was going on inside his head.

Go in, a voice dared him. *Do it.*

He entered in a filmy, sallow light. No one was at the

urinals or sinks. The groom was in a closed stall. A pungent smell filled his nostrils, marijuana.

'That you, love?' the groom's affectionate voice called out.

Every wicklike nerve in Campbell's body stood at attention. He mumbled something barely audible.

'Better get in here, hon,' James Voskuhl gulped, 'If you want the end of this bone.'

Phillip Campbell pushed open the door.

The groom looked up, bewildered, the tip of a joint on his lip. 'Hey, man, who the hell are you?'

'I'm the one who kills useless worms like you.' With that, he fired. Just once.

James Voskuhl's head snapped back. A splatter of red sprayed against the tile. The groom rocked once, then crumpled forward in a heap.

The echo of the gun blast seemed to concuss the entire room. It left an effluvium of cordite that mingled with the pot.

A strange calm took over Phillip Campbell, a fearlessness. He pulled the groom's head back and set him upright.

Then he waited.

The sound of the outer door opening and echoes of the distant party rushing in went right through him.

'That you, Vosk?' a woman's voice called out.

It was her. The bride.

'What're you smoking in there – tar?' Kathy giggled. She went over to the sinks, and he heard the sound of running water coming on.

Campbell could see her through a crack in the stall. She was at the sink, wide, cat-shaped glasses, thrashing a comb through her hair. A vision came to him. How he would set this up. *What the police would find.*

It took everything he had to control himself – to let her come to him.

'You better save me a hit or two, mister,' the bride called out.

He watched her dance over to the stall. *So close now. So unbelievably delicious. What a moment.*

When she opened the door, it was her *look* that meant everything to him.

The sight of James, red drool leaking from his mouth. The startled recognition of the killer's face suddenly clicking in; the gun aimed right at her eyes.

'I like you better in white, Kathy,' was all the killer said.

Then he squeezed the trigger – and a blinding white flash exploded through the green cat's-eye-shaped lens.

Chapter Fifty-Two

I was in early Monday morning, feeling a little nervous about my first contact with Raleigh after our dancing-and-dining experience, wondering where all this was going to go – when one of the task force Inspectors, Paul Chin, rushed up to me. 'Lindsay, there's a woman in Interrogation Room Four I think you should check out.'

Ever since a physical description of the assailant had hit the airwaves, people were calling in with fake sightings and dead-end leads. One of Chin's jobs was to follow them up, no matter how unlikely.

'This one a psychic or a police buff?' I asked with a skeptical smile.

'I think this one's the genuine article,' said Chin. 'She was at the first wedding.'

I almost leaped out of my chair after him. At the front of the squad room, I spotted Raleigh coming in. *Chris.*

For a moment, a tingle of pleasure rushed through me. He'd left about eleven, after we ended up polishing off both bottles of wine. We ate, chewed over our separate stints on the force, and the ups and downs of being married or single.

It had been a sweet evening. Took the heat off from the case. It even got my mind off Negli's. What scared me a little was the tremor inside that it could be something more. I caught myself staring at him Friday night, while he helped out with the dishes, thinking, If times were different . . .

Raleigh ran into me, carrying coffee and a paper. 'Hey,' he smiled. 'Nice vest.'

'Chin's got a live one in four,' I said, grabbing his arm. 'Claims to have a physical sighting. You want to come along?'

In my haste, I was already by him, not even giving him a second of recognition. He put down his paper on our civilian-clerk's desk and caught up on the stairs.

In the cramped interrogation room sat a nicely dressed, attractive woman of about fifty. Chin introduced her to me as Laurie Birnbaum. She seemed tight, nervous.

Chin sat down next to her. 'Ms Birnbaum, why don't you tell Detective Boxer what you just told me.'

She was frightened. 'It was the beard that made me remember. I didn't even think of it all week. It was so horrible.'

'You were at the Brandts' wedding?' I asked her.

'We were guests of the Weils,' she replied. 'My husband works with Chancellor Weil at the university.' She took a nervous sip from a cup of coffee. 'It was just a brief thing. But he gave me the chills.'

Chin pushed down the record button of a portable recorder.

'Please, go ahead,' I told her, soothingly. Once again, I felt close to *him* – the bastard in the red beard.

'I stood next to him. He had this graying red beard, like a goatee – the kind they wear in Los Angeles. He looked older, maybe forty-five, fifty, but there was something about him. I'm not saying this right, am I?'

'You spoke to him?' I asked, trying to communicate that even though she didn't do this every day, I did. Even the male detectives admitted that I was the best at Q and A on the floor. They joked that it was 'a girl thing'.

'I had just come in from the dance floor,' she said. 'I looked up, and there he was. I said something like, "Nice affair . . . bride or groom?" For a moment, I thought he looked kind of appealing. Then he just sort of glared at me. I took him for one of those arrogant investment-banker types from the Brandt side.'

'What did he say to you?' I said.

She massaged her brow, straining to recall. 'He said, in the weirdest way, that they were *lucky*.'

'Who was lucky?'

'Melanie and David. I may have said, "Aren't they lucky?" meaning the two of them. They were so stunning, and he replied, "Oh, they're *lucky*." ' She looked up with a confused expression on her face. 'He called them something else . . . *chosen*.'

'Chosen?'

'Yes. He said, "Oh, they're lucky . . . you could even say they were chosen." '

'You say he had a goatee?'

'That's what was so strange. The beard made him seem older, but the rest of him was young.'

'The rest of him? What do you mean?'

'His face. His voice. I know this must sound strange, but it was only for a moment, as I came off the dance floor.'

We got as much as we could from her. Height, hair color. What he was wearing. Everything confirmed the sparse details that we already had. The killer was a man with a short, reddish-gray beard. He was in a tux. The tux jacket he had left behind in the Mandarin Suite.

A fire was building inside me. I felt sure that Laurie Birnbaum was credible. *The beard. The tux.* We were piecing together his face. 'Is there anything more, anything at all that stands out to you? Some physical characteristic – a mannerism, perhaps.'

She shook her head. 'It happened so quickly. It was only when I saw the drawing of him in the *Chronicle*.'

I looked at Chin, conveying it was time to call down an artist to firm up the details. I thanked her, made my way back to my desk. We'd get a sketch from her, and one from Maryanne Perkins at Saks.

The murder investigation had entered a new phase. It was very hot. We had a stakeout operational outside the Bridal Boutique at Saks. One by one, we were contacting the names on the list, anyone who had ordered a wedding dress in the past several months.

My heart was pounding. The face I had imagined, my dream of the red-bearded man, was starting to fill in. I felt we had him contained.

My phone rang. 'Boxer,' I answered, still shuffling through the names in the Saks wedding folder.

'My name's McBride,' a deep, urgent voice said. 'I'm a homicide detective. In Cleveland.'

Chapter Fifty-Three

'I got a homicide here that fits the pattern of what you've been dealing with,' McBride explained. 'Gun shot wounds, both of them, right between the eyes.' He described the quick, but grotesque deaths of Kathy and James Voskuhl, killed at their wedding at the Rock and Roll Hall of Fame in Cleveland. This time, the killer didn't even wait for the wedding to end.

'What kind of weapon your guy use in Napa?' McBride asked.

'Nine millimeter,' I told him.

'Same.'

I was reeling a little bit. *Cleveland?* What the hell was Red Beard doing in Ohio? We had just made the breakthrough, found out where he was casing his victims. Did he know that? If so – *how?*

Cleveland was either a copycat killing, which was entirely possible, or this case had just broken wide open and could lead anywhere.

'Did your victims end up in sexually explicit positions, McBride?' I asked.

The officer grunted. 'Yeah. Got the crime-scene photos here in front of me. Nasty. They're sexually explicit all right.'

'Can you get me a close-up of their hands?'

'Okay, but why the hands?'

'What were they wearing, McBride?'

I heard him shuffling through photos. 'You mean rings?'

'Good guess, Detective. Yeah.' I was praying that it wasn't our guy. Cleveland . . . it would shatter everything that made me feel we were getting close to him. Was Red Beard taking his killing act across the country?

A minute later, McBride confirmed exactly the thing I didn't want to hear. 'There are no wedding bands.'

The bastard was on the move. We had a stakeout going where we thought he might show up and meanwhile he was 2,000 miles away. He'd just murdered a couple at their reception in Ohio. Shit, shit, shit.

'You said the bodies were found in a sexually explicit position?' I prompted McBride.

The Cleveland cop hesitated. He finally said, 'The groom was shot sitting on the john. We found him there. Sitting up, legs open. The bride was shot in the stall, too, as she was coming in. There was enough of her brains on the inside of the door to confirm it. But when we found her, she was kneeling down. Uh, her face was stuffed between his legs.'

I was silent, forming the image in my mind, hating this

cruel, inhuman bastard more every day.

'You know . . . fellatio-style,' McBride managed. 'There's a few things my investigators want to ask you.'

'Ask me yourself. I'm gonna be there tomorrow.'

Chapter Fifty-Four

Six-thirty the next morning, Raleigh and I were on our way to Cleveland, of all places. McBride met us at the plane. He wasn't how I had imagined him. He wasn't flabby, middle-aged, Irish-Catholic. He was intense, sharp-boned, maybe thirty-eight, and black.

'You're younger than I thought.' He smiled at me.

I smiled back. 'And you're definitely less Irish.'

On the way into town, he brought us up to speed. 'Groom's from Seattle. Had something to do with the music business. Worked with rock bands. Producer . . . marketing guy. Bride grew up here in Ohio – Shaker Heights. Father's a corporate attorney. Girl was cute, a redhead, with freckles and glasses.'

He pulled a manila envelope off the dashboard and tossed it over to me in the passenger's seat. Inside were a series of glossy eight-by-elevens of the crime scene: stark, graphic, somewhat resembling old photos of gangland rubouts. The groom was sitting on the stall with a surprised expression and the top of his head blown off. The bride was slumped over his lap, curled in a pool of blood, hers and his.

The sight of the couple filled me with a cold dread. As long as the killer was in northern California, I felt we had him contained. Now he was on the loose.

We grilled McBride about the venue – how the victims might have ended up in the men's room and what security was like at the Hall of Fame.

Each answer I heard convinced me even more that it was our guy. But what the hell was he doing *here*?

We pulled off the highway at Lake Shore Boulevard. A modern skyline rose all around us. 'There she is,' McBride announced.

From a distance, I saw the Rock and Roll Hall of Fame glinting up ahead like a jaggedly cut jewel. A twisted killer had struck in the city's most celebrated venue. By now, he might already be back in San Francisco. Or Chicago, New York, Topeka . . . Planning another gruesome double murder. Or maybe he was in a hotel room across the square, watching us arrive.

Red Beard could be anywhere.

Chapter Fifty-Five

It was the third time in two weeks I had to go over a harrowing double-murder scene.

McBride walked us up to the second floor and through an eerie, empty atrium devoid of pedestrian traffic to a men's room blocked off by crisscrossing yellow crime tape and cops.

'Public bathroom,' Raleigh said to me. 'He's getting nastier each time.'

This time there were no bodies, no horrifying discoveries. The victims had long been transferred to the morgue. In their place were grim outlines of tape and chalk; gut-wrenching black-and-white crime photos taped to the walls.

I could see what had happened. How the groom had been killed first, his blood smeared on the wall behind the toilet. How Red Beard had waited, surprised the bride as she came in, then moved Kathy Voskuhl into the provocative position between her husband's legs. *Defiled her.*

'How did they both end up here in the middle of their wedding?' Raleigh asked.

McBride pointed to a crime-scene photo on the wall. 'We found a smoked-down joint next to James Voskuhl. Figured he came here to cop a buzz. My guess is the bride went up to join him.'

'No one saw anything, though? They didn't leave the reception with anyone?'

McBride shook his head.

I felt the same smoldering anger I had felt twice before. I hated this killer, this savager of dreams. With each act I hated him more. The bastard was taunting us. Each murder scene was a statement. Each one more degrading.

'What was security like that night?' I asked.

McBride shrugged. 'All exits except the main one were closed down. There was a guard at the front desk. Everyone from the wedding arrived at the same time. A couple of half-assed guards were floating around, but generally at these affairs, they like to keep a low profile.'

'I saw cameras all around,' Raleigh pressed. 'They must have some film?'

'That's what I'm hoping,' said McBride. 'I'll introduce you to Sharp, Head of Security. We can go over that now.'

Andrew Sharp was a trim, wiry man with a square chin and narrow, colorless lips. He looked scared. A day ago he had a fairly cushy job, but now the police and the FBI were all over him. Having to explain things to two outside cops from San Francisco didn't help matters. He brought us into his office, popped a Marlboro Light out of a pack, and looked at Raleigh.

'I got a meeting with the Executive Director in about eight minutes.'

We didn't even bother to sit down. I asked, 'Did your guards notice anyone unusual?'

'Three hundred guests, Madam Detective. Everyone congregated in the entrance atrium. My staff doesn't usually get involved a whole lot except to make sure no one with too much to drink gets too close to the exhibits.'

'What about how he got out then?'

Sharp wheeled in his chair, pointing to a blowup of the museum layout. 'Either the main entrance, here, where you came in, or one we left open off the back verandah. It leads down to the Lake Walk. There's a café there during the summer. Mostly it's blocked off, but the families wanted it open.'

'Two shots fired,' I said. 'No one heard anything?'

'It was supposed to be a high-class crowd. You think they want my guards milling around? We keep two, three guys, to make sure overzealous guests don't wander into restricted areas. I should have guards patrolling the corridors down by the rest rooms? What ya gonna take, toilet paper?'

'Security cameras?' Raleigh asked.

Sharp sighed. 'We've got the exhibition halls covered, of course. The main exits . . . a remote sweep of the Main Hall. But nothing on the corridor where the shooting took place. Nothing in the crapper. Anyway, the police are scanning tape with members of each family as we speak. It would make it a helluva lot easier if we knew who on earth we're looking for.'

I reached into my briefcase and took out a copy of a bare-bones artist's sketch of a red-bearded man. It showed a thin face with a jutting chin, hair combed back and a lightly shaded goatee.

'Why don't we start with him.'

Chapter Fifty-Six

McBride had to be back in the office for a press briefing on the investigation. I needed to figure out why the killer had come to Cleveland, and what, if any, connections there were to our murders back in San Francisco. The next step was to talk to the parents of the bride.

Shaker Heights was a posh, upper-end suburb in the height of midsummer bloom. On every street, green lawns led up to graceful, tree-sheltered homes. One of McBride's men drove me out, while Raleigh went back to the Lakefront Hilton to meet with the family of the groom.

The Koguts' home was a warm, redbrick Normandy under a canopy of tall oaks. I was met at the door by an older sister of the bride, who introduced herself as Hillary Bloom. She sat me down in a comfy, picture-filled den: books, large-screen TV, photos of the two of them as kids, weddings. 'Kathy was always the rebellious one,' Hillary explained. 'A free spirit. It took her a while to find herself, but she was just settling down. She had a good job – a publicist for a firm in Seattle, where she met James. She was just coming around.'

'Coming around from what?' I asked.

'Like I said – she was a free spirit. That was Kathy.'

Her parents, Hugh and Christine Kogut, came into the room. For the third time, I witnessed the glazed, bewildered shock of people whose lives had been shattered.

'She was always in and out of relationships,' her mother eventually admitted. 'But she also had a passion for life.'

'She was just young,' her father said brokenly. 'Maybe we spoiled her too much. She always had an urge to experience things.'

From her pictures – the wispy red hair and dare-me eyes – I could see the same joy for life the killer had obviously seen in his first two victims. It made me feel sad, weary.

'Do you know why I'm here?' I asked.

The father nodded. 'To determine if there was any connection to those other horrible crimes out West.'

'So, can you tell me, did Kathy have any connection to San Francisco?'

I could see a cast of grim recognition creep its way onto their faces.

'After college, for a while, she did live there,' Christine Kogut said carefully.

'She went to UCLA,' Hugh told me. 'For a year or so after, she stayed in Los Angeles. Tried to catch on with one of the studios. She started out with a temp job at Fox, then she got this publicity job in San Francisco, covering music. It was a very fast life. Parties, promotions, no doubt a lot worse. We weren't happy, but for Kathy, she thought it was her big break.'

She lived in San Francisco. I asked if they had ever heard of Melanie Weil or Rebecca Passeneau.

They shook their heads.

'What about any relationships that might've ended badly? Someone, who out of jealousy or obsession, might've wanted to do her harm?'

'Recklessness always seemed like a basis for Kathy's relationships,' Hillary said with an edge.

'I did warn her.' Her mother shook her head. 'She always wanted to do things on her terms.'

'Did she ever mention anyone special from the time she lived in San Francisco?'

Everyone looked at Hillary. 'No. No one special.'

'No one stands out? She lived there for quite a while. She didn't keep up with anyone after she left?'

'I seem to remember her saying she still went down there every once in a while,' her father said. 'On business.'

'Old habits are hard to crack,' smirked Hillary, with a tightening of her lips.

There had to be some connection. Some contact from the year she had spent there. *Someone* came all the way here to see her dead.

'What about anyone from San Francisco invited to the wedding?' I asked.

'There was one girlfriend,' her father said.

'Merrill,' said her mother. 'Merrill Cole. Shortley now. I think she's at the Hilton, if she's still here.'

I pulled out the artist's sketch we had of the killer's possible appearance. 'It's only a rough likeness, but do you know this man? Is it someone who knew Kathy? Did you see anyone like this at the wedding?'

One by one, the Koguts shook their heads.

As I got up to go, I told them if anything came to mind, regardless how small or insignificant, to get in touch with me. Hillary walked me to the door.

'There is one more thing,' I said. I knew it was a long shot. 'By any chance, did Kathy buy her wedding dress in San Francisco?'

Hillary looked at me blankly and shook her head. 'No, from a vintage shop. In Seattle.'

At first, the answer deflated me. But then, in a flash, I saw that this was really a connection I was looking for. The first two murders had been committed by someone stalking his victims from afar. That's why he found them in the way he did. Tracked them.

But with this one, Kathy, she had been chosen in a different way.

I was certain that whoever had done this had known her.

Chapter Fifty-Seven

I drove straight to the Hilton on Lake Shore Boulevard and was able to catch Merrill Shortley just as she was packing her things, about to depart to the airport. She turned out to be stylish, maybe twenty-seven, with shoulder-length, chestnut brown hair tied back in a bun.

'A group of us were up all night,' she said, apologizing for the swollen lines around her face. 'I'd like to stay on, but who knows when they'll finally release the body. I have a one-year-old at home.'

'The Koguts told me you live in San Francisco.'

She sat on the edge of the bed across from me. 'Los Altos. I moved down two years ago when I got married.'

'I need to know about Kathy Kogut in San Francisco,' I explained. 'Lovers. Breakups. Someone who might have a cause to do this.'

'You think she *knew* this madman?' Her face was clenched.

'Maybe, Merrill. You can help us decide. *Will* you help us?'

'Kathy hooked up with guys,' Merrill said after a pause. 'She was always free about things in that way.'

'Are you saying she was promiscuous?'

'If you want to see it that way. Men liked her. There was a lot of energy going on back then. Music, film. Alternative stuff. Whatever made her feel alive.'

I was getting the picture. 'Does that include drugs?'

'Like I said, whatever made her feel alive. Yes, Kathy did recreational drugs.'

Merrill had the pretty, but hard-edged face of a street survivor who had now remade herself as a soccer-mom.

'Anyone come to mind who might've wanted to hurt her? Someone who was overly fascinated? Maybe jealous when she moved on?'

Merrill thought a bit, shook her head. 'I don't think so.'

'You two were close?'

She nodded. At the same time, her eyes hooded.

'Why did she move away?'

'She landed a great job. Must've seemed like she was finally climbing the ladder. Her father and mother always wanted that. It's the Shaker Heights thing. Look, I really have to catch a plane.'

'What are the chances Kathy was running away from something?'

'You live the way we lived, you're always running from something.' Merrill Shortley shrugged and looked bored.

There was an attitude, a coldness about Merrill I didn't like. She still surrounded herself with the cynical aura of a dissolute past. And I had the suspicion she was withholding. 'So what'd *you* do, Merrill? Marry the dime-bag mambo king of Silicon Valley?'

She shook her head. Finally, she smiled thinly. 'Fund manager.'

I leaned forward. 'So you don't remember anyone special? Someone she might've kept up with? Been scared of?'

'Those years,' Merrill Shortley said, 'I have a hard time remembering anyone special at all.'

'This was *your friend*,' I said, my voice rising. 'You want me to show you what she looks like now?'

Merrill stood up, stepped over to the dresser, and began to pack a leather bag with toiletries and makeup. At some point, she stopped and caught a glimpse of herself in the mirror. Then she looked over her shoulder and caught my eye. 'Maybe there was this one guy Kathy was into. Big shot. Older. She said I'd know who he was – but she wouldn't give me a name. I think she met him through the job. As I remember, he was married. I don't know how it ended. Or who ended it. *Or if it ever did.*'

My adrenaline began to flow. 'Who is he, Merrill? He might have killed your friend.'

She shook her head.

'You ever see this man?'

She shook her head again.

I pushed on. 'You're the one friend from back then she invites to her wedding and you never met him once? You don't even know a name?'

She gave me a cool smile. 'She was protective. She didn't

tell me everything. Scout's honor, Detective. I assume he was a public figure.'

'You see her much in the past couple of years?'

Merrill shook her head again. She was being a real bitch. New money in Silicon Valley.

'Her father told me she still used to come to town. On business.'

Merrill shrugged. 'I don't know. Look – I have to go.'

I yanked open my bag and removed one of the crime-scene photos McBride had given me, the one of Kathy, wide-eyed, slumped in a bloody heap in front of her husband.

'Someone she *knew* did this. You want to be met at the plane and thrown in a holding cell as a material witness? You can call in your husband's lawyer, but it'll still take him two days to get you out. How would the tech-fund crowd react to that news? I'm sure I could get it in the *Chronicle*.'

Merrill turned away from me, her jaw quivering. 'I don't know who it was. Just that he was older, married, some big-time SOB. Kinky, and not nice about it. Kathy said he played sex games on her. But whoever he was, she was always quiet about it, protective. The rest you'll have to do on your own.'

'She still continued to see this guy, didn't she?' I was starting to put it together. 'Even after she moved to Seattle. Even after she met her husband.'

She gave me the slightest smile. 'Good answer, Inspector. Right up to the end.'

'How close to the end?'

Merrill Shortley picked up the phone. 'This is four-oh-two. Checking out. I'm in a rush.'

She stood up, slung a Prada bag over her shoulder, an expensive-looking raincoat over her arm. Then she looked at me and said dryly, 'To the very end.'

Chapter Fifty-Eight

'No wonder the bride didn't wear white,' Raleigh frowned and said, as I told him about my interview with Merrill Shortley.

McBride had set us up for dinner at Nonni's, an Italian place on the lake, a short walk from our hotel.

Raleigh's interview with the groom's parents had yielded nothing eventful. James Voskuhl had been an aspiring musician who had floated on the edge of the music scene in Seattle, finally hooking his way into representing a couple of upcoming bands. He had no known connection to San Francisco.

'The killer knew Kathy,' I said. 'How else would he find her here? They had a relationship.'

'*Right up to the end*,' he mused.

'To the *very* end,' I answered. 'Meaning, maybe here, in Cleveland. These weren't choirgirls. Merrill said this guy was older, married, kinky, predatory. It fits the pattern of the murders. Someone she knew in San Francisco must have seen Red Beard. *Somebody knows.* Merrill claims that

Kathy was protecting her lover, possibly because he was a celebrity.'

'You think this Merrill Shortley has more to add?'

'Maybe. Or the family. I got the feeling they were holding something back.'

He had ordered a '97 Chianti and when it came he tilted his glass. 'Here's to David and Melanie, Michael and Becky, James and Kathy.'

'Let's toast them when we catch this pathetic bastard,' I said.

It was the first time we'd been alone in Cleveland, and suddenly I was nervous. We had an entire evening to fill, and no matter how we kept steering back to the case, or joked how 'this wasn't a date', there was this pull, this bass chord twanging inside me, telling me that this was no time to start anything with anyone, not even handsome and charming Chris Raleigh.

Then why had I changed into a baby-blue sweater and nice slacks instead of staying with the chambray shirt and khakis I'd worn all day?

We ordered. I had osso bucco, spinach, a salad; Raleigh, a veal paillard.

'Maybe it was someone on her job?' Raleigh said. 'Or connected with her job?'

'I told Jacobi to check out her firm in Seattle. Her father said she still came down to San Francisco on business. I want to see if that's the case.'

'And if it isn't?'

'Then either she was hiding something, or they are.'

He took a sip of wine. 'Why would she go through with a wedding if she was still involved with this guy?'

I shrugged. 'They all said Kathy was finally settling down. I'd like to see what she was like back then, if this is what they meant by settling down.' I was thinking that I wanted another talk with the sister, Hillary. I remembered something she had said. *Old habits are hard to crack.* I had thought she was talking about drugs, parties. Did she mean Red Beard?

'McBride tells me tomorrow morning we should be able to review some film at the museum.'

'The guy was *there*, Raleigh,' I said with certainty. 'He was there that night. Kathy knew her killer. We just have to find out who he is.'

Raleigh poured a little more wine into my glass. 'We're partners now, aren't we, Lindsay?'

'Sure,' I said, a little surprised by the question. 'Can't you tell I trust you?'

'I mean, we've been through three double murders, which we're committed to solving; I backed you up with Mercer – I even helped clean up after dinner at your place.'

'Yeah, so?' I grinned. But his face had a cast of seriousness to it. I was trying to figure out where he was going.

'What do you say, maybe it's about time you started calling me Chris.'

Chapter Fifty-Nine

After dinner, Chris and I walked down by the tree-lined lakefront toward our hotel. A cool, misty breeze lapped at my face.

We didn't say much. That same nervous apprehension was tingling on the surface of my skin.

Occasionally, our arms brushed. He had his jacket off, and there was a solid outline to his shoulders and arms. Not that I was noticing superficial things like that.

'It's still early,' he said.

'Five-thirty, our time,' I replied. 'I could still catch Roth. Maybe I should bring him up to date.'

Raleigh grinned. 'You already called Jacobi. I bet he was probably in Roth's office before he hung up the phone.'

As we walked, it was as if this unbearable force were pulling me close, then pushing me away. 'Anyway,' I said, 'for once I don't feel like calling in.'

'What do you feel like?' Raleigh asked.

'Why don't we just walk.'

'The Indians are playing. You want to sneak our way in . . . in the fifth inning?'

'We're cops, Raleigh.'

'Yeah, that would be bad. You want to dance, then?'

'*No*,' I said, even firmer. 'I don't want to dance.' Every word seemed charged with a hidden, electric message. 'What I'm starting to feel like . . .' I turned to him, 'is that I'm having a hard time remembering to call you *Chris*.'

'And what I'm starting to feel like,' he answered, facing me, 'is I'm having a hard time trying to pretend that nothing's going on.'

'I know,' I muttered breathlessly, 'but I just can't.'

It sounded really stupid, but as much as I wanted him, there was a greater hesitation inside holding me back.

' "I know . . . but I just can't." What does that mean?'

'It means, I'm feeling things, too. And that part of me wants to go with those feelings. But right now, I just don't know if I can. It's complicated, Chris.' Every nerve in my body was on alert.

We found ourselves walking again, the breeze from the lake suddenly cooling the sweat that had broken out on my neck.

'You mean it's complicated because we're working together?'

'*That*,' I lied. I'd dated guys on the force once or twice.

'*That* . . . and what else?' Raleigh said.

A thousand desires inside me were screaming to give in. What was going through my mind was crazy. I wanted him to touch me; and I didn't. We were alone on the waterfront. At that moment, if he held me, if he bent and kissed me, I don't know what I would've done.

'I *do* want to,' I said, my fingers reaching for his hand, staring into his deep blue eyes.

'You're not telling me the whole story,' he said.

It took everything I had to hold off confessing. I don't know why I didn't. A deep part of me wanted him to want me, and to keep thinking I was strong. I could feel the heat from his body, and I thought he could feel the wavering resolve in mine. 'I just can't right now,' I said softly.

'You know, I won't always be your partner, Lindsay.'

'I know that. And maybe I won't always be able to say no.'

I don't know if I was disappointed or relieved to see our hotel up ahead. I was sort of happy I wouldn't have to make a decision – when Raleigh took me by surprise. He leaned over without warning and pressed his lips on mine. The kiss was so soft, as if he were gently asking, 'Is this okay?'

I let the kiss linger, warmly. *Soft hands . . . soft lips.*

It wasn't as if I hadn't imagined this happening. Now here it was, out of the blue, and I was giving in. But just as I was starting to give him myself, the fear caught up to me – the fear of the inescapable truth.

I dropped my head, slowly pulled away.

'That was nice. For me, anyway,' Raleigh said, our foreheads coming to rest against each other.

I nodded, but said, 'I can't, Chris.'

'Why are you always holding back, Lindsay?' he asked.

I wanted to say, *'Because I am deceiving you.'* Tell him everything that was going on. But I continued to deceive, though I did it with the greatest yearning I had felt in years. 'I just want to nail Red Beard,' I answered.

Chapter Sixty

The next morning, Detective McBride left a message for us to meet him in Sharp's office at the Hall of Fame.

Something had come back on the film.

In a sparsely decorated conference room, the museum's Security Chief, McBride, and several members of the CPD Homicide staff sat facing a wide-screen video monitor on a walnut cabinet.

'At first,' Sharp began self-importantly, 'we were just randomly going through the tape with members of the families, stopping on anyone who didn't look familiar. Your sketch,' he turned to me, 'helped narrow it down.'

He flicked a handheld controller toward the screen. 'The first clips you're gonna see are the main entrance.'

The screen lit up, standard black-and-white surveillance footage. It was so weird and strange. Several gaudily dressed guests seemed to be arriving at once, many of them outfitted as famous rockers. One was Elton John. His date had teased his hair dyed in various light and dark shades, Cyndi Lauper-style. I recognized a Chuck Berry, a Michael

Jackson, a couple of Madonnas, Elvis, Elvis Costello.

Sharp fast-forwarded, the film advancing like individual, edited stills. An older couple arrived dressed in traditional evening wear. Behind them, almost tucked into their backs, came a man who was clearly shying away from the camera, averting his face.

'*There!*' Sharp said.

I saw him! My heart pumped madly in my chest. Goddamn Red Beard!

It was a horrible, grainy likeness. The man, sensing the direction of the camera, quickly hurried by. Maybe he came there earlier, scouting for security cameras. Maybe he was just smart enough to avoid a direct shot. Whatever it was, he sneaked into the crowd and disappeared.

A ball of anger knotted in my chest. 'Can you back up, home in?' I said to Sharp. 'I need to see his face.'

He leveled his remote and the image channeled into a higher magnification.

I stood up. I was staring at a partially obscured shot of the killer's face. No eyes, no clear feature. Only a shadowy profile. A jutting chin. And the outline of a goatee.

There was no doubt in my mind that this was the killer. I didn't know his name; I could barely see his face. But the fuzzy image I had first sketched together in my mind with Claire was now clear in front of me.

'Is that the best you can do?' Raleigh pressed.

A member of the museum tech staff replied, 'Might be able to get it technologically enhanced. On this rough footage, this is what we have.'

'We pick him up again later on,' Sharp said.

He quickly fast-forwarded and stopped at a wide-angle view of the Main Hall, the wedding reception. They were able to home in on the same tuxedoed man standing at the edge of the crowd, observing. When the image was magnified, though, it became grainy and lost its resolution.

'He's purposely avoiding looking at the camera,' I whispered to Raleigh. 'He knows where they are.'

'We ran these shots by both families,' Sharp said. 'No one places him. No one can identify who he is. I mean, there's a chance it's not him. But considering your sketch . . .'

'It's him all right,' I said firmly. My eyes burned on the grainy screen. I was also sure we were looking at Kathy Voskuhl's mysterious lover.

Chapter Sixty-One

Hillary knew. I was almost sure of it. But why she would conceal such a thing related to her sister's death, I couldn't imagine. *Old habits are hard to crack,* she had said.

I wanted another shot at her, and I reached her by phone at the family house in Shaker Heights.

'I had a chance to speak to Merrill Shortley,' I told her. 'Now I just need a few details cleared up.'

'You realize this is a very stressful time for my family, Detective,' Hillary replied. 'We told you what we knew.'

I didn't want to come on too strong. She had lost her sister in a horrible way. Her parents' home was filled with mourners and grief. And she was under no obligation to talk to me at all.

'Merrill told me a few things about Kathy. Her lifestyle . . .'

'*We* told you all that,' she replied defensively. 'But we also told you that after meeting James she had begun to settle down.'

'That's what I want to talk to you about. Merrill recalled

there *was* someone she was seeing in San Francisco.'

'I thought we told you, Kathy dated lots of men.'

'This one went on for a long time. He was older. Married. Some kind of big shot. Possibly famous.'

'I wasn't my sister's keeper,' Hillary complained.

'I need a name, Ms Bloom. This man could be her killer.'

'I'm afraid I don't understand. I already told you what I know. My sister didn't exactly confide in me. We lived very different lives. I'm sure you've put two and two together already – there was a lot I didn't approve of.'

'You said something to me the first time we talked. *Old habits are hard to crack.* What sort of habits were you referring to?'

'I'm afraid I don't know what you mean. The Cleveland police are handling this, Inspector. Can't we just let them do their job?'

'I'm trying to help you, Ms Bloom. Why did Kathy move away from San Francisco? I think you know. Was someone abusing her? Was Kathy in trouble?'

Hillary sounded frightened. 'I appreciate what you're trying to do, but I'm going to hang up now, Inspector.'

'It's going to come out, Hillary. It always does. An address book, her phone bill. It's not just Kathy. There are four others, back in California. They were just as hopeful about the rest of their lives as your sister. Just as deserving.'

There was a tiny sob in her voice. 'I have no idea what you're talking about.'

I felt I had one last chance. 'Here's the really ugly truth about murder. If I've learned one thing as a homicide detective, it's that the lines don't stay fixed. Yesterday you were an innocent victim, but now you're in this, too. This killer will strike again, and when he does, you will regret you didn't tell me for the rest of your life.'

There was a heavy silence on the line. I knew what it meant. It was the struggle inside Hillary Bloom's conscience. Then I heard a click. She had hung up the phone.

Chapter Sixty-Two

Our flight back to San Francisco left at 4:00 p.m. I hated, *hated* to leave without a name. Especially when I felt we were so close.

Somebody famous.

Kinky.

Why were they protecting him?

Anyway, we had accomplished a lot in just two days. It was clear to me that all three murders were committed by the same person. We had a strong lead tying him to San Francisco, a possible identity, a confirmed ID. The trail was warm here, and would grow ever hotter when we got home.

Both investigations would proceed locally. Cleveland would contact the Seattle police force to do a search and seizure on the bride's home. Maybe something in her personal effects, an address book, an e-mail in her computer, would divulge who her San Francisco lover was.

Waiting to board our plane out of Cleveland, I called my voice mail for messages. There was one each from Cindy and Claire inquiring about my trip, *our case.* Reporters pushing for my comments on the Cleveland crime. Then I heard the throaty voice of Merrill Shortley. She had left her California number.

I punched the number as fast as I could. A housekeeper answered, and I could hear the wail of a baby crying.

When Merrill got on, I could tell that some of her cool veneer had cracked. 'I was thinking,' she began, 'there was something I didn't mention yesterday.'

'Yes? That's good to hear.'

'This guy I told you about – the one Kathy was hooked up with in San Francisco? I was telling you the truth. I never knew his name.'

'Okay, I hear you.'

'But there were some things . . . I said he didn't treat her well. He was into intense sex games. Props, scenarios. Maybe even a little filming. Problem was, Kathy liked the games.'

There was a long pause before Merrill went on. 'Well . . . I think he pushed her, forced her to do more than she was comfortable with. I remember marks on her face, bruises on her legs. Mostly it was her spirit that was broken. None of us were exactly bringing home Tom Cruise then, but there was a time when Kathy was real scared. She was in his control.'

I began to see where this was heading. 'It's why she moved away, wasn't it?' I said.

I could hear Merrill Shortley sigh on the other end. 'Yes, it was.'

'Then why did she continue to see him from Seattle? You said she was involved with him. Right up to the end.'

'I never said,' Merrill Shortley sounded sad, 'that Kathy knew what was good for her.'

Now I saw Kathy Kogut's life take on the shape of tragic inevitability. I was sure she had fled San Francisco, tried to escape from the grip of this man. But she couldn't break free.

Was that true of the other murdered brides?

'I need a name, Ms Shortley. Whoever this was, he might've killed your friend. There are four others. The longer he's out there, the greater the chance he'll do it again.'

'I told you, I didn't know his name, Detective.'

I raised my voice above the din in the terminal. 'Merrill, *someone* must know. You were with her for four years, you partied together.'

Merrill hesitated. 'In her own way, Kathy was loyal. She said his name was well-known. He was some kind of celebrity – someone I would know. She was protecting him. Or maybe protecting herself.'

My mind raced to the film and music businesses. She was into a bad scene. She was over her head, and like people who feel trapped, she ran. She just couldn't get far enough away.

'She must've told you something,' I pressed. 'What he did, where he lived – where they would meet. You guys were like sisters?' *Wicked sisters?*

'I swear, Inspector. I've been racking my brain.'

'Then someone else must know. Who? Tell me!'

I heard Merrill Shortley let out a mirthless laugh. 'Ask her sister.'

Before we boarded, I beeped McBride and left a detailed message on his voice mail. Kathy's lover was probably someone famous. It was why she had moved away. The profile fit the pattern of our killer. Her sister, Hillary, might know the killer's name.

On board, all I could think about was that we were getting close. Raleigh was there beside me. As the plane rose, I leaned into his arm, surrendering to total exhaustion.

All my physical troubles seemed a million miles away. I remembered what I'd said to Claire. I told her that finding this bastard gave me the resolve to go on. The red-bearded man in my dream who had gotten away would not be free for much longer.

'We're going to get him,' I said to Raleigh. 'We can't let him kill another bride and groom.'

Chapter Sixty-Three

E ight the next morning, I was at my desk and calling Cleveland.

There were several ways I could go with this investigation. Hillary Bloom was the most direct, assuming, as Merrill implied, she was able to give us a name. It was clear that, in a twisted way, she was trying to save her family the added pain of having Kathy publicly branded as some kind of pathetic sexual victim, cheating on her husband-to-be right up until their vows.

Sooner or later a name would emerge. From her, or from Seattle.

Before I did anything else, I called Medved's office and rescheduled the blood treatment I had canceled. I would see him at five o'clock today. After a brief wait, the receptionist said the doctor would meet me there himself.

Maybe it was good news. Truth was, I *was* feeling a little stronger. Maybe the treatments were beginning to do their work.

It was hard picking up where I left off in San Francisco.

The best leads were now in Cleveland. I read some reports on the evidence Jacobi was tracking down; held a meeting of the Task Force at ten.

Actually, the most promising leads – the hair and the Bridal Boutique at Saks – had come from my meetings with Claire and Cindy. I couldn't resist calling Claire a little before noon.

'Bring me up to date,' she said excitedly. 'I thought we were partners.'

'I will,' I replied. 'Get Cindy. Meet me for lunch.'

Chapter Sixty-Four

The three of us leaned against the side of a stone wall in City Hall Park, picking at salad sandwiches we had bought at a nearby grocer's. *The Women's Murder Club meets again.*

'You were right,' I said to Claire. I passed her a copy of the security photo showing Red Beard sneaking into the Cleveland wedding.

She stared at it, her eyes focusing intensely. Claire looked up only when the confirmation of her physical supposition brought out a curious half-smile. 'I only read whatever that bastard left behind.'

'Maybe,' I said, tossing her a wink. 'But I bet Righetti would've missed it.'

'This is true,' she allowed with a satisfied beam.

It was a bright, breezy June day; the air was fragrant from a crisp Pacific breeze. Office folk worked on their tans, secretaries gabbed in groups. I recounted what I had found in Cleveland. I never mentioned what took place by the lake between Chris Raleigh and me.

When I finished with Merrill's shocking revelation, Cindy said, 'Maybe you should've stayed out there, Lindsay.'

I shook my head. 'It's not my case,' I explained. 'I was only there on a consult. Now I'm running point between three jurisdictions.'

'You think Merrill Shortley has more to tell?' asked Claire.

'I don't think so. If she knew, I think she would have told me.'

'The bride must have had other friends here,' said Cindy. 'She was in publicity. If this guy was famous, maybe she met him through her job.'

I nodded. 'I have someone checking that out. We also have the Seattle PD combing through her apartment.'

'Where'd she work when she lived here?' Claire asked.

'An outfit called Bright Star Media. Apparently, she was connected into the local music scene.'

Cindy took a sip of iced tea. 'Why not let me have a go at it.'

'You mean like you did at the Hyatt?' I said.

She grinned. 'No, more like Napa. C'mon . . . I'm a reporter. I sit all day with people trained to find the dirt on anybody.'

I bit into my sandwich. 'Okay,' I mumbled. 'Be my guest.'

'In the meantime,' Cindy inquired, 'can I run with what we have so far?'

Much of it was classified. If it came out, it would point back to me. 'You can run with the similar pattern of murder in Cleveland. How we found the bodies. The bride's background here. Absolutely *no mention* of Merrill Shortley.' In that way, I hoped the killer would sense that we were closing in on him. It might cause him to think twice about killing again.

When Cindy went over to a nearby ice-cream cart to buy a gelato, Claire took the moment to ask, 'So how are you feeling? You okay?'

I shrugged. 'Queasy. Light-headed. I was told to expect it. I'm having a blood treatment this afternoon. Medved said he'd be there.' I shut up when I saw Cindy on her way back.

'Here,' our young friend announced brightly. She was carrying three ices.

Claire clutched her chest and pretended she was going into cardiac arrest. 'I need gelato about as much as Texas needs a warm breeze in August.'

'Me too,' I laughed. But it was mango, and with the infection attacking me inside, it seemed like wasted caution to refuse.

Claire ended up taking hers, too. 'So what you specifically haven't told us,' she said, with a slow roll of her tongue, 'is what went on between you and Mr Chris Raleigh in Oh-hi-oh.'

' 'Cause there was nothing to tell,' I said.

'One thing about cops,' Cindy laughed, 'is you would think they would learn how to lie.'

'You writing for the gossip page now?' I asked. Against my will, I felt my face blush. Claire and Cindy's greedy eyes bore down on me, driving home that it was pointless to resist.

I pulled a knee up on the edge of the wall and sat yoga-style. Then I took them through where things stood: the long, slow dance in my apartment; the anticipation of sitting next to him on the plane; the nervous walk down by the lake; my own doubts, hesitation; the inner conflicts holding me back.

'Basically, it took every bit of self-control not to rip his clothes off right there on Lakefront Walk,' I concluded – and laughed at how it must have sounded.

'Girl, why didn't you?' Claire said, wide-eyed. 'Might've done you some good.'

'I don't know,' I said, shaking my head.

But I did know. And though she tried to smile through it, Claire knew, too. She squeezed my hand. Cindy looked on, not knowing what was going on.

Claire joked, 'I'd give up losing twenty pounds to see Cheery's expression if the two of you got picked up for going at it in the woods.'

'Two San Francisco cops,' announced Cindy in a news-caster tone, 'in pursuit of the Bride and Groom killer, were discovered *au naturel* in the bushes by the Cleveland waterfront.'

The three of us choked with laughter and it felt *so good*.

Cindy wagged a finger at me. 'That, Lindsay, I would've *had* to print.'

'From now on,' Claire giggled, 'I can see things growing pretty humid in that squad car.'

'I don't think that's Chris's style,' I defended him. 'You forget, the man's into *The Shipping News*.'

'Oh . . . it's Chris now, huh?' mooned Claire. 'And don't be so sure about that. Edmund plays three instruments, knows everything from Bartok to Keith Jarret, but he's risen to the occasion in some very unexpected places.'

'Like where?' I laughed, the surprise caught in my throat.

She coyly shook her head. 'I just don't want you thinking that 'cause a man keeps himself with a certain dignity, there's any dignity when it comes to that.'

'C'mon,' I exhorted, 'you put it in play. Let's hear.'

'Let's just say that a few John Does aren't the only things that have been stiff on our examining tables.'

I almost fumbled my gelato onto the ground. 'You've got to be kidding. You? And Edmund?'

Claire's shoulders jiggled in delight. 'As long as I've gone this far . . . once we did it in a parterre box at the Symphony. After a rehearsal, of course.'

'Whatta you guys do? Just go around leaving your mark like poodles?' I exclaimed.

Claire's round face broadened with delight. 'You know, it was a long time ago. But as I think of it, that time in my office at the coroner's Christmas party . . . that wasn't so long ago.'

'As long as we're baring our souls,' injected Cindy, 'when I first got to the *Chronicle* I had this fling with one of the senior guys from Datebook. We used to meet down in the library, in the far reaches of the Real Estate section. Nobody ever went there.'

Cindy scrunched her face, abashed, but Claire cackled with approval. I was amazed. I was learning the hidden, suppressed side of a person I had known for ten years. But there was a little shame building in me as well. *I didn't have a list.*

'So,' Claire said, looking at me. 'What's Inspector Boxer got to share from her closet?'

I tried to recall a single moment when I'd done something totally crazy. I mean, when it came to sex, I didn't think of myself as someone who held back. But somehow, no matter how hard I searched my memory, my passion always ended up between the sheets.

I shrugged, empty-handed.

'Well, you better get started,' Claire remonstrated. 'When I'm drawing my last breath, I won't be thinking about all those fancy degrees or conferences I spoke at. You only have a few times in your life to really cut loose, so you might as well take 'em when they come.'

A little tremor of remorse knifed through me. At that moment, I didn't know what I wanted more: my place on the list – or a goddamn name for Red Beard. I suppose I wanted both.

Chapter Sixty-Five

A couple of hours later, I sat in my hospital smock in the hematology clinic.

'Dr Medved would like a word with you before we start,' said Sara, my transfusion nurse.

I felt a stab of apprehension as she unpacked an IV setup for my treatment. Truth was, I had been feeling okay. Not much pain or nausea other than the incident in the ladies' room last week.

When Dr Medved walked in with a manila folder under his arm, his face was friendly but unconfiding.

I smiled weakly. 'Only good news?'

He sat across from me on the ledge of a counter. 'How are you feeling, Lindsay?'

'I wasn't feeling so bad when I saw you before.'

'Fatigued?'

'Only a little. End-of-day kind of thing.'

'Sudden nausea? Queasiness?'

I admitted I *had* vomited suddenly once or twice. He made a quick notation on a chart, paged through some other medical charts in the folder. 'I see we've undergone four packed red cell transfusions so far . . .'

My heart was racing, the longer he took. Finally, he put down the folder and looked squarely into my face.

'I'm afraid your erythrocyte count has continued to decline, Lindsay. You can see the trend line here.'

Medved passed me a sheet. Leaning forward, he took a pen out of his breast pocket. The paper had a computer graph on it. He traced the pattern with his pen. The line went steadily down. *Shit.*

'I'm getting worse,' I said hoarsely.

'To be frank,' the doctor acknowledged, 'it's not the trend we were hoping for.'

I had ignored that this might happen, burying myself in the case, sure that the numbers would improve. I had built this view on a natural trust that I was too young and energetic to be truly sick. I had work to do, important work, a life to live.

I was dying, wasn't I? Oh, God.

'What happens now?' I managed to say. My voice came out as a whisper.

'I want to continue with the treatments,' Medved replied. 'In fact, increase them. Sometimes these things take a while to kick in.'

'Super hi-test,' I chuckled glumly.

He nodded. 'From this point on, I'd like you to come in three times a week. And I'm going to increase the dosage by thirty per cent.' He shifted his weight off the counter. 'In and of itself, there's no immediate cause for alarm,' he declared, in a marginally uplifting tone. 'You can continue to work – that is if you feel up to it.'

'I *have* to work,' I told Medved.

Chapter Sixty-Six

I drove home in a daze. One moment I was battling to unravel this damned case, and the next I was fighting for my life.

I wanted a name. I wanted it now more than ever. And I wanted my life back. I wanted a shot at the whole deal – happiness, success, someone to share it with, a child. And now that I had met Raleigh, I knew there was a chance that I could have these things. If I could hold out. If I could will the good cells into my body.

I went into my apartment. Sweet Martha was all over me so I took her for a short walk. But then I moped around, alternating between a resolve to fight through this mess, and sadness that I couldn't. I even contemplated making a meal. I thought it would calm me.

I took out an onion, and cut two desultory slices. Then I realized how crazy it all was. I needed to talk to someone. I wanted to shout, 'I don't fucking deserve this!' and this time I wanted someone to hear it.

I thought of Chris, his comforting arms around me. His

eyes, his smile. I wished I could tell him. He would come in an instant. I could rest my head on his shoulder.

I called Claire. She could tell from my first tremulous sound that something was terribly wrong.

'I'm scared,' was all I said.

We talked for an hour on the phone. At least – *I* talked.

I went back and forth with Claire in a numbed state – panicked by the impending nearness of Negli's next stage. Then Claire reminded me of what I had said when I first told her about the disease. That nailing this bastard gave me the will to fight on. It separated me from being just another person who was sick. I had a special purpose.

'Has that changed for you, Lindsay?' she asked softly.

'No. I want to get him more than ever.'

'Then that's what we're going to do. You, me, little Cindy. We're here to help you fight. We're your support, darlin'. Just this one time, don't try to do it all yourself.'

In an hour, she had calmed me enough, so we could say goodnight.

I curled up on the couch. Martha and I snuggled under a blanket and watched the movie *Dave* – one of my favorites. When Sigourney Weaver visits Kevin Kline in his new campaign office at the end, it always makes me cry.

I fell asleep, hoping for a happy ending in my own life.

Chapter Sixty-Seven

The next morning I went at it stronger than ever. I still believed we were close, maybe just hours from a name for Red Beard.

I checked in with Roth's contact, a Jim Heekin on the Seattle police force. Heekin said they were sorting through the bride's possessions as we spoke. If something came up he would let me know immediately.

We got a reply back from Infortech, where Kathy Voskuhl had worked in Seattle. In the three years she held her job as a junior account manager, there was no record of any reimbursements for business trips to San Francisco. Her job was to work with developing clients in Seattle. If she repeatedly went down there, she was on her own.

Finally, I called McBride. The Koguts were still claiming that they knew nothing more. But yesterday he'd met with the father, who seemed ready to give in. It was wrenching that some desperate attempts to hold together their daughter's virtue was clouding their judgment.

Since I was a woman, maybe one more try from me

would push them over the edge. I placed a call to Christine Kogut, the bride's mother.

When she came on, her voice was different – remote, but freer, as if she were in a less tormented state. Maybe I just hoped she was.

'Your daughter's killer is running free,' I said immediately. I could no longer hold back. 'Two other couples' families are suffering as well. I think you *know* who was hurting Kathy. Please, Mrs Kogut, help me put him away.'

I heard her take in a long breath. When she spoke, grief and the release of shame trembled in her voice. 'You raise a child, Detective, she is always part of you. You love her so much and you think there is always that part that will never go away.'

'I know,' I said. I could feel she was teetering. *She knew his name, didn't she?*

'She was this beautiful thing . . . she could make anyone love her. A free spirit. One day, we thought that some other free spirit would shape her into the kind of person she was meant to be. We cultivated that freedom in our children. My husband insists we always favored Kathy. Maybe we helped bring it all on.'

I didn't say a word. I knew what it was like to finally give up what you were holding inside you. I wanted to let her reach that point on her own.

'Do you have children, Detective?'

'Not yet,' I told her.

'It's so hard to believe, that your baby can be the cause of so much pain. We begged her to break free. We even got her the new job. Moved her ourselves. We thought, if she could only get away from him . . .'

I was silent, letting her go at her own pace.

'She was sick, like an addict is sick, Detective. She couldn't stop herself. But what I don't understand is *why* he would hurt her so badly. He took away all that was pure about her. Why did he need to hurt our Kathy?'

Give me the name. Who is he?

'She was mesmerized by who he was. It was as if she had no self-control when it came to this man. She shamed us right up until the end. But even now . . .' her voice lowered '. . . I still wonder how someone who loved my daughter could possibly kill her. I'm afraid that I don't believe it. That's partly why I wouldn't tell you.'

'Tell me now,' I said.

'I think she met him at the opening of one of his films. He told her he had a face like hers in mind when he dreamed up one of his characters. His *heroine*.'

It was then that Mrs Kogut told me.

My body went numb.

I knew the name. Recognized it. He was famous – Red Beard.

Chapter Sixty-Eight

I sat there, ratcheting the possible connection through my mind. Things were starting to piece together. He was one of the minority partners at Sparrow Ridge Vineyards, where the *second* couple had been dumped. He had known Kathy Kogut for years in San Francisco. Preyed on her. He was older. Married.

Famous.

By itself, the suspect's name proved nothing. He had merely known the last bride. He had a circumstantial connection to the crime scene of the second killings. But based on the descriptions of Merrill Shortley and the grieving Christine Kogut, he had the brutal temperament, and maybe the motive, to commit these vicious murders. The conviction built up inside me that this *was* Red Beard. I grabbed Raleigh.

'What's going on?' he asked, startled. 'Where's the fire?'

'I'm going to start one in here. Watch.' I dragged him into Roth's office. 'I have a name,' I announced.

They looked at me in wide-eyed surprise.

'Nicholas Jenks.'

'The writer?' Raleigh gaped.

I nodded. 'He was Kathy Kogut's lover here in San Francisco. Her mother finally gave it up.' I walked them through the not-so-random connections he had with at least two of the victims.

'This guy's ... *famous*,' blurted Roth. 'He made those movies, blockbusters.'

'That's exactly the point. Merrill Shortley said it was someone Kathy was trying to conceal. The guy's got two connections, Sam.'

'He's got connections, all right,' Roth cried. 'Jenks and his wife are invited to all the big affairs. I've seen his picture with the Mayor. Wasn't he part of the bid to keep the Giants here?'

The air in Cheery's office became heavy with the weight of dangerous possibilities and risk.

'You should have heard how the Koguts described him, Sam,' I said. 'Like some kind of animal. A predator. I think we're going to find he had something going with *all three girls*.'

'I think Lindsay's right, Sam,' Chris said.

We watched Roth slowly clicking the facts into his head. Nicholas Jenks was famous. A national figure. Untouchable. The Lieutenant's face twisted as if he had swallowed a bad clam.

'You've got nothing right now,' he came back. 'All of it. It's beyond circumstantial.'

'His name has popped up in connection with four dead

people. We could get face to face, like I would with anyone else. We could talk to the District Attorney.'

Roth held up a hand. Nicholas Jenks was one of San Francisco's most prominent citizens. Implicating him on a murder charge was dangerous. *We'd better be right.* I didn't know what Cheery was thinking. Finally, there was the slightest relaxation in his neck, only a tight swallow, but in Roth-speak, it was a go-ahead.

'You could talk to the DA,' he agreed. 'Call Jill Bernhardt.' He turned to Raleigh. 'This *can't* get out until we have something really firm.'

Unfortunately, Assistant District Attorney Jill Bernhardt was stuck in court. Her secretary said she wouldn't be out until the end of the day. Too bad. I knew Jill a little, liked her. She was tough, with dazzling smarts. She even had a conscience.

Raleigh and I got a cup of coffee, going over what we should do next. Roth was right. As far as a warrant was concerned, we had nothing. A direct confrontation could be dangerous. A guy like this, you had to be sure. He would fight back.

Warren Jacobi shuffled in, a self-satisfied smirk puffing up his face. 'Must be raining champagne today,' he muttered.

I took it as another sardonic zinger aimed at Raleigh and me.

'For weeks I can't even get a bite on this shit.' He sat down and cocked his head toward Raleigh. '*Bite . . . champagne . . .* that works, Counselor, doesn't it?'

'Works for me,' Raleigh said.

Jacobi continued, 'So yesterday Jennings comes back with three places that had sold a few cases of the bubbly in question. One of them's this accountant in San Mateo. Funny thing is, his name's on file. Ends up he did two years up in Lampoc for securities fraud. Kind of a reach, isn't it? Serial killing, securities fraud . . .'

'Maybe the guy's got a thing against people who file joint returns,' I said, and smiled at Jacobi.

He puckered up his face. 'The other's some woman manager at 3Com who's stocking up for a fortieth birthday bash. This Clos du Mesnil is a real collectible. It's French, I'm told.'

I glanced up, waiting for him to get to the point.

'Now the third one, that's what I mean by *raining* . . . big auction house, Butterfield and Butterfield. Three years back, sold two cases of the eighty-nine. Went for twenty-five hundred per case, plus commish. Private collector. At first they wouldn't give out the name. But we squeezed. Turns out he's a big shot. My wife, she happens to be a fan. Read every one of his books.'

Raleigh and I froze. 'Whose, Warren?' I pressed.

'I figure, I check it out I can be a hero, bring home a signed copy. You ever read *Lion's Share* by Nicholas Jenks?'

Chapter Sixty-Nine

Jacobi's statement felt like an elbow to my solar plexus. At the same time it removed all doubt for me.

Kathy Kogut, Sparrow Ridge, the Clos du Mesnil champagne. Jenks was now tied into all three murders.

He was Red Beard.

I wanted to run and confront Jenks, but I knew I couldn't. I wanted to get up close, glare in his smug eyes, let him know I knew. At the same time, a suffocating tightness swept up in my chest. I didn't know if it was a flash of nausea, Negli's, or the release of my bottled-up rage. Whatever it was, I knew I had to get out.

'Let's go,' I said to Raleigh in a pleading voice.

He looked stunned and confused, as I rushed out.

'Hey, I say something wrong?' I heard Jacobi say.

I grabbed my jacket and purse and ran down the steps to the street. My blood was rioting inside me – angry, accusing, scared. A cold sweat had broken out all over me.

I ran out into the cool day, started to walk fast. I had no idea where I was going. I felt like a foreign tourist wandering in the city for the first time. Soon, there were crowds, stores, people rushing by who knew nothing about me. I wanted to lose myself for a few minutes. Starbucks, Kinko's, Empress Travel. Familiar names flashed by.

I felt drawn by a single, irrepressible urge. *I wanted to look in his eyes.*

On Post, I found myself standing in front of a Borders bookshop. I went inside. It was large and open, bright with merchandised stands and shelves of all the current books. I didn't ask, I just looked. On a table in front of me, I spotted what I was searching for.

Lion's Share. Maybe fifty copies – thick, bright blue, some stacked, some propped up.

Lion's Share by Nicholas Jenks.

My chest was exploding. I felt in the grip of unspeakable, but undeniable right. A mission, a purpose. This was why I was an investigator. *For this very moment.*

I took a copy of Jenks's book and looked at the back cover. I was staring at the killer of the brides and grooms. I was sure of it. It was the cut of Nicholas Jenks's face, sharp as a stone's edge, that told me. The blue eyes, cold and sterile, controlling.

And one more thing.

The red beard was flecked with gray.

Book Three

Red Beard

Chapter Seventy

J ill Bernhardt, the tough, savvy Assistant District Attorney assigned to the Bride and Groom case, kicked off her Ferragamos, and curled her legs up on the leather chair behind her desk. She fixed her sharp blue eyes directly at my face.

'Let me get this straight. You think the Bride and Groom killer is Nick Jenks?' she asked.

'I'm sure of it,' I said.

Jill was dark, disarmingly attractive. Curly jet-black hair framed a narrow, oval face. She was an achiever, thirty-four, a rising star in Bennett Sinclair's office.

All you needed to know about Jill was that as a third-year prosecutor, it was she who had tried the La Frade case, when the Mayor's old law partner was indicted on a RICO charge for influence peddling. No one, including the DA himself, wanted to submarine his or her career by taking on the powerful fundraiser. Jill nailed him, sent him away for twenty years. Got herself promoted to the office next to Big Ben himself.

One by one, Raleigh and I laid out Nicholas Jenks's connections to the three double murders: the champagne found at the first scene; his involvement in Sparrow Ridge Vineyards; his volatile relationship with the third bride, Kathy Voskuhl.

Jill threw back her head and laughed. 'You want to bust this guy for messing up someone's life, be my guest. Go try the *Examiner*. Here, I'm afraid, they make us do it with facts.'

I said, 'We have him tied to three double murders, Jill.'

Her lips parted into a skeptical smile that read, *Sorry, some other time.* 'The champagne connection might fly, *if* you had him nailed down. Which you don't. The real-estate partnership's a non-starter. None of it pins him directly to any of the crimes. A guy like Nicholas Jenks – public, connected – you don't go around making unsubstantiated accusations.'

With a sigh, she shifted a tower of briefs aside. 'You want to take on the big fish, guys? Go back, get yourself a stronger rod.'

My mouth dropped at her hard-edged reaction to our case. 'This isn't exactly my first homicide, Jill.'

Her strong chin was set.

'And this isn't exactly my first Page One case.' Then she smiled, softened. 'Sorry,' she said. 'It's one of Bennett's favorite expressions. I must be spending too much time around the sharks.'

'We're talking about a multiple killer,' Raleigh said, the frustration mounting in his eyes.

Jill had that implacable, prove-it-to-me resistance. I had worked with her on murder cases twice before, knew how tireless and prepared she was when she got to court. Once, she had invited me to go 'spinning' with her during a trial at which I was a witness. I gave up in a sweat after thirty grueling minutes but Jill, pumping without pause, went on at a mad pace for the full forty-five. Two years out of Stanford Law, she married a rising young partner at one of the city's top venture firms. Leapfrogged a squadron of career prosecutors to the DA's right hand. In a city of high achievers, Jill was the kind of girl for whom everything clicked.

I passed her the security photo from the Hall of Fame, then Nicholas Jenks's photograph.

She studied them, shrugged. 'You know what an adversarial expert witness would do with these? It's pupshit. If the cops in Cleveland feel they can convict with this, be my guest.'

'I don't want to lose him to Cleveland,' I said.

'So come back to me with something I can take to Big Ben.'

'How about a Search and Seizure,' Raleigh suggested. 'Maybe we can match up the champagne bottle from the first crime scene to the lot he purchased.'

'I could run it by a judge,' Jill mused. 'There must be someone out there on the bench who thinks Jenks has done enough to bring down the structure of literary form to the point where they'd go for it. But I think you'd be making a mistake.'

'Why?'

'Some two-time crack whore, *her* you can bring in on suspicion. You bring in Nicholas Jenks, you better arraign. You alert him that you're on to him – you'll spend more time fending off his lawyers and the press than making your case. If he's it, you're gonna have one shot and one shot only to dig up what you need to convict. Right now, you need more.'

'Claire has a hair in her lab from the second killing – the DeGeorges,' I said. 'We can make Jenks give us a sample of his beard.'

She shook her head. 'With what you have, his compliance would be totally voluntary. Not to mention, if you're wrong, what you might lose.'

'You mean by narrowing the search?'

'I was talking politically. You know the game rules, Lindsay.'

She riveted those intense blue eyes directly at me. I could envision the headlines, turning the case back against us. Like the screw-ups with O.J. Simpson, or Jon Benet Ramsey. In both cases, it seemed the cops were as much on trial as any possible defendants.

'Look, if the guy's guilty, I'd like to tear him apart as much as you,' Jill told us. 'But all you're bringing me is an unlucky preference in champagne and an eyewitness on her third vodka and tonic. Cleveland's at least got a prior relationship with one of the victims, bringing up a possible motive, but right now, none of the jurisdictions have enough to go on.'

Jill got up, smoothed her navy skirt, then leaned on her desk. 'Look,' she finally admitted, 'I've got two of the biggest headline grabbers in the city looking over my every move. You think the District Attorney and the Mayor want to pass this thing on?' Then she fixed unflappably on me. 'What's the litmus test here? You're sure it's him, Lindsay?'

He was linked to all three cases. The desperate voice of Christine Kogut was clear in my mind. I gave Jill my most convincing nod. 'He's the killer.'

She got up and made her way around the desk. With a half-smile, she said, 'I'm gonna make you pay if this blows off any chance of getting my memoirs in print by forty.'

Through the sarcasm, I saw a look flare up in Jill Bernhardt's eyes, the same resolute look I had seen when she was spinning. It hit me like a spray of Mace. 'Okay, Lindsay, let's make this case.'

I didn't know what made Jill tick. Power? An urge to do right? Some manic drive to outperform? Whatever it was, I didn't think it was far from what had always burned through me.

But, listening to her cogently mapping out what we needed to indict, a tantalizing thought took hold of me.

I thought about getting her together with Claire and Cindy.

Chapter Seventy-One

A t an old-fashioned steel desk in the dingy halls of the *Chronicle*'s basement library, Cindy Thomas scrolled through four-year-old articles on microfiche. It was late. After eight. Working alone, in the underbelly of the building, she felt as if she were some isolated Egyptologist scraping the dust off of long-buried hieroglyphic tablets. She now knew why it was referred to as 'the Tombs'.

But she felt she was onto something. The dust was coming off secrets and something worthwhile would soon be clear to her.

February . . . March, 1996. The film shot by with indistinguishable speed.

Someone famous, the Cleveland bride's friend had said. Cindy pushed the film onward. This was how stories were earned. Late nights and elbow grease.

Earlier, she had called the public relations firm Kathy Kogut had worked for in San Francisco, Bright Star Media. News of their former staffer's death had reached them only that day. Cindy inquired about any feature films

Bright Star might've had an association with. She was disappointed when she was told the firm didn't handle films. The Capitol, she was told. The concert palace. That was Kathy's account.

Undeterred, Cindy plugged Bright Star's name into the *Chronicle*'s data bank. Any subjects of articles, names, companies, reviews written in the past ten years were recorded there. To her mild delight, the search came back with several live responses.

It was assiduous work, and discouraging. The articles covered a period of more than five years. That would tie in with the time Kathy was in San Francisco. Each article was on a different microfiche cassette.

It required going back into the files. Requisitioning. Three items at a time. After four sets, the night librarian handed her the clipboard, saying, 'Here, Thomas, it's all yours. Knock yourself out.'

It was quarter past ten – she hadn't heard a peep from anyone in over two hours – when she finally came upon something interesting. It was dated February 10, 1995. *Arts Today* section. FOR LOCAL BAND, SIERRA, NEW FILM TAPS INTO A HIT.

Cindy's eyes shot down the text, fast-forwarding to anything that stuck out: plans for their album, an eight-city tour. Quotes from the lead singer.

'*Sierra will perform the song at tomorrow night's bash at the Capitol to kick off release of the film* Crossed Wire.'

Her heart stood still. She zoomed ahead to the following day's *Arts* section.

She consumed the article almost in a single suspended breath: . . . *took over the Capitol. Chris Wilcox, the star, was there.* A photo, with a dishy actress. *Bright Star . . . other recording stars in attendance.*

Her eyes traveled over the three accompanying new photos. In tiny print, underneath each shot, she noticed the photographer's name: *Photography by Sal Esposito. Property of the* Chronicle.

Photography! Cindy jumped out of her seat at the microfiche desk and hurried back through the musty, ten-foot-high stacks of bundled, yellowing editions. On the other side of the Tombs was the *Chronicle's* photography morgue. Rows and rows of unused shots.

She had never even been in here – didn't know how it was laid out.

Creepy, creepy place, especially this late at night.

She recognized the aisles were chronological. She followed the signs at the end of each aisle until she found February 1995. She ran her eyes along the outside of the stacked plastic bins dated the tenth.

When she spotted it, it was on the highest shelf. Where else? She stepped up on the lower shelf, on her tiptoes, and wiggled the bin down.

On the dusty floor, Cindy frantically leafed through folders bunched up in elastic. As if in a dream, she came upon one marked in large black letters: *'Crossed Wire' Opening – Esposito.* This was it.

Inside were four contact sheets, several black-and-white glossies. Someone, probably the reporter, had written the names of each person, in pen, at the bottom of each shot.

Her eyes froze as she came upon the photo she was hoping for. Four people were toasting the camera, with arms locked. She recognized Kathy Kogut's face from the photos Lindsay had come back with. Red hair, curly. Trendy, in-laid glasses.

And next to her, smiling into the camera, was another face she knew. It took her breath away. Her fingers trembled with the realization that she had the hieroglyphics at last.

It was the trimmed, reddish-colored beard. The narrow, complicit smile – as if he knew where all this might one day lead.

Next to Kathy Kogut was the novelist Nicholas Jenks.

Chapter Seventy-Two

I was totally surprised when Cindy appeared at my door at half-past eleven. With a look of wide-eyed elation and pride, she blurted, 'I know who Kathy Kogut's lover was.'

'Nicholas Jenks,' I replied. 'C'mon in, Cindy. *Down*, Martha.' She was tugging at my Giants nightshirt.

'Oh God,' she wailed loudly. 'I was so pumped up. I thought *I* had found it.'

She *had* found it. She had beaten McBride and Seattle, two squads of trained investigators as well as the FBI. I looked at her with genuine admiration. 'How?' I asked.

Too restless to sit, Cindy stalked around my living room, as she took me through the steps of her amazing discovery. She unfolded a copy of the news photo showing Jenks and Kathy Kogut at the movie opening. I watched her circle the couch, trying to keep up with herself: Bright Star . . . Sierra . . . *Crossed Wire* . . . She was hyper. 'I'm a good reporter, Lindsay,' she said.

'I know you are.' I smiled at her. 'You just can't *write* about it.'

Cindy stopped, the sudden realization of what she had overlooked hitting her like a pie in the face.

'Oh God,' she moaned. 'That's like being in a shower with Brad Pitt, but you can't touch.' She looked at me, half-smiling, half like nails were being driven into her heart.

'Cindy,' I reached out and held her, 'you wouldn't have even known to look for him if I hadn't clued you in on Cleveland.' I went to the kitchen. 'You want some tea?' I called out.

She collapsed on the couch and let out another wail. 'I want a beer. No, not beer. Bourbon.'

I pointed to my small bar near the terrace. In a few moments, we sat down. Me, with my Nocturnal Seasonings, Cindy, with a stiff glass of Wild Turkey, Martha comfortable at our feet.

'I'm proud of you, Cindy,' I told her. 'You did crack the name. You scooped two police forces. When this is over, I'm gonna make sure you get a special mention in the press.'

'I *am* the press!' Cindy exclaimed, forcing herself to smile. 'And what do you mean, "When this is over." You have him.'

'Not quite.' I shook my head. I explained that everything we had, even stuff she didn't know – the vineyard, the champagne – was circumstantial. We couldn't even force him to submit a hair.

'So what do we need to do?'

'Tie Nicholas Jenks solidly into the first crime.'

Suddenly, she began pleading. 'I have to run with it, Lindsay.'

'No,' I insisted. 'No one knows. Only Roth and Raleigh. And one more . . .'

'Who?' Cindy blinked.

'Jill Bernhardt.'

'The Assistant District Attorney? That office is like a colander trying to sail across the Pacific. It's nothing but leaks.'

'Not Jill,' I promised. 'She won't leak this.'

'How can you be so sure?'

'Because Jill Bernhardt wants to nail this guy as much as we do,' I said, with conviction.

'That's all?' groaned Cindy.

I sipped a soothing mouthful of tea, met her eyes. 'And because I invited her to join our group.'

Chapter Seventy-Three

The following day we met after work for a drink at Susie's; it was Jill's first introduction to our group.

All day, I couldn't fix on anything other than the thought of confronting Jenks with what we knew and bringing him in. I wanted to accelerate everything – bring about a face-to-face confrontation. I wanted to let him know we had him. *Goddamn Red Beard.*

As we waited for drinks, I threw out a couple of new developments. A search of Kathy Kogut's home in Seattle had uncovered Jenks's name and phone number in the dead bride's phonebook. A trace by Northwest Bell had turned up three calls to him in the past month – including one three days before the Cleveland wedding. It confirmed what Merrill Shortley had told us.

' "Right up to the very end", ' Claire quoted. 'Creepy. Both of them, actually.'

We ran Jenks's photo by Maryanne Perkins of Saks as part of a photospread with five others. We desperately needed something that pinned him to the first crime. She paused over his likeness for a few seconds. 'It's him,' she declared. Then she paused. 'But then it's hard to tell. It was so quick. And far away.'

The thought of a defense attorney cross-examining her didn't sit well. It was no surprise to me that Jill agreed.

It took no longer than a single margarita for her to make a seamless introduction into our group.

Claire had met Jill a few times when she testified at trials. They had developed a mutual respect for each other's rise through their male-dominated departments.

We asked Jill about herself and she told us she was Stanford Law, and her father was a corporate attorney back in Dallas. No interest in the corporate thing. That was for her husband, Steve, who was running a venture fund for Bank America. They lived in Burlingame – affluent, exclusive – took rock-climbing treks in the desert at Moab. No kids. 'It just doesn't fit, right now,' she said.

Jill seemed to live the epitome of the fast, successful life. At the same time, there seemed to be something missing. Maybe she was tired from the grind, the pace of her accomplishments.

When our drinks arrived, Claire and I toasted Cindy's ingenuity in coming up with Jenks's name in such a short time. And beating two Police Departments to the punch.

Claire raised a glass to her. 'You're pretty good for a rookie, honey. But you're still not the king.' She smiled at me.

'So I'm thinking,' Jill said, looking around the table, 'I know I can hold my own at dinner parties and all . . . but that's not why you asked me in, is it? Seems like we have all the angles covered here: the press, the force, Medical Examiner. Just what kind of a group is this?'

I answered, since it was I who had invited her in. 'Women. Climbing the ladder in their careers. Law enforcement.'

'Yeah, with soft, pushover types for bosses,' grinned Cindy.

'Well, I qualify there,' said Jill. 'And it doesn't hurt that each of you seems to have some connection with the Bride and Groom cases.'

I held my breath. Jill could blow this whole thing if she wanted to but she was here.'We have been sort of working together,' I admitted.'Outside the investigation.'

Over margaritas, I explained how we had originally gotten together. And how we had come upon this case, trying to solve it, sharing what we knew, freelance. How it had become a sort of bond. How things had just gotten a bit deeper.

Jill arched her eyebrows.'I assume you're sharing all this with the investigation?'

'Of course,' I insisted. 'Well, sort of.' I told her how we were giving Cindy only what the Department was about to release to the press-at-large. How there was a thrill in cutting through the Department, advancing the case.

'I know it's a different game when everything starts to get legal,'I said.'If any of this makes you uncomfortable . . .'

We were all sort of hanging there, awaiting her response. Loretta came and we ordered another round. We were still hanging – waiting on Jill.

'How about I let you know when things start to get uncomfortable,' she said eventually, opening her blue eyes wide. 'In the meantime, you're gonna need a lot stronger corroboration if we want to take this thing to court.'

The three of us breathed a sigh of relief. We tilted our near-empty glasses toward our new member.

'So, this outfit have a name?' Jill inquired.

We looked around, shrugged, shook our heads. 'We're sort of a women's murder club,' I said.

'Lindsay's deputized us,' grinned Claire.

'The Margarita Posse,' Jill threw out. 'That has possibilities.'

'Bad-ass bitches,' giggled Claire.

'One day, we're all gonna be running things,' Cindy said. 'Homicide Chicks,' she came back, with a satisfied grin. 'That's who we are. That's what we do.'

'Just shut me up if I start to roar,' laughed Jill.

We looked around the table. We were bright, attractive, take-no-shit women. We were going to run things – some day.

The waitress brought our drinks. We raised four glasses toward one another. 'To us.'

Chapter Seventy-Four

I was driving home, really pleased at having brought Jill into the group, but it didn't take long for the thought to worm its way in that I was still *withholding* from my friends.

My beeper sounded.

'What're you doin'?' Raleigh asked, when I buzzed him back.

'I was headed home. *Beat.*'

'You up for talking just a little? I'm at Mahoney's.' Mahoney's was a dark, crowded bar near the Hall that was usually thick with off-duty cops.

'Already ate,' I told him.

'Meet me, anyway,' Raleigh said. 'It's about the case.'

I was only a few minutes away. Mahoney's was on Brannan. To get to Potrero, I had to go right by it.

I found myself a little nervous again. I was scared we were no longer playing things by the book. The book was, partners didn't get involved. Nor people with their lives ebbing away. I knew that if I let things go, anything could happen. This wasn't some casual fling we could go at for a night and try to rationalize away the next day. As much as I wanted him, I was holding back. Scared to let it all come out. Of letting myself go. Of dragging him in.

I was relieved when I saw Raleigh waiting for me outside the bar. He came up to my car. I couldn't help noticing that he looked good, as usual.

'Thanks for not making me go in,' I said.

He leaned on the edge of my open window. 'I looked into Nicholas Jenks,' he said.

'And?'

'The guy's forty-eight. Went to law school, but never finished. Started writing novels his first year. Wrote two books that didn't go anywhere. Then this twisted thriller, *Crossed Wire*, hit. So he bagged the law for good.'

'Sounds like a good career move,' I said, pushing the hair out of my eyes.

'There's something you should know. More than five years ago, cops were called out to his home in a domestic dispute.'

'Who made the call?'

'His wife. His first wife.' Raleigh leaned in closer. 'I pulled up the report. First-on-the-scene described her as pretty beat-up. Bruises up and down her arms. Large bruise on her face.'

A thought flashed in my head. Merrill Shortley, on Kathy's boyfriend: '*He was into intense sex games.*'

'Did the wife file?' I asked.

Chris shook his head. 'That's as far as it went. Never

pressed charges. Since then, he's cashed in, big-time. Six huge bestsellers. Movies, screenplays. New wife, too.'

'That means there's an old one out there who might be willing to talk.'

He had a satisfied expression on his face. 'So, can I buy you a meal, Lindsay?'

A hot bead of sweat burned a slow path down my neck. I didn't know whether to get out or stay in. 'Chris, I already ate. Had a commitment.'

'Jacobi,' he grinned. He could always get me with that smile of his.

'Sort of a woman's thing, a group of us. We meet once a month. Go over our lives. You know, nanny problems, personal trainers, country homes. Affairs, things like that.'

'Anyone I know?' Raleigh smiled.

'Maybe one day I'll introduce you.'

We sort of hung there, my blood slowly throbbing in my chest. The hair on Raleigh's forearm gently grazed against mine. This was driving me insane. I had to say something. 'Why'd you call me out here, Chris?'

'Jenks,' he replied. 'I didn't tell you everything. We ran a firearms check on him with Sacramento.' He looked back with a glint in his eye. 'He's got several registered. A Browning twenty-two caliber hunting rifle, a Renfield thirty-thirty. A Remington forty-point-five.'

He was leading me on. I knew he had struck pay dirt.

'There's also a Glock Special, Lindsay. Nineteen-ninety issue. *Nine millimeter.*'

A rush of validation shot through my veins.

Chris frowned. 'He has the weapon of choice, Lindsay. We've got to find that gun.'

I made a fist and brought it down against Raleigh's in triumph. My mind was racing. Sparrow Ridge, the phone calls, now a Glock Special. It was all still circumstantial, but it was falling into place.

'What're you doing tomorrow, Raleigh?' I asked with a smile.

'Wide open. Why?'

'I think it's time we talked to this guy face to face.'

Chapter Seventy-Five

H igh on the cliffs above the Golden Gate Bridge, 20 El Camino del Mar was a stucco, Spanish-style home with an iron gate guarding the terracotta driveway.

Red Beard lived here – Nicholas Jenks.

Jenks's home was low, stately, surrounded by decorously trimmed hedges and bright, blossoming azaleas. In the driveway's circle, there was a large iron sculpture, Botero's *Madonna and Child*.

'Fiction must be good,' whistled Raleigh, as we stepped up to the front door. We had made an appointment through Jenks's personal assistant to meet him at noon. I had been warned by Sam Roth not to come on too hard.

A pleasant housekeeper greeted us at the door and took us back to a spacious sunroom, informing us Mr Jenks would be down in a short while. The lavish room seemed straight out of some designer magazine – with rich Jacquard wallpaper, Oriental chairs, a mahogany coffee-table, shelves of mementos and photographs. It opened onto a fieldstone patio overlooking the Pacific.

I had lived in San Francisco all my life, but never knew you could come home every night to this kind of spectacular view.

While we waited, I examined photos arranged on a side table. Jenks with a series of well-known faces: Michael Douglas, the top guy from Disney, Bill Walsh from the 49ers. Others were with an attractive woman I took to be his new wife – sunny, smiling, with strawberry-blonde hair – in various, exotic locations, on beaches, skiing, a Mediterranean isle.

In a silver frame, there was a four-by-six of the two of them in the center of an enormous, lit-up rotunda. The dome of the Palace of Fine Arts. It was a wedding photo.

It was then that Nicholas Jenks walked in. I recognized him immediately from his photographs.

He was slighter than I had imagined. Trim, well-built, no more than five-ten, wearing an open white dress-shirt over well-worn jeans. My eyes were drawn immediately to the reddish, gray-flecked beard.

Red Beard, it's good to meet you, finally.

'Sorry to put you off, Inspectors,' he said with an easy smile, 'but I'm afraid I get cranky if I can't get my morning pages in.' He held out his hand, noticing the photograph I was still holding on to. 'A bit like the set of *Marriage of Figaro*, wasn't it? Myself, I would've gone for a small civil ceremony, but Chessy said if she could snare me in a tux, she'd never ever doubt my commitment to her.'

I wasn't interested in being charmed by this man, but he was handsome and immediately in control. I could see what some women found attractive about him. He motioned us to the couch.

'We were hoping,' I said, 'to ask you a few questions.'

'About the Bride and Groom killings – my assistant advised me. Crazy . . . terrible. But these acts, so incredibly desperate, cry out for at least a small measure of sympathy.'

'For the victims,' I said, placing his wedding photograph back on the table.

'Everyone always goes to the plight of the victims,' Jenks said, 'but it's what's inside the killer's head that puts cash in the account. Most people figure these acts are simply about revenge. The *sickest* kind of revenge. Or even subjugation, like most rapes. But I'm not so sure.'

'What's your theory, Mr Jenks?' Chris asked. He made it sound as if he were a fan.

Jenks held out a pitcher of iced tea. 'Something to drink? I know it's a hot one, though I've been holed up in the study since eight.'

We shook our heads. I took a manila folder out of my bag and placed it on my lap. I remembered Cheery's admonition: 'Keep it light. Jenks is a VIP. You're not.'

Nicholas Jenks poured himself a tall glass of tea and went on. 'From what I've read, these killings appear to be a form of rape, the rape of innocence. The killer is acting in a way that *no one can forgive*, in the most sacred setting of our society. To me, these killings are the ultimate act of purification.'

'Unfortunately, Mr Jenks,' I said, ignoring his bullshit, 'we didn't come up here seeking your professional advice. I have some questions related to these killings we'd like to run by you.'

Jenks sat back in his chair. He looked surprised. 'You make that sound awfully official.'

'That's entirely up to you,' I said. I took out a portable cassette tape-player from my bag. 'You mind if I turn this on?'

He stared at me, his eyes shifting suspiciously, then he waved his hand, as if it were of no concern.

'So where I'd like to start, Mr Jenks, is with these killings. Do you have any specific knowledge of any of the crimes other than what you've read in the papers?'

'Knowledge?' Jenks paused, nominally reflecting. Then he shook his head. 'No. None at all.'

'You read there was a third killing? Last week. In Cleveland.'

'I did see that. I read five or six papers every day.'

'And did you also read who the victims were?'

'From Seattle, weren't they? One of them, I remember, was some kind of concert promoter.'

'The groom,' I nodded. 'James Voskuhl. The bride actually lived for a while in town, here. Her maiden name was Kathy Kogut. Do either of those names mean anything to you?'

'No. Should they?'

'So you never met either of them? Any interest you had in this case was just like anyone else's . . . morbid curiosity.'

He fixed his eyes on me. 'That's right. Morbid curiosity's my business.'

I opened my manila folder and took out the top photo. He was playing us, just as he had been playing us by leaving dead-ending clues along the way.

I slid the photo across the table. 'This might sharpen your memory,' I said. 'That's Kathy Kogut, the bride who was murdered the other night. The man next to her, I believe, is *you*.'

Chapter Seventy-Six

Slowly, Red Beard picked up the photo and stared at it. 'It is me,' he declared. 'But the lady, though quite beautiful, I don't recognize. If I can ask, where's this picture from?'

'The San Francisco opening of *Crossed Wire*.'

'Ah,' he sighed, as if that classified something for him.

I watched the gears in his brain start to shift for the right response. He was definitely smart, and a pretty good actor.

'I meet a lot of people at these events. It's why I try to avoid them. You say this was that girl who was killed in Cleveland?'

'We were hoping this was someone you might've remembered,' I replied.

Jenks shook his head. 'Too many fans, not much appetite to meet them, even the really pretty ones, Detective.'

'The price of fame, I imagine.' I took the photo back, thumbed it for a moment, then slid it back in front of him.

'Nevertheless, I have to come back to this particular fan. I'm curious why she doesn't stick out for you. From *all those other fans.'* I withdrew a copy of a Northwest Bell phone bill from my folder and handed it to him. On it were several highlighted calls. 'This is your private number?'

Jenks held the copy of the bill. His eyes dimmed. 'It is.'

'She called you, Mr Jenks. Three times in just the past few weeks. Once . . . *here*, I circled it for you . . . for a whole twelve minutes only last week. Three days before she was married, then killed.'

Jenks blinked. Then he picked up the photo again. This time he was different: somber, apologetic. 'Truth is, Inspector,' he said, 'I was *so, so* sorry to hear what had taken place. She seemed, in the last month, so full of anticipation, of hope. I was wrong to mislead you. It was foolish. I *did* know Kathy. I met her the night of the photo there. Sometimes, my fans are rather impressionable. And attractive. At times I, too, to my detriment, can be an impressionable man.'

I wanted to lunge across the table and rip Nicholas Jenks's impressionable face off. I was certain he was responsible for six vicious murders. Now he was mocking us, and the victims. Goddamn him.

'So you're admitting,' Raleigh interjected, 'that you *did* have a relationship with this woman.'

'Not in the way you're insinuating,' Jenks sighed. 'Kathy was a woman who hoped to satisfy her own vague artistic aspirations through an association with someone engaged in the act of creating. She wanted to write herself. It's not exactly brain surgery, but I guess if it was so damn easy we'd all have a book on the bestseller list?'

Neither of us responded.

'We spoke, maybe met, a few times over a couple of years. It never went beyond that. That's the truth.'

'Sort of mentoring?' Raleigh suggested.

'Yes, that's right. Good choice of words.'

'By any chance,' I leaned forward, no longer able to control my tone, 'were you *mentoring* Kathy in Cleveland last Saturday, the night she was killed?'

Jenks's face turned granitelike. 'That's ridiculous. What an inappropriate thing to say.'

I reached into the folder one more time, this time taking out a copy of the security photo of the killer arriving at the Hall of Fame. 'This is a security photo from the night she was killed. Is that you, Mr Jenks?'

Jenks didn't even blink. 'It might be, Detective, *if* I had been there. Which I categorically was not.'

'Where were you last Saturday night?'

'Just so I understand,' he said stonily, 'are you suggesting *I'm* a suspect in these crimes?'

'Kathy Kogut talked, Mr Jenks.' I glared at him. 'To her sister. To her friends. We know how you treated her. We know she left the Bay Area to try to get away from your domination. We know things were going on between you right up to the wedding night.'

I wouldn't take my eyes off Jenks. There was nothing in the room but him and me.

'I *wasn't* in Cleveland,' he said. 'I was right here that night.'

I ran the whole body of evidence by him. From the bottle of Clos du Mesnil left behind at the Hyatt to his involvement in the real-estate trust that owned Sparrow Crest Vineyards to the fact that two of the murders had been committed with nine-millimeter guns, and according to the state, he owned one.

He laughed at me. 'This is not what you're basing your assumptions on, I hope. I got that champagne ages ago.' He shrugged. 'I don't even recall where it is. It's probably at our country home, in Montana.'

'You *can* locate it, I assume?' Raleigh asked, then explained that it was a sign of respect that we were asking him to turn it over voluntarily.

'Would you mind supplying us with a hair sample from your beard,' I asked.

'*What!*' His eyes met mine with a churlish defiance. I imagined the look Melanie Brandt might have seen as he attacked her. What Kathy Kogut saw as he raised his gun to her head.

'I think,' Nicholas Jenks finally answered, 'that this fascinating interview has come to an end.' He held out his wrists. 'Unless you're intent on taking me away, my lunch is waiting.'

I nodded. 'We'll need to follow up. On your whereabouts. And on the gun.'

'Of course,' Jenks said, standing up. 'And should you need any further cooperation – feel free to request it through my attorney.'

I assembled the photographs back into the folder. Raleigh and I got up. At that moment, the attractive strawberry blonde from the photographs walked into the room.

She was undeniably pretty, with gentle, aquamarine eyes, a pale complexion, long, free-flowing hair. She had a tall dancer's body, and was dressed in thigh-length tights and a Nike T-shirt.

'Chessy!' Jenks exclaimed. 'These are officers from the San Francisco Police Department. My wife, Inspectors.'

'Sorry, Nicky,' Chessy Jenks apologized. 'Susan's coming over. I didn't know you had guests.'

'They were just leaving.'

We nodded stiffly, moved toward the door. 'If you could locate what we talked about,' I said to him, 'we'll send someone by to pick it up.'

He gazed right through me.

I hated to leave without taking him in, and to have treated him with kid gloves. But we were still a few steps away from an arrest.

'So,' Chessy Jenks smiled and said, 'has my husband finally gone homicidal?' She went up to Jenks, clasped his arm in a teasing way. 'I always told him, with those creepy-crawly characters he writes about, it was inevitable.'

Could she know? I wondered. She lived with him, slept with him. How could she not be aware of what was going on inside his head?

'I truly hope not, Ms Jenks,' was all I said.

Chapter Seventy-Seven

'What did she mean by that?' Chessy Jenks went up to her husband, confused, after the Police Inspectors left the house.

Jenks brushed her away. He paced over to the large French doors leading out to the Pacific.

'Idiots,' he muttered. 'Amateurs. Who the hell do they think they're dealing with?'

He felt a prickly, stabbing heat racing over his shoulders and back. They were stupid, tiny-minded. Beetles. That's why they were cops. If they had any brains, they'd be doing what he was doing. Living high over the Pacific.

'That's why they dig landfills,' he replied distractedly. 'A place for cops to feel at home.'

Chessy picked up the wedding photo from the coffee-table and set it back in its rightful spot. 'What did you do now, Nick?'

Why did she always drive him to this? Why did she always need to know?

She came over, looked at him with those lucid, patient eyes.

As always, his anger leaped up in a flash.

He didn't even realize he had hit her.

It was just that suddenly his hand hurt and Chessy was sprawled on the floor – and the bamboo table on which the wedding pictures were had toppled over – and she was holding her mouth.

He shouted. 'Don't you know when to keep away from me? What do you need, a road map?'

'Uh-uh, Nick,' Chessy said. 'Not here . . . not now.'

'Not here, what?' he was shouting. He knew he was shouting, losing control. That the staff might hear.

'Please, Nick,' Chessy said, pulling herself off the floor. 'Susan will be here soon. We're going to lunch.'

It was the notion that Chessy thought she could just sit there and judge him that really set him off. Didn't she see who she really was? Just some blonde with freckles he had picked out of a cattle call and turned into God's gift to Martha Stewart.

He grabbed her by the arm and put his face inches from her beautiful terrified eyes. 'Say it!'

The arm he held was trembling. A tiny stream of mucus ran out of her nose. 'Jesus, Nick . . .'

That's what he liked, her fear of him, even though she never showed it in public.

'I said, say it, Chessy.' He twisted her arm behind her back.

She was breathing heavily now, sweat forming under

her T-shirt. Her little tits poked through. When she glared back at him, with her paltry defiance, he twisted harder, digging his fingers into her arm. He shoved her toward the bedroom, her bare feet stumbling along.

In the bedroom he kicked the door shut.

Who did the lead cop think she was? Coming in here . . . accusing him like that. In her cheap Gap ensemble. What a fucking insolent bitch.

He dragged Chessy into the clothes closet. *Hers*. It was dark in there. Only the dark and her sobs and the pervasive smell of her perfume. He pushed her forward against the wall, rubbed himself against her buttocks.

He pulled Chessy's gym shorts down, her panties along with them. 'Please!' she cried. 'Nicky?'

He found the familiar place where her small cheeks parted. He was very hard and he pushed himself in deep.

He was driving himself inside Chessy. 'Say it,' he gasped. 'You know how to make it stop. Say it.'

'Ruff,' she finally murmured in a tiny whisper.

Now she was loving it, as she always did. It wasn't bad – it was good. They all ended up wanting and loving it. He always picked them so well.

'Ruff,' she whimpered. 'Ruff, ruff. Is that what you want, Nick?'

Yes, that was part of what he needed. It was all he expected from Chessy.

'You love it, Chessy,' he whispered back. 'That's why you're here.'

Chapter Seventy-Eight

We kept a close watch on Jenks's movements with a surveillance team of three cars. If he made a move to dump the gun, we'd know. If he moved to kill again, we hoped we could stop him. No matter how clever he was, I didn't see how he could plan and execute another murder right now.

I wanted to speak with someone who knew him, who might be willing to talk. Raleigh had mentioned an ex-wife, a history of violence between them. I needed to talk with her.

It wasn't hard to track Joanna Jenks down, now Joanna Wade. A search through the police files had her maiden name listed as part of the domestic complaint she had filed against her husband years before. A Joanna Wade was currently residing at 1115 Filbert Street on Russian Hill.

It was an attractive, limestone townhouse on the steepest part of the Hill. I buzzed, identified myself to the house-keeper who opened the door. She informed me Ms Wade was not at home.'*Ehersizing,*'she said.'*Gold's Gym. On Union.*'

I found the gym around the corner between a Starbucks and an Alfredson's market. At reception, a buffed, pony-tailed staffer informed me Joanna was in Exercise Room C. When I asked what Joanna Wade looked like, the staffer laughed. 'Think blonde. And kiss-ass fit.'

I wandered in, and through a large observation window, spotted a tai-bo class in Exercise Room C. About eight women sweating in Lycra and jog bras were kicking their legs out, karate-style, to loud music. I knew that tai bo was the latest exercise craze, the biggest burn. Any one of these women looked as if they could take a resisting suspect up against a wall, then beat the patrol car back to the precinct with breath to spare.

The only blonde was in front. Trim, sculpted, pushing herself hard and barely breaking a sweat. It was her class.

I hung around until she finished up, and most of the class had rushed out. She toweled off the sweat on her face.

'Great workout,' I said, as she headed my way.

'The best in the Bay Area. Looking to sign up?'

'Maybe. First, I thought I could ask you a couple of questions.'

'Try Diane up front. She can tell you the whole deal.'

'I wasn't talking tai bo.' I flashed her my badge. 'I'm talking Nicholas Jenks.'

Joanna stared at me, flapping her blonde ponytail off her shoulders to cool her neck. She smirked. 'What'd he do, get caught shoplifting one of his books out of Stacey's downtown?'

'Can we talk?' I asked.

She shrugged and led me over to a changing area that was unoccupied. 'So what could I tell you about Nick that you couldn't find out from one of his own jacket flaps?'

'I know it was several years ago,' I said, 'but you once filed a domestic complaint against him.'

'Listen, in case the paperwork didn't catch up, I dropped the charge back then.'

I could see the terror of the moment exploding all over again for her. 'Look,' I said genuinely, 'no one's trying to dig up old wounds, Ms Wade. I'd just like a read on your ex-husband.'

'Up to his old tricks again?'

I could see her sizing me up. Was I an ally or a foe? Then she let out a capitulating breath and looked right at me.

'If you're here about Chessy, I could've warned her – if he hadn't been such a creep about how he dumped me. How did he put it: "*I write through her, Jo. She inspires me.*" You ever read his books, Detective? She didn't have to inspire him by holding a job down while he went off and found himself, did she? She didn't have to read his drafts, deal with his rages when he got rejected, tell him every night how much she believed in him. You know where he met her, Detective? In the makeup room at *Entertainment Tonight.*'

'What I'm asking, Ms Wade,' I said, 'is how violent is Nicholas Jenks?'

There was a pause while she looked away. When she turned back, her eyes had filled up as if she were about to cry.

'You come in here after all these years and make me go through this again. What do you want me to say? That his mother didn't love him? That he's a screwed-up, dangerous man? Life with Nick . . . it's so hard. He's holding something in and God only knows when it's going to come out. I used to ask myself why? What had I done? I was just a kid.' Her eyes glistened.

'I'm sorry.' I truly felt for her. For both Mrs Jenkses. I couldn't even imagine what it was like to wake up and find myself married to someone like him.

'I need to ask,' I said, 'what are the chances things with your ex-husband have intensified? Become more serious?'

She looked stunned. 'Is Chessy all right, Detective?'

'*Chessy's* all right,' I nodded, making it clear I felt there were others who might not be.

She waited for me to blink. When I didn't, she gave me a mirthless laugh. 'So I guess we're talking a lot deeper than pilfering a book from Stacey's bookstore?'

I nodded again. Woman to woman now, I said, 'I need to ask you a crucial question, Ms Wade.'

Chapter Seventy-Nine

What I asked Joanna Wade was this: 'Is Nicholas Jenks capable of murder?'

I couldn't tell her the reason, but it didn't matter. Joanna was a quick study. I saw the shock in her eyes. After she calmed, I watched her go through a thoughtful evaluation.

Finally, she looked at me and asked again: 'Have you read his books, Detective?'

'One, *Fatal Charm*. Tough book.'

'He lives with those characters, you see. Sometimes I think he forgets it's only what he does for a living.'

I saw the self-judging look in her eyes. I leaned in closer. 'I don't mean to hurt you, but I have to know.'

'Could he kill? Is he capable of murder? I know he's capable of completely debasing another human being. That's murder, isn't it? He's what they call a sexual sadist. His father used to beat his mother in their bedroom closet as an aphrodisiac. He preys on weakness. Yes, the famous Nicholas Jenks humiliated me. But let me tell you the worst thing, the very worst. He left me, Detective. I didn't leave him.'

Joanna leaned back and gave me sort of a compassionate smile. 'I've seen Chessy around a few times. Luncheons, benefits. We've even spoken a bit. He hasn't changed. She knows I know exactly what she's going through, but it's something we can't share. I see the fear; I know how it is. When she looks in the mirror, she no longer recognizes the person she once was.'

My blood was at boiling point. Through the tough veneer, I saw a glimpse of the woman Joanna Wade had been – young, needful, confused. I reached out and touched her hand. I had my answer. I closed my pad, ready to get up, when the other woman surprised me.

'I thought it was him. I immediately thought of Nick when I heard about those terrible crimes. I remembered his book, and I said, "It could be him." '

I stopped Joanna. 'What book?'

'That first thing he wrote – *Always A Bridesmaid*. I figured that's what brought you here, what connected him to the murders.'

I stared at her, confused. 'Just what are you talking about?'

'He wrote it before we met. I was lucky enough to come in for the second unpublished one which, I'm told, he recently sold for two million. But this book, I'd totally forgotten about. It was about a student in law school who discovers his wife with his best friend. He kills them both. Ends up going on a rampage.'

'What kind of rampage?' I asked. What she said next took my breath away.

'He goes around killing brides and grooms. A lot like what happened.'

Chapter Eighty

That was a piece of the puzzle I needed. If Jenks had premeditated these crimes, mapped them out in some early book, it would constitute unimpeachable knowledge. No longer circumstantial. With everything else we had, I could definitely bring him in.

'Where can I find this book?' I asked.

'It wasn't very good,' Joanna Wade replied. 'Never published.'

Every nerve in my body was standing on end. 'Do you have a copy?'

'Trust me, if I did I would have burned it years ago. Nick had this agent in town, Greg Marks. He dumped him when he got successful. If anyone would have it, it might be him.'

I called Greg Marks from the car. I was really humming now. I loved this.

The operator connected me and after four rings, an answering tape came on: *You've reached Greg Marks Associates . . .* I cringed with disappointment. Damn, damn, damn!

Reluctantly, I left him my pager number. 'It's a matter of great urgency,' I said. I was about to tell him why I was calling, when a voice cut in on tape: 'This is Greg Marks.'

I explained I needed to see him immediately. The marina wasn't too far; I could be there in ten minutes. 'I have an engagement at One Market at six-fifteen,' the agent replied curtly. 'But if you can get here . . .'

'You just stay right there,' I told him. 'This is police business, and it's important. If you leave, I'll arrest you!'

Greg Marks worked out of his brownstone, a third-floor loft with a partial view of the bridge. He answered the door, a short, balding man, smartly dressed, in a Jacquard shirt buttoned to the top. He looked at me suspiciously.

'I'm afraid you haven't picked a popular topic with me, Detective. Nicholas Jenks hasn't been a client for over six years. He left me the day *Crossed Wire* hit the *Chronicle*'s bestseller list.'

'Are you still in touch?' I wanted to make sure anything I asked him wouldn't get back to Jenks.

'Why? To remind him how I babysat him through the years when he could barely use a noun with an adjective; how I took his obsessed midnight calls, stroked that gigantic ego?'

'I'm here about something Jenks wrote early on,' I interrupted. 'Before any big deals. I spoke to his ex-wife.'

'Joanna?' Marks exclaimed, with surprise.

'She said he had written a book that never got published. She thought it was called *Always A Bridesmaid*.'

The agent nodded. 'It was an uneven first effort. No real

narrative power. Truth is, I never even sent it out.'

'Do you have a copy?'

'Packed it back to him as soon as I turned the final page. I would think Jenks must, though. He thought the book was a suspense masterpiece.'

'I was hoping I wouldn't have to go through him,' I said, without conveying the basis of my interest. I leaned forward. 'How do I get my hands on a copy of that novel, without going to Jenks directly?'

'Joanna didn't save it?' Marks rubbed a finger across his temple. 'Jenks was always paranoid about people ripping him off. Maybe he had it copyrighted. Why don't you check into that?'

I needed to run this by someone. I needed to run it by the girls.

'Do you want to hear something really scary about Jenks?' the agent said, then.

'Not really, but please go ahead.'

'Here's the idea for a book he always wanted to write. It's about a novelist who is obsessed – the kind of thing Stephen King does so well. In order to write a better book, a *great* book, he actually murders people to see what it's like. Welcome to the horrible mind of Nicholas Jenks.'

Chapter Eighty-One

This was why I had become a homicide detective. I rushed back to the office, my head whirling with how to get my hands on this lost book, when the next bomb-shell hit.

It was McBride.

'Are you sitting down?' he asked, as if he were about to deliver the coup de grâce. 'Nicholas Jenks was here in Cleveland the night of the Hall of Fame murders. The son-of-a-bitch was here.'

Jenks had lied right to my face. He didn't even blink.

It was now clear, the unidentifiable man at the Hall of Fame had been him after all. He *had* no alibi.

McBride explained how his men had scoured the local hotels. Finally, they uncovered that Jenks had been at the Westin, and amazingly, he registered under his own name. A desk clerk working there that night remembered him. She knew it the minute she saw Jenks – she was a fan.

My mind raced with the ramifications. This was all McBride needed. They had a prior relationship with the victim, a possible sighting at the scene. Now, Jenks was placed in his town. He had even lied under questioning.

'Tomorrow, I'm going to the District Attorney for an indictment,' McBride announced. 'As soon as we have it, I want you to pick Nicholas Jenks up.'

The truth hit me like a sledgehammer. We could lose him to Cleveland. All the evidence, all those right hunches, wouldn't help us. Now, we might only be able to tag on a concurrent life sentence at a second trial. The victims' families would be crushed. *Mercer would go ballistic.*

I was left with an absolutely demoralizing choice: either pick Jenks up and hold him for McBride, or make our move now with less than an airtight case.

I should run this up the ladder, the voice sounded in my head.

But the voice in my heart said, *Run it by the girls*.

Chapter Eighty-Two

I got the three of them together on an hour's notice.
    'Cleveland's ready to indict,' I told them. Then I dropped
the bombshell about the book *Always A Bridesmaid*.

'You've got to find it,' Jill declared. 'It's the one link we
can tie in to all three crimes. Given that it was unpublished, it's as good as exclusive knowledge of the killings. It
might even parallel the actual crimes. You find that book,
Lindsay, we put Jenks behind bars. For ever!'

'How? Joanna Wade mentioned a prior agent and I went
to see him. *Nada*. He said to check out the office of
copyrights. Where is that?'

Cindy shook her head. 'Washington, I think.'

'That'll take days, or more. We don't have days.' I turned
to Jill. 'Maybe it's time for a Search and Seizure. Blow in on
Jenks. We need the gun. Now, this book. And we need
them now.'

'We do that,' Jill said nervously, 'we might bungle this
whole investigation.'

'Jill, you want to lose him?'

'Anyone know about this yet?' she asked.

I shook my head. 'Just the first team – you guys. But when Mercer finds out, he'll want to jump in with everything he has. Cameras, microphones, the FBI waiting in the wings.'

'If we're wrong, Jenks'll sue our ass,' Jill said. 'I don't even want to think about it.'

'And Cleveland'll be waiting,' said Claire. 'Make us look like a bunch of fools.'

Finally, Jill sighed, 'All right . . . I'm with you, Lindsay. If you can't think of another way.'

I looked at all three of them to make certain we were unanimous. Suddenly, Cindy blurted: 'Can you give me another twenty-four hours?'

I was puzzled. 'Why?'

'Just until tomorrow. And I need Jenks's Social Security number.'

I shook my head. 'You heard what I said about McBride. Anyway, for what?'

She had that same look as the other night, when she burst into my apartment – holding the photo of Jenks and Kathy Kogut, the third bride. 'Just give me until tomorrow morning. Please.'

Then she got up and left.

Chapter Eighty-Three

The following morning, Cindy sheepishly pushed open the glass doors leading to the office of the San Francisco Writers Guild. This felt a lot like the day at the Grand Hyatt. At the reception desk, a middle-aged woman with the punctilious air of a librarian looked up at her. 'May I help you?' she asked.

Cindy sucked in a deep breath. 'I need to find a manuscript. It was written quite a while ago.'

The word copyright had set her off. She had written short stories in college. They were barely good enough to get into the school's literary journal, but her mother had insisted, 'Get them copyrighted.' When she investigated, it turned out it took months, and was way too costly. But a friend who had published told her about another way she could register documents locally. He told her that all the writers did it. If Nicholas Jenks had wanted to protect himself in his salad days, he might've gone the same route.

'It's sort of a family thing,' Cindy told the woman. 'My

brother wrote this history, going back three generations. We don't have a copy.'

The woman shook her head. 'This isn't the library. I'm afraid that whatever we have here is restricted. If you want to find it, you'll have to have your brother come in.'

'I can't,' Cindy said solemnly. 'Nick is dead.'

The woman softened, looked at her slightly less officiously. 'I'm sorry.'

'His wife said she can't locate a copy. I'd like to give it to our dad, a sixtieth birthday present.' She felt guilty, foolish, lying through her teeth like this, but everything was riding on getting this book.

'There's a process for all of this,' the woman replied sanctimoniously. 'Death certificate. Proof of next-of-kin. The family lawyer should be able to help you. I can't just go letting you in here.'

Cindy thought swiftly. This wasn't exactly Microsoft here. If she had found her way to the crime scene in the Grand Hyatt, tracked Lindsay to the second crime, she ought to be able to handle this. Everyone was counting on her.

'There must be a way you can let me take a look – please?'

'I'm afraid not, dear. Not without some documentation. What makes you even think it's registered with us?'

'My sister-in-law is sure it is.'

'Well, I can't just go giving out registered documents on someone's hunch,' she said, with finality.

'Maybe you can at least look it up,' Cindy proposed. 'To see if it's even here.'

The dachshund-nosed defender of the free press finally relaxed. 'I guess I can do that. Do you have any idea when?'

Cindy felt an adrenaline surge. 'Yes, about ten years.'

'And the name?'

'I think it was called *Always A Bridesmaid*.' She felt a chill just saying the words.

'I meant the name of the author, please.'

'Jenks,' Cindy said, holding her breath. 'Nicholas Jenks.'

The woman peered at her. 'The mystery writer?'

Cindy shook her head, faked a smile. 'The insurance salesman,' she said, as calmly as she could.

The woman gave her a strange look, but continued to punch in the name. 'You have proof of relationship?'

Cindy handed her a piece of paper with Jenks's Social Security number on it. 'This should be on his registration.'

'That won't do,' the woman said.

Cindy fumbled through a zipper in her knapsack. She felt the moment slipping away. 'At least tell me if it's here. I'll come back later with whatever you want.'

'Jenks,' the woman muttered skeptically. 'Looks like your brother was a bit more prolific than you thought. He's got *three* manuscripts registered here.'

Cindy wanted to let out a shout. 'The only one I'm looking for is called *Always A Bridesmaid*.'

It took what seemed like several minutes, but the stony resistance of the woman finally weakened. 'I don't know why I'm doing this, but if you can verify your story, there seems to be a record of that manuscript's being here.'

Cindy felt a surge of validation. The manuscript was the final piece they needed to crack a murder case and put away Jenks.

Now, she just had to get it out.

Chapter Eighty-Four

'I found it,' exclaimed Cindy, her voice breathless on the phone. '*Always A Bridesmaid!*'

I pounded my desk in elation. This meant we could definitely make our move. 'So what does it say, Cindy?'

'I *found* it,' Cindy went on. 'I just don't actually *have* it.' She told me about the Writers' Guild. The book was there, but it would take a little coaxing to actually get it in our hands.

In fact, it took barely two hours, starting with a frantic call to Jill. She had a judge pulled out of chambers, who signed our court order mandating the release of Jenks's manuscript *Always A Bridesmaid.*

Then Jill and I ran down to meet Cindy. On the way, I made one more call, to Claire. It seemed fitting that all of us should be there.

Twenty minutes later, Jill and I met Cindy and Claire in front of a drab building on Geary, where the Writers Guild maintained its offices. Together, we rode to the eighth floor.

'I'm back,' announced Cindy, to a surprised woman

behind the reception desk. 'And I brought my documentation.'

She eyed us suspiciously. 'Who are these – cousins?'

I flashed the clerk my badge and also presented the
officially stamped search warrant.

'What's going on with this book?' the woman gasped.
Clearly feeling that matters were now out of her authority,
she went inside and came back with a supervisor who read
over the court order.

'We only hold them for up to eight years,' he said with
some uncertainty. Then he disappeared for what seemed
like ages.

We all sat there, in the stark reception area, waiting like
pacing relatives for a baby to be born. What if it had been
thrown out? Ten years was a long time.

Finally, the supervisor came out with a dusty bundle
wrapped in brown paper. 'In the back of the bins,' he
sighed, with a self-satisfied smile.

There was a coffee shop right down the street. We took a
table in the back and crowded around with anticipation. I
plopped the manuscript down on the table, peeled off the
brown-paper wrapping.

I read the cover. *Always A Bridesmaid – A novel by
Nicholas Jenks*.

Nervously, I opened it and read the first page. The
narrator was reflecting on his crimes from jail. His name
was Phillip Campbell.

What is the worst thing, the novel began, *anyone has ever
done?*

Chapter Eighty-Five

We split up the book into four sections. We each paged silently through our section, searching for some scene or detail that would parallel the real-life crimes.

Mine was about this guy's life, Phillip Campbell. His picture-perfect wife, catching her with another man. He killed them both – and his life changed for ever.

'Bingo!' Jill spoke up suddenly. She read out loud, bending back the sheaf of paper like a deck of cards.

She described a scene with Phillip Campbell – *'breath pounding inside, voices ringing in his head'* – stealing through the corridors of a hotel. It's the Grand Hyatt. A bride and groom are in a suite. Campbell breaks in on them – and kills them without having a second thought.

'In a single act,' Jill read from the manuscript, *'he had washed away the stench of betrayal, and replaced it with a fresh, heretofore unimagined desire. He liked to kill.'*

Our eyes locked. This was beyond creepy. Jenks was crazy – but was he also crafty?

Claire was next. It was another wedding. This time, the scene is outside a church. The bride and groom are coming down the steps, rice is being thrown to shouts of congratulations, applause. The same man, Phillip Campbell, is waiting at the wheel of the limo that will take them away.

We looked at one another, stunned. It was how the second murders were committed.

Jill murmured, 'Holy shit.'

Claire just shook her head. She looked sad and shocked. I guess we all were.

A long-suppressed cry of satisfaction built up in my chest. We had done it! We had solved the Bride and Groom murders!

'I wonder how it ends?' Cindy mused, fanning to the end of the book.

'How else?' said Jill grimly. 'With an arrest.'

Chapter Eighty-Six

I rode up to Jenks's house with Chris Raleigh. We barely spoke, both of us brimming with anticipation. Outside, we were met by Charlie Clapper and his CSU team. They would grid-search the house and grounds as soon as we took Jenks in.

We rang the bell. Each second I waited, my heart pounded harder. Every reason I became a cop was grinding in my chest. This was it.

The door opened and the same housekeeper answered. This time, her eyes went wide as she took in the convergence of police cars.

I flashed my badge and hurried past her. 'We need to see Mr Jenks.'

We found our way back to the sitting room where we had met only two days before. A startled Chessy Jenks met us in the hall. 'Inspector,' she gasped, recognizing me. 'What's going on? What are all those cops doing out front?'

'I'm sorry,' I said, meeting her eyes. I *was* sorry for her. 'Is your husband at home?'

'Nick!' she cried, realizing in a panic why we had come. Then she ran along with us, trying to block me, shouting. 'You can't just come in here like this. This is our home.'

'Please, Mrs Jenks,' Raleigh implored.

I was too wound up to stop. I wanted Nicholas Jenks so bad it hurt. A second later, he appeared, coming in from the back lawn overlooking the Pacific. He was holding a golf club.

'I thought I told you,' he said icily, looking perfectly unruffled in his white shirt and linen shorts, 'the next time you need something from me you should contact my lawyer.'

'You can tell him yourself,' I said. My heart was racing. 'Nicholas Jenks, you are under arrest for the murders of David and Melanie Brandt, Michael and Rebecca DeGeorge, James and Kathleen Voskuhl.'

I wanted him to hear every name, to bring to mind every one of them he'd killed. I wanted to see the callous indifference disintegrate in his eyes.

'This is insane.' Jenks glared at me. His gray eyes burned with intensity.

'Nick!' cried his wife. 'What are they talking about? Why are they here in our house?'

'Do you know what you're doing?' he hissed, the veins bulging on his neck. 'I asked you, *do you have any idea what you're doing*?'

I didn't answer, just recited the Miranda.

'What you're doing,' he raged, 'is engaging in the biggest mistake of your little life.'

'What are they saying?' His wife was pale. 'Nick, please tell me. What is going on?'

'Shut up,' Jenks spat out at her. Suddenly, he spun back toward me with a vicious fire in his eyes. He lunged forward with his fist and swung at me.

I cut his feet out from under him. Jenks fell across an end table to the floor, photos falling everywhere, glass shattering. The writer moaned loudly in pain.

Chessy Jenks screamed, stood there in a paralyzed state. Chris Raleigh cuffed her husband and dragged him to his feet.

'Call Sherman,' Jenks shouted at his wife. 'Tell him where I am, what's happened.'

Raleigh and I pushed Jenks out to our car. He continued to struggle and I saw no reason to be gentle.

'What's your theory on the murders now?' I asked him.

Chapter Eighty-Seven

After the last news conference had ended, after the last flashbulb had dimmed, after I had rehashed, for what seemed the hundredth time, how we had narrowed in on Jenks, after a beaming Chief Mercer had been chauffeured away, I hugged Claire, Cindy, and Jill. I then passed on a celebratory beer, and wandered back to the Hall of Justice.

It was well past eight and only the prattle of the night-shift interrupted my being alone.

I sat at my desk, in the well-earned silence of the squad room, and tried to remember the last time I felt this *good*.

Tomorrow, we would begin meticulously compiling the case against Nicholas Jenks: interrogating him, accumulating more evidence, filling out report after report. But we had done it. We had caught him just as I hoped we eventually would. I had fulfilled the promise I made to Melanie Brandt that horrible night in the Mandarin Suite at the Grand Hyatt.

I felt proud of myself. Whatever happened with the

Negli's, even if I never made Lieutenant, no one could take this away.

I got up, stepped over to the freestanding blackboard that listed the cases we were working on. Under *Open Cases*, somewhere near the top was her name: *Melanie Brandt*. I took the brush and rubbed her name, then her husband's, until they disappeared, until the blue smear of chalk was no more.

'I bet that feels good.' Raleigh's voice sounded behind me.

I turned. He was there, looking smug.

'What are you doing here?' I asked. 'So late.'

'Thought I'd straighten up Roth's desk, steal a few brownie points,' he said. 'What do you think, Lindsay? I came to find you.'

We were in a corner of the squad room and there was no one around. He never had to move. I went to him. Nothing in the way. No reason to deny this.

I kissed him. Not like before, not just to let Chris know I was interested. I kissed him the way I had wanted him to kiss me that night on the tree-lined lakefront in Cleveland. I wanted to steal the breath right out of him. To say, '*I wanted to do this from the first time I saw you.*'

When we finally pulled apart, he repeated with a smile, 'Like I said, I bet that feels good.'

It did feel good. Right now, it all felt good. It also felt unavoidable.

'What are your plans?' I smiled at him.

'How loosely are we talking?'

'Specifically, right now. Tonight. The next several hours, at least.'

'I thought I would come back, straighten Cheery's desk, and see if you wanted me to take you home.'

'Let me get my purse.'

Chapter Eighty-Eight

I don't know how we got all the way to my apartment in the Potrero. I don't know how Chris and I talked and drove and ignored what was tearing at us inside.

Once we got through my doors, there was no stopping it. I was all over Chris; he was all over me. We only got as far as the rug in the foyer, kissing, touching, fumbling for the buttons, the zippers, breathing loudly.

I had forgotten how good it was to be touched like this, to be held, to be desired by somebody I wanted, too. Once we touched, we knew enough to take our time. We both wanted it to last. Chris had what I needed more than anything else – *soft hands*.

I loved kissing him, loved his gentleness, then his roughness, the simple fact that he was concerned about my pleasure as much as his own. You never know until you try it out – but I loved being with Chris. I absolutely loved it.

I know it's a cliché, but that night I made love as if it might never happen again. I felt Chris's current, warming me, electrifying – from my womb to my thighs to the tips of my fingers and my toes. His grasp was all that held me together, kept me from breaking apart. I felt a trust for him that was unquestioning.

I held nothing back. I gave myself to Chris in a way I never had to anyone before. Not only with my body and my heart; these were things I could pull back. I gave him my hope that I could still live.

When I cried out, tremors exploding inside me, my fingers and toes stiff with joy, a voice inside me whispered what I knew was true.

I gave him everything. He gave it back.

Finally, Chris pulled off me. We were both tingling, still on fire.

'What?' I gasped for breath. 'Now what?'

He looked at me and smiled. 'I want to see the bedroom.'

Chapter Eighty-Nine

A cool breeze was blowing in my face. Oh God, what a night. What a day. What a rollercoaster!

I sat wrapped in a quilt out on my terrace, overlooking the south end of the Bay. Nothing was moving, only the lights of San Leandro in the distance. It was quarter of two.

In the bedroom, Chris lay asleep. He'd earned some rest.

I couldn't sleep. My body was too alive, tingling, like a distant shore with a thousand flickering lights.

I couldn't help but smile at the thought: It *had* been a great day. 'June seventh,' I said aloud. 'I'm gonna remember you.' First, we found the book. Then we arrested Jenks. I never imagined it could go any further.

But it had. It went *way* further. Chris and I made love that night twice more, the last three hours a sweet dance of touching, panting, loving. I didn't want his hands to ever leave me. I didn't ever want to miss the heat of his body. It was a new sensation. For once, I had held nothing back, and that was very, very good.

But here, in the dark of the night, an accusing voice

needled me. I was lying. I hadn't given it all. There was the one, inescapable truth that I was concealing.

I hadn't told him about Negli's. I didn't know how to. Just as we had felt such life, how could I tell him I was dying? That my body, which a moment ago was so alive with passion, was infected. In a single day, it seemed that everything in my life was transformed. I wanted to soar. I deserved it. I deserved to be happy.

But he deserved to know.

I heard a rustling behind me. It was Chris.

'What are you doing out here?' he asked. He came up behind me, placed his hands on my neck and shoulders.

I was hugging my knees, the quilt barely covering my breasts. 'It's gonna be hard,' I said, leaning my head on him, 'to go back to the way things were.'

'Who said anything about going back?'

'I mean, like partners. Watching you across the room. Tomorrow we have to interrogate Jenks. Big day for both of us.'

His fingers teased my breasts, then the back of my neck. He was driving me crazy. 'You don't have to worry,' he said. 'Once the case is made, I'm going back. I'll stick around for the interrogation.'

'Chris,' I said, as a chill shot through me. I had gotten used to him.

'I told you, we weren't going to be partners for ever.' He bent down, inhaling the smell of my hair. 'At least, not *those* kind of partners.'

'What kind does that leave?' I murmured. My neck was

on fire where his hands caressed me. Oh, let this go somewhere, I begged inside. Let this go all the way to the moon.

Could I just tell him? It was no longer that I couldn't find a way. It was just, now that we were here, I didn't want it to end.

I let him take me into the bedroom.

'This keeps getting better and better,' I whispered.

'Doesn't it? I can't wait to see what happens next.'

Chapter Ninety

I had just gotten to my desk the following morning and was flipping through the *Chronicle* to get to the continuation of Cindy's article on Jenks's arrest when my phone rang.

It was Charlie Clapper. His Crime Scene team had spent most of the night going through everything in Jenks's house.

'You make a case for me, Charlie?' I was hoping for a murder weapon, maybe even the missing rings. Something solid that would melt Jenks's sneering defiance.

The CSU leader let out a weary breath. 'I think you should come down here and see.'

I grabbed my purse and the keys to our work car. In the hallway, I ran into Jacobi. 'Rumors say,' he grunted, 'I'm no longer the man of your dreams.'

'You know you should never believe what you read in the *Star*,' I quipped.

'Right, or hear from the night-shift.'

I pulled myself to a stop. Someone had spotted Chris

and me last night. My mind flashed through the red-hot copy that was probably running through the office-rumor mill. Behind my anger, I knew that I was blushing.

'Relax,' Jacobi said. 'You know what can happen when you get caught up in a good collar. And it *was* a good collar.'

'Thank you, Warren,' I said. It was one of those rare moments when neither of us had anything to hide. I winked and hit the stairs.

'Just remember,' he called after me, 'it was the champagne match that got you on your way.'

'I remember. I'm grateful. Thank you, Warren.'

I drove down Sixth to Taylor and California to Jenks's home in Sea Cliff. When I arrived, two police cars were blocking the street, keeping a circle of media vans at bay. I found Clapper – looking tired and unshaven – catching a few minutes' rest at the dining-room table.

'You find me a murder gun?' I asked.

'Just these.' He pointed to a pile of guns in plastic bags on the floor.

There were hunting rifles, a showcase Minelli shotgun, a Colt automatic .45 pistol. No nine millimeter. I didn't make a move to examine them.

'We went through his office,' Clapper wheezed. 'Nothing on any of the victims. No clippings, no trophies.'

'I was hoping you might've come across the missing rings.'

'You want rings?' Clapper said. He wearily pushed himself up. 'His wife's got rings. Plenty of them. I'll let you go through them. But what we did find was this. Follow me.'

On the floor of the kitchen, with a yellow *Evidence* marker on it, was a crate of champagne. Krug. Clos du Mesnil.

'That we already knew,' I said.

He kept looking at me, as if I had somehow insulted him with the obvious. Then he lifted a bottle out of the open case.

'Check the numbers, Lindsay. Each bottle's registered with its own number. Look here, four-two-three-five-five-nine. Must make it go down all the more smoothly.' He took out a folded-up green copy of a *Police Property* voucher from his chest pocket. 'The one from the Hyatt was from the same lot. Same number.' The CSU man smiled.

The bottles *were* the same. It was solid evidence that tied Jenks to where David and Melanie Brandt were killed. It wasn't a weapon, but it was damning, no longer circumstantial. A rush of excitement shot through me. I high-fived the pale, heavy-set CSU man.

'Anyway,' Charlie said, almost apologetically, 'I wouldn't have brought you all the way out here for just that.'

Clapper led me through the finely furnished interior of the house to the master bedroom. It had a vast picture window looking out on the Golden Gate Bridge. He took me into a spacious closet. Jenks's.

'You remember the bloody jacket we found at the hotel?' In the rear of the closet, Charlie squatted over a large shoe-rack. 'Well, now it's a set.'

Clapper reached behind the shoe-rack and pulled out a crumpled Nordstrom's shopping bag. 'I wanted you to see how we found it.'

Out of the bag, he pulled balled-up black tuxedo trousers. 'I already checked. It's the other half of the jacket at the Hyatt. Same maker. Look inside, same style number.'

I might as well have been staring at a million dollars in cash, or a ton of stolen cocaine. I couldn't take my eyes off the pants, imagining how Nicholas Jenks would squirm now. Claire had been right. She'd been right from the start. The jacket hadn't come off the victim. It had always belonged to Jenks.

'So whad'ya think, Detective?' Charlie Clapper grinned. 'Can you close your case or what? Oh yeah,' the CSU man exclaimed, almost absent-mindedly. 'Where'd I put it?'

He patted his pockets, searched around his jacket. He finally found a small plastic bag.

'Straight out of the sucker's electric razor,' Charlie announced.

In the bag were several short red hairs.

Chapter Ninety-One

Claire said, 'I've been expecting you, honey.' She took my arm and led me back into the lab to a small room lined with chemicals. Two microscopes were set up side by side on a granite-block counter.

'Charlie told me what he came up with,' she said. 'The champagne. Matching pantalones. You got him, Lindsay.'

'Match these,' I held out the plastic bag, 'we put him in the gas chamber.'

'Okay, let's see,' she said, smiling. She opened a yellow envelope marked *Priority Evidence*, and took a Petri dish identical to the one I had seen after the second murders. It had *Subject: Rebecca DeGeorge, #62340* in bold marker written on the front.

With a tweezer, she placed the single hair that had come from the second bride onto a clear slide. Then she inserted it under the scope. She leaned over it, adjusting the focus, then caught me by surprise, asking, 'So how're you feeling, woman?'

'You mean Negli's?'

'What else would I mean?' she said, peering into the scope.

In the rush of apprehending Jenks, it was the first time in the past few days that I had really thought about it. 'I saw Medved late last week. My blood count's still down.'

Claire finally looked up. 'I'm sorry, Lindsay.'

Trying to sound upbeat, I walked her through my regimen. The increased dosage. The higher frequency. I mentioned the possibility of a bone-marrow transplant.

She gave me a broad smile. 'We're gonna have to find a way to get those red cells of yours shaken up.'

Even in the laboratory, I must've started to blush.

'What?' asked Claire. 'What're you hiding? Trying unsuccessfully to hide?'

'Nothing.'

'*Something's* going on – between you and Mr Chris Raleigh, I bet. C'mon, this is *me* you're talking to. You can't pull that blue-wall-of-silence stuff.'

I told her. From the first kiss at the precinct to the slow, torturous ride home to the burst of heat right there on the foyer floor.

Claire grasped me by my shoulders. Her eyes were as bright and excited as mine. 'So?'

'So?' I laughed. 'So . . . it was awesome. It was . . . *right*.' I felt a chill of doubt come over me. 'I just don't know if I'm doing the right thing. Considering what's going on.' I hesitated. 'I could love him, Claire. Maybe I already do.'

We stared at each other. There wasn't much more to say.

'Well,' Claire's eyes returned to her microscope, 'let's see what we have here. Hairs from his chinny-chin-chin.'

The three hairs from Jenks's razor were set on a cellular slide. She loaded it into a scope. The two scopes were side by side.

Claire looked first, leaned over, as she focused the new one in. Then she went back and forth. 'Mm-hmm,' she uttered.

I held my breath. 'What do you think?' I asked.

'You tell me.'

I leaned in. Immediately, I remembered the first hair, the one from inside Rebecca DeGeorge's vagina. Thick, reddish-gray, a white filament twisted around its base like the coil of a snake.

Then I looked at the hairs from Jenks's razor. There were three of them, shorter, clipped, but each had that same reddish hue, that same coil of filament around them.

I was no expert. But there was no doubt in my mind.

The hairs were a perfect match.

Chapter Ninety-Two

Nicholas Jenks was in a holding cell on the tenth floor of the Hall of Justice. He was headed to arraignment later today.

His lawyer, Sherman Leff, was with him, looking as if this were all just a formality, and the scales of justice were resting on the shoulders of his English-tailored suit.

Jill Bernhardt accompanied Raleigh and me. Jenks had no idea what was coming his way. We had the champagne, the tuxedo pants, matching hairs from his beard. We had him in the suite with David and Melanie Brandt. I couldn't wait to tell him all the good news.

I sat down across from Jenks and looked him in the eye. 'This is Assistant District Attorney Jill Bernhardt,' I said. 'She's going to be handling your case. She's going to convict you, too.'

He smiled – the same gracious, confident and condescending glint as if he were receiving us in his own home. *Why* does he look so confident? I wondered.

'If it's all right,' Jill said, 'I'd like to begin.'

'Your meeting,' Sherman Leff said. 'I've no objection.'

Jill took a breath. 'Mr Jenks, in an hour you are going to be arraigned for the first-degree murder of David and Melanie Brandt at the Grand Hyatt Hotel on June fifth. Shortly after, I believe a Cleveland court will do the same for the murders of James and Katherine Voskuhl. Based on what the Medical Examiner has just uncovered, I believe you can expect a Napa Valley court to follow through as well. We have overwhelming evidence linking you to all three of these crimes. We're sharing this with you, and with your counsel, in the hope that your response to this evidence might spare the city, the families of the deceased, and your family, the further humiliation of a trial.'

Sherman Leff finally cut in. 'Thank you, Ms Bernhardt. As long as consideration is the spirit of the day, we'd like to begin by expressing my client's deep regret for his emotional outburst toward Inspector Boxer at the time of his arrest. As you might imagine, the shock and the suddenness of such an accusation, so totally preposterous after he had fully complied with your questioning, in his own home . . . I'm certain you can understand how the wrong emotions might take hold.'

'I do deeply regret that, Inspector,' Jenks spoke up. 'I realize how this must look. My being less than forthcoming about my relationship with one of the deceased. And now you seem to have stumbled upon that unfortunate book.'

'Which,' Leff interjected, 'I must advise you, we will be

making a motion to suppress. Obtaining it was an unjustified intrusion into my client's private domain.'

'The warrant was totally justified,' Jill said calmly.

'On what grounds?'

'On the grounds that its existence was revealed during follow-up questioning necessitated by your client's false testimony concerning his whereabouts when Kathy Voskuhl was killed.'

Leff hung in midmotion, stunned.

'Your client *was* in Cleveland, Counselor,' I sprang on him. Then I said to Jenks, 'You were registered under your own name at the Westin Hotel. You stayed two nights, coinciding with the Voskuhl murders. You said you were at home, Mr Jenks. But you were *there*. And you were at the Hall of Fame.'

Jenks's smile disappeared and his eyes flicked around the room. He swallowed, and I could see the knot sliding down his throat. He was retracing his alibis and lies. He looked at Leff, somewhat apologetically.

'I *was* there,' he admitted. 'I *did* conceal it. As it happens, I was in town to address a local readers' group. You can check – the Argosy Bookstore. I didn't know how to explain it. Coupled with knowing Kathy, it seemed so incriminating. But let me make this clear. You're wrong about the wedding. I was nowhere near it.'

My blood rose. I couldn't believe this guy. 'You had a reading? When, Mr Jenks?'

'Saturday afternoon. At four. A small group of very loyal fans. The Argosy was very kind to me when I first started out.'

'And after that?'

'After that I do what I always do. I went back to the hotel and wrote. I took a swim, had an early dinner. You can ask my wife. I always spend the evenings alone when I'm on the road. It's been written up in *People* magazine.'

I leaned across the table. 'So this was all some bizarre coincidence, right? A woman with whom you've denied having a sexual relationship for years is brutally murdered. You just happen to be in town. You just happen to lie about being there. Your likeness just happens to be caught by a security camera at the scene. Is that how it goes, Mr Jenks?'

Leff placed a cautionary hand on Jenks's arm.

'*No!*' his client snapped, his self-control clearly chipping away.

Then he became calmer and wiped the sweat off his brow. 'I lied for Chessy – to preserve my marriage.' He straightened himself up in the wooden chair. His alibi was collapsing. 'I'm not a perfect man, Detective. I slip. I deceived you about Kathy. It was wrong. The answer is yes, what you assume to be true is. We *were* lovers on and off for three years. It continued well into her relationship with James. It was folly. It was the desperate thrill of a fool. But it was *not* murder. I did not kill Kathy. And I did not kill the others!'

Jenks stood up. For the first time, he looked scared. The panic of what was happening was clearly sinking in.

I leaned forward and said, 'A bottle of champagne was left in the suite at the Hyatt where the Brandts were killed.

It matched the same lot you purchased at an auction at Butterfield and Butterfield in November nineteen-ninety-six.'

Leff objected, 'We know that. Surely the unfortunate coincidence of my client's taste in champagne doesn't implicate him in this act. He didn't even know the Brandts. That wine could have been purchased anywhere.'

'It could have, yes – however, the registration numbers on the bottle from the Hyatt matched those from the rest of the lot we uncovered at your home last night.'

'This is getting absurd,' Jenks said angrily. 'This sort of bullshit wouldn't even make one of my books.'

'Hopefully, this will be better then.' From under the table, I pulled out the Nordstrom's shopping bag holding the balled-up tuxedo pants. I tossed them on the table in front of everybody's eyes. 'You recognize these?'

'Pants . . . what kinds of games are we playing now?'

'These were found last night. In this bag. In the back of your bedroom closet.'

'So? What're you saying – they're mine? Joseph Abboud. They could be. I don't understand where you're going.'

'Where I'm going is that these pants match the tuxedo jacket that was found in the Brandts' suite. They're a suit, Mr Jenks.'

'A suit?'

'It's the pants to the jacket you left in their hotel room. Same brand. Same style number. Same size.'

A deepening panic began to sweep over his face.

'And if all that still falls short of your usual material,' I said, fixing on his eyes, 'then how's this? *The hair matched.* The hair you left inside poor Becky DeGeorge matches hairs taken from your house. It belonged to you, you animal. You convicted yourself.'

Jill leaned forward. 'You're going away, Jenks. You're going away until the appeals finally run out and they come to stick a loaded needle in your arm.'

'This is insane,' he cried. He was leaning over me, veins in his neck swelling, shouting in my face. 'You bitch! You're setting me up! You fucking ice-bitch! I didn't kill anyone.'

Suddenly, I found that I couldn't move. Seeing Jenks unwind was one thing. But there was something else going on. I felt pinned to my chair. I *knew*, but I couldn't fight it – it was the Negli's.

I finally got up and went to the door, but my head swirled and the room tilted. My legs began to buckle. Not here, I begged.

Then I felt Raleigh supporting me. 'Lindsay . . . you all right?' He was looking at me, worried, unsuspecting. I saw Jill there, too.

I leaned against the wall. I begged my legs to work. 'I'm okay,' I whispered, holding onto Raleigh's arm.

'I just hate that bastard,' I said, and walked out of the interrogation room. I was white, very weak, swaying. I barely made it to the ladies' room.

Inside, I felt faint, then nauseated, as if some angry spirit were trying to claw its way out of my lungs. I closed my eyes, leaned over the sink. I coughed, a raw burning stinging in my chest, then I shook and coughed some more.

Gradually, I felt the spell recede. I took a breath, opened my eyes and shuddered.

There was blood all over the sink.

Chapter Ninety-Three

Four hours later, in District Criminal Court, I felt well enough to watch Nicholas Jenks be arraigned for murder.

A buzzing crowd filled the halls outside the courtroom of Judge Stephen Bowen. Photographers flashed cameras blindly, reporters surged for a glimpse of the sullen, shaken, bestselling writer.

Raleigh and I squeezed through, took a seat behind Jill in the front row. My strength having returned, the riot in my chest subsided. *I wanted Jenks to see me there.*

I saw Cindy, sitting in the press section. And in the back of the courtroom, I spotted Chancellor Weil and his wife.

It was over before it began. Jenks was led in, his eyes as dead and hollow as a crater on the moon. The clerk read the docket, the suspect rose. The bastard pleaded Not Guilty. What were they going to argue – that all the evidence was inadmissible?

Leff, the consummate showman, was unusually respectful, even demure before Judge Bowen. He made a pleading case for release on recognizance based on Jenks's stature in the community. For a moment, the killer's accomplishments even swayed me.

Jill fought him head-on. She graphically detailed the savagery of the murders. She argued that the suspect had the means and the lack of roots to flee.

I felt a surge of triumph rippling through me when the Judge struck his gavel and intoned, 'Bail Denied.'

Chapter Ninety-Four

Now, we were celebrating.

It was the end of the day, a day for which I had long waited, and I met the girls for a drink at Susie's.

We had earned this. Nicholas Jenks had been arraigned. No bail. No consideration of the court. The four of us had pulled it off.

'Here's to the Women's Murder Club,' Cindy cheered, with her beer mug in the air.

'Not bad for a collection of gender-impaired public servants,' Claire agreed.

'What did Jenks call me?' I shook my head and smiled. 'A fucking ice-bitch?'

'I can do ice-bitch,' Jill said, grinning.

'To the ice-bitches of the world,' Cindy toasted, 'and the men who cannot thaw us out.'

'Speak for yourself,' said Claire. 'Edmund thaws me just fine.' We all laughed and clinked beers.

'Still,' I said, letting out a deep breath, 'I'd like to turn up a murder weapon. And I want to nail him to the second crime.'

'When I'm through with him,' Jill tugged at her beer and said, 'you won't have to worry about him serving time for the second crime.'

'You see Jill chop down his lawyer's bail request?' Cindy said, with admiration. 'You see the look on his face?' She made her fingers into scissors. 'Snip, snip, snip, snip, snip. Straight for the testicles. That man was left standing there in his suit with a two-inch dick.' Cindy's cherubic nose twisted as she said, *Snip, snip, snip.*

'And yet,' I said, 'without a weapon, his motive still needs work.'

'Damn his motive, child,' Claire exclaimed. 'Let well enough alone.'

Jill agreed. 'Why can't his motive simply be that he's a sick bastard? He's had a history of sexual sadism for years. He's brutalized three women that we know of. I'm sure more will come out as the trial moves on.'

'You saw him, Lindsay,' Jill went on. 'He's crazed. His little perfect world gets rocked, he goes insane. This morning, he was about to plant a death grip on your throat.' She grinned toward the group. 'Lindsay just sort of glares up at him like, *Get the fuck out of my face.*'

They were about to raise a glass to me – the tough hero cop who would always carry the tag that she was the one who nailed Jenks – when the realization shot through me that I could never have done it without them. It wasn't my steel nerves that had taken over in the interrogation room, but the grip of my disease squeezing the life out of me. I had kept it concealed – not shared it even with the ones who had become my closest friends.

'That wasn't about Jenks,' I said.

'Sure seemed like it.'

'I don't mean the confrontation. I mean what happened after.' I bit my lower lip. 'When I almost collapsed, that wasn't about Jenks.'

They were still smiling, except Claire, but one by one the gravity in my eyes alerted them.

I looked around the table and told them about the Pac Man-like disease that was eating my red blood cells. I'd been fighting it for three weeks now, I said, with transfusions. And yet my blood count was deteriorating. I was getting worse.

I started strong, my voice firm, because it'd been part of my life for a while now, but when I finished, I was speaking in a hushed, scared tone. I was blinking back tears.

Jill and Cindy just sat there, rocked in disbelieving silence. Then, there were three hands reaching out for me – Cindy's, Jill's, then last and warmest, Claire's. For a long time, no one said anything. They didn't have to.

Finally, I smiled, choking back tears. 'Isn't it just like a cop to go and shut down a party just when it's going good.'

It broke the tension, cut through the sudden pall.

They never said, *We're with you.* They never told me, *You're gonna be all right.* They didn't have to.

'We're supposed to be celebrating,' I said.

Then I heard Jill's voice, out of the blue, solemn, confessing. 'When I was a little girl, I was real sick. I was in a brace and hospitals between the ages of four and seven. It broke my parents, their marriage. They split up as soon as I got better. I guess that's why I always felt I had to be stronger and better than anyone else. Why I always had to win. 'It started in high school,' she went on.

I wasn't sure what she was referring to.

'I didn't know if I would be good enough. I used to . . .' She unbuttoned the cuffs of her blouse, rolled the sleeves up over her elbows. 'I've never showed these to anybody except Steve.'

Her arms were marked with scars. I knew what they were – self-inflicted slashes. Jill had been a cutter.

'What I meant to say was, you just have to fight it. You fight it, and fight it, and fight it . . . and every time you feel it getting stronger, you fight it some more.'

'I'm trying,' I whispered, my voice choking. 'I really am trying.' Now I knew what propelled her, what was behind that steely gaze. 'But how?'

Jill's hands were holding mine. There were tears in our eyes.

'It's like with Jenks, Lindsay,' she said. 'You just don't let it win.'

Chapter Ninety-Five

*I*n the cold, cramped cell, Nicholas Jenks paced anxiously. He felt as if dynamite were about to explode at the center of his chest. How could they destroy his name, attack him with those wild allegations, disgrace him all over the news? He wasn't guilty. He was innocent!

It was dark and he was freezing. The cot in his jail cell wasn't fit for a monk. He was still in the damp clothes he'd been wearing when they had brought him in. Sweat began to break out on his palms.

He'd make the little Inspector-bitch pay. One way or another, he'd get her in the end. That was a promise.

What was his fucking poodle of a lawyer doing? When would Leff get him out of there?

It was as if all reason had been sucked out of his world.

What the hell was going on?

Or, at least, Phillip Campbell thought to himself, That's what Jenks *ought* to be feeling. What he thought the bastard would be saying in his mind.

Campbell sat in front of the mirror. *Time for you to go away. Your work is finally done. The last chapter's been written.*

He dabbed a wet cloth in a bowl of warm water. It was the last time he would ever have to play the part.

So how does it feel, Nicholas?

He pulled out the pins that held in his hair and let his locks shake out.

How does it feel to be a victim, a prisoner? To feel the same degradation and shame you cast on others?

Slowly, he wiped the dark makeup off his eyes, dabbing with the cloth, feeling a smooth sheen begin to return to his face.

How does it feel to be helpless and alone? To be kept in a dark space? To feel betrayed?

One by one, Phillip Campbell tugged at the hairs of the reddish beard on his chin, until the fake hairs came out and a new person was revealed.

Not able to recognize in the mirror the person you once were?

Scrubbing the face until it came clean and smooth. Unbuttoning the shirt, Nicholas's shirt, and soon, from underneath a bodysuit, a well-defined woman's body came to life: the outline of breasts, shapely, smooth legs, arms rippling with lean strength.

She sat there, newly revealed, a bright glow in her eyes. *This is rich.*

How does it feel, Nicholas, to be royally fucked? The tables turned for once.

She couldn't restrain the thought that it was fitting and funny, that in the end he had been trapped by his own twisted mind. It was more than funny. It was absolutely brilliant.

Who's laughing now, Nick?

Book Four

The Whole Truth

Chapter Ninety-Six

The night following Jenks's arraignment, Chief Mercer had gotten the skybox at PacBell from one of his wealthy buddies. He invited several of us, including me, Raleigh and Cheery, to a Giants game. It was a warm summer evening. They were playing the Cards. My father would have loved it.

I didn't really want to go, didn't want to feel on display as the cop who'd caught Jenks, but Mercer insisted.

And it was Mark McGwire and all, so I put on a windbreaker and we went along for the ride.

All evening long, Chris and I kept sneaking looks at each other. There was a special energy in the box, a glowing ring around just him and me.

The game was background noise. In the third, Mighty Mac hit one off Ortiz that went out of sight and almost landed in the Bay. The stadium cheered wildly, even for a Card. In the fourth, Barry Bonds tied it with a shot of his own.

Chris and I couldn't stop watching each other. We had

our legs up on the same chair, like school kids, and every once in a while, our calves brushed together. *Jesus, this was better than the ball game.*

Finally, he winked at me. 'Want something to drink?' he said.

He went over to the bowl of drinks, which was elevated from the seats, and I followed. The others didn't look back. As soon as we were out of sight, he placed his hands on my thighs and kissed me. 'You want to hang around?'

'Still beer left,' I joked.

His hand brushed against the side of my breast, and I felt a tremor. *Soft hands.* My breath quickened. A flicker of sweat broke through my neck.

Chris kissed me again. He drew me in close, and I felt the cadence of a heart, pounding between us. I didn't know if it was his or mine.

'Can't wait,' he said.

'Okay, let's get out of here.'

'No,' he shook his head. 'I meant I *can't* wait.'

'Oh Jesus,' I gasped. I couldn't hold back. My whole body was heating up to the boiling point. I glanced down at Cheery and the two Mill Valley types. *This is crazy, Lindsay.*

But everything lately was crazy, everything speeding out of control.

It seemed as if every natural force in the universe was driving Chris and me to find a secluded spot. There was a bathroom in the skybox, barely large enough to put on makeup in. We didn't care.

Chris led me inside while the baseball crowd roared at something. We could barely squeeze in. I could not believe I was doing this here. He unbuttoned my blouse, I unfastened his belt. Our thighs were pressed tightly onto each other's.

Gently, Chris lifted me onto him. I felt as if a shooting star had exploded in my veins. Chris was up against the counter; I was in the palms of his hands, squeezed into this tiny space, but we were in a perfect rhythm.

A crowd roar echoed in from outside – maybe McGwire had hit another, maybe Bonds had robbed him – who cared. We kept rocking. Chris and I. We were both breathing hard. My body was slick with sweat. I couldn't stop. Chris kept it going, I gripped on tight, and in a moment, we both gasped.

Two hero cops, I thought.

It was the best – the freest, the most excited I had ever felt. Chris rested his forehead on my shoulder. I kissed his cheek, his neck.

Then the strangest thought took hold of me. I began to laugh, a mixture of laughter and exhausted sighs. We were pinned there, spent, a few feet from my boss. I was giggling like a damn fool. I was going to get us caught!

'What's so funny?' Chris whispered.

I was thinking of Claire and Cindy. And what we had just done.

'I think I just made the list,' I said.

Chapter Ninety-Seven

The next day, Jenks asked to meet again. Jill and I went to see him on the tenth floor. We wondered what was up.

This time, there was no cat and mouse, no bullshit at all. Leff was there, but he rose – humbly – as soon as we came in.

Jenks looked far less threatening in his gray prison outfit. The worried look on his face was a clear message.

'My client wants to make a statement,' Leff said, as soon as we sat down.

I was thinking, This is it. He wants to make a deal. He's seen how ridiculous it is to play this game.

But he came out with something unexpected.

'I'm being framed,' Jenks announced.

It took about a half-second for Jill's eyes to bump into mine.

'I have to hear this again,' she said. 'What's going on?' She looked at Jenks, then at Leff.

'We've got your client tied to all three crime scenes;

we've got him in Cleveland at the time of the last murder; we've got his lying about a prior relationship with Kathy Kogut, one of the last victims; we've got his book detailing an astonishingly similar criminal pattern; we've got his facial hairs matched to one found in another victim's vagina. And you're claiming *he's being framed*?'

'What I'm claiming,' Jenks said, ashen-faced, 'is that I'm being set up.'

'Listen, Mr Jenks,' Jill said, still looking at Leff, 'I've been doing this eight years. I've built cases on hundreds of criminals, put over fifty murderers behind bars myself. I've never seen such a preponderance of evidence implicating a suspect. Our case is so airtight it can't breathe.'

'I realize that,' sighed Jenks. 'And that I've given you every reason to find my plea implausible. I've lied about being in Cleveland, my relationship with Kathy. On the others, I can't even account for my whereabouts. But I also know set-ups. I've mapped out more of them than anybody. I'm a master at this. And I can assure you, someone is setting me up.'

I shook my head with disbelief. 'Who, Mr Jenks?'

Jenks actually looked scared. 'I don't know.'

'Someone hates you enough to set all this up?' Jill couldn't hold back a snicker. 'The little I know of you, I might buy that.' She turned to Leff. 'You looking forward to presenting this case?'

'Just hear him out, Ms Bernhardt,' the lawyer pleaded.

'Look,' Jenks said, 'I know what you think of me. I'm guilty of many things. Selfishness, cruelty, adultery. I have

a temper, sometimes I can't hold it in. And with women . . .
you can probably line up a dozen of them who would help
put me away for these murders. But clear as that is, I did
not kill these people. Any of them. Someone is trying to set
me up. That's the truth. Someone has done a brilliant job.'

Chapter Ninety-Eight

'You buy any of that shit?' Jill smirked at me, as we waited for the elevator outside Jenks's holding cell.

'I might buy that he somehow believes it,' I told her.

'Give me a break. He'd be better off going for insanity. If Nicholas Jenks wants to narrow down a list of people who might want to set him up, he might as well start with anyone he ever fucked.'

I laughed, agreeing that the list would be long. Then the elevator door opened and, to my surprise, out walked Chessy Jenks. She was dressed in a long, taupe summer dress. I immediately noticed how pretty she was.

Our eyes met in an awkward, silent moment. I had just arrested her husband. My Crime Scene team had ripped apart her house. She would have every reason to look at me with complete disdain – but she didn't.

'I'm here to see my husband,' she said in a shaky voice.

I stiffly introduced her to Jill, then I pointed her to the visiting area. At that moment, she seemed about as alone and confused as anyone I had ever seen.

'Sherman tells me there's a lot of evidence,' she said.

I nodded politely. I don't know why I felt something for her, other than she seemed a young, vulnerable woman whose fate was to fall in love with a monster.

'Nick didn't do this, Detective,' Chessy Jenks said.

Her outburst surprised me. 'It's only natural for a wife to want to defend her husband,' I acknowledged. 'If you have some concrete alibi . . .'

She shook her head. 'No alibi. Only that I know my husband.'

The elevator door had closed, and Jill and I stood there waiting again. As in hospitals, it would take minutes for it to go down and come back up. Chessy Jenks made no move to walk away.

'My husband's not a simple man. He can be very tough. I know he's made enemies. I know how he came at you. From the outside, it must be very hard to believe this, but there are times when he's also capable of tenderness, incredible generosity, and love.'

'I don't mean to sound unsympathetic, Ms Jenks,' Jill stepped in, 'but under the circumstances you really shouldn't be talking with us.'

'I have nothing to hide,' she came back. Then she looked downcast. 'I already know what you know.'

I was dumbfounded. *I already know what you know?*

'I spoke with Joanna,' Chessy Jenks continued. 'She told me you'd been by. I know what she told you about him. She's bitter. She's got every right to be. But she doesn't know Nick like I do.'

'You should review the evidence, Ms Jenks,' I told her.

She shook her head. 'Guns . . . maybe, Detective – if that's all there was. But a knife? That first murder – slicing that poor couple to bits. Nick can't even fillet a fish.'

My first thought was that she was young and deluded. How had Jenks described it? *Impressionable* . . . but something struck me as curious. 'You said that you and Joanna talk?'

'We have, Detective. A lot more in the past year. I've even had her over – when Nick was away, of course. I know she was bitter after the divorce. I know he hurt her. But it's sort of our own support group.'

'Your husband knew about this?' I asked.

She forced a smile. 'He didn't even mind. He still likes Joanna. And, Detective, she's still in love with him.'

The elevator came and we said goodbye. As the door closed, I looked at Jill. Her eyes were wide and her tongue was puffing out her cheek.

'Whole fucking family gives me the creeps,' she shuddered.

Chapter Ninety-Nine

I knew it the minute Medved walked in the office. I saw it in his face. He didn't have to say a word.

'I'm afraid I can't be very positive, Lindsay,' he said quietly, meeting my eyes. 'Your red count continues to decline. The fainting spells, the fatigue, blood in your chest. The disease is progressing.'

'Progressing?' I whispered.

Medved nodded, soberly. 'Stage Three.'

The words thundered in my head, bringing with them the fears of the increased treatments I dreaded. 'What's the next step?' I asked weakly.

'We can give it one more month,' Medved said. 'Your count's twenty-four hundred. If it continues to decline, your strength will start to go. You'll have to be hospitalized.'

I could hardly comprehend what he was saying. A month. That was too close. Too fast. Things were just starting to work out now that Jenks was arrested. Everything else, everything I wanted to hold onto, was resolving, too.

A month – four lousy weeks.

When I got back to the office, a few of the guys were standing around, grinning at me. There was a beautiful bouquet of flowers on my desk. Wildflowers.

I smelled them, taking in the sweet, natural scent, and read the card. *There's a hill of these where I have a cabin up at Heavenly. Tomorrow's Friday. Take the day off. Let's go there.*

It was signed *Chris*.

It sounded like what I needed. The mountains. Chris. I would have to tell him now that the truth would come clear soon.

My phone rang. It was Chris. 'So?' No doubt someone in the office, playing Cupid, had alerted him that I was back.

'Haven't opened your card yet.' I bit my lip. 'Too many others to sort through.'

I heard a disappointed sigh, let it linger just a moment. 'But on the chance you were asking me away, the answer is I'd love to. It sounds great. Let's be on the road by eight.'

'Late riser,' he said. 'I was hoping we'd beat the morning rush.'

'I was talking tonight.'

I had a month, I was thinking. Mountain air, running streams and wildflowers is a good way to begin.

Chapter One Hundred

We spent the next two days as if we were in a beautiful dream.

Chris's cabin was funky and charming, a redwood A-frame ski chalet on Mason Ridge overlooking Heavenly. We hiked in the woods with Sweet Martha, took the tram to the top of the mountain, and walked all the way down. We grilled swordfish on the deck.

In between, we made love in the comfort of his large, four-poster bed; on the sheepskin rug in front of the wood-burning stove; in the chilly thrill of the outdoor shower. We laughed and played and touched each other like teenagers, discovering love again.

But I was no starry-eyed adolescent. I knew exactly what was taking place. I felt the steady, undeniable current rising inside me like a river spilling over its banks. I felt helpless.

Saturday, Chris promised me a day I would never forget.

We drove down to Lake Tahoe, to a quaint marina on the California side. He had rented a platform boat, an old puttering wooden barge. We bought sandwiches and a bottle of Chardonnay, and went out to the middle of the lake. The water calm and turquoise, the sky cloudless and bright. All around, the rocky tips of snow-capped mountains ringed the lake like a crown.

We moored, and for a while, it was our own private world. Chris and I stripped down to our suits. I figured we'd kick back, enjoy the wine and the sun, look at the view, but Chris had sort of an expectant dare-you look in his eye. He ran his hands through the frigid water.

'No way,' I said, shaking my head. 'It's got to be fifty degrees.'

'Yeah, but it's a dry cold,' he teased.

'Right,' I chortled. 'You go, then. Catch me a coho if you see one swim by.'

He came toward me with playful menace in his eyes. 'You can catch one yourself.'

'Not a chance.' I shook my head in defiance. But I was laughing, too. As he stepped forward, I backed to the rear of the craft until I had run out of room.

He put his arms around me. I felt the tingle of his skin on mine. 'It's sort of an initiation,' he said.

'An initiation for what?'

'Exclusive club. Anyone who wants to be in it has to jump in.'

'Then leave me out,' I laughed, squirming in his strong arms. With only weak resistance, he yanked me up on the cushion seat in the stern of the boat.

'Shit, Chris,' I cried as he took hold of my hand.

'Geronimo works better,' he said, pulling at me. I screamed, '*You bastard!*' and we toppled in.

The water was freezing, a total, invigorating rush. We hit the surface together and I screamed in his face, '*Goddamn you!*' Then he kissed me in the water, and all at once I felt no chill. I held onto him, at first for warmth, but also because I never wanted to let him go. I felt a trust for him that was so complete, it was almost scary. The water was fifty degrees, but I was burning up.

'Check this out,' I dared him, kicking free of his grasp. There was an orange boat marker bobbing fifty yards away. 'Race you to that buoy.' Then I cut out, surprising him with my speed.

Chris tried to keep up with steady, muscular strokes, but I blew him away.

Near the buoy I slowed, waited for him to catch up.

Chris looked totally confounded. 'Where'd you learn to swim?'

'South San Francisco YMCA fourteen-, fifteen-, sixteen-year-old Division Champ,' I boasted. 'No one else could keep up. Looks like I still have it.'

Moments later, we had guided the boat to a private, shady cove near the shore. Chris cut the engine, and put up a canvas shade around the cabin that was supposed to protect us from the sun. With bated breath, we crept inside, blocked off from anyone's view.

I let him slowly unfasten my bathing suit, and he licked beads of water off my arms and breasts. Then I kneeled down and unbuttoned his shorts. We didn't have to speak.

Our bodies were saying everything. I lay back, pulling Chris onto me.

I had never felt so connected to another person, or a place. I arched against him, silently, the lake lapping gently at our sides. I thought, If I speak, it will change everything.

Afterward, I just lay there, tremors of warmth radiating through my body. I never wanted this to end, but I knew that it had to. Reality always gets in the way, doesn't it?

Chapter One Hundred and One

S ometime that evening, I found myself starting to cry.

I had made spaghetti carbonara, and we ate in the moonlight on the deck with a bottle of Pinot Noir. Chris put a cello concerto by Dvořák on the stereo, but eventually we switched to the Dixie Chicks.

As we ate, Chris asked about where and how I had grown up.

I enlarged on what I had already told him about my mom, and how my dad had left when I was just a kid; how Mom had worked as a bookkeeper at the Emporium for twenty years. How I had practically raised my sister.

'Mom died of breast cancer when she was only fifty.' The irony of this certainly wasn't lost on me.

'What about your father? I want to know everything about you.'

I took a sip of wine, then told him how I'd only seen him twice since I was thirteen. At my mother's funeral. And the day I became a cop. 'He sat in the back, apart from everybody else.' Suddenly, my blood became hot with long-buried feelings. 'What was he doing there?' I looked up, my eyes moist. 'Why did he spoil it?'

'You ever want to see him?'

I didn't answer. Something was starting to take shape in my head. My mind drifted, struck by the fact that here I was, maybe the happiest I had ever been, but it was all built on a lie. I was blinking back the impact of what was going through my mind. Not doing real well.

Chris reached over and grasped my hand. 'I'm sorry, Lindsay. I had no right to . . .'

'That's not it,' I whispered and squeezed his hand. I knew it was time to really trust him, time to finally give myself over to Chris. But I was scared, my cheeks trembling, my eyes holding back tears.

'I have something to tell you,' I said. 'This is a little heavy, Chris.'

I looked at him with all the earnestness and trust my worried eyes could manage. 'Remember when I almost fainted in the room with Jenks?'

Chris nodded. Now he looked anxious. His forehead was furrowed with deep lines.

'Everyone thought I was just freaked out, but it wasn't that. I'm sick, Chris. I may have to go into the hospital soon.'

I saw the light in his eyes suddenly dim. He started to speak, but I put my finger to his lips.

'Just listen to me for a minute. Okay?'

'Okay. I'm sorry.'

I poured out everything about Negli's. I was not

responding to treatments. Hope was fading. What Medved had warned only days before. I was in Stage Three, serious. A bone-marrow transplant might be next.

I didn't cry. I told him straight-out, like a cop. I wanted to give him hope, to show him I was fighting, to show him I was the strong person I thought he loved. When I was done, I clasped his hands and took a monumental breath. 'The truth is, I could die soon, Chris.'

Our hands were tightly entwined. Our eyes locked. We couldn't have been more in touch.

Then he placed his hand gently on my cheek and rubbed it. He didn't say a word, just took me and held me in the power and softness of his hands and drew me to him.

And that's what made me cry. He was a good person. I might lose him. And I cried for all the things we might never do.

I cried and cried, and with each sob he pressed me harder. He kept whispering, 'It's all right, Lindsay. It's all right. It's all right.'

'I should've told you,' I said.

'I understand why you didn't. How long have you known?'

I told him. 'Since the day we met. I feel so ashamed.'

'Don't be ashamed,' he said. 'How could you know you could trust me?'

'I trusted you pretty quickly. I didn't trust myself.'

'Well, now you do,' Chris whispered.

Chapter One Hundred
and Two

I think we rocked all night. We laughed some, cried some.
I don't even remember how I woke up in bed.

The following day, I barely left his touch. With all that
was threatening, all that seemed so uncertain, I felt so safe
and sure in his arms. I never wanted to leave.

But something else happened during that weekend –
apart from Negli's, apart from Chris and me. Something
gripping, invading my sense of comfort and security.

It was something Jacobi had said that planted the
thought.

One of those thrown-out remarks you pay no attention
to, but which somehow get filed away in your mind. Then
it comes back at the oddest time, with more force and logic
than before.

It was Sunday night. The weekend was over. Chris had
driven me home. Hard as it was to leave him, I needed to be
alone for a while, to take inventory of the weekend, to figure
out what I would do next.

I unpacked, made some tea, curled up on my couch

with Her Sweetness. My mind wandered to the murder case.

Nicholas Jenks was behind me now. Only the countless reports to fill out remained. Even though he was still ranting about being set up. It was just more insanity, more lies.

It was then that Jacobi's words snaked into my brain.

'Good collar,' he'd said, early Tuesday morning. He had that annoying, persistent look in his eyes. 'Just remember,' he'd called after me, 'it was the champagne match that got you on your way. Why do you think Jenks left that champagne?'

I was barely paying attention. Jenks was locked away; the case was a slam dunk. I was thinking about the night before, and Chris. 'I don't know, Warren. We've been over this. Heat of the moment, maybe.'

'You're right,' he nodded. 'That must be why he didn't ball up the jacket and take it with him, too.'

I looked at him, like, 'Why are we going through this now? Jenks needed a clean tux jacket to get out of the hotel undetected.' The DNA match on the hair made it all academic, anyway.

Then he said it. 'You ever read the whole book?' he asked.

'Which book?'

'Jenks's book. *Always A Bridesmaid*.'

'The parts that matter,' I replied. 'Why?'

He said, 'I don't know, it just sort of stuck with me. Like I said, my wife happens to be a fan. There were some copies of the manuscript around, so I took one home. It was interesting how it all came out in the end.'

I looked at him, trying to figure out where all this was heading.

'It was a set-up,' Jacobi said. 'This Phillip Campbell guy, he gets off. He pins the whole thing on someone else.'

Days later, Warren's words came creeping back into my mind. *A set-up. He pins the whole thing on someone else.*

It was ridiculous, I told myself, that I was even dignifying this scenario by running through it in my mind. Everything was solid, airtight.

'I must be an idiot,' I said aloud. 'Jenks is clinging to any story he can to wiggle his way out of this.'

I got up, brought my tea into the bathroom, began to wash my face.

In the morning I would tell Cheery about my disease. I had some free time coming. I would face this thing head-on. Now that the case was complete, it was the right time. *Now that the case was complete!*

I went into the bedroom, ripped the tags off a *Little Bit of Heaven* T-shirt Chris had bought me. I got into bed and Martha came around for her hug. Memories of the week-end began to drift into my head. I closed my eyes. I could hardly wait to share it with the girls.

Then a thought from out of the blue hit me. I shot up, as if I'd had a nightmare. I stiffened. 'Oh no. Oh Jesus, no,' I whispered.

When Jenks lunged at me at his house, he had swung with his left hand.

JAMES PATTERSON

When he'd offered me a drink, he'd picked up the pitcher with his left hand.

Impossible, I thought. This can't be happening.

Claire was certain David Brandt's killer had been *right-handed*.

Chapter One Hundred
and Three

J ill, Claire and Cindy looked at me as if I were insane.

The words had barely tumbled out of my mouth. 'What if Jenks is right? What if someone *is* trying to set him up?'

'That's a crock!' snapped Jill. 'Jenks is desperate, and only moderately clever. We've got him!'

'I can't believe you're saying this!' exclaimed Cindy. 'You're the one who found him. *You're* the one who made the case.'

'I know. I know it seems crazy. Hopefully, it *is* crazy. Please – just hear me out.'

I took them through Jacobi's comment about the book; then my lightning bolt about Jenks's left-handedness.

'Proves nothing,' Jill said.

'I can't get past the science, Lindsay,' Claire said with a shake of her head. 'We've got this goddamn DNA at the scene.'

'Look,' I protested, 'I want the guy as much as anybody. But now that we have all this evidence – well, it's just so *neat.* The jacket, the champagne. Jenks has set up complicated murders in his books. Why would he leave clues behind?'

'Because he's a sick bastard, Lindsay. Because he's an arrogant prick who's connected to all three crimes.'

Jill nodded. 'He's a writer. He's an amateur at actually *doing* anything. He just fucked up.'

'You saw his reactions, Jill. They were deeper than simply desperation. I've seen killers on Death Row still in denial. This was more unsettling. Like *disbelief.*'

Jill stood up, her icy-blue eyes spearing down at me. 'Why, Lindsay? Why the sudden about-face?'

For the first time I felt alone and separated from the people I had most learned to trust. 'No one could possibly hate this man more than me,' I declared. 'I hunted him. I saw what he's done to these women.' I turned to Claire. 'You said the killer was right-handed.'

'*Probably* right-handed,' she came back.

'What if he simply held the knife in his other hand?' proposed Cindy.

'Cindy, if you were going to *kill* someone,' I said, 'someone larger and stronger, would you go at him with your opposite hand?'

'Maybe not,' injected Jill, 'but you're throwing all this up in the face of facts. Evidence and reason, Lindsay. All the things we worked to assemble. What you're giving me back is a set of hypotheticals. "Jenks holds his pitcher with his left hand. Phillip Campbell sets someone up at the end of his book." Look, we have the guy pinned to three double murders. I need you firm on this.' Her jaw was quivering. 'I need you to testify.'

I didn't know how to defend myself. I had wanted to nail Jenks as eagerly as any one of us. More. But now, after being so sure, I couldn't put it away, the sudden doubt.

Did we have the right man?

'We still haven't uncovered a weapon,' I said to Jill.

'We don't need a weapon, Lindsay. We have his hair *inside* one of the victims!'

Suddenly, we were aware that people from other tables were looking at us. Jill sat back down. Claire put her arms around my shoulders. I slumped back against the cushion of the booth.

Finally, Cindy said quietly, 'We've been behind you all the way. We're not going to abandon you now.'

Jill shook her head. 'You want me to let him go, guys, while we reopen the case? If we don't try him, Cleveland will.'

'I don't want you to let him go,' I stammered. 'I only want to be one hundred per cent sure.'

'I *am* sure,' Jill replied, her eyes ablaze.

I sought out Claire, and even she had a skeptical expression fixed firmly in my direction. 'There's an awful lot of physical evidence that makes it pretty clear.'

'If this gets out,' Jill warned us, 'you can toss my career out with the cat litter. Bennett wants this guy's blood on the Courthouse wall.'

'Look at it this way,' Cindy chuckled, 'if Lindsay's right, and you sent Jenks up, they'll be studying this case as a

"How *Not* To" for twenty years to come.'

Numbly, we looked around the table. It was as if we were staring at the pieces of some shattered, irreplaceable vase.

'Okay, so if it's not him,' Claire sighed, 'then how do we go about proving who it is?'

It was as if we were all the way back at the beginning – all the way back at the first crime. I felt awful.

'What was the thing that nailed our suspicion on Jenks?' I asked.

'The hair,' said Claire.

'Not quite. We had to get to him before we knew who it belonged to.'

'Merrill Shortley,' Jill said. 'Jenks and Merrill? You think?'

I shook my head. 'We still needed one more thing before we could take him in.'

Cindy said, '*Always A Bridesmaid*. His first wife.'

I nodded slowly.

Chapter One Hundred and Four

Over the next few days, I went back over everything we had on Joanna Wade.

First, I reread the domestic complaint she had filed against Jenks. I looked at pictures of Joanna taken at the station, bruised, puffy-faced. I read through the officers' account of what they found at the scene. Exchanges laced with invectives. Jenks swinging wildly, clearly enraged. He had to be subdued, had resisted arrest.

The report was signed by two officers from Northern, Samuel Delgado and Anthony Fazziola.

The following day, I went back out to visit Greg Marks, Jenks's former agent. He was even more surprised at my visit when I told him I was here on a different aspect of Jenks's past. 'Joanna?' he replied, with an amused smile. 'Bad judge of men, Inspector, but a worse judge of timing.'

He explained that their divorce had been finalized only six months before *Crossed Wire* hit the stands. The book sold nearly a million copies in hardcover alone. 'To have put up with Nicholas through all the lean years, then come away with barely more than a cab fare,' he shook his head. 'The settlement was a pittance compared to what it would've been if they had filed a year later.'

What he told me painted a different picture of the woman I had met in the gym. She seemed to have put it all behind her.

'She felt used, dropped like worn baggage. Joanna had put him through school, supported him when he first started writing. When Nick bagged law school, she even went back to her job.'

'And afterward,' I asked, 'did she continue to hate him?'

'I believe she continued to try and *sue* him. After they split up, she tried to sue him for a lien against future earnings. Non-performance, breach of contract. Anything she could find.'

I felt sorry for Joanna Wade. But could it drive her to *that* kind of revenge? Could it cause her to kill six people?

The following day, I obtained a copy of the divorce proceedings from County Records. Through the usual boilerplate, I got the sense it was an especially bitter case. She was seeking three million dollars judgment against future earnings. She ended up with five thousand a month, escalating to ten if Jenks's earnings substantially increased.

I couldn't believe the bizarre transformation that was starting to take over my mind.

It had been Joanna who had first alluded to the book. Who felt cheated, spurned, and carried a resentment far deeper than what she had revealed. Joanna, the tai bo instructor who was strong enough to take down a man twice her size. Who had misled me about her relationship with Chessy. Who even had access to the Jenkses home.

It seemed crazy to be thinking this way. More than preposterous . . . it was impossible.

The murders were committed by a male, by Nicholas Jenks.

Chapter One Hundred
and Five

The next day, as we shared a hot dog and a pretzel in front of City Hall, I told Chris what I had found.

He looked at me in much the same way the girls had a few days before. With shock, confusion. Disbelief. But he didn't get negative.

'She could've set the whole thing up,' I said. 'She knew about the book. She lobbed it out there for us to find. She knew Jenks's taste – in champagne, in clothes – about his involvement with Sparrow Ridge. She even had access to the house.'

'I might buy it,' he said, 'but these murders were committed by a man. Jenks, Lindsay. We even have him on film.'

'Or someone made up to look like Jenks. Every sighting of him was inconclusive.'

'Lindsay, the DNA was a match.'

'I spoke to the officers who went to the house when he beat Joanna,' I pressed on. 'They said, as enraged as Jenks was, she was dishing it right back to him, just as strong.

They had to restrain *her* as they took him away in the car.'

'She dropped the charges, Lindsay. She got tired of being abused. She may not have gotten what she deserved, but she filed and started a new life.'

'That's just it, Chris. *She* didn't file. It was Jenks who left her. His agent, Greg Marks, told me. She sacrificed everything for him. He described her as a model of co-dependency.'

I could see Chris was unconvinced. I had a man in jail with almost incontrovertible evidence against him. And here I was, unraveling everything. What was the matter with me?

Then, out of the blue, something came back to me, something I had filed away long ago. Laurie Birnbaum, a guest of the Weils at the Brandt wedding had described the man she saw in these words: 'The beard made him seem older, but the rest of him was young.'

Joanna Wade, medium-height, right-handed, the tai bo instructor, was strong enough to handle a man twice her size. And Jenks's nine millimeter – he said he hadn't seen it in years. *At the house in Montana.* The records showed he bought the gun ten years ago, when he was married to Joanna.

'You should see her,' I said, with rising conviction. 'She's tough enough to handle any of us. She's the one link who knew about everything: wine, clothes, *Always A Bridesmaid*. She had the means to pull it all together. The photos, the sightings, were all inconclusive. What if it was her, Chris?'

I held his hand – my mind racing with the possibilities – when I felt a sudden, awful tightness in my chest. I thought it was the shock of what I had just proposed, but it hit me with the speed of an express train.

Vertigo, nausea. It swept from my chest to my head.

'Lindsay?' Chris said. I felt his hand bracing my shoulder.

'I feel kind of weird,' I muttered. The sweats followed, then a rush, then a terrible light-headedness. As if armies were marching and clashing in my chest.

'Lindsay?' he said again, this time with real concern.

I leaned into him. This was the scariest sensation. I felt both momentarily robbed of strength and then back in control; lucid, then very woozy.

I saw Chris, and then I didn't.

I saw who killed the brides and grooms. And then it faded away.

I felt myself falling toward the sidewalk.

Chapter One Hundred
and Six

I found myself coming to on a wooden park bench in Chris's arms. He held me tightly while my strength returned.

Orenthaler had warned me. It was Stage Three. Crunch time in my body. I didn't know which held more apprehension for me: going on chemo and gearing up for a bone-marrow transplant, or feeling my strength eaten away from the inside.

You can't let it win.

'I'm okay,' I told him, my voice getting stronger. 'I knew this would happen.'

'You're trying to do too much, Lindsay. Now you're talking about reopening a whole new investigation.'

I took a deep breath and nodded. 'I just need to be strong enough to see this through.'

We sat there for a while, the color in my face reviving, the strength in my limbs returning. Chris held me, cuddled me tenderly. We must've looked like two lovers trying to find privacy in a very public place.

Finally, he said, 'What you were describing, Lindsay, about Joanna – you really think it's true?'

It could still add up to nothing. She had not lied about her separation from Jenks, and about her current relationship with him and Chessy. Had she concealed a bitter hatred? She had the knowledge, the means.

'I think the killer is still out there,' I said.

Chapter One Hundred
and Seven

I decided to take a huge risk. If I blew it, it could knock the lid right off my case.

I decided to run what I suspected by Jenks.

I met him in the same visiting room. He was accompanied by his lawyer, Leff. He didn't want to meet, convinced there was no longer a point in talking with the police. And I didn't want to convey my true intent and end up feeding their defense arguments, if I was wrong.

Jenks was sullen, almost depressed. His cool and meticulous appearance had deteriorated into an edgy, unshaven mess.

'What do you want now?' he sneered, barely meeting my eyes.

'I want to know if you were able to come up with anyone who would like to see you in here,' I said.

'Pounding the lid on my coffin?' he said, with a mirthless smile.

'Let's just say, in the interest of doing my duty, I'm giving you one final chance to pry it back open.'

Jenks snorted skeptically. 'Sherman tells me I'm about to be charged in Napa with two more murders. Isn't that great? If this is an offer of assistance, I think I'll take my chances on proving it myself.'

'I didn't come here to trap you, Mr Jenks. I came to hear you out.'

Leff leaned over and whispered in his ear. He seemed to be encouraging Jenks to talk.

The prisoner looked up with a disgusted glare. 'Someone's running around, intent to look like me, familiar with my first novel. This person also wants to see me suffer. Is it so hard to figure out?'

'I'm willing to hear any names,' I told him.

'Greg Marks.'

'Your former agent?' I asked.

'He feels like I owe him my fucking career. I've cost him millions. Since I left, he hasn't gotten a worthwhile client. And he's violent. Marks belongs to a shooting club.'

'How would he have gotten his hands on your clothing? Or been able to get a sample of your hair?'

'You find that out. You're the police.'

'Did he know you'd be in Cleveland that night? Did he know about you and Kathy Kogut?'

'Nick is merely proposing,' Leff cut in, 'that other possibilities do exist for who could be behind these crimes.'

I shifted in my seat. 'Who else knew about the book?'

Jenks twitched. 'It wasn't something I paraded around. Couple of old friends. My first wife, Joanna.'

'Any of them have any reason to want to set you up?'

'My divorce, as you may know,' Jenks sighed uncomfortably, 'was not exactly what they call "mutually agreeable". No doubt there was a time Joanna would've been delighted to find me on a deserted road while she was cruising along at sixty. But now that she's back on her feet, with a new life, now that she's even gotten to know Chessy . . . I don't think so. No. It isn't Joanna. Trust me on that.'

I ignored the remark and looked firmly in his eyes. 'You told me your ex-wife has been to your house.'

'Maybe once or twice.'

'So she'd have access to certain things. Maybe the wine? Maybe what was in your closet?'

Jenks seemed to contemplate the possibility for a moment, then his mouth crinkled into a contemptuous smile. 'Impossible. No, it isn't Joanna.'

'How can you be so sure?'

He looked at me as if he were stating an understood fact. 'Joanna loved me. *She still does.* Why do you think she hangs around, cultivates a relationship with my new wife? Because she misses the view? It's because she cannot replace what I gave her. How I loved her. She is empty without me.

'What do you think,' he said, 'Joanna's been holding specimens of my hair in a jar ever since we were divorced?' He sat there, stroking his beard, while his face softened a little. 'Someone has it in for me, but not Joanna. She was just a little clerk when I met her. She didn't know Ralph Lauren from J.C. Penneys. I gave her self-esteem. I devoted myself to her, and she to me. She sacrificed everything for me, even worked two jobs when I decided to write.'

It was hard to think of Jenks as anything other than the ruthless bastard who was responsible for these horrible crimes, but I kept at him. 'You said the tuxedo was an old suit. You didn't even recognize it. And the gun, Mr Jenks, the nine millimeter. You said you hadn't seen it in years, that you thought it was kept somewhere at your house in Montana. Are you so sure this might not have been planned for some time?'

I could see Jenks subtly shifting his expression, as he came around to the impossible conclusion.

'You said that when you started writing, Joanna took a second job to help support you. What sort of job was it?'

Jenks stared up toward the ceiling, then he seemed to remember.

'She worked at Saks.'

Chapter One Hundred
and Eight

Slowly, unavoidably, I was starting to feel as if I were on the wrong airplane, heading to the wrong city.

Against all logic, I was growing surer and surer that Nicholas Jenks might not be the killer. *Oh brother!*

I had to figure out what to do. Jenks in handcuffs was the lead picture in both *Times* and *Newsweek*. He was being arraigned in Napa for two additional murders the following day. Maybe I should just stay on the wrong plane, get out of town, never show my face in San Francisco again.

I got the girls together. I took them through the mosaic that was starting to come clear: the acrimonious contest over the divorce; Joanna's sense of being discarded; her direct access to the victims through her contacts at Saks.

'She was an assistant store manager,' I told them. 'Coincidence?'

'Get me *proof*,' Jill said. 'Because as of now, I have proof against Nick Jenks. All the proof I need.'

I could hear the worry and frustration in her voice. The whole country was watching this case, watching her every move. We had worked so hard to sell Mercer and her boss, Bennett Sinclair, that it was Jenks. And now, after all that – to propose a new theory and suspect.

'Authorize a search,' I told Jill. 'Joanna Wade's house. Something has to be there. The missing rings, a weapon, details on the victims. It's the only way we'll ever pin it down.'

'Authorize a search on what basis? Suspicion of new evidence? I can't do that without blowing this case wide open again. If we show we're not even sure, how can I convince a jury?'

'We could check where she worked,' proposed Cindy. 'See if she had specific access to information on the brides.'

'That's circumstantial. It's crap,' Jill cried. 'One of my neighbors works at Saks. Maybe she's the murderer.'

'You can't go through with this,' argued Cindy, 'if we still have doubt.'

'*You* have doubt,' said Jill. 'What I have is everything in place for a slam-dunk conviction. To you, it's a story, you follow it where it leads. My whole career is on the line.'

Cindy looked stunned. 'You think I'm here for just the story? You think I sat on every lead, agonized over not being able to go to copy, just so I could wind up with the book rights later on?'

'C'mon, girls,' said Claire, her arm on Cindy's shoulder. 'We have to be together on this.'

Slowly, Jill's intense blue eyes grew calmer. She turned to Cindy. 'I'm sorry,' she said. 'It's just that when this gets out, Leff will plant more doubt in that jury's mind.'

'But if they turned out to be right,' said Claire. 'We can't back down now just because it's bad tactics. There *could* be a murderer out there, a multiple murderer.'

I said to Jill, 'Authorize a search. C'mon, Jill.'

I had never seen her look so upset. Everything she had achieved in her career, everything she stood for, was being placed squarely on the line. She shook her head. 'Let's try it Cindy's way. We'll start with Saks, check Joanna out there.'

'Thank you, Jill,' I said. 'You're the best.'

She sighed resignedly. 'Find out if she's had any contact with anyone who had access to those names. Connect Joanna with those names, and I'll get you what you want. But if you can't, be prepared to fry Jenks.'

From across the table, I took her hand. She gripped mine. We both exchanged a nervous smile.

Jill finally joked, 'Personally, all I hope you come back with is the hot item to be featured in next year's Christmas catalog.'

Claire laughed loudly. 'Now that wouldn't be a total loss, would it?'

Chapter One Hundred
and Nine

The following day, the day Nicholas Jenks was set to be arraigned for the murders of Rebecca and Michael DeGeorge, I set out to track down a new killer.

I couldn't let Jenks know we were looking that closely at Joanna. Nor did I want Joanna to know we were focusing suspicion on her, either. And I didn't want to face Mercer's or Roth's reactions.

With all this going on, it was my Medved day, too. Shit, shit, shit. After that spell in the park with Chris three days before, I had gone for a blood test. Medved called back himself, told me he wanted me to come in. Being called in again like that scared me. Like that first time with Dr Roy.

That afternoon, Medved kept me waiting. When he finally called me in, there was another doctor in his office – older, with white hair and bushy white eyebrows. He introduced himself as Dr Robert Yatto.

The sight of a new doctor sent a chill through me. He could only be there to talk about the bone-marrow procedure.

'Dr Yatto is Head of Hematology at Moffett Hospital,' Medved said. 'I asked him to look at your latest sample.'

Yatto smiled. 'How are you feeling, Lindsay?'

'Sometimes okay, sometimes incredibly weak,' I answered. My chest felt tight now. *Why did I have to go through this with someone new?*

'Tell me about the other day.'

I did my best to recount the reeling spell I'd had in City Hall Park.

'Any emissions of blood?' Yatto asked, matter-of-factly.

'No, not lately.'

'Vomiting?'

'Not since last week.'

Dr Yatto got up, came across the desk to me. 'Do you mind?' he asked, as he cradled my face in his hands. He expressionlessly squeezed my cheeks with his thumbs, pulled down my eyes and peered into my pupils, under my lids.

'I know I'm getting worse,' I said.

Yatto released my face, nodded toward Medved. Then, for the first time since I had started seeing him, Medved actually smiled.

'It's not getting worse, Lindsay. That's why I asked Bob to consult. Your erythrocytic count has jumped back up. To twenty-eight hundred.'

I gave a double-take to make sure I had heard right. That it wasn't some kind of wishful dream I was playing out in my own head. 'But the spells . . . the hot and cold flashes? The other day, I felt like a war was going on in me.'

'There is a war,' Dr Yatto said. 'You're reproducing cells. Fighting off bad ones. The other day, that wasn't Negli's talking. That was you. That's how it feels to heal.'

I was stunned. My throat was dry. 'Say that again?'

'It's working, my dear,' Medved said. 'Your red blood count has increased for the second time in a row. I didn't want to tell you in case it was an error, but as Dr Yatto said, you're building new cells.'

I didn't know whether to laugh or cry. I stammered back, 'This is real? I can trust this?'

'This is *very* real,' Medved said, with a nod.

I stood up, my whole body shaking with disbelief. For a moment, all the inner hopes and joys that I had suppressed – a chance at my career, running on Marina Green, a life with Chris – came tumbling through my brain. For so long, I had been so scared to let them free. Now, they seemed to burst out of me.

Medved leaned forward and warned, 'You're not cured, Lindsay. We'll continue the treatments, twice a week. But this is hopeful – more than hopeful. This is good.'

'I don't know what to say.' My body was totally numb. 'I don't know what to do.'

'If I were you,' Dr Yatto said, 'I'd bring to mind the one thing you might've thought you'd miss most, and go do that today.'

I wandered out of the office in a haze. Down the elevator, through the sterile lobby, into a flowered court-yard that overlooked Golden Gate Park.

The sky was bluer than I'd ever seen it, the air off the Bay sweeter and cooler and more pure. I stood there, just hearing the beautiful sounds of my own breaths.

Something crept back into my life that had been away, something I never thought I would embrace again.

Hope.

Chapter One Hundred and Ten

'I have something to tell you.' I phoned Chris, my voice ringing with urgency. 'Can you meet me for lunch?'

'Sure. You bet. Where?' No doubt he thought I had something important to break on the case.

'Casa Boxer,' I said, with a smile.

'That urgent, huh?' Chris laughed into the phone. 'I must be starting to have a bad effect on you. When should I come?'

'I'm waiting now.'

It took him barely fifteen minutes to arrive at the door. I'd stopped on the way at Nestor's bakery and picked up some freshly baked cinnamon buns. Then I popped a bottle of Piper-Heidsieck that I had saved in my fridge.

Never in six years had I bugged out on a case in the middle of the afternoon. Especially one of this magnitude. But I felt no guilt, none at all. I thought of the craziest way I could break the good news.

I met him at the door, wrapped in a bedsheet. His big blue eyes went wide with surprise.

'I'll need to see some ID,' I grinned.

'Have you been drinking?' he said.

'No, but we're about to.' I pulled him into the bedroom.

At the sight of the champagne, he shook his head. 'What is it you want to tell me?'

'Later,' I said. I poured him a glass, and began to unfasten the buttons of his shirt. 'But trust me, it's good.'

'It's your birthday?' he said, smiling.

I let the bedsheet drop. 'I would never do this for just my birthday.'

'*My* birthday, then.' He grinned.

'Don't ask. I'll tell you later.'

'You broke the case!' he exclaimed. 'It *was* Joanna. You found something that broke the case.'

I put my fingers to his lips. 'Tell me that you love me.'

'I do love you,' he said.

'Tell me again, like you did at Heavenly. Tell me that you won't ever leave me.'

Maybe he sensed it was Negli's talking, some crazy hysteria, or that I just needed to feel close. He hugged me. 'I won't leave you, Lindsay. I'm right here.'

I took his shirt off – slowly, very slowly – then his trousers. He must've felt like the delivery boy who had stumbled into a sure thing. He was as hard as a rock.

I brought a glass of champagne to his lips, and we both took a sip from it.

'Okay, I'll just go with this. Shouldn't be too difficult,' he said huskily.

I drew him to the bed, and for the next hour we did one

thing I knew I would have missed most in the world.

We were in the middle of things when I felt the first terrifying rumbling.

At first it was so weird, as if the bed had speeded up and was rocking faster than us; then there was a deep, grinding sound coming from all directions, as if we were in an echo chamber; then the sound of glass breaking – my kitchen, a picture frame falling off the wall – and I knew, *we* knew.

'It's a goddamn quake,' I said.

I had been through many of these – anyone who lived here had – but it was startling and terrifying every time. You never knew if this was the Big One.

It wasn't. The room shook, a few dishes broke. Outside, I heard the bleat of sudden horns and triggered car alarms. The whole thing lasted maybe twenty seconds – two, three, four vibrating tremors.

I ran to the window. The city was still there. There was a rumble that sounded like a massive hump-back whale breaching underground.

Then it was still – eerie, insecure as if the whole town were holding on for balance. I heard more wailing sirens, the sound of voices shouting on the street.

'You think we should go?' I asked.

'Probably . . . we're cops.' He touched me again, and we melted into each other's arms. 'What the heck, we're Homicide, anyway.'

We kissed, and once again we were locked into a single, intertwined shape. I started to laugh. The list, I was thinking. The skybox at the Giant's match. Now an earthquake.

This sucker's starting to get pretty long.

My beeper suddenly went off. I cursed, rolled over, glanced at the screen. It was the office.

'Code one eleven,' I told Chris. Emergency Alert. 'Shit,' I muttered, 'it's just an earthquake.'

I sat up, pulled the sheet over me, called in on the phone next to the bed.

It was Roth buzzing me. Roth *never* buzzed me. *What was going on?* Immediately, I transferred to his line.

'Where are you?' he asked.

'Dusting off some debris,' I said, and smiled toward Chris.

'Get in here. Get in here fast,' he barked.

'What's going on, Sam? This about the quake?'

'Uh-uh,' he replied. 'Worse. Nicholas Jenks has escaped.'

Chapter One Hundred
and Eleven

As he sat shackled to the seat of the police van on the way back from Napa, Nicholas Jenks watched the impassive eyes of the patrolman across from him. He plotted, schemed. He wondered how much it would take to buy him his freedom.

One million? Two million? After all, what did the fool take home? Forty grand a year?

He figured the steely-eyed officer was someone above reproach, whose commitment to his duty was unquestioned. If he were writing it, that's who he would have put in the car with him.

Five million, then, he smirked. If *he* were writing it. That notion possessed a cold, punishing irony for him. He *had* written it.

Jenks shifted in his restraints – wrists cuffed, torso strapped to the seat. Only minutes earlier, he had stood in the red brick courthouse in Santa Rosa, while the prosecutor in her little Liz Claiborne suit pointed her finger at him. Over and over, she accused him of things only a mind as cultivated as his would think up and do.

All he could do was stare coldly while she accused him of being this *monster*. Sometime, he'd like to lock her in the law library and show her what he was really capable of.

Jenks caught a glimpse of the sky and the sun-browned hills through the narrow window on the rear door and tried to get a fix on their bearings. Novato. Just hitting Marin.

He pressed his face to the steel restraining wall. *He had to get out.* If he were writing it, there would always be a way out.

He looked at the guard. So what was the story. Joe Friday? What happened next?

'You married?' he asked.

The policeman stared through him at first, then he nodded.

'Kids?'

'Two,' he revealed, even breaking a slight smile.

No matter how hard they tried to resist, they were always fascinated to talk with the monster. The guy who killed the honeymooners. They could tell their wives and friends, justify the miserable six hundred a week they brought home. He was a celebrity.

'Wife work?' Jenks probed.

The cop nodded. 'Teacher. Business Ed. Eighth grade.'

Business Ed, huh? Maybe he would understand a business proposition.

'My wife used to work,' Jenks grunted back. 'My first wife. In retail. My current wife worked, too, in television.

'Course now, she only works *out*.'

The remark produced a snicker. The tight-assed bastard was loosening up.

Jenks saw a landmark he recognized. Twenty minutes from the Golden Gate Bridge. There wasn't much time left.

He glanced out the window at the patrol car following them. There was another in front. A bitter resignation took hold. There was no way out. No elegant escape. That was only in his books. This was life. He was screwed.

Then, out of nowhere, the police van lurched violently. Jenks was hurled forward in his seat, directly into the guard across from him. For a second, he wondered what was going on, then the van lurched again. He heard a rumbling.

It's a fucking quake!

Jenks could see the lead police car swerve to avoid the charge of another car. Then it skidded off the road.

One of the cops yelled, 'Shit,' but the van continued on.

Jenks spun around in panic, trying to hold onto anything that was fixed in the compartment. The van was bucking and jolting.

The police car following them jumped over a sudden hump in the highway, and, to his total amazement, *flipped*. The driver of Jenks's van looked behind him in shock. Then suddenly the other cop in front screamed for the driver to stop.

An 18-wheeler was breached in their way. They were headed right toward it. The van swerved, and when it did, the road buckled again. Then they were out of control – flying.

He was going to die here, Nicholas Jenks was sure. Die here, without anyone ever knowing the whole truth.

The van crashed into the stanchions of a Conoco station. It screeched to a stop, spinning twice on its side. The officer across from him was hurled against the metal wall. He was writhing and moaning as he looked at Jenks.

'Don't move,' the officer panted.

How the hell could he? He was still shackled to the seat.

Then came this horrid, wrenching sound, and they both looked up. The towering steel light above the station split like a redwood and crashed down on them. It smashed through the door of the van, striking the officer sitting in the back and probably killing the guard on impact.

Jenks was sure he would be killed – all the smoke, the screams, twisting of metal.

But he wasn't. He was clear. The streetlight had torn a hole in the side of the car, ripped his restraints right out of the seat. He was able to kick himself free, even with shackled hands and feet, and push himself through the gaping hole.

People were running in the street, screaming and in a panic. Motorists pulled off the road, some dazed, others jumping out of their vehicles to help.

This was it! He knew if he didn't run he would replay this moment for the rest of his life.

Nicholas Jenks crawled out of the van, dazed and

disorientated. He spotted no cops, only frightened passers-by streaking past. He limped out, and joined the chaotic street scene.

I'm free! Jenks exulted.

And I know who's setting me up. The cops won't get it in a million years.

Chapter One Hundred
and Twelve

It took about three minutes for Chris and me to throw on some clothes and head back to the Hall. In the rush, I never told him my news.

By disaster standards, the quake was nothing much – unless you had spent the past five weeks tracking down the country's most notorious killer. Most of the damage ended up confined to shattered storefronts and traffic accidents north of the city, but as we pushed our way through the clamoring throng of press in the Hall's lobby, the quake's biggest news crackled with the fierceness of a live wire:

The Bride and Groom killer was free.

Nicholas Jenks had managed to flee when the police van taking him back to jail flipped over outside Novato, the result of a chain of automobile accidents caused by the tremor. The policeman guarding him had been fatally injured. Two more, in the front seat of the overturned van, were hospitalized.

A huge Command Center was set up down the hall

from Homicide. Roth himself took charge. The place was crawling with brass from downtown and, of course, the press.

An APB was released, Jenks's description and photo distributed to cops on both sides of the bridge. All city exits and highway tolls were being monitored; traffic slowed to a crawl. Airports, hotels, and car-rental ports were put on alert.

Since we had tracked Nicholas Jenks down originally, Raleigh and I found ourselves at the center of the search.

We placed an immediate surveillance on his residence. Cops spread out all over the Sea Cliff area, from the Presidio to Lands End.

In searches like this, the first six hours are critical. The key was to contain Jenks in the grid where he had bolted, not let him contact anyone who could help his escape. He had no resources – no funds, no one to take him in. Jenks couldn't stay on the loose, unless he was a lot craftier than I thought he was.

The escape left me stunned. The man I had hunted down was free, but I was also left conflicted. *Were we hunting the right man?*

Everyone had a theory about where he might head – the wine country, east into Nevada. I had my own theory. I didn't think he'd go back to the house. He was too smart, and there was nothing to be gained there. I asked Roth if I could borrow Jacobi and Paul Chin, to play out a hunch.

I took Jacobi aside. 'I need you to do me a big favor, Warren.' I asked him to do surveillance outside Joanna

Wade's apartment on Russian Hill. Then I asked Chin to do the same outside the house of Jenks's former agent, Greg Marks.

If Jenks really believed he was being set up, those were two places he might go.

Jacobi gave me a look as if I were sending him out on another champagne lead. The entire corps of Inspectors was following up leads. 'What the hell, Lindsay . . . why?'

I needed him to trust me. 'Because it struck me as funny, too,' I said, begging his support, 'why Jenks would leave that damn tuxedo jacket behind. I think he might go after Joanna. Trust me on it.'

With Warren and Paul Chin in place, there was nothing I could do except monitor the wires. Six hours into the search, there was still no sign of Nicholas Jenks.

Chapter One Hundred and Thirteen

Around four, I saw Jill pushing her way through the crowd buzzing outside my office. She looked ready to kill somebody, probably me.

'I'm glad you're here,' I said, grabbing her. 'Trust me, please, Jill.'

'Cindy's downstairs,' she said. 'Let's go talk.'

We sneaked out, and were able to find her amid a throng of reporters clawing at anyone who came down from the third floor. We called Claire, and in five minutes we were sitting around a table at a coffee shop just down the block. Jenks's escape had thrown all of my speculations into disarray.

'You still believe he's innocent?' Jill pressed the issue immediately.

'That depends on where he turns up next.' I informed them how I had stationed a couple of men around the homes of Greg Marks and Joanna Wade.

'Even now?' Jill shook her head and looked close to blowing. 'Innocent men don't run from police custody, Lindsay.'

'Innocent people might,' I said, 'if they don't believe the justice system is being just!'

Claire looked around with a nervous swallow. 'Ladies, it strikes me we're entering into very sensitive territory here, all right? We've got a manhunt trying to locate Jenks – he could be shot on sight – and at the same time, we're talking about trying to firm up a case against someone else. If this comes out, heads will roll. I'm looking at some of those pretty heads right now.'

'If you *really* believe this, Lindsay, you need to take it to someone,' Jill lectured me. 'Roth, Mercer.'

'Mercer's away. And right now, everybody's focused on locating Jenks. Anyway, who the hell would believe this? As you say, all I have is a bunch of hypotheticals.'

'Have you told Raleigh?' asked Claire.

I nodded.

'What does he think?'

'Right now, he can't get past the hair. Jenks's escape didn't help my case.'

'I knew there was something I liked about that guy.' Jill finally smiled thinly.

I looked at Claire for support.

'It's hard to argue your side of things, Lindsay,' she sighed. 'That said, your instincts are usually good.'

'So then bust in on Joanna, like Lindsay proposed,' said Cindy. The more I was around her, the more I loved her.

Things had suddenly gotten very sticky in the way of accountability. I turned to Claire. 'Is there anything we might have missed that could implicate Joanna?'

She shook her head. 'We've been through all that. All the evidence points the finger *directly* at Nicholas Jenks.'

'Claire, I'm talking about something that was there, right in front of us, that we just didn't see.'

'I want to be with you on this, Lindsay,' Claire said, 'but like I said, we've been through it. Everything.'

'There's got to be something. Something that could tell us if the killer is male or female. If Joanna did it, she's no different than any killer I've tracked down. She *left* something. We just haven't seen it. Jenks left something – or someone left it for him – and we found him.'

'And we ought to be out looking for him now,' Jill said sternly, 'before we end up with Couple Number Four.'

I felt alone, but I just couldn't surrender. It wouldn't be right. 'Please,' I begged Claire, 'go through everything one more time. I really think we've got the wrong man.'

Chapter One Hundred and Fourteen

In the dim light of the makeup mirror, the killer sat transfixed by soft blue eyes that were about to become gray.

The first thing was to smear her hair until all the blonde had been dyed away, then brush it back *smooth*, a hundred times, until it had lost its luster and shine.

'You forced me into this,' she said to the changing face. 'Forced me to come out one more time. I should have expected as much. You love games, don't you, Nick?'

With a cotton swab, she applied the base, a clear, sticky balm with a glue-like smell. She dabbed it over her temples, down the curve of her chin, in the soft space between her upper lip and her nose.

Then, with a tweezer, she matted on the hair. Tufts of reddish brown.

The face was almost complete. But the eyes . . . anyone could see they were still hers.

She slipped out a pair of tinted contacts from the case. Moistening them, stretching her lids to insert each one.

She blinked, well satisfied with the result.

The familiarity was gone. The change was complete. Her eyes now reflected a steely, lifeless gray.

Nicholas's color.

She was him.

Chapter One Hundred and Fifteen

Claire's call woke me out of a deep sleep.

'Come down here,' her voice commanded.

I blinked groggily at the clock. It was ten after five in the morning. 'Come down *where*?' I moaned.

'I'm at the damn office. In the damn lab. The guard at the front counter will let you in. *Come right now.*'

I heard the urgency in her voice and it took only seconds for me to come to my senses. 'You're at the lab?'

'Since two-thirty, sleepyhead. It's about Nicholas Jenks. I think I found something, and Lindsay, it is a mindblower.'

At that hour, it didn't take me more than ten minutes to get to the morgue. I parked in the circular area outside the coroner's entrance reserved for official vehicles and rushed in, my hair uncombed, dressed only in a sweatshirt and jeans.

The guard buzzed and let me through. He was expecting me. Claire met me at the entrance to the lab.

'Okay,' I said, 'my expectations are high.'

She didn't answer. Only pressed me up against the door

of the lab, without a word of greeting or explanation.

'We're back at the Hyatt,' she started on. 'Murder Number One. David Brandt is about to open the door. Pretend you're the groom,' she said, placing her hand on my shoulder and gently easing me down, 'and I'll be the killer. I surprise you as you open the door, and stab – *right-handed* – not that it makes any difference now.'

She thrust her fist in the space under my left breast. 'So you fall, and that's where we find you, later, at the scene.'

I nodded, letting her know that I was following along so far.

'So what do we find around you?' she asked, wide-eyed.

I made a mental picture of the scene. 'Champagne bottle, tuxedo jacket.'

'True, but that's not where I'm headed.'

'Blood . . . a lot of blood.'

'Closer. Remember, he died of a cardiac, electro-mechanical collapse. We simply assumed he was scared to death.'

I stood up, gazed down at the floor. Then suddenly I saw it as if I were there with the body.

'Urine.'

'Right!' exclaimed Claire. 'We find a small residue of urine. On his shoes, on the floor. About six cubic centi-meters' worth, that I was able to save. It seemed logical that it belonged to the groom – voiding is a natural response to sudden fear, or death. But I was thinking last night, there were traces of urine in Cleveland, too. And here, back at the Hyatt, I never even had it tested. *Why would I?* I always assumed it was from David Brandt.

'But if you were here, crumpled on the floor, and I was the killer standing above you, and the pee was *here*,' she said, pointing to the floor around me, 'who the hell's urine would it be?'

Our eyes locked in one of those shining moments of epiphany. 'The killer's,' I said.

Claire smiled at her bright student. 'The annals of forensic medicine are rich with examples of murderers "getting off" when they kill, so *peeing* isn't so far-fetched. Your nerves would be on end. And good old compulsive me, obsessed down to the last detail, refrigerates it in a vial, never knowing what for. And the thing that makes this all come together is, *urine can be tested.*'

'Tested? For what?'

'For *sex*, Lindsay. Urine can reveal one's sex.'

'Jesus, Claire.' I was stunned.

She took me into the lab to a counter with two microscopes, some chemicals in bottles, and a device I recognized from college chemistry classes as a centrifuge.

'There aren't any flashing gender signs in urine, but there are things to look for. First, I took a sample and spun it down in the centrifuge with this KOH stain, which is something we can use to isolate impurities in blood cultures.' She motioned for me to look in the first scope.

'See these tiny, filament-like branches with little clusters of cells like grapes? It's candida albicans.'

I looked at her blankly.

'Yeast cells, honey. This urine's laced with high deposits

of yeast. Boys don't get them.'

I started to smile, but before I could say anything, she dragged me on. 'Then I put the other sample under the scope, and brought it up three thousand mag. Check this out.'

I lowered myself over the scope and squinted in.

'You see those dark, crescent-shaped cells swimming around?' Claire asked.

'Uh-huh.'

'Red blood cells. Lots of them.'

I lifted my head off the scope and looked up.

'They wouldn't show up in a man's urine. Not to anywhere near this degree. Not unless they've got a bleeding kidney, which to my knowledge, none of our principals show any signs of.'

'Or,' I shook my head slowly, 'unless the killer was menstruating.'

Chapter One Hundred
and Sixteen

I stared at Claire as the news settled in my mind. Nicholas Jenks had been telling the truth all along.

He wasn't in the room when David and Melanie Brandt were killed that night. Nor in Napa. Probably nowhere near the Hall of Fame in Cleveland. I had hated Jenks so much I couldn't see past it. None of us had been able to get past the fact that we wanted him to be guilty.

All the evidence – the hair, the jacket, the champagne – had been an incredible deception; Jenks was a master of the surprise ending, but someone had set the master up.

I put my arms around Claire and hugged her. 'You're the best.'

'You're damn right I am. I don't know what it proves,' she answered, patting my back, 'but the person standing over that poor boy at the murder scene was a woman. And I'm just as sure that she stabbed David Brandt to death with her right hand.'

My mind was spinning. Jenks was loose, hundreds of cops on the chase – and he was innocent.

'So?' Claire looked at me and smiled.

'It's the second best news I've heard today,' I said.

'Second best?'

I took her hand. I told Claire what Medved had shared with me. We hugged again. We even did a little victory dance. Then both of us got back to work.

Chapter One Hundred
and Seventeen

Upstairs at my desk, I radioed Jacobi. Poor guy, he was still sitting outside Joanna Wade's home at the corner of Filbert and Hyde. 'You all right, Warren?'

'Nothing that a shower and a couple of hours' sleep wouldn't improve.'

'Tell me what's going on.'

'What's going on,' Jacobi recited, as if he were resentfully going over his log. 'Four-fifteen yesterday afternoon, target comes out, struts down the block to Gold's Gym. Six-ten, target re-emerges, proceeds down block to Pasqua Coffee, comes out with plastic bag. I suspect it's Almond Roast. Goes into the Contempo Casuals boutique, comes out empty. I gotta figure the new fall stuff hasn't arrived yet, Boxer. She makes her way home. Lights go on on the third floor. Is it chicken I smell, I don't know – I'm so fucking hungry I might be dreaming. Lights go out about ten twenty-five. Since then, she's been doing what I'd like to be doing. Why you got me out here like a rookie, Lindsay?'

'Because Nicholas Jenks is going to try to find his

ex-wife. He believes she's setting him up. I think he knows that Joanna is the murderer.'

'You trying to cheer me up, Boxer, bring meaning into my life?'

'Maybe. And how's this . . . I think she's guilty, too. I want to know immediately if you spot Jenks.'

Chris Raleigh came in about eight, tossing a surprised look at my bleary eyes and disheveled appearance. 'You should try a brush in the morning.'

'Claire called me at five-ten. I was in the morgue at five-thirty.'

He looked at me funny. 'What the hell for?'

'It's a little hard to explain. I want you to meet some friends of mine.'

'Friends? At eight in the morning?'

'Uh-huh. My girlfriends.'

He looked completely confused. 'What am I not following here?'

'Chris,' I seized his arm. 'I think we broke the case.'

Chapter One Hundred and Eighteen

An hour later, I got everyone together on the Jenks case, hopefully for the last time.

There had been a few alleged sightings of Nicholas Jenks – in Tiburon down by the Marina, and south of Market, huddled around a gathering of homeless men. Both of them proved false. He had eluded us, and the longer he remained free, the greater the speculation.

We got together in a vacant interrogation room that Sex Crimes sometimes used. Claire smuggled Cindy up from the lobby, then we rang down for Jill.

'I see we've loosened the requirements,' Jill commented, when she came in and saw Chris.

Raleigh looked surprised, too. 'Don't mind me – I'm just the token male.'

'You remember Claire, and Jill Bernhardt from the District Attorney's office,' I said. 'Cindy, you may recall from Napa. This is the team.'

Slowly, Chris looked from one face to another, until he

settled on me. 'You've been working on this, independently of the Task Force?'

'Don't ask,' said Jill, plunking herself down in a wooden chair. 'Just listen.'

In the cramped narrow room, all eyes turned to me. I looked at Claire. 'You want to begin?'

She nodded, scanned the group as if she were presenting at a medical conference. 'On Lindsay's urging, I spent all last night going through the three case files; I was looking for anything that would implicate Joanna. At first, nothing. Other than coming to the same conclusion I had before that, from the pronounced downward angle of the first victims' wounds, the killer was right-handed. Jenks is *left-handed*. But it was clear that it wouldn't stick.

'Then something struck me that I had never noticed before. At both the first and third crime scenes there were traces of urine. Individually, I guess neither the Medical Examiner in Cleveland nor I ever thought much of it. But as I thought through the crime scenes in my head, the *locations* of these deposits didn't make any sense. Early this morning, very early, I rushed down here and performed some tests.'

There was barely a breath in the room.

'The urine we found at the Grand Hyatt demonstrated large deposits of yeast, as well as atypically large counts of red blood cells. Red blood cells in that amount appear in the urine during menstruation. Coupled with the yeast, there's no doubt in my mind that the urine was a woman's. A woman killed David Brandt, and I have no doubt we'll find a woman was in the stall in Cleveland, too.'

Jill blinked back, dumbfounded. Cindy's bright red lips parted in an incredulous half-smile.

Raleigh just shook his head.

'Jenks didn't do it,' I said. 'Joanna must have. He abused her, then he dumped her for his new wife, Chessy, just as he was about to strike it rich. Joanna tried to sue him twice, unsuccessfully. Ended up with a settlement many times smaller than she would have gotten a year later. She watched him gain celebrity and wealth, and a new, seemingly happy, life.'

Chris looked amazed. 'You really believe a woman could physically pull this off? The first victims were stabbed, the second were dragged twenty, thirty yards to where they were dumped.'

'You haven't seen her,' I replied. 'She knew how to set Jenks up. She knew his tastes, his investments, and had access to his possessions. She even worked at Saks.'

Cindy chipped in, 'She was one of the few people who would've been aware of *Always A Bridesmaid*.'

I nodded toward Jill. 'She had the means, the motive, and I'm damned sure she had the desire.'

A really heavy silence filled the room.

'So how do you want to play this?' Chris finally said. 'Half the force is looking for Jenks.'

'I want to inform Mercer, try to get Jenks brought in without someone killing him. Then I want to go ahead and pierce Joanna's cover. Phone calls, credit cards. If she was in Cleveland, something will tie her there. I think you'd agree now,' I said to Jill, 'we have enough to authorize a search.'

Jill nodded, at first hesitantly, then with more resolve. 'It's just impossible to believe that after all this, we now have to defend that bastard.'

Suddenly, there was a loud rap on the glass window of the door. John Keresty, an Inspector on the Task Force, broke in on us.

'It's Jenks. He's just been sighted. He's up in Pacific Heights.'

Chapter One Hundred
and Nineteen

Raleigh and I leaped up, almost as one, racing back to the Command Center.

It appeared Jenks had been seen in the lobby of a small hotel called the El Drisco. A bellboy spotted him, free of his cuffs. Now he was on the streets, somewhere up in Pacific Heights.

Why there? My mind ratcheted through the possibilities. Then it became clear.

Greg Marks lived up there.

I radioed Paul Chin, who was still sitting surveillance on the agent's apartment. 'Paul, be on the alert,' I told him. 'Jenks may be headed your way. He was seen in Pacific Heights.'

There was a beep on my cell phone. It was Jacobi. Everything was happening at once.

'Boxer, there's an All Available Units on Jenks up in the Heights about a mile from here. I'm headed up there.'

'Warren, *don't leave!*' I shouted into the receiver. I still believed Joanna was the murderer. I couldn't leave her unmonitored, especially with Jenks on the loose. 'Stay at your post.'

'This takes precedence,' Jacobi argued. 'Besides, nothing's happening here. I'll call a radio car to relieve.'

'*Jacobi!*' I shouted, but he had already signed off and was on his way to the Heights. I turned to Chris. 'Warren's left Joanna's.'

Suddenly Karen, our civilian clerical, shouted for me. 'Lindsay, call for you on One.'

'We're headed out,' I hollered back to her. I had strapped on my gun, grabbed the keys to my car. 'Who is it?'

'Says you'd want to talk to him about the Jenks case,' Karen said. 'Says his name is Phillip Campbell.'

Chapter One Hundred and Twenty

I froze, fixed on Raleigh, then I lunged back toward my desk.

I signaled Karen to patch it through. At the same time, I hissed under my breath to Raleigh, 'Start a trace.'

I waited in a trance; seconds could mean the difference. The breath was tightening in my chest. Then I picked up.

'You know who this is,' Nicholas Jenks's arrogant voice declared.

'I know who it is. Where are you?'

'Not a chance, Inspector. I only called to let you know, whatever happens, I didn't kill any of them. I'm not a murderer.'

'I know that,' I told him.

He seemed surprised. 'You do?'

I couldn't let Jenks know who it was. Not with him on the loose. 'I promise, we can prove it wasn't you. Tell me where you are.'

'Hey, guess what? I don't believe you,' Jenks declared. 'Besides, it's too late. I told you I'd take this into my own hands. I'm going to solve these murders for you.'

Jenks could hang up any moment and we'd lose him. This was my only chance. 'Jenks, I'll meet you. Anywhere you want.'

'Why would I want to meet you? I've seen enough of you to last a lifetime.'

'Because I know who did it,' I told him.

What he said next jolted me.

'So do I.'

And then he hung up.

Chapter One Hundred and Twenty-One

Sixth ... Market ... Taylor ... the streets shot by, the top hat on the roof of Chris Raleigh's car flashing wildly.

Ellis.

Larkin.

We shot up Hyde, climbing through the lights, then rocked over the bumps as we careened over Nob Hill. In a matter of minutes, we arrived in Russian Hill.

Joanna lived on the top floor of a townhouse on the corner of Filbert and Hyde. We were no longer waiting to flush her out. Jenks was loose; he had probably homed in on her. Now it was a matter of preventing more killing.

We slowed, cut the lights as we wove through the quiet, hilly streets. The house had been unguarded for maybe fifteen minutes. I didn't know if Joanna was up there. Or where the hell Jenks was.

Chris pulled to the curb. We checked our guns, and decided how to proceed.

Then I saw a sight that tore the breath from my lungs.

Chris saw it, too. 'Christ, he's here.'

From a narrow alley two houses away, a man in a beard and baggy sports coat emerged. He looked both ways as he hit the street, then he made his way down the block.

Raleigh pulled out his gun and reached for the door. I looked closer in disbelief, grabbed onto him. 'Wait. Look again, Chris.'

We both gaped in amazement. He had the same look: the short, reddish-gray hair, the same unmistakable beard.

But it wasn't Jenks.

The figure was thinner, fairer; the hair slicked back hiding a longer length, not cut short. I could see that much.

It was a woman.

'That's Joanna,' I said.

'Where's Jenks?' Chris grunted. 'This just keeps getting creepier.'

We watched the figure slink down the block as a frenzy of possibilities ran through my mind. This *was* creepy.

'I'll follow her,' Chris suggested. 'You go upstairs – make sure it's her. I'll radio for support. Go on, Lindsay. Go!'

The next moment, I was out of the car, crossing the street toward Joanna's apartment. Chris eased the Taurus down the block.

I pushed random buttons until a woman's angry voice replied. I identified myself, and a gray-haired woman emerged from the apartment next to the front door. She announced that she was the landlady.

I badged her, got her to locate a key pronto. Then I told

her to get back in her apartment.

I had my gun out, took off the safety. A film of hot sweat was building up on my face and neck.

I reached Joanna's apartment on the third floor. My heart was pounding. '*Careful, Lindsay,*' a voice inside me said, then came a cautioning chill. Could Nicholas Jenks be here?

I had certainly entered enough hostile environments during my police career, but none worse than this. I inserted the key, turned, and when the lock caught, pushed the door with my foot.

It swung open, revealing the bright, stylishly decorated apartment of Joanna Wade.

'Anyone here?' I shouted.

No one answered.

There was no one in the living room. Same for the dining room, kitchen. A coffee mug in the sink. The *Chronicle* out and folded to the Datebook section.

No sign that I was in the home of a psycho. That bothered me.

I moved on. More magazines – *Food and Wine, San Francisco* – on the coffee-table. A few yoga posture books.

In the bedroom, the bed was unmade. The entire place had a relaxed, unforbidding feel.

Joanna Wade lived like any ordinary woman. She read, had coffee in her kitchen, taught exercise, paid her bills. Killers were preoccupied with their victims. This didn't make sense.

I turned into the master bath.

'Oh, damn it!' The case had taken a last, irrevocable turn.

On the floor, in her workout tights, was Joanna Wade.

She was leaned against the tub looking at me, but not really – actually, she was still looking at her killer. Her eyes were wide and terrified.

He had used a knife. Jenks? If not him, then who?

'Oh, Christ,' I gasped. My head was spinning and it *hurt*.

I hurried over to her, but there was nothing I could do. Everything had twisted again. I knelt over the dead woman as a final, shuddering thought filled my mind:

If it wasn't Joanna, who was Chris following?

Chapter One Hundred and Twenty-Two

Within minutes, two blue-and-whites screeched to a stop outside. I directed the patrol officers upstairs to the grisly body of Joanna, but my thoughts had turned to Chris. And whoever he was following.

I had been up in the apartment for ten, maybe twelve minutes, without a word from him. I was worried. He was following a murderer, and a murderer who had just killed Joanna Wade.

I ran downstairs to an open patrol car and called in what had happened to Command Central. A riot of doubts was crashing in my mind. Could it somehow have been Jenks, after all? Could Jill have been right? Was he manipulating us, right from the start? Had he set everything up, even the sighting in Pacific Heights?

But if it was him, *why* would he kill her now? Was Joanna's death something I could have prevented? What in hell was going on? Where was Chris, damn it!

My cell phone finally beeped. To my relief, it was Chris.

'Where are you?' I bleated. 'You had me scared to death. Don't do that to me.'

'I'm down by the Marina. The suspect's in a blue Saab.'

'Chris, be careful. It's *not* Joanna. Joanna's dead. She was stabbed a bunch of times in her apartment.'

'Dead?' he muttered. I could feel the frantic question slowly sinking into his mind. 'Then who is driving the Saab up ahead of me?'

'Tell me where you are exactly.'

'Chestnut and Scott. The suspect just pulled up to the curb. The suspect is getting out of the car.'

Somehow, this sounded familiar. *Chestnut and Scott?* What was down there? In the tumult of green-and-whites screeching up in front of Joanna's building and reporting in, I raked my mind for a connection.

'He's heading away from the car, Lindsay. He's starting to run.'

Then it hit me. The photo I had picked up at Jenks's house. The beautiful and unmistakable moonlit dome. The Palace of Fine Arts.

It was where he had been married.

'I think I know where he's going!' I shouted. 'The Palace of Fine Arts.'

Chapter One Hundred and Twenty-Three

I hopped into one of the parked radio cars and took off with the siren blaring all the way to the Presidio.

It took me no more than seven minutes, with traffic wildly shifting out of my way, to speed down Lombard over to Richardson to the south tip of the Presidio. Up ahead, the golden rotunda of the Palace of Fine Arts loomed powerfully above a calm, gleaming pond.

I saw Chris's blue Taurus pulled up diagonally across from the tip of the park and jackknifed mine to a halt next to it. I didn't see a sign of any other cops.

Why hadn't any backup arrived? What the hell was going on now?

I clicked my gun off safety and made my way into the park underneath the giant rotunda. No way I was waiting.

I was startled by people running toward me, away from the rotunda grounds.

'Someone's shooting,' one of them screamed.

Suddenly, my legs were flying. 'Everyone out! I'm San

Francisco police!' I yelled, as I bumped through the people rushing by.

'There's a maniac with a gun,' someone sobbed.

I ran around the pond alongside a massive wall of marble colonnade. There was no sound up ahead. No more shots.

Leading with my gun, I rounded corners until I was in sight of the main rotunda. Huge Corinthian columns soared above me, capped with ornate, heroic carvings.

I could hear voices in the distance: a woman's mocking tone. 'It's just you and me, Nick. Imagine that. Isn't it romantic?'

And a man's, Jenks's: 'Look at you, you're pathetic. As always.'

The voices echoed out of the huge dome of the main rotunda.

Where was Chris? And where was our backup?

Cops should have been here by now. I held my breath, straining to hear the first police siren. Every step I took, I heard my own footsteps echoing to the roof.

'What do you want?' I heard Jenks's cry reverberating off the stone. Then the woman shouting back, 'I want you to remember them. All the women you fucked.'

Still no sign of Chris. I was tight with worry.

I decided to go around the side of a row of low arches that ran down to the voices. I ducked around the corner of the colonnade.

Then I saw Chris. Oh, God! He was sitting there, propped against a pillar, watching everything unfold.

My first reaction was to say something like, 'Chris, get down, someone will see you.' It was one of those slow-motion perceptions where my eyes were faster than my mind.

Then my body was seized with horrible fright, nausea, and sadness.

Chris wasn't watching, and he wasn't hiding.

The front of his shirt was covered with blood.

All my police training gave way. I wanted to scream, to cry out. It took everything I had to hold it in.

Two dark bloodstains were soaking through Chris's shirt. My legs were paralyzed. Somehow I forced myself over to him. I knelt down. My heart was pounding.

Chris's eyes were remote, his face as gray as stone. I checked for a pulse and felt the slightest rhythm of a heartbeat.

'Oh, Chris no.' I stifled a sob.

When I spoke, he looked up, eyes glimmering as he saw my face. His lips parted into a weak smile. His breath wheezed, heavy and labored.

My eyes filled with tears. I applied pressure to the holes in his chest, trying to push back the blood. 'Oh Chris, hang in there. Hang in there. I'll get help.'

He reached for my arm. He tried to speak, but it was only a weak, guttural whisper.

'Don't talk. Please.'

I raced back toward the patrol car and fumbled with the transmitter until I heard Dispatch. 'Officer down, officer down,' I shouted. 'Four-oh-six. I repeat, four-oh-six!' – the statewide call for alarm. 'Officer shot, rotunda of the Palace of Fine Arts. Need immediate EMS and SWAT backup. Possible Nicholas Jenks sighting. Second officer on the scene inside. Repeat, four-oh-six, emergency.'

As soon as the dispatcher repeated the location back to me with a 'Copy,' I threw down the transmitter and headed back inside.

When I got to him, Chris was still holding on to small breaths. A bubble of blood popped on his lip. 'I love you, Chris,' I whispered, squeezing his hand.

Voices rang out ahead in the rotunda. I couldn't make them out, but it was the same man and woman. Then there was a gunshot!

'Go,' Chris whispered. 'I'm holding on.'

Our hands touched.

'I've got rear,' he muttered with a smile. Then he pushed me away.

I scurried ahead, my gun drawn, glancing back twice. Chris was watching – *watching my back*.

I ran in a low crouch all the way down the length of the row of columns closest in, clear up to the side of the main rotunda. The voices echoed, intensified. My eyes were riveted.

They were straight across the basilica. Jenks, in a plain white shirt. He was holding one arm, bleeding. He'd been shot.

And across from him, holding a gun and dressed in men's clothes, stood Chessy Jenks.

Chapter One Hundred and Twenty-Four

S he looked like a bizarre disfigurement of the beautiful woman she was. Her hair was matted and dyed a shade of gray and red. Her face still carried the marks of her disguise, a man's sideburns and flecks of a grayish-red beard.

She was holding a gun tightly, pointing it directly at him. 'I have a present for you, Nick.'

'A present?' Jenks said, in desperation. 'What the hell are you talking about?'

'That's why we're here. I want to renew our vows.' Chessy took a small pouch out of her jacket and tossed it at his feet. 'Go ahead. Open it.'

Nicholas Jenks knelt, stiffly, and picked up the pouch. He opened it, the contents spilling into his palm. His eyes bulged in horror.

The six missing rings.

'Chessy, Christ,' he stammered. 'You're out of your mind. What do you want me to do with *these*?' He held out a ring. 'These will put you in the gas chamber.'

'No, Nick,' Chessy said, shaking her head. 'I want you to swallow them. Get rid of the evidence for me.'

Jenks's face twitched in apprehension. 'You want me to *what*?'

'Swallow them. Each one is someone you've destroyed. Someone whose beauty you've killed. They were innocent – like *me*. Little girls on our wedding days. You killed us all, Nick – me, Kathy, Joanna. So now give us something back. *With this ring, I do pledge.*'

Jenks glared and shouted at her. 'That's enough, Chessy!'

'I'll say when it's enough. You love games, so play the game. Play *my* game this time. *Swallow them!*' She pointed the gun. 'No sense pretending I won't shoot, is there, dear?'

Jenks took one of the rings, raised it to his lips. His hand was shaking badly.

'That was Melanie, Nicky. You would've liked her. Athletic . . . a skier . . . a diver. Your type, huh? She fought me to the end. But you don't like us to fight, do you? You like to be in total control.'

She cocked the gun and leveled it at Jenks's head.

Jenks put the ring in his mouth. With a sickened expression, he forced it down his throat.

Chessy was losing it. She was sobbing, trembling. I didn't think I could wait any longer.

'Police,' I yelled. I stepped forward, two hands on my .38, leveling it at her.

She spun at me, not even showing surprise, then back to

Jenks. 'He has to be punished!'

'It's over,' I said, carefully advancing toward her. 'Please, Chessy, no more killing.'

As if she suddenly realized what she had become, the sickening things she'd done, she looked at me. 'I'm sorry . . . I'm sorry for everything that happened – except this!'

Then she fired. At Jenks.

I fired, too – at her.

Chessy's slender body flew backwards, hitting the wall hard and crumpling against it. Her beautiful eyes widened and her mouth sagged open.

I looked and saw that she'd missed Jenks. He was staring at her in disbelief. He didn't think she could do it, didn't think she hated him that much. He still believed he controlled Chessy, and probably that she loved him.

I hurried to her, but it was too late. Her eyes were already glazed and the blood was streaming from her chest. I held her head and thought that she was so beautiful – like Melanie, Rebecca, Kathy – and now she was dead, too.

Nicholas Jenks turned toward me with a gasp of relief. 'I told you . . . I told you, I was innocent.'

I looked at him in disgust. Eight people were dead. The brides and grooms, Joanna, now his own wife. *I told you I was innocent.* Is that what he thought?

I swung, my fist catching him square in the teeth. I felt something shatter as Jenks dropped to his knees. 'So much for your innocence, Jenks!'

Chapter One Hundred and Twenty-Five

I was running and I realized that I no longer knew exactly what I was doing, where I was. Somehow my instincts brought me back to where Chris had been shot.

He was still up against the pillar in the same position. He looked as if he'd been waiting for me to return.

I rushed up to him, knelt down as close as I could get. I could see police and the EMS medical crew finally arriving. What had taken them so long?

'What happened?' Chris whispered. I could barely hear him.

'I got her, Chris. Chessy Jenks was the killer.'

He managed to nod his head. 'That's my girl,' he whispered.

Then Chris smiled faintly and he died on me.

I never would have imagined, or dreamed, that Chris would be the first to die. That was the most terrible and dreadful shock. It was unthinkable, impossible to believe.

I put my head down close to his chest. There was no

movement, no breath, just a terrifying stillness. Everything seemed so unreal.

Then the medics were working on Chris, doing heroic, but useless things, and I just sat there holding his hand.

I felt hollowed out and empty and incredibly sad. I was sobbing, but I had something to say to him; I had to tell Chris one last thing.

'Medved told me, Chris. I'm going to be okay.'

Chapter One Hundred
and Twenty-Six

I couldn't go near my office at the Hall. I was given a one-week leave. I figured I'd take another of my own time on top of that. I sat around, watched some videos of old movies, went for my treatments, took a jog or two down by the Marina.

I even cooked, and sat out on the terrace overlooking the Bay, just as I had with Chris that first night. On one of those nights, I got really drunk and started playing with my pistol. It was Sweet Martha who talked me off the ledge. That, and the fact that if I killed myself, I would be betraying Chris's memory. I couldn't do that. Also, the girls would never have forgiven me.

I felt a hole tear at my heart, larger and more painful than anything I had ever felt, even with Negli's. I felt a void of connection, of commitment. Claire called me three times a day, but I just couldn't speak for very long, not even to her.

'It wasn't you, Lindsay. There was nothing you could've done,' she consoled.

'I kind of know that,' I replied. But I just couldn't convince myself it was true.

Mostly, I tried to persuade myself I still felt a sense of purpose. The Bride and Groom murders were solved. Nicholas Jenks was shamelessly milking his celebrity status on *Dateline* and *20/20*. Negli's seemed to be in remission. Chris was gone. I tried to think of what I would do next. Nothing very appealing came to mind.

Then I remembered what I had told Claire when my fears of Negli's were the strongest. *'Nailing this guy was the one clear thing that gave me the strength to go on.'*

It wasn't just about right or wrong. It wasn't about guilt or innocence. It was about what I was good at, and what I loved to do.

Four days after the shooting, I went to Chris's funeral. It was in a Catholic church, out in Hayward, where he was from.

I took my place in the ranks, with Roth, Jacobi. With Chief Mercer, who was dressed in blues. But my heart was aching so bad. I wanted to be up near Chris. I wanted to be next to him.

I watched his ex-wife and his two young boys struggling to keep it together. I was thinking about how very close I had come to their lives. And they didn't know it.

Hero cop, they were eulogizing him.

He was a marketing guy, I smiled. And then I started to cry.

Of all people, I felt Jacobi grasp my hand. And of all the improbable things, I found myself holding his back. 'Go ahead,' he seemed to be saying. 'Go ahead and weep.'

Afterward, at the graveside, I went up to Chris's ex-wife, Marion. 'I wanted to meet you,' I said. 'I was with him when he died.'

She looked at me with the fragile courage only another woman could understand.

'I know who you are,' she said, with a compassionate smile. 'You *are* pretty. Chris told me you were pretty. And smart.'

I smiled and took her hand. We both squeezed hard.

'He also said you were very brave.'

I felt my eyes well up. Then she took my arm and said the one thing I wanted most to hear.

'Why don't you stand with us, Lindsay.'

The Department gave Chris a hero's burial. Sad, mournful bagpipers opened the service. Row after row of cops in dress blues. A twenty-one-gun salute.

When it was over, I found myself walking back to the car, wondering what in God's name I was going to do next.

At the cemetery gates I spotted Cindy and Jill and Claire. They were waiting there for me.

I didn't move. I stood there, my legs trembling badly. They could see that if they didn't make the first move, I could break down.

'Why don't you ride back with us?' Claire said.

My voice cracked. I could barely utter the words. 'It was supposed to be me, not him,' I said to them. Then one by one they all came up and hugged me.

I put my arms around all of them and melted into their

embrace as deeply as I could. All four of us were crying. 'Don't ever leave me, guys.'

'*Leave?*' Jill said, with wide eyes.

'None of us,' promised Cindy. 'We're a team, remember? We will *always* be together.'

Claire took hold of my arm. 'We love you, sweetie,' she whispered.

The four of us walked arm-in-arm out of the cemetery. A cooling breeze was blowing in our faces, drying our tears.

At six o'clock that night, I was back at work inside the Hall of Justice.

There was something important I had to do.

In the lobby, almost the first thing you see, there's a large marble plaque. On it are the names and dates of all the men and women who wore the uniform of the SFPD and died in the line of duty. Tonight, a mason is working on the plaque.

It's an unwritten rule on the force, you never count them. But tonight, I do so. There are ninety-three, starting with James S. Coonts on October 5, 1878, when the SFPD was first formed.

Tomorrow there will be one more: Christopher John Raleigh. The Mayor will be there; Mercer, too. The reporters who cover the city beat. Marion and the boys. They will memorialize him as a hero cop. I will be there, too.

But tonight, I don't want speeches or ceremonies. Tonight, I want it to be just him and me.

The mason finishes up the engraving of his name. I wait

while he sands the marble, vacuums away the last particle of dust. Then I walk up, and run my hand over the smooth marble. Over his name.

Christopher John Raleigh.

The mason looks at me. He can see the pain welling in my eyes. 'You knew him, huh?' he says quietly.

I nod, and from somewhere deep in my heart, a smile comes forth. *I knew him.*

'Partner,' I say.

Epilogue

Coup de Grâce

Chapter One Hundred and Twenty-Seven

I have come to learn that murder investigations always have loose ends and questions that cry out to be answered. Always.

But not this time.

I was home one night about a month after we buried Chris. I had finished dinner for one, fed and walked Her Sweetness, when there was a knock on the door – a single, authoritative rap.

I hadn't buzzed anyone up from downstairs, so I went and looked through the peephole before I opened up. I couldn't believe my eyes. It was Nicholas Jenks.

He had on a blue blazer over a white shirt and dark gray slacks. He looked as arrogant and obnoxious as ever.

'Aren't you going to let me in?' he asked, then smiled as if to say, 'Of course you are. You can't resist, can you?'

'No, actually I'm not,' I told him. I walked away from the door. 'Get lost, asshole.'

Jenks knocked again, and I stopped walking. 'We have nothing to talk about,' I called loud enough for him to hear.

'Oh, but we do,' Jenks called back. 'You blew it, Inspector. I'm here to tell you how.'

I froze. I walked back to the door, paused, then opened it, my heart beating fast. *You blew it.*

He was smiling, or maybe laughing at me. 'I'm celebrating,' he said. 'I'm a happy fella! Guess how come?'

'Don't tell me – it's because you're a bachelor again.'

'Well, there's that. But I also just sold North American rights to my latest book. Eight million dollars. Then the movies paid four. This one's non-fiction, Lindsay. Guess the subject, take a stab?'

I wanted desperately to punch Jenks out again. 'And I'm the one you have to share your news with? How goddamn sad for you.'

Jenks continued to grin. 'Actually, I came here to share something else. And you *are* the only one I want to share this with. Do I have your attention yet, Lindsay? You blew it big-time, babe.'

He was so creepy and inappropriate that he was scaring me. I didn't want him to see it. What did he mean, I *blew* it?

'I'd offer you a drink, but I hate your guts,' I smirked.

He threw up his hands, imitated my smirk. 'You know, I feel exactly the same thing toward you. That's why I wanted to tell you this, Lindsay, *only you.*' He lowered his voice to a whisper. '*Chessy did what I told her to do,* right up until the very end. The murders? We were playing a terrible, wonderful game. Tragic husband and wife kill happy, innocent husbands and wives. We were *living* out the plot of a novel. My novel. *You really blew it, Lindsay.* I got away clean. I'm free. I'm *so* free. And now, I'm richer than ever.'

He stared at me, then he started to laugh. It was probably the most sickening sound I'd heard in my life.

'It's true. Chessy would do anything I wanted her to do. All of them would – that's why I picked them. I used to play a game where they barked like dogs. They loved it. Want to play, Lindsay? Ruff, ruff!'

I glared at him. 'Don't you feel kind of inadequate – playing your father's old games? Joanna told me about that.'

'I took things way past anything my father ever imagined. I've done it all, Inspector, *and I got away with it.* I planned every murder. Doesn't that make your fucking skin crawl? Doesn't it make *you* feel inadequate?'

Suddenly, Jenks was putting on plastic gloves he had in his jacket pockets. *What the hell?*

'This is perfect, too,' he said. 'I'm not here, Lindsay. I'm with this sweet little liar of a bitch in Tahoe. I have an alibi bought and paid for. Perfect crimes, Inspector – my specialty.'

As I turned to run, Jenks took out a knife. 'I want to feel this going inside you, Lindsay. Deep. The coup de grâce.'

'Help!' I screamed, but then he hit me hard. I was shocked at how fast he moved, and how powerful he was.

I slammed into a living-room wall and almost fainted. Martha instinctively went after him. I'd never seen her bare her teeth before. He lashed out and cut her shoulder. My poor dog fell over, whining horribly.

'Stay away, Martha!' I screamed at her.

Jenks picked me up and threw me into my bedroom. Then he shut the door.

'There was supposed to be another Bride and Groom murder while I was in jail. New evidence was going to slowly reveal itself. It would become clear that I was innocent – framed. Then I'd write the book! But Chessy turned around and double-crossed me. I never respected her more, Lindsay. I almost loved her for it. She showed some goddamn guts for once!'

I crawled away from Jenks, but he could see there was nowhere for me to go. I thought I might have a broken rib.

'You'll have to kill me first,' I told him, in a hoarse whisper.

'Glad to oblige,' he grinned. 'My pleasure.'

I crawled hand over hand toward my bed, the side facing a window on the Bay.

Jenks came after me.

'Stop, Jenks!' I yelled, at the top of my voice. 'Stop right there!'

He didn't stop. Why should he? He slashed back and forth with the knife. Christ, he was enjoying this. He was laughing. Another perfect murder.

I reached under the bed to where I'd fastened a holster and revolver, my home-security system.

I didn't have time to aim, but I didn't have to. Nicholas Jenks was stunned, the knife poised over his left shoulder.

I fired three times. Jenks screamed, his gray eyes bulged

in disbelief, then he collapsed dead on top of me. 'Burn in hell,' I whispered.

I called Claire first – the Medical Examiner; then Cindy – the best crime reporter in San Francisco; then Jill – my lawyer.

The girls came running.

Headline hopes you have enjoyed 1st TO DIE, and invites you to sample James Patterson's latest compelling thriller, 2nd CHANCE, out now from Headline.

The Choir Kids

Chapter 1

Aaron Winslow would never forget the next few minutes. He recognized the terrifying sounds the instant they cracked through the night. His body went cold all over. He couldn't believe that someone was shooting a high-powered rifle in this neighborhood.

K-pow, k-pow, k-pow . . . k-pow, k-pow, k-pow.

His choir was just leaving the Harrow Street church. Forty-eight young kids streamed past him onto the sidewalk. They had just finished their final rehearsal before the San Francisco Sing-Off, and they had been excellent.

Then came the gunfire. Lots of it. Not just a single shot. A strafing. *An attack.*

K-pow, k-pow, k-pow . . . k-pow, k-pow, k-pow.

'Get down . . .' he screamed at the top of his voice. 'Everybody down on the ground! Cover your heads! Cover up!' He almost couldn't believe the words as they left his mouth.

At first, no one seemed to hear him. To the kids, in their white blouses and shirts, the shots must have seemed like firecrackers. Then a volley of shots rained through the church's beautiful stained-glass window. The depiction of Christ's blessing over a child at Capernaum shattered, glass splintering everywhere, some of it falling on the heads of the children.

'Someone's shooting!' Winslow screamed. Maybe more than one person. *How could that be*? He ran wildly through the kids, screaming, waving his arms, pushing as many as he could down to the grass.

As the kids finally crouched low or dove for the ground, Winslow spotted two of his choir girls, Chantal and Tamara, frozen on the lawn as bullets streaked past them. 'Chantal, Tamara, get down!' he screamed, but they remained there, hugging one another, emitting frantic wails. They were best friends. He had known them since they were little kids, playing four-square on blacktop.

There was never any doubt in his mind. He sprinted towards the two girls, grasping their arms firmly, tumbling them to the ground. Then he lay on top of them, pressing their bodies tightly.

Bullets whined over his head, just inches away. His eardrums hurt. His body was trembling and so were the girls shielded beneath him. He was almost sure he was about to die. 'It's all right, babies,' he whispered.

Then, as suddenly as it had begun, the firing stopped. A hush of silence hung in the air. So strange and eerie, as if the whole world had stopped to listen.

As he raised himself, his eyes fell on an incredible sight. Slowly, everywhere, the children struggled to their feet.

There was some crying, but he didn't see any blood; no one seemed to be hurt.

'Everyone okay?' Winslow called out. He made his way through the crowd. 'Is anyone hurt?'

'I'm okay . . . I'm okay,' came back to him. He looked around in disbelief. This was a miracle.

Then he heard the sound of a single child whimpering.

He turned and spotted Maria Parker, only twelve years old. Maria was standing on the whitewashed wooden steps of the church entrance. She seemed lost. Choking sobs poured from her open mouth.

Then his eyes came to rest on what had made the girl hysterical. He felt his heart sink. Even in war, even growing up on the streets of Oakland, he had never felt anything so horrible, so sad and senseless.

'Oh, God. Oh, no. How could you let this happen?'

Tasha Catchings, just eleven years old, lay in a heap in a flowerbed near the base of the church. Her white school blouse was soaked with blood.

Finally, Reverend Aaron Winslow began to cry himself.

Book 1

The Women's Murder Club – Again

Chapter One

On a Tuesday night I found myself playing a game of crazy-eights with three residents of the Hope Street Teen House. I was loving it.

On the beat-up couch across from me sat Hector, a barrio kid two days out of Juvenile; Alysha, quiet and pretty, but with a family history you wouldn't want to know; and Michelle, who at fourteen had already spent a year selling herself on the streets of San Francisco.

'Hearts,' I declared, flipping down an eight and changing the suit, just as Hector was about to lay out.

'Damn, badge lady,' he whined. 'How come each time I'm 'bout to go down, you stick your knife in me?'

'Teach *you* never to trust a cop, fool,' laughed Michelle, tossing a conspiratorial smile my way.

For the past four months I'd been spending a night or two a week at the Hope Street House. For so long, after the terrible bride and groom case earlier that summer, I'd felt completely lost. I took a month off from Homicide; ran down by the Marina; gazed out at the Bay from the safety of my Potrero Hill flat.

Nothing helped. Not counseling, not the total support of my girls – Claire, Cindy, Jill. Not even going back to the job. I had watched, unable to help, as the life leaked out of the person I loved. I still felt responsible for my partner's death in the line of duty. Nothing seemed to fill the void.

So I came here . . . to Hope Street.

And the good news was, it was working a little.

I peered up from my cards at Angela, a new arrival who sat in a metal chair across the room, cuddling her three-month-old son. The poor kid, maybe sixteen, hadn't said much all night. I would try to talk to Angela before I left for the night.

The door opened and Dee Collins, one of the House's head counselors, came in. She was followed by a stiff-looking black woman in a conservative gray suit. She had Department of Children and Families written all over her.

'Angela, your social worker's here.' Dee kneeled down beside her.

'I ain't blind,' the teenager said.

'We're going to have to take the baby now,' the social worker interrupted, as if completing this assignment was all that kept her from catching the next CalTran.

'No!' Angela pulled the infant even closer. 'You can keep me in this hole, you can send me back to Claymore, but you're not taking my baby.'

'Please, honey, only for a few days,' Dee Collins tried to reassure her.

The teenage girl drew her arms protectively around her

baby, who, sensing some harm, began to cry.

'Don't you make a scene, Angela,' the social worker warned. 'You know how this is done.'

As she came towards the girl, I watched Angela jump out of the chair. She was clutching the baby in one arm and a glass of juice she'd been drinking in the other hand.

In one swift motion she cracked the glass against a table. It created a jagged shard.

'Angela,' I leapt up from the card table, 'put that down. No one's going to take your baby anywhere unless you let her go.'

'This *bitch* is trying to ruin my life,' she glared. 'First, she lets me sit in Claymore three days past my date, then she won't let me go home to my mom. Now she's trying to take my baby girl.'

I nodded, peering into the teenager's eyes. 'First, you gotta lay down the glass,' I said. 'You *know* that, Angela.'

The DCF worker took a step, but I held her back. I moved slowly towards Angela. I took hold of the glass, then I gently eased the child out of her arms.

'She's all I have,' the girl whispered and then started to sob.

'I know,' I nodded. 'That's why you'll change some things in your life and get her back.'

Dee Collins had her arms around Angela, a cloth wrapped around the girl's bleeding hand. The DCF worker was trying unsuccessfully to hush the crying infant.

I went up and said to her, 'That baby gets placed somewhere nearby with daily visitation rights. And by the way, I didn't see anything going on here that was worth putting on file . . . *You*?' The caseworker gave me a disgruntled look and turned away.

Suddenly, my beeper sounded, three dissonant beeps punctuating the tense air. I pulled it out and read the number. *Jacobi, my ex-partner in Homicide. What did he want?*

I excused myself and moved into the staff office. I was able to reach him in his car.

'Something bad's happened, Lindsay,' he said, glumly. 'I thought you'd want to know.'

He clued me in about a horrible drive-by shooting at the LaSalle Heights Church. An eleven-year-old girl had been killed.

'Jesus . . .' I sighed, as my heart sank.

'I thought you might want in on it,' Jacobi said.

I took in a breath. It had been over three months since I'd been on the scene at a homicide. Not since the day the bride and groom case ended.

'So, I didn't hear,' Jacobi pressed. 'You want in, *Lieutenant*?' It was the first time he had called me with my new rank.

I realized my honeymoon had come to an end. 'Yeah,' I muttered back. 'I want in.'

Violets are Blue

James Patterson

'Makes Kay Scarpetta's lot look positively fairytale' *Mirror*

This is James Patterson's sixth No. 1 bestseller in a row, and perhaps his best.

Around noon, I got a call on my cell phone. 'Just checking in,' the Mastermind said. 'How is San Francisco, Alex? Lovely city. Will you leave your heart there? Do you think it's a good place to die?'

The Mastermind of ROSES ARE RED is back – and he's hot on Alex Cross's trail. His cold, taunting threats leave Alex angry and deeply concerned for his family's safety.

Meanwhile, Alex is drawn into his most bizarre investigation yet. Two San Francisco joggers are found dead – bitten and hung by their feet to drain the blood. Further murders in California, and then on the East Coast as well, completely baffle Alex and the FBI. Is this the work of a cult, of role players, or even of modern-day vampires? Desperate to stop the deaths, Alex teams up with Jamilla Hughes, a savvy woman detective, and the FBI's Kyle Craig. But Alex has never been closer to defeat, or in greater danger. In a shocking conclusion, he must survive a deadly confrontation – only to learn at last the awful secret of the Mastermind.

Praise for James Patterson:

'A master of the suspense genre' *Sunday Telegraph*

'James Patterson's gift to thriller fans is D.C. homicide detective and psychiatrist Alex Cross' *Washington Times*

'Brilliantly terrifying . . . so exciting I had to stay up all night to finish it' *Daily Mail*

0 7472 6691 3

headline

2nd Chance

James Patterson with Andrew Gross

Lindsay Boxer, San Francisco's only woman homicide detective, is back in 2nd Chance – the mind-blowing new thriller in the international No. 1 bestselling Women's Murder Club series.

I moved in closer and knelt over the body. Tasha's blouse was soaked with blood, mixed with falling rain. Just a few feet away, a rainbow-hued knapsack still lay on the grass. Bullet holes were everywhere, splintered glass and wood. Dozens of kids had been streaming out to the street . . . All those shots, and only one victim.

The tragic end of the honeymoon murder case left Lindsay Boxer unsure if she could ever return to work. But when a little girl is shot outside a San Francisco church, she knows it's time to reconvene the Women's Murder Club. Working with reporter Cindy Thomas, assistant DA Jill Bernhardt, and medical examiner Claire Washburn, Lindsay starts to track a mystifying killer who quickly turns his pursuers into his victims.

Acclaim for James Patterson's novels

'Unputdownable' *The Times*

'Makes Kay Scarpetta's lot look positively fairytale' *Mirror*

'A master of the suspense genre' *Sunday Telegraph*

0 7472 6693 X

headline

The Beach House

James Patterson and Peter de Jonge

The blockbuster of the summer is an unforgettable story of wealth, betrayal, sex and murder.

The second that Columbia law student Jack Mullen steps down from the train at East Hampton, he knows that something is very wrong. As he greets his family, his kid brother Peter lies stretched out on a steel gurney, battered, bruised – dead. The police are calling the drowning an accident. Jack knows that's wrong. Someone wanted his brother dead.

But the establishment says otherwise. Jack tries to uncover what really happened on the beach that night, only to confront a wall of silence; a barricade of shadowy people who protect the privileges of the multi-billionaire summer residents. And when he discovers that his brother had nearly $200,000 in his bank account, Jack realises Peter wasn't just parking cars to make a living . . .

The Beach House is a breathtaking drama of revenge and sexual intrigue – with a plot so absorbing and a finale so shocking it could only have come from the unique mind of James Patterson, writing with his co-author of *Miracle on the 17th Green*, Peter de Jonge.

Praise for James Patterson

'I can't believe how good Patterson is. I have never begun a Patterson book and been able to put it down' Larry King, *USA Today*

'A master of the suspense genre' *Sunday Telegraph*

'James Patterson does everything but stick our finger in a light socket to give us a buzz' *New York Times*

0 7553 0017 3

headline